*A Banner
with a
Strange Device*

A Banner with a Strange Device

A Novel by
ARONA McHUGH

Doubleday & Company, Inc.
Garden City, New York

A BANNER WITH A STRANGE DEVICE, Arona McHugh

Grateful acknowledgment is made to the following
for the use of copyrighted material:

BREGMAN, VOCCO AND CONN, INC.
Lines from *Good Morning Blues* by James Rushing, Count Basie and Ed Durham. Copyright ©
1938, 1959 by Bregman, Vocco and Conn, Inc.
Reprinted by permission.

ALFRED A. KNOPF, INC.
Lines from "Peter Quince at the Clavier." Copyright 1923, 1951 by Wallace Stevens from *The
Collected Poems of Wallace Stevens*. Reprinted
by permission.

ROBBINS MUSIC CORPORATION
Lines from *I Got It Bad and That Ain't Good*.
Words by Paul Webster, music by Duke Elling-
ton. © Copyright 1941 Robbins Music Corporation, New York, N.Y. Reprinted by permission.

INFEL-VERLAG
"Herbsttag" from *Translations* by Rainer Maria
Rilke. Reprinted by permission.

To Miriam Lipman, my mother, with love.

*A Banner
with a
Strange Device*

Part One

One

The sky over Cambridge this morning in May was a meticulously enameled blue; sunlight filtered cheerfully through the fresh green of old, tapestried trees; the passing lilac flowers though now rusted and crumpled exuded still the faint incantative scent of all springs and in the gardens the prim, waxen tulips waned, their once stiff, upright petals opening out wider, lax, melting, making ready to go.

In Langdell the first-year class of Harvard University Law School was taking its one and only year's exam in Property. Four hundred and ninety-nine members of this class sat in the large amphitheatrical lecture hall, their heads bent, their pens rushing like witches' brooms over the rustling, rapidly turned blue book pages. An hour and a half had gone by since the proctor first said *go*, the exam was slated to last four hours; they smiled, they knew, they wrote like men who were bargaining with the devil for more time.

The five-hundredth man in the class had, at nine o'clock, looked over the seven questions on the mimeographed sheet and, realizing that his atheistic stay in that church full of reverent worshipers was to be short, carefully and slowly inscribed on the cover of his blue book some of the barren particulars of his place in this round world; he was Michael Adam Wainscott, a sometime member of this class and the day was noday, May 1948. There was no space for his age, which was twenty-six or the painful question as to what a man, supposedly in the prime of the age of reason, was doing making ready to flunk an important exam. After that, he had uncapped his fountain pen and made a stab at answering one or two of the questions. Several futile circuits of his pumpkin head had been made in search of the slightest tittle of information concerning the others until finally at ten-thirty a satiric bugle blew the minor, dying fall notes of retreat somewhere in that same chaotic mind and he capped his pen, turned the gutless bluebook in to the proctor and left.

He wandered purposelessly into the fair, windless day, across Kirkland and Cambridge Streets into the College Yard and bumbled along until he came to the steps of Widener, where he sat down. All around him the day shone and gleamed in a green so pure and clear, so rendingly fresh, so burnished and enhanced by holyspring sunlight that it was blinding. In no state to relish such triumphant, innocent vitality he closed his eyes and sat brooding like a thin-blooded, homeless mole out in a raging sleetstorm. I studied, he thought defensively, I did study for the damn exam. But it had not been enough, that last-minute cramming, not enough to make up for a whole year's slighted work, classes cut, notes not taken, important points not thoroughly comprehended.

Reaching into the pocket of his green corduroy jacket he took out cigarettes and a book of matches and, opening his eyes, tried to tear off the match and light it with his right hand only. He'd been managing to accomplish this and other one-handed feats, quite successfully since 1945 but today, nothing worked. He could tear off only half the match, and then, after several unsuccessful attempts to strike it, he managed it at last, by bracing the matchbook against the stone step, but the flame flickered out before he could get it to the cigarette and burned his fingers in the bargain. Damn it, he thought, noticing that a passing girl, a nice-looking one too, had stopped, her eyes full of curiosity and sympathy, to watch his struggle and was about to offer help, blast and damn that exam which had gotten him all unnerved. Reluctantly, he withdrew his left hand from his pocket and lighted the cigarette at last, frowning at the girl who turned away hastily. So there was one unknown girl who'd seen his war souvenir and more, undoubtedly, would have to be exposed to what he still considered a monstrous imperfection. His hand was really all right now and he'd have to stop keeping it hidden so shame-facedly. All things considered he'd been damn lucky; a hand that shattered and burned by an exploding grenade three years ago could've come out much worse. But the surgery done immediately to repair the tendons cut in forearm and wrist had been expert and although the skin grafting had been a long, discouraging process, now, for all necessary intents and purposes he had a normal left hand and, most of the time, he knew that people really didn't notice it and that he was just being supersensitive. But Christ, sometimes, when he looked at this unlikely, drawn, horny, ragtag-colored thing which was his left hand, he felt a sense of utter disassociation. It seemed more like the paw of some weird animal than a human hand. Although grudgingly he had to admit that in the past year there'd been a big improvement and, by next year, the doctors had told him, it would look almost completely normal, except for the color which would never be quite the same as before. It was something he would have to learn to live with, he thought now, finishing his cigarette, like the fact that he had just flunked an exam and thereby, perhaps, a career.

Food, Mike thought dismally, might help interrupt this dangerous and futile self-shriving although he didn't feel hungry. Still, eating would be a good idea because his parents were leaving today for a weekend in Westport and Minta might just not've bothered to replenish the larder. They always seemed to assume that he had enough money and he hated to disillusion them but, like all other GI Bill veterans, he was rich the first part of the month and beggarly from the fifteenth on. Anyway, he could still afford coffee. He cut across the Yard and out to the Square and Hayes-Bickford where he drank coffee and ate two crullers. Then, still in search of some vacuum-filling distraction, he crossed the street and browsed through the Coop, looking at new books, reading snatches here and there and fetching up finally before the rack in the rear which contained new issues of literary magazines and scholastic quarterlies. An article in the *New Critics Review* on Faulkner caught his eye because it was written by Bill Dunne, an old friend of his parents', and he paused to scan it, leaning against a counter, turning the pages rapidly and mumbling mechanical sorrys as people tried to squeeze by him. He began to feel cheerful for the first time that morning, as he read on, and, at one point, having lost his way in a miasmic, evil-smelling swamp of symbolical analysis, he gave vent to an unrestrained crow of laughter, tossed the magazine back on the rack and got on the subway to Boston, still distracted with his vision of literary hacks like Dunne fighting their way through the Spanish moss, rooting around in the bog of Southern myth looking for ridiculous meanings.

The train finally came up into the light of day and they were running onto the bridge over the river. Mike looked down at the sailboats and sculls, graceful on the glistening, sun-dappled water. The spring day shimmered on his eyes and quickened, at last, his sluggish blood and marrow while the earth turned and unrolled for him, millennia of spring. Smoking hot off creation, primeval ooze and slime, 140 million years of reptilian monsters lumbering along but after the horror of tyrannosaurus rex, grew the first flowering plants and after awhile, more believable animals and finally, mirabile dictu, people, to whom spring was fertility rites, human

5

sacrifices and death dances. And was it so different, even now? The old garlanded the young with laurel and sent them off to be butchered for whatever cause was fashionable at the moment and the young, in their turn, lay in wait, then pulled the venerable's beards, plucked out their rheumgummed eyes, mocked at their impuissance and hard-earned wisdom and sent them off to rot and die, unloved and unwanted. I'll start with the Renaissance, Mike thought, walking down the Charles Street platform, the green and silver Elizabethan season, all pink and white and maypole colored, announced by the musick of bawdy catches and heraldic trumpets and I'll leave off just before the papier-mâché Easter bunnies, jaundiced marshmallow chicks, newtgreen jelly eggs and cellophane grass, because we're about to come full circle to where the world will smoke again, split asunder in mushroom clouds of fire. The fatal secret of all beginnings and endings has been discovered and not even tyrannosaurus could live on a radiated planet, still less humans like me who might have hoped to reach crabbed age and see the spring in a new century.

He went down the steps of the station, through the underpass and began the slow climb up Beacon Hill, his old green book bag, heavy with unread books on the law, slung over his shoulder. On this day in May, Mike Wainscott, madly trying to squeeze a left-hand brain into a right-hand profession, quite rightly sprouted asses' ears. Now, his father, of course, had known it all along.

"Law School!" Sam Wainscott had said incredulously, "when, with free tuition, expenses, a pension and not a care in the world, you could be over in Paris, having yourself a time. Registered for sinecure courses and . . ."

"And painting masterpieces, I suppose," Mike'd interrupted coldly, "when I can't paint, or writing another *Sun Also Rises* when I can't write. And, actually spending most of my time in cafés talking grandly about integrity and art with a lot of other fakes."

"I thought that a lot of your poetry was very good and those prose sketches you did for the *Scrivener* showed a fine sense of language."

"That was just kid stuff," Mike had said impatiently. "Every kid writes poems and stories and thinks he's going to be a writer. If they have any sense they give it up. There's nothing more pathetic than someone who's always talking and dreaming of what he'll write someday and never does because he didn't have the talent in the first place."

"How do you know you haven't got talent?" Sam Wainscott had

6

demanded. "You've really never given it a chance. I thought you had some promise and I ought to know."

"Thanks a lot, Sam," Mike'd said blandly, "but I think maybe you're kind of prejudiced."

There'd been a lot more conversations like that one ever since Mike'd finished off his B.A. a year after getting the ruptured duck and they always ended up the same way, and Mike had gone to Law School. And he didn't like it but damned if he'd admit it. Of course, he thought now, pausing before the door of his house on Mount Vernon Street while he fished in his pocket for the dogtag chain which now served as keyring, if I really cared about showing Sam, I'd've worked at it. No courage of convictions. But if I'm flunked, he thought, opening the door and starting up the stairs, washed out, what then? You deserve it but can't actually believe it'll fall on you, like death and misfortunes which are for other people. Immature bastard who can't accept consequences. Never mind about that immature, that lousy psychologisch word. Maybe I am but is it such a surprising human condition especially when you're Sam Wainscott's son, his only child. What were his chances, anyway? There were two more exams to go, next week, one long four-hour one in Torts and a shorter one in Criminal Law. There was still time, time to stay up all night, time to round up and copy the notes from classes he'd cut out of sheer boredom. If only he had back all those wasted hours of self-indulgent lolling at Lamont listening to poetry records instead of going to classes or keeping up with his work. What a schizoid simpleton to've fallen between two stools like that. Could they kick you out for failing one course? He couldn't remember. Probably the other 499 characters in his class knew vital items like that. Only he, with a quarterwit mind fixed on higher things like Eliot's dry voice saying "I will show you fear in a handful of dust," only he was unaware of the facts of survival. And how had he done in the water under the bridge exams? Let's see. Civil Procedure? Well, he'd written a lot. Probably made that. Agency. Not so good. Contracts. Oh, ugh! Still, might've managed to squeeze through on that, because although some blank spots, it'd been the first exam and he'd made an effort to overcome the yawning tedium which had attacked him in the first class back last fall. They can't flunk me, he thought. I'll do better next year. I'll concentrate. I'll burn all my poetry books to propitiate the legal gods. I'll cover sheets of foolscap with fine, copperplate script at every exam.

In the living room he dropped his book bag on top of the piano and prowled through the dining room, the kitchen and even poked his head into the sacred precincts of Sam's study. He went on up the stairs, looked into the bedrooms and Minta's studio. Not a soul around. Had they gone? No, there was his mother's little suitcase lying on her bed, open, half-packed. Well, it was only twelve-thirty. He went to the phone in the downstairs hallway, dialed a number and asked to speak to Miss Jean Donnelly.

"Jean," he said and, as always, when he heard her voice on the phone, wondered why the hell he kept seeing her. It was what his father called the wrong-side-of-the-blanket Boston accent; a superimposition of the generally sloppy, loose, imprecise American speech habits on top of the tart, earshriveling vibrations of the Yankee twang.

"Hi, baby. Mike. Listen, Jean, I think it'd be better if I call you before you come over here. They're not starting out as early as I thought."

As expected she was aggrieved because hadn't she asked to be let off at three so they could spend more time together and why couldn't she come over anyway? Was he ashamed of her?

Mike listened, thinking of Sam's little homily delivered after an accidental meeting one night in the Bellevue taproom. Oh, he'd been polite and even charming to Miss Donnelly and bought them drinks but later Mike'd heard how sad it was that a man of such intelligence and worldliness had whelped a son afflicted with the most atrocious taste in women.

"It is not bad enough," Sam had declaimed dramatically while Mike'd tried not to laugh, "that she be skinny and have those protruding eyes the color of skim milk and wear too much rouge, but, to pile Ossa on Pelion, she has a voice worse, far worse than a seagull. I would, even so, forgive her all those abominations but to smear Vaseline on her eyelids, that I cannot possibly countenance. That you do is to your eternal shame."

"You are, aren't you?" she was saying.

"Oh relax," Mike said, trying not to be nasty. After all, he hadn't seen her for a week and a half and, although his father's criticisms were unfortunately too true, she made a good enough bed in this season of indecision. "I've explained all this before Jean. My private life is my affair. Even though I do live here."

"Then you ought to get a place of your own," she said resentfully. "I hate all this sneaking around and waiting for your folks to go away weekends. We're too old for that."

"So you keep telling me," Mike said glumly. "So let's not ruin this weekend, huh? Now, when you leave the office call me here.

They'll probably be gone by three but sometimes there are last-minute crises at the magazine and Sam can't get away."

She made a dissatisfied, giving-in sort of sound and Mike hung up and went into the kitchen, thinking what a drag it was the way he somehow always managed to hurt Jean's feelings. If only she wasn't so damnably sentimental and could see their relationship the way he did; a pastime, sexually and socially expedient, but no. There was the continual, transparent lamentation about how much her religion meant to her and what a sin she was committing by sleeping with him. He'd been secretly amused the first few times she'd voiced this plaint because her virginity had been lost long before he met her. Of course, to a great love, a flyboy, killed in the war. In time, this wearisome display of her tortured conscience began to exasperate him and he'd finally told her he could no longer bear to add to her burden of guilt. And naturally, with big martyr eyes she'd answered, but I love you Mike, and so there they were on the same old carousel and the only way to get off was either to be brutal or marry her. He'd have to be a bastard someday soon, he supposed, because marriage to her was out. Too bad, because in many ways the relationship was convenient.

He was getting hungry and still no sign of Minta, Sam, or lunch. He opened the refrigerator door, scowled at the bottle of imported Chablis that stood up green, elegant, and beaded with cold drops on the upper shelf, ran his eye over the cold chicken in aspic, the Bel Paese and fruit and slammed the door shut. The makings of a real charming, little continental lunch there and a lot of it too. Had they been expecting him after all? He went over to the stove and hefted the percolator experimentally. Just the way he'd left it this morning, half-full. He set the gas going and was reaching into a cupboard to get his jar of peanut butter when the front door opened and banged shut.

"Mike, darling," his mother said, "how lovely, you're home for lunch. I just ran out to get some French bread and lettuce." She dumped an armload of paper bags on the boneclean pine table. Mike looked at her as she moved across the room, a tall, slender woman, her gray-streaked, brown hair pulled tightly back into a large bun at the nape. She kissed him lightly on the cheek. "How was the exam?"

"Pretty fair," Mike muttered, unscrewing the cap of the jar.

"Michael!" Araminta Wainscott said indignantly, "you're not going to eat that barbaric peanut butter when I have a wonderful lunch all ready. I won't let you. I can't imagine what possesses you to persecute your tastebuds so."

"I like peanut butter," Mike said. "That's why I bought a jar. I'd never get any if I left it . . ."

"You have plenty of time to eat it when I'm not here," his mother interrupted decisively. She looked at him with her beautiful, deep, brown eyes, eyes so exactly like his that Mike was often startled when their glances clashed. Now, as he gave in and put the peanut butter back, Mike thought of all the young painters who had, over a period of years, been enchanted by the wide-spaced, innocent, melting sweetness of Araminta's eyes. And he remembered the wrenching discovery that Sam knew all about Minta's admirers but'd been too busy himself to care and which came first, the stylish pseudo-litry girls who flocked around handsome Sam, or Minta's paint-daubed satellites, and the hell with it, he'd anesthetized himself against it, long ago.

Now, as he turned the gas off and poured himself a cup of coffee, he said crossly, "Why can't we ever have some beer in this house?"

"Beer and peanut butter," Araminta Wainscott said, rubbing garlic all over the teakwood salad bowl. She shook her head. "You know that Sam and I don't drink beer," she added patiently. "I don't know how you can stand it, but if you want it, you'd better get it yourself."

Mike looked around the kitchen; at the walls, one all mellow redbrick, the other three, rough, white plaster, the copper pots hanging on hooks above the stove, the brown pottery and red iron casseroles, the shelf of herbs and spices, the wideboarded, sanded and polished floor, the simple wooden table and benches, the wormy chestnut cupboards fitted with not only every variety of European china, pottery, glassware, and cutlery but also a collection of bottled and packaged delicacies, stuff he wouldn't put in his mouth, but all imported from the old world and purchased at a staggering sum from S. S. Pierce.

"Yeah," he said, "beer and peanut butter. A couple of good, old American customs. But I suppose they'd be out of place in a kitchen that's a chichi copy of a French farmhouse. You'd think that Sam never spent a good part of his youth drinking beer with the Lost Generation, the way he shudders at the word now. Oh, but don't tell me, that was Spanish, French, German, or Danish beer, unlike common ordinary American non-atmospheric beer."

Araminta grimaced delicately at the romaine lettuce she was shredding. "Darling, do stop sounding like one of those wartime big industry ads. I should think you'd be above that our boy is fighting for a slice of mom's blueberry pie and a new car every year bosh. Our kitchen is not remarkable and it's much more Early American than French. Though we did attempt to make it look as much as possible like the kitchen of the cottage at Meudon where we lived the first few years we were married. It was your first home and we have wonderful memories of it."

"Yeah, I know," Mike said, "it was all like a Renoir painting."

"Well, it was," Araminta Wainscott said, blinking suddenly. "We were awfully happy and the world was very exciting then and we knew so many wonderful people who were doing important, creative things and we were so delighted to be there and away from the stuffy dullness of our parents' homes. And you were such a charming little baby even though it was very difficult for us because we didn't have much money and there was no hot water and I had to boil every bit we used and I was always washing diapers it seemed to me. And we never thought we'd have a son who'd grow up and make fun of and dislike everything we liked and lived for."

Oh sure, Mike thought cynically, it sounds like such a pastoral idyll but she overlooks how they got lost along the way. But aloud he said:

"Sorry, Minta, guess I'm just a boor."

His mother smiled, happily mollified. "You're not a boor, darling. You had a difficult time in the war and Sam and I understand that, though I confess we are baffled by some of your activities and ideas since your return. But we know what it's like. Your father had the same kind of confusions after the first war, although of course he wasn't wounded as you were."

Mike felt a grin coming on and turned to look out the window so his mother wouldn't see it. No point in hurting her feelings again. He enjoyed needling his father because Sam was always good for rugged battle but Minta wasn't fair game. It'd be damn funny if they didn't blame all his peculiarities on the war. It was in the tradition wasn't it that all young men suffered from the war? Got lost and isolated and acted like a Hemingway character. At least, in their war that'd been the pose. And then, all the sad, young men who'd been risking their necks as officers in the ambulance service got lost in the Paris cafés and wrote books about how society diddled them with false values. Imagine how they would have felt if they'd been diddled into being a drafted private in the infantry, Mike thought, amused. The ambulance drivers of his father's war'd had all of the advantages of the officer caste and none of its drawbacks. A genuine infantry private of the U.S., British, French, and probably German armies of the World War I days, you'd have some respect for, because not only did they risk and lose their lives, but also they lived eternally in mud and lice and were treated like real dogs by their officers. In his war, Mike mused, relations between officer and enlisted had been better (particularly in combat, where they were all cannon fodder), yet in rear areas and stateside the EM were still subject to a large measure of robot discipline and pridegalling, off-limits to EM crap. Of course, Sam had warned him that it was unwise of an intelligent young man to submit himself to the military without the protection of rank but since taking orders had bothered Mike far less than having to give them he'd resigned himself for the duration to being treated like a noncomposmentis field darky.

How ironic it'd been then when he was overseas, and had managed to be one of the few survivors of a decimated platoon and a stricken company to discover himself willy-nilly, Tech Sergeant Wainscott and exceedingly responsible. In that crucible, even he, who'd feared it, melted easily into command and suddenly became the authoritative type he'd never wanted to be. Until they straggled back to civilization again, and he'd been expected magically to revert to his serf status below stairs. Then he had thought of Sam, far away back home and grudgingly acknowledged that it might not be bad to have the extra pay, privileges and respect since the burdens had fallen on him anyhow. But even if I had gone to OCS and been a second lieutenant in the infantry, he thought now, sipping his cooling coffee, Sam wouldn't have understood Lieutenant Wainscott any more than he did Sergeant Wainscott.

The difference in the two wars, particularly for Americans, was so enormous you couldn't even compare them. Sam's war represented a completely different era when officers as a matter of course came from the upper classes and had university educations and the private soldiers were always from down below. And, naturally, a war like that, precipitated by the assassination of an Austrian archduke would have plenty of room for glamorous volunteers full of noblesse oblige, attached and not accountable, Richard Harding Davis figures, dilettantes in search of adventure. My war, Mike thought, didn't start off in style, being fought by gentlemen and their vassals for obscure reasons which somehow turned into an abattoir; mine was started by maniac scum, a plague of rats and cockroaches, which were everywhere and had to be fought long and hard by a grim machine. So I was the real thing, I know what being a soldier means, the uniform I wore was not a fancy collection of spurious symbols, rakish, dashing, and false, my medals and ribbons are real, hardwon, bloodred, dirt common, I've been there and that's something Sam can never truly say. The hell with it, he thought, so Sam and Minta don't want to probe any deeper or try to figure out why I can't stand their way of life. They prefer to fall back on that old cliché, the war, a war and an experience they can never understand. Let them. Forget it.

"What's all the fuss about lunch, Minta?" he asked casually.

"Oh didn't you know? No, of course, how could you? You were studying last night when he called but Bill Dunne is in town, he was speaking over at Harvard last night and he wanted to see Sam today at his office, so we invited him for lunch and he's driving down to Westport with us."

"Sometimes," Mike said tiredly, "life is too coincidental to stand. What's that carpetbagger doing over at Harvard?"

"Perhaps you'll find out at lunch if your manners improve by then," Minta said in a nursery nanny tone which ill befitted her, considering.

"Maybe I won't stay for lunch," Mike said sourly.

"Bill Dunne is a fascinating, intelligent, charming man and I don't understand your antipathy," Araminta said crisply. "Besides, he's anxious to see you, he told Sam. Hasn't seen you since you went into the Army."

"Has it been that long?" Mike asked in mock astonishment. "Why it seems to me that it's impossible to get away from the guy. Everywhere you look his name is on some collection or anthology or literary rehash. Or else, an article, typically entitled, Our Younger Writers, Do They Measure Up?"

Minta tossed salad vigorously. "Bill Dunne is one of our oldest friends," she said finally, "and if you're going to be rude, perhaps you'd better not stay. I like him very much and I won't have him insulted."

"Mmmm," Mike said, "I know. Well, I'll behave. Don't worry Minta." He turned and went into the living room, flinging himself angrily into a chintzy maple chair. So what, he thought, remembering how his mother had looked when he'd said that, yes I do know. Am I supposed to forget all about it and be nice, well-mannered, civilized, because they are, because they don't know what it means to love, or to be as I was, a thin, leggy dolt who didn't appreciate the advantages of having sophisticated parents.

For years, he'd wondered why they didn't get divorced. Half the boys in all the schools he'd gone to had divorced parents and he'd always thought that at least those other boys knew where they stood. Because in those simple days it had seemed so black and white; mothers and fathers who loved each other did not want other people to love. Later when he was older and had lived down some of the resentment and bitterness, he'd been able to see them in perspective, to figure out their complications and to understand that of course they'd never get divorced, no matter how strong the provocation might appear, not even that one time when Sam was never there but Bill Dunne always was. And he'd been home from school a lot because of sickness and old enough then, to clothe the formerly confusing skeletons with flesh. Wretchedly sure then that Sam and Minta would really get divorced and Minta would marry Bill Dunne but it hadn't happened. All blown over and he'd never known why and Bill Dunne had married someone else, his second wife, and now he had a third one or perhaps a fourth, Mike couldn't remember.

He might have saved himself some real heartache back there when he was twelve years old, if only he'd dug Sam and Minta the way he did now. Because what did love have to do with it for crissakes? If you were two people with just a small fund of love to spend, you didn't really waste it on others. You saved it for yourself and your work and since fond regard for yourself required that your life be a perfect picture, you squeezed out a small amount to retain, however loosely the third panel of your reverent self-altar piece. And since Sam and Minta were the same sort of people exactly, whose careers and ambitions formed the central and most important section of their lifelong masterpiece, the whole damn triptych would fall down if one of them left the other.

Oh, they were productive and successful enough he had to admit. Minta was a pretty good painter. She'd run through periods of cubism, surrealism, expressionism, and surrealistic formalism and these paintings were shown in galleries, respectfully reviewed and, sometimes, even bought. This was what she considered and spoke of as her *real* painting. What she actually made money on were commissioned portraits of children and adults and paintings of children sans commission, in interesting clothes, Victorian, Edwardian, and Empire costumes which were always sold but dismissed casually by her as her egg-money painting, and everyone she knew agreed with her except Mike, who thought that her paintings of children were the best things she did. But he was a reactionary.

His father, Mike supposed, could be considered successful. Not financially, of course, but Mike couldn't think of any phase of writing, publishing, or journalism in the last twenty years that Sam had somehow not been involved in, starting in 1919 when he'd come to Paris as a foreign correspondent for one of the New York papers, met Minta who was studying painting there, married and settled there and later when he was editing an excellent literary magazine and running a small, private press. In 1930 the magazine had died of financial starvation and they'd moved to London where Sam had worked for a British book publisher for eight years, coming back to the States as an editor in one of the Boston publishing houses, the year before the war began in Europe. Sam'd been one of these uncanny editors who could smell genius, talent, promise, even best-sellers, miles away and coax and delve and quarry the very best out of his writers. He'd been especially good with lady novelists. Of course, he'd kept his hand in the journalistic pie by writing vast numbers of articles all during the tense thirties in Europe. And now he was the big chief on the *Pilgrim*, a respectable, literary monthly.

And these were his parents; his handsome, imposing father and his beautiful, charming mother, both intelligent, witty, well-read, well-educated, well-bred, full of good taste, social graces, brains and talent and, Mike always added when he thought about it, one-track minds. Those wonderful Wainscotts who led such fascinating lives. They had to have everything, Mike thought bitterly, including me, to make the full, rich, creative life picture complete, but after awhile it turned out I was an awkward shape, so I got painted out and shoved into the shadowy background. He'd wanted a pet, a dog, a cat, even. Too much trouble and mess and smell and then he'd gotten shipped off to school early and that had ended the pet problem. He'd wanted to have a brother or a sister, someone who wasn't an adult who belonged to him. Well they'd had no time for that obviously and, since they'd had brothers and sisters of their own, they'd never known how lonely it was being an only child. But if you had to be the only one at least you could have a real home, a house with porches, cellars, attics, a big yard, trees to hang swings from, and a neighborhood peopled by boys like him, with whom he could play games, fight and be friends. Not apartments in Paris, London, or Boston or strictly supervised, rigidly disciplined European schools, with the only two humans closest to him, either removed by distance or self-absorption. Well that was what he had wanted and since it wasn't part of their myth he'd never gotten it.

Their code, he thought, which together, perhaps with a trace of self-conscious laughter but, nevertheless, deep down taking it all quite seriously, they'd evolved in the first years of their life together. And this myth which had been part of their time had been taken wholly to their hearts so that although the times changed they had not, they lived on with the myth and it became a way of life. Perhaps they'd even talked out the ethics of it, Mike didn't know, but whether it was verbally dogmatized or not, they could live no other way. They could take lovers because they had the freedom to be individuals and it was in the tradition, the not being tied down by middle-class morality or dull, graceless people's standards. But they did it together, they believed in it together, they never disagreed with one another in any way about how they wished to live and that was why no third person could dent that united front, not their son or any of their lovers. Now, of course, Mike thought, sitting and looking at the cubist painting on the wall, the cottage at Meudon transformed to gray and purple planes and angles, they were getting old and if there were any more lovers, he didn't know about them. Now, there were only old friends coming to lunch. And nobody even remembered old passions, except Mike, the reactionary, the prude.

He heard the door open and a moment later, Sam Wainscott, a black Homburg set at a rakish angle on his handsome, leonine head, came into the room.

"Ah, the son and heir," he said, pulling his hat off and scaling it onto the piano, "are we to be honored with your presence at lunch?"

Mike nodded, without speaking. The ways of genetics were strange, he thought. Sam Wainscott was the very model of a man. Even at the age of fifty he was muscular, broad-chested, tall, erect, and with not an extra ounce of fat on him. Even the lines on his forehead, the web of crow's feet around the blue eyes and the totally iron-gray color of his mass of neatly trimmed, vigorous curls did not make him look older but merely more distinguished and overwhelming than he had at thirty and forty. But the sperm and the egg which had met to form Mike had bypassed all this source of enduring, masculine good looks including the strong face and stanch Roman nose and bestowed on him everything that made Araminta so delicately beautiful. Her perfectly shaped round head looked a little too small atop Mike's long, gangling body, her straight dark hair, lovely cameo-like face, large dark eyes framed in long, sooty black lashes, all transferred to Mike and slightly changed by the addition of Sam's firm square chin and straight, wide mouth just made him look, he'd decided when he was completely grown up and knew his face wouldn't change any more, like a wet seal or a neurotic cocker spaniel.

"Where's Bill?" Araminta asked coming in from the dining room with a bundle of Italian straw place mats in her hand.

"He'll be up soon," Sam said. "Went back to the hotel to check out. I guess a highball before lunch won't take the edge off the wine. How about you, Mike?"

"Why not?" Mike said indifferently.

Sam looked annoyed. "Don't break your neck. I know you'd rather have beer."

"I've resigned myself to accepting bourbon as a substitute," Mike said silkily.

"Oh stop posturing," Sam said sharply. "In spite of all this apparent preference for beer I've noticed that every time we go away and you have one of your parties my liquor stock is considerably lowered."

"Bourbon on the rocks for me," Minta said. "I'll get it when I've finished setting the table."

"If you don't want my friends whose tastes are better than mine to drink your liquor why don't you say so?" Mike demanded of Sam.

"As you well know," Sam said irritably, "I am not objecting to you or your friends drinking whatever's available. What I dislike is hypocrisy."

So he goes around and measures the bottles before and after Mike thought, accepting the drink from his father with a mutter of thanks. Well, damn him anyway. He must remember tomorrow to take all the bar stuff out of here, and buy a cheap bottle of blended rye, even though his check hadn't come yet. Christ, was he never going to have enough money of his own so he wouldn't have to suffer these parental indignities. He fished a toothpick from his pocket, poked at his teeth and waited for Sam to rise to the bait. "I suppose," he said slyly, "Bill Dunne was telling the Harvard lads all about the Lost Generation. He was getting too fat for that sort of thing, last time I saw him."

Sam grimaced at the toothpick. "Where do you unearth these gorilla habits?"

"It's a good habit," Mike said, full of injured innocence. "Stops tooth decay. You know," he added, returning to the fray, "I just read an article of Dunne's on Faulkner. It was terrible. You aren't going to print one of his lousy articles, are you?"

"Why yes, as a matter of fact we are," Sam said, trying hard obviously to ignore his misbegotten son's boorishness. "He's just finished a lecture tour of universities and colleges which have writing programs. Been talking to the younger generation of writers. Perhaps we might call them apprentice writers. He's quite enthused, perhaps not about them, but he certainly has many positive ideas about what this trend means. That's what this article is about. He thinks this might even be the opening salvo of a new book."

"Holy hat," Mike said, sitting up with sudden energy. "So he's found a new baby, a new gold mine, the embryonic writers. Oh Jesus, don't tell me any more about him. What a profession for a man to follow, a parasite of writers, a professional Boswell to whole generations of writers. When one dies off or there's no more new material on them, off he marches to capture more and newer writers so he can keep putting out books and articles. Why, the man's a bloodsucker. He's dangerous."

"It seems to me," his father commented acidly, "you're more worked up about this than you ought to be considering that you're an embryo lawyer, not a writer."

Mike lowered his eyes and lit a cigarette with his good hand. "Ah I don't care," he said slumping back in his chair and pulling the bored expression down over his face. "People like that just make me sick, is all."

"If you want to bait Dunne you can try it at lunch, on him," Sam Wainscott said authoritatively. "Not on me. He's more than a match for you. And Mike, when are you going to start using your other hand? It's all right now. You shouldn't be ashamed of it."

"Sure, I know," Mike said, chewing on his thumbnail. "It's the red badge of courage and I ought to write a book about how I got it and how everybody else who has two good hands is a sybaritic coward and doesn't know what the word honor means."

Without waiting for an answer he got up and went upstairs to the bathroom. When he came down again, Bill Dunne was there, a short chubby man, with curly gray hair, a bronzed face and a perennially boyish grin, capering around the living room with a drink in his hand, talking a blue streak to Sam and Minta, who were sitting together on the sofa, laughing appreciatively.

"Mike!" Dunne said delightedly, springing forward. "The young Clarence Darrow. How the hell are you, boy?"

"Hi, man," Mike said giving him a limp handshake.

"And when do you cross the bar, eh?" Dunne asked, grinning.

"When there's one clear call for me," Mike said coldly, dropping into a chair.

"I don't know," Bill Dunne said, shaking his head. "You young fellas today. If I had that GI Bill, I tell you, I wouldn't be wasting it in Law School."

Mike yawned. "I know," he said finally, "you'd be in Paris. Well,

I've been there. I was born there, remember. I've seen a lot of Europe, before and after, and believe me it doesn't look near as good now as it did in the twenties. Part of it's bombed to hell and everybody's poor. And they hate Americans. I like it here."

"Mike," his mother said warningly and then, as he looked at her sullenly, she smiled and added in a softer voice, "I forgot to tell you but Sally Brimmer, well, of course, that's not her name now, I forget her married name, called you this morning. She's only just gotten back from California. Staying with her brother, I believe she said. I wrote the number down on the phone pad."

"No kidding," Mike said. He sat up. "Sally. She's back? For good? Or just a visit?" He heard the excitement in his voice and tried to control it. "I mean, that's fine." He stood up. "I'll go call her. There's a session tomorrow and she might want to go. Better tell her." He backed awkwardly out of the room, still talking.

Out in the hallway, dialing the number he heard Bill Dunne say, "Now, what hit him? First he's as droopy as a Salvador Dali watch and then he springs up like a jack-in-the-box."

Mike heard his father laugh in that man of the world way and he cursed all three of them in there, especially Bill Dunne, that fat little pot, bulging out of the blue flannel blazer he affected.

"Mrs. Mayhew please," he said to the oddly accented woman's voice at the other end of the line. Maid, he supposed. Staying with her brother, Minta'd said. Must mean Dudley was out of the Medical Corps, probably married, like to get a look at the kind of woman Dudley might marry, still, the Army might've changed Dud, might even have become a possible mate for a reasonable facsimile of a woman.

While he waited he heard them all laughing and Bill Dunne talking away like a machine gun. Gossip, he thought, that's all they do. Their greatest amusement is tearing their friends to pieces. Just have friends so they can analyze them for hours at a time. And, after ripping them apart it was even more fun to put them back together again with all the guts taken out. You'd think at their age they might begin to act like . . .

There was a noise on the phone but it was only the maid again sounding dubious. Mrs. Mayhew was about to leave the house, could he say who was calling please, she was in a great hurry. Mike gave his name furiously, as he always did, when asked to identify himself to the impersonality of the telephone.

This time it was Sally and the moment he heard her voice he

realized why he could never stand Jean's telephone voice or any other woman's for that matter.

"Darling," she was saying, her voice so rich, warm, husky, and full of caressing overtones, "Mike, I'm terrible. I've been meaning to call you ever since I got back. I knew you were returned from the wars because Dud said he caught a glimpse of you on the street one day although you didn't see him and he didn't . . . Well, never mind all that . . . What have you been doing? It's so good to hear you."

"Good to hear you too," he said, while the gulf of six years yawned wide and impossible and he wondered what the hell to say to her. Why, anyway, now that he thought clearly about it, had she bothered to call him after all this long time without a word, not even one to throw at a dog and the way things had ended between them . . . What d'you want Sally, he ought to say, you never thought of me for six long years, although I thought about you plenty, why bother me now, for what? But her voice melted away the six years and he said jokingly, "Been a damn long time since I heard from you. Didn't you know you were supposed to write to our boys in service?"

"Yes, I was very awful about that," she said contritely. "Always been bad about letters. Was I married the last time you saw me? Oh Lord, I'm so dismally old."

"No. Si wrote me. I was sorry to hear about . . . uh . . . Mayhew. Tough break," he added awkwardly.

"Yes," Sally said and there was a pause. "It happened so close to the end of the war too. It was one of those suicidal kamikaze planes. Made a direct hit, they said, right where he was. Well, dammit, I meant to be cheeful. You're all right, aren't you? Didn't lose anything? Or are you just full of psychic traumas?"

"Sam and Minta think I am," Mike said loudly. "Hemingway told them it's the thing to get from wars. One of my hands was fouled up in Belgium but it's okay now and otherwise I'm all whole and well. What've you been doing in California all this time?"

Satisfiedly, he noted with one ear, that the conversation in the living room had ceased, which must mean they'd heard him.

"I'm terribly well educated now," Sally was saying. "Went to Berkeley and got a B.A. in English. Aren't you impressed?"

"Hey now. Si and Tom will be happy as hell to see you. They're back here too. Working on M.A.'s over in Cambridge. You can all have litry conversations."

"Sounds lovely," Sally drawled. "I'd love to see them. Oh it'll take years to catch up. Are they all married and producing children?"

"Tom is. No children. Si is engaged in a half-ass sort of way."

"You mean he has a mistress?" she said with the old, amused chuckle. "I knew he always wanted one. And you?"

"Celibate," Mike answered briefly. Thanks to you, he thought, or wouldn't you remember. "Where is this place you're staying?"

Sally laughed. "Dudley's now a resident at Bay Colony. He also procured a mangy walkup apartment on Revere Street but apparently found that batching it with only the occasional company of this incomprehensible cleaning woman who greeted you on the phone, was a bore, so he sent for me. I'm to warm his home and hearth. So far, as you can perhaps imagine, it's awfully like living in an igloo. However, it was sort of sheer necessity. I was dreadfully broke and he more or less sent an ultimatum. Oh, he didn't quite state it like that but I'm clever at reading between lines. So far, I'm simply miserably bored."

Ah, so that's it, Mike thought. I'm the straw to be clutched by the bored and disoriented prodigal. But it was no use lying to himself. He did want to see her. Even the sound of her name had made him jump like a schoolboy. And he was different now and so perhaps she was too. Why brood about the irretrievable past? "You might try going back to school," he said, "like all of us veterans. It's the fashionable thing to do this year. Get a graduate degree."

"Perhaps. Although I really don't think I want to. I'm simply not bluestocking material. What I'd like to do is find a job singing. Had one in California just before I was uprooted. Little group, quite bad really, played in all sorts of awful places, terribly shabby and junky the whole thing but sort of fun for me. I always like to sing. But Mike darling, I'm in a fearful rush. I'm to meet my aunt for lunch. When can I see you? I'm free tonight."

"That'd be great," Mike said, thinking quickly and wondering if he broke the date with Jean, but no, it would be impossible and quite unfair, "I'm afraid not," he added regretfully. "I'm unfortunately committed to something else and I see no way out of it. But look Sal, there's a weekly session on at the Bat Club, these days. In fact, you might be able to line up a job contact there. It's tomorrow afternoon and I'm having some cats up beforehand for a few balls. Si and Tom'll be here and some others. About two. Can you come?"

"I reckon you've got a girl," Sally drawled. "What's she like?"

"Just a girl."

"To pass away the time in Venezuela?"

"Right."

"Mmm," Sally said. "Well it would be divine to come to your party but I'm already going to the session. You remember Dick Fitzgerald, Mike, don't you? He closed in on me at the Cinnamon Room the other night and I had to promise I'd go to the session with him and meet him beforehand for a drink."

"Are you," Mike asked sternly, "by any chance, talking about an overbearing, pretentious opportunist named Jazzbo Fitzgerald who writes for the *Tatler?*"

"He did say he was working for a newspaper," Sally said. "I wasn't really listening. Why, what's the matter with him? As I remember him, he was kind of a sweet little college boy and he used to tell me very seriously that I sang almost as well as Billie Holiday and on occasion . . ."

"Well he isn't any more," Mike interrupted flatly. "He stinks. Man, is he awful. You can't go meet him tomorrow Sally. He'll write about you in his nowhere paper."

"I don't see how I can get out of it, darling, much as I'd . . ."

"Bring him up here," Mike interjected decisively. "That way, he'll forget about interviewing you. There'll be people he knows milling around, and free drinks even if it isn't Sam's best bonded bourbon."

"But if you don't like him," Sally said dubiously.

"I hate his guts," Mike said, "but I'd sacrifice anything to see you and save you from his poisoned pen. Come on, baby. He'll be happy as hell to come. Just don't tell him that Sam won't be here."

"I'm afraid," Sally said amusedly, "that I lost track of this conversation sentences ago. Please, Michael, I'm just an alien here now. What has your father's whereabouts to do with . . ."

"The Jazzbo," Mike said, "is a man of parts. He believes in getting places through persistent battering of good connections. To him Sam's an entree into the literary world. He's just itching to get me to introduce him to my old roué parent. Hints around about it every time I see him."

"Does he know you don't like him?"

"Sure," Mike said, "but he has a hide like a stegosaurus."

"Well I guess you love me more than honor," Sally said laughing. "It's very noble and brave of you darling and I'm so glad you warned me. I hope you won't be frightfully rude to him though since I'm to be responsible."

"I won't talk to him," Mike said calmly, "he'll understand."

"See you tomorrow then," Sally said. "I'm looking forward to it."

"Me too," Mike said. He heard the click and hung up.

"We're in the dining room," Minta called. "Everything's ready."

"Coming," Mike said. But he sat for a moment looking at the telephone. She was back and so was he and perhaps this time . . . Aah whatdya doing, he asked himself, waiting for the sunrise? He got up and went in to eat lunch.

"I think," Bill Dunne was saying as Mike slid quietly into his chair, "the funniest part of the whole affair was when Sheila was there in Paris at the beginning of the war, with all those kids on her hands. I mean, my God, there were kids from three or four different marriages there. You know, all in some school or other and had to be gotten back to the States and poor, goddamn Sheila got stuck with the lot of them." He stopped eating chicken and started to count on his fingers, laughing. "There were her two by her third husband who was with the Free Poles in London, and then there was Zephyre, what a hell of a name for a pretty little girl, who was her second husband, Dickie, you remember him, well, Dickie's child by Dottie Sloane."

"Wasn't she that featherbrained heiress who persisted in believing that she could paint?" Araminta interrupted curiously. "And bought that whole gallery outright just to show her amateurish messes?"

Bill nodded. "That's the one. Her father was a beer baron. Well Dottie'd married someone else by that time and was back in the States and Dickie was supposed to have custody or anyway be responsible for Zephyre until she got out of school but he'd been in Italy and got interned there, and poor Sheila was getting frantic cablegrams from Dottie to for Christsake get Zephyre out of France. What a picnic. And there was someone else too, oh yes, there was Sheila's third husband's child by his first wife, who was an Austrian. The boy was an American though because they'd been living over here when he was born and anyway, the father was a naturalized American now I come to think of it."

"What was he doing with the Free Poles then?" Mike demanded contemptuously. They were a lost generation all right he thought disgustedly and not because of what society had done to them but because they were so damn woolly-headed.

"Well, he was born a Pole," Bill Dunne said. "Came from a very good old aristocratic Polish family, in fact. And America wasn't in the war then and he wanted to fight. Anyway, Sheila got all those kids back here but it must have been the wildest embarkation in history, not to mention getting them all to Le Havre, or wherever. It's a wonder her hair didn't turn gray overnight. But she's fantastic. On the trip back with all those children to see to and only one nursemaid, she wrote half her novel, *Strange Midnight*."

"She must've had a lot of them," Mike muttered sourly.

"Huh," Bill Dunne paused, fork in midair. "Oh," he laughed, "I see."

"More wine?" Sam asked. He was smiling. "Pretty witty that boy of mine, eh Bill? In fact, if I understand Mike aright, I agree with him about Sheila. I thought her first stories in the twenties and thirties showed an enormous talent but then she began to overplay her hand. Got too sentimental and Riviera in the chichi season."

The lunch was as continental as Mike had expected. Even an Early American cherry wood table could be transformed, he reflected, by Italian straw place mats and Quimper ware. But he was hungry and he ate quickly, wanting to get out of there.

"Go easy on that wine, boy," his father cautioned him. "It's not beer you know. You don't gulp it."

Mike sent the old gourmet a beetle-browed glance which went unnoticed, deliberately turned his glass practically upside down inside his mouth and poured himself some more.

Araminta brought in the fruit, cheese, and coffee. Bitter Italian coffee of course in demitasse cups and a small bottle of anisette.

Mike refused coffee and cheese and, watching his mother and father and Bill Dunne conscientiously peeling their apples, he took a large one and bit into it with an exaggeratedly gusty crunch.

His mother was recalling the time when they'd been so hungry on the train coming up from Rome and at lunch time they'd stopped in La Spezia and bought a darling little basket lunch from the peddler on the platform; cold chicken and ham and lovely Italian bread and tangerines and this really awful American from Montana, who couldn't speak a word of any language and barely any English really and made absolutely no attempt to, anyway, this fool kept thinking there was a dining car aboard and of course there wasn't. And finally just when the train was ready to pull out of La Spezia, he asked us and we told him he'd better buy something at the station and then there was this terribly funny last minute flurry with him shouting at the boy on the platform, what do you have, and the train was on its way and the Italian of course was looking blank, so mercifully Sam took a hand and leaped to the window, shouting *Panini*, and grabbed the money from this cowboy's hand and threw it and the boy threw one of those sandwiches, you know, half a loaf of bread with cheese and ham inside which Sam caught by some miracle. So this cliché Westerner was fortunately fed. He had an actual ten-gallon hat, I swear, and he wore it. He was going to Monte Carlo of course, to gamble."

24

Mike felt his eyes glazing all through this little colorful vignette of European travel but he munched steadily on his apple, finished it and lit a cigarette.

"Say, Bill," he said politely as soon as soon as his mother paused for breath, "I understand you've been going around talking to young writers. What did you say to them?"

"Well now, Mike," Dunne said, mopping at his mouth with a napkin, "I don't know how much you know about these writers' programs that have sprung up at schools since the war, but it was mighty interesting. I learned a hell of a lot on that trip although I can't say what I saw and heard made me too happy."

"You don't say," Mike said, pursing his lips and nodding sagely. "Why, what's going on?"

"Oh they had a few writers' workshops here and there before the war," Bill Dunne said, leaning back and unbuttoning his jacket, "but they didn't amount to a hill of beans. Of course there was Professor Baker at Harvard but that was playwriting. But you know, after the war, there was the GI Bill and a lot of boys and girls too thought they'd like to be writers, and they found that at some schools, which leaped right into the fray, you see, elaborating their writing programs, they could go to college, get a degree, be taught to write by published writers and get tuition and pay for it, all at the same time. Besides writing, the students read masterpieces of literature and critical analysis of the masterpieces all of which is supposed to teach them how to write a work of correct genius. Then in the weekly workshop meetings, they apply this critical analysis to each other's work which is usually worth about as much as alchemist's gold because they get so critical they don't write. They sit around and eat their own entrails."

"I don't know if that's quite fair, Bill," Sam Wainscott said. "I've seen some of the work put out by graduates, teachers, and students at these schools and a good deal of it is excellent, technically especially, very competent."

"I grant you that," Bill Dunne said shrugging. "I'll even go so far as to say that one quarter of the people there will be writers, maybe no geniuses, but good, solid ones. The rest of them won't. And I'll wager that the good writing will come out only after they've left school. A lot of them don't leave, you see. They stay on and teach Freshman Comp, and they try to write on the side but academic pressures compel them instead to work on an advanced degree and so they do pedantic research instead. I think it kills something in a creative writer when he has to spend all his time reading criticism and teaching it and reading a whole classful of stories every week and judging them."

"You mean he may as well be an editor," Sam Wainscott said ruefully.

"Sure," Bill Dunne said, grinning, "and everybody knows no good editor can write a good, live novel. Besides," he added holding out his demitasse cup so that Minta could refill it, "life on a campus is too sheltered. It's still those cloistered ivy walls no matter how times have changed."

"Yeah, but what did you tell them?" Mike asked loudly. He had taken his toothpick out again and was poking around in his teeth. "Did you tell them they were doing great work or did you tell them they'd never be as good as the Lost Generation?"

"Stop being funny, Mike," his father said crisply.

"I'm not being funny," Mike said. "I'm dead serious. I want to know what he told all those starry-eyed young hopefuls. Did you give them tips on how to be good writers or did you cut them to ribbons by telling them there'd never be another Hemingway?"

Bill Dunne and Sam exchanged glances and Araminta stood up and began to clear the table. Mike looked down at the cigarette he was lighting and, slowly, he brought his bad hand out of his pocket and drew the cigarette from his lips. He waited, his eyes still down, then he heard his mother sigh and her footsteps moving toward the kitchen.

"I don't know what we're all getting so serious about," Bill Dunne was saying cheerfully. "I'll tell you what I told them, Mike, sure, near as I can remember, although you'd get it better if you read my article. I told them that to be a writer is like any other creative activity. A gamble. You can't be sure, but you've got to take chances, believe in yourself, work at it, don't sit around and talk about it. Get around, see the world, see people, and how they act. I told them that it's hard work and lonely work and it doesn't often pay and it's full of disappointments and frustrations and most of the time it's easier to do almost any other kind of job. And as for the Lost Generation, if you're referring to the writers who were young when your father and I were, sure I talked about them. What the hell, I knew them when they were getting started, after a war, just like now, and I said that those men weren't afraid to take chances, they had guts and what's more, I put it to them, pulling no punches, that I didn't think that this generation had the same kind of guts. You kids are all security conscious. You're all spending your youth working toward jobs that'll pay you pensions when you're sixty instead

26

of living while you're young. Now I think there's something wrong with that." He paused and gulped at his coffee, still smiling, but his eyes above the russet apple cheeks were serious.

Mike shook his head. "Seems to me you have a hell of a lot of nerve telling stuff like that to guys who grew up in a depression, graduated into a war and have nothing to look forward to but death by radiation."

"They wanted to know and I told them," Bill Dunne said stubbornly. "And for the most part they took it well." He laughed reminiscently. "Kinda funny. One fella up in back somewhere at one of the Midwestern schools, shouted out, when I was telling them about how we all managed to get over to Europe and live there after the last war, Sounds swell, Bill, but weren't papa and mama paying the passage? That got a big laugh but I squelched that by saying that most of us had no money and a damn sight more opposition from our parents to the idea of expatriation than they did and still we managed to make it. And Uncle Sugar wasn't paying our bills then either."

"So what's Europe," Mike said coldly. "You think you have to live in Europe to get the right kind of experience to be a writer. That's crap and you know it. Look at your favorite man, Faulkner. Stayed right to home in Mississippi. What's the matter with here?"

"No one said the United States was a bad place for a writer," Sam said smoothly. "You have a great knack for distortion, Mike. In those days, Europe was a splendid place for struggling young artists, not only financially but also because there were great men there and a stimulating ferment of new ideas. You have no conception of how hidebound and provincial most of the United States was when we were young. Perhaps Europe is not the same now as it was then. I don't know. So many incredible holocausts have happened there since our time. And yet, many young people are going there now to live, write, and paint. It must still hold some attraction."

"Oh listen," Mike said heatedly, "you people believe that if you don't go helling around drinking absinthe in cafés on the Left Bank and living and talking about La Vie Art, you'll end up a dullard in suburbia feeding your lifeblood into a washing machine. You all think you're pretty sophisticated burning your candle at both ends not only so it won't last the night but so it leaves a stink when it goes out, but good old sentimental, hackneyed, Henry Wadsworth Longfellow, sitting right over there in Cambridge, wrote the worst poem in the world on the same gospel. Art for art's sake and it was just as phony then as it was in the yellow nineties, in your heyday and as it is now."

"He did?" Bill Dunne said pulling his ear and grinning slyly over at Sam. "You mean that art is long life is fleeting balderdash?"

"No, I don't," Mike said. "I mean a poem called 'Excelsior' in which 'the shades of night are falling fast as through an Alpine village passed, a youth who bore mid snow and ice, a banner with a strange device, excelsior.' And this boob is told by everybody in town not to risk his neck in the pass because he'll get clobbered by a storm which is about to set all the glaciers moving and start avalanches and even a girl tries to get him to stay with her in the hay, but on he goes stubbornly, and naturally he's found next morning lifeless but beautiful of course, and still clutching his goddamned dimwitted banner."

"I didn't know that poem had anything to do with art," Bill Dunne said laughing. "Read it as a kid and I always thought it had something to do with God and goodness. Or maybe that's how my teacher explained it. She was a saintly old lady with a tea apron and a pompadour."

"That's the way I work it out," Mike said gruffly, suddenly embarrassed. "It's like Hemingway's leopard in the snows. No one knows what he was seeking at that altitude. It's complicated and mystical." He stopped for a minute, realizing that they were both staring at him as if they'd never seen him before. He knew he ought to shut up altogether because he was betraying himself and not making sense either, not to them certainly. But, although he tried, biting his lips in an effort to stop the words, he couldn't.

"Yes, certainly it has something to do with God," he said, speaking slowly and carefully, his eyes fixed on a row of breadcrumbs he was lining up, "because a person who creates is close to whatever God is. But the higher you climb the farther away from the ground and the realities you get. Without earth to put your feet on, without human warmth near you, the colder and crazier you get, and eventually you die of it. It's too high, too freezing, too pure, too dazzling for mortal eyes or for leopards or for boobs with banners. The best artists and writers and composers and the most holy and truly good men have made it up there and seen a bit and maybe even lived to tell a little but they're as high as they can go and then they freeze to death and it's the end. Now, maybe you cats who pay lip service to genius and creativity might say that brief glimpse of the highest was glory, but for me and the majority of my fellow ants, the price is too great. For everyone who gets to the top and touches the sun, just before he's blinded, there are thousands who've fallen on the lower slopes with stones in their mouths."

"I gather," Bill Dunne said quietly, "that you don't think it's worthwhile even to hike up the foothills."

"No, I don't," Mike said standing up. "In fact, I consider the whole notion almost a death wish. I want to live with my feet on solid ground. I don't believe in the special nature of the artist, or his opium dream they call vision. I don't believe in climbing lonely icy heights with a tattered symbolic banner. I want to stay down in the valley and huddle around in the warmth with the rest of the sheep and eat bread and peanut butter and drink beer and just live out all the life I've got left like an ordinary guy who is glad of his common clay."

"There were some writers," Sam Wainscott said sharply, "who managed to scale the heights and yet keep in touch with humanity and the earth. Shakespeare for one."

"Are you going to tell me he was happy?" Mike asked incredulously. "The guy who wrote *Lear* was happy? Besides he was a genius. For every ten thousand who delude themselves there's one genius."

"Happiness!" his father exclaimed contemptuously. "How the hell do you know what it is? You don't, can't, because it's an utterly individual matter, because we're all, still, thank God, born unique, in spite of timid skrimshankers, like you, who yearn for the herd. And of course, you presume, in your halfbaked manner to know whether Shakespeare was happy or not, when, to scholars who've spent their lives immersed in him and his work, he remains an unrecorded mystery. But, naturally," he added, twisting his lips, "I was forgetting that you know all. There's one thing you don't know though, with all your huckster talk about happiness, and that is, that to try to stamp out an essentially God-given talent is ruinous, not to anyone else, but to yourself. I've told you before that I thought you had such a talent. A way of using words, of creating life on paper. I knew it needed development but that it was definitely there and might be miraculously good someday. Instead of working on it, you're fighting it, making a criminal mistake. Because if you crush that ability and force yourself into another way of life for whatever crazy, stubborn reason, you will wake up one day when it's too late, all cold and dead inside, no matter how warm and comfortable you are on the outside. You'll ignore what I say now, no doubt, with your smug let's-all-be-well-adjusted-kids-in-the-ingroup-together assurance, but you wait."

In the sudden dead silence that followed, Mike, struggling against an overmastering impulse to pick up something (in fact his hand had closed tight on an apple) and fling it at his father, noticed that Dunne had left the room, presumably in decent embarrassment and that Minta was standing in the doorway, looking pained.

"Sam," she said warningly. "Don't relapse into senile Victorianism, please. Mike must live his own life."

"I know," Sam said in a grim, subdued voice. "But what good is all the living I've done if I can't transmit a simple fact to him? I found out early what I was. He's older and hasn't any idea. By the time he does it'll be too late. I've had a good life because I was lucky enough to know in time who Sam Wainscott was and what suited him. All I want is, well, something of the same for him."

"Listen," Mike yelled, outraged, "don't try to talk over my head as if I were two years old. It's damn decent of you, Sam, to keep dreaming that I have talent. The only trouble is, all this concern comes too late. I'm glad you consider you've had a good life if it helps you but you were so absorbed in living it you didn't give a damn about mine. And that's just the point. God-given talent for Christ's sake! You all believe desperately in that, don't you? You'd be out of business if you didn't. You'll keep right on mouthing these outworn shibboleths because it's too late for you to be honest. To look around and see millions of trashy, pretentious, empty books, remaindered for twenty cents, carted away for pulp, the imbecilic daubs on canvas multiplying rapidly all over the country as more people can afford to buy paint and brushes and the refuse from the junk heap and the magpie's nests that's called sculpture, all vomited forth by God-given talents, for you to look around, I repeat and see all this mass delusion for what it is, would kill you. It's too late for you. But not me. I don't want to live a vicarious dream in some bad book I write. Or spend my days in some pawnshop fantasy of fame while real life passes me by. The hell with it. At least my kids, if I have any, will know that their old man didn't just spawn them into the world and then forgot about them while he went helling off in pursuit of a batch of raddled, overpainted muses."

Nobody said anything at all and Mike walked out the door, turning around to add in a now conventional, controlled voice, "Well, *arrivederci*, as they say in La Spezia, have a good weekend."

Two

          Up in his room Mike pushed the dormer windows wide and leaned out, looking down at the sloping tumble of roofs and chimneypots, flowered backyard gardens, jumble of brick and Bulfinch, cobble and church spire and Georgian, quaint historical landmark spiraling down to meet the river; old brown, garnet and gold city like a landscape done in aquatint and smoke. A view of Bruges or was it Delft? No, not enough yellow although the light was Dutch enough. The pale, blue spring sky ballooned around him and the sun was warm on his head. It was better than Paris.

Sam and Minta had moved into this house when he was eighteen and he had imperviously overridden their protests about how important it was for him to live at college, left his third of a suite at Eliot House cheerfully and commandeered this attic room for his first, only, and permanent home. He'd painted the plaster walls himself and furnished the place with pieces from his Grandmother Wainscott's house in Stockbridge. Araminta, after remarking plaintively how strange it was to have a son who actually *liked* the silver cord had, in unwontedly motherlike style, made some yellow curtains for the room and shopped around for weeks to find a rug of a brilliant burnt-orange color. Mike, who'd merely wanted any old rug to put his bare feet on when he got out of bed, had protested that the color didn't matter.

"This is basically my house," Araminta had retorted, "and even if I never go into your room, just knowing that, above my head, is a stark, monastic, totally white-walled cell, simply reeking of poverty and abstinence and full of battered old furniture that your father used to death when he was a boy, will give me cold chills. You would probably prefer to sleep on a straw pallet on a stone floor but you won't do it in my house."

And now, after nine years, there lay the rug as bright and warm as a cannel coal fire and there, by the window was a scarred, inkstained pine desk which had been Sam's and the curtains, still a jaunty yellow although somewhat limp and, jammed into a big, old, Victorian mahogany bookcase that would be worth his life to move, a microcosm of books. Childhood favorites, like E. Nesbit, John Masefield, *Wind in the Willows*, *Knights of the Golden Spur*, all of Stevenson, Carroll, Kipling, Cooper, Arthur Ransome, all of the books illustrated so sumptuously by N. C. Wyeth and Howard Pyle from *King Arthur* to *Robin Hood* and accounts of the Lafayette Escadrille and World War I aces, were on the upper shelves while the lower ones reflected his undergraduate courses and changing literary tastes. Last year Minta had given him another, more modern bookcase and he had made an attempt to arrange some of his books in sequence, starting out bravely with several volumes of the *History of English Literature*, then *Canterbury Tales*, Shakespeare, Donne, Milton, but about that time, he'd realized there'd be no place for his law books, and there were always new volumes coming in, so he'd given up and the new bookcase had become as disorderly as the old one and now there were even books stacked on the floor.

It seemed to him, looking around his room now, cataloguing all its familiar items that, indeed nothing, after nine years had changed, and yet he knew that the air of permanent reassurance in his attic was spurious. He was different now, and because of this, Sam and Minta, for the first time in his life, seemingly, were reacting to him, disapprovingly, it was true, but nevertheless, he aroused some response. Before the war, it seemed, their whole attitude had been one of distance, of carefully controlled sanitary unemotionalism which manifested itself in seeing that he was kept as far away from them as possible, as if they were plague carriers who might infect him dangerously if he got anywhere near them. Only once, before he went into the Army, had Sam come close to indicating a sort of angry concern, but that had been short-lived. Now, however, since he'd returned from the wars, so obviously become a dull, middle-class type, their disappointment was very apparent. Right this minute, downstairs, they were probably discussing him and without any mental effort at all, he knew how the dialogue sounded. Sam would be saying that he thought Mike must be retarded going to jam sessions just as he'd done at twenty, sneaking girls in on weekends when they were away (he'd never told them, of course, but keen to sin as they were, they had guessed about Jean), living at home at his age, Sam'd be snorting. Why he should get an apartment of his own, he should be married, but that would be too much of a risk for him to take. My

God, he's the most cautious, cagy, conservative kid I've ever run across and my son to boot.

Mike sat down in the big, fat, overstuffed easy chair by the book-case and lolled, remembering how sometimes in the Army, in barracks and ruined buildings, in tents and hospitals and holes in the ground, dirty, sick, and scared, stiffening up his sinews without respite, surrounded by many men in the same condition, he'd thought about his attic room on Mount Vernon Street and it had seemed then, a haven of quiet and beauty, that he would not live to see again. And yet, he had survived, through many miracles. He'd made it, he was here, with everything he cared about right around him, he was happy and he didn't want to move for years. Boston was a great city and, after a peripatetic childhood and four years of being pushed around in the war's chess game, if he never traveled again it would suit him fine. Make no moves, he thought, volunteer for nothing, turn no pages in the book of Mike Wainscott. No commitments, no marriages, no apartment hunting, no packing or unpacking, no search for clay-footed high adventure. "Soldiers are citizens of death's gray land," Siegfried Sassoon had written, "drawing no dividend from time's tomorrows." Yes, Mike thought, in defiant, silent answer to Sam, but now, I have my dividend. I've been saved, Sam, with plenty of tomorrows and I'm going to relax and wallow in them.

He looked at his watch and remembered then, with a wry grimace, the particularly unrelaxed tomorrow he'd just let himself in for. Never should've called Sally, dammit! Just knowing she was back in town, that he'd be seeing her tomorrow and again, after that, perhaps many times, would wreck his evening with Jean. He'd be thinking of Sally and the whole night'd be lousy and Jean would catch on. Then don't think about it addlepate. But it was no use. The whole thing had started up in him again the moment he'd heard Sally's incantative voice.

And he remembered her as he sat there, staring abstractedly at his scarred hand, that symbol of his adulthood, not only Sally and how he'd loved her that painful year but also, with relentless clarity, the young, inept Mike of six and a half years ago. He saw himself and all of them, Sally, Ben Merritt, Si, Dudley, Tom Baring, as if, like Ben, they were all no longer living but frozen forever in bronze, life-size figures on a memorial frieze, caught in a moment of time, that crazy, desperate year, the first year of the war.

In the fall of that year when he was a junior and there was the draft and Pearl Harbor was two months away, Mike was damn fed up with the war in Europe just from listening to Sam and Minta mourning about Paris being defiled by the Nazis. He was tired of hearing news bulletins blasting forever on the radio, tired of Sam fruitlessly pulling strings to get over as newspaper or magazine war correspondent, and irritated beyond endurance by Sam's conviction that America would enter the war and that, therefore, Mike should try to avoid the draft by joining the Field Service. Well that was how Sam had put it, draftdodging, but it'd been perfectly clear to Mike that his father expected all good Hemingway kids, the minute they heard the blast of a trumpet, to drop all their boring sober-sided peace-time pursuits and run fast as their legs could carry them, to the nearest war and glory. But not in any mundane way, in badly fitting olive drab with sergeants barking at you and the Articles of War hanging over your head. No. With style and glamour and hell's own amount of dash.

"You get drafted and stuck in the infantry, boy," Sam'd warned, "you'll take guff from the officers and get your head blown off before you've had time to memorize your rank and serial number. Volunteer for the Field Service. I know some people who can help you. You'll see enough action, be doing something worthwhile and you might even live."

The old fancy uniform, ambulance act, Mike'd thought disgustedly, he wants me to get in on it too. "Well, gee Sam," he'd said innocently, "I was kinda thinking of volunteering for the Air Force if we do go to war. I mean, this war, I think that's the romantic place to be."

Sam hadn't thought this a bit funny since, according to him, a flier's life was more dangerous than that of a foot soldier and demanded a small amount of mechanical and mathematical ability which Mike did not have. This discussion had been terminated by Minta's rushing in soothingly to say that surely if Mike was drafted they wouldn't waste all his knowledge of languages and Europe in the infantry and Sam had, typically, retorted with magnificent irony that, certainly not. They would put Mike in Intelligence because he knew so much and parachute him behind enemy lines and that would be the end of him, a damn fool who wouldn't take advice.

In order to avoid that kind of talk and the spectacle of Sam being glum because he couldn't sit in his trench coat drinking brandy and braving the blitz with morituri te salutamus quips, Mike had begun to spend a lot more of his free time at Harvard. In his sophomore year he'd been seized by inspiration, and as soon as his classes had been over and any necessary library studying done, he'd taken

34

off for Mount Vernon Street, his typewriter and his great future as poet and short story writer. But, in the fall of '41, with his creative frenzy somewhat abated and his ivory tower room assaulted by the sounds of Adolf Hitler, Winston Churchill, and Franklin Roosevelt calling for action on the radio, he'd discovered that he was wandering around Harvard as friendless as the melancholy legend of the guy who'd called Reinhardt. Not that he'd ever been a social specimen. By the age of twenty he'd gotten accustomed to this difficulty, this basic shyness of his, which overwhelmed him with people and caused him to withdraw instead of pressing forward; why the hell would anyone want to know a misfit like him who couldn't even articulate a commonplace without tripping over his tongue? Of course, he'd had a few friends at Andover. Once he got used to people he was fine but most of those guys had gone to other colleges and Dick Samuels who'd come to Harvard with him had left at the end of their sophomore year. Dick had been his best friend. Wanted to be a writer too but had decided that writers needed vast experience in all kinds of living in order to write and that going to college was a waste of time. Mike had lost touch with the few men he'd known in Wigglesworth and Eliot when he'd lived there and didn't care and so except for some nodding, class-conversation acquaintances, he was damnably lonely.

One red and gold October day when, leaf-like and autumnally depressed, he was drifting down the steps of Widener Library and wondering if, in order to emerge from this inhuman vacuum he was living in, he oughtn't to volunteer for the Marines, or the Army Air Force, or come back to live at Harvard or join Dick Samuels on the bum and knowing he didn't want to do any of those and above all bursting to talk, he caught sight of a guy named Tom Baring who'd sat next to him in Contemporary Poetry, sophomore year. They'd exchanged words about assignments and notes, a few cracks about Ezra Pound and the instructor's veneration of him and Baring, who looked kind of like a grownup Boy Scout, tall, blond, regular-featured with a flat, clear, Midwestern voice and a happy smile, seemed intelligent and friendly enough when they talked but as soon as the class ended, he'd shoot out the door in a tearing hurry. Once they were discussing Laura Riding, just before class started and when they had to break off at the entrance of their instructor Mike, surprised and pleased to find another person who had read her poetry, had suggested they have coffee afterwards and talk some more, an unusually outgoing move for him and one that he regretted immediately. Baring had said very politely that he'd like to but he

had a job and perhaps some other time. And that had been it because Mike, feeling guilty and lazy with Sam paying his bills, figured
that a working student probably had better things to do with his
time than frivoling it away talking about obscure lady poets. But this
outcast day, seeing Baring again, providentially in his path, he determined to try again and advanced purposefully down the steps toward him, setting his face into a convivial grimace which withered
when he realized that Baring was in company. Quick as a flash Mike,
never one to intrude himself as the awkward third, lifted his arm in
lazy salute, and was about to pass on when Baring stopped him with
what seemed like a genuinely warm hello and introduced him to
the tall, spindle-shanked, bat-eared, odd-looking type who was with
him.

"My roommate, Si Hunnicutt. He's been wanting to meet you."

"Me!" Mike was genuinely astonished. Why this Si character who
looked like the living embodiment of the bumpkin schoolmaster,
Ichabod Crane, should want to meet him, was a mystery.

"You didn't tell me the cat thinks he's a leper," Ichabod said
merrily to Tom, "I just thought he was a poet."

"Absolutely." Tom Baring grinned at Mike's obvious puzzlement.
"A true one. Sat in Cloud-Cuckoo Land all semester scribbling great
verse instead of notes and never realized I was reading over his
shoulder. I liked the stuff that came out in the *Scrivener*," he added
turning to Mike, "especially since I'd seen some of it in process of
creation but I never mentioned it to you. Since I was eavesdropping
it didn't seem fair."

Mike writhed inwardly a little during this conversation, particularly
since some of the early drafts of those poems he'd been writing in
class contained some embarrassingly personal material which he had
later pruned out. He managed however to mumble his thanks and
then, impelled by his loneliness, blurted out his dissatisfaction with
the editors of the *Scrivener*, perversely determined as they were to
reject his best work and print only the stuff he thought fourthrate.

"Wainscott," Si Hunnicutt intervened briskly, "say no more. God
has listened to your plea and sent me to rescue you from those
latter-day dodos. I"—and he drew himself up grandly till he looked
like an attentuated whiskbroom—"am, this year, on the editorial
board and I think your woodnotes wild are the best things to appear
on its pages in aeons. And if you think what they've printed is
lousy I am ravening to see what you think is good. Do you have
anything on hand now?"

Cautiously, Mike admitted that two complete poems were even

then in his possession, and although he thought they might still need some polishing, if Si wanted to see them . . .

"Killer," Si said heartily and incomprehensibly. "We'll go over to your house and read them."

"It'll have to be a beer joint, I'm afraid," Mike said diffidently. "I don't live over here."

"Christ no, Wainscott, that won't do. It'd be an insult to any writer to read his work in all that sophomoric racket."

"We'll have to use our pad then," Tom Baring said, "since you're so full of standards. Though you won't get much time there."

Si flailed his long windmill arms around indignantly. "Baring, for Godsakes, it's the middle of the week. How the hell could that chick manage to get out of school in the middle of the week? I mean, on weekends, well, I'm human too, I can manage to cut out for a few hours on the Lord's day, but if he's going to start bringing her in during the week . . . it's just the bloody damn end. Feet must be put down. On his butt preferably."

"She got it fixed up somehow," Tom said calmly. "I don't dig it myself but that's what he told me last night. He wants the rooms from three to five. I've been meaning to tell you."

"So as the feller said, the very rich 'are different from you and me' and innocent as I was, I never believed it till now. Look," Si appealed to Mike who stood by baffled but intrigued, "you're an old Bostonian, aren't you? Do all your best families have these bad cases of overactive libidos?"

"Never mind," Tom cut in, "it's sour grapes, sport. If you were Sally's boy all your roommates would be living in the subway station. Come on, we might as well go over there now. We've only got about an hour and a half."

"Well look," Mike said hurriedly, "I don't know what this is all about but I don't want to put anyone out over a few poems, I mean. You could always read them in the library or some other time. I mean, there's no hurry."

"The hell there isn't," Si said firmly. "I want to show my hand on that magazine, pronto. Anyhow, we live there too. We pay rent, plebeian as we are, and besides, you ought to get a gander into this situation. It's not every day a poet can run into something Faulknerian like this."

"You're dramatizing, Si," Tom said as they walked along toward Lowell House. "I roomed with Ben for a semester last year and he's a good joe. Just that he's got a lot of miserable problems."

"Okay," Si said resignedly, "it's just a nice, sweet, star-crossed love situation, normal as apple pie, with that ghostly brother of hers thrown in for added flavor. The hell with it. Only one of these days I'm going to tell him that I'd like to study on occasion and if he wants to screw his first cousin, seventeen times a week, he'd better get himself a single room."

All along, Mike was wondering why he'd never seen Hunnicutt around before, because with a face and personality like that, he'd be hard to miss and it came out that Si had spent a year at Tufts, his father's old college, before transferring to Harvard, where he'd had to start all over again as a freshman.

"So," Tom Baring said, "in spite of all his inveighing against sophomoric behavior he's still one of them."

"I'm two years older," Si said huffily.

"I don't know if I'd ever've transferred if it meant beginning all over again," Mike said dubiously. "I mean other schools are probably as good."

"Come come, Wainscott. You're uttering heresy. No you're probably right but you see my old man's a doctor and I was slated to inherit the family stethescope. So I go to his college and I'm in premed and one day, I read "Ode to a Nightingale" for my Eng. Comp. and Lit. class and I am sent way out. A sandbag of doubt hits me on the head and I realize that biology, chemistry and kindred witchcraft leaves me trembling with ennui, whereas, 'Forlorn, the very word is like a bell,' freezes me to my seat, and I decide to bow out. Flourish of trumpets. Hunnicutt then decides if he's going to study literature it had better be in the grand manner. Of course my father didn't like my switching but after some thought he realized that the human race'd be better off if I did."

Once they'd climbed the stairs to the third-floor suite, taken off jackets and disposed of books, Si clapped a pair of enormous black-rimmed glasses on his long, pointed nose and disappeared into the bedroom to read Mike's poems. Tom went out somewhere and Mike, sitting uneasily at one of the three desks in the study, wondered what the hell possessed him, handing over his most intimate thoughts, his poetry, that way to this total stranger, this breezy fellow who seemed to have no scruples at all. Glad I'm not his roommate, Mike thought. I'd hate to have him discuss my sex life so publicly. Not that he'd had any at that point, still, Si probably would've considered that strange too.

Now how long did it take to read two poems anyway? The funny bastard was probably doubled up in there, laughing himself sick. Mike cursed Si under his breath and vowed to himself that it was the last goddamn time he'd give anything he'd written to anyone, personally. Hereafter, he'd just hand it in to the *Scrivener* office or mail it out. No waiting around for reactions.

In the midst of all these distraught sensitivities, he suddenly noticed a photograph on one of the desks. It was a snapshot of a girl in a bathing suit, standing by a dinghy at the edge of some body of water. Her long fair hair was blown back by the wind and a lovely smiling face was tilted up to the sun. He picked up the photograph and was inspecting it closely when Tom Baring came back.

Mike, embarrassed at being caught snooping, dropped the framed picture back on the desk hastily and tried to make a joke. "Who's this junior Venus de Milo belong to? Lucky old Si?"

Tom laughed. "Si wouldn't be in there perusing your poems man, if she were his girl. He'd be running around in a circle chasing his tail and yipping. No, that's our other roommate Ben Merritt's girl, Sally. Sally Brimmer, the one Si's making all the noise about Ben taking up here. Isn't she a beauty?"

"Sally Brimmer," Mike repeated slowly. "You know, I've heard that name before but I can't remember where."

"Oh sure," Tom said casually. "If you've been around Boston much you probably have. Well-known old family I gather. Perhaps you know her brother. He's over at the Med School now but he used to live in the house here. Or, if you dig jazz you might've seen her at some of the sessions. She sings sometimes. Pretty fine style. Real feeling."

Si came out of the bedroom just then and Mike found that, contrary to his supersensitive expectations, Si's attitude was refreshingly and honestly critical.

"Not bad, Wainscott, though a trifle eclectic. For instance, I definitely trace overtones of Eliot in this one on music, impressions, I gather, of a girl singing."

"Oh yes," Mike remembered writing it during the summer when his parents had a cottage on the Cape and he'd been attracted to the daughter of a nearby family, an affection which the girl hadn't noticed and he hadn't expressed. He'd walked along the beach and thought of the girl and of the mermaids not singing to him and had turned it around till he'd gotten a wish fulfillment in his poem: a mermaid with the face of this girl singing to him. A stupid concept and he'd almost forgotten the girl. How could one remember anything that never really happened?

"You know," Si was saying, "there's nothing like a little frustrated desire to help out a poem, I always say. Hmm, I could probably do a whole paper on that subject. What d'you say, Tom?"

"It's been done. By other crackpots."

"I'm not very original really," Mike said. "In fact, I *was* reading Eliot at that time."

"Nobody is when they start out," Si said paternally. "But these are good anyway. The one about Cape Ann in the hurricane is tremendous and not at all derivative. I'll take both of them if I may and rush them into print for the next issue. And you can now classify me as a genuine admirer, with some reservations, of course. So anytime you have more I'd like to see them."

"What kind of reservations?" Mike asked curiously. This flip character who had grasped the deliberately obscure essence of his music poem was not only keen to literary nuances but also uninhibited enough to disclose some truths about the general nature of his work.

"Wouldn't be Si if he didn't have reservations," Tom the mediator said, with a smile.

"Sure," Si agreed quickly. "I'm supercritical constantly. Means nothing. Part of my style. Even had reservations about being born, I've been told. Everybody was damned annoyed with me, I took so long."

"You don't have to be polite," Mike said. "I'd really like to know what throws you off about my stuff."

"I can't help it if the cat is too aware of overtones," Si said, interpreting a warning grimace from Tom. He turned to Mike. "Well, since you ask, I think there's a kind of painful inwardness in all the poems. Uh, it's, if you'll forgive my saying so, as if you see life as a bad dream because you don't want to know any other way of seeing it."

"Hell," Tom protested. "That's his vision. If that's the way he sees things, that's it."

Si shook his head. "No that's not what I mean. I wouldn't question if it were just that. It's kind of, as if . . . oh hell! There's practically a smugness, as if he says, I stop here and what's beyond this can't be worth my while and I think the boy's too talented for that type of fearful, self-imposed limitation. The stuff's a little too isolated and, what the hell's the word that super-intellectual friend of yours uses, Tom? Orgone?"

"Arcane," Tom said, grinning, "which you very well know. Don't play the hayseed with me."

"Anyway," Si said, ignoring Tom's gibe, "I like your work now but I think it will just peter out if it keeps on that way and with your talent it'd be a crime."

Mike thought of saying, well, thanks a lot and what do you suggest I do about it, before completing a dignified exit when the outer door banged open and the room was suddenly feverishly noisy with the arrival of a large, muscular whirlwind who was Ben Merritt.

Ben had obviously been drinking and just as plainly it had not made him happy. He acknowledged Si's introduction of Mike with a brief handshake and an unintelligible mutter, threw his books contemptuously on the floor and sank into the only armchair after producing from the pocket of his dirty white corduroy pants a pint of blended rye whiskey which he silently offered around. When the bottle had been returned after some polite sipping, Ben tipped his head back and took a long swallow. A trickle of whiskey ran down his unshaven chin and he rubbed at it carelessly with the back of his hand.

So this, Mike thought, with a ridiculous jealousy, is that girl Sally's guy; and then, why not, he's the male animal incarnate, and he looked, with the sullen resentment of the cerebral male, at this superb physical specimen and thought, why dammit, he looks like he might be a boxer or a truckdriver or a longshoreman, anything but a Harvard junior, cousin to a girl from an old Boston family which must mean he is too.

"Do any of you have money?" Ben asked suddenly. His voice and accent, Mike noted, were completely, identifiably Boston-Harvard, and yet there was a strange, almost undetectable nuance in the familiar, patterned speech, a kind of actor's overemphasis, so perfect that it was almost a mockery.

"I ask," Ben continued moodily, "because I'm to meet Sally in half hour and I haven't two cents. If neither of you has it could you possibly pass the hat around because the hellish alternative would be my goddamn cousin Dudley."

"You mean to say you're going to go all the way over to the Med School and pull Dud out from the insides of a cadaver just to touch him for money?" Si inquired sardonically. "Christ, you must be desperate."

"I don't have to go anywhere," Ben said sullenly, shooting a dark glance at Si. "The gummy bastard was up here awhile ago looking for me, but I was warned in time and took off. What a hell of a note, having him turn up here today, just when Sally's coming. It's one of those rotten coincidences that today was the Haddock's anniversary lunch and, naturally, being a paid-up member in good standing he wouldn't miss it, or an opportunity to check up on me. I'm damn tired of seeing that long, psalm-singing face and listening to his pompous advice and sermons on how I'm making a mess of things and hurting my mother. And the hypocrisy of him. Pretending he's concerned about me. Why we've always hated each other's guts. But every chance he gets now he sneaks back here to spy on me so he can report to my stepfather. I know he does. There's no other way that old spider could be so disastrously well-informed about me. I've cut classes all day," Ben added savagely, "and run around trying to borrow money. You people are my last resort. If I can't get it from you I'll be forced to ask him and God, he might follow me down here and of course I can't let him know that Sally's here. He'll know something's up and it will ruin everything. And I don't want anything to go wrong. Not today. Of all days." And Ben slumped back, his head drooping, his arms folded, his eyelids closed, the very picture of a bound Gulliver, hopelessly beaten by the Lilliputian nastiness of a world he never made.

In spite of his instinctive, envious dislike of Ben Merritt, Mike found himself unwittingly moved by the kind of simple, naked intensity of the guy's outburst. At first glance, Mike thought ironically, Ben seemed the least likely candidate for anyone's sympathy. Certainly no man ought to feel sorry for one so physically well-endowed and yet, when one looked at him more attentively, it was easy to see that Ben's damnable handsomeness was dissipated by a small, weak, petulant mouth, that his perfect man's body housed childish emotions and that his looks and physical strength were of no use to him whatsoever in coping with the more crafty and subtle varieties of human intelligence. Interested spectator that he was, Mike looked interrogatively to Tom and Si for guidance, but found none. Tom appeared depressed and compassionate but silent and Si, peering at Ben over the tops of his tented fingers like an impervious judge, bland.

"Not that I want to disillusion you, Ben," Si said coolly after a short, uncomfortable silence, "but even if you should demean yourself to ask Dud for money, I doubt if he'd give it to you. Why waste your time? And neither Tom nor I have a cent to spare. It's too close to the end of the month, man. The whole house'll be broke. This is a hell of a time to borrow money."

Ben heaved himself up in the chair and leaned forward, elbows on knees, nursing the half-filled whiskey bottle between his huge hands. The expensive, gray, cashmere sweater he was wearing looked effete on his cofferdam chest, the wool pulled tight across the shoulders and arms. He got up and began to pace back and forth, running his hand through a tangled mass of dark, curly hair. The room seemed to shrink away to the size of a cage and Ben was the restless beast prowling, full of a furious and barely restrained power.

"Dudley has money," Ben said bitterly, kicking any books and wastebaskets in his path. "Dudley always has money. And why wouldn't he? He never spends it on anything, the cosy bastard. Did you ever see him take out a girl?" he demanded suddenly, whirling on Tom and Si who were staring at him now with outright curiosity. "No, and I'll tell you why. Because he's a walking coffin nail and no girl, of her own free will, would go out with him. And yet, he has more money than anyone, rich as Croesus, just like my stepfather, both of them blasted pinchpennies." He stumbled over a sofa pillow, fallen off the couch and booted it viciously against the door. "My mother would give me more money but he won't let her, that damnable, stinking husband of hers. And it's not his money, it's my mother's. He has no right to it. And because of him, I'm made to look ridiculous and everyone thinks that there's something the matter with me that I have to go around with my hand out all the time. And don't you think that my stepfather and Dudley don't make every effort to see that's what everyone thinks." He stopped, glaring around at them and took a long thirsty swallow from his pint bottle. "Do you know," he said, his voice suddenly quiet and sad, "if I don't get some money I can't take Sally out tonight. I haven't even a clean shirt for Godsakes. No money to get my laundry out. Been walking around all day like this, while all the supercilious bastards who've never seen chest hair before, raised their eyebrows. I could take Sally to eat in the Dining Hall but where can I take her afterwards? She'd like to dig the band at the Congo tonight. I know she would. Getting her out of that caterwauling school wasn't easy but I had to do it. I had to see her and tell her and now dammit we'll have to sit in the station."

"Tell her what, Ben?" Tom intervened gently.

Ben rubbed his forehead dazedly and frowned as if he'd forgotten what had been said and then, looking suspiciously at Si and Mike, shook his head. "Dudn't matter now. Tell you too, Tom. Later. Ah, Sally's a wonderful girl. She's sit in the station but I don't want her to."

"Why the hell do you have to sit in a station waiting room when you have a car?" Si demanded bluntly.

Ben thought for a moment and then said dejectedly, "No gas."

Tom got up. "You go take a shower, Ben," he advised kindly.

43

"I'll get your laundry out. Give me the ticket. I can dig up enough for that."

"Well," Si said casually, stretching his arms over his head, "I guess the only thing I can do is go borrow some money from John Dudley Brimmer, that Midas cousin of yours. I won't tell him it's for you. You can pay me when you get your stipend and I'll pay him."

"That's the boy," Tom said encouragingly. "If anyone can do it, you can."

"God yes," Ben Merritt's face became almost happy. "Why didn't I think of that before. You're the only one he acts halfway human to. I don't know how you do it."

"The only way to deal with a clam," Si said merrily, "is to steam him open. Works every time. Will ten be enough? Never mind, I'll make it twenty."

"God what a relief," Ben Merritt exclaimed and went off to take his shower, leaving Mike alone again. Logically, he knew he ought to leave. He'd concluded his business with Si and there was no further reason for sticking around. But that one brief glimpse of Ben Merritt and his attendant woes had fascinated Mike. And most of all, he wanted, if at all possible, to meet the girl in the photograph and find out why her name was so familiar. I could wait a few minutes more, he thought shamefacedly. It wouldn't be right to go without saying goodbye to Si and Tom anyhow.

"Mission accomplished," Si announced on his return, bouncing briskly into the armchair. "Twenty smackers given over without a word or a question. It's not such a much to you, Wainscott, because you don't know the cat but wait till you see him. John Dudley Brimmer is the last living relic of the Ice Age. The priceless part of the whole thing, of course, is that he gave me the money to furnish his cousin whom he really despises, with the wherewithal to wine and dine and furnish sexual refreshment for his sister, the latter to occur in this very room," he glanced at his watch, "in approximately forty-five minutes with little, if any, buildup or I don't know two oversexed characters when I see them. And the cream of the jest as it were is that the lender of these useful moneys doesn't even know his sister is in town for these purposes and it is precisely for these perverse reasons that I took the beggarly job on. Not because I want to further the path of true love like noble old Tom. No, it appeals to all the rotten, pandering instincts I have."

Mike glanced around uneasily.

"Oh he won't hear me," Si assured him. "The shower's going. He's standing under the cold water trying to sober up. Isn't he something?

Not a brain in his head. Everything he's got is concentrated in his pants. Tom sees him as a misguided scion of wealth, a victim of a terrible childhood. Ben himself could give you all the details any time you'd want them. He's always feeling sorry for himself, but in reality, whatever happens to him is his own fault. You know, he was on the football team for the last two years, but the dumb sonovabitch can't even keep in training. Gets drunk all the time and his academic record is terrible. So they warned him and finally this year they pitched him off the team. Tom started coaching him in English and history last year which is why he rooms here but as a student he is nowhere. Now watch, he'll come out of the shower naked as when he emerged from the womb because he's just the kind of fool who always forgets to take a towel to the bathroom. At least that's what he says. My theory is that he's nothing but a blatant exhibitionist. So at least once a day, everyone is treated to the sight of his marvelous physique which gives him the upper hand, he thinks, over us badly built boys who can at least pass an exam. I think it's a family trait myself because Sally's the same way."

"She's very lovely," Mike said nodding toward the photograph. "Is she like him?"

"Oh she's got more brains," Si said. "Only she takes care not to let them show. But that's all she bothers to conceal. God!"—he lay back in his chair and lolled his tongue out for a moment—"she really is a lush piece. I mean, my God, she's about seventeen or something ridiculous like that and the only men who don't break out in a sweat over her are very far gone queers. The thing is, she's got everything. You know, charm, sophistication, wit, style, personality, a beautiful voice, a beautiful body, a sensational face, money, brains, breeding, ah what the hell, a terrific woman. But it's almost impossible to explain her because then you'd have to explain her passion for this musclebound cousin of hers and that would lead us further into the swampy morass of that whole, screwed up family including her godawful brother. No, I guess the best thing is just to see her."

"I'd like to," Mike said, trying not to sound too eager.

"Hm," Si looked amused. "If a mere picture can stun you what will the real thing do? I suppose it's the extra sensitivity of the poet. Well, stick around, Wainscott. If you dig the true jazz mayhap we could contrive to run into them over at the Congo tonite." Sensing Mike's bewilderment he added airily, "Dixieland, man, boogie, blues, Bixe, Louis, Bessie, and all like that."

"I'm afraid I don't know much about popular music," Mike

said apologetically. "I mean, I've heard Glenn Miller and Artie Shaw . . ."

"That's just dance music," Si'd interrupted, "commercial stuff. Now the Congo is a hep little spot over on Columbus where they have a little three-piece group and all the good musicians from the big bands going through town come over and sit in after hours. Perfect place for you to get educated. How about it? Of course," he grinned, a trifle maliciously, "Tom'll think it smacks of horning in on Ben's date but they won't notice anyway. Too busy feeling each other up under the table."

And that had been the beginning. After two years of a dreamy social isolation at Harvard, suddenly, in the space of one autumn afternoon and evening, he'd moved out of the detached and fearful world of his imagination, out onto a stage, into a play and he had been one of the leading actors.

The music had started it. The moment he heard those loud, wild, free trumpet notes falling like a shower of bright, poignant arrows all over the little, dark cave of a club, that night, he got tremendously excited. And Si, watching him, smiled and said, "You got the call, boy, you're a righteous man."

In the uninhibited warmth of this blue and smoky world Mike found a kind of beauty and passion which had heretofore been his only when he was writing. He was all relaxed and rocking with the music and Si and Tom were two guys he wished to hell he'd known years ago and in between sets they were all talking their heads off about every damn thing under the sun, particularly this new, marvelous stuff, this jazz of which Mike knew nothing but was avid to learn and drinking immense amounts of beer, getting so thirsty from talking, when suddenly he saw Ben Merritt come in with the girl in the photograph. Ben and Sally came and sat at their table and Mike was introduced and while he was still saying How do you do, he not only remembered where he'd seen her before but also he fell in love with her. It was as easy and unblushingly naïve as that.

Sally was wearing a white wool dress with a hooded collar and her bright hair hanging down, newlywashed and flyaway and subtly perfumed. It was just soap probably, Mike thought, sitting next to her, his nostrils twitching with the wonderful smell of her, his eyes resolutely fixed on the empty stand, on his beerglass, on Si's face, anywhere so he wouldn't have to betray himself by staring mesmerized at her lovely face. He sat rigid, his right hand clutched desperately around his glass because her chair was so close to his that his elbow might have (and would have) brushed burningly against the jutting prow of her breasts, if he moved an inch.

Si made a joke about her being dressed like an unfrocked Trappist monk and Ben looked surly and ordered drinks in a loud voice.

"We're both quite drunk," Sally announced clearly. "We're having a party because Benjie's going away. Did he tell you?" She leaned her head on Ben's shoulder, her full white eyelids drooping and reached up to stroke his face, her fingers moving sensuously over his cheek, mouth, and neck. "He's going to Canada to join their Air Force. I'm glad you're all here so you can tell him how stupid he is, wanting to be a premature hero and get his silly neck broken." Even in the dim light Mike saw that her long eyelashes were wet.

"What the hell do you want to do that for?" Tom said exasperatedly. "My God, we're not even in the war!"

"We will be," Ben said somberly and looked at each of them in turn. "We will be and you'll all get it sooner or later. My idea is to get it sooner."

"You're crazy," Si said. "There's every chance we won't be and I, for one, intend to hold on to my skin as long as I'm allowed."

"I can't stomach it any more," Ben cried in fury. His voice was so loud that even the opening blasts of brass from the stand couldn't quite drown it out and several people at nearby tables turned around to stare. "I hate my life, do you understand that? I hate cosy guys like you Hunnicutt and my cousin Dud and my stepfather. All so smug and knowing. What have I got to stay around here for? I've as good as flunked out and I don't care. Playing football was all I was good at and now I've been kicked off the team. I'm always broke and I have to go begging to my stepfather who hates my guts. I can't stay around here and watch the life being crushed out of my mother, because every time she sees me she knows there'll be some sort of trouble. I've always wanted to run away and now I'm old enough to do it and there's a damn good reason."

"Take it easy, man," Tom said softly. "We could get you straightened out and back on the team in no time. And you don't want to leave Sally, do you?"

"Sally understands," Ben said looking at her fondly. "Don't you baby?" He put his arm around her, his large hand cupped around her breast.

"Oh I understand, dammit," Sally said, unmistakably crying, "but I can't stand to have you go. Don't go, Benjie, I'll die if you go. You'll get killed. You'll never come back."

The more they argued and urged him to change his mind, the

more double bourbons Ben ordered, and tossing them off almost as quickly as they appeared, seemed to be armored stubbornly against any of the pleas of love or reason. He'd be leaving next week with a group of other volunteers from Harvard. Nor did he want to change his mind. The hell with them all. Cowards.

"'We would not die,'" he mumbled indistinctly, his blue eyes blazing up with a strange, fanatic light, "'in that man's company that fears his fellowship to die with us.'"

Mike, who never expected to hear even a line of Robert W. Service's cross this athletic joker's lips, was galvanized.

"Member, Tom, we were reading Shakespeare last year, that was the only play I liked."

"I remember," Tom said smiling like a particularly pleased Socrates.

"I learned it," Ben said, contemplating this fantastic feat in fuddled awe. "First time ever wanted memorize poetry. 'We few, we happy few, we band of brothers; For he today that sheds his blood with me Shall be my brother. Be he ne'er so vile, This day shall gentle his condition; And gentlemen in England now abed Shall think themselves accurs'd they were not here And hold their manhoods cheap whiles any speaks That fought with us upon St. Crispin's day.'"

"One might know," Si sneered, "that the first piece of poetry you ever learned would go to your head. Have you never heard of propaganda, man?"

"Fuck you," Ben said and stumbled off to the men's room and didn't come back. Mike and Tom went to look for him and found him, passed out and snoring on the floor. They carried him to the car and Sally suggested that Si and Tom had better take him to Lowell House and she would go sleep at her aunt's. So Mike found himself walking with her up the steep slopes of Beacon Hill.

"What's your name anyway?" she asked toward the end of their silent walk when she caught her heel on a rough place in the sidewalk and he held her arm to keep her from falling. "I heard it once but that was before I got giddy and completely miserable."

Mike, who'd been brooding about his failure to find a cab outside the Congo and their subsequent interminable wait in the subway, told her his name, wondering if she'd remember.

"My mother painted you," he blurted, "in Paris, a long time ago, when you were a little girl. I remember seeing you there then, a couple of times. We played together. You probably have forgotten all about it."

48

"Oh God," Sally Brimmer said, laughing hoarsely in the silence of Louisburg Square, "are you that Mike Wainscott? Of course, I remember. You were such a funny, solemn, little boy who didn't dare say boo. And there was a French maid who watched us all the time as if we were going to do illicit things and called you Michel. You had short pants and a beret and I thought you were the dullest little boy I'd ever known. And I hated having to sit for that painting. It's hanging right there in my aunt's house and I shudder each time I look at it. Why on earth did your mother, who I vaguely remember liking, want to paint me as some sort of little Renoir. My parents thought it was marvelous but how I hate to even see myself in that blue and white striped bustly taffeta with a wax parrot, ye gods, on my finger."

"Oh one of Minta's ideas, I suppose," Mike said uneasily. "I remember her raving about how she'd found the perfect Renoir child to paint and what great luck because"—he lapsed satirically into his mother's voice—"she'd just discovered those marvelous clothes and the wax monster in the Flea Market."

"Parents are weird, aren't they?" Sally Brimmer said laughing up at him. "You're still a solemn little boy, Michel, but since we've found each other after all these years you ought to kiss me goodnight before I go into that awful house and hope not to wake my horrid uncle." He felt her softness pressing against him and before he knew it, he was kissing her hard.

"Stupid Benjie," Sally said after awhile, leaning against him, "passing out and no goodies, no love for me. That's why I let you kiss me, Michel, because I'm sad and you're sad too, I can tell. And also, I can tell you don't know much about kissing girls. But I could teach you lots about that. I'm very expert if I don't care about anything. And after Benjie goes, I won't care about anything at all. I shouldn't even be here now," she said lowering her voice conspiratorially. "I should be in school. But Benjie forged a note in his mother's handwriting and I should be back by tomorrow morning. But I won't be. I won't go back till Benjie goes." She giggled a little. "Oh won't my aunt be scandalized to see me in the morning. It's lucky I have a key to the house because otherwise I'd have to sleep at your house and your mother'd be awfully surprised to see me too."

"I'm sure she wouldn't mind," Mike said awkwardly, "and I'd like it very much." He stood there wanting to kiss her again and wondering if she'd let him.

"Ah well," Sally said, swaying a little in the doorway of the staid house in Louisburg Square, "praps I'll come and visit you sometime then and we'll play together again with no French maid to watch us this time. But no, I won't be able to, because if Benjie goes, I'll die, I'll be dead, I can't stand to live. . . ."

To his horror she began to sob, the sounds echoing loudly in the quiet square. "You'll wake your uncle," he said uneasily, taking the key from her hand. Noiselessly he opened the door and pushed her inside the dimly lighted foyer. She quieted down immediately and, like a thief in the night, Mike stealthily closed the door behind him and ran. He had no wish to meet her fearsome uncle, outraged and scandalized at the spectacle of some young man he'd never seen before escorting his drunken niece who should've been safely locked in her cubicle at school. It would've been an impossible situation to explain, Mike reflected slowing up when he was safely onto Mount Vernon Street, and could only be funny in the movies.

He hoped that magical night, as he quietly climbed the stairs to his attic, that he hadn't dreamed it all and that when he saw Sally again she'd remember kissing him as no girl had ever kissed him before. Surely he'd never kissed a girl that way in his whole life. But then he'd never been so impassionedly in love before. His head whirling with liquor, jazz, and Sally, he sat down at his desk and, at top speed, wrote a sonnet to her, full of words like fire and wine and white-swan-breasted and incandescent which, when he found it many years later and reread it before well-deserved destruction, struck him as so incredibly Swinburnian that he wondered if he actually had written it or had the spirit of some extraordinarily bad *fin de siècle* poet taken demonic possession of him that night.

But then, he'd only been twenty and burning with love; first, dedicated and only love and he mailed a copy of the sonnet to Sally in anonymous cowardice.

"But of course I knew you wrote it," she said a little condescendingly, after Ben had gone off to join the RCAF and Mike was allowed the fantastic privilege of seeing her on the weekends she came up from school. "It would have to be you, Michel. You're the only poet type I know. Funny boy." She looked at him critically. "I know absolutely nothing about poetry of course and I must say I'm awfly flattered even though it's quite corny, isn't it? I mean, it isn't very modern."

"No," Mike admitted. "But I don't feel very modern about you."

They were dancing somewhere and he was trying not to hold her too close. Her body pressed up against his drove him into such a wild frenzy that he could barely control himself. But he hadn't been taking her out for too long and surely it would be too soon . . .

50

"Yes," she said and moved closer to him, swaying against him in time to the music, "I noticed. You're wildly old-fashioned, aren't you, Mike? Why are you afraid to get close to me?"

"You know why."

"There're ways," Sally said reasonably, "of doing things about that."

His parents, as they often were, had been away that weekend and she knew it. So they went to his house and when they sat on the edge of his bed and she took his hands and placed them on her breasts Mike had known the agonizing embarrassment of the long dreamed of moment happening too soon. But Sally was calm about it. Plenty of time, she said. And so there was; many weekends for a long wonderful winter and spring. All the while he knew that as he grew more serious she remained as casual as she'd been in the beginning.

"I want to marry you," he said one cold February night when they were lying naked and warm together in his bed.

"Don't be silly, darling," she said as if soothing a fretful child. "I don't love you the least little bit although I like you very much. I love Benjie and have for years but he's not here now. You knew that, Mike, you can't pretend you didn't. I'll be eighteen in May and praps then the war'll be over and I can marry Benjie."

"The war won't be over in May."

"Then you'll be drafted," Sally went on, "and I'll make my debut. I'm to have a big outdoor June party and another one during the fall season and I'll be going to thousands of parties and dances and balls and assemblies and teas and dinners and we won't see one another any more in any case. Then, the war'll be over and Benjie will come back."

"I suppose you like all that debut and society jazz."

"It will pass the time away," Sally said indifferently, "and I do like fun of whatever sort. Of course there'll be too many other girls involved to suit me but one must take the bitter with the sweet and so on. D'you know, it's weird but most girls hate me."

"Because they're jealous probably."

"No, I think it's more subtle than that. I think I'm considered a sort of traitor to my sex because I won't imprison my body in all these uncomfortable chastity belts and feel pinched and miserable as they do in the name of convention and mince around uttering little shocked shrieks about things that are quite natural and lovely. And their dates run after me and then they act as though I'm a tramp who's surreptitiously given them doses of Spanish fly. The men I mean. And the conversations they have about sex at school seem so utterly childish to me," Sally said wearily. "There are some decent girls of course. I have two friends at school but one of them comes from California and the other is Swedish and they won't be bowing to society with me."

"Never mind about all that," Mike said impatiently. "I'm telling you that I love you, Sally. So much that it hurts. How can you go to bed with me all the time like this and not care? I never heard of a girl like you. You're so damn young and yet you know so much."

"I know," Sally said frankly. "I've heard it's not the way for girls to be but I don't see why if you find sex fun you shouldn't go ahead and have as much as you want. Nothing to do with love. I've always had this feeling, you see. It was as if I was always on fire. So when I was fifteen and Benjie and I had sex for the first time it seemed the only right and expected thing."

"So I'm just a stopgap till he gets back?"

"Oh you're nice too," Sally said agreeably. "But you get too intense. Why don't you just let it be pleasant like this while it goes on and not fret so much?"

"What if Ben doesn't come back?" Mike asked hollowly.

"Then I spose I'll marry someone," Sally said negligently, "simply to get away. When I finish school I have nowhere to go except my aunt's house and I couldn't bear it there. But it wouldn't be you, Mike, much as I like you."

So they hadn't talked about it any more and a few months later it became very obvious that she was seeing someone else. She was never at home when he called nor did she answer the letters he wrote to her at school or to her aunt's house. In June, he received an invitation to her party. It came to Lowell House, addressed to him in care of Tom. He threw it in to the wastebasket immediately upon opening it and Si, whose pleasure at receiving a similar invitation was evident, took him to task.

"So you had a few blissful months with the most desirable chick in town," he said irritably, "and instead of being grateful you're going around wasting away because she doesn't want you any more. She's that kind of girl, man, and you had full warning beforehand. If Merritt hadn't gone away at that precise moment you'd never have gotten near her but he did and your shy, retiring, poetical temperament challenged all her highly developed feline instincts. But the end was inevitable. By next year, Merritt will have, once too often, gone out to fly and forgotten to take whatever vital aeronautical equivalent of a towel he needs, with him, like a parachute, and that'll be the end of him or else she'll finally use her intelligence instead of her sex drive and realize that he's a nothing and will remain a nothing even if he inherits money, and she'll marry someone else. Mrs. Millionaire Polo Player with her picture in all the magazines. Either surrounded by her children, at least six of them, all dressed in hunting clothes and tally-ho-ing their heads off or else pouring coffee in the drawing room of her lovely mansion and swearing she smokes a certain brand of cigarette, the fee for which advertisement helps to pay the grooms' salaries. Christ, Wainscott, come off it. I hear this party is going to be an enormous splash. Her miserly uncle is crazy to marry her off to the right type so he's got to launch her well."

"I suppose," Mike sneered, "that the Navy character you introduced her to, the one she's always getting photographed with, is a Social Register foxhunter with a vault full of inherited stocks."

"Joe's got a head full of brains," Si said reprovingly, "and he's a much more hardened character than you, Wainscott. Also older. To him, Sally is a lovely unexpected break in the war. Weird, you know, I never expected they'd get together. I just happened to meet her when I was with him and some spark must've been set off because he called her up and it's become a great thing."

"The hell with him," Mike said bitterly and he had not gone to Sally's party. Once, after that, he'd seen her at a session. She'd come with his hateful successor, Lieutenant Joseph Mayhew, USN, who, Mike had to admit grudgingly, seemed like a superior type for a Navy officer; nevertheless, he left almost immediately upon their arrival because just the sight of Sally being casual and friendly to him made him so wretched he wanted to go home and commit suicide.

In July, word had come that Ben Merritt's plane had been shot down over the English Channel, all the crew missing, presumably dead. Every now and then, during that long, hot summer, while he skulked up in his attic, writing reams of tortured poetry, Mike considered sending Sally a consolatory note about Ben's death, but he never did it. It would've been a mere convention if not a downright farcical lie.

In August Minta had decided that she simply must paint at Rockport and insisted that he come with her. There, he'd lain gloomily on the sand, wishing that some engulfing wave would come and carry him out to sea or that an eagle would swoop and rend his flesh. One evening after he'd contemptuously refused to accompany Minta and her friends on a two-day boat trip up to the Isle of Shoals, he was wandering indifferently down Rockport's main street looking for a place to eat and met Sally coming out of a shop. She'd been at Bar Harbor visiting and was driving back to Boston.

He was silent, only able to look at her, as she rattled on, seemingly quite at ease and full of high spirits, talking about a job offered to her in the fall, singing with Vance Paley's band at the Cinnamon Room of the Hotel Trimount. Her uncle and her brother were opposed but she thought she might do it anyhow. They went to eat clams somewhere and he told her, haltingly, how sorry he'd been to hear about Ben's death.

"No you weren't," she lashed back tartly, "you were like all those other jealous, mean-spirited, little men who mocked him. Let's get drunk, shall we, and go swimming without bathing suits?"

Afterwards, back at the cottage, their bodies still damp and tingling from the raw, cold nightwater, he made love to her wishing he could hate her enough not to want to. For the rest of his life he'd remember that night and the smells of late summer roses, crushed dewy grass and saltsultry breeze drifting through the bedroom window and how he'd hated himself for still going crazy about her, hating her cheerful, pliable, uncaring willingness to give him her marvelous body and have it mean nothing.

"You love this Navy character, Mayhew?"

"No."

"You keep seeing him all the time."

"Because he interests me. In fact, he fascinates me. He's one of the most truly impervious men I've ever known."

The smell of her hair, the feel of her soft, smooth, rounded body, her magical voice, a cigarette shared between them.

"You sleep with him all the time?"

"Of course. He makes marvelous love."

"As good as the great Ben?"

"No. No one does."

"But of course you have to make absolutely sure?"

"Why do you care, Mike?"

"I can't stop being in love with you. It drives me nuts. Why can't it be like this all the time?" Her head on his shoulder, his hand caressing her.

"Oh you'll find someone else to love, Mike. I know how it is. I felt like that about Benjie. I never gave a damn about anyone else when he was here and when he was alive, even though not here, I still didn't. But now he's dead and I imagine I'll find someone else. But not to love. I don't want to love anyone any more. It's too painful."

"So you'll do it with any man and you don't care."

54

"Don't be childish, Michael. That's one reason I stopped seeing you. You're like a little boy about some things."

Anyone else, Mike thought, lying there hopelessly, his mouth against her breast, any other man, would be only too damn happy to take what she gave so lavishly, but he had to be the wretched fool who wanted her love, her soul and her spirit too. And he wondered then, if she could give that to anyone, or indeed, was it there at all? And perhaps that'd been why she thought she loved Merritt; because he'd wanted no more of her than she could give any man nor could he repay in any other coin. It had been a perfect reciprocity of the flesh. Fie on it, Mike thought and mockingly, fie on thee for being so literary even at one of the most inexplicably sad moments of your life. How did one explain unrequited love to the beloved who did not want it? "Tis an unweeded garden that grows to seed; things rank and gross do possess it merely."

He'd never seen Sally again after that summer night. In October, instead of returning to school, he volunteered for the Army. Letters from Si and Tom before they were drafted, occasionally informed him of her doings. How she'd been singing with Paley's band and how good she was, and how, a little later, family pressure had forced her to give it up and shortly after that, she'd run off with Joe Mayhew.

"It seems I was wrong and she has good taste after all," Si wrote. "By this time you undoubtedly couldn't care less, at least, I hope so."

Three

Downstairs, the phone rang and rang. Mike started out of his trance and leaped down the steps two at a time. By the time he got to it, Sam was there, being suave.

"For you," Sam said, handing over the receiver. And in a stage whisper, "Batten down your eardrums."

It was Jean and she'd decided to get her hair done, an operation which would hold her up till five. Did he think, she asked sarcastically, he'd be ready to see her by then?

"Sure," Mike said cheerfully, listening with half an ear to his father who was burrowing in the hall closet muttering about voices that raised the hackles on his spine. "Fine, baby. I have studying to do anyhow. You might call just before though. No, still here. No, nothing exciting. Right, see you." He hung up quickly.

"Your eagerness to see that girl is touching," Sam Wainscott remarked, coming out of the closet laden with coats.

"She's all right," Mike said defensively.

"She's mediocre," Sam said evenly, "and what's more you know it."

"So'm I," Mike said.

His father favored him with an appraising glance. "Well, far be it from me to contradict you," he said. "If that's what you want, it's a wide open field."

"Listen Sam," Mike said awkwardly. "I'm sorry about what I said before. I mean, I'm flattered you thought so well of me."

"It's all right, Mike. I am, perhaps, too arrogant about what is important and what is not. But you have to do what you think best. Just try to stop acting like an adolescent. I can't put up with rudeness."

"Yup," Mike said. "Well, have a good time." He turned and started up the stairs again and reached the landing just as the phone rang. If it's Jean again, he thought furiously as he raced back down, changing her mind, I'll tell her to go to hell. I don't want to see her now. But fortunately, it was Si Hunnicutt.

"Say Bo," Si said breezily, "what the hell happened to you? You were slated to turn up for lunch here today, remember?"

"Oh Jesus," Mike said. "I clean forgot. Damn sorry, Si. Hope no preparations were made."

"No trouble," Si said easily. "Caroline's usual spaghetti. All it means is we have it for supper too. What's the matter? Exam go to your head?"

"I guess," Mike said. "I was nowhere."

"I figured," Si said. "Ah but you should've been here. Tom and I spent the whole morning having a brilliant discussion on Eliot and the signs of the zodiac and Tarot cards. You'd've been electrified. It all started, see, with Tom showing up to study, looking like a pair of ragged claws, you know from reading New Criticism all night. Caroline, blessed be the innocent, wanted to know about the claws and we told her about the crab and she said, you mean Cancer the Crab, because she was reading her daily horoscope in the *Tatler* and Cancer is the sign she was born under. Anyway, Tom's hair stood on end, because being a minister's son, he's familiar with all aspects of the occult, and it was immediately obvious to him, as it had not been to me, that a girl who knows zodiac signs and believes in horoscopes doesn't just depend on newspapers. And by God, if he wasn't right. She had an actual pack of Tarot fortunetelling cards at the bottom of her little brass trunk and after a little persuasion she brought them out, since we'd never really seen the Hanged Man. Wouldn't tell our fortunes though. Claims she's forgotten how."

"I thought you were supposed to be studying," Mike said laughing, "for exams."

"This is studying, man," Si said righteously. "We figure that any ingenious interpretation of Tarot and the 'Wasteland' can be worked into any course exam or paper. I tell you, laddie, you don't know all the crossword puzzle thrills you miss, shut up with Blackstone this way.

"But I did not call to lobby. What time do we convene at your stately home tomorrow? I couldn't remember and Caroline is afraid we might be too early. She hates to break in on boudoir scenes. I told her you wouldn't care but she said Jean would. She pretends to be dewy-eyed about love, you see, but all the time she is watching the progress of your tender affair, hawklike, because she conceives of it as a deadly parallel with ours."

"Is she listening to you?" Mike asked chuckling.

"Of course," Si said imperturbably.

"I happen to know," Mike said, "that there's no parallel at all. You can tell her that. I'm not going to marry Jean and you are going to marry her."

"True," Si said casually. "But don't let on to her. Suspense is essential with these redheads. Say, listen, Mike, to go from ridiculous to ridiculous, I ran into that sniggering character you persist in knowing, Gordie Bruce, who ought to have with Wallace bled, it'd be good for his manners, and I find that he too is gracing your gathering tomorrow. Would you really do this to your old tried and true friends?"

"Gordie's all right," Mike said. "He's just young."

"He's a little snot," Si said firmly. "You ought to stop collecting stray cats, Mike."

"I used to be a stray cat once, myself," Mike said. "I still have a fellow feeling."

"Man," Si said, "that exam really put you down there with Gorki. Should I wear a black armband tomorrow?"

"Maybe you should," Mike said, "because the Jazzbo is going to be here too."

"You're out of your goddamn mind," Si said calmly. "You couldn't commit an act of treason like that. I've known you too long. You're trueblue. Why, it'd be like opening the gates to the Trojan horse."

"Nevertheless," Mike said, "I decided that this little group is getting too inbred. We need new blood."

"New blood!" Si made a derisive noise. "Why didn't you ask the whole Jukes family and be done with it? Chrissakes, you better go to bed and put a cold compress on your head."

"I had to ask him," Mike said. "Tell you why tomorrow."

"All right," Si said mournfully. "But I warn you, I'm going to bring my ear trumpet and the first word that joker addresses to me, up it goes."

"Fair enough." Mike rang off and climbed back upstairs. It was probably churlish of him not to have told Si about Sally but hell, after the morning he'd spent, the marvels of exaggeration Si'd create about Sally's reappearance did not bear thinking about. Why Si could laugh your life away for you because he was so damn unerring. He could even make you see yourself through his eyes and there you were, a flat piece of cardboard, a display-window humpty dumpty, with not a serious, tragic, or real emotion to your name. No, tomorrow would be soon enough for that.

It'd be an odd gathering tomorrow, no doubt about it, but a made-to-order show for lucky Si, whose wry view of the world as a ridiculous comedy in which he himself played the buffoon while friend and foe alike strutted and postured ludicrously saved him, seemingly, from all those embarrassing emotions that other, less armored folk were heir to. Only sometimes he went too far and then the Punch and Judy operator was metamorphosed into the smiler with the premeditated knife beneath the cloak, and it was then that you wondered how you could consider such a sadistic monster a lifelong friend. But disapproval of Si never lasted. Pretty soon he'd be prancing around making dull old life funny again. The only victim of comedy-turned-malice who'd never forgiven Si was Dud Brimmer and that'd been pre-war and maybe in this new world it didn't count any more.

Funny now, trying to remember the first time he'd seen Sally's brother. Yes, it was that same fall before Pearl Harbor, wasn't it, when, with Ben Merritt gone to join up, Si, an expansive master of the revels, had some kind of crowded noisy gathering going at the suite in Lowell House not only every Saturday after football games but also every other night in the week.

Yes, it was a soft foggy night just before Thanksgiving vacation, because there'd been a note in the mail from Sally that morning, the first indication since they'd met, that she knew he was alive. She'd be home for the holiday and could he call?

With his hot and lickerish blood bubbling and seething at the thought of seeing his heart's desire in a mere few days he arrived at Si's *Walpurgisnacht*, blundered across the floor of the study room stepping on hands and bowling over beer glasses, listened to Muggsy Spanier and Joe Turner blasting from the phonograph, drank warm beer and was pricked by the gadflies of twenty varied conversations:

"Turn that volume up will you? It's Teagarden in 'Serenade to a Shylock.' I want you to hear that riff. Gutty as hell . . ."

" 'O Mamamamamamamama, where did you stay last night . . . ?' "

Sally hasn't got a man now with Ben gone. She wants me. Me.

"The capitalistic system is doomed I tell you. It depends on war to keep going. Well how the hell would you know about the suffering working class. Your uncle was in the Hoover cabinet."

A loud, gravelly, Southern mountain voice. "Ah don't wanna reed ee-levun hundred pages just to find out that people ah bawn,

59

get married, have babies and die. That's awl that there *War and Peace* is about."

His opponent, a tall, husky, wild-haired specimen in a leather jacket, clawing the air fervently. "You don't see *life*, that's all. The immense . . . uh . . . mystery of it all. Now take the whole groping mysticism of Mother Russia . . ."

"Well, that's where Ah stand. And, Ah don't mahnd telling yew although Ah hate Reds, Ah don't blame the Bolsheviki, if that's the kind of people that the Russian upper class was made of."

"No, no. You aren't looking deep enough. Tolstoy understood that human life and values are . . . are . . . abiding . . . bigger than uh . . . uh . . . ideas, wars . . . , uh . . . symbolized by the Russian winter which uh . . ."

"Look out for Chrahst's sake, you're on mah foot . . . Mah Gawd!"

Mike moved quickly out of the way as beer splashed from the glass of the impassioned lifelover who was wringing his hair in the anguish of trying to think and articulate at the same time, and Si appeared proffering a solicitous towel and, with many sly winks and nods (he enjoyed the clowns who turned up at his pad, Mike and Tom were convinced, far more than they enjoyed themselves) dragooned him into a heated discussion on religion.

Trying to look as though he knew what the Manichean heresy was but really thinking about Sally, Mike was therefore the first in that busy voluble crowd to sight the tentative-looking character in the doorway.

"Somebody looking for you, Si."

"Where? Oho! Miching Malicho! By the pricking of my thumbs, John Dudley Brimmer this way comes. Ah, now for some fun. Sally's brother, you know."

"Oh yes." Mike Wainscott, exaltedly in love, trying to appear casual. Might not be a bad idea to get to know this lovely mysterious girl's brother. But Dud Brimmer apparently was politely uninterested in Si's efforts to entangle him in theological discussion and after a few minutes Si left him sitting on the couch by the door and came back looking disgruntled.

"He'll just sit and drink awhile, he said. I wanted to introduce him around. But no. I'm sick of these empty vessels who never participate."

"Doesn't he talk?"

"The laconic Spartans were fulminating windbags compared to him. Hey, Pete, come on over here."

The cool-faced fellow who loped over to them in the conventional white bucks was introduced as Pete Howle, a name which Mike recognized because all the week before Si'd been crowing about going to the coming-out party of Howle's sister Betsy where he'd lapped up oceans of champagne as well as, to hear him tell, captivating all feminine hearts with iridescent persiflage.

"Dud looks even more solemn tonight than he did at Betsy's do last week," Howle commented in what Mike's father referred to as a pure Cold-Roast-and-Hasty-Pudding accent.

"No, I can't agree with you there Pete," Si said gleefully. "On the dance floor he needed only a band of crepe and a hat to put it on. Why the hell does he go to these affairs if they leave him so cold?"

"Oh I think he feels it's sort of a family obligation. He doesn't honor many by his appearance, which doesn't break any of the girl's hearts but the families . . ."

A flying wedge of armchair football strategists descended on Howle then to reconstruct in tedious detail each move of last week's game against Dartmouth and Si who scorned football went off to get more beer. Mike, left alone, wondered if he ought to go over and introduce himself to this enigmatic brother of Sally's. Dud Brimmer had not moved an inch from his position at the end of the couch nor had he talked to anyone. He simply sat there upright, drinking his beer, seemingly aloof from the noise swirling around him, scanning the room and its occupants with a complete lack of expression.

Halfheartedly Mike started in Dudley's direction and then an embarrassing picture of himself charging up to this reserved, icy-eyed type with a glad hand and a hailfellow grin, saying Hello there Dud, you don't know me but I know Sally, overwhelmed him, and he turned abruptly and went to the bathroom instead.

Si, with a fresh supply of cold beer, was now dodging through the rooms, replenishing glasses while simultaneously conducting a running defense of atheism: he announced loudly that he'd have more respect for a guy who declared himself Napoleon Bonaparte than for one who claimed affiliation with an organized religion, a bellwether sally which brought forth groans, cheers, hoots, and offers to defenestrate him then and there.

"Listen," Si shouted, pouring beer recklessly onto floor, shoes, and Dudley Brimmer's neatly pressed pants, "if He returned to this world right now, He'd deny the whole mixed and dubious ancestry which foisted divinity onto him. Godsakes! Half Jew, half bird! Any right-thinking cat'd keep quiet about it."

"Well," Mike commented when Si plumped down beside him a few minutes later, "Brimmer actually smiled at that last one."

"Ah, it wasn't original," Si said dismissingly. "Fascinated by our representative from Greenland's icy mountains, are you, Wainscott? Well, you are not alone. John Dudley Brimmer is my greatest unsolved case. I take opium and play a violin some nights just to repress my curiosity about him for a few hours. Now look at him over there! You know why he hasn't budged since his arrival? Because they're having a hot pornographic discussion in that corner and he's just soaking it all up. You ought to see his eyes now. They're weird. And the more smut flying around, the bigger the eyes get. If eyes could be said to slaver, his do."

"Are you implying that that stiff-looking Brahmin is some kind of an auditory voyeur?"

"Implication, hell!" Si's eyes glittered. "Did you ever run into a situation, Mike, where you know damn well, down in your bowels, there's something definitely peculiar, and you're the only one who sees it and you get to feeling you're crazy? It's like having a strong sense of smell and you know there's gas leaking somewhere or a dead rat in the cellar and no one else smells it but you."

"Sooo. You suffer from olfactory hallucinations, Mr. Hunnicutt. A most interesting symptom."

"Crown me with thorns, I expect it," Si said resignedly. "All I know is, here's this weird icicle, Brimmer, intelligent as hell under the frost, loaded with loot and an entree into society, working the way they have to do in Med School, a peon's day, and how has he been spending all his free time? Obsessedly gumshoeing around after his cousin and his sister, trying to catch them out. When they were all together at home on vacations he probably stayed up all night, watching their bedroom doors."

"Well, I dunno," Mike said. "I don't think it's so abnormal for a brother to behave like that. She's still pretty young. Even if Merritt is a cousin."

"Let me just tell you one thing, Wainscott, and if you don't detect Mephistophelean cunning you're a far less sensitive poet than I took you for. One of Merritt's troubles was an inability to hold too much liquor without going to pieces. And, if you have the hound of heaven trailing you every time you want a piece, drinking helps. Your kindly, self-appointed guardian cousin who knows all, then passes the word about your alcoholism to stepdaddy who cuts your allowance. No ski trips with Sally all snuggly in the lodge. See? And while you're muddling around trying to get out of your trap you don't have to go hungry and thirsty. Good old Cousin Dudley will always take you out to dinner and see to it that you get plenty of your favorite poison. Then you come reeling home, stinking of Johnny Walker and your roommates know that you were scrounging their cigarettes only that afternoon."

"Nobody could be that much of a bastard, Si. You're almost accusing Brimmer of driving his cousin into joining up."

"Well, you figure it out," Si said, getting up briskly. "I'm going back to my philosophy of religion class where the problems are simple. For example, if God created the earth in six days and nights, how come he let the dinosaurs stay around slobbering in the swamps for over a hundred million years. You know, first He's in a rush, then He's got millenniums to waste. There's a flaw in the logic there somewhere."

The party hurtled on heedlessly and noisily till midnight. Mike with a lot of beer under his belt, found himself astonishingly expansive, talking away glibly to a variety of people he didn't know well at all, and enjoying every minute of it, till he noticed, amazed, that the rooms seemed to be emptying out. There was a lot of laughter coming from the bedroom however and going in to get his coat before starting the trip across the river, he found Si sitting rather lopsidedly on one of the bunks, telling dirty jokes to Dud Brimmer and Pete Howle who were completely convulsed. Dud, in particular, presented an astounding contrast to his earlier solemnity, rocking back and forth in the throes of his mirth, his face red, his glasses misted by hilarious tears. Tom Baring seated on the other bed, packing his pipe, was the only one unaffected by the ear-splitting merriment.

"Don't know how you do it, Si," Pete Howle drawled, after a moment taken to collect himself. "Known this feller here," he indicated the still shuddering Dud, "for years and never, to my knowledge, seen him laugh like this!"

"Oh that's easy enough," Si said negligently, still poker-faced. "Oh I dig you, Dud, yessir." Nodding his head wisely. "All I have to do is read Poe. You know, Dud, before I met your sister I used to think that all your family died in the House of Seven Gables and that you alone escaped. I discount Ben of course," he added airily, "because . . ."

Mike, remembering it all now, could even hear as he'd heard then, the tinkle of shattered glass and the silence, and see the beer, spilling and frothing on the floor and Dud, white-faced, his smile frozen, calmly reminding Si that he must mean the House of Usher and Si smiling and saying he stood corrected, and then Tom asking Si to apologize and Dud protesting that it was unnecessary.

And Tom pushing Si into the bathroom and telling him to go sober up and Dud leaving, still calm and polite, trailed by Pete Howle and then Si shouting with his head dripping wet from being under the faucet.

"Where d'you come off, Baring, asking me to apologize to that ghoul? You think I meant that crack about Poe as a joke? Maybe you didn't get the point, but that whited sepulchre Brimmer did and I'm glad I said it. Oh sure, when he wanted me to tell him what Ben was doing then I was a friend. Then, he couldn't do too much for me. Invitations to dinner at his club, loaned me dough, to his aunt's for tea, theatre tickets he couldn't use, I got. Then Ben leaves. Bang! I don't see Brimmer for a month of Sundays until tonight. This absence after such assiduous friendliness is suspicious to me and I begin to wonder if, after all, there isn't something to that poor blockhead Merritt's story."

"Oh you're nuts," Tom said disgustedly. "All Dud's supposed hounding of Ben was for Ben and Sally's own good. They're hamstrung by a mess of a will and half the time Dud was acting as a buffer between Ben and his stepfather, protecting him, just to save his future and Sally's too, for that matter. Why for Godsakes, if it hadn't been for Dud, Ben would've flunked out after his freshman year through sheer apathy. Dud hired me to coach him."

"Oh Beelzebub!" Si moaned. "Never mind all the Gothic trappings about evil wills and cruel stepfathers. Baring, will you never admit of the Devil? Dud and Ben hated each other. People do hate, you know. It's even normal. What's not normal is your steadfast, serenely dippy refusal to recognize bastardly behavior in others."

"You're wrong there," Tom said curtly, "because I think you behaved like a bastard to Dud tonight and I'm not repressing it either. The sad truth of the matter is that Dud really liked you. He's a damn lonely guy who's all locked up inside himself. So he'd come here, pretending, I'm sure, that it was because of Ben, but actually to get some social life, to get away from the medical shop talk of a career he's not even sure about. And since you're so damn uninhibited you're one of the few people he felt at ease with. So, because of some manufactured paranoiac notion of yours you went and put the shiv into him. If you had one empathic bone in that jackanapes body of yours, you'd've realized that the reason he prob-

64

ably hasn't turned up here since Ben left is that he thought with Ben gone we didn't like him enough to ask him over. I didn't notice you calling him up either."

"Hearts and flowers," Si sneered, flamboyantly playing an imaginary violin. "Poor dear Dud, all he wants is to be entertained. Well, I can do that all right, but raise him from his ancestral dead, no, that I won't do." And he rushed off to McBride's for a drink—to wash all that, as he put it, saintliness out of his mouth, leaving Tom and Mike to kill half a fifth of whiskey found in Ben Merritt's desk while they discussed who was more eccentric, Si or Dud. They went on after that to a typical, undergraduate, middle-of-the-night session, ranging through sex and Freud to who was the greatest living American writer. Tom naturally thought Hemingway and this led to Mike's giving vent to boyhood memories and opinions of life with his parents, those eternal residents of the seacoast of Bohemia.

"It must've been great." Tom was unabashedly envious. "Living all over Europe the way you did. Knowing famous people. My youth was so damned ordinary. Plain, simple, and Midwestern. Summers in New Hampshire—good old American outdoor boy stuff. And in Cedar Rapids when there was no school or studying and I got bored with playing baseball or collecting stamps, I'd sit out under a tree in the back yard and read books and envy the characters because things happened to them and nothing ever happened to me. I wanted adventure, excitement, hair-raising escapades in glamorous, foreign lands. Did you ever read any of B. Gwinnett Brown? He was a nineteenth-century journalist. Wrote a slew of books, mostly short pieces on travel in Europe, with nice little watercolor illustrations done by himself."

"Did I?" Mike was highly delighted. "Griefstricken women in furs disappearing into the Istanbul night. Polish noblemen losing all their fortunes at Monte Carlo and staggering out to put a bullet through their brain. Sinister croupiers with bloodless spidery hands. My grandmother Wainscott had a whole set and I went through the entire lot the summers I stayed there. Trouble was, I should have read them the way you did, not knowing a damn thing about Europe. By the time I got to Brown, his Europe was long dead and gone: all those comic-opera uniforms and situations and useless titles, all melted away, ignored and forgotten. My Europe was just a miserable bore!"

But Tom, that pleasant sound friend, who complained of an ordinary childhood, didn't really believe him and somehow Mike found himself telling about all the different boarding schools he'd gone to.

"I never fitted in. Didn't have a category. Kids love categories. Bad at team sports and athletics in general. And I just didn't know how to act with people my age. Anyway, I started off on these rounds when I was about eight or nine because they'd moved to an apartment in Paris and there wasn't room for me if Minta was to have a studio. On vacations I had to sleep on an army cot in the living room. It was supposedly good for me to live away at school because I was too shy and dependent on them. Better for me and for them. Particularly Minta. For the first five years of my life, apparently, she had only a few hours a day to paint and frequently not even that. She could hardly wait for me to grow up."

The French school, the Swiss school, and then later, when Sam'd been working for Brick and Bartlett in London, the English school. Bloody little English snobs with their soccer, and cricket and the simplicity of their reactions to an American who spoke English with a French accent. Who was not really upperclass or rich although the school fees were expensive. American expatriates and everyone knew the wild lives they led. And having sinus infections, colds, and earaches all the time until finally a severe case of bronchitis had caused the headmaster to recommend to Sam and Minta that their son was falling so far behind that perhaps a change of climate . . . All imaginary, Sam'd said, but at fourteen Minta'd brought him back to the States because that was all they could do with him.

Hot summer Stockbridge with his Grandmother Wainscott deaf and vague, his hostile Aunt Millicent and his mama's-boy priggish cousin, Neddy, and Minta going back to England again. Sam would have his vacation when she got back and they were going to Spain. (She'd only gotten as far as southern France, it happened, because the Civil War broke out that summer and Sam had gone over the border to do some freelance article writing, and left her behind. She might as well have stayed another month in the States, with him, Mike'd always thought afterwards.) Part of the summer to wait through with these unknown relatives before going to Andover.

"You'll be a real American boy, Mike," Minta had said, the facile tears rising in her rich, brown eyes. "At last. I mean, darling, don't look so forlorn. You'll love it. You'll see."

But he'd not been fooled. He'd been sullen. Having hated all the other schools, why should this one be different? He was as strange in America as he'd been everywhere else.

"Why can't you live here, why can't you?" he'd shouted. "I don't want to go to boarding school. I want to go to a day school and come home every afternoon."

"And find me with my hands all floury from baking cookies, I suppose?" Minta'd laughed a little but they'd both known it was not funny. "No, darling. I'm not that sort of person. I can't be. I don't understand you, Mike. Most boys your age are glad to be away from their parents."

What had he cared for most boys? If they wanted to break away from their parents, it was because they'd had their parents around before, and he never had. He'd glared at her in hatred because he could not bring himself to say, "Don't go back, stay here, so I can have someone who cares about me, a real family, so I won't always be alone."

Oh, she'd understood all right but had pretended not to. She'd talked a lot about the creative urge and how difficult it was for a woman.

"It's all very well for a man," Minta'd said rather sourly. "No one expects them to give up their little hobbies and sports for a child and particularly never their careers. But a woman is supposed to simply put away her essential self in lavender as soon as she has a baby and utterly devote herself to child rearing until the child has no further need of her. At which time she will gracefully retire to a shelf and bother no one. Oh no, darling, it's not that I don't love you because I do and I've always felt simply torn and had to force myself often, to send you off, so I could turn back to my easel. But it wouldn't be of benefit to you or to me or Sam if you had a mother, embittered and useless, because she'd had to give up what she likes to do best and is good at, for you."

"There are things you can accept with your head but not your heart," Mike had, in telling Tom Baring, said later. "Perhaps she was right but I never thought her painting was worth what it did to me. There are an awful lot of second-rate painters in the world but each child has only one good mother. Going to Andover, it turned out, was damn good for me. Began to feel as if I belonged somewhere for the first time in my life."

Tom thought it was too bad they couldn't've changed places at some point in their boyhood, but anyway, they agreed, the moving finger had writ and made them what they were and what did it matter since soon they were to die. Tom was not too sure of this but Mike convinced him that wars were getting worse and killed more people. They became melancholy as the night waned and the war loomed and Ben Merritt's whiskey disappeared.

"He'll die, that's for sure," Tom said darkly. "It's almost certain death being a pilot these days."

"Then I can marry his beautiful girl," Mike said. The whiskey on top of beer had gone to his head and loosened his tongue. "Before I die too. I love that girl and I'm bound to have her. Come fill the cup, Tom, and in the fire of spring . . ." He began to sing, " 'For fourteen years I courted Sall-eeee . . . Heigh-ho you rolling river . . .' "

"Everyone wants a beautiful woman before they die. But not Sally. She's a witch. Anyway, you're drunk, Mike."

"So I am." Mike was pleased. "How are you?"

"Getting there." They killed the bottle and, after awhile, Tom said reasonably, "Well, if we're going to die we shouldn't hold a grudge against poor old Si. Let's go tell him."

"He won't die." They walked slowly and blunderingly along Mount Auburn Street, in the damp, November night.

"Then Dud won't either."

"How you know?"

"Because they're Scrooge and Marley, that gloomy comic turn. Si's Scrooge, always Bah-humbugging. And Dud's Marley. Dead to begin with."

"Now who's making snide cracks?"

"Careful of those steps. Lead down to hell and McBride's Raths-keller. Let's tell Si about B. Gwinnett Brown. Just his speed. You know, Brown ought to be revived. Take people's mind off the lousy present."

"Probably out of print. I don't see Si here, do you?"

"I hear him. He's in back, having a fight."

They'd had to drag him away from a violent argument with a couple of patriots from the Business School who wanted to bash his head in, and so they'd never told him about Button Gwinnett Brown, that night or any other.

The tricks of memory. B. Gwinnett Brown, that long-dead bimbo with his walrus moustache: the steel-engraved picture behind tissue paper facing the title page of every volume of the two-shelf set. And he had not thought of him from that drunken night in 1941 to this spring afternoon six and a half years later and never reread him as he'd planned. And what had happened to all those men at Si's party that night? Si Scrooge and Dudley Marley, of course, had not died; and only Ben, the doomed and driven, had not returned and one would never know the hows and whys of his going. Then Sally and the war had happened to him, and between the two of

68

them, that old Mike was gone, irrevocably and utterly and just as well too. And that Southerner with the grating voice who didn't want to read 1100 pages to find out that people were born, married, procreated, and died? And all those others, talking so intensively about Ah Life that foggy night in Lowell House. How many of them had been killed halfway through the book and how many were now living out their 1100 pages? War and peace, Mike thought. I'll take peace and Button Gwinnett Brown.

Revive him, he'd said to Tom. B. Gwinnett Brown, the little cake dipped in tea that opened up vistas of a peaceful dreaming past. What a subject for a thesis. He would give it all to Si or Tom, Mike thought gleefully. A chance to discover someone new. Wasn't that the quest of all M.A.'s and Ph.D.'s in English? Get them away from those wornout fields of Joyce and Melville in which every stone had been not only turned but pulverized. Mike dashed out of his room and hurtled down the stairs. Had they gone? No, Minta was standing before the hall mirror, adjusting a scarf.

"Mike," she said, "we were wondering if we should disturb you to say goodbye. Please open the windows and air the place out before we come back, darling, would you mind? It always reeks of spilled stale beer and inferior face powder after one of your parties."

"Your mother has always been an advocate of plain living and high thinking." Sam emerged from the kitchen, carrying a magnum of Moet champagne.

"Say, Sam, do you still have any copies of B. Gwinnett Brown?"

"B who?"

"Gwinnett Brown. The cat who wrote all those travel pieces in the eighties."

His father stared at him. "Why? Was he involved in a precedent setting lawsuit?"

"No, no," Mike said impatiently. "I just want to reread him is all. He's the answer to a Ph.D.'s prayer. Can't you just see it? *The World of B. Gwinnett Brown.* Everything's the world of, nowadays. Parts of it publishable in the *Pilgrim*. Little-known unappreciated writers of America series."

"Hmmm." Sam hoisted his gigantic bottle again. "How did you do in your exam this morning?"

"Marvelous well, thank you," Mike lied. "Sure to get an A."

"Then the unearthing of the literary bones of this better-forgotten scribe will not be your work?"

"It's for Si or Tom. I'm going to be a wealthy, secure, cigar-smoking corporation lawyer. Don't you think it has possibilities, Sam?"

"For S. J. Perelman perhaps. Your Cousin Ned might have kept your grandmother's set. Why don't you go see him? He goes to the same Law School you do."

"God, no. I'd rather go to a secondhand bookstore if I want dust and mold."

"We really ought to have him over for dinner sometime," Minta said. "And, by the way, someone named Gordon Bruce called and said not to disturb you if you were studying. It wasn't important, he said, and he'd see you tomorrow."

A horn bleated three times out in the street.

"That's Bill," Sam said. "We'd better go or he'll have some official of the Preserve the 19th-Century Tranquillity of Beacon Hill on our heads." Cradling the bottle carefully, he started down the stairs.

"Goodbye darling," Minta said kissing him lightly. "Have a good time."

Casting a final goodbye over the stairs, Mike turned and went into the kitchen. The only way a guy could get a decent cup of American coffee around here was to brew it himself. Minta and Sam of course had a special espresso machine they'd brought back from Europe. Right now though there was no time to fill up the percolator and wait. Instant coffee was pretty barbaric, even he would admit that, and he didn't use it often but he kept a jar around for emergencies and as a symbol, like the peanut butter and beer.

He looked at his watch. Quarter of four. Now what had Gordie wanted? Si was undoubtedly right about Gordie but what could one do? Somehow he'd become Gordie's little tin god ever since that night during the war when he'd run into him, young, drunk, and miserable, in the Bat Club. Mike remembered how Gordie's veneer of pseudosophistication, a mixture of leering sexual allusion and cocktail party wisecracks lifted bodily from *New Yorker* stories which made him sound incredibly callow, had not disguised his real bitterness at being turned down by the Army. Mike'd forgotten all about Gordie until last year when he'd come back and gone down to dig a session at the old Bat and there was Gordie, older now, but with the same style. Working his way through college he'd quipped and the college turned out to be, Gordie'd shamefacedly confessed, that odd school, Marplot. Mike'd been interested in Marplot, Boston's sole and abortive adventure in progressive adult education, but Gordie'd sluffed off his questions and talked fast about other subjects.

Poor kid, Mike'd thought, how lousy to be a snob without a kingdom and he supposed he should've despised Gordie for his flimsy character but instead he'd felt even more sympathetic. And anyway, how could you cut someone who thought you were great? It would take a damn secure ego to squelch such wholehearted admiration and this, Mike admitted to himself, he did not have.

Of course he didn't go out of his way to encourage Gordie but last week when he'd run into him sitting glumly at a table with a beautiful little chick, he'd asked them over for a ball before the next week's session. It was really the girl who'd inspired the invitation. She was very young, small and rather delicate, with a crop of curly, black hair and enormous, melancholy, brown eyes, eyes made even more magical by the thick, long, deepblack eyelashes that fringed them. It was not so much her looks that had intrigued Mike but her expression of eager expectancy. She looked as though she thought something wonderful might happen to her any minute, which was, Mike'd recognized from the height of his age, a typical youthful phenomenon, but with this girl it was not quite the same. There was a kind of shadow of troubled wistfulness cast over the anticipation, as if, at the same time, she was afraid that nothing would ever happen at all. Obviously nothing at all had been happening as she sat there with Gordie whose back had been turned to her and who seemed to be feeling his own deprivations keenly. It would be nice to take a girl like this one out, Mike had thought idly, smiling at her (what was her name, something Biblical and beautiful) because you could really show her a good time. Her eyes would open wide at the most ordinary social manifestations of the adult world and she'd be very impressed. Of course, she was Gordie's girl, and then, there was Jean but still . . . So, he'd asked them over and when he'd seen the little chick smile as if the wonderful thing she'd been waiting for had happened and how Gordie looked pleased although he'd tried to be casual about it, he'd been glad. And the hell with Si and the jokes about his sad friends.

Mike poured the boiling water into a mug, mixed it with the coffee powder and carried it upstairs to his room. Four o'clock. There'd be a little time to get some licks in on his typewriter before Jean came and maybe, if something good came out on paper, he'd feel better when he saw her. He put the coffee mug down on the desk beside his covered typewriter, the only machine he'd ever had the slightest use for. It was an old, 1929 model, Royal portable, its metal sides cerulean blue and some of its yellowed keys devoted to cedillas, accents *grave* and *égue*, and pound-sterling signs. It wasn't in very good condition but Mike was reluctant to turn it in for a newer model. He'd bought it for twelve dollars, secondhand, when he was a freshman and on it he'd written all of the poems and stories that Sam had thought showed so much promise.

Next to the coffee mug he ranged an opened pack of cigarettes, a small silver ashtray stamped with the coat of arms of the city of Bremen, a lighter, of Swedish make which had fallen out of the pocket of a dead German soldier and an old Waterman fountain pen. Slowly he sat down in the chair by the desk, uncovered his typewriter and, pulling open the lower drawer, dredged out a thick pile of typewritten paper. The top sheet was blank except for two lines. Self-consciously, he read them. THE FLAG-FILLED AIR, A Novel, by Michael Wainscott. Carefully, he placed the bundle of manuscript, top sheet down, on the desk beside the typewriter and riffled through some of the bottom sheets. Let's see. He'd done ten pages last time, the other day when he should have been studying for that damned Property exam. The very last sheet on the bottom was numbered 510. Picking up pages 500 to 510 he began to read, occasionally penciling in corrections. When he'd finished he frowned and threw the pages down on top of the pile. Lousy, he thought, bad. About one paragraph in the whole ten pages is any good. He sat staring balefully at the manuscript and chewing on his thumbnail. It was ridiculous. He was wasting his time, building up hopes and shirking his work and classes for this, this sandcastle that he'd thought, at its beginning, might be a good war novel.

He scowled, pushed back his chair impatiently and prowled around the room, hands deep in his pockets. What the hell was the matter with him anyway? Was he some kind of schizoid? To deliberately decide to say goodbye to a writing career, to select a stable profession like the law which would give him a steady income, and a regular, ordinary life, the sort of life he'd never had and always wanted, and then, then, to start to write a novel. He was crazy, that's all there was to it, a crazy, immature jerk.

He'd thought it all over while he was there in the hospital, receiving final treatments on his hand. The doctors had suggested he exercise his fingers. Typing, they'd said, would be a good way. So he'd spent his time writing some new stories, rewriting old ones, mailing them out. All during the fall semester of his delayed senior year he'd done the same thing. But the stories didn't sell, they were no damn good and nobody wanted them. He'd even tried a couple of agents who'd given him the usual gimmicks in their rejecting letters about how good his stories were but how there was no market for them. Try them again with other kinds. What other kinds, Mike'd thought bitterly, this is the only kind I can write. When one agent had been more honest than the others and written that she thought an agent ought to like the work of authors she represented and she didn't like his, he'd decided finally to throw in the towel. She was one of the best in the business, he knew from his father, and if she didn't like his work it was just plain bad. There was no point in continuing to delude himself. Sure, he could've shown some of the stuff to Sam. But actually, Mike had never contemplated showing what he wrote to his father. He'd succeed on his own or not at all because that way he'd be sure to know if his work amounted to anything. Otherwise there'd always be lurking doubts as to how much of his acceptance he owed to Sam and his influence.

No, if he'd continued believing himself to be a writer, it would have been an exercise in self-deception and he'd turn out to be exactly like all those old phonies he'd seen around all his life. People who had maybe written one book and talked all their lives about writing another. Never did. Writers who lived off their friends and family and wrote about one story every four years which they probably couldn't sell. Writers who were shabby, who lived in one-room, coldwater tenements, whose children grew up in slums, whose wives divorced them because there was never any money to pay bills and who yet talked proudly of the gospel of true creativity, who wouldn't bend a knee to Hollywood or the advertising agencies, no sir. Writers, on the other hand, who did bow to commercialism and tormented themselves always as having betrayed their gift to Mammon. Writers who, in despair at all the impossibles, committed suicide. And the most miserable of the lot, the Sunday writers, who worked at jobs they hated during the week and flogged themselves to the typewriter nights and weekends, who couldn't enjoy a minute of their spare time, who lived wretchedly in the present, nagged eternally by some demon vision of future fame which consistently eluded them. If you had the talent, Mike'd reasoned, it would be recognized and you wouldn't have to throw away your whole life in the agonizing effort of making the world heed your choked cry, *I'm a writer*.

So he'd taken and passed the entrance exam after getting his B.A., registered at the Law School and begun to attend classes. In a way, it'd been a relief not to think about all the marvelous books he was going to write someday; it was good to be able to sit down and read a novel or poetry or short stories when he'd had some hours to spare from studying and not have to flay himself with the thought that he ought to utilize his free time writing. But, at the same time, there was an odd emptiness about his life. He'd always written. Ever since he was nine he'd done some sort of scribbling, poetry for a long while, and humorous skits and short stories and a hell of a lot of very long, literary papers when he was an undergraduate. And the thought that never again would he involve himself in the strange, enkindling excitement of having words and ideas in his head and after much labor, see them come out on paper, had created a peculiar sadness. But he'd remained resolute.

And then, one brisk, golden afternoon, late in October, he'd come home from classes and started looking through his desk, for his Army serial number which he'd forgotten, for a wonder, after living intimately with it for years. There'd been some VA forms to fill out. But, in the mass of papers, he'd found a small notebook, and, opening it, he'd felt a prickle, a shiver, along his spine, because it contained some hastily scrawled notes about a year of his life in the Army overseas.

The camp in England, D-Day, Normandy, the platoon, officers and men, detailed descriptions of arms, terrain, seasons, how people looked at certain times, then blank spaces and then, two lines, written in a stiff cramped hand:

Rain and cold and the bitter fir trees of Hurtgen Forest. Old Ernie Hemhorroid is here with us—dashing, glamorous war correspondant—Bah!

Then, many pages, shadowy, in places almost illegible, in pencil, written in the hospital:

I wouldve died there with the mines exploding every step and the murderous fire—I wouldve died as 7500 men like me did in 21 days in that inferno—There is no hell but hurtgen and no heaven and if there is God he shows his face only sometimes in the goodness of man but this is not gods time. The devil is impartial. In Hurtgen he slaughtered germans and gis alike—I did not die there I was saved by my wound. They say Ive been brave and will be recommended for the S Star above and beyond the call of duty in the 10th day—Did I know I couldnt have lasted 11 more days and thus went out to get them to end it all because I did not care. It was unbearable impossible fiendish. There was no way out but death, no way out of hurtgen. The dr said this morning that I was lucky because the way the bullet hit it couldve killed me instead it went into my shoulder and didnt even shatter a bone. It was dug out and I am as good as new and can go back on the line by the middle of dec.

Haha I said thank you very much. O I know he said with a sharp look you dont think youre lucky. No I said I was hoping for a blighty wound. He didnt understand but let it pass. Considering what others got by way of wounds in Hurtgen he said youre lucky. Yes I know I said theres never any ideal wound is there? But the point is you dont want to push your luck too far. If I had my way he said all the men with intelligence enough to run the world after the war is over would be allowed one taste of combat and then if they survived that theyd be retired behind the front for the rest of the war. Were losing all our best men, the casualty rate for 1st and 2nd lts. very high, mostly all college trained.

No matter where you are therell always be some utopian dreamer. He was youngish too and a yale med school product. Havent you heard of democracy I said. Leaving the ignorant masses to man the foxholes isnt good democratic practice. Where dyou think you are in platos republic? He gave me the old song about how if intelligent rational men ran the world thered be no need for anybody to be at war but I told him that intelligent men had been around for years producing no appreciable change in the state of things—except possibly figuring out newer and more deadly weapons—and how about you people? Would you retire all of your educated doctors behind the lines to save their minds for the future? We are behind the lines he said. Up to your ass in blood I said and if any aid stations and hospitals happen to be in the way of a bomb they get it too—Well he said philosophically were supposed to heal war or peace anyway.

I said whos to bell the cat, decide whos intelligent enough not to fight?—itll get to be a racket—theyll fix iq tests. That idea made me laugh so hard he told me to take it easy I wasnt out of the hospital yet.

He was looking over my chart and servicerecord and of course wanted to know why I hadnt gone to ocs or gotten myself a desk job and I said I used to be an idealist—Strikes me he said youve led a pretty charmed life anyhow coming over on D-day and still here and not wounded till now. Youre not looking close enough I said or youd see all my tdy stints noted with g2, (as my mother said I know languages so well) the company clerk time because for awhile we had only men who were more scared of words than of germans. You couldve stayed in that he said why didnt you? I asked to go back I said by this time weary of him. Why was he wastinghis time with me anyhow his ivy league conscience was bothering him perhaps sending a harvard man back into the line when because doctors are powerful beyond othermortals just as well not. There were ways. I'd heard about them. After all there was only something like 1/16 of an inch difference between a shot muscle and a good one and he could send me on to the general hospital to take a lot of xrays and tests just to make sure that Wainscotts throwing arm wouldnt suddenly go to pieces in a pinch when he was ready to lob a grenade at five nazis about to cut him down in the flower of his youth but I didnt ask him. He has his conscience and I have mine. Anyway he has a good case. If a guy has a chanceto stay out of combat and doesnt hes a fool and I hoped he wouldnt ask me why and he didnt fortunately.

Because I was planning to write the great american war novel of this war the real novel of men in combat the kind of novel that hadnt been written in america only in france england and germany a novel like sassoons fierce unpleasant war poetry full of sights and smells or barbusses en feu not a tale of ambulancedrivers frisking around in rear areas with nurses and for this I needed experience first hand. I had to be right in there with it down in it breathing it skinned by it parboiled by it but now after Hurtgen I see that I will probably be killed by it and not live to write it and now after Hurtgen I wonder if its worth writing about or indeed if anything is worth doing. Words are stupid and meaningless in actuality powerless to influence events. There are no words to describe how one felt when dan rooney m/sgt disappeared in a mortar burst and came down like a fourth of july rocket in scraps and pieces one of the 2 tommyguns he was firing remained intact, Guns being more enduring than the frail humans who man them and no words can make him or all the others whole and live again—All my socalled art or piety or wit cannot lure them back so if Ive been saved from sure death in Hurtgen by a minor wound for that great literary purpose Ive changed my mind, no thank you—capt. david chilton mo is going to send me back to my outfit The nazis are about ready to cry kamerad dont you think he says finally going away—

The next entry had been dated: 17 Dec. 1944. Fog, rain, haze, snow on the trees and a bombardment like the end of the world. How wrong you were, Captain Chilton, the Germans are pounding the hell out of us and I am back in time for the winter offensive along the Ardennes. Right there in the social swim, I never miss a peak event. Ay, now I am in Ardennes, the more fool I. There's a mess going on and nobody seems to know what, except that it isn't good. I've had it now, I'm sure.

Yeah, Mike had thought cynically, scanning the last entry and throwing the notebook aside, he'd gone downstairs to brew himself a pot of coffee. Some fouled up mess all right. He'd measured out the coffee and set the percolator on the gas. The snow and the cold and the Bulge and those hills in Luxembourg which had looked a little like the Christmas vacations when he went skiing around Stockbridge. And the old castles reminding him of the Limbourg's paintings of winter. Yes, but I was lucky again, he'd thought, I was not in Bastogne or Saint-Vith or in the forward outposts and I was not taken prisoner and I didn't even get wounded again until February at the Prum River and even there, in spite of all indications to the contrary, I didn't lose my hand. *Christ,* he'd thought, *I'm alive!* I lived. Compared to that miracle Christ's resurrection was as believable and simple as the building of a house. Operation Christ-Rose the insane Nazis had called the Ardennes offensive but they didn't rise ultimately. It was us, us goddamn dirty dogfaces, and it wasn't just because we had more and better weapons but because we were free men who could take initiative and risks and fight like hell for our lives and maybe because we were still old-fashioned enough to basically believe all those old tales of our youth and to act on them. The Minute Men firing behind trees at the solid red British square, the Davy Crocketts and Dan'l Boones, the Leatherstockings and the pioneers who fought off Indians, even the stereotyped cowboys and U. S. Cavalry.

Abstractedly, Mike'd heard the bubbling perk of the coffee in its pot, poured himself a cup and suddenly with the smell of the fresh-made coffee, all his senses had been alerted: inextricably mixed, a tangle of ghostly odors flooded his nostrils and each smell had a sound and then the pictures had come, at first like an old film, pocked and torn, moving jerkily, slowly and then faster, a stream of images: the smell of sweat and latrine stinks and burning, burning metal, burning flesh, death in musty plaster, death in mud and snow. Had there been a smell to snow? Yes, then afterwards the air would be clear and potable but all that winter he'd had a cold which had been as well because some of the smells had been so overpowering. Then earlier smells of the damp European cold and wet leaves and earlier than that crushed apples when Mike Wainscott summered in Normandy and men running and men hiding and towns burning and rivers of gasoline for all those OD tanks, trucks, jeeps, command cars, halftracks and rivers of blood and the sodden bloody dead, and the frozen bearded dead and Mike Wainscott running and jumping over dead men, friends. The stink of the planet Earth in those years must have been noisome in outer space, Mike had thought, sitting at the kitchen table, forgetting to drink his coffee. In the other galaxies they must've worn gas masks and fumigated the streets of the faraway stars. And here in 1947 I am washed, he had thought, I am well fed, warm and clothed, my body and brain are intact, nevertheless once I have looked into the hollow eyes, the noseless, fleshless face of Azrael the Angel of Death and with his blood-gobbeted hands he has marked me, indelibly and forever.

The coffee had grown cold at his elbow, he'd forgotten about it, forgotten where he was: he'd heard voices, American voices, that weird range of regional accents, an almost Cockney twist in Philadelphia, the clipped seventeenth-century English of Maine, the similarities of New Orleans and Brooklyn, the tidewater voices, the backwater voices, the range and the plain and the prairies and the mountains and the delta voices. The voices of the men in his platoon in his company. The outofdate slang, the grousing, the bitching, the steady cursing, the jokes. And he'd seen them, too, all together again, green new troops to be blooded on D-Day, welded by fire and courage into a good fighting unit, notwithstanding all their losses and the criminal mistakes of higher strategy, brave men, now mostly dead. The platoon, the company, the regiment, the division, filled up with replacements and by the time of the Ardennes, it'd been a wholly different outfit. If they'd only stayed alive awhile longer, Mike had thought absently lighting a cigarette. His mind had begun to run very fast and presently he'd gotten up and gone upstairs, uncovered his typewriter and rolled a sheet of paper into it. I'll just jot down an outline, he'd thought, bending down and picking up the little notebook, maybe ten pages, it'd be a shame to let all those damn notes go to waste, and then, it was self-conscious, ridiculous, pompous, but after all, he *had* lived and might even hand himself down to posterity through his children sometime, and if he couldn't make the voices of his friends in the company be heard again, no one could and there must be some remnant, he'd thought furiously, they can't've died like a batch of stupid, pointless insects, silently. Once they were men and bestrode the earth with the sun on their heads. But anyway, just ten pages . . .

Hah! Ten pages, just an outline! In October, a lamb led to slaughter, he'd thought that and here in May he was the burdened possessor of 510 pages and it was just a first, rough, messy draft, not even finished, though a hundred times he'd sketched out the ending in his mind. But say he finally did finish it, working on it half-time and neglecting and perhaps losing out on Law School altogether. What would he be left with? An unwieldy mass of words that would take a tremendous amount of work to put it into even a shapeless shape. Cutting and cutting then, taking each sentence and going over it with sandpaper and a fine tooth comb, weeding and selecting more exact words, fitting them in, polishing, making the sentences and paragraphs fit together smoothly, making them say precisely what he wanted them to say, so that the words matched the idea, the feeling and the motion. The words must cover and clothe his people, their talk, their actions, their thoughts, as their own skins once had, they must be the only words. If he could do this, his men would live, be seen as he had seen them, their dead voices would waken and be heard and . . .

And he couldn't do it, he couldn't do it. He didn't have the patience, nor, why not face it, the ability. The pages he had just read over were lifeless, boring and ugly. It was a herculean task and he'd never do it. And if by some incredible miracle he did waste a couple of years of his life and literally weep and fast and pray over the goddamn thing and complete it but no one in the end wanted it, what then?

He groaned and flung himself into his easy chair and on a sudden impulse reached out a hand to the bookcase, pulling out a black-bound book, the title of which was obliterated by years of handling. He opened to the first page and read the words:

"In the late summer of that year we lived in a house in a village that looked across the river and the plain to the mountains . . ." and all the way through the famous first chapter. He read hungrily, seizing on each word, shaking it around in his head like a dog with a bone, worrying each perfect sentence and finally, wretchedly slamming the book shut and throwing it down on the floor. How did he do it, Mike wondered, how did he manage it? No matter how one might scorn his legend and his aristocratic war, it was genius and no amount of scoffing at mystical leopards could change that. He had done it. It was fixed there permanently for all to see. The mermaids won't sing to me, Mike thought bleakly.

He sat there for awhile with his eyes closed and thought of Bill Dunne and his father. My God, they probably went through the same thing once. Everyone in those days had been creative. Poets, writers, painters. Dunne had started out as a poet, Mike knew. And

Sam? Sam must've done something, stories, perhaps even a novel, although he'd never mentioned it. Had it hurt when they'd bowed and accepted reason? A second place as he'd have to do someday. But not now, not yet. He'd have to keep trying. Having gone so far he could not go back. It was like Bastogne, he thought and smiled a little, he was surrounded, surrounded by five hundred and ten pages of messy manuscript. He reached into his bookcase again and, picking out the Oxford Book of English Verse, checked in the index and flipped through the pages. Here it was.

"In Xanadu," he read, "did Kubla Khan, a stately pleasure dome decree Where Alph the sacred river ran through caverns measureless to man down to a sunless sea." And on, relaxed, through the familiar surreal landscape until he came to it, the place where he always felt a little chill of delight and a kind of heightening of all sensations, as if he could see right into people's heads and the veins on every leaf on a tree yards away . . .

> I would build that dome in air,
> That sunny dome! those caves of ice!
> And all who heard should see them there,
> And all should cry, Beware! Beware!
> His flashing eyes, his floating hair!
>
> Weave a circle round him thrice,
> And close your eyes with holy dread,
> For he on honey-dew hath fed,
> And drunk the milk of Paradise.

Mike closed the book quietly. My God, if only he could! He got up and went over to his desk, rolled paper into the typewriter and began to tap the keys, at first tentatively with many long unseeing pauses, then faster, with more power, his fingers scarcely stopping, his eyes now fixed on the paper, now on the keys, not noticing the growing dimness in the room, nor hearing the telephone ringing again in long, loud, imperious peals downstairs.

Four

"It's the last concert of the season," Frances Merritt had said on the phone that morning. "You really ought to go, Sally. And I thought we might have lunch in one of those lovely red and blue Swedish places."

Sally had hesitated, smothering a sigh. Friday afternoon Symphony in her present mood, ye gods, and all those people she didn't want to see who'd be there. Yet she was so very fond of Aunt Fan and since she'd been back there'd been little opportunity to see her alone. Neither she nor her aunt could expand and talk like human beings when her uncle Ben Merritt was around exuding his constant cold disapproval.

"It's an all-Beethoven program," her aunt had pressed eagerly. "With Serkin."

Oh well, Sally'd thought, yielding to her aunt's hopeful tone, if smorgasbord décor and music give her some kicks why be a churl?

"Shall we go in my car?" she'd asked.

"Car!" Frances Merritt had exclaimed, pronouncing the word as if it were a profanity. "Heavens, no. It's a wonderful day."

Of course, Sally thought now, walking over to the house in Louisburg Square, how very un-Boston and forgetful of me to suggest driving to lunch and Symphony. In California one drove everywhere, even around the corner to buy a newspaper, but in Boston it would be a flamboyant, nouveau riche sin to drive when one had two good legs and the weather was seemly. Perhaps it was just as well, really, considering that the streets of this city were as spare and bony and independent as the original inhabitants were supposed to have been. The first time she'd gotten trapped in one of those traffic jams downtown Sally had felt wildly homesick for the spaces and vistas of California. I shouldn't have come back, she thought now, walking up the front steps to the familiar door. I should've stayed there and found a job or another husband or gone to New York, but not come here. I'm out of tune here, always was and now it's worse.

Had Mike thought she was hideously presumptuous calling him casually like that after all this time and the really bald way she'd jilted him? If so his voice had not betrayed it. He'd sounded pleasant, warm, and friendly and, except for his refusal to ditch this obviously dull girl, quite interested. Surprising that he hadn't married though, but fortunate because after three weeks here, her boredom was unutterable. And even if an encounter with Mike produced no revived passion, at least he was sure to know some interesting new people.

As usual, Aunt Fan was not quite ready and Sally sat, smoking, in the upstairs sitting room. Nothing ever changed in this house. All the furniture was exactly the same, highly polished, unbudging. It was peculiar after five years to find herself sitting in the same chair by the same sunny window looking out at an unchanged garden. Time had moved on and she was no longer the same girl who'd run away to New Hampshire and married Joe Mayhew but this house, where she'd spent too many dreadful vacations from school, so many flagging, dreary days, this house had not turned a hair.

It's so darned gracious, Joe'd said, looking around superciliously, so blastedly exactly what it is and I hate what it stands for and so do you, my love, although you haven't come to terms with it yet. But I'm going to take you away from all this unostentatious, smugly limited perfection because it's not for you. You're too vivid, you clash with all these antiques. What have these centuries of hallowed, mercantile tradition to do with you? You're a tropical kind of flower, born to unfold slowly and languorously in the sun. He'd said all this mockingly and Sally'd laughed because she'd thought him very amusing then. She'd been childishly flattered at the attentions of a man so much older than she, who'd been so incredibly clever as to've graduated from Harvard at twenty and done it, under the, to her, insuperable handicap of working his way through. She'd never known a man so brilliant and cynical who, in his twenty-eight years had done so much. None of the boys she'd known had gone to sea as a deckhand or worked on fishing boats. The tales of his lurid experiences on ships and in ports of South America and Europe had fascinated her. And then, just when she'd categorized him as a kind of rough-and-ready Jack London type, he'd told her about the two years he'd spent as a Rhodes Scholar at Oxford: wearing cap and gown, taking bicycle trips through England, spending cloistered hours reading in the ancient libraries, his walking trips on the Continent with a knapsack on his back, eating bread and cheese by the side of poplar-shaded roads in France. She remembered now, painfully, an amazing evening when she'd sat spellbound for two hours in a restaurant while he'd discoursed in detail on the medieval mind in terms of its cathedral architecture as compared with the thought of the Renaissance as embodied in its churches and art. Finally, confused and made resentful by the names and references which were utterly unknown to her, she'd said, with tears in her eyes:

"Why do you tell me all this? You know perfectly well I don't understand a quarter of it!"

Because he wanted her to know of his interests and because he'd always suspected, and the tears of frustration proved it, that she was not the mere flibbertigibbet she looked, but had a wonderful intelligence, which could become highly cultivated.

"And will you be my tutor?" she'd asked, not quite sure, being a simple-minded girl of eighteen, whether she should feel patronized or honored.

"If your highness will condescend so far," he'd said smiling, and they'd both laughed and it'd all been a delightful joke.

After the war, he'd said, going on with the game, as part of her education, he'd show her England, France, and Italy, his way, to correct the bad impressions she'd received as a child of the corrupt expatriate set. But naturally, it'd been just light chatter and not to be taken seriously. The war'd thrown everything out of kilter. It was a kind of Never-never Land where one had as much fun as one could, knowing it was all very temporary. Joe Mayhew had been the most interesting man she'd run into since Ben had gone away. He didn't worship her or want to wrap her in cotton wool the way Mike had. She'd gotten dreadfully impatient with Mike after meeting Joe. Poor Mike with his romantic, cloudy, poetic adoration, how could he compare with a handsome strong-minded confident man? Joe had shown her some articles he'd written in learned journals and, rather diffidently, his published thesis on the political influences in Milton's *Paradise Lost*, all of which had been most impressive but at that time, way over her head.

Now, sitting in her aunt's armchair, Sally stubbed out her cigarette impatiently. What an arrant fool she'd been to come back. Not only was her life impossibly boring and inhibited but also, every time she came into this damn house now, she was beset by a wolfpack of rending memories. On the Adam mantelpiece there was a framed photograph of Benjie. She picked it up and stared at it. It was horribly lifelike. Really, it was unfair to the living to keep these inanimate images around. Probably every time Aunt Fan looked at it, saw the head full of curls, the broad shoulders, the sweet smile, the rounded, cleft chin, she cried. Six years of bitter, hopeless tears rising to her eyes and yet, she kept the thing around to harrow up her soul. God, thought Sally, dropping the photograph back on the mantel, he's been dead so long and that big body you can still see in the cold, flat picture, the body I used to feel so close and warm against mine, was burned up or drowned ten fathoms down and is all gone.

Down the hall was the bedroom where the damned old devil, her Grandfather Brimmer had lain dying. Remembering her grandfather now, Sally thought, lighting a fresh cigarette, I shall never hate anyone, as long as I live, as I hated him. That vile old man with his alternate rages and cold, vengeful silences, the exact cruelty of his words and his proficiency at making Aunt Fan jump like a scared rabbit at his every command. The hurt bewildered look on her face. That crazy, proud, spiteful old man who, living, had the absolute power to turn at least six people's lives to waste and now, even though dead eight years, could still strangle his heirs in the coils of a complicated and bitter will. Sally'd often wished she believed in the oldtime religion, in heaven and hell, because it would've pleased her immensely to imagine Grandfather Brimmer roasting for eternity in the hottest, deepest fires.

"My dear," her aunt, rushing in, tall, thin, and harried-looking. "I am so sorry. Everything went wrong this morning. You're looking splendid." She kissed Sally on the cheek. "I'll put on my hat and a bit of lipstick and we can go."

Sally watched with some amusement while her aunt clapped a black velvet beret straight down on her gray hair and scrabbled frantically in her bag searching for the lipstick.

"Aren't you supposed to tilt the beret a bit, Auntie? Or would that be too frivolous for Friday afternoon? Well, at least you haven't reverted to one of those awful hats. Really, it's become a national joke. Any magazine article about Boston always refers to those terrible hats the Boston ladies wear to Friday afternoon Symphony."

"It is rather silly," Frances Merritt said abstractedly, adjusting the beret, "because they're not actually such museum pieces. Simply not in the latest fashion but quite plain and serviceable."

"That's a terrific picture of Benjie," Sally said abruptly. "When was it taken?" I hope she doesn't cry, she thought, but I can't spend my life avoiding his name when I'm with her.

Her aunt frowned. "The summer before he went away, I think. When we took that two weeks' trip to Canada. You know, I always

84

liked that picture particularly. That was just how Will Driscoll, his father, looked, when I first met him." She sighed. "Poor Benjie. Your grandfather could never forgive him for looking so completely like the man he hated. Benjie seemed to have no Brimmer features at all. Of course his eyes were blue but large, just like his father's."

Sally laughed. "Not like those beady Brimmer eyes which stare right through you and find you dreadfully wanting."

"Not eyes to charm with, no," her aunt said. "But it was often said that no one would dare try any malfeasance after a pair of those good Brimmer eyes had riveted holes in a swindling mind. How is Dudley, by the way?"

"Speaking of riveting eyes? He's as peculiar as ever. Did he tell you why he wanted me to come back here and live with him? He's scarcely spoken two words to me."

"I think that's one of the reasons," Frances Merritt said carefully. "He's quite aware, I'm sure, that you hardly know each other. It's very unfortunate and all your grandfather's fault for insisting upon bringing him here when he was a mere child of eight. I remember saying then that it was monstrous to separate a boy of that age from his family. But he insisted that the only male Brimmer heir, I remember his emphasis on Brimmer, should be raised in the Brimmer tradition and not in some helterskelter, rootless, foreign manner."

"Life would've been much simpler if my father hadn't decided to be an expatriate," Sally said as they walked at a brisk clip down the Common toward Boylston Street. "Why did he anyway? Before he began to drink so much he just seemed to do a lot of partying and all those sporty things, skiing and racing cars and polo and tennis that he could as well have done here."

"What you really mean is that your father made things unnecessarily difficult for his children, don't you?"

"Oh Auntie, really." Sally stopped in confusion and then, picking her words carefully, added, "I didn't mean to sound so horridly cold-blooded and critical. I was quite wild about Jack and very shattered when he died; but to be perfectly honest, I hate having to hang around with my tin cup, dependent on the good opinion and offices of Dudley and I wouldn't have had to if Jack'd been more sensible. If I'm wrong, you might tell me."

"Oh no," her aunt said calmly, "you're perfectly right. My brother and I, both, managed quite unwittingly to do disastrous things to our children. Our initial mistake was in thinking your grandfather was basically human and when we found out our error it was really too late."

"It must've been pure hell being Grandfather Brimmer's children. It was bad enough being a grandchild."

"All those things you said about your father," Frances Merritt said, "were, in a sense, quite true. He would've been happy enough living here if his father had not been such a tyrant. But they quarreled continually. The First World War was very welcome to my brother. Just like my poor Ben. He couldn't have been a playboy over here, Sally, you're wrong about that. He was slated to learn how to run textile mills and he knew it and loathed the idea. At any rate, he defied my father and even though his allowance was cut off he had a small income from my mother's property and he managed on that. I'm sure that after a few years he would've given in and come home, but then, of course, he met your mother and married her and then he couldn't. She wasn't wanted."

"Really?" Sally asked incredulously. "I never knew that. I always thought Jack and Maddalena didn't want to come back and when I came here I could quite see why. What was the matter with Maddalena anyway? I mean I know she had the wrong religion but—"

"Your grandfather was a mass of prejudices, Sally. And aside from hating Catholics, Jews, Negroes, and all non-Anglo-Saxons, he despised people without money. If your mother's title had been accompanied by a great deal of property or money he might have overcome some of his other objections to her. But it wasn't, so he remained adamant and punitive."

"You know," Sally said as they entered the Swedish restaurant, "Grandfather Brimmer was one of the few perfectly consistent characters I've ever heard of. Mean all the way through. I've never heard anyone say anything really good about him. Except grudgingly that he was honest and shrewd."

They circled the smorgasbord table and sat down with heaped-up plates.

"In his time," Frances Merritt said consideringly, "the patriarchal tyrant was common enough, on all levels. 'Run and hide, children, papa's home.'" She smiled wryly. "However there's no doubt that he was a dreadful mixture of emotional impoverishment, driving ambition and ruthless egoism. And of course it's easy enough for us to forget this now, but in three generations by a combination of hard work and shrewd marriages, the financial and social position of the Brimmers was established. He could never forgive my brother Jack or me for marrying the wrong people and spending money instead of earning it. Mmm, these meatballs are so excellent." She looked around the restaurant happily. "I do love the color scheme here. I've been trying to persuade your uncle to have the kitchen redone in the Swedish manner. I'm sure the servants would benefit from a gayer kitchen."

"Well, it's your house," Sally said bluntly. "If you want to remodel the kitchen why can't you?"

Her aunt smiled a little. "The young are always so clear-eyed. Sally, don't you know that none of the money or property is really mine? I forfeited all rights to it when I married Will Driscoll. Your uncle controls it all and when he dies, I presume Dudley and the trustees will take it over."

"I knew all that," Sally said, rather embarrassed. "I thought perhaps by this time it might've changed."

Frances Merritt shook her head. "Oh no. Your grandfather was not the sort of man to let people escape from their just penances simply because he died."

Sally toyed with a bit of herring on her plate. Her aunt, at least, had changed, she thought. She doesn't look hurt and unhappy any more. There she sits with her long, narrow face, sharp-boned, her long narrow nose and rather sallow skin, her uncompromising gray hair drawn back in a bun, as thin and angular and flat-chested as ever, looking a little older, more lines in her forehead and her throat beginning to get that ropy look, but smiling and pleased about small details, serenely discussing all the awful things that'd been done to her.

"This is sort of a personal question, Auntie, and so of course if you don't want to answer you needn't, but if Benjie's real father had lived, d'you suppose you'd ever have regretted it, what you gave up by marrying him. Or do you now?"

"No," her aunt said promptly. "There are only two things in my life that I regret. One is that Will Driscoll died so young. The other was that I allowed myself to marry a second time, because my father insisted. You'd have to have seen me when I was young to understand, in a sense, how important Will Driscoll was to me. Basically, I was a very plain girl. All the Brimmer women were plain. And I was shy and awkward and at twenty-one, withering unmarried on the vine, with my father saying at every opportunity that no one would marry me except for his money, when, just after the war was over I was doing some work in this canteen on Marlborough Street and I met Will Driscoll. He was the handsomest man I'd ever seen."

"Yes," Sally murmured, remembering, "if he looked like Benjie, he must've been."

"He paid a good deal of attention to me," her aunt said thoughtfully, "the first time such a thing had ever happened to me. There were pretty girls all over the place but he chose me. Of course, I foolishly had to tell him I didn't see why and was astounded to find that he thought I looked kind and sympathetic. He'd been badly wounded at Château Thierry, and he didn't want to spend all his time admiring the looks of egotistical females. I began to see more and more of him, much against my father's wishes. Father said that if we married he would cut me off and I knew he meant it. I remember Will counseled me to think about it carefully because I might regret choosing him instead of the money. But I didn't. He remained in the Army you know, and his salary as a captain was small and I was so radiantly happy with him and when little Will . . . Ben . . . was born and of course I've never had luxurious tastes . . . Oh dear, I've talked too much. Shall we have seconds? I do believe I could do with some more of the meatballs and this delightful, spicy little fish."

They had ordered cake and coffee and Sally, glancing at the time, had suggested that they'd better take the subway to Symphony Hall and postpone the famous walk or they'd be late, when her aunt said suddenly:

"I've always been very fond of you, Sally, and often wished I could be more of a mother to you. You lost yours so young. But then, you see, there was always Benjie and so much of my time was spent trying to shield him from your grandfather's hostility and to control Benjie's own hostility toward his stepfather and grandfather."

"Maddalena wasn't much of a mother," Sally said casually, sipping at her coffee. She had a sudden vision of her mother, beautiful, blonde, very curved, calling her *carrissima mia* and showering perfumed kisses on her for a few, brief minutes before going out somewhere. "Jack was better. He used to play with me a lot and take me out to wonderful places and buy me marvelous dolls and toys. But then he got to be sick so often. I didn't know until I was about seven that he was sick from drinking too much." They were always going away somewhere, taking trips, but one day it was just known with flat finality that this latest absence was to be forever. Jack, the terror of the highway, lolloping along that hairpin road in southern France, with her mother beside him. Oh well, all that spilled champagne . . .

"You know," Frances Merritt was saying, "your mother's tradition was so different from ours. She might very well have thought it quite natural to send a boy away from his family and back to the home of his forefathers. A great mistake, the whole concept."

"It wasn't such a great mistake for Dud," Sally said, rather viciously slashing into her cake. "He got all the booty."

"Nevertheless, I do feel I should have tried to spend more time with him. It was hard, because your grandfather decided to take Dudley in hand, to erase, he said, the dreadful effects of his early years."

"I suppose," Sally said reflectively, "it's no wonder that Dud's peculiar then. Being raised by Grandfather Brimmer would do it. Have you seen his apartment, Aunt Fan? Now why in the world when he has all that money would he want to live in a seventy-five-dollar-a-month, furnished by someone else's bad taste, three flights up place like that?"

"I don't believe he notices his surroundings," her aunt said. "He seems to care only about his work."

Sally rose and slipped into her scarlet wool spring coat. "Isn't there some fine, healthy girl who'd be mad to marry the rich young Dr. Brimmer and mother a lot of fine, healthy children?"

"Of course there is. I've introduced him to many suitable girls since he's been back. It's been an effort for me because we've lived quite quietly since Benjie, well, since the news came. But I tried for Dudley and it didn't do a bit of good. He seemed utterly uninterested in any of the girls he met. Your Uncle Ben actually is quite concerned because neither of you are married. You're the last of this particular line, you know."

"No issue," Sally said smiling. "Ever the man of finance. Well, I'm sure that Dud will see to it. He's very canny about money. Even if he waits till he's forty-five to marry and produce, he'll do it. As for me, since I have no fortune, it doesn't matter."

"Isn't that the Animal Rescue League over there?" Sally asked as they walked along the sinuous darkbrown deadend alleyway where even on a bright day like this the sun had trouble finding its way. "Do you do any more work with them, Auntie, or have other noble causes taken you away?"

"I've been contributing some time to the Salvation Army," Frances Merritt said. "Their Evangeline Booth home and hospital, you known, for unwed mothers. I've been trying to persuade Dudley to interest some of his colleagues. It doesn't pay much, of course, and most young obstetricians apparently want to get rich. I think I may have interested a woman doctor who's quite wonderful, a German, one of those people who came here to escape the Hitlerian persecution. Her husband is a very highly regarded psychoanalyst, and she's very enthusiastic and hardworking for Planned Parenthood."

"Birth control!" Sally said incredulously. "In this state?"

"We've been working very hard to put a referendum on the ballot in this coming election," her aunt said warmly. "Dr. Asch is utterly fearless about speaking to some of the most hidebound people. Very frank. She and her husband have rented one of those big old houses in the Back Bay and she has turned the basement into a sort of art gallery."

Sally laughed. "Auntie, you've been dabbling around with reformers and arty people again. What does Uncle Ben say to this?"

"He has his interests and I have mine," her aunt said calmly.

So they had compromised, Sally thought, while they waited on the subway platform, and perhaps that's why she's so much more serene. But what a sad and ludicrous marriage it's been. She remembered once trying to explain her Aunt Fan and Ben Merritt to Joe and how really peculiar it'd sounded. No wonder he'd been derisive.

"If that *mariage de convenance* has been consummated, I'll eat my uniform," he'd said. "But how could she do it? How could an enlightened, liberal, intelligent, sweet, and lovely lady like your aunt yoke herself to a walking account book?"

"She did it for Benjie," Sally'd said depressed, because Benjie had been reported missing then, and it'd all seemed so pointless.

Joe had snorted. "Well I never met your cousin but from all I've heard of him he'd have made out a lot better if he'd kept his born name and his mother had gone to work to support him and not saddled him with a stepfather like that, a name that didn't belong to him and a lot of spurious social and financial advantages tied up in strings of hatred. Still when it comes to inherited moneys all you people have a blind spot. And I suppose this miserable stick of an uncle of yours didn't object at all?"

"Oh no," Sally'd said, surprised at the naïveté of the question, "why should he? Grandfather was very good, Aunt Fan says, about judging people's attitudes toward money and Ben Merritt apparently had as much respect and reverence for money as he did. So, instead of my father who didn't want to and died before things could change, Ben Merritt actually got to be in charge of most of the Brimmer money."

Sitting beside her aunt on the rocking subway car on their way past Arlington and Copley to Symphony, Sally wondered irritatedly why these unbidden snatches of conversation with Joe Mayhew kept flashing across her mind since she'd returned. Perhaps it was because so very little in California had reminded her of him. They'd been there together such a short time. And now her aunt, eerily enough, was talking about him too.

"I was so pleased," Frances Merritt said feelingly, "when I heard you'd decided to go to college. I've always thought women should have an advanced education. I knew that Joe would inspire you. Such a fine mind."

"It was something to do while he was away," Sally said. "Then, of course, he never came back and it was all I had to do. And it was fun. And, you know, I was majoring in English but I've always been interested in clothes and art in a dabbly, dilettante sort of way, so I took art history and painting courses too and some in clothes design. This dress I'm wearing, for instance, is one I designed myself. Found a terrific Italian dressmaker lady who was beautifully intuitive and she'd make up some of my wild ideas."

"That lovely dress?" her aunt exclaimed. "I kept admiring it during lunch and meant to tell you but I was talking so much I forgot. It looks so simple and graceful, with that nice, round, gathered neckline, and the gray silk is lovely."

"I'm not too satisfied with this kind of flashy scarlet cummerbunded waistline," Sally said deprecatingly. "It's a little too gimmicky I think now."

And now that she'd switched her aunt to the safe subject of clothes perhaps she'd not talk about Joe any more. There was no need to tell Aunt Fan exactly why she never wanted him to cross her mind again. Let her put it down to conventional grief and go on thinking how virtuous I was to occupy my widowed time in intellectual and creative pursuits. She'll never know how extremely close I came, in that first year after Joe'd gone when I learned nothing I didn't know before about drinking and men, to being kicked out, to never getting all that valuable higher education.

But then, everyone'd been that way during the war. What difference did it make? At the end of that semester, when the grades came out, the dean of women had called her in and told her that she might very well flunk out if her average wasn't pulled up, a long way up. The dean had suggested that perhaps she might move out of her apartment. The apartment for an undergraduate student had after all only been permitted because she was married, with a husband who might reappear at any moment, but now, with no husband, perhaps it would be as well to take a room in a girls' dormitory on campus. She'd study more profitably, the dean'd said. Sally had refused. She was not going to live in a dorm with a lot of bleating children, she was too old for that. The dean had said it was terrible about the war and do try to fix up your grades my dear and let Sally alone. And, rather than go back to Boston, she had cut out all social distractions for a whole semester and had done well enough to stay around for three more years and earn the degree. There'd been no further communication from the dean of women about her unorthodox apartment and if the dean'd known that Sally was considered one of the best and most available lays on campus she'd probably sighed and put it down to conventional grief and the terrible war.

The subway car rocketed into Symphony and they descended and climbed the stairs to Huntington.

"You know Sally," her aunt said unexpectedly, "I used to hope that someday you and Benjie . . . but then . . . oh, the war," she sighed.

Sally wondered if her aunt knew. No, she couldn't have. If she'd even remotely suspected, the idea would've been brushed away as ignoble. No, one could never imagine one's own beloved son . . . If you remembered children when they were small and innocent, it would be difficult to accept them properly as grownup humans, with strong drives. She knew we cared about one another. But she'd probably thought of it as young, rosepink love and been blind to its real basis, the thing that drew us together like magnetized scraps of iron.

Dud had known, of course. He'd caught them at it, down in the old boathouse at Nahant, one summer afternoon when she was fifteen and he and Benjie had engaged in a silent, horrible struggle which had ended when Benjie threw Dud in the water and not another word had ever been said about it.

They slipped into their seats at Symphony Hall, Sally keeping her eyes averted from the familiar faces, the heads turned in her direction, the eyes bright with curiosity. Her aunt's face, rapt with attention, was turned toward the musicians. Perhaps I could sneak into the ladies' room and stay there all during intermissions, Sally thought, remembering all the eyes, and avoid them all. But that wouldn't do, no, it was always crowded in there too. She closed her eyes and concentrated on the opening bars of the Sixth Symphony.

At the intermission Sally fled up the stairs and smoked her cigarette with the balcony sitters and the students from the rush seats. But, although she was not buttonholed on her way back through the downstairs lobby, she overheard enough snatches of conversation, to know that her past history was being exhaustively discussed.

"I can't bear it," she said to her aunt, sliding thankfully into her seat. "If I see one more of the girls I went to school with in one of those ghastly maternity smocks accompanied by her smirking mother, I shall scream and throw a foaming fit."

"They're all having babies. You ought to be thinking about it yourself."

"An immaculate conception, Auntie?"

Her aunt looked reproachful and a bit uneasy. "I meant, naturally, that you ought to be married again."

The only fault Aunt Fan had, Sally thought, stifling a yawn, was an almost complete lack of humor. "Away with marrying. No, seriously, I'm sort of bored with loss. I just want to have a good time."

"At least you haven't married a saxophone player," Frances Merritt said reflectively. "Your uncle was always afraid of that."

"According to that awful Howle woman, the one whose daughter looks like a monolithic pillar, whatshername, Betsy, I did much worse. I just overheard her telling some perfectly strange female, obviously as a sequel to the complete history of the crazy, scandalous behavior of the Brimmer family, that I had eloped to New Hampshire, carrying only a toothbrush in my pocket, with a clam-digger from the Cape Bogs who, it'd always been suspected, was part Portygee. And that ghastly hag knows perfectly well that Joe's family was unimpeachable Plymouth Rock. Not Midwestern robber baron vulgarians like hers."

"You needn't descend to her level," Frances Merritt said, frowning. "No matter what the provocation. To be ancestry-proud is quite as unintelligent as to be purse- or race-proud."

"Oh, I know," Sally said sulkily. "But I hate being talked about in that malicious way. So damn small town."

"Ah," her aunt said happily as the orchestra members began to file back into their places and the soloist commandeered the piano. "Now we shall hear the 'Emperor' played as it should be."

After the concert was over they walked home, all the way down Huntington to Copley Square, down Boylston to Arlington, through the Public Garden, across Charles to the Common and then over the Hill. Sally realized, as she tried to match her aunt's brisk strides, that she felt warm and slow. Too much drinking and not enough exercise, she thought, I'm beginning to puff like an old woman.

"Auntie, do you still have the place in Nahant? Because if you do and aren't using it, I'd like the key. Want to do some swimming."

"Of course. We haven't used it for quite a few years. We generally

93

rent it out to three very pleasant schoolteachers from the Fourth of July."

It was settled that Sally should have use of the cottage till the end of June which would not put out the teachers. Frances Merritt was curious to know what she was planning to do the rest of the summer but Sally remained evasive. No need to explain the possibility of a job with Vance's band, not, at least, till it was more of a certainty. She'd know about it for sure in a few weeks and then the hue and cry would be on since neither her brother nor her uncle would care for the idea of revived society singer, one little bit. It's their own fault, she thought spitefully, they ought to settle money on me right now, a good, sizable sum, if they don't want me to set up as a public spectacle. But actually, to be ravingly truthful, earning money was not the real reason for taking the job if it was finally offered. She liked to sing. Simple as that but impossible to explain to her family.

A tall, strapping milkmaid type was flouncing down the steps from the first-floor landing as Sally entered the Revere Street apartment house and since the stairs were narrow she leaned against the newel post and waited, appraising this latest example of the awful things women did to themselves; the rather regal carriage and robust sturdy body denigrated by stupidly stuffing them into a sausage-tight, flamboyant red-black-and-green-flowered print sheer, nice legs ruined by toeless, ankle-strapped, clumpy-heeled shoes, marshmallow pretty, blue-eyed face overpowered by bramble-bush permanent, carrion red nails, toes, and lips and, most distasteful of all, an overwhelming scent of too much strong, sick-making perfume at five-thirty in the afternoon.

On her way up to the third floor now, Sally wondered if Dudley would be home and hoped fervently that he was not. Living with her brother, she'd found in the three weeks since her return, was, in many ways, similar to living in a boarding house whose only other occupant used words as if they cost money. On some uncomfortable occasions they would meet in the kitchen or the hallway or collide at the bathroom door and then it would be necessary to say something in order to extricate themselves but in the main, her brother spoke to her only when absolutely necessary and she replied in kind. She wouldn't have minded actually if these few essential conversations didn't perforce consist entirely of money, a commodity which Dudley apparently found as painful to dispense as she to receive but since he was in charge of her allowance and paid all the bills of their rooming house, their communications for three weeks had been solely of this boring financial nature.

In California she'd received a punctual allowance check each month from Dudley's bank but one day after her arrival in Boston he'd taken her to his bank and set up an account for her. He'd then explained in a precise dissertation that although she could write as many checks of whatever amount she wanted on her account, he'd expect the present money to last quite a time. He'd pay all the bills and leave a small, cash fund in the house for basic necessities. Should she wish to eat there a good deal she could supplement this with her money. He usually ate at the hospital. He liked to have eggs, bacon, bread, fruit, and coffee around for breakfasts. A woman came in to clean several times a week and she could do any laundry Sally wanted unless she preferred to send hers out as he did. He didn't expect to see much of her as he was very busy at the hospital or studying. Sally could go and come as she pleased and if she wished to have people in, even when he was home, by all means, she could use the living room freely, since he used his bedroom as a study as well as sleeping quarters and it was at the other end of the apartment with a good soundproof door and walls so that social noises would not disturb him. In actuality, she'd have the run or the entire apartment most of the time. Feel free to use the liquor in the living-room cabinet. He liked Scotch but perhaps she'd like to augment the bar with her own selection . . . (I can buy it from the expense account he's setup for me, Sally'd thought, at this point, really a most superior boarding house.) Well, that seemed to be about all, except that she should notify him when the funds in her account got low. Next year, when she received her income from the trust she could, if she pleased, move out and set up her own place, but since he was responsible for her until then, he deemed this the best arrangement. Since then, she'd hardly seen him at all.

What he did with himself in his free time was an utter mystery. Sometimes, to her surprise, he would turn up at some family occasion but usually for the briefest possible time. "You doctors are always so busy," the hostess would murmur plaintively as he politely took his departure, and to Sally, "Your brother is so involved with his work one never sees him." To this she could only smile and nod. She supposed he was.

And why Dudley had taken this apartment, why he wanted her to come and live with him (wanted, hell! commanded would be more accurate) remained, after three weeks, a complete enigma. Why couldn't he have let her stay on in California for that one more year? He certainly couldn't have wanted her there as a companion. Then what? A hostess? This idea admittedly had crossed her mind before arrival, but a week with Dudley had clearly indicated its absurdity. For now, as far as she could tell, he was even more solitary than he'd been years ago. Finally, she'd decided that perhaps her brother and her uncle wanted to marry her off before she got too old or declassé running around doing heaven knows what with oddballs out in raffish California but if this were so, their efforts in three weeks were pitiful. If Dudley knew any seemly, suitable men he'd made no arrangements for her to meet them and although her aunt had given a dinner party for her it'd been mostly family or old friends of the family. The few men her age she'd seen since her return were either married, engaged or uninteresting.

I hope I can last out this year, Sally thought now, searching in her bag for the apartment key. Then when I get my money I'll go to New York, get an exciting job, do something extraordinary, different, meet men who are interesting, live a vital life, get me out of this vegetable torpor. Of course, she thought wryly, turning the key in the lock, before the year's over I might go quite insane either from ennui or from living with this shadowy, walled-in brother of mine.

She walked into the living room, peeling off her coat and stopped short at the sight of her brother who sat quietly in a chair, a drink in his hand and rather incorrectly dressed, for him, in a white T-shirt and a pair of white hospital pants.

"Hello," he said, regarding her over the edge of his glass. "Want a drink?"

Sally stared at him. How odd he looked. Quite unfamiliar in fact. Was it his negligee attire? She sank down in a hideous overstuffed chair, electric green in color, shiny round the arms and seat and overwhelmed with ropy fringe and murmured that she'd adore a drink. Curiously, she examined him as he mixed the Scotch and water and courteously handed the cold glass to her. Of course! He was not wearing his glasses. Made him look peculiarly naked and strange and, rather uncomfortably, she felt those unprotected eyes raking her, up and down. Damn odd eyes too. Probably simple myopia. Anyway it was always sort of a shock to see the actual eyes, usually framed and—in a sense—hidden by glasses. Ever since she could remember, her brother had worn glasses, even as a small boy. He sat down again now looking at her in that same dogged, fixed way and she wondered what made her want to wriggle.

"And what," Dudley said, crossing his legs and essaying a smile that made her blood run cold because it was so miserable an effort, "has my pretty little sister been doing today? Beautiful dress, my dear, sets off your charms and so on."

Why he's boiled, Sally thought, in sudden recognition, annoyed with herself for not catching on immediately, wouldn't you know that drinking would bring out this clumsy gallantry. How stupid of him. Briefly, she described her afternoon, watching him all the while with a slight distaste. Not that he was actually ugly or anything, but no woman could find him handsome or physically stimulating, that was for sure. Impersonally, she could say that he wasn't badly built, a little narrow in the chest perhaps and sort of squat in the seat, although he was tall enough. But his face, which was all that big, bony Brimmer nose and high forehead, accentuated by the close-cut hair, was really terribly hatchety and now, without glasses, those pale seagull eyes, naked and blinking, and the thin, grim mouth—dear God, he looked really sort of like a bird of prey. If only the face and manner expressed some warmth, Sally thought, it might offset that vulturous head but even half-drunk all he seemed able to summon up was this oafish coyness and cold, rather lecherous stare. It was ridiculous, of course, to feel that one's own brother was X-raying one through clothes but it was a sensation with which she was familiar, and, as a brother, Dudley might as well have been a strange man for all she knew of him.

"Yes," he repeated, wagging his head and pouring more Scotch into his glass with a generous but slightly shaky hand, "a very charming dress. You always did dress well. You know, Sally, you're too young to remember this, I suppose, but you were such a beautiful little girl, you really looked like one of those expensive dolls, all pink and white and your hair was cut in bangs like one of those blonde Dutch dolls and I remember you were always dressed in little frilly dresses, with dots and ribbons and ruffles. Pink or blue."

"How nauseating," Sally said drily.

"You don't remember of course," Dudley went on, unheeding, "how I used to call you my beautiful, little golden princess. I loved your hair. Liked to pick you up and carry you. Smelled sweet."

He stared at the floor and Sally wondered just how much he'd drunk. It was really surprising to find that one of the impenetrables that lay hidden under that reserve was this revolting maudlin streak. Smelled sweet, indeed! She flared her nostrils in distaste and suddenly became aware of the persistent odor of that damn perfume which had followed her all the way upstairs. My God, whatever that passing woman had drenched herself with, it was hideously strong.

Poison or tear gas was nothing to this. Must've poured it on herself. Bad enough to leave the clogging smog of it trailing through hallways but when it began to permeate people's apartments that was really too much. She sniffed the air delicately. Yes, it was right here in the living room. She had, in fact, been aware of it all along but the strange behavior and appearance of Dudley had distracted her. Of course it'd probably drifted in from outside when she'd opened the door. Idly, she wondered what kind of scent it had been, probably some distilled henbane called Assignation or one of those sordid sensational names and perhaps the woman had been on her way to an actual assignation. She didn't remember having seen her around before but that wouldn't signify since she rarely spoke to or noticed any of the inhabitants of the building. Of course there was always the possibility that she was just a visitor, but oughtn't there to be a law against visitors so heavily scented?

"Yes," Dudley was saying, his voice soft, rather blurred and sad, "I was always a very ugly little boy, everyone thought so and it seemed so strange that I had a sister who looked like you. I remember looking in the mirror at myself, scrawny, big-nosed, ugly, with glasses, even as a boy. Remember, your nurse in France used to call me little monkey. A little wizened monkey of a boy, the monkey and the beautiful little Infanta, who was you. But you didn't like me, you know, you used to push me away, you didn't want me to touch you, you used to scream and then everyone would accuse me of teasing you. Because I was so ugly, I frightened you, I suppose."

"You'll get frightful scars on your psyche from brooding about things like that," Sally said. "I don't remember anything at all about it."

She couldn't stop smelling that perfume. It was giving her a headache. She got up decisively and opened a window. Her brother looked at her inquiringly.

"I thought it was rather cool," he said. "Or are you inferring that I ought to get the fumes of Scotch out of my head?"

"It wouldn't be an utterly odd idea," Sally said crisply. "I've never seen you drink so much. What are you celebrating?"

"The end of an affair, my dear," her brother said. He raised his glass. "The beginning of a new Dudley. You didn't know the old one very well, did you? But I've always cherished a strong, although inexpressible, affection for you."

"Oh no," Sally said. She stared at him. "That awful perfume. And I thought it was just coming in from the hallway."

"Yes," Dudley said, wrinkling his nose. "It is pretty overwhelming, isn't it? But then, she was just here. Left right before you came, in fact. You might have encountered her."

"Yes," said Sally blandly. "Who is she?"

"Let's just say tactfully that she's rather the college widow of the hospital. I can see by your face that you are horrified by my lack of taste, but then, your nostrils will be troubled no longer. She will not return here again."

"She scarcely seemed your type," Sally said, trying to be tactful.

Dudley refilled his glass. "The truth of the matter is, actually, that I am not her type, poor girl," he said ruefully. "I'm afraid I rather puzzled her."

Well, that explains it all, Sally thought. That hefty number threw him over and so he sat down and got drunk and maudlin. What a silly bore. She wondered how much of his life was lived in this subrosa fashion. Brief affairs and then, a little quiet, solitary drunk full of self-pity, because he was ugly and had always been so.

"You see," Dudley was saying, "doctors shouldn't drink much, if at all. But sometimes it helps me to relax." He shook his head. "Still I don't like the idea of solitary drinking."

Sally rested her chin in her hand and stared at him. Was that why he'd wanted her to come back? So she could sit and drink with him when he'd been thrown over by another girl and didn't want to drink alone? Of course, and then, the perfect victim, she'd have to listen to weepy, distorted stories of how cruel, she, as a three-year-old child, had been to him. Impossible, she thought, this is absolutely too crazy.

"Sally," Dudley said solemnly, "you don't know how glad I am that you came home just now. I've been wanting to talk to you for so long, but I . . . it's been difficult."

"It's a phenomenon I've noticed," Sally agreed. "Whisky loosens the tongue." Casting about in her mind for some excuse to leave the room or even the house, but there seemed no way to do it, so she sat back and sipped at her now flat drink and resigned herself.

"I feel we could be friends," Dudley said earnestly, blinking his shortsighted eyes. "I need to have someone I can feel close to, can talk to. I've never felt close to anyone. And you always seemed to prefer Ben to me. Everyone did, I suppose."

"I loved Ben," Sally said. "And not as a brother."

Dudley tilted his head and gave her an odd look. "Oh yes, I know," he said. "But he was all wrong for you. My little golden princess.

God, I remember the day I found you in that boathouse. I wanted to kill that rotten bastard."

Sally felt her face getting red, but she said steadily, "What you won't seem to understand is that it wasn't simply a one-sided thing, that I wanted exactly what he wanted. And if you don't mind, I mean, I'm glad you're relaxing and all, but I'd rather not talk about it."

"But you have to talk about things that bother you, get them out of your system," her brother explained, sitting up with sudden energy. "That's been one of my troubles my analyst says. And that incident of you and Ben always weighed on me. A normal, brotherly im . . ."

"Analyst?" Sally broke in impatiently. "Did I hear you right?"

"I'm undergoing psychoanalysis," Dudley said, beaming at her benevolently as if he'd just given her a splendid present. "This is almost the end of my third month. That's actually the reason I wanted you to come back. Because of course one of the basic reasons for my undergoing this was my difficulty relating to people and I felt I ought to get out of myself more in order to help my analysis along. I'm alone a good deal even in the hospital. And it will help me in my career also. I took this medical residency because I'm quite undecided about a field of specialization and because it was all that was available at the hospital I wished most to train in."

Sally curled up in her chair and held her empty glass out to him. If I'm to be his home confessional, she thought, I may as well drink. It was bad enough before when he was walled up but now he was all out to relate to people and she was his first lesson. Once again, she thought wistfully of how free she could be if it were next year and she had her money. But he had it all now, he could withhold it or give it as he chose and now, for a year, she'd have to sit like patient Griselda and listen to the sounds of ice thawing around him.

"How nice for you," she said politely, accepting the refilled glass and watching him pour himself another stiff one. "And that highly scented girl," she added, "is she puzzled by you because you don't relate?"

Her brother laughed, a short nasty cough of a laugh, a mingling of rheum and despair. "Possibly. I've never related very well to women, particularly not experienced ones. She left, because, to be blunt, I am quite impotent and she got bored."

There was a dreadful silence and Sally did not dare look up from her embarrassed study of the terrible flowered carpet. After awhile she was aware of choked, explosive sounds. It was ghastly hearing a man cry, even if it was a brother you didn't like very much.

"Don't, Dud," she said uncomfortably. "I'm sure the therapy will help you."

"It's all right," her brother said, looking up finally. "Foolish of me to get worked up. Simply that I've never talked about it to anyone before you, except, of course, my analyst. It's hard . . . to say it."

"I daresay it wasn't the wisest thing in the world to get involved with a Bay Colony nurse, then," Sally said, realizing it was malicious and yet, unable to help herself. All that money, she was thinking, for him, for a stick, a man who can't even do what a man should do.

"No," Dudley said bleakly, "but it happened right after I'd begun my analysis and I was so sure, so confident. And there'd be no problem of marriage. And I could never marry, of course, not until I straighten this out."

"Oh I quite see that," Sally said coolly.

"I've always been this way," Dudley said miserably. "Oh it's not that I haven't tried. God," he added suddenly energetic, "what a hell of a subject to be talking about to one's sister."

Privately, Sally agreed but she said soothingly, "Oh I quite understand, darling."

"Yes, well it's never worked, no matter what. Today was one of my days to see the doctor, and we talked about the kind of women I have always ended up trying to go to bed with. I had thought it was very logical because with those women, not whores you know, but who like sex and are willing, at any rate, there is no virginal resistance to break down. But in the process of the free association, I became aware that it wasn't at all logical but self-destructive, because I don't respect such women and so their easiness doesn't help me at all."

"In fact, what you need is a virgin," Sally drawled, "one with few, if any, sexual desires." The words flashed across her mind in the form of a classified advertisement and she repressed a smile.

"That was not actually mentioned," Dudley was saying, deadly serious. "But my analyst did say that he wondered why I simply did not find a girl I liked and enjoyed talking to that I could just take out and forget about the sex. Someone rather unawakened, innocent who would build up my confidence and not expect things of me until I was ready for them. Of course, he didn't actually describe a girl this way, but it's obvious that any girl uninterested in sex would have to be innocent and probably quite young. Although of course she'd have to be intelligent. Emptyheaded girls are an abomination." He held up the bottle of Scotch and looked at it closely. "Enough for one more apiece."

"Not for me, thanks. And don't you have to go on duty?"

"I have a good head for liquor, you know, Sally," Dud said, pouring the remainder of the whisky into his glass. "Sometimes a little high in hospital, nobody ever knows, but don't want anyone to catch on. Analysis helps me to cut down some though, be a little stronger. You hold your liquor well too," he said eying her shrewdly, "must be inherited. Ben now, he couldn't do it. Easy, sloppy drunk," he added contemptuously.

Sally decided to let that pass. It was true that her brother drank well. If it were anyone else, she thought, he'd be lying on the floor, snoring by now, having obviously drunk almost the entire quart by himself in one afternoon. "Our late father," she could not resist saying, "wasn't awfully good at holding his liquor so perhaps it's not inherited."

Dud frowned. "I know. He'd been at it too long, that's why. Begins to tell after awhile. That's why I want to stop."

"Your analyst sounds a bit cynical," Sally said, changing the subject. The thought of her father and of the way he'd lived and died invariably depressed her. "Did he mention how you were to go about initiating this adolescent relationship?"

"He simply helped me see matters in a different light," Dudley said coldly. "This whole notion is all my idea really and it seems inherently sensible to me."

Sally shrugged. "Oh I daresay it's sound enough in an antiseptic, therapeutic laboratory sort of way. There's always the human element though, you know. You'd need to like the girl and she'd have to reciprocate somewhat. Girls aren't guinea pigs even though they are young."

"Naturally," Dudley said exasperatedly. "I understand that. It might take awhile to find the right sort of girl. That's where you come in."

This time Sally could not control herself and gave a great shout of laughter. "Oh Dud, really. You're not seriously sitting there, even drunk as you are, and suggesting that I, I, do anything as unspeakable as that. Parade girls around in front of you so you can pick one to build up your confidence. My God, well darling, really, what sort of a madam do you think I am?"

"You're making it sound quite different from the way I'd meant it," Dudley said stiffly. "I suppose I should have known you'd take it in this ribald way. It was a mistake, I see now, to tell you anything, but you were the only one who could help me and I thought . . . never mind. If you can forget what I said, please do so."

Dammit, thought Sally, now I've set his therapy back weeks. The whole thing was so sad and ludicrous and yet, here she was, his sister, stuck with his awful, burdensome confidences. She sighed.

"I'm sorry, Dud," she said trying to make her voice sound contrite, "I'll try to help you of course, but darling, I simply don't know any girls, young or old. I've been away so long. In any case, I understand from Aunt Fan that not only she, but all the mamas in Boston are throwing girls at your head, virgins all, no doubt. Why not pick one of them?"

"Precisely," Dud said, sitting up straight, "pre-cisely, ex-actly, the kind of girls I don't have in mind. I've been meeting marriageable girls from good families since I was in day school. I've gone to multitudes of coming-out parties, and similar mating-meeting occasions. That's the crux of the whole matter. None of those girls would do."

"Perhaps I'm awfully obtuse . . ." Sally began.

"No, no," her brother said eagerly, "If you'll only listen. When I was in college there were girls around whom I thought it might be nice to know. You know, attractive, intelligent, not girls who made debuts or whose families one knew, but you see I never dared approach any of them. Somehow, it was easier to go to the dances and parties one was invited to among people one knew. And I was never a conspicuous success there. But I was always afraid that somehow I'd be married before I knew it and the whole incredible truth would come out. Well, that's beside the point. I tried with the kind of women you know about and I ran away from the kind of girl who'd marry me, no matter how ugly and dull I was, because I was rich Dudley Brimmer. And I never learned actually how to be at ease with girls."

"Not even in the Army?" Sally asked.

"More of the same," her brother said brusquely. "More Peggy M . . . I mean girls like that nurse you saw, who got bored and two Australian girls who wanted to marry me because I could take them to the States."

"Poor lamb," Sally said.

"You wouldn't be doing anything more than Aunt Fan," he went on unheedingly "if I met girls casually when you had them up here. And you know all sorts of people, Sally. You meet them easily. I don't. And, well, there's all the jazz people you know . . ."

"You know them too," Sally interrupted. "Knew them before I did."

"I can't do it. Mike and Si and Tom were your friends and Ben's, not mine. I never felt comfortable with them. Si thought I was an amusing stuffed shirt, useful to borrow money from."

"But you liked them?"

"Yes, but they didn't like me."

"You never made any effort, Dud," Sally said wearily. "How do I know, if I manage to bring around some youthful jazz-digging bohemian, that you won't freeze the hell out of her?"

"I won't," Dudley said. "I must change, Sally, I must, I have to, I can't go on like this. And now, you see, I have my analysis and that will help. Talking to you like this is a beginning, don't you see? I'd never have done it before."

"I'd like to help, Dud," Sally said untruthfully, getting up, "but I simply can't see how I'm going to run across this special type you want. Now let's see"—she began to tick off on her fingers—"she must be young, innocent, intelligent, interesting, pretty enough to arouse you so that after a three-year asexual courtship your confidence is all built up but she herself must have no corresponding desires and above all she must be lacking in the usual female desire to get married and when it's convenient for you she must vanish."

"I didn't say any of that."

"You implied it. My God, Dud, it's the most cold-blooded thing I've ever heard of."

"I might fall in love with her," he said stubbornly, "and then, when the other thing is cleared up, of course, I'd marry her."

"Oh Lord," Sally sighed, "this hypothetical she." She walked across the room and stood looking down at him. "Dudley, if there's one thing I do know about you, it's that you were brought up by our saintly granpa who believed that the Brimmers were the Lord's anointed. I don't believe you'd ever marry anyone whose family wasn't as close to sanctity as the Brimmers and their ilk."

"Not true," he said dully, "I'm not a snob. You . . . you don't know me at all, Sally."

"Perhaps. I don't mind being proved wrong. But I don't much care for the role of accessory in the corruption of the innocent."

"Cruel," he muttered, "you always were, cruel and proud, and you hated me, you always did. Or else you're the bitch they always said but I never believed. If not, you wouldn't say those things to hurt me after all I've told you. Don't ask you to do anything terrible, just meet a few girls, be friendly . . ." His voice trailed off and then he said, clearly and laconically, "I'd make it worth your while."

Sally felt oddly cold. "Whatever do you mean?"

"You know what I mean." He smiled at her cynically and reached up, taking her hand. "I want you to like me, Sally. I want us to be friends. We will be, won't we? You're the only person besides Aunt Fan that I've ever felt fond of. Want to work on that feeling. You're always so"—he stumbled a bit and then pronounced carefully—"un-in-hibited, relaxed, about your emotions. People like you, make friends. That's all I want." He pressed her unenthusiastic hand tightly. "Not much to ask, is it? And I'm the one who can settle more money on you after next year. Give you lots of money, anytime I want to, after you're twenty-five. You know that?"

"I know that," Sally said. The palm of his hand was unpleasantly moist and she felt again that sensation of distaste. "What about before I'm twenty-five?"

"Bigger allowance," he said thickly, regarding her, his eyelids drooping.

Sally drew her hand away casually. "That would be very useful," she said coolly. "And now, shouldn't you take a nap?"

"Good idea." He stumbled to his feet and lurched down the hallway to his bedroom.

Sally heard a heavy thump and the creak of bedsprings. She went to the bathroom and washed her hands slowly and carefully with a cake of deodorant soap.

Five

Marplot College stands on one of the lower slopes of Beacon Hill; not the picturesque and carefully kept one facing the Charles River, nor the still grandiose representative one that fades off into the lower Common and Public Garden, but the down-at-the-heel one, the tradesman's entrance one that declines into Cambridge Street, the slummy tenements of the West End and the honky-tonk tinsel of Scollay Square. And Marplot itself is, in the Boston-Cantabrigian, Ivy League canon concerning good schools and colleges, a wrong one, an off-beat place, shabby, unaccredited, and unrecognized.

Marplot was an upstart of a college, founded in the exciting, new, intellectual freedom of the twenties by a group of eccentric radicals who believed that education in Massachusetts was too rigid, formalized, and expensive. These latter-day Bronson Alcotts argued that the lecture series at the Ford Hall Forum, the Boston Public Library, Museum of Fine Arts, and kindred institutions were not sufficient to feed the desire for education and culture so manifestly rife in the populace. Because the myriad colleges and universities, those stars in the crown of the Commonwealth, had such high standards regarding entrance exams, tuition fees, required subjects, class hours, course of study, and all the apparatus connected with getting a degree (which was after all not the important thing was it, since a person could have one of those BA certificates and not be in the least cultured,) it was blatantly obvious, Marplot's founding visionaries maintained, that many people who wanted an education in the city were put off, frightened, too poor and too hard-working to get it.

But Marplot was to be more than a center of adult education whose fees per course were to be low enough for almost any ordinary workingman's pocket. It was destined, from the beginning, to be a place for the meeting of minds, an institution of such Socratic and Platonic principles that it would revive the now dogmatized, conventionalized concept of the Athens of America. The classes would not be composed of musty scholars mouthing stale knowledge to yawning hundreds in vast lecture amphitheaters, but would, instead, be true seminars; small groups of shining-eyed people, old, young, and middle-aged who came to sip the pure waters of learning. Neither the learning nor the sippers of it would be corrupted by that commercial, ignoble necessity, that marketplace commodity, the degree. At Marplot the pure in mind would receive knowledge of all kinds from men and women who need not be sterilely academized by Ph.D.'s in order to impart it. The teacher would teach out of sheer love and the student would learn because he really wanted to. One would not take classes at Marplot in order to attain prestige, social status, the right kind of husband or wife, a profession or a salary. No, one would go, because God was Knowledge, because the mind of man was a wonderful thing and what went into your head was better than money in the bank.

So Marplot in its early days awarded no degrees, conformed to no academic standards, went its own sloppy, tousled, ungirdled, smiling, nature-girl way and, in the renaissance air of the twenties, flourished enough to move out of the three-story, old, brick, family residence it had occupied and have a building especially designed and created to express its own unique personality.

The unenlightened tourist wandering around Beacon Hill and passing by the new Marplot building would not have known that an exciting, new, intellectual ferment was going on inside because the exterior superficially conformed to the red brick, white-doored, white-pillared Boston-Harvard notion of architecture proper for colleges. The founders had thought it would be ridiculous to deny history and plant a modern building in the midst of one of the few areas left, not only in the city, but in the entire United States, which remained an unspoiled remainder of that gracious period. The Georgian façade was, however, somewhat marred by large, modern, bald windows which might have passed muster in a wider building but since Marplot was limited as to ground space it had to rise, rather narrowly to five stories and thus, it had a spindly, big-eyed air, like an underfed child. The interior, on the other hand, tried to be as modern as possible but since neither the monetary backers, the prophetical founders or the German expressionist stage set designer they'd hired could agree on what was modern, the end result very much resembled a Dada collage, which seemed satisfactorily avant-garde to Marplot's movers and shapers but when it was unveiled to the public the jaundiced eye roving over the place might easily have become unfocused.

The first sight to meet this eye was the ground-floor lobby. It curved, waved, and undulated in turquoise and was surmounted by white plaster friezes, dubiously Greek, and looked exactly like a badly misshapen piece of reject Wedgewood.

Those whose minds were unfettered and whose eyes were unjaundiced could pass easily through the lobby and find, in one of the billows opposite the entrance, a semi-elliptical door, which, when opened, funneled them into the auditorium which was like the interior of a hollow eggshell done in grape purple, its seats sloping amphitheatrically to a stage. All around the sides of this egg were white and pink marble statues of characters in Greek mythology, all executed rather daringly by a young Boston sculptor who subsequently moved to New York because the commissions at Marplot were the only ones he'd ever received in Boston. His representations of Europa and the Bull, Pan, and Leda and the Swan, were, from the very beginning, a thorn in the side of Boston and thus a joy to the administration of Marplot, dedicated as they were to the true, the free and the beautiful. At first, the city censor had ordered that the statues be removed and exiled beyond the territorial limitations of the city. Marplot stanchly refused to comply and in the end, a compromise was reached. The offending portions of the statues were chastely draped in toga-like lengths of white silk. They stayed that way until the hullabaloo of prudery was over and then they were unveiled. Periodically, they were pounced upon again and again they would be shrouded, or occasionally, wrathfully removed. But somehow they always found their way back, a little grimier each time, but still defiantly proclaiming that truth is beauty and so on.

The ground floor also contained administrative offices which were difficult to work in due to their peculiar inefficient shapes and, on the second floor Marplot got down to business with classrooms and a library. Now the library was designed most particularly to prove that the ordinary library housing a musty collection of books, patrolled by sentinel, martinet librarians, ever alert to pounce on the slightest whisper, patronized by solemn students writhing in concentrated agony over assigned readings, was, to put it mildly, an utter and complete absurdity. Marplot's library, therefore, had only one wall, the one that faced the stairs and corridor leading to the classrooms. One side was all window, and one side really was a wall but it was a building wall and as such quite necessary but in any case one would never notice it because it was completely covered from floor to ceiling by shelves of books, gaily jacketed, brightly colored, exceedingly decorative and full of uncut pages. The fourth side of the library consisted of a row of white Doric columns which were twice yearly decorated with fresh laurel wreaths. Originally it had been decided to place boxes of earth at the foot of each column with ivy planted in each box so that in time the library would come to look like a sylvan glade but this airy notion was abandoned just in time when somebody remembered the traditionally collegiate symbolism of ivy.

If one troubled to glance through the insterstices of the abortive sylvan glade one could see signs of another building wall but actually it was only half a one since part of it was taken up by stairs so that, if you were going to the library, you could get there without resorting to the stairs on the classroom side. The wall facing the classrooms had a door in it, far to the left, so as not to interfere with what was happening on the wall, which was covered from door to windows with a mural in birchbark white, red and black and depicted exactly the life Keats had described in his "Ode on the Grecian Urn," heifer lowing to the skies and all. How charming, the romantic might say upon viewing it, but a closer inspection of the mural might give such a one a rather nasty turn because the young Boston painter who created it and later blew his brains out, due to lack of recognition, had been inspired, not only by Picasso and cubism but also by African primitives and surrealism, so that the heifer lowing to the skies, for example, had two heads, one black and one red, one elongated with a cone-shaped eye and one, many-faceted, with five open mouths and a tiny, little, red eye like a hippopotamus' floating in the center of one of the mouths.

For the rest, the library had plain white pine tables, unpainted, benches to match and some red leather and chromium tubed chairs scattered around by the windows and in corners. Down the center of the room marched another row of Doric pillars and the two rows of pillars between them supported the library's half ceiling. The other half of the room was open, it would be in keeping to say, to the sky but the sky was three flights up and anyway the Boston sky was, on the whole, anything but classically Mediterranean even in the warm seasons. Therefore, half of the library was open to the third-floor ceiling, thoughtfully painted azure to simulate sky.

Since there was no use trying to study in a room which patently did not believe in study and which served as a corridor half the time there was nothing distracting about the curving flight of wrought-iron stairs leading up from the center of the library to the students lounge. Naturally, there was also a wrought-iron railing for the students in the lounge to lean on and look down into the library and at the Grecian Urn mural. And there were always exciting things going on in the library; stimulating, creative discussions, for instance, or little groups reading poetry aloud to one another from the books they pulled easily off shelves. Such words as stack pass, library card, or reserves were anathema in the clear, cerebral air of Marplot. Books were to be read for love, understanding and discussion and one should not, the school's prospectus proclaimed, have to wait till class time to do so or to take down steamtable notes. The moment of incandescence should be the moment of vocalization or question. So, in Marplot's Library in those days one could hardly get a line read before someone was starting a discussion on it.

By the time they got to the third floor everyone involved in Marplot's expressive building was rather tired and the money had dwindled alarmingly with no prospect of more and there were still more classrooms and the painting and sculpture studios to be equipped as well as boring things like bathrooms and faculty offices, so that the student lounge on the third floor was ecstatically simple. What walls there were were pale, pale green adorned by a few Japanese prints. Everywhere else was rice paper and bamboo screens so that if you wanted to be private, have a tête-à-tête, or take a nap you could simply enclose yourself. The floor was covered with straw matting, there were low tables scattered around, in the corners were piles of cushions and thick straw mats to sit on or unroll if you felt sleepy and behind one screen was a small hotplate, a cupboard and a table where the school had one of the students sell tea and coffee every afternoon and evening.

Beyond that, Marplot became conventional. The classrooms were unattractive; small, poky rooms with armrest chairs in an uneasy clutter, a dais and desk for the teachers, and blackboards. And all the walls of the top-floor rooms were brownish buff, cheap in wholesale quantities. There was a studio with a skylight on the fifth floor where painting and sculpture were taught on alternate days and evenings. A partition of beaverboard was supposed to keep these two plastic arts separated but somehow easels, canvas, and turpentine seeped in among plaster, wood, and stone, and resulted in a horrible jumble at least once a week. But who cared about that. What mattered was the spirit of Marplot.

And the courses one could take, ah the courses! Classes were given either morning, afternoon, or evening but there were far more evening than day courses. There were classes in every major or minor literature. There were languages, history, economics, philosophy, psychology, Oriental and Western religions, classes in directing, acting and play production, classes in how to start businesses, how to manage money, how to be fashion designers, how to write stories for highpaying slick magazines or how to be foreign correspondents, how to write great novels or poetry, how to write movie scripts, how to be radio announcers. There was, of course, Art, history as well as studio, and jewelry design and, a class, very popular with suburban ladies, on how to recognize and refurbish antiques. A perusal of Marplot's catalogue detailing these and the many, many more courses, taught by so many eminent men, all knowing either the magic secret of success or the totality of plumbed and unplumbed depths of knowledge from civilized and uncivilized times, would fair make a prospective student's head reel and the fees were not at all prohibitive, even if one just had an ordinary job, and it would be so worth it, one would get so much out of it. One would meet interesting people, nay, even fascinating, exciting people, people whose lives were not humdrum, bounded by office, home, and family. People who had lived in Europe, who were free souls, people who were well educated and of the upper, rich, leisured class but yet who loved teaching so much they could tear themselves away from their fabulous lives for one night a week and come to inspire the eager searchers at Marplot. Then, too, there was always the chance that one could improve oneself. Knowledge was, after all, power. Perhaps there would be a better job in the offing if one took the class in Speech Improvement or the class in Play Reading-Aloud or the class in Modern Dance, how much more graceful it might make one, more attractive to men, or the class in Music Appreciation, one could go to Pops or the Esplanade concerts or even Symphony and feel quite at home there, the meaning quite plain. Besides it would be something new and different, a change, a break in the monotony, sometimes even a chance. So in the beginning they flocked to register.

And Marplot did not deceive them. The men and women who taught the courses either were very interested in the new educational experiment or did like to teach and welcomed a larger audience for their subjects or else were glad, simply, to pick up a little extra cash. If many people's lives were not changed, if most of the students did not receive all they'd hoped for, it was not Marplot's fault. And it was to their credit that some of those who came and took the courses did get exactly what they'd wanted, a small glimpse of what was good about the life of the mind.

But, by the early thirties things changed and the sky turned gray over Marplot. People no longer had the money to pay for interesting courses. If they wanted to learn they went to the public libraries and read free books. Most of the time they were too busy trying to get enough to eat and some coal for the furnace to worry about learning. And, by then, it became very obvious that middle-aged and older people had neither the time nor the money for Marplot and younger people had neither the money nor the desire. For if there was any money at all to be spared for education, it was quite plain to the younger pragmatic generation that it must go to the coffers of schools which offered degrees or trades and professions, tickets to salaried jobs.

And the very air over Beacon Hill had changed. Boston itself had never accepted the new wind of art and freedom but a few brave souls had dared there and for a short time Beacon Hill had sported its own small, repressed Greenwich Village, its bad, miniscule copy of the Left Bank in Paris. There'd been artists in studios and little theatre playhouses, some galleries in empty stores, a few arty teashops and cellar cafés, some defiant beards and bookshops. Cold Roast Boston and Depression Boston wanted no more of that or of Marplot. To one group which still had its thriftily invested money and its long heritage, Marplot was simply a ridiculous, unseemly, not at all well-bred modernday version of the sort of lunacy that periodically sprang up in Boston, ran its course and blessedly died a natural death. One simply ignored these rashes; Bronson Alcott and the Temple School, The Newness and Brook Farm, mesmerism, head bump readers, strange religions and philosophies, reformers, outré vulgar personalities who would not stay in their place, they had all disappeared just as Marplot and those ghastly batikclad sandaled girls and bearded soi-disant artists would go away. The other group, if they thought of Marplot at all, connected it derisively with those nude, indecent statues and the bunch of nuts who lived in the neighborhood or went to school there.

So Marplot's founders, trying to weather their own personal storms, sadly, were forced to give up the ghost and were succeeded by a group of more practical people who looked cynically around and saw that all the other colleges and universities in the area still charged the same tuition and their classes were not empty. Cannily, they then decided, that though it might take some doing, there was still a need for a more inexpensive college in Boston but what was wanted was a cutrate Liberal Arts college which awarded degrees.

So, all through the thirties and early forties Marplot struggled along trying to gain respectability and security. Its library was walled in, its book collection augmented, its courses were diminished little by little until there remained only the orthodox, austere, required subjects as a bedrock. The painting and sculpture studio was turned into labs, the faculty all had degrees, the lobby was no longer turquoise but a dull gray, the grape purple of the auditorium had faded to an unobtrusive puce, the statues remained permanently veiled and the mural in the library was curtained except for state occasions so that the students who really studied there now would not be distracted.

The tuition, however, remained low, by Eastern standards. In truth, they had no excuse to raise it because Marplot did not offer much and the degree it now doled out was sniffed at on the Eastern seaboard above the Mason-Dixon line. Marplot, in fact, was not yet an accredited school although many students who could not afford other schools or who suffered from some academic flaw in their secondary education turned up there, registered their intentions of matriculating and took what they could by way of classes. The majority of the courses were still given in the evening because three quarters of the students were employed fulltime in the days, and a good proportion of these sturdy souls spent six years of their lives going to Marplot after work five days a week. The day students could manage the degree in the conventional four years although it was apparent to them as they worked along that what they'd get in the end would go unnoticed in the world, academic or otherwise, and many of them, after two years at Marplot, if they wanted to major in a special field or get more out of college, scraped together money for train fare and room rent and departed for the Midwest and the land grant state universities where, for the same tuition fees, they could really go to college. Still, for those who couldn't or wouldn't leave, Marplot was a haven; the only college in Massachusetts which the poor, working student could afford.

When the war ended in 1945, the GI Bill students began to pour into Marplot, bringing with them the ever welcome government money and, after years of limping along, the school now began to have the wherewithal to refurbish itself and improve its faculty, library, and curriculum. Refreshed, Marplot threw itself again into the struggle for accreditation and now, three years after the war, it looked as though the long, Sisyphean effort was to be rewarded. Marplot's exhausted administration rejoiced. The majority of the student body was delighted. But to a small group of vipers within Marplot's bosom it was a matter of supreme indifference whether Marplot attained academic respectability or not, because, no matter how you cut it, the school was still a dump, a joke, a monstrous travesty of a college and to have to admit that you went there, especially to a Harvard man, was to brand yourself irrevocably inferior and poor.

On this particular lovely May Saturday, Gordon Bruce, the ringleader of this Marplot-is-the-place-where-when-you-have-to-go-there-they - have - to - take - you - in - but - if - you - like - it - you're - irredeemably-square group, had come to his detested Alma Mater about eleven o'clock in the morning, to study in the library. Once there, his studying resolved itself into a half hour of hanging around the circulation desk, talking to his chick, Deborah, who worked there and fifteen minutes devoted to perusing a battered library copy of *Studs Lonigan*. He had to, he thought, he had to flee to reading the damn book as a refuge, away from Deborah's prissiness, her smug virginity. Goddamn the girl! He'd come specially early to the library. Needn't have come till she got through at one o'clock and then picked her up for a bite somewhere before they went on to Mike's. But he'd dragged his ass out of bed early on Saturday morning, an unthinkable move ordinarily, just so he could get some time alone with Deborah and here she was, being stubborn again. Over the top of his book, Gordie could see Deborah sitting at the library desk doing something with catalog cards. He stared at her balefully. For half an hour he'd argued with her, in whispers, at the desk, but she'd just shaken her head. What the hell kind of girl was she anyway? He slammed the book shut. He was sick of reading about Studs. The cat was nowhere. He got up, feeling in his pocket to make sure he had cigarettes and matches, and sauntered toward the library door. Deborah raised her head inquiringly as he went past the desk and gave him a timid smile. He didn't smile back. Let her think that he was cutting out alone, it would serve her right. He went out and climbed the steps to the lounge, lighting a butt as he went.

The lounge had lost its simple, aesthetic Japanese character long ago and was now contemptuously referred to as the Wreck Room. It was now prevailingly dingy gray and had a full complement of walls, an old, battered piano with yellowed keys, a shaky, scarred Ping-pong table, a few benches, a lot of folding chairs and some very hard wooden ones. Some day the lounge would bloom again when Marplot had completed its more pressing obligations toward books, faculty, and courses but right now, two loaves of bread were barely enough and to trade one in for a lily would smack too much of an earlier Marplot and its nonsense with Grecian Urn murals. The depression Marplotters who ran the school now didn't even want to think about the parlous waste of money that that sickening picture represented.

Gordie made straight for one of the last remnants of the earlier Marplot, a decrepit red leather and chrome chair which might very well tip one onto the floor if sat on too carelessly, and, well aware of the antique's peculiarities, lowered himself into it gingerly. Once you figured out the balancing act, he thought, it was far more comfortable than any other seat in the damn room. He looked around the room irritably and, noticing that his cigarette had gone out, lit it again and threw the burned-out match on the floor, even though an ashtray, one of those standing ones, wafting a stale, month-old smell of ashes and butts, leaned tipsily at his elbow. God, what a shithouse, he thought, blowing smoke, will I be glad to get shut of this place. And of Deborah, that little bitch, that damned tease.

He closed his eyes to shut out the sight of the Wreck Room. Thank God he was the only one here so he didn't have to make conversation with any moron who happened to be around. What a perfect setup, he thought bitterly, the building almost empty, school all over, no more classes, the last final had been held this morning and by eleven o'clock when he'd arrived most of the students taking it had gone. Only three students, grind, fools, in the library. At noon, May Rogers who was working with Deborah this morning would leave and at one, the library would be officially closed by Deborah and the school would then be closed till Monday. Only old Ed the janitor, or custodian, as he preferred to be called, would then be left in the whole damn building and he was so fat and had so much trouble with his feet that he'd just stay down in the furnace room sleeping and unless somebody bothered him, he wouldn't start crawling up the stairs till two o'clock. But even if Ed were wandering around the building, highly unlikely though that was, it wouldn't matter, because Deborah also had the key to the Staff Ladies Room on the third floor right behind the lounge and Ed wouldn't dare go in there unless he pounded on the door first. Anyway, they could lock it behind them. Oh, of course, Deborah didn't think so. She claimed that Ed could walk right in with his key and he would too because he'd think all staff ladies had gone but that was ridiculous and just one of Deborah's excuses. He'd heard so many of them in the past four or five months that he was damn good and sick of them. Gordie sighed dispiritedly and pulled on his cigarette. The Staff Ladies Room had a nice little couch in it and if Deborah would say yes, they could leave the library a few minutes before one, no one'd be there by then, Deb could unlock the ladies room door, they'd slip in, lock it behind them and in fifteen minutes they could be out of there with not a soul the wiser. Maybe twenty minutes. By one-thirty, he figured, they'd be having lunch somewhere. It was a perfect opportunity, practically the only perfect one he'd had in this case, and by God, he wasn't going to pass it up. They'd never be likely to have another chance like this, not before he left anyway, and if he didn't make Deborah once before he left, he'd never have any respect for himself again. Well, anyway, until the next girl, but still it would rankle. No, by Christ, he wasn't going to let her get away with it.

It wasn't bad enough, Gordie reflected aggrievedly, to let his emotions get tied up for six months with a girl whose naïveté and innocence about ordinary facts of life at the age eighteen, no, she was nineteen now, was well-nigh astounding, incomprehensible in this day and age, but she also had to be a girl who came from an out-of-this-world, orthodox, Jewish family. Gordie had gone with innocent girls before, that was really not much of a problem, but for crissakes, you had to have some place to work in and since Deborah's father would apparently go off the deep end if he knew his daughter had taken up with a Gentile, there was no opportunity to educate Deborah on the sofa of her family's living room when the parents were asleep as it was often possible to do with other girls. Other girls also had parents who went away for weekends or vacations, thoughtfully leaving a house free for parties and full of available bedrooms, but not Deborah's family, who seemed to have nothing to do but sit around and keep hawklike eyes on Deborah. So, in all the time he'd been going with her, the closest he'd ever gotten to her house was to meet her on the beach in Winthrop, where she lived, a few hot Sundays this month, and, if all the stories he'd heard from her concerning her father's violent temper and religious mania were true, it was about the closest he wanted to come. If a man was so far gone in this modern world and in this country as to start slapping his daughter around and ripping the house apart because she had spent twenty minutes standing in front of her door talking to some lad from her high school, whose only crime was not being Jewish, Gordie could see why it would not be healthy to get within six feet of such a character. But still, it definitely cut down the area of operation. Even if a girl were a hell of a lot more sophisticated than Deborah you had to work with a certain amount of finesse. They preferred beds and sofas or, at least, cars.

At the thought of cars, Gordie sighed and permitted himself the despondent luxury of regret. If only his father hadn't died, if only his father and mother'd been smarter, he wouldn't be sitting here now, like some kind of a two-bit square trying to figure out ways of seducing a girl that, under other circumstances he probably would never have met, or been bothered with, if he had.

When Gordie was younger and heard people refer to his obstetrician father as a "society doctor" he'd thought it was a compliment. Only later did he learn that the term was not flattering; that it meant physicians who took only patients capable of paying steep fees, who devoted no time to clinics and who, very possibly, sanctified and performed so-called therapeautic abortions at whopping prices. But then, after his father's sudden death of heart failure at the age of fifty, Gordie'd learned a lot of surprising things. Such as that, while he and his sister were raised much like children of really rich families, they were not rich. That the large, well-furnished house on beautiful grounds in one of the most exclusive sections of Newton, the two cars, the various maids, cooks, and gardeners who worked for them, the summer cottages at the best North Shore and Cape resorts, the expensive camps and private day schools, the European and Caribbean trips his parents took, everything had depended on his father's earnings. The Bruce family had lived through the Depression as though it had not existed, as though there were no old age, tomorrows, incapacitation and winters of flesh and spirit, until that terrible day when Gordie was fourteen.

He'd had to leave St. Paul's in the middle of his sophomore year and go to public high school and his sister Peggy would never get to Miss Folsom's School where her mother had gone. And Mrs. Bruce couldn't explain any of it; why the house, furniture, and cars had to be sold, why they must live in a miserable little three-room apartment in the Back Bay and above all why they had lived beyond their income, spent up all her sizable inheritance, invested and saved nothing and were left with only a rapidly dwindling insurance.

After a bewildered year, it became apparent that someone would have to go to work until Gordie graduated from high school and so his mother, who'd never worked anywhere and who was trained only to be a good wife and charming hostess, took a job at a ladies specialty store on Tremont Street. Standing on her feet all day catering to horrid women who'd never had a tenth of the things she'd had, ruined her disposition and her charm. She came home each night, lachrymose, exhausted, and complaining, and since she could not cook or be domestic and was too listless, miserable, disorganized, and bereft, in her words, to learn, Gordie and his sister did the shopping on their way home from school and straightened up the constricted, shabby little apartment. There was hardly enough room for the three of them to turn around in and Gordon had to sleep on a daybed in the living room. Gordie's sister who was learning cooking in school made the suppers which Gordie could never think of without nausea, consisting as they usually seemed to of white sauce and lumpy biscuits.

There was no money at all for college, not even for a small, insignificant one. Gordie's mother had told him that plainly. He would have to go to work. She would not be able to go on killing herself in this awful job much longer. It was making her old before her time. She was sorry because she'd expected him to go to Harvard in the family tradition and if his father had lived they'd've wanted for nothing and here she'd broken down and left the sentence unfinished. But what would he do, Gordie'd wondered bewilderedly, what kind of work? He wasn't trained. His mother didn't know. She wasn't brought up to work either but had to do it, willy-nilly, and it was harder for her being so much older and used to an easier life. Gordie'd been raised to respect and obey his mother and to consider her word as law and, like most boys, he'd imitated his father's attitude toward women and to his father, his mother had been someone to cherish and protect, therefore, he supposed at that time, that he must do it too. His mother obviously expected him to assume his father's role of wage-earner. Peggy, his sister, was only ten years old and she couldn't earn any money. Before he'd even finished high school, Gordie'd begun to feel a terrible sense of responsibility and a corresponding fear.

He'd kept on with his academic course in high school because he couldn't stand to think that his life was to be like the lives of other boys in his school who were learning trades and office skills in preparation for a wageslave existence. Many of them even had afterschool jobs now. One day, in desperation, several months before graduation, he'd had a talk with his English teacher about chances for getting a college scholarship. Previously he'd despised those jerky grinds in his Latin and Math and Chemistry classes who were going to college on scholarships, guys who did nothing but study and, whose life at college would be more study, interspersed only with work for the money to eat. Going to college like that would be worse than illiteracy, Gordie'd thought, knowing that for his former St. Paul's classmates, college would be like all the books. They'd go only to Ivy League colleges, the ones that counted, have allowances and cars, live in the right houses, join the right clubs, meet the right people, get started on careers that led somewhere, have a decent social life. They'd be *in*. The thought of having to work his way through college on a scholarship and possibly, while he was waiting tables, meeting some of his old prep-school classmates, mortified him. And yet, he couldn't reconcile himself to a life as an office clerk, getting a penny-ante salary, being a shabby, white-collar jerk all his days, either.

Gordie's English teacher had looked over his grades and listened to his halting, embarrassed remarks and then had said, disapprovingly: "Well, Bruce, I'm afraid you don't have a chance. If you wanted a scholarship you should have tried to raise your marks a long time ago. What did you plan to study?"

English, he supposed, Gordie'd said with hauteur, feeling the shock of a man who has at last humbled himself to ask for something he knows is beneath him and finds to his surprise that it is, instead, far above him.

"English!" the man had said scornfully. "Unless you want to study education along with it you might as well forget it. It's useless. You'll never earn a penny. Now, if you'll take my advice, you'll get a job days and take a few courses at BU at night. You seem to have a certain facility in composition writing and maybe you could study journalism. BU has a pretty good school."

"BU!" Gordie'd exclaimed, touched now to the very quick and then, as the teacher had looked at him quickly, he'd added in a politer voice, "I mean I wasn't thinking about going there."

"Okay, Bruce," this bastard had said irritably, "I know you transferred here from St. Paul's but you asked for my advice and I gave it to you. We can't all go to Harvard, you know."

Gordie had told himself that he didn't care. If he couldn't go to college the way people like him ought to go then he'd rather not go at all. And his mother agreed with him.

Anyway it didn't matter about going to college, not really, because of the war and Gordie figured he'd be called up and since he didn't want to go into the Army anyhow and had nothing else to do but go to work at some indefinite, demeaning occupation, the day after high school graduation, he went down to the Navy recruiting offices to enlist. And the Navy had rejected him because when he was five years old, before he could remember, he'd had rheumatic fever and been left with a slight heart murmur. All the doctors who'd seen him had assured his parents that its presence would probably never trouble him, that he would undoubtedly live a long, energetic life with it and be as athletic as he liked and he himself had forgotten all about it. The Navy doctors agreed. Probably never cause you a bit of difficulty if you lead an ordinary life, they said, but we can't risk you for combat. So then Gordie'd tried the Coast Guard and finally volunteered for the Army but even there the answer had been finally and irrevocably *no*.

The night that he'd been turned down by the Army, Gordie'd stood outside the recruiting station at five o'clock of a cool June evening and felt even more hollow, alone, rejected, and deprived than he had the day his father died. Then, he'd lost his father whom he loved, he'd lost a way of life which was the only one he'd known, one whose smiling blessedness now seemed to him as unreal as if it never existed, but now, now he had lost a whole world. Now, he was really shut out. The whole mainstream of life rushed by him. An entire segment of masculine experience was forbidden to him. He was isolated, naked, stripped of all self-esteem, not a man with a man's birthright to bear arms and serve his country but a cripple to be pushed aside as unfit. He'd walked aimlessly along the narrow streets because he did not want to go home. There was nothing to go home for or even to live for. There was nowhere to go. Whatever was in store for him in the future he knew it could not be anything good or anything he wanted. He'd stared the lousy, drab inevitability of his future in the face and it made him sick. Everything had been taken from him. He was the most useless piece of trash ever allowed to be born and grow up thinking he had a chance. He'd tried to get drunk enough to pass out someplace and forget for a while the pain that ate him up inside but even that pleasure was denied him because he looked too young to be served liquor and some places where they questioned his age he'd bitterly observed soldiers, sailors, and Marines who looked even more boyish than he did, drinking their heads off while bartenders smiled.

Doggedly however he'd gone from one dive to another, sometimes managing to get a lousy highball of bad barwhisky and ginger ale and frequently, nasty refusals, and thinking oppressedly about his mother. She'd be glad as hell that her darling boy was never to be taken from her. In fact, she'd even suggested that if he were drafted he could plead dependency. So she could retire and he could spend the rest of his life plugging away like a nobody to pay her back for those two years of standing on her feet and being a shopgirl. And now there was no way out. Even the Army wouldn't have him. He was stuck, trapped. For the rest of his life he, the boy nobody else wanted, would be coming home to his mother, to be her comfort and support. But goddamit, not now, not tonight.

He'd been dragging himself through a tangled network of little streets behind the Bradford Hotel when he'd heard music coming from someplace close by. The sound of wailing trumpets and wild drums had come to him all the way down the street and he'd followed it and tracked it down to a dimly lit cellar. It was a small place, smoky and dark with a tiny bar, a few tables and booths and three or four guys playing music on a little dais at the other end. The bartender hadn't questioned his age and he'd sat at the bar finally getting drunk and hazy but still quite able to feel the compelling power of the music. He'd liked popular music, swing, they called it then, and had danced to Glenn Miller records but this stuff was altogether different. It had power and sensuousness and he'd felt all worked up and at the same time calmer. One of the musicians, an easy, smiling Negro, had gotten up and sung something although it sounded more like shouting than singing. Gordie hadn't been able to catch all the words of the song but it was the saddest goddamn thing he'd ever heard and he felt every note because the guy was saying all the things that he, himself, Gordie the rejected zero, was feeling. Everyone was kicking him around, he was just as no-account as the guy in the song was, doors were slammed in his face, he couldn't get a drink in a decent place, he didn't have a girl to love him, why would any girl love a 4-F when there were uniforms all around. Gordie'd wanted to put his head down on the bar and bawl. His eyes had stung, what with thick smoke, no air and sadness. The steady, driving beat of the drums, the blue trickle of the brass, the mournful, minor chords of the piano, the lamentations of the singer brought all of Gordie's melancholy to a head. He'd rubbed his eyes, gulped at his drink which collided with the misery choking his larynx and ended up letting out a couple of crazy, strangled coughs. For a few seconds he'd had trouble getting his breath and then some soldier had pounded him on the back. Gordie'd muttered his thanks casting angry glances at the uniform. Then, suddenly, he'd wanted to talk to someone, uniform or no, and he'd asked the soldier what the song was.

"Just blues," the man'd said offhandedly. "Makes them up as he goes along. Pretty good isn't he? This the first time you've been here?"

Gordie'd admitted that it was and the next thing he knew he'd been spouting off to the soldier who seemed like a hell of a nice fellow, well-informed about this kind of music, intelligent and above all spoke with an accent that Gordie recognized immediately. The guy's name was Mike Wainscott and he hadn't seemed to care about Gordie was a civilian but Gordie had to tell him anyhow.

"It's the blues, man," Mike'd said wisely. "The best way to get over them is to listen to people who really know what the blues are. Like that cat up there singing. Sure you feel lousy being turned down but what can you do about it? If you want to know what it's like to be turned down every day of your life try being one of the dark-skinned boys for awhile."

Gordie hadn't known much about a lot of the things Mike said that night. He'd never thought particularly about Negroes one way or another but they sure could play music and he liked the way this Mike talked. He'd felt a lot better when he finally left the bar that night, it was called the Bat Club, and Mike'd said that he had a week more left of his furlough and why didn't Gordie come around to listen to more music the next night and they'd meet.

Everyone'd seemed to be asleep by the time Gordie'd gotten home that apocalyptic one in the morning but the next night when his mother had come home from work, there'd been a scene touched off by her suspicious questions. She had, it seemed, been worried, lain awake. Heard him come in. What had he meant by causing her all this needless fretting? Instead of staying up all night long, doing god knows what horrible things, he should've been up bright and early job-hunting. The querulous tirade had gone on for a few minutes before Gordie'd summoned up enough courage to cast aside his gentlemanly instincts, so carefully nurtured in him, a relic of another age that had nothing to do with them now. Now he thought we're going to be, we are, like all sorts of shoddy, poor, frustrated, igno-rant people, fighting among ourselves for our right to exist. He'd then breathed deeply and raised his voice to a shout, and in shocked dis-belief, his mother'd paused in the middle of a word. Her children, no one, had ever spoken to her so. What Gordie'd said had been, he remembered afterwards, wondering how he'd dared, blunt, crude and, as his mother'd said later, lower-class.

"I'll get a job all right," he'd said, "but not to support you. You're not an old woman and you're not crippled. Not a 4-F like me," he'd added, grinning horribly at his startled mother and sister who'd gazed at him in fearful fascination as if toads instead of words were hopping out of his transformed mouth. "It's wartime now, Mother dear, and you could get a good job easily. You could learn how to type and work in some defense plant office or something. I suppose you think you're going to retire and I'm going to work and that's it. Well, it isn't. I'll get a job but it'll be for me, for me to dress up if I can without a uniform and take out girls, if I can get any."

His mother had finally recovered her tongue and set up some sort of wail about his ingratitude and if only his father were alive but Gordie hadn't waited to hear the end of it. He'd rushed off to the Bat Club. It'd been embarrassing to have to ask Mike for advice about jobs, a guy he'd just met but Mike'd bought a lot of drinks for him and that had helped and the music was more primitive and bloodstirring than the night before and Gordie'd felt the fever of his independence rising in him. He had dared and he'd have to dare further in order to consolidate his gains and after a couple of hours it'd been easy to ask Mike and Mike'd been cheerful and reassuring and said he'd ask his father.

By the time Mike had left Boston, Gordie had a job as a sort of office boy at Houghton Mifflin. He'd used Mike's father's magic name and although it wasn't much of a job, Gordie'd had high hopes then of perhaps getting ahead in publishing. His job didn't pay much either but the work was more interesting than it would be in an insurance company. Nights and weekends he immersed himself in the fascinating jazz world which enlivened blacked-out Boston, and there he'd met some people he thought might be great to know if they'd ever act like they knew he was alive. For instance, there was that beautiful Sally Brimmer who was real society and had made a big debut the year before. Gordie had maneuvered an introduction and managed to be witty and keep her laughing for a full fifteen minutes before competition interrupted. And there was never another chance. Too many other guys around. Anyway, what did he have to offer someone like her? Maybe if his life had turned out the way it should've and he'd be going to Harvard and still living in Newton, it'd be different. So when he'd seen her around he'd say hello or smile at her, and that's all, and sometimes, he could tell, she wouldn't even remember him, but she'd always smile back. After that of course she made the papers by eloping with that kind of snooty, supercilious Navy character who was always with her. Gordie couldn't figure how a girl who had all those advantages of money and background could throw herself away on an unimportant nobody. Why did some guys have all the luck? She must've been a pretty strange girl anyway, Gordie'd thought, because you never saw her with the kind of people a girl like her ought to hang around with. The rumor went that she was more than friendly with some of the musicians and didn't give a damn about their color either. She'd been pretty chummy too, with some of those friends of Mike's, the ones that Gordie'd tried hard to know without much success until he realized that they were a stuffy boring lot. It had made him sick to see how impressed they were with themselves. Acourse most of the men were Harvard and upperclassmen and all fit and able to go into service which they did a lot of griping about and Gordie supposed that they pretty much despised him because he was none of these things. Well, a fat lot he cared. He was no dumb young punk like they thought he was and when he saw them he was careful to talk airily about St. Paul's and since they were English or History Lit majors, he'd always make a point to refer to books he was reading or had read or got to see around the publishing house. He'd been glad when he started getting to know different people who came to the sessions and he didn't have to keep up the pretense of acquaintance with these jokers because he used to come to the clubs alone in the beginning after Mike'd left and there was nobody to sit with but them. Pretty soon, they'd all disappeared from circulation and he didn't see them again till after the war. But just the same without having to put up with their pained looks, because he didn't know a damn thing about literary history and philosophy, he knew he'd have to go to college. By this time he'd been desperate enough not to care where he went, just somewhere to learn a little.

As it happened he hadn't gone for another year and then the only place he'd found within his means was Marplot. BU was too expensive. He'd decided that he wanted to study journalism but anyway you had to take some liberal arts before you went into the journalism school and those little necessary things could be gotten at Marplot cheaper. The first two years, he'd gone nights, because he was working all day and it'd been rough, even though it was only a cruddy little college.

His mother, finding that no amount of tears or sick headaches could affect her son who had suddenly changed from a nice, well-behaved, gentlemanly boy to a selfish, cynical, rude, young man that she could barely believe was her son, had sighed and accepted the inevitable. She'd taken typing and shorthand at a business school in the mornings and worked selling wedding gowns at Conrads in the afternoons. When her course was over, she'd found a job, immediately, in one of the offices of the Charlestown Navy Yard. Although she'd still groaned about having to associate with people she'd never have noticed in her life before at least there was a decent salary and new clothes. Pretty soon there was enthusiasm for a well-done job and her bit for the war effort and in no time at all she was making friends with her co-workers who played bridge just as well as rich women. And what do you know, he suddenly had a self-sufficient mother, and could concentrate on his own future.

Having worked for a year as an office boy at Houghton Mifflin, Gordie was promoted to a clerical post at a higher salary. But by this time he'd achieved a comprehensive view of the publishing business and was correspondingly disillusioned. It was too dull and slow-moving for him and he'd yearned for something else but what else was there? And the office was close to Marplot. When work was done he could eat a leisurely supper someplace on the Hill and then have plenty of time to study or socialize till classes began. But he'd chafed continually at the thought of the time and money he was wasting there in those unhallowed halls. Half the time if any new person he met asked him if he went to college he'd lie and say he didn't rather than confess he went to a sewer like Marplot. And the most bitter ignominy of all was to have to go to Marplot nights. To sit in those dimbulb classes full of earnest, greasy idiots who were all almost middle-aged anyway, some of the guys were almost bald, all those office workers with their cheap, shiny blue suits, men and women both, all exhausted and whitefaced from a day's work, full of bad breath and BO, with tired eyes, full of pretenses and phony ambitions. Who did they think they were kidding anyway, with their intense notetaking and discussions after class with the instructors. Of course there were some younger ones like himself but they were all misfits, German refugees who spoke with impenetrable accents and had brooding eyes from all the horrors they were supposed to have suffered or female, mousy wallflowers who lived under their parents' thumbs and wanted to have someplace to go after work. The day students were a much more normal crowd. Gordie'd run into a few of them who'd stayed around the library late studying. They were all more his age, with his interests, kind of lively and like college kids anywhere except with less money.

Still, grudgingly, Gordie'd had to admit he was learning a few things and some of the instructors weren't bad. He'd had a good course in modern European history with a teacher he could really respect who taught over at BU days. While he was taking that class he'd decided that he was going to be a foreign correspondent. He'd pictured himself dashing around Europe in a trench coat watching governments fall and civil wars begin. But then, the modern European history cat had gotten a dollar a year job in Washington and the guy who took over the class was a pedantic cretin who taught history in a suburban high school daytimes and the whole zest went out of the class for Gordie.

Nevertheless, his inspiration had lasted long enough to take him over to the BU registrar's office. With a better paid job now and thirty-six Marplot credits under his belt he could transfer and at least, for crissakes, hold his head halfway up when people asked what college he went to. But the registrar's office had been pretty snippy considering who they were and handed out all kinds of salty jive about how he'd lose credits if he came to their high-toned school as nowhere Marplot was still unaccredited. He'd be damned if he'd start all over again!

Back at Marplot for his third year Gordie'd resigned himself to being a middle-aged man before he ever got through there and into BU's journalism school. He'd be the oldest cub reporter in the newspaper business. Probably have gout by then too. So if he had to wallow in one rut at least he might change his daily tedium and on a chance he had gone down to the Boston *Tatler* to see if maybe he could get some kind of job there to give himself some newspaper experience. He'd landed a menial copy boy deal which galled him but at least he was around a newspaper and someday . . . The paper had a morning edition so Gordie'd worked on the evening shift and went to school days which had made him feel a little better. He'd found he could concentrate on his classes better in the bright light of morning and while his day classmates were squares at least they were his contemporaries. And now he could even get his biology requirement out of the way. Even that wasn't so bad early in the day. Cutting up earthworms at night in a lab might, he realized, have knocked him out of college altogether.

One of his few good classes that semester was one in the English novel and it was in that class that he'd first met Deborah. He'd noticed her right away because there were only about three pretty girls in the day classes and two of them seemed to be spoken for. Acourse, she was not too lush a piece, with few curves to be seen, and those few well hidden under unprepossessing clothes and for a while he'd been repelled by what he thought were her piano legs until one day she'd cast off those ugly wool knee socks she'd persisted in wearing and appeared in nylons and he'd been delighted to notice that she had terrific legs for such a small girl. So he'd maneuvered her into conversation one day, after class, ostensibly about some assignment and found, at first, that it was awful talking to her because she didn't seem to know how to make the conventional chitchat that was usually a standard part of a girl's repertoire. But then they'd gotten to talking about books and there she'd brightened up amazingly. After a few more classroom conversations he'd decided that she was pretty smart when it came to books and fantastically dumb about life. So he'd begun to educate her, feeling a fine sense of power because she was so innocent. In her whole eighteen years she'd had about one date with a boy and the way her eyes opened wide when Gordie casually mentioned the most elementary facts concerning males and females delighted him, at first. He guessed she thought he was pretty wonderful and sophisticated and this pleased him so much that he neglected to notice, for a while, that he was kind of falling for her.

Since the awful night at the Bat Club when Gordie had felt that no girl would want him because he was 4-F he'd really had wonderful luck in finding jelly roll. In fact, it wasn't bad being one of the few men around when all the other cats had gone into service. Girls whose boyfriends were overseas or who'd been too young to have boyfriends when the war began and now had grown up to find the romantic world depopulated of men, seemed to have a desperate feeling that maybe all their prospective and future mates would be killed and they'd live and die, unsatisfied and unknowing old maids. Eat, drink, and be merry for tomorrow—the motto'd been for everybody and it'd been a good time, a wild time, Gordie thought, but it had definitely begun to change by the fall of 1945 when all those boatloads of decorated, scarred heroes had begun to clot the harbor waters. Then the girls'd begun to change too. They no longer wanted loose, promiscuous, fun sex, with no strings, just for kicks. No, they were all out to marry the cats who'd come back for a taste of mom's blueberry pie and now they thought twice about giving out to just anybody. Well, that was all right with Gordie. Maybe those serious veterans wanted to get married and get tied up in domestic strings but not him. He was just a boy who had to start making his way in the world and what chiefly galled him when you began to see men around Boston again in quantity was not that he was having competition in the skin game but that in all those wartime years when the world had to go on while the men had gone off soldiering he'd not been able to grab himself a plush job or the beginnings of a decent career. That was the time to have done it, he'd told himself disgustedly because now all those little squares'd be back operating and getting ahead and there he'd still be, a jerk, only an older one with naught to show for his years.

He'd've probably not had a damn thing to do with Deborah, even at Marplot, if it hadn't been for that funny combination of it being 1947 with men all over the joint marrying up girls and getting themselves re-established in jobs and colleges, loaded with that damn sugar coated GI Bill and this one girl he'd been having successfully for a year, up and marrying a joe she used to know who'd gotten out of the Marines and the desperate feeling that he had to get on in the world, make a success of himself and here he was, still a jerk, with no background and frigging away his time at Marplot. So the first thing that struck him when he met Deborah was her amazing bookishness. If there was one thing he couldn't stand was a girl who'd read more books and was more literary than he was. Especially someone like her who was non compos mentis about everything else. He'd started off being lofty with her, throwing names of writers around, but when she'd responded eagerly, he'd found himself in deep water. Hemingway he could handle but who were the Georgian poets? One night she'd recited all of "J. Alfred Prufrock" to him, just like that, from memory and this annoyed him so much he got all of Eliot's collected poems out of the library and read them. Every name she'd mention he'd hunt up and read, whether he liked them or not. Except he balked at this German poet, Rilke. He had enough English and American poets and writers to catch up on without these weird continentals. He borrowed some books from her and occasionally went out with her of an afternoon on book-hunting expeditions in secondhand bookstores. This seemed to be the greatest treat of her life although she didn't have a penny for anything else. He hated to admit it but meeting her was one of the best things that'd happened to him because she got him going, reading important things, people he ought to know about, instead of just flipping through magazines or required reading for courses, or people you liked to read, like Hemingway. Of course, he'd introduced her to things, Thomas Wolfe for instance. And Farrell. And O'Hara. But Jesus, every time he thought he was one up on Deborah, having read all of Thomas Wolfe before she had (she was slow on American writers) she'd turn up innocently outdistancing him by reading something like literary criticism. She'd been so interested in Wolfe and the other American writers she just had to get some books by the critics to see what they thought. So acourse he'd had to dig into that too and what a goldmine! He'd pictured himself running into those snotty friends of Mike's someday and being able to throw out opinions about writers that he'd garnered from these critics.

In the beginning he had not intended to make any passes at Deborah. It would take, he figured, too much time and effort. They would just have this great platonic relationship, all very high-minded, and talk about books and things. And jazz of course. He'd taken her to a couple of sessions and loaned her a few books like *Young Man with a Horn* and brought some of his records to a school party for her to listen to because there'd been a borrowed phonograph to play them on and there was no other chance since he couldn't go to her house. But that party, now, it'd been a Christmas party, he remembered, had been a damn mistake, because they'd both drunk a lot of punch and he'd kissed her and suddenly realized that he was pretty hungry because his other girl had taken off with the Marine a month before and he got all excited and that was the end of any high-minded ideas for him. The party had happened in December and now it was the end of May and for over five months now he'd been lusting for Deborah and getting precisely nowhere and it just couldn't go on, he thought now, sitting in the Wreck Room.

Because he was going away. A break, a real break for the first time since his father had died, had come his way, and he'd landed a job on a newspaper in Portland, Maine, as a cub reporter. It was his big chance and the glimmering, glittering image of the trench-coated sophisticated, dashing, foreign correspondent was coming closer and clearer. And all he needed to crown the glory of his onrushing future was to have Deborah, to have her at last and release the wild, pent-up frustration of years of being rejected, turned-down, and kicked around. He was coming into his own and it was about time. Nobody would look pained when he said anything now, people wouldn't ignore him, he wouldn't have to be a menial office or copy boy any more. Or a young jerk or punk. He was a man now, with a man's job and a career in the offing and he'd show everyone. But a man who went with a girl for eight months and never got to go to bed with her wasn't much of a man.

He stubbed out his second cigarette and got up, smiling a little. Deborah didn't know he was going away. He'd only found out himself the other day and he had a feeling that, when he told her, she'd do anything he wanted her to because he knew that she'd hate like hell for him to go. It was funny about her, he thought, sauntering down the stairs to the library. He was the first boy she'd ever kissed and, at first, when he'd kissed her, she'd pushed him away and then, he'd gone a little further and started touching her and she'd been scared to death but he'd persisted and inside of five months he'd gotten her so that she liked it and didn't object. In fact, she even responded very nicely. And he also knew that she wouldn't have let him do all that to her if she wasn't sort of in love with him. But still, crazy as she was about him, she'd go no further than conventional necking. He'd managed to get his hand between her legs a few times although she'd been very upset when it'd happened. Whether it'd aroused her or not he couldn't tell because she'd folded herself away from him like a clam inside its shell afterwards. Then, he'd hit on the brilliant notion that she was the kind of girl with whom words had more power than actions, because, although she liked to be kissed, petted and fondled, he hadn't been able to get close enough for real sexual arousal, so he'd discussed the whole thing with her. But even that hadn't worked. She'd gotten stubborn. So now, he would play the trump card. It'd better work, Debby old girl, he said to himself as he opened the library door, because if it doesn't, I won't have a scruple in the world. I'll just get you drunk and seduce you. On Boston Common or in an alleyway if I can't find any other place.

Six

"Ah hell," Gordie said disgustedly. "You'll be a smug virgin all your life, Debby. You're just too goddamn frigid to be anything else."

They sat, after their silent, meagre drugstore lunch of Cokes and hamburgers, on the sunwarmed grass of the Common, their backs to the Shaw Memorial, sharing a chocolate peanut bar for dessert.

"Well, what do you care if I am?" Deborah demanded. "I'll never see you again. You said so." She took slow, careful bites of her half of the chocolate bar, finished it, neatly crumpled the paper and put it into her purse.

"Always a reason for holding out," Gordie sneered. He threw himself down full-length on the grass. "Oh, sure," he said. "I know how little teases like you work. The idea is to keep a guy frustrated and he'll keep coming around. Well, dammit, you're right. I came around, fool that I was. And what the hell good did it do me. I just got frantic, frustrated, and wild. But this, today, tops everything. Listen, Deb, d'you think any man would put up with what you did to me today?"

"It was your idea," Deborah said. "Suppose someone had seen us. It's all right for you. You're going away. But I'd've been expelled."

"Oh crap," Gordon said. He lit a cigarette and deliberately put the pack back in his pocket, not looking at Deborah.

"May I have one, please?"

"Oh, buy your own," Gordie snapped. "What's the use of wasting cigarettes on you? You don't even inhale."

"Never mind," Deborah said turning her head away. She stared blindly down the length of the Common. It was such a beautiful day and, this morning, had held such promise. But Gordie had spoiled it and now he was being so disagreeable that probably the rest of the afternoon would be worse. And the sun kept right on shining.

"What do you care if you get kicked out of that lousy little school?" Gordie said. "It's not worthwhile going to in the first place."

"It's all I can afford," Deborah said stiffly. "And I don't care what you say about it, Gordie, they have been good to me. They gave me a scholarship when I couldn't have scraped up any money at all to go the first year. And they've given me jobs and . . ."

"The hell with it," Gordie interrupted. "Be a grateful little slave all your life. Who cares? Only you're just throwing your money away because a degree from Marplot is worth about as much as this candy wrapper. All I know is I'm damn glad to be well out of it, the phony, pretentious school and all the little girls, phony and pretentious too, who'll neck and let a man feel them up and go into the ladies lounge and lie down on the couch and the minute the guy opens up his pants and shows them what a man is like after a little frigid tease has gotten him all excited, they jump two feet away and act like it's all a terrible mistake and he's a disgusting animal. What the hell did you think it was, for crissakes? A rattlesnake? Jesus," he snorted, "I've never seen a girl look so scared. And when I asked you to at least for crissakes to help me out! My God, that's the least a girl can do if she won't let a man get into her. But no! You acted as if you'd vomit. It's nice," he said bitterly, flinging his cigarette butt at a curious squirrel, "swell, groovy, that a cat my age has to go off and screw himself in a john, a ladies' john at that." He sat up, reaching over and turned Deborah's face toward him. "Look at me," he demanded. He held her face between his hands. "Damn you," he said. "You look like you might be so passionate. And when I kiss you, I always think, this one time, maybe you will be. But you're always the same. Cold as a witch's tit."

For a moment they stared into each other's eyes. Deborah saw her mop of nervously disarranged curly black hair, her small heart-shaped face, dwindle, till she was nothing but a pair of brown mournful headlamps grotesquely distorted and made ludicrous by two scornful gray funhouse mirrors. She pulled herself away.

"I'm sorry, Gordie," she said carefully. "I didn't mean to be unfair. It's just that I'd never . . . well, you know . . ."

"Oh, I know," Gordon said wearily. "You've never seen a man. But good Christ, Deborah, you've got to learn sometime. What the hell are you going to do if you get married?"

"Marriage is different," Deborah said. "I mean, if that's what married people do, then, of course, it would be"—she searched for the word—"right."

"Oh it would?" Gordie said. "That little ceremony would make it okay to admit you have sexual feelings huh? Tchah," he added disgustedly, "you're hopeless. I thought you'd be different. Not like all these other female sheep. You've got more intelligence. But you're no different from all the other little square chicks. Why let me neck you and kiss you when, after I get all horny, you're going to push me away and say, That's enough now, go away you dirty little boy? You're a damn hypocrite, Deb, because I know you like it. You just won't admit it."

"Of course I like you to kiss me, Gordie. I like you. Can't you like a person and want to kiss them without the other thing?"

"No," Gordie said explosively. "Not with a man you can't. With a boy or a fruit maybe you could get away with it. But a man wants a woman that way or not at all. And if it scares you and makes you sick you better not get into any more necking sessions because some other cat might wring your neck getting left the way you always leave me."

"What about love?" Deborah asked timidly.

"Love is Sex," Gordie said. "That's all it is. What did you think it was? Marriage? Flowers and candy and being taken out to the movies? Saying sweet words to each other? But never giving in till he gives you a ring and a square little house. Sure you think so. What I should have done is to tell you I loved you and asked you to marry me. Then I bet you'd've opened your legs to me."

"No, I wouldn't've," Deborah said stoutly. "Because I would have known you didn't mean a word of it and that would be much worse, having you lie."

"What do you mean, lie? I'm an honorable-looking, clean, upstanding American type. Plenty of girls'd think I was okay to marry. Why, if I said I wanted to marry you, wouldn't you believe me?"

"Oh, this is all silly," Deborah said. "I couldn't marry you anyway, so there's no point in being theoretical."

"Oh, the Jewish thing," Gordie said dismissingly. "You know damn well you don't care about that. You can't sit there and tell me you wouldn't marry a cat because he wasn't Jewish."

"I *don't* care about it," Deborah said. "But my parents do. And then there's another thing." Deborah clasped her knees and stared at him solemnly. "The other person, the one I might marry, he might care, or his parents would. I'd hate to get my feelings hurt because of something for which I'm not responsible."

"If you mean me," Gordie said modestly, "I'm no snob."

Deborah smiled.

"What does that mean for crissakes?" Gordie demanded. "You think I am? You think I wouldn't marry you for a reason like that? And maybe that's why you won't let me get . . ."

"No, no, no," Deborah interrupted. "I know you can't marry anyone and you don't want to. It has nothing to do with that. Let's not talk about it any more. Let's go."

"I tell you, Deb, if you're saving it till you're married you're making a big mistake. Maybe you'll never get married."

"Women can get into all sorts of trouble with sex if they're not married," Deborah said primly.

"Sure they can." Gordie patted his jacket pocket. "But only if they fool around with careless cats. I'm always careful. In fact," he laughed bitterly, "right here I have a little boxful of what prevents trouble. Bought them before I came to school today, thinking something would happen. Oh, I don't suppose they'll go to waste though."

"I'm sure there are lots of girls in Portland," Deborah said bitingly.

"Everywhere," Gordie said casually. "Only I didn't want lots of girls. I wanted you." He put his arm around her and, pulling her toward him, kissed her.

"Don't tell me you don't want it," he murmured after a few minutes. "With a mouth like that you can't be cold. You're just scared that's all. Once we do it you'll wonder why you passed it up so long."

"Yes, but then you'll go away and I'll feel worse."

"You're sorry I'm going, aren't you?" he asked softly. "Well then, be nice to me, baby, be nice to me. Come on," he said coaxingly, holding her close, her head against his shoulder, "think about it, will you? Promise me, baby. Only three more weeks and I'll be gone up to a cold, lonely bed in Portland and nothing'll be left of us, not even a nice memory."

Afterwards, as they climbed the Hill, Deborah regretted her promise. Not that she was committed to say yes, but having gotten her softened up to the point of thinking about it, Gordie would ruin their last three weeks by never letting up. It would be all like what had happened this noon in the lounge. It was funny too because before it was always so sweet and tender with kisses and nuzzlings and nice things said, that was the part she liked, and why it had to go on and become unpleasant but if, as Gordie said, that's the way it always was with men, then she didn't want any of it.

And yet, she did like Gordie, Deborah thought, very much, and would miss him when he went away. When he wasn't being nasty about sex he was so exciting to be with. In the beginning, she'd been humbly proud that such a paragon of worldliness had chosen her; had wanted to kiss her and tell her she was pretty and exciting; had considered her worthy to walk beside and talk to. She supposed she might've eventually gone to bed with him if all her original bedazzlement had continued but as time had gone on she'd become aware that just as Gordie considered Marplot degrading, so also he thought that he was slumming among his fellow students. He made it plain that he was a proud exile from the Ivy League and when the wheel of fortune turned he'd be leaving this Bowery of the educational world and go back where he belonged. To Deborah, for whom going to college at all was miraculous, a goal attained at considerable trouble and struggle, this attitude of Gordie's had at first been bewildering, but after awhile she'd begun to resent it. He needn't think he was going to treat her like a little slum tart he'd picked up, somebody to have sex with but at the same time was so ashamed of that, although he talked all the time about his friends and his full, rich life with intelligent, well-educated people, in all the eight months she'd known him, he hadn't made the slightest effort to introduce her to any of these marvelous people. But today, finally, she was going to meet some of these lofty friends of his and she'd been excited for a whole week, looking forward to this afternoon and her encounter with this worldly jazz crowd of Gordie's, these Olympian friends who had been in the war, were painters, writers, graduate students, had lived in Europe and, of course, had all been to Harvard. This great moment of meeting people who were not square, was not, Deborah decided, going to be ruined by Gordie's sulks. And so she had promised to think about doing what Gordie wanted before he left and that had made him jolly again.

They arrived at Mike's house and Gordie leaned on the bell marked *Samuel Wainscott*. "Busy, busy," he said grinning like a salacious chipmunk.

"Perhaps they're not here yet. We might be too early." Deborah stood on the first step glancing up at the fanlighttopped white door with its brass codfish knocker. She was beginning to feel anxious. What in the world would she ever say to all these people? How should she act? Of course they would think she was a young ninny and they'd pity Gordie having to drag this albatross of a shy, backward child, around with him. "Maybe they're not home," she said hopefully.

"Oh, they're home all right," Gordie said, smirking. "Only they're still in bed, way way upstairs, that's all, and Mike's probly getting dressed now to answer the buzzer."

"In bed! But it's almost two o'clock."

"Don't be so naïve, baby," Gordie said affably. "When Mike's family goes away on weekends, Jean Donnelly, that's Mike's girl, comes over to stay with him. If your family would ever go way once in a while and you weren't such a smug little virgin, that's what we'd do. I'd seduce you all over the goddamn house for two days and one night, like Mike's probly been doing to Jean. And they have two floors. Oh God," he sighed, pulling out a cigarette, "what a lucky sonovabitch that Wainscott is, having a family like his. Only I'd just as soon not go to bed with Jean. Too damn long, flatchested, and scrawny." He leaned on the bell again, lighting his cigarette, and grinned at Deborah's obvious discomfort.

"Well, if they're in bed," Deborah said, trying to sound as if it was a perfectly ordinary everyday occurrence, "perhaps we should come back later." She wasn't going to rise to Gordie's bait. This was the way sophisticated people behaved and thought nothing of; living with each other and sleeping together and so on, whereas the people her own age at school were all engaged in what Gordie called the little squares sparring match, girls trying not to give in to boys and boys trying to make them. Kid stuff, Gordie said. And no wonder he thought so if he had friends like these. Deborah wondered what Mike's girl was like and felt a little sorry for her. Everyone knowing she went to bed with Mike on weekends when his family was away and men speculating about her body. She wouldn't like to have people talking about her like that.

The buzzer sounded. They went up the stairs, past small empty niches set in the whitepaneled walls. Sunlight shafted in rainbow prismatic layers through a skylight, high up, blinded them.

"I've never known anyone who lived in one of these old houses on Beacon Hill," Deborah whispered as they started up toward the second floor. "Wouldn't it be wonderful, Gordie, to live right up here, in the middle of Boston and never have to do any of that awful traveling on subways and trolleys?"

"Killer," Gordie said. "Down with the dull suburbs. Well, maybe next year I'll get a job on a Boston paper and a place up here and you can be my mistress. How about that mess, baby?" He grinned at her wickedly. "Think you'd like that?"

"Maybe," Deborah said. Perhaps it wouldn't be so bad if one lived with a man in a house like this and never saw one's family again. It might even be fun and sex would be fun. It wouldn't just be all this hole in the corner sneaking about and furtive caressing in dark hallways. After all, one didn't really need to be married. People in books seemed to get along quite well without it and have a very good time. She and Gordie could have parties and serve drinks and it wouldn't be dull and strife-torn as marriages usually seemed to be, because they'd each be quite independent, he working, she going to . . .

"Mike!" Gordie called when they'd reached the top of the stairs and were standing in a long hallway all painted white, the walls of which were hung with more modern pictures than Deborah had ever seen outside of an art book.

"Up here," a lazy voice said and, looking up, Deborah saw Mike's sleek seal-like head hanging above them from the next landing. "Oh, it's you, Gordie, with the pretty little chick. Jean and I'll be down in a minute. Why don't you two go on into the living room and sit down. I'll get some drinks together."

Deborah had never seen a living room quite like the Wainscotts'. It was so filled with color and light and contained so few of the conventional living room eyesores that she exclaimed involuntarily, clasping her hands, "Why it's more like an Impressionist painting than a room."

"How about that," Gordie said noncommittally, sinking onto a low, modern, gray sofa, dotted here and there with winepurple and bluegreen corduroy cushions. "Are you," he wondered, "going to go around making square, little, intellectual remarks like that all afternoon?" His face conveyed blasé disapproval.

But Deborah was too excited to care. She walked around the room, her hands clasped behind her back. Now what made this living room so different? The ceiling was high, the windows long, the walls painted pale gray and all the woodwork white. For one thing, she thought, gratefully, there was no wallpaper, as in ordinary people's parlors, and then there were no overstuffed chairs and sofas upholstered in heavy maroon plush, and no lace curtains and no thick silk drapes smothering the windows. The curtains here were a heavenly mulberry color and were drawn back all the way to let in the wonderful afternoon light. There was a grand piano filling the space between two windows. It was bare of the ornaments, photographs, and fringed scarves which in Deborah's experience always seemed to adorn pianos. She looked respectfully at an array of sheet music. Bach, Mozart, Schubert. Imagine playing Bach.

"Does Mike play?" she asked in a low voice.

Gordie, who was flipping through a *New Yorker*, did not look up. "I don't know," he said. "It's all too longhair for me."

"Then it must be his mother," Deborah said, remembering suddenly how her mother used to play on the old out-of-tune upright, which had gone into storage along with practically all their other furniture, never to be seen again because they hadn't been able to pay the bill. Her mother'd been trying to learn that Rachmaninoff prelude, the "Bells of Moscow" it was called, just before they'd moved, but had never quite mastered it and now there was no piano and there never would be and that was the end of Rachmaninoff or any other music around her house except for the radio which offered precious little and got on her father's nerves anyhow.

"Uh-uh," Gordie said, "his mother's a painter."

"Oh really." Deborah was impressed. She stared at the canvases on the walls. They seemed to be mostly squares and angles. She couldn't recognize much of anything in them. The Museum of Fine Arts had few paintings of this sort but she had seen enough reproductions in books. Picasso and Braque and Cubists, wasn't it? "Then she must have done all those paintings out in the hall too, I suppose?"

Gordie didn't answer. He was tearing avidly through *The New Yorker* and when he finished, she knew, he'd look up and scornfully question the author's temerity. Whether it was a story or an article or a review it didn't matter. Gordie always said, Jesus, who the hell told him he could write?

The whole wall opposite the sofa was taken up by bookshelves reaching from floor to ceiling and each white painted shelf was jammed with brightly jacketed books. Deborah had been saving the books for the last and now she stood like an acolyte at the altar, before the middlebank of shelves, tipping her head back and scanning the titles. So many books, she thought, and she had read so few of them. If only she were here alone and could just pick out an armful and sit down and read. The books seemed to catch and hold all the light in the room. She could see their varicolors reflected in the window glass and in the polished wood of the piano. Oh how fine it would be to have such a library. She had just begun to buy a few books herself, haunting secondhand bookshops all over Boston, and spending afternoons in ecstasy at remainder sales in Gilchrist's and Jordan Marsh. But she never had enough money and just the other day she'd had to let a copy of *Look Homeward, Angel* slip right through her fingers; standing there in this shop up on Huntington Avenue near Symphony Hall, turning pages and reading snatches of Wolfian lyricism in regretful misery, knowing that if she paid the demanded seventy-five cents for it, there wouldn't be enough left over for carfare home.

The bell rang and Gordie looked up. "Well, the joint's beginning to jump finally," he said hopefully.

Deborah turned away from the bookshelves and walked carefully across a thick mulberry-colored rug. She sat down in an armchair covered with nicely faded chintz. Now the ordeal was about to begin. What would she ever say or do? How'd she been fool enough to want to meet a lot of strange people and run the risk of being stared or laughed at or, worse, completely ignored. Desperately, she fixed her eyes on the rug as she heard footsteps from the floor above. The tap of heels. That must be Mike's girl. It was a wonderful rug. Not a pattern on it. Just a solid glowing stretch of color. It would be splendid to sit down on it before the bookshelves and read, her back turned to the room. She longed for a cigarette and wished she'd taken Gordie's boorish advice and bought some of her own. Now she'd have to ask him and perhaps he'd be as rude about her wasteful lack of inhalation, before all these people, as he'd been earlier. How mortifying!

"Hi," Mike said, appearing around the door. "Sorry we took so long. Jean's in the kitchen making drinks." He smiled at Deborah, a smile which lightened his thin, solemn face.

Deborah thought that he was really quite nice-looking in that brown corduroy jacket and white sweater. His dark hair looked as if it had just been freshly plastered down with water.

"Nice to see you again," he said to her. "Your name's Deborah, isn't it? For a while I thought it was Tamar, confusion of Biblical female names and all, but I finally decided it couldn't be. Hope you've been making yourself at home in the regrettable absence of the host."

Gordie grinned at him knowingly. "Oh, we understand," he said meaningfully. "Your family being off in the fair green privies of Connecticut and all." He laughed.

"Ah yes, privies." Mike said. He was looking at Deborah as he said this and she noted that one corner of his mouth was twisted slightly. Now what was a privy, she wondered, something to do with a toilet, she had a vague feeling but wasn't absolutely sure and, in any case, Mike didn't seem to join in Gordie's laughter and oddly enough Gordie was serenely unconscious of the lack of response.

"Well," Mike said, looking at Gordie's *New Yorker*, "I see you've found your spiritual home."

"I . . . I've been looking at your books," Deborah said falteringly, wondering why she was saying it at all.

"Quite a collection, isn't it?" Mike said. "Mostly products of the old man's toil in creative vineyards. Some of those twenties novels are completely unreadable nowadays. I think Sam must keep them around as examples of what not to do."

Deborah smiled at him politely as if she knew exactly what he meant and agreed with him. She reminded herself of Alice, how the animals do go on, only it wasn't quite like that, because really although she was uncomprehending it must mean he didn't think she was a complete dodo or he wouldn't have bothered to talk to her in this friendly way.

"Which ones?" she asked shyly. "I mean the unreadable ones. I seem to have read so few of them that I couldn't . . ."

"My chick thinks," Gordie intervened, in a proprietary tone, "that your living room here looks more like an Impressionist painting than a room."

Deborah felt herself blushing. "I didn't mean," she began hastily, but Mike was laughing and looking at her approvingly.

"*Touché*," he said. "That's exactly what I've thought all along but was never able to phrase it so well. I must tell that to Minta. That's my mother," he added to Deborah. "She, in fact, looks more like a Modigliani painting than a woman."

Gordie sniggered and Deborah thought how strange it was to hear someone talk that way about his mother. There were sounds of feet and voices coming up from below.

"I think that's Si," Mike said heading toward the door. "I detect vibrations from that twang. There's some cigarettes in that blue leather box, Deborah. The monstrosity with fat cherubs tooled into the top."

"He's very nice," Deborah said to Gordie after Mike had gone out. Gratefully she opened the box on the table and took out a cigarette. For some reason Gordie got very gallant and sprang over to strike a match.

"He's very literary," Gordie said with pride. "A great guy. Knows some of the damnedest people though. This cat Si"—he lowered his voice—"that's coming now, well he's really nowhere. You'll see."

Deborah drew on her cigarette, hoping that she was inhaling and wondering if she would ever learn to blow smoke out of her nostrils. Gordie had now gone back to his *New Yorker*, looking completely unconcerned, and Deborah leaning back in the chair thought how odd it was that after all this time, when he'd been talking about these great friends of his, he should suddenly act as if they were not really friends at all but the kind of impossible people he consigned to the limbo of nowhere. But what difference did it make anyway?

Here the people were, coming in, she heard loud laughter in the hall and, at least, no matter what Gordie said, he knew them, while she was a stranger. She sat up stiffly in the chair, her ankles crossed and tried to copy Gordie's indifferent face. This chair now, she thought, searching frantically for distraction, chintz didn't really belong in a modern room, did it, but this one seemed fine. Because everything here was in harmony. How at home one could feel in a room like this. Fool, she had just, in her abstraction, dropped an ash on the beautiful rug even though there was a very handsome little blue and white pot on the table which seemed to serve as an ashtray. Hastily she bent down and brushed the ashes out of sight under the chair.

"What the hell are you doing, baby?" Gordie asked irritatedly. "This is Jean Donnelly, Mike's chick. Deborah Miller, Jean."

Overcome with confusion Deborah straightened up and said how dyoudo in a subdued mutter to the tall thin girl with the prominent blue eyes who had come silently into the room bearing a tray of drinks.

Jean Donnelly, wearing a gray suit, a pink sweater, a strand of pearls, high-heeled ankle strap sandals and an utterly, uninteresting face, nodded coolly in Deborah's direction.

"Rye whiskey, ice and water," she announced plunking the tray gracelessly down onto the coffee table. "Not a bottle of mix in the house. I happen to like a little ginger ale but Mike of course thinks the best people drink it straight or with water. Anyway, Gordie, I'm glad you're here. This is going to be an awful party." She sat down beside him on the sofa and took a long gulp of her drink.

"Who's all coming?" Gordie picked up a glass and sipped at it. Deborah wondered if she were to be offered one and decided that no matter how nice Mike seemed he must be remiss about girls. How could he like her? The affected way, now, she was holding a long unlighted cigarette waiting for Gordie to strike the match, the big cloud of smoke she blew out . . .

"Oh, all sorts of Mike's terrible friends," Jean said leaning back and crossing her long thin legs. Skirt's too short, Deborah thought critically, bony knees. "That clown Si who thinks he's so witty. Caroline's not too bad of course, but she's sort of, well, too arty, you know, Gordie." Jean brushed at her carefully permanented hair. Every curl in place, Deborah thought, uncomfortably, remembering her own tousled mop, and shrinking inside her sweater and skirt.

"And to make matters worse," Jean continued tipping her head back against the sofa, "that girl, Sally Brimmer, the one everyone talks about all the time, is back in town and she's coming and Mike's all worked up about it. He doesn't say anything but I can tell. Gordie, you knew him a long time ago. Tell me honestly. Did he have a thing with her?"

"Oh, I don't know, baby." Gordie was trying to look all-knowing and bland at the same time and Deborah, feeling disgusted and left-out, wished that she had not come. Anyway, she thought, I'm going to have a drink. The other two did not notice her arrival before them or her departure in the direction of the bookshelves with a full glass. They were deep in conversation. Sinkingly, Deborah considered, that if two people could so successfully ignore her, how would it be when there were more? It was too awful to contemplate. She sipped on her drink. So far, her only experience with drinking had been at the few Saturday afternoon jam sessions Gordie had taken her to. The first time he'd ordered a Coke for her and a rum Coke for himself and Deborah had tasted his, curious to see what difference the rum made. At first, disappointingly, it had seemed to taste just like her own plain Coke, but after a few sips, she'd found herself able to talk more easily and at the next round she'd ordered a rum Coke for herself, while Gordie'd grinned wisely and said she was starting down the primrose path. In the middle of this first primrose rum-Coked step, Deborah had noticed delightedly how much more comfortable she felt, how much easier it was to rock with the music and feel part of the scene. Why, the world wasn't too terrifying after all and people not so awfully hostile and she didn't even feel that awful constriction in her throat when she had to talk, that came from the fear of saying something silly which would arouse laughter, particularly from Gordie.

She wanted to feel sure of herself like that all the time. Still, of course, they could never afford more than one rum Coke or at the most two for her, at the sessions, and naturally, she never wanted to get drunk. Her father got into this terrible state at the idea of her wearing lipstick and he still didn't know she smoked. She had to hang her clothes out to air when she came home and he would undoubtedly kill her if she ever came into the house reeling.

But here she was at this party, feeling stiff and shy, and that awful girl of Mike's was being plain rude and ignoring her and acting as though she was some sort of little beetle and Gordie was no help. Deborah took a big swallow of her drink. I'm going to enjoy myself, she thought defiantly. She took another gulp. Whiskey had a much more unpleasantly medicinal taste than rum, and there wasn't even any Coke to sweeten it up, but never mind, if Jean Donnelly likes to mix hers with ginger ale and Mike thinks water is better, I'm on his side. The day isn't completely lost and more people are coming and if Jean didn't like them, then they were obviously wonderful people. Deborah moved down to where the bookshelves ended at the windows. Working through the books slowly would take quite a while and perhaps by then Mike would come back . . . She heard the bell ring several times and the sound of voices approaching from the kitchen but she kept her back turned and pretended to be completely absorbed.

The funny part of it was that actually she forgot to pretend and so when Gordie said suddenly, in her ear, "What the hell, baby, let's not be so exclusive. Let's get out of our square little intellectual shell, huh?" She jumped and turned around, embarrassedly noting that there were now quite a lot of people in the living room. Beyond Gordie, she saw that Mike, standing beside a tall, odd-looking, large-eared fellow, was smiling over at her.

Gordie waved a hand in front of her eyes. "Wake up, baby."

"Gordie," Deborah said, "look at this." She held the book open. "Look what it says. *To Sam Wainscott from James Joyce.*" She riffled the pages excitedly. "It's printed in Sylvia Beach's bookshop in Paris. It must be a first edition of *Ulysses* and autographed to Mike's father. Isn't that terrific?"

Gordie looked nervously around and said in an undertone. "Don't get so intense, baby. Mike's father is an editor you know, and he used to live in Paris and knew all those cats. Nothing to get excited about."

"Oh, but Gordie," Deborah protested, her voice rising, "I mean, Joyce was one of the greatest writers of the twentieth century. Having an autographed copy of one of his books is . . . is . . ." She stopped helplessly suddenly aware of a silence in the room and of Gordie's disapproving face. Her cheeks felt hot and she slipped *Ulysses* back into its place on the shelf. Everyone must've heard her making a fool of herself. What a little rube they must think her, getting worked up about something the sophisticated person took in his stride. No wonder Gordie never wanted to take her any place. She turned around, her eyes lowered.

"So you found the prize Joyce," Mike was saying, handing her a fresh drink. "Good for you. Sam's damn proud of it of course and it's pretty valuable but in an excess of unostentation he acts as if it's any other book. If you're interested in autographed first editions there're quite a few here, Dos Passos, MacLeish, Hemingway, and so on. Come over here. I'll show you some."

"I suppose it's silly," Deborah said, wondering if his light, friendly tone masked amusement. "I mean, I've never known any writers and it's kind of terrific to come across well . . ."

"You think there's something sacred about writers?"

"Oh yes," Deborah said fervently. "Don't you?"

"The printed word is holy to Debby" Gordie intervened. "Instead of movie actors she's had pictures of Hemingway and that British cat, I forget his name, who wrote that autobiography with the salty title, on her bedroom walls since she was fourteen."

"Robert Graves," Deborah mumbled, raging inwardly. Never, never again would she confide any of her ridiculous private secrets to sneaky Gordie. How could he drag out and blat such embarrassing things around in front of all these strange people. "*Goodbye to All That* is the title."

"Hey, he's very good," Mike said, his face quickening. "Although," he added disparagingly, "you can have Hemingway, after *Farewell*. Not to mention personally, and that goes for most writers. Wild egomaniacs, most of them."

"Well, I guess you'd know," Deborah said humbly. "But still, to me, it seems so marvelous. Being a writer, I mean."

Mike shrugged. "It's a bum's life sustained by empty illusions. Well, anyway, here's the Dos Passos and here's a Cummings, *Enormous Room* and some MacLeish poems . . . and . . ."

"And by their deeds ye shall know them," the skittery, elephant-eared character, Deborah had noted before, erupted now in a blast that made her jump.

"No," said this peculiar-looking personage, holding up his hand, "don't say a word. Just let me adore you. I don't know whose little China figurine you are or where you came from or even, what your name is, but you are a pure ray of light cast into the pit of fathomless darkness which is at present the so-called mind of Mike Wainscott. Do you know, do you realize, young woman"—he folded his long arms together like a mandarin—"how long I have know this abysmal renegade? No, you can't know but it's been aeons, an eternity of, I thought, faithful friendship. But alas, I was deceived. He never thought me a friend. No, because if he did, he would have told me that in his very own home he had an autographed first edition of Joyce. Nursing it to his viperish bosom. But completely cognizant of the fact that I, his old companion in arms, was writing my M.A. thesis mainly on Joyce, did he notify me of this? No. He let me blunder on blindly . . ."

144

"This is Si Hunnicutt," Mike cut in, introducing Deborah. He snorted. "Don't mind him. He goes on this way all the time."

Si didn't much look like Deborah's idea of a graduate student, particularly not one immersed in Joyce. Such a wonder should surely be wearing a goatee and dark glasses or at the very least a slouch hat, the brim turned down all the way round. But Si, with his gawky, perpetual-motion arms and legs, thatch of flying hay-colored hair, long, inquisitive nose, ruddy face and small bright blue eyes, was unmistakably a red and yellow fantastic. He should have a cap and bells, she thought, and stand the mocking court before and before she knew it the words were out. She clapped a guilty hand over her mouth but it was too late. Horrified, she began to stammer apologies but Si and Mike were shouting with laughter and did not hear her. Over on the sofa where he again sat with Jean Donnelly, Gordie raised his head, looked at her in cold irritation and then turned away. He thinks I've done something idiotic she thought wretchedly, and oh I have.

"Well, there you are," Mike said finally. "I always thought that court jester's act would catch up with you someday, Si." He put his hand on Deborah's shoulder. "An overwhelming whiff, isn't it? Almost as powerful as sulphur and brimstone."

Si grinned broadly. "Oh, I don't know. I always figured myself in the butternut brown of the Yankee peddler. Purveyor of wooden hams and nutmegs and all that. You never can tell about women," he confided to Mike. "This one now looks as though she might make tinklings with her feet, which is all to the good, but as lagniappe she senses auras too."

It was the drink, Deborah thought. She would never have said anything at all, still less something so personal and ridiculous about a man she didn't even know, if she hadn't guzzled her first one and been well through her second.

"For Heavens sakes, Si," said a tall, redheaded girl in black-rimmed harlequin glasses, "I could hear that windy howl of yours all the way into the kitchen. What's so funny?"

"This," Si said to Deborah, "this Gorgon with the long strands of hair messily straggling out from her stylish pony tail, is my true-love, Caroline Lamb. She's a poor uneducated artist creature but mine own."

Deborah thought she'd never seen a person look quite so much like one of those fashion magazine creations as this tall, elegant girl and, studying Caroline's simple, straight black jersey dress, carelessly belted with some sort of gold chain, she once again became unhappily conscious of her own schoolgirl attire.

"Oh, you paint," she said politely. "How interesting."

"Paint!" Si howled. "No, thank God, she doesn't pretend to do that any more. I wouldn't have her in the house if she did. My God, she might turn into an elder statesman."

"The connection fails me," Mike said poker-faced.

"Painters are always elder statesmen," Si said, as if speaking to a child. "Any fool knows that. It's an understandable transition. Painters, you see, dwell in a primeval universe, a nonvocal, nonrational one of neo-impressionist futurism and formalistic surrealism with only a cloudy shadow of maggots in the neurotic artist's psyche to disturb the general green murk and . . ."

"I work for Filene's," Caroline said firmly to Deborah raising her voice so that it drowned out Si's. "Advertising, window dressing, fashion sketches. Fascinating but poorly paid. Oh, this is Ella Baring," she added indicating a small blonde girl who had just come up to them, looking exactly, Deborah thought, like a Christmas card angel. "She's really a painter."

Ella Baring no more resembled Deborah's notion of a painter than Si, a Joyce graduate student. She felt immediately comfortable with this healthy, pleasant-looking girl who was dressed much like herself, in sweater, skirt, and ankle socks.

"I heard you," Ella announced, smiling cheerfully at Si, "and painters are not always elder statesmen. Sometimes they're political idealists. Like Picasso."

"Now there," Si said, "you have a classic example of the maggots I spoke about. And here"—he pointed to Mike—"is another. Hiding autographed firsts of *Ulysses*. Why I could probably write my whole thesis around your father and Joyce in Paris."

"No you couldn't," Mike said. "Your field is American Lit, remember? Besides you've changed your goddamn topic so often I can't keep up with you. Anyway, Sam never knew Joyce that well. Just followed him down the street at a safe admiring distance."

"Managing to get his autograph by osmosis, eh?" Si jeered. "Honest to God, boy, maybe I'm a provincial but at least I'm not strangling in *déja vue*. Instead of wasting your time learning to justify man's inhumanity to man because Justice Pinwheel in 1837 in Galena, Illinois laid down the precedent that there have to be witnesses to prove liability, knowing fullwell that nine tenths of the world is afraid to stick its neck out, you ought to . . ." He interrupted himself to drain his glass and hand it to Caroline.

"Castigation," he added smoothly, "always makes me thirsty and you are the chosen handmaiden of the Lord. A lot of whiskey and very little water please."

Watching Caroline stalk off toward the kitchen, her lips compressed, Deborah thought how depressing it was to know that no matter how imposing and elegant a girl looked, somewhere there was always a man who could, with no effort at all, deflate her.

"As I was saying, Wainscott, away with this preparation of yours to play *diabolus avocati* to the meek so they won't inherit the earth. Take Deborah to some Joyce classes and clear your head." He winked at Deborah. "You'd like to go over to Harvard and participate in the phallic rites of Bloomsday, young one, wouldn't you? But then, of course"—Si lowered his voice to a concerned, conspiratorial whisper and nodded in the direction of the sofa where Jean Donnelly sat apparently absorbed in dialogue with Gordie— "your lachrymose dolly might get jealous if you took another girl to a lecture."

Mike looked grim. "It's not so funny you cracker-barrel Mencken, you. I've been having a hell of a time with her ever since she found out Sal was coming."

"And of course Bruce is the perfect source for confidences," Si said. "Knows nothing and tells all."

Deborah was fortunately rescued from the awkward silence that followed by Ella Baring who exchanged humorously commiserating glances with Mike and led Deborah over to the piano bench to meet her husband.

"Do you . . . uh . . . paint like Mike's mother?" Why did Si have to have such a loud voice, Deborah wondered painfully, trying not to hear, behind her, his explosive, "Oh no, not him! Well, for Godsakes, she needs to be taken in hand. Why don't you . . ."

". . . old-fashioned," Ella Baring was saying comfortably. "I paint people, mostly."

"As a matter of fact," Tom Baring said, "my wife is an artist arrivée. She's having her first show. The opening's tomorrow. If you're interested in painting you might like to come."

"Why yes," Deborah said. She strained her ears but Si seemed to have stopped talking about Gordie. "I mean I don't know much about art but I'd love to come. You must be very excited. Having your work on display, I mean."

"Oh sort of," Ella said languidly.

"How blasé we are," her husband said teasingly. "I might get taken in if I didn't know you've had insomnia for a week now."

"You're a liar," Ella said, unruffled. "Of course," she explained to Deborah, "I think it's wonderful, but you see, I'm really awfully unknown and if it weren't for this woman doctor, Jenni Asch, who's interested in encouraging young artists and has turned part of her house into a gallery, I'd never be showing at all. I'm sharing the show with two others." She fished around in her handbag. "I've got an invitation around here someplace."

Deborah gazed respectfully at the square of gray pasteboard decorated with red and yellow blocks, read the wildly staggered calligraphy and was suddenly stricken with worry. "Is it very—uh—formal?" she stammered. "I mean, you dress up and things?"

Ella seemed to understand. She looked approvingly at Deborah's black-and-white saddle shoes and then at her own which were exactly the same. "Oh, I know," she said ruefully, "getting decked out is such a bore. You know, I'm really rather in a quandary myself about what to wear. I hate conventional girly clothes and yet I don't want to be one of those poseurs who dresses the part of the seedy, eccentric, flamboyant artist to the hilt. Paint-stained blue jeans and turtleneck sweaters are fine for the studio but that gallery tomorrow will simply be reeking with prosperous German burghers and I think I ought not to look too bizarre. You know, Tom, I don't even have a dress."

"Well, why don't you make something tonight," he suggested. "We could go over to Si's and use Caro's sewing machine, after the session."

"We're broke," Ella said mournfully, chewing on her thumbnail. "At least there isn't enough to buy any material. Not if we're going to eat this week. I wonder if Caro would sell me that applegreen silk she bought at the remnant sale. It'd be just the thing for one of those simple Chinese shaam-type dresses. I could pay her back when we get the check from my father."

Deborah had been listening to the Barings uneasily, wondering if perhaps it was a family discussion which she shouldn't really be part of. On the other hand, she found herself strangely fascinated because it was the first conversation of its kind, she'd ever heard. In her experience, no matter how poor you were you never admitted it, and you certainly didn't discuss ways and means so casually in front of perfect strangers. She remembered suddenly the time when she was in high school and had taken her first babysitting job for a woman across the street and the woman and her husband were just stepping out the door and then her mother had appeared saying that the whole arrangement had to be canceled. Her father didn't want the neighbors thinking that his daughter had to be a servant maid. Outraged and apologetic, Deborah had gone home grinding her teeth at the thought of a father who wouldn't let his daughter earn a few cents of her own, even though most of the food in the house at the time hadn't been paid for at the local grocery store and, in fact, there was a constant danger that there might not be any food at all if the long overdue bill wasn't paid soon.

"Sometimes I wonder," Tom Baring was saying gloomily, "if this skimpy living that's as much a tradition among artists and scholars as the fourflusher's living on credit is, doesn't get to be a bad habit after a while. At first we can't afford it and then maybe we don't try to. Besides, if an artist is successful he's looked on with suspicion by his ragged fellow conformists in Bohemia."

"You're always depressed when your GI Bill check runs out," Ella said dimpling at him. "Some artists have made money in their lifetime. But if they're completely honest about their work and don't make concessions to the public's changing tastes or flatter the buyers, they lose it. Like Rembrandt. And I'd rather have had his genius than all the money the dealers and collectors have made on him since he died. D'you think you can borrow a dollar or so from Si, Tom? I really must buy a pair of stockings for tomorrow. I haven't any at all. I just remembered."

Tom sighed. "I just borrowed five from him so we could go to the session, and buy gas and beer for tomorrow. What d'you need stockings for? You're one of the artists. You can receive all the homage and plaudits in puttees and it will be quite acceptable. Anyway the mob'll be so drunk on the punch they won't notice your legs."

"Oh, I don't think Dr. Asch provides things like that, do you?"

"She'll produce something for the inner man," Tom said wisely. "She's a gemütlich type. Perhaps even some ritz little canapés."

"Oh nonsense," Ella said. "You're just teasing. It's not going to be fancy at all, Deborah. You just come in whatever clothes you have on hand." She paused for a brief second, exchanged a glance with her husband and then said casually, "Perhaps you'd like to come over to our house beforehand. We're having sort of a picnic lunch. All people you've met here. About one-thirty."

Deborah hesitated wondering if Gordie'd been invited although not daring to ask. And if he hadn't she'd be there alone with all these strange people. But Ella Baring seemed so nice and kind and would surely not make her feel out of it and she wanted intensely to go.

"Thank you," she said shyly, taking her courage in hand. "I'd love to come."

"Fine," Ella Baring said. "I'll write the address on the invitation."

Of course Gordie would be coming, Deborah thought, as she tucked the card into her small leather purse, that was why she'd been asked, wasn't it? Still, it was odd that Ella hadn't simply said oh you'll be coming with Gordie and he knows where it is and, even more peculiar, at this party of his dear friends, that no one, except Jean Donnelly, seemed to be paying much attention to Gordie, not even Mike, who was still talking rapidly, in low tones, to Si, and now that a sudden silence had fallen on the Barings, she heard Si say:

"If we don't get this show on the road, man, we're going to be awful damn late for the session."

"We're waiting for Sal," Mike said. "She's coming with the Jazzbo."

"Oh God, my earplugs," Si groaned. "Ah the bell! Hear it not, Wainscott, tis the knell that summons thee to heaven and me to hell. What kind of sacrifices do I have to make so you can see an old flame anyway?"

"Oh shut up, Si, please," Caroline said, appearing hastily from the back of the apartment. "Jean is in an awful state, gibbering out in the kitchen and that smirky Gordie is just egging her on. Mike, why don't you go out and talk to her and I'll answer the door."

"She's always salty lately," Mike said shortly. "What difference does it make? I'll get the bell myself."

Caroline gazed after him exasperatedly. "If that isn't just typical male," she exclaimed.

"Unless the divine Sara has degenerated considerable since last I saw her," Si interjected callously, "you'll understand why."

"That's not the point," Caroline said impatiently. "Sally's not his girl any more and from what I've heard she treated him very shabbily anyway. But Jean is. Well, I'm not mad for her really, you know, but it was pathetic, honestly, the way she was going on. Threatening not to go with us to the session, to leave Mike forever, tears in her eyes. Imagine getting into a wild dither like that because of an old girl. It's all that snide Gordie's fault, I'm sure. He's such a liar."

"I don't suppose Sally can help it," Tom Baring said ruminatively, "but it's almost supernatural, this perennial faculty of hers for setting people on their ears even before she steps in the door." He smiled at Deborah who was trying to hide her flushed face behind some sheet music. "How about another drink, Deborah? And while I'm at it, I'll try some missionary work out in the kitchen."

"Why bother?" Si said shrugging. "Mike'd be relieved if Jean walked out. So would everyone else. The girl's a drag and a bore. Why not admit it? The trouble is, due to Mike's inertia and her masochistic passion for him, she won't hold to her threat. I'm damn glad Sally's turned up."

"Well, I'm not," Tom said. "Jean may be a bore but she's not a Lorelei. Mike doesn't need to have his dreams haunted again. Somebody solid to pull him out of his rut would be a hell of a lot better for him."

"There's no passionate imagination in you, Baring," Si jeered. "Sal, at least, could wake him up."

"I'm awfully curious to see Sally," Ella said. "She sounds really fabulous."

"Sounds obnoxious to me," Caroline said briefly. "In fact, I know I'm going to loathe her." She tossed her head and pitched her voice a little higher. "Frankly I'm a little fed up with all this corny adoration. Just because she chooses to come down from her exalted position and slum around with jazz people and perennial Harvard men."

"Malice and envy," Si said reprovingly from the sofa, "will get you absolutely no goddamwhere, Caro. Besides"—he let out a sudden wild hoot of laughter—"Sal's had a mixed-up childhood and you know what that means."

Deborah felt as if she had somehow blundered into the midst of a very close family who were having an argument understandable only to themselves and perhaps their ancestors. My, they must all have known each other for a long time and see one another a lot, she thought, a little jealous, and was pleased to see Gordie ambling across the room toward her.

"Well," he said beaming, "Sally baby just showed with the Jazzbo, so we can cut out soon. She looks terrific. Real fine tan and all. They're in the kitchen."

"How exclusive," Caroline said coldly. "And I suppose we go into the kitchen to be presented at court."

"No bitchery, please," Si said getting up. "I'm going to get another drink. You can come along if you want."

"We're both coming," Ella said decisively. "Don't be silly, Caroline. You don't want to leave Jean alone. She's probly crying into the whiskey right in front of Sally and the men are standing around helplessly."

"Oh well, I spose so," Caroline said sulkily.

"I see you've been taken up," Gordie said a little bitterly to Deborah when they were alone in the living room. "All those characters drag me way down, they're so damn pretentious. But I noticed that you were hanging on every word that Si was handing out."

"I thought he was very interesting," Deborah said, wondering if she was going to see this famous Sally that all the talk was about. "Who, exactly, is Sally?" she asked Gordie in a low voice.

"Sally Brimmer."

"I never heard of her."

"My God," he was genuinely surprised. "How do you get so ignorant, baby? Living in Boston all your life?"

There was a sudden commotion of people in the room, and Mike was saying, "I guess you've met everyone here, Sal, no, there's Deborah," and she was being introduced to a vividly beautiful girl in a sleeveless turquoise dress who drawled Hello at her in the richest, huskiest voice Deborah had ever heard. Behind her, a tall fellow with a disdainful expression under his lank blond hair turned out to be Dick Fitzgerald, or the Jazzbo, who pumped her hand listlessly. Deborah read his reviews in the *Tatler* faithfully and was very excited at the thought of meeting someone whose opinions about movies, popular bands, and other forms of entertainment were printed under a byline every few days for all the world to see, but she had no chance to say how much she liked his work because he'd turned boredly away from her and sat down on the sofa, peeling off his gray flannel jacket to reveal shockingly bright fireman's red suspenders over a dazzlingly white shirt.

"Killer," Gordie said admiringly at the suspenders and walked over to sit beside him. Deborah heard him say, "Portland Signal," a cigarette plastered to his lower lip, dangerously waggling with each word he uttered while the smoke poured up in a cloud blinding him and anyone who was close to him. Deborah supposed it was the way journalists smoked. Gordie always threw himself so heartily into any new role.

"They're a fine pair, aren't they?" Si said in her ear. "The Fourth Estate. Let it be a lesson to you. The path of scholarship, however cloistered, at least protects one from such vulgarities. Say, Sal"—he reached out and annexed the beautiful girl who was wandering past them—"what the hell's the idea of bringing him here? Before we could stop him he was pouring himself drinks from Mike's father's best scotch which he unearthed from some godknowswhere, but then why should we be surprised, a ferret can't really help himself. Now, he's sulking because Sam isn't around and no opportunity for a cushy job pitch. He shouldn't be encouraged or have you been away too long?"

Covertly, while Sally and Si talked, Deborah studied the famous Sally Brimmer. If it was true that Mike was still in love with her, as all his friends seemed to think then, of course, it explained Jean Donnelly because, reasoned Deborah with simple admiration, to a man who had once had this girl, all others must henceforth seem pointless facsimiles. Deborah knew that she was staring rudely, fascinated by this girl who, with her long, wavy real gold hair and rich, warm tan, glowed, in the midst of Boston's tentative, changeable spring like some mythical, pagan goddess of summer, all sun-ripened and sea-robed, floating casually to the shore of a sea-washed Grecian isle. But she isn't actually Grecian perfection, Deborah thought, abandoning fancy, because her nose is a bit too beaky and her arms a little too round and wasn't she really somewhat buxom and top heavy for those long slim legs, so that technically she could not be considered a real beauty and it all came down to what people, men particularly, called sex appeal. But whatever it was as soon as Sally came into the room, Caroline didn't look elegant any more, only pale and awkward, her dress a little too self-consciously weird and Ella Baring seemed more like a lost, big-eyed, button-nosed waif than the serenely, lovely seraph of an hour ago. As for herself, Deborah thought hopelessly, although the liquor had previously made her feel almost brilliant in conversation and brightened up her solemn, pinched face, well now, she knew herself to be a dwindling candle. Her saddle shoes had turned to enormous sabots, and her skirt and sweater to sackcloth. She knew her nose was shining and that all her lipstick had worn off. And what's more, self-conscious or not, she knew this Sally, although apparently concentrating closely on Si's fast, frothy flow of quips was looking at her speculatively. Why me, Deborah thought defensively and wished there were someplace to go. She looked wildly around the room but they all seemed to be involved in tête-à-têtes.

"How's Dud?" Si was asking. "I hear you two are developing into a charming brother-sister relationship."

Sally raised an eyebrow. "It's a mere matter of convenience," she said coolly. "We see one another as little as possible. He has this medical residency at Bay Colony, you know, and spends most of his time there, presumably."

"Say," Si exclaimed, "I know a cat who's doing a medical res. there too. Matt Berman. We used to work a board job at Tufts together. Ran into him recently. He's got a pad around here. Mayhap Dud knows him."

"Oh darling," Sally said handing Si her empty glass, "you know perfectly well that if Dud knew God he'd never mention it. Do get me another drink, Si, please. All this renewing auld acquaintance is very dehydrating."

Left marooned with Sally, Deborah made a great business of lighting a cigarette but the matches kept either dying or burning her fingers. She waited for this glamorous girl to murmur an excuse and drift off but instead Sally Brimmer flicked a lighter under Deborah's cigarette and waited patiently until the interminable nervous puffing finally succeeded.

"You're very pretty," Sally said, "and you look so damn young too. How old are you, anyway?"

"Nineteen," Deborah said.

"Perfect," Sally drawled incomprehensibly. "Are you attached to any of these males here?"

"I came with Gordie, Gordon Buce, I mean Bruce. He's over there talking to Mr. Fitzgerald."

"Oh yes." Sally negligently blew smoke at Gordie and regarded him as if he were under a microscope. "I've seen him here and there but I didn't remember his name. He rather presumptuously asked me why I bothered to come back to Boston since he finds the city utterly unworthy and is shaking its vile dust from his feet."

"Yes," Deborah said looking at the floor. Suddenly she felt very miserable. He was really going away, it was true, and she would be alone. The only girl in the world without a boy.

"Actually you know," Sally said critically, "he's rather awful but at nineteen it's very easy to get intense about the weirdest people." She laughed. "Don't look so shocked."

She can't be too much older than I am, Deborah thought, but not wanting to continue this embarrassingly personal kind of conversation, she did not demand Sally's age in return but praised her tan.

"I was soaking up sun in California three weeks ago," Sally said. "And I'm desperate to go swimming here but the weather keeps changing."

"The water's icy," Deborah said. "I live in Winthrop and last Sunday I tried to wade and nearly lost my toes to frostbite."

"How handy of you to live in Winthrop. I have a summer place in Nahant. Perhaps we can go swimming together sometime before the beaches get clogged up with summer types."

"Well," Deborah began hesitantly, "I . . . I . . . why that'd be very nice." She wished that Gordie had finished telling her about who this girl was and why she was someone important. Even if she wasn't famous it was still bewildering, this friendliness from a girl who was so obviously utterly different from herself.

"Sally, baby," the Jazzbo said, coming up behind her and hugging her, "there's talk in the town that you might sing at the session today and if that's so don't you think we ought to be cutting out."

"I did say I might," Sally said disengaging herself. She smiled at Deborah. "I'll see you. Must get my bag."

"Man," said Gordie coming up with Deborah's jacket, "isn't she the sexiest? Look at that rear wiggle. What was she talking to you about?"

"Oh, swimming and tans and things," Deborah said vaguely. What an awful leer on his face and his mouth got so loose.

They were going to the session in the Barings' car and, as Gordie steered her down the hill to where it was parked, she said hastily, "What makes her, Sally I mean, so special, Gordie?"

"She's special all right," Gordie said. "Oh would I love to have that just once. Don't get mad, baby. She's just one of those women every man wants to have."

"So I gathered," Deborah said. "But you seemed to think I ought to know something about her. As if she were an actress or something?"

"Well, I don't know," Gordie said, "where you been all your life Debby, I swear. Why man, Sally baby's top drawer. One of those Brimmers. Except her name isn't Brimmer any more cause she married some Navy cat named Joe Mayhew who was killed in the war. Made news because she eloped with him. Big coming-out party during the war and practically right after that she elopes with this cat who wasn't even rich. But long before she was digging jazz and sang blues sometimes at the sessions. That was in all the papers too but maybe you're too young to remember. Anyway she just blew into town after being on the Coast for hell's own amount of time."

"Is that all?" Deborah asked, disappointed.

"Well I've just told you the main facts," Gordie sniggered as he helped her into the car. "There's other things, like rumors that she's a nympho, that means real oversexed baby, and . . ."

"I don't believe a word of it," Deborah said. "You always exaggerate about women. She was very nice to me and suggested we ought to go swimming together sometime. She has a cottage in Nahant."

"Oh come off it," Gordie said. "What would you two have in common?"

"It's the truth," Deborah said stubbornly. "I didn't suggest it. She did."

"Well, they do say that nymphos are underneath Lesbians," Gordie reflected, which thought seemed to cheer him and confused Deborah more than ever. She made a note to look up the word lesbian in the dictionary since certainly she wasn't going to ask Gordie.

"And in California," he was going on in that maddening sneering obscure way, "they have some weird goings on, so I've heard. So you just watch out with that swimming stuff."

"What are you talking about?" Deborah inquired indignantly.

"Nothing. Forget it. I don't believe it anyhow. She couldn't be. Not from what I've heard and seen." He turned to Deborah and added nastily, "You really made a hit today, didn't you my sweet little virgin? All because you swarmed around dropping these pretentious, little culture vulture remarks. Well, I want to tell you, baby, these cats might seem real great to you but you want to watch them. That Si, boy! And even Mike. Oh sure," he said addressing the empty front seat, "I drag little Debby up out of that pathetic ignorance and then she gets to be a real gone chick and forgets all about ofay Gordie who never got his just reward. But don't think I'll forget it," he said looking at her angrily. "You're not going to make a fool out of me."

"I'm not trying to," Deborah said. "What's the matter with you anyway?"

"Nothing," Gordie said. "Only if anyone gets into you, it's me first. That's all." He leaned back and smiled at her as Tom Baring opened the front door of the car. "There's still lots of time before I go," he added softly. "Remember, Debby. You promised."

Deborah sighed, a small sigh. "Oh yes," she said. "I remember."

Seven

When Matthew Berman woke up that Saturday afternoon around three he lay half-drowsing for a while waiting for the prevailing mood of the day to assert itself. After a few minutes he made out that it was going to be a good day although there were some unpleasant connotations around the edges, but all in all, the weather of his shrunken day promised to be fair and this made getting out of the sack easier. He sat up, swinging his legs over the side of the bed and mooched into the bathroom, barefooted and still in the underwear he'd been too tired to take off this morning at 8:30.

He stared at his darkly unshaven face in the medicine-cabinet mirror, wondering if he would ever win this perpetual battle for enough sleep. Probably not as long as he was a resident. Maybe not all his life. Doctors weren't supposed to sleep. Still, he'd become accustomed to crazy sleeping hours during med school and internship and would undoubtedly get back into the groove again by next year. It was that plush year and a half with the Occupation forces in Germany that had undone him temporarily for the spartan life. All that Yes sir, here, and Bitte Herr Kapitan there and the big social life in schone München and skiing trips to Garmisch any weekend he cared to go. Maids to pick up after him, serve him meals, draw his baths; great leaves in Paris, Rome, and Switzerland, and a stunning variety of women to choose from. Oh yes, he thought, stripping off his grubby underwear and turning on the shower, to be an officer in the American Army in the Europe of 1946 and 1947, made you the topdrawer aristocrat of the world. It'd been a great feeling, and many times in the past year while he was sweating through this Medical Residency at a pittance salary, persistently bedeviled by the knowledge that he'd made a mistake choosing that particular specialization, however lucky and clever he was to have wangled anything at the Bay Colony, almost every other day, in fact, since

September, he'd wondered if he oughtn't to have stayed in the Army wallowing in that rich life for at least another year.

He soaped his body vigorously and banged furiously on the pipe because the plumbing in this place was so insane that you could get marooned here for as much as twenty minutes without any water. There was a loud clanking and suddenly a niagara. He was almost scalded and then abruptly the water became freezing cold but at least he'd washed the soap off. He turned off the shower and stepped out on the tiled floor which he remembered vaguely had been white when he moved in. The dirty floor reminded him of something. That obligatory cloud hovering around the perimeter of his fine waking mood. Oh Christ, of course! His family. Coming to see him and the new apartment and everything looked like hell. Bare of furniture, dirty, and his clothes strewn all around, and no point running around to remedy the unremediable because all of them, aunt, uncle, and brother would be here by the time he finished dressing, on their way home from a bar mitzvah in Brookline, to see the kind of dump on Joy Street that Matthew had to pay out good money for. He groaned and looked around the bathroom seeing it with his Aunt Sophy's eat-off-the-floor brand of housekeeping eyes. Well, what difference did it make? Sophy and Moe were okay, he could handle them, but his brother would be impossible if you were receiving him in Buckingham Palace. Families, he thought bitterly, wadding up his wet and grimy bathtowel and stuffing it into the swollen, dirty clothes bag behind the bathroom door, now if he'd stayed in the Med Corps, that would be a situation he'd never have to meet.

Except, of course, paradoxically, Saul, his brother, was one of the reasons he had not stayed. He could not have left Sophy and Moe stranded with the problem of what Saul had become. Not that he'd been a fat lot of help, but at least he was around, just in case. Well, naturally, he didn't pretend his return was completely motivated by altruism. If he'd stayed in the Army, he would have gone to hell as a doctor. His practice there in Germany had been all of the minor-bellyache, penicillin-shot school. Not learning a damn thing. Eventually he'd have had to get out and take a residency someplace and the longer he delayed the harder it would've been to leave. Maybe he'd never have left. He'd've ended up like that colonel, what was his name, who'd been Regular Army for years and had long ago forgotten whatever medicine he knew. Some nights he'd play bridge all night and then take Benzedrine during the day to stay awake and Nembutal the next night to quiet him down enough to sleep.

No thank you, thanks very much, but no. Matthew glanced in the mirror again. Well, even if he did look exhausted and like a Mafia bandit, at least he didn't resemble the doped up, weird-eyed fish which Colonel Whatever, there in Munich, had become. I've got to squeeze sometime for the barber, Matthew thought. When a man had a thick head of black hair which sprang into curls and waves when he wasn't looking, he had to keep getting it cut or he'd begin to look like a crooner and not a doctor and people'd begin to suspect him of having dirty fingernails to match the wild mop of hair. Sometimes patients got the damnedest prejudices. Once, when he was interning some cranky old man'd told him straight out that he didn't trust doctors who had long curling eyelashes like a woman. Old bastard wouldn't even let him get near the bed. Now there was popular ignorance for you. What the blazes was he supposed to do about his eyelashes for Godsakes? He began to shave quickly, squinting into the mottled mirror and grimacing at the stubbornness of the thick bristle.

So now, let's see, it was almost Saturday night and for a wonder he was off duty. No plans either. It was hard to make plans because the hospital required a certain fluid dedication on the part of its residents which was what made the Bay Colony one of the best hospitals in the United States to train in, still once in a while, it was nice to be human and get out of the white coat. Anyway, he was going to be human tonight. Just lie around on his ass and make merry while Dud Brimmer would have the duty. Yeah, but first he'd have to cope with the family. Well, it was only right. It'd been about three weeks since he was last there. The idea was to have dinner with them in a restaurant and after that they'd probably take off and then the night would brighten. A little telephone call to Peggy Morgan. She was a good sport and when he'd first come back they'd had some good shacking. But then he started getting swamped in work, study, and sleep, and they'd lost touch. He figured she was tied up with somebody from the way she talked when he'd run into her at the hospital but Peggy never stayed put for any length of time so maybe by now she'd be free. He rinsed off his face and went pulling drawers out in the bedroom bureau looking for some clean clothes. The only clean shirt he could find had a button missing but fortunately it was one of the lower ones.

He padded barefoot into the living room and sat down in the one easy chair to put on his shoes and socks. Great woolly curls of dust lay in the corners and around the edges of the worn rug and there was a hole in the toe of one of his socks. I need a mistress, he thought, a nice pliant sort of girl who could clean apartments, sew, be consistently eager to jump into bed when he was around but able to occupy herself chastely and usefully when he wasn't, some paragon who had her own income, would be quiet when he wanted to listen to music or study and, above all, a girl who definitely had no thought of marriage. In a word, a wishfulfillment girl, an impossible girl, the kind of girl every guy dreamed about but could never get, which accounted for all this marriage going on.

Speaking of music where were those new records? If he put one on now there'd be a few uninterrupted minutes before the family came after which goodbye music appreciation. He poked around in the bedroom litter and finally located the unopened package on top of the bureau all the time. Vivaldi, he thought, that's the boy for today, "The Seasons," and we'll start off with the spring side. He found some rather acidulous orange juice which had been standing for God knew how long in the small refrigerator, poured himself a large glass, flicked the switch of the phonograph and sat down again in the armchair, leaning back luxuriously to smoke, drink, and listen. Ah peace, quiet, solitude, nothing to do. Great. It was for moments like these, granted they were all too few, that he had primarily taken this apartment. Naturally, he was considered crazy by his family. Maybe it *wasn't* sensible but the rent wasn't much, and it gave him a chance to have some privacy once in a while, the kind of thing you didn't get in residents quarters in hospitals. Couldn't expect his Aunt Sophy, for one, to understand that a man his age had to have a place to take a woman occasionally or just be alone to listen to music without a lot of racket. Most of the residents his age had wives stashed around town and even if they didn't get home much at least there was somewhere of their own to go when they could and some sex, a good meal and companionship when they got there. So this apartment was a luxury that an old bock of twenty-eight could just now afford and he was going to treat himself to it as long as his money held out.

Now take Dud Brimmer, for instance. No, you take him as the nurses down at the hospital would say who all disliked him because they claimed he looked through them when he was talking to them as if they were bedpans or something. Matthew grinned at this image particularly when he thought of some nurses who'd fit the description pretty well. And some of the other residents didn't like him either. Thought he was a snob and trying to freeze them out which wasn't the case at all. Oh sure, Dud was hard to know, after all, they'd been at Fitzsimons General together during their first six months in the Medical Corps, and in that time Dud hadn't been exactly what you'd call friendly. But then, he'd been the same with everybody, and you could, if you had eyes in your head at all, see that he just didn't seem to know how to break out of that shy shell. Matthew'd been subjected to plenty of characters in his time, who were on a higher plane than he, financially, socially, intellectually, and some of them'd made damn sure you knew it, but Dud wasn't one of those. Anyway, back there at Fitzsimons, Matthew'd seen no reason why Dr. Brimmer and Dr. Berman should be bosom buddies because even though they both came from the same city, were the same age and in the same profession, Dud's Boston and his were worlds apart. It was simple and all boiled down to, would a guy like this invite you to dinner at his family's home or, by the same token, would you invite him to yours, and since, automatically, the answer would be a definite no, in both cases, there you were.

So it was a little weird after almost two years of going their separate ways in the Army to find themselves fellow Medical Residents at the Bay Colony. Matthew'd expected, when they'd first met, back in September, that there'd be the same kind of distance but waddya know, the ice was breaking up. Dud had seemed positively eager to talk. Good to see a familiar face was how he'd put it, but for Brimmer it was an earth-shaking statement. Matthew kind of knew what he meant too. Most of the other residents looked so young and those two years they'd been in the service seemed to have dropped them out of the real world altogether.

That night, when they'd run into each other in the Residents Lounge, Matthew'd had some records with him and, by God, if it didn't turn out that Brimmer really knew his music. Humanity had burst out all over him while he discoursed about what he called baroque and rococo music, the composers of which were then unknown names to Matthew. Like Vivaldi. Dudley was also a Bach fancier and, at that time, Bach was not only hard for Matthew to take, but kind of tied up in his mind with dreary, religious music. Mozart had been Matthew's boy then. Still, a guy ought to keep an open mind and it wouldn't do to curdle the new, friendly Brimmer so he'd listened intently. After that, it had kind of become a habit when they'd had a few free minutes to mosey around record shops to see what they could pick up and then take them back to Dud's place for a few drinks while they listened. So, all of a sudden, they were kind of friends and one afternoon, Brimmer'd invited him to come along for tea at his aunt's house, where a famous cellist, was on hand, and an assortment of the kind of people Matthew'd never dreamed he'd get to know.

He supposed now, as he sat there dreamily in his chair, listening with half a contented ear to the Vivaldi, that in spite of being exhausted half the time, having no steady girl and not liking his residency, this year had been a pretty good one, because all during it and notwithstanding its discomforts, he'd had a feeling of motion, expansion, in almost every direction. He knew that, at the hospital, he was learning something every minute and if only he could direct himself into a suitable channel he'd be in clover. And through Dudley and his kind of standing invitation to take tea at Mrs. Merritt's (and he'd even been invited there for dinner, which showed how wrong he'd been about Dudley before in his parochial youth) he'd been meeting a real fine class of people. Frances Merritt, Dudley's aunt, was such a really great lady, so fine and intelligent, gracious and unprejudiced that Matthew shuddered every time he thought of her in conjunction with his own aunt. Then, of course, he'd be ashamed of himself because Sophy after all had never had Frances Merritt's advantages and what a bastard he was to think like that considering that, after his own mother died, Sophy'd raised him. And she had a heart of gold too. Still, she was so damned ignorant and materialistic compared to a woman like Frances Merritt who went around in a cloth coat all the time, an old tweed, while his aunt who was a pauper compared to the Merritts, had to have yet, a Persian lamb coat.

Maybe it was a family or caste quality, that lack of ostentation, because Brimmer's apartment was not the sort of establishment you connected with inherited wealth. Just the same, the first time he went there, Matthew, living in hospital at the time, had been damned impressed at the idea of a resident having a six-room place like this all to himself. It'd be a great place to have parties, Matthew'd thought, and certainly, a never-ending round of tail, but what Brimmer did with it, remained a mystery because he never threw a party to Matthew's knowledge, and if he had a girl she was the best kept secret in town. He didn't seem to want a roommate either, and after Matthew'd been to the Merritt house in Louisburg Square he could see that the seventy-five dollars a month Dudley paid for this shabby apartment of his was no strain on him. He needed somebody to help pay his rent like he needed an extra nose. No, Matthew figured, Brimmer was just one of those guys who liked a lot of solitude. For one thing, he really *listened* to music. It'd really been an education, this past year, Matthew mused, to be exposed to Dudley's record collection. They'd just sit up there and have a couple of drinks, good stuff, bonded bourbon or Scotch and put their ears to work. It wasn't always music though. Sometimes they talked a hell of a lot of medicine. Brimmer didn't like his residency either and was casting around to find some other specialty but he wasn't getting frantic about it, the way Matthew felt *he* was. But if you had his dough you'd never really have to brood about your future.

The Vivaldi sung itself silkenly to a stop and Matthew got up and turned it over. Yes, indeed, he thought, Dr. Matthew Berman has received quite an education since his return to his hometown. Musical, medical, and personal, including some insight into that mysterious being, himself. Well, so what? Wasn't it about time? I'm not a bad guy, he thought righteously, I just want to get ahead in the world. Somebody has to have some luck in my family. My brother and my mother sure as hell never had any. Although it wasn't luck either. It was being smart, cool, uncommitted, until the right thing came and then you chose it and moved fast with it. And I have been lucky, he thought, walking over to the windows and peering out, because I have this talent for saying the right thing to the right person at the right time. I could be a good doctor, with a tongue like sandpaper and all my medical skill would avail me not a damn thing. Because doctors worked with people. The personal relationships were very important. Someone like Brimmer now, so reserved and withdrawn and putting people's backs up right away without even meaning to, could depress the hell out of a sick person and, as for the clinic outpatients they avoided him if they could. But not me, I'm a house afire, the patients ask specially for me, I'm their dream boat.

Matthew walked around the room nervously jingling the change and keys in his pants pocket. Irritably, he thought of his brother, and of Sophy and Moe, who expected him to help and were wondering why he didn't get on the stick. That was just the trouble, the reverse of the coin. If the right people liked him so did the wrong ones and what's more they all expected, needed, wanted help. His patients liked him because he helped them, but more, they liked him because he was interested in them, too damn quick to care, to show sympathy. I'm too eager to please, he thought, to have people like me. What I need is a little of Brimmer's detachment. What went on with Brimmer, anyway? The hell with personality. Jesus, any fool could have that. Or looks. Any gigolo, drugstore cowboy and twobit jerk could be good-looking. What Brimmer had was much more solid. Money, social position, brains, security. And yet . . . Well, it didn't pay to go poking around in every tangled skein you ran across. Just wait, keep your nose clean and on the right side of the world, away from crazies and weirdos and bloodsuckers, the wiseguy remarks to yourself, watch the wheel spin around and play the shrewd game of good guy. And above all, don't get sensitive. Thin skins were only for the affluent or the lonely nuts.

A little discretion wouldn't hurt either, boy, he told himself sourly. If he'd learn to keep his mouth shut concerning vulnerable areas in his own life, he'd never have gotten into that stupid argument with Gregor, although you couldn't really call it an argument since who could argue with an analyst even off duty, Gregor all through it having remained unruffled. Nevertheless, because of it he'd had to play proud since then and thus deprive himself not only of the Asch's cook, Hannelore's, culinary talents, but also the flattering friendship of Gregor and Jenni.

Jenni Asch had taken a shine to him the very first time they'd met at Frances Merritt's teatable and although he'd heard her name at Bay Colony he hadn't actually realized just who she was. He'd accepted her invitation to come for brunch the following Sunday because he was always looking for a decent meal and lo and behold had found himself meeting Gregor, her husband, who was *the* Gregor Asch, one of the most well-known of Freud's pupils. In fact it was Gregor's books, rather than Freud's which had converted Matthew, in college, to a halfass belief in the subconscious. Eating his head off at the great Gregor Asch's elbow Matthew felt that he'd come a long way from Mattapan, although geographically it was Gregor who'd come a long way from Vienna and Munich. Still even here in Boston, Gregor and Jenni remained first-rate examples of the cosmopolitan intellectual and it was Matthew Berman who had, in his own native city, taken a couple of giant steps across a gulf, into Gregor Asch's dining room.

Later, by snooping around at Bay Colony, he'd realized that Jenni Asch was not just Gregor's wife and a funny-looking German lady doctor, but one of the best obstetricians and gynecologists in the city, who, not only had a practice full of wealthy ladies who swore by her, but also chose deliberately to devote her time to patients who couldn't pay her a penny. In addition to that, she had her finger in every artistic, musical, and reformer pie in town and naturally enough she was associated with Frances Merritt in that Planned Parenthood hopeless cause.

In the beginning, Matthew'd not understood why two such stimulating, brilliant and influential people of another generation and a completely different background from his, liked him, invited him over consistently and practically considered him a member of the family, urging him to drop in any time he was free and tired of hospital food and life. Then, of course, it had come to him, one night, while listening to Jenni talk about the vast advances in knowledge concerning causes and cures in human sterility and how she wished they had known all this years ago, that, of course, Jenni and Gregor both loved babies and children but were themselves childless. So, in some obscure way, which was probably as clear as daylight to Gregor, if not to Jenni, her frustrated maternal impulses had caused her to latch on to Matthew Berman, a twenty-eight-year-old orphan who wasn't quite sure of his next move, one autumn afternoon in Louisburg Square. Which had been his great good fortune until he realized that when people adopt you they also feel entitled to grub around in your life like a family.

Jenni and Gregor were swell people but they had a little bad habit of passing out free advice. There was the matter of his future. Jenni thought Matthew ought to go in for OB-GYN work and try for a residency in it, next year. There was even a possibility that one might open at Bay Colony and if Matthew wanted she would try . . . Matthew didn't know. He couldn't remember having had any special affinity for obstetrics. He was basically much more interested in Gregor's profession than in Jenni's and he was fascinated listening to Gregor talk about the queer caperings of the human mind, but he could afford neither the time nor the money for analytic training. This was how his argument with Gregor had started.

They had been sitting around after dinner at the Asches' relishing some excellent Armagnac and the talk had turned to a conference Gregor had just attended in New York where one of the biggest problems raised had been the immense need for more doctors trained in psychiatry. And Gregor had then turned his speculative eye on Matthew.

"Don't look at me," Matthew had protested.

"It is very interesting," Gregor had pursued ruminatively, "that you can afford to possess a *pièd-a-terre* which you use very little but have no money for the training in which you are most interested and at which, I believe, you might be very good."

"Look," Matthew had said reasonably, "you know I can afford that apartment because my father left me a small amount of money.

It isn't enough to keep me going for the five or six years I'd need if I went into psychiatry. I can manage a three-year residency and that's it. After that, I'll be starting off in the world penniless at the age of thirty-two or thirty-three and I've got to make it. I just can't afford any time beyond that."

Gregor had then gone on to deliver a little impromptu lecture on how convenient an excuse lack of money was and depend on it if you found someone saying he had not the money to do what he supposedly wanted very much to do, granted he was not disabled, and blind, then the reason was not lack of money but some kind of psychic conflict. This was the sort of standard analytic gambit Matthew was used to from Gregor so he'd remained cool and shrugged noncommittally.

"But perhaps you wish to make financial success quickly in order to be married," Gregor had continued smoothly.

"Oh, I don't know," Matthew had said startled by this sudden change of tempo. "I don't have any plans that way now. But maybe by that time I will."

"You have never met or known any girls in your life you wished to marry?"

Matthew'd been amused. "Are you going to send me a bill, Gregor?"

"Nonsense. This is one of the imbecilities of the analyst's life. From you, I expect a more sensible reaction."

"I'm sorry, Gregor. I was just joking anyhow."

"It is too late in life for me," Gregor had grunted, "to remotely comprehend the American sense of humor. Particularly since it seems so often one of the few socially acceptable masks for intense hostility. 'Kidding' "—he'd pronounced the word with distaste—"I believe it's called. But I digress. Have you not thought that for a man of sense, of normal drives, it is peculiar that by the age of twenty-eight on his way to twenty-nine he has never met a girl to be serious about?"

"Hell, no," Matthew'd said loudly. "I've been too busy all my adult life trying to get somewhere. It hasn't been easy. If it hadn't been for the government and the war I might never've been able to finish Med School. And I paid for it with two years of time which I could've used to a lot better advantage. But I'm not kicking about it. Not only because one has to pay for what one gets but also because it was part of my citizen's obligation and I was a lot better off than plenty of other guys. So, that's why I've had neither the time, money, or above all, the inclination to get responsibly linked up with a girl. I know that most residents are married when they're twenty-two, have four kids and live in packing-cases, but maybe I have better sense than they do. I've had enough struggle to last me for a good long while and I'd like to relax a bit and have something to offer my wife when I do get married. Anyway, Gregor, I don't know what deep neurosis you're reading into this but believe me it's not uncommon. There're plenty of men who don't get married or find the right woman till they're established and in their middle or late thirties."

"Naturally, I am aware, Matthew, of the drive to power and also that it cannot be satisfied as conveniently and temporarily as the young male's libido. But you are not as self-sufficient and controlled as these very ambitious men usually must be. And you are warm, interested in people and friendly. The sort of man who is likely to fall deeply in love many times from youth onward. Nor do you have any substitutes such as a big, pleasant family. Yes, it is very peculiar . . ."

"If you're not analyzing me now, Gregor, I'd like to know what you are doing?" Matthew had tried to keep his voice amused but some irritation had crept in in spite of his efforts.

"I assure you I do not present conclusions to my patients in this manner." Gregor had folded his arms and looked somberly at Matthew. "Tell me, you know that if you undertook psychiatric training you must yourself be analyzed and perhaps this is one of the reasons you don't wish to?"

"I'm not afraid of it, if that's what you mean," Matthew'd said annoyed. "But I don't think I need it either. Anyway, why talk about it? Analysis or no analysis it's all part and parcel of a career I can't afford. And the same goes for love since you brought it in. When I'm set up, I'll get a wife and live like everyone else."

"I must disagree with you," Gregor had said politely. "You will not."

Matthew had sat up straight in his chair, keeping a tight grip on the arm. I must remain cool, objective, he'd thought. I respect Gregor, he's a famous man who has somehow taken an interest in me. Gregor's too big a man to pry out of malice, to take advantage of what I told him in a weak moment when I was drinking furiously after an impossible, depressing two hours with my brother Saul.

"Gregor," he'd said, feeling kind of good that his voice came out straight with no shakes, "I admit that I forced a lot of family skeletons on you at the Kollmers' party and I'm sorry I banged your ear like that, but it still doesn't give you the means to predict my future."

Gregor'd regarded him steadily. "I do not possess powers of extrasensory perception, no. But I have a great background of experience which, in addition to my knowledge of the mind's workings, can help to see signposts where others might not. I speak to you of love and you pooh-pooh me and drench me with economic and social interpretations. But love is a very basic instinct. Falling in love is not solely accomplished to satisfy one's libido. It also happens because the human needs to find in adult life the close warmth, the sense of belonging in someone else's heart and the desire to take someone into his, the need to drive away the loneliness which is the human condition, all this that he has had if he was lucky as a child, with good, loving parents, brothers and sisters, friends and pets. All this is natural. But far too frequently something happens to destroy or anesthetize in the human the ability to love, though he might wish to do so, though he may love others in mass, help them, as long as he is not deeply committed to them. But the most deeply personal relationship of all, he shuns like bubonic plague. I do not say that such a person cannot live a fulfilled life at some time. I am prepared for miracles. Yet from all my experience I am dubious."

Jenni who'd been called away to the hospital during dinner had returned while Gregor was talking, peered into the room, waved at Matthew and gone away again. He'd wished intensely that she'd come back and stop this whole lecture, put on a record, tell them about the delivery, anything to stop her husband from overstepping the bounds of friendship which he was going to do in no time at all. And yet, Matthew had thought bitterly, I brought it on myself just by talking too much.

Gregor had been packing his pipe and finally began to puff away like an old Viennese uncle. He had refilled his and Matthew's glasses, put on a record of Mozart Horn Concertos and sat down again, staring bemusedly at the smoke from his pipe drifting up to the ceiling.

"So where's all this leading to?" Matthew'd asked harshly. "You're not going to just let me dangle, Dr. Asch, after all that buildup, are you? You've got something in mind?"

"It was not I," Gregor'd pointed out carefully, "who came to you and asked you to tell me your problems. Normally, since you are not a patient, I would ignore those things you told me. But you are quite close to us. At the hospital, Jenni finds you are considered a very brilliant young man. You have an excellent record, you please all your supervisors, you are immensely skillful, responsible. But, strangely enough, you are pervaded with a sort of inertia. You do not like your present residency yet you make no move to obtain another. You thought seriously of remaining in the Army in spite of all its obvious drawbacks to your medical future. It is curious. Then, the day you have drunk a little too much and all your controls are relaxed you present me with answers to many puzzling things. You ask me questions about your brother whom you think is mentally disturbed but refuses to come and see me and you explain all his difficulties. You talk about your parents, your father's flagrant philandering, your mother's mysterious death. In so doing of course you tell me a good deal about yourself. After all that, you are sober and ashamed of telling me and hope I will have forgotten. I am trained not to forget such things, I like you and I am concerned about you . . ."

"In the first place," Matthew had interrupted angrily, "I didn't say that Saul's troubles stemmed from what happened to our mother. It's what happened to him in the war. In the second place, I was very clear, no matter how much I'd drunk, that nobody ever found out whether my mother's death was an accident or not. She used to take sleeping pills all the time because she had insomnia and one night she just took too many. That's all."

"And it is not reasonable to suppose," Gregor'd said in that damn knowing way of his, "that such an accident might have been planned."

"Oh, reasonable!" Matthew'd begun to shout unavoidably. "A woman who commits suicide because she and her husband don't get along and because he chases around isn't reasonable."

"Of course," Gregor'd said quietly. "But it is the uncertainty of it all that still bothers you. And if it was so, that she was not reasonable, what of it? Either way you are still ashamed of it and yet why? It was none of your doing and you are not responsible."

Matthew had gotten up then, feeling as though his head might burst open unless he got out of there fast. He'd not trusted himself to speak, to say goodbye to Jenni. He'd just marched to the closet, got his coat and taken off. Since then, Jenni had called him to apologize for Gregor, to invite him back to dinners and he'd simply refused. So of course he hadn't heard a word from them since then.

Matthew sat up straight suddenly. Of course. Why hadn't he seen it before? He'd walked out on Gregor and Jenni that night because Gregor had put into words just what Saul believed. And it was lousy hearing this old lie from someone who was objective and intelligent, someone he respected as much as he did Gregor. Saul, who'd been twelve when their mother died was firmly convinced that she'd killed herself because of their father's doings and he'd never taken a cent from the old man and had refused to see him. He'd even gotten sore at Matthew for occasionally writing letters to him and for taking money for college and Med School from him. Of course, to Saul, with his kind of intense, extreme thinking, a woman who killed herself because of an unhappy marriage was not off balance, just a victim of love's evil. To Matthew, it meant that his mother, whom he couldn't remember now too well, had been pretty damn unstable if she'd done it on purpose. He didn't think she had. It'd been an accident and you didn't hold grudges against a man who was your father because of accidents.

Hell, Matthew thought, looking at his watch, where are those people? His whole night off would be shot if they didn't show soon. And speaking of grudges why was he holding one against the Asches? What a damn fool he was. Here were two people who liked him, whom he liked, who could do a lot for him, who had helped make this past year very pleasant for him, who'd been kind and put themselves out for him, and he was behaving like a sulky child. I'd better make my peace with them, he thought shamefacedly, that is, if they haven't decided by this time that I'm an ingrate and a fool.

He went to the phone and dialed the house number. Jenni should be finished with her afternoon office hours by now, at least he hoped so. It'd be a little harder to talk to Gregor.

"Matthew," Jenni's voice, slightly cracked and as shrill as if she were talking to a deaf person. "You have been neglecting us."

"I know. I called to—er—apologize for walking out on both of you that way and for being rude."

"But of course, I understand. Gregor is sorry also. He was going heavily, abstractly onward in search of truth and he did not mean to hurt your feelings, I know."

"Anyway, I've been damn busy," Matthew added gratuitously.

"Yah, yah, that I know. But tomorrow afternoon can you come? There is to be a little party at the gallery. Three young painters show. And one of them, Ella Baring the wife of an acquaintance of yours. On your recommendation, I go to look at her work and I think she is so talented. So it is due to you and you must come. I want to send you an invitation but Gregor said to not bother you until you are ready and it must be left up to you."

"He's too damned smart," Matthew said laughing.

"Sometimes, even he irritates me, knowing so much," Jenni said cheerfully. "The opening is at four tomorrow but you may come earlier."

"Well—uh—I'm not much on art, Jenni," Matthew said uneasily. "You know that."

"You know well enough to tell me to see her work. And it is good."

"All I did was go to a poker game at Si Hunnicutt's apartment, a guy I used to know at Tufts, and he had one of her paintings there. So I thought about you, that's all. But I hardly know the girl and I'll feel like a fool looking at paintings when I don't know a damn word to say about them."

"So if you wish to remain a narrow mind all your life, I cannot help you. But you make me impatient, not even to try. Because you are a doctor you need not be stupid about other things."

"Okay, okay," Matthew said. He could see why anti-birth control people ran the other way when they saw Jenni coming. "I'll come. Do I have to wear a tuxedo?"

"Imbecile. Your usual clothes. Tomorrow then, at four or earlier."

Matthew sat by the telephone for a few minutes after Jenni'd rung off wondering if maybe he should call Dud Brimmer and tell him about this art show. This was more up Brimmer's alley than his. Jenni wouldn't mind. Matthew dialed the hospital resident's quarters first, but they said Dr. Brimmer was expected on duty at midnight and wasn't around now. Probably sleeping at his own place, then, Matthew thought. By this time must be up though. He picked up the receiver again and had started to dial before he suddenly remembered, stopped himself and put the phone down.

He and Dud had not seen much of each other for the past month. The work load at the hospital had grown very heavy and neither of them had had a damn minute for anything but sleep, clinics, conferences, rounds, patients, problems, study, the whole thing. Then, in the midst of all this frenzy, Dud's sister, a war widow apparently, had come back to Boston from out West and was living in his apartment. The fact that Brimmer had a sister he'd never mentioned in all this time was peculiar, although for that matter, since when did Berman go around brandishing *his* happy sibling relationship if he could help it. But Dud's sister must be pretty goddamn devoted to him to come all the way across a continent to make a home for him in that place. While wealthy men often disregarded creature comforts it was very rare for rich women to do it. Elegant town houses and servants was more like it.

Matthew'd expected to see less of Brimmer anyhow after the sister's arrival and frankly it was just as well because a female version of Dudley would be catastrophic. She'd probably be domineering and snobbish and either too intellectual or mad for animals.

Finally, for Godsakes, the long-awaited bell rang and a few seconds later his family bustled in full of good cheer and all dressed up, his aunt kissing him and darting suspicious eyes around at one and the same time. His brother, Saul, was full of more than good cheer.

"Boy, that was a well-stocked bar they had there," he said, slapping Matthew on the back, a manner of greeting which he disliked and which Saul knew he disliked.

"Such a pig your brother," Sophy said. "Scotch he drank, nothing but Scotch would he have, one right after another."

"What the hell," Saul said, "it was free, wasn't it? Some spread, Bud, you should've been there."

He settled himself with difficulty in the easy chair and Matthew cleared some medical books off the couch to make a place for his aunt and uncle and they began to talk about the bar mitzvah.

"It was so nice," his aunt was saying. "A catered affair. The boychik did so well. He wasn't nervous or anything."

"Not like you, Bud," his brother said jovially.

It was like Saul to bring up painful experiences. Matthew'd stammered and faltered all the way through his bar mitzvah speech, horribly embarrassed, wishing he were any other place, and had, for three agonizing minutes, forgotten it altogether. His first public appearance after having crossed the threshold from boyhood to religious manhood and he'd messed it up.

Now, before the war, Matthew thought, sitting silently and looking at his brother, I could have told him off when he made cracks like that, but then, before the war, he probably wouldn't have made them. Because ever since they were kids, they'd been pals, in spite of the fact that they were utterly different from each other. Saul'd been the big, husky, popular, athletic brother Matthew'd looked up to, who'd taken care of him and taught him things. And later, after their mother's death, they'd clung together fiercely, putting up a united front against the rest of the world.

Matthew remembered even now, with a kind of a wonder, how much he'd admired his brother; the way he'd worked while he was in high school at part-time jobs and how when he'd graduated in the height of the depression what a hustler he'd been, taking all kinds of jobs, driving trucks, a shipping clerk down in the garment district, working on construction jobs with the WPA, short-order cook in hash joints, anything to make a buck. And, at the same time, working out in the gym every night, learning how to box, because as he said he was a natural for it, and it'd be the fastest way to put himself into the big money. He was right too. Down at the gym people had their eyes on him, he'd gotten himself a manager and by the time Matthew had graduated from high school, Saul was getting some small, local bouts. There'd been a running argument around the house for a while, Matthew remembered, because to Sophy, the fight game was only for bums and no-goodnicks. Then there'd been another fight when Matthew had wanted to go to college and on to Med School and their father out there in Chicago, now remarried and making good in the liquor business, offered to foot all the tuition bills for the four college years. Saul'd said that Matthew was a lousy traitor if he took a cent from that racketeer, he didn't believe that crud about the liquor business, which was all racketeer ridden anyhow and Saul, the crazy sonovabitch, had been willing, just to keep his kid brother from contamination, to support Matthew himself, kick in all his fight gold and work at other jobs besides. Well, for Christ's sakes who could've let him do a crazy thing like that? His manager'd sure thought it was a lousy idea because Saul was getting good, better all the time, more bouts coming his way, but still he hadn't been making enough to send a brother through college. Matthew'd refused Saul and accepted his father's offer for four years' tuition money. Books and living expenses he'd have to work for and Saul could contribute if he wanted to and maybe later he might help with Med School because the old man didn't seem anxious to do anything about that.

Saul'd sulked for a while and finally admitted to his stubborn self and Matthew that maybe it was okay to take money for college from their skunk of a father but only on the understanding that later on, one or both of them would pay every cent back, but by the time he'd started Tufts, Saul'd forgotten the whole grudge because he'd won an unimportant fight in Boston Garden against some puncher from Worcester and the papers began to mention Saul Berman as a fighter to watch. Of course, his aunt was always around keening about Saul getting beaten up and when his nose got broken in the next and bigger fight, she cried all night, but none of it worried Saul because he was, in all brotherly honesty, one of the handsomest men around and the slight break in his nose merely heightened his masculine good looks.

"Putting on the dog," Saul was saying now. "Throwing a party like that for a thirteen-year-old boy. Goddamnedest waste of money."

"So," his aunt retorted, "if my brother wants to spend money it's his money and it's his only son and he's an older man already. I'd do the same and so would you, Mr. Smarty, if you got married when you were in your forties and you had just one child, one son . . ."

Matthew saw his brother's face getting red and rushed in. "How about taking a tour through the apartment, Sophy? Isn't that what you came for?" He wished his aunt wouldn't be so tactless but still he knew damn well that Saul was a trial to live with and she had to put up with it all the time so he supposed that sometimes she just walked hard on the eggs and broke them and to hell with it.

"I don't know," his aunt said, momentarily diverted, shaking her head, "what there's to look at? For this, you had to use up your inheritance money. Why didn't you buy yourself a nice car?"

"He should've refused the dough altogether, will or no will," Saul said loudly. "Let that bitch of a wife have it all. After all, when a pimp dies, the whore is entitled to . . ."

"Now that," Sophy said firmly and furiously, turning on him, "is enough. No more. Not another word. After all, he was your father and now he's dead. At least have a little respect for the memory of the dead."

"Oh sure," Saul sneered. "A guy can be the worst lowlife in the world but when he dies, all of a sudden, he's some kind of a saint."

"Come on," Matthew said, herding his aunt before him. "Maybe you can give me a few tips on fixing up the place. Nothing like a woman's touch, you know. How about you, Moe?" He turned to his uncle who'd been sitting quietly in the middle of all this, leafing through a newspaper. Moe, now, was a nice little guy, always quiet and calm, and Matthew liked him and the way he sat imperturbably through the storms of Saul's and his wife's talk.

"Later," he said, giving Matthew a sympathetic smile. "Meanwhile I've got this." He produced a bottle of Napoleon brandy from his coat pocket. "Expensive schnapps," he announced beaming, "I was going to bring it out for the party but they had so much schnapps there, all kinds, I figured I'd bring it to you instead."

Matthew got some glasses for them and went back to the bedroom where his aunt was poking around in corners and chattering along to him about curtains and how she could run some up for him on the sewing machine and did he have to sleep under a miserable-looking army blanket like that, didn't he have enough money to buy himself a nice blanket, at least, some cheerful color . . . He kept standing there, not really listening and occasionally saying, yes, and you're so right, Sophy. Anything, he thought, anything to keep them in here and away from Saul. Back there, in the living room, for a second, he'd almost forgotten and his hands had itched to give his brother a real poke in the nose. But losing his temper with Saul was no solution. And what was the solution, wise guy, he asked himself as he leaned against the wall and nodded obediently in tune with his aunt's voice. What could anyone do for a man like his brother now? How would it be possible to find again the brother he had loved, the good-natured, generous, happy-go-lucky brother that he'd been.

In those days, everyone had loved Saul and Saul, without reservations, except for their father, had returned this love. Men, women, dogs, and babies had bloomed in the warmth of Saul's gusto, his obvious, sensual joy in just walking around, eating, drinking, having his name plastered on the sports pages, owning and driving a fast red convertible, wearing expensive suits, giving presents to people and having beautiful girls to go out with any time he wanted. But for a wife, Saul did not want any of those fancy, rootless creatures that clustered around fighters and show business people. No, he wanted a nice girl and so he'd married one, a girl from the neighborhood, whose father had a business on Chauncy Street, making workingmen's clothes. Rose was a pretty girl but Matthew'd found her incredibly dull. But for Saul, she'd been great, had worshiped him, gone to all his fights, cheering loudly, dressed up to the nines. And Saul, naturally, returned all her admiration. His conversation after his marriage, when it was not concerned with his fights, tended to consist of catalogs of what Rose'd said, worn, bought to furnish their apartment, and cooked for their supper. Matthew'd decided that it was a good thing he was too busy at college to see much of his brother, who was getting to be a real complacent bourgeois in spite of his raffish profession and acquaintances. And even that one link with a rather exciting and non-respectable life wouldn't last long, because Rose's father and mother wanted him to quit and go into the business. Matthew'd known that this eventually would happen if Saul did not make the real big time in boxing because his brother wanted to make a lot of money and have a big family of children and, as he sometimes said, he wouldn't like his kids to have a father with a smashed-up face. Matthew'd supposed it was inevitable that he and his brother drift apart, being so different, and, if Saul would be happy manufacturing workingmen's clothes and being married to a nitwit, well who was he to criticize?

In January of 1942 Saul came back from winning a fight in Chicago which had boosted him up the ladder a little further toward his manager's dream of a match with the heavyweight who was the number one contender for the title, but in April, classified 1-A and with no important matches looming, Saul had shocked everybody by volunteering for the Army.

Saul's wife had not spoken to him for a week. Why, why, was all she'd seemed to be able to say, with red eyes, why does he have to do this to me now? He's married. He could take a job in a defense plant. Maybe by the time they draft him the war will be over. Then she'd wail again and Sophy would comfort her and weep a bit herself.

Saul'd been bewildered by them. "What's the matter with you people?" he'd ask. "Somebody in the family's got to go. Bud's studying to be a doctor and he's got to finish. They need doctors. So it's me. You think I'm going to sit on my ass and wait for them to get me? Not me. I want to get my hands on a few of those Nazi bastards."

Moe, usually so uncommunicative had sided with Saul. "It is right, that he should volunteer to fight for a country like this and not wait to be asked. Wars, I don't like, Solly, killing, I hate, but I am proud you should want to go."

After basic training Saul'd been chosen to go to Infantry OCS at Fort Benning, which had surprised Matthew a little. Somehow he'd never thought of his brother as officer material and, in fact, when Saul'd come home on furlough before going overseas, Matthew found himself feeling very jealous of him as handsome as the hero of a war movie in his greens and pinks with the gleaming second lieutenant bars and the Georgia suntan. Then they'd started getting V-mail from Saul with an APO number and Sophy and Moe'd speculated nervously and endlessly about where he could be until the spring of 1944 when they found out. Saul had been with the 36th Division and in the fighting along the Rapido River he'd been wounded so severely that his right leg had to be amputated.

That year, 1944, had been Matthew's last in Med School and so he'd scraped some more money out of his father and been rooming in the Med students dorms which was why he'd gotten all the bad news of that year filtered through Sophy's clotted tears and some undoubted distortions. The substance of it, however, had been common enough.

Rose had met a Navy dentist, stationed availably at the Fargo Building, and written Saul a dear John letter asking for a divorce. Like all deadly wartime letters this one did not catch up with Saul until the war was over for him and it'd been followed almost immediately by another, written as soon as she'd heard he was wounded. This second cancel-all-I-said-before, I-was-just-lonely-for-you letter had suffered no delay. It'd gone straight to First Lieutenant Berman's hospital bed because now there was no trouble finding him. He'd have to stay put for a good long while. He didn't bother to answer either letter, but merely had allotment payments to his wife stopped and transferred to Sophy.

Rose had obtained an uncontested divorce, married her dentist and gone to live with him in Los Angeles and Saul'd come back with an artificial leg. The government sent him to school to learn a good, sit-down trade and now he worked as a linotype operator for the Boston *Beacon-Journal*, and drove the nice, new, specially equipped car given by a grateful country to World War II amputees. He was still big and good-looking but that once happy, handsome face was now almost disfigured by a permanent scowl and bitter lines, and one of his few amusements was drinking too much. For a while, after he'd returned, according to Sophy, he was drunk all the time and, because he hadn't learned to navigate too well then on his substitute leg, he was always falling down and strangers in bars would pick him up. Now, he knew how to walk okay and was wise enough to avoid humiliation, so he'd drink only enough to give him a buzz on, and then come home late, stumbling and swearing and Sophy who anxiously waited up for him would run to the door to help him and spend the rest of the night crying. He wouldn't go near a boxing match and he hated women.

Back in the front room now, Matthew watched his brother, leaning back in the easy chair, his voice loud and cynical, his face flushed from too much Scotch and brandy, and experienced an overwhelming hopeless, impatient anger. Four years, Matthew thought, this stubborn, screwed-up ignoramus who wants to destroy himself, lost his leg four years ago and time hasn't helped him to change or adjust. Now, he's settled in his rut of misery. Talk to him, Matthew, Sophy'd pleaded and he'd tried. But it had been like reasoning with barbed wire and eventually Matthew'd been sickened by the sound of his own sensible, calm advice. He'd begun to feel that truthfully he was a pompous ass. What right, after all, did he have to patronize Saul? He hadn't lost a leg, a wife, and a career, all in one mortal blow.

"All right," Saul would say nastily, "so you're a doctor but I'm not sick and I don't need your goddamn advice. Go peddle your pills."

And when Matthew had asked him to go see Gregor Asch, Saul's reaction had been savage, snarling, and succinct, "If that refugee headshrinker could give me another leg, I'd go. So get off my back will you, Bud, and don't mention that crap to me again, because one leg or not, I can still pound the shit out of you."

So that was it. He'd never talked personally to Saul since then. In fact they'd scarcely exchanged any kind of word.

"Well and who was it that got the treatment at the bar mitzvah," he asked now, briskly, after he'd complimented his uncle on the excellence of the brandy. The best thing to do, Matthew figured, was to keep away from any even remotely touchy topic and Saul seemed to have already demolished the bar mitzvah.

"What's the matter with you, Matt?" Sophy cried. "I told you a thousand times already, your young cousin Lenny. You're getting so absentminded at that hospital, forgetting about your family. Not even calling up."

"He's getting too good for Mattapan," Saul jibed. "He's probably got his mind on some rich Newton babe."

"Listen," Matthew said coldly, "you come into Boston to go to work every day. If you're so crazy to see me, why don't you call me?"

Saul grinned maliciously. The only pleasure he seemed to get out of life, nowadays, besides drinking, was seeing how far he could push people, Matthew reflected, annoyed with himself for rising to the bait.

"Sure, Bud," Saul said, "it's a deal. Only I'll let you know ahead of time because I wouldn't want to break up anything you had on with a broad. Or you could always bring your broad along."

"Sorry," Matthew said lightly, "afraid I don't have a girl right now. Too busy." And if I did, he thought, you'd never see her. Once, before he'd correctly gauged the new, postwar Saul, he'd taken a girl to his aunt's house and Saul'd started right off insulting her.

"I almost forgot," Sophy was saying, taking a paper-napkin-wrapped package from her purse, "I brought you some knishes, Matt. Such a shame, I was thinking, you weren't there and you like them so much."

The little pastry wrapped meatballs were very good. Matthew wolfed down four of them and it occurred to him that he was damn hungry.

"Thanks a lot, Sophy. They're swell. But you know I have to eat some dinner. How about us going to Chinatown. Or did you eat too much at the party?" After dinner, he thought tensely, I'll definitely try to get hold of Peggy. Boy, do I need relaxation, in a bad way.

"Nah," Saul was saying. "Let's see, it's five-thirty now. I could go for some Chinks pretty soon."

Sophy nodded and Moe said he wasn't too hungry but if he had another schnapps he'd get an appetite and anyway all that noodle, rice, Chinese mishmash always left him feeling empty. So Matthew poured another brandy all around and just then the bell rang.

He wondered who it was, while he pressed the buzzer and went to open the door. People didn't drop in on him too much. He was so curious he stepped out into the hallway and looked down over the stairs. There was no one in sight and then a woman's voice called questioningly, "Dr. Berman?"

"I'm Dr. Berman," he said, as he saw the blonde head come up over the stairwell. It was dim there in the hallway but even so he could see that she was probably the most beautiful female he'd ever run across. Did she live in this building and if she did where the hell had he been all this time?

"How do you do," she said coolly and held out her hand. "This is rather an informal sort of introduction but I'm Sally Mayhew, Dud Brimmer's sister and I fear that I'm the bearer of evil tidings."

He took her hand automatically and shook it, stammering something gallant and polite like, "Huh! Wassamatta?" (Dud's sister! The catastrophe!) and slapped his forehead to stir his staggered brain.

"My dear man. Is it really that much of a shock? I'm afraid I exaggerated. Dud has not died, he's simply incapacitated and cannot go on duty tonight. He wondered if you could possibly and kindly take over for him?"

Matthew pulled himself together. "Oh. I'm sorry to hear that. Well, sure, sure I could."

"That's good of you. I thought perhaps you might have terribly important plans." She turned back toward the stairs.

"Oh—er—no—nothing," he assured her quickly. "Dud always makes up the time and I can do whatever I was going to to one night as well as another." Now what the hell does she care, he thought. She obviously wanted to get away fast after performing an unpleasant duty and he wanted to keep her there, just to look at her a little more and listen to that voice.

"How convenient of you," she drawled but she'd turned back again and was leaning against the railing, regarding him attentively, her head a little to one side, one eyebrow raised, an almost exact replica of her brother's interrogative mannerism. "You mean he's done this sort of thing before?" There was a very slight note of annoyance.

"Oh, only a few times." Matthew was absurdly glad that she was still standing there talking. "He seems to have these recurring attacks of gastroenteritis. But I suppose you know about that."

"No," she said looking at him thoughtfully, "I didn't."

"Well, it's nothing to worry about," Matthew said hastily. "I mean I guess for a while there he thought he might have an ulcer but then he had himself looked at and it wasn't."

"Don't you get a little tired of covering for him when he has these, ah, inexplicable digestive attacks, Dr. Berman?"

"Well, it's only been a few times," Matthew said defensively. "He doesn't make a habit of it and he always, as I say, pays back. And even if they are—uh—just psychosomatic, they can hurt like hell." He was puzzled by the coldness of her tone. Christ, he thought, she sounds as if she didn't like him.

Almost as if she'd read his thoughts, Sally Mayhew said, "I'm afraid I'm quite ignorant. My brother and I, you see, Dr. Berman, don't know each other very well."

"Say Bud," Saul's voice at the door. "What's up?" He limped over the threshold. "Anything the matter?"

"I have to go on duty tonight," Matthew said shortly. "Mrs. Mayhew just came to tell me her brother's sick." He introduced them.

"Oh then you are interrupting your plans," Dud Brimmer's sister said after acknowledging Saul's gruff hello with a gracious smile. "I'm sure Dudley wouldn't want that. Is there someone else we can call on?"

"Waddya keeping the lady standing out in the hall for, Bud?" Saul said impatiently, interrupting Matthew's polite it's quite all rights. "Where are your manners? Maybe she'd like to come in and sit down and have a drink of brandy."

Now why the hell doesn't he mind his own business, Matthew thought savagely. As if his luck wasn't bad enough already, having this lush-looking dish appear at his door when his family was there and God knows if he'd ever get an opportunity like this again, but now Saul wanted to invite her in, no doubt so he could tell her that she was a nice-looking broad and Sophy could give her the once over and ask her a lot of personal questions. The one good thing was that she would certainly refuse. She'd been itching to get down those stairs and now was her chance. But no, she thought it was an absolutely divine idear, and the next thing he knew, Saul, grinning triumphantly, was leading her through the door and helping her off with a little velvet jacket and there were more introductions.

Saul had sunk back, still grinning like a fox, in his chair and it was left to Matthew to run around pulling out a chair and trying to start the foredoomed conversational ball rolling while his lousy brother just sat comfortably saying nothing but looking at Dud

Brimmer's sister all the time, his eyes narrowing, watching the way her hips moved and taking in every detail of her fine legs and the full, firm curves of breasts clearly outlined under the thin material of her blouse.

Matthew tried to concentrate on that blouse of hers while he was hunting desperately around in the kitchen for a glass and, finding nothing but an old cheese glass, had to go back, get his own, and wash it out, so he wouldn't have to think about how he hated his damn brother and his stinking luck and keep himself from listening to the halting, forced conversation that was going on out in the living room between his aunt and Sally Mayhew. It looked as if it was made of foam, that blouse. He'd never seen anything like it before. Kind of a creamy color and of some material that was soft, sheer, and clinging and rippled in rows and rows of very small ruffles all down the front and around the wrists. He knew he didn't care about the blouse by itself although he always did like a nicely dressed woman, no, it was those beautiful, goddamn breasts so full and ripe underneath it. When Saul had taken off her jacket, he'd had an immediate sharp, strong desire to put his hands on them. It was a feeling he'd never experienced that fast before about a woman but then he couldn't remember having ever run into a woman that beautiful, that perfect, and that completely sexual. Her sexuality was emphasized by her clothes, but not in an obvious way. According to conventional standards of sexily dressed women, she was all bundled up and yet she was more overwhelmingly sensuous in that blouse and a wide velvet skirt with a high waistline than any half-naked babe with a tight skirt and everything showing.

He started to fill her glass, watching her as he did so. She was sitting down now, her legs crossed and peeking out under the skirt he saw a foam of lace and ruffles the exact color of the blouse, caught here and there with knots of cherry-colored ribbon. She looked like a princess and he couldn't stop gaping at her, so he poured too much and the brandy spilled over on the table. Then he realized that everybody was looking at him and his uncle said drily, "Maybe Mrs. Mayhew would like her schnapps now, Matt," so he closed his mouth and handed her the glass hoping nervously that it wasn't too full, that she wouldn't stain her blouse.

"It's lovely brandy," she said.

They were all trying to make polite conversation. Moe commented on the fine weather they were having. Sophy complimented her on her clothes. Then there'd be a lame, little silence. Then Matthew'd have to rush in with something, completely pointless, delivered in a low mutter which trickled off into nothingness. Dud Brimmer's sister remained completely poised, with her ankles crossed neatly now, sipping delicately at her brandy, her shining head inclined politely at whoever was speaking. She volunteered no questions of her own and her answers to any of their comments were pleasant and brief. But every now and then, she'd look over, in a puzzled sort of way, at Saul. And that excellent brother of his, of course, said hardly anything. He had enough to do trying to see what was underneath all those ruffles.

Christ, Matthew thought tiredly, what a bunch, himself included. Maybe Saul was giving her the once-over but he wasn't alone. He wished she'd go away. What could she possibly think of them, everybody X-raying her like that, like a bunch of rubes, glomming a jewel. His aunt, now, sitting there on the couch, plump, well-corseted, in her anonymous best black dress, her white hair neatly permanented and arranged like the hairdresser wanted it, her round face with its short, broad nose, watchful and curious, she, who had worked, as an immigrant girl, twelve hours a day on the sewing machines of various sweatshops, was mentally fingering the black velvet and the sheer stuff of the blouse and so was his uncle, the cutter, the man who'd worked in the garment industry since he'd come to this country as a thirteen-year-old boy. Both of them sat there, their faces saying plainly to him who knew them so well: A rich, blonde shicksa who comes to see Matt, just drops in on him, what kind of nice girl would come to see a fellow in his apartment. This, in spite of all the great elaborate pains he'd gone to, explaining about her brother's illness, trying to indicate as obviously as possible that she was a stranger to him.

"It's a shame about your brother," Sophy was saying now to Sally Mayhew. "Did he have to have a doctor?"

Everybody laughed a little embarrassedly at this and then Sophy wanted to know what was so funny and what was the matter, didn't doctors get sick too, like everybody else and when they did, what happened?

"I'm sure Dudley will be quite well tomorrow," his sister said. She'd taken out a cigarette and Matthew bounded over to light it for her, aware that Saul was smirking contemptuously at his trigger-like eagerness. For once, he didn't mind his brother's sick effort to make him feel ashamed of having two legs and being fast on them, because she gave him a sensational smile and he was close enough to her to smell some delightful, dizzying perfume.

"Too bad you had to put yourself out, coming all the way over here," Sophy said with that kind of bland rudeness which infuriated Matthew because he knew it was her way of fishing for information.

"Why it wasn't far," Sally Mayhew said rather amusedly. "And the telephone is so terribly impersonal, don't you think?"

Sophy looked dashed and Matthew thought she'd probably never been put so neatly in her place before. Serves her right, he thought vengefully, while another uncomfortable silence ensued and he searched desperately for something, anything to say. But Dud Brimmer's sister was ahead of him, dropping a little bombshell into the room.

"I've been wondering where I'd seen you before, Mr. Berman," she said, turning to Saul so that he was forced to stop his inventory of her pectoral muscles, "and now I've just remembered. You used to box, didn't you? Or perhaps you still do? I've been away so long I wouldn't know."

Oh no, Matthew thought, resting his head on his hand, not this too. Now what will Saul do, he wondered, tensed, what the hell can he do when a perfect stranger and a voluptuous doll at that smiles nicely at him and asks him in a throaty, bestBoston voice, the kind of question no relative or friend would dare ask. Why he had the whole family so damn scared it wasn't safe to mention so much as a cardboard box in his presence. So he could be rude, that's what he could do, rude, snarling, and lousy.

"Me?" Saul said roughly, "In the fight game. God forbid!"

"But I'm almost sure," she began frowning a little, ". . . of course, I could be wrong, but I thought that you're the Saul Berman I saw fight Billy Bang in the Garden, oh years ago, just before the war, I think, and I saw several other bouts too. Names I can't remember."

"You sound like you were a fan of this guy Berman's." He continued to look her over boldly as he said this and then added loudly, "So you like the fights, huh?"

"Why yes," she said. "At least I used to. I went with my cousin and he was very interested in boxing. He thought you were awfully good."

They were looking at each other in a strange, intent kind of way. The conversation had suddenly become narrowed down, personal and full of intimate overtones.

"I keep telling you. I don't do any fighting."

"But you did," she said smiling composedly.

"You're pretty sure I'm that old beat-up pug?" Saul was smiling now and he looked like his old self for a minute.

Sophy and Moe exchanged wondering glances and Moe shrugged.

Matthew slumped back in his chair. For once, nobody would have to rush in and change the subject and fix up hurt feelings. She was more than a match for him. But, dammit, why did it always happen this way? What the hell did they see in him? He's a lout, that's all, Matthew thought angrily, he always was, even before when he was a good-natured happy lout and I liked him. And yet, when Saul was around all the girls looked at *him* and his brother might as well have been the Hunchback of Notre Dame. Even if he called them broads, their eyes all lighted up in that special way, just like this one now and who would've thought that Dud Brimmer's sister would go for that type. No, he must be wrong, she really must have seen him fight, but how incongruous, a girl like that being interested in boxing.

"Oh, I was quite sure when I first saw you and heard your name," Sally Mayhew was saying casually. "But I wanted to be absolutely certain."

"After all," Saul said, "you could be wrong. People in the audience don't see fighters that close. And it's a long time ago." He stopped enjoying himself then, right after the words came out and memory caught up with him.

"No, I remember quite particularly," she said in that cool, positive voice, "because Ben . . . my cousin . . . looked quite a bit like you. A rather remarkable resemblance actually and he'd done some boxing in school and college and I think he rather envied you."

"Huh," Saul sneered, "that's a good one." He leaned forward and looked at her darkly. "Well, you're right, that was me, and it's nice you remembered, but I don't box any more. I got a nice job on the *Beacon-Journal*, regular hours, everything just peachy."

"Such a good paper," she said graciously.

"Yeah," said Saul, "but I don't read it."

"Oh," she said, not in the least ruffled by his rudeness, "I thought perhaps reporters had to read their own copy occasionally."

"I'm only a stiff down in the linotype room," Saul said aggressively. "Reporters have to run around too much. A one-legged bastard like me has to sit down. Maybe you oughta tell your cousin that."

"I'm afraid that's impossible, you know," Sally said politely and sweetly, managing to make the sweetness hit Saul right in the teeth like a spoonful of very cold ice cream. "He died in the war."

Saul winced and drew back in his chair. "That's tough," he said. "A lotta good guys got it. But it's my turn to envy him. My idea is, if you're gonna die, you better do a good job of it, instead of a half-ass one, like I did."

"Solly," Sophy said in a warning, strangled voice.

Saul ignored her. "That's the way I feel about it," he said seriously to Sally Mayhew. "Your cousin is better off."

"I think you're wrong," she said crisply. "At least you're here and he isn't. There's a great difference."

"I'd as soon not be."

She looked at him thoughtfully and then set down her empty brandy glass and stood up. Matthew, with an inward groan of relief, went to get her jacket. As he held it out for her she faced Saul and said quietly,

"I still think you were very lucky, Mr. Berman. Death is so horribly final."

"It's the only solution for a basket case," Saul said scoffingly. "You may think you'd rather have a guy around no matter if he's only half there but I don't think you know what you're talking about, if you don't mind my saying so." He got to his feet, however, slowly and ponderously and shook hands with her, which was unusual for him. Nowadays, he wouldn't get out of a chair for anyone and what was more peculiar he gave her a big smile, the kind he used to have on tap all the time.

"Mr. Berman," she said and her voice was warm and soft, "if you don't mind *my* saying so, you hardly look like a basket case to me." She turned away. "Well I must go. It's been so nice, meeting you all." And Matthew was escorting her to the head of the stairs.

"Do you want me to walk down with you? The stairs are kind of steep. Might turn your heel."

"No thank you, I shall be quite all right. Thank you for the brandy and for helping Dudley."

"Oh, that's okay." Matthew ran his fingers through his hair, nervously. "I'm—uh—sorry about my brother. He gets a little—uh—bitter sometimes."

"Very understandable, I'm sure," she said briskly and started down the stairs. "Goodbye Dr. Berman."

"Goodbye," he said miserably. If only he'd had a little nerve. He could've asked her if she and Dud would like to come over for a few drinks and some music sometime. But no, after that wonderful little session with his relatives, chances were she'd as soon forget she ever saw him. He went back into the apartment and slammed the door with unnecessary force.

The family restrained themselves admirably until they were settled in the Oriental gloom of the Green Dragon Inn waiting for sub-gumfooyong.

"She's a model, maybe, Matt?" Sophy asked, firing the first salvo.

"If you mean Mrs. Mayhew," Matthew said shortly, "I don't know."

"How could she be a model?" Saul jeered. "Those damn fool fashion magazines you're always reading, Sophy, all the women in them look like consumptives. That girl was really stacked and I do mean built."

"There are other things you could model besides dresses," Sophy said.

Saul said nothing. A dreamy look came over his face and he licked his lips a little.

"Such clothes," Sophy said enviously. "Alone, a blouse of ecru chiffon like that must cost anyway eighty to a hundred dollars and those petticoats with the little red ribbons, everything of the best. And velvet, a velvet suit like that must cost, how much would you say, Morris?"

"Who knows?" Matthew's uncle said impatiently. "Expensive! A piece of velvet like that, real heavy material, thick pile, a lot of money that's all. I guarantee you she didn't buy them in a store. They're custom made. From one of the good designers."

"She lives with her brother," Sophy went on, "but she's a Mrs. Is she divorced?"

"I understand her husband was killed in the war," Matthew said. He ate two oyster crackers carefully. How long was this imbecilic inquisition going on?

"No kidding," Saul said. "Now howdya like that? The cousin she mentions but the husband she forgets about."

"I don't see what's so unusual about it." Matthew said. "Any reason she should tell complete strangers her sad story?"

"And all the time I thought she was married," Saul mused. "A beautiful piece of black velvet like that wandering around loose. And you knew it too. Well, that explains a lot."

"So where does she get all the money for clothes like that?" Sophy was at it again. "A poor widow. You know her well, Matt?"

Matthew sighed and wondered what good words would do. "Now listen," he began patiently, "I don't know her at all. I met her this afternoon for the first time just like you did. And I suppose she has money for clothes like that because her family's rich. They're what you'd call society or something. Now that's all I know about her. So could we please talk about something else?"

"A society girl," Sophy said, her eyes widening. "So you've been too busy with a society girl shicksa to visit your own family. What's the matter, there aren't enough Jewish girls for you, you have to run around with . . ."

"Oh for Godsakes, Sophy! Don't you believe a word I say?"

"Oh my ass," Saul said violently. "So maybe you don't know her but you can't blame Sophy for thinking you do. If I ever saw a kid with his first case of hot pants, you were it, Bud. Every time you looked at her you drooled and you couldn't keep your eyes off her."

Matthew bit his lip and tapped his foot under the table. He's trying to goad me, he thought. It isn't enough the bastard fouled me up with the loveliest girl I've ever seen he has to grind the salt in too.

"Well, maybe I did stare at her," he said finally, feeling good that he was keeping his voice down, "but at least I didn't run my eyes up and down her as though she was some stripper at the Old Howard."

"Well, what the hell's the matter with that?" Saul wanted to know. "When you come right down to it there's not too damn much difference between a broad like that and one of the babes at the Old Howard. They're just women. The trouble with dames like that is that pussyfooting bastards like you always think they should be put up on the wall like a painting with a Touch Me Not sign on 'em. Sure, I looked her over and believe me I was sitting at a much better angle than you were. That peekaboo blouse wasn't showing me just ruffles. And you want to know something else? She knew what I was doing and she liked it too, a hell of a lot better than those schoolboy mooneyes you were turning on her."

"Oh you're full of shit," Matthew said, irritated beyond bearing. "If you think you're so good why don't you ask her for a date?"

"Solly, Matty," Sophy interrupted plaintively. "Such language, you don't have to use."

"Don't be such a wiseguy," Saul said sharply. "Or maybe I will. That'd spoil your nice little game, wouldn't it?"

"She wouldn't go out with you."

"You wanna bet on that?"

"Sure, I'll bet on it."

"I wouldn't want you to lose, Buddy boy. After all, you're my own dear brother. Anyway," he added in a different tone, "you don't give a damn whether I go out with her or not. You just don't want your high-class buddy at the hospital, her brother, to see what kind of a roughneck brother *you've* got. You're a lousy little snob, Bud."

"So here's the food already," Moe interrupted pacifically, "so maybe we can eat now boys and stop all this. This is no way for brothers to talk to each other."

"He's a little snobbish bastard," Saul said sullenly, "you know it and I know it." He pushed his heaped-up plate away petulantly. "I don't want this junk," he said. "This isn't food. I want a good steak. Something you can sink your teeth into."

There was a complete silence and everybody ignored him and ate, although Sophy looked as though every mouthful choked her. Saul lit a cigar and gave Moe his plate.

"You eat it," he urged. "I'm sorry Sophy, I'm a loudmouth. But I just haven't got any appetite all of a sudden." He turned to Matthew, his voice a little less strident. "I was only kidding about that girl, Bud. She's not my speed. But just let me give you a word of advice. A guy like you is a pushover for a girl like that. Oh, I don't blame you, she's something all right, but if you do go after her, just watch yourself, that's all I have to say, watch yourself or you'll be up shitcreek."

He blew smoke at his brother, as if he were some kind of damn oracle, Matthew thought bitterly, but why ruin the rest of the meal for Sophy and Moe who had him on their hands all the time.

"Thanks, Dorothy Dix, I'll remember that."

But with the tea and almond cookies Sophy got on another pitch Matthew couldn't stand. "I want you to come to supper Friday night, Matt," she said. "There's a nice girl. I know her mother. She'll come and you'll meet her. She's very nice, an older girl, smart, a BU graduate, a librarian."

"I know," Matthew said "and she hasn't caught a husband yet and she's twenty-seven years old and her parents are getting worried. And your wonderful nephew the doctor doesn't have a wife either. What could be better? Her father probably has a small amount of money he'd be glad to invest in helping a young doctor get started and of course she's a raving beauty."

"Don't get your hopes up," Saul said grinning. "I saw her once."

"What about you?" Matthew retorted. "Why don't you take her out? Why am I always the target? You do have two nephews you know, Sophy."

"Me," Saul said innocently. "This girl doesn't want me. She wants a professional man, a doctor, an engineer, you know, somebody with nachus. You think with her education her family'd let her throw herself away on a joker like me who only went through highschool?"

"You'll come Friday night and meet her Matt?" Sophy said hopefully.

"No," Matthew said firmly. "I will not meet her Friday night or any other night. If I happen to come for supper some night and find a girl there you're trying to sic on me I'll turn right around and walk out. I'll find my own girl."

"Sure," his aunt said bitterly, "a shicksa."

Saul was laughing for a change and Moe looked bored.

"Sophy, honest to God," Matthew said heatedly, knowing it was a lost cause before he started, "can't you realize how damfool prejudiced you sound. I never can understand why Jews should be as narrow and bigoted as the anti-Semites are. It just adds to the problem."

"That's why," Moe said. He shrugged and passed a cigar to Matthew, after lighting one himself. "Corona-Corona," he said. "They don't want you so you don't want them. Foolishness!" He sighed. "A Jew lives somewhere long enough he becomes like the people in the place. Trouble is, nobody lets them live there long enough. Look at Germany. Always some madman like Hitler comes along." He smiled and patted Matthew's arm reassuringly.

He's a good man, Matthew thought, feeling better, feeling fond of his family for the first time since they'd showed up and Moe is so eminently sane and reasonable, only why the hell can't he straighten Saul out? Why can't someone? "Look Sophy," he said, "every one of these girls you pick out for me is under the thumb of her family. Naturally she has trouble finding a husband. Who wants to marry a family?"

"Hear, hear," Saul said. He was reaching for the check and looking at the clock on the wall.

"It's the war," Sophy said sadly, "so many boys were killed."

"Yeah," Saul said nastily, "hardly a dentist is now alive."

Matthew shot Sophy a warning glance and she said hastily that she and Moe were going to see a movie at the Metropolitan and did they want to come? Matthew thought he'd better go home and sleep some more since he had to go back to work and Saul, who seemed restless, muttered something about maybe looking in on a poker game down in the South End and would Sophy and Moe mind if he didn't pick them up when the movie was over? They looked relieved, Matthew thought, and said they'd walk to the movie because Sophy wanted to windowshop on the way.

"Such a nice night," Sophy said, "and if we go up Summer Street we can see Filene's and Jordan's windows."

"That's the long way around," Moe objected but he laughed and they went off almost gaily, leaving Saul and Matthew standing on the sidewalk by the car.

"I'll drive you home Bud," Saul said.

He doesn't even see, Matthew thought, that they're glad as hell to get rid of him. They looked like two kids going off on a holiday. The self-centered bastard. "No thanks," he said. "I'm going to walk too. I need some exercise and air. Don't get much these days. Anyway, if you're going to the South End it'll put you out of your way."

"My way," Saul said vacantly. "Oh . . . yeah. Well . . ." He shrugged. "Suit yourself." He opened the car door and slid cumbersomely in behind the wheel.

"Bye." Matthew turned away.

Saul poked his head out of the window. "Just remember what I told you, Bud. Keep your pants buttoned." He laughed and started up the car.

"You go to hell," Matthew said loudly, not caring that passing people were staring. "And next time I come home I'd appreciate it if you weren't around."

"Temper, temper, Doctor," Saul said mockingly and the car leaped away from the curb.

Jesus Christ, Matthew thought, clenching his fists in impotent fury as he marched angrily along the streets not even seeing where he was going, one of these days he's going to go too far, that's all, and I won't care that he's crippled or what people say, I'm going to knock him down. And that'll be great, he thought realizing that he must've almost run, because suddenly he was crossing Washington Street, that'll be swell, just what he wants, to make me an animal like him. Dr. Berman who's supposed to be helpful to suffering humanity, a man with education, professional prestige and brains, a somebody, pushing over his one-legged brother. Boy, Saul'd love that, and how he'd laugh. I'll just have to stay away from him, Matthew thought, waiting for the light to turn green on Tremont, that's all.

He walked through the Common. Sally Mayhew. He said her name over to himself. Sally Brimmer Mayhew. Was Sally her real name or a nickname? What was Sally the nickname for? Sarah. Sarah Mayhew. He'd never liked the name Sarah before. But suddenly Sarah became the most beautiful girl's name in the world. Although Sally was still better. And she lived on Revere Street and he knew her brother but that, that was all. She hadn't even looked at him. Oh it would've been okay if she'd ignored him because he wasn't anybody important. But she hadn't looked at him because Saul was there. It was funny the way they'd talked, two perfect strangers, she, a lady and he, a, well, he'd said it himself, a roughneck. Almost as if they'd shared a secret.

Bosh, Matthew thought, I'm just depressed. He reached his doorway. Even if they hadn't been there, he wouldn't have a chance with her anyhow. Besides what did he care? He'd seen good-looking girls before. What made her so special? He dragged himself into his apartment and flopped on the couch, his arms folded under his head. What a great day it'd turned out to be, so lousy he could almost taste it. And yet, maybe there'd've been a chance. He pictured himself, being alone when she came. He'd've asked her right in, of course, no making her hang around on the doorstep. God, what an unsure Johnny come lately he must've seemed. Offered her a drink. Played a record maybe. Talked. She had a beautiful voice. She'd've asked him about being a doctor because they'd be discussing her brother. She'd be interested and smile . . . oh hell . . . shut up, he told himself. Then they'd go on to other things, his mind pursued and he couldn't stop it, the theater, music, books, had she been doing anything interesting since her return to Boston, had she liked California, maybe she'd like to see a play with him . . . It was all stupid and useless but at least he'd've made a showing. She would not have put him down as some sort of a lowclass schmuck with no manners which is what he looked like now and who could wonder, seeing the family he came from. But why did she look at Saul like that? He certainly had no manners and unless she was blind she couldn't have avoided noticing the street-corner loafer way he took her in. She should've been outraged. Instead she'd talked to Saul as if he were an old and valued friend. He groaned aloud, remembering Saul's boorishness . . . Hell! Forget about it. There were other beautiful girls, girls who showed right away they thought he was pretty much something. After all, being a doctor wasn't just like being a shoeclerk. The hell with it, maybe he would see her again, with no Saul around. And that bastard, what cool nerve he had talking as if he could take out a girl like that. A girl like Sally Mayhew would laugh in his face. But fantasies were part of Saul's problems he supposed. Why even pay attention to his talk?

She was a pretty funny girl anyway. Nice and polite and friendly to a rude slob like Saul and acting very cold, almost bitchy about Dud being sick. Could Saul have been right and not just trying to bolster his ego when he'd said that she liked the dirty way he was looking at her? Impossible. She was a million light-years away from him. She'd merely been gracious and friendly because she had good manners and felt sorry for him and he, like a typical crude animal had mistaken her civilized ladylike behavior for something else. Why did I have to have a brother like him, Matthew thought bitterly. Somebody I have to be ashamed of all the time. And it wasn't as though, war or no war, Saul couldn't've made something decent of his life. He'd been smart enough as a boy, a pretty good student. If my mother had lived Matthew thought, Saul might not've ended up in this pickle. But after she died all he wanted to do was get out of school fast, make a lot of money, be a big shot, be independent of our father. And all the things she'd cared about, music, education, religion, becoming a person of some consequence, a decent guy, Saul had turned away from, and if she could see him now, her wonderful boy, she'd be horrified. He'd turned out to be an over-sexed, crude, loudmouth just like the old man, Matthew thought smiling at the irony of it, the father he'd hated.

Matthew began to think about going on duty and his cheerlessness increased. If you could help some of them who looked at you with begging eyes, if you could do something more than eke out or temporarily alleviate the pain, but you had to turn away. Because the medical wards were full of people dying of diseases for which there was no cure. Not yet. Maybe someday. Who could wait that long? The patients couldn't and he couldn't. If I go into obstetrics, he thought, I can probably get that residency in the fall, Jenni will recommend me, it won't be so hopeless. There'll be life, a life the doctor helps bring forth. He might even be pretty good at it and Jenni sure as hell could teach him a lot. He remembered back to his internship days and some of the deliveries when he was on emergency. The time when the cord was wrapped around the baby's neck and it'd been touch and go and he'd had to handle it alone and it'd turned out fine and what a sense of accomplishment he'd had. The residency would be three years and then he could really make a lot of money. Christ, he thought, with a surge of panic, I've been stalling for too long. I've got to make out, be somebody that a girl like Sally Mayhew couldn't put down with a look. Yes, that was it, and suddenly he felt great with the weight of indecisiveness gone. He'd talk to Jenni tomorrow at that gallery party. And if no residency was available at Bay Colony well there were other hospitals in the area or even in other cities. Even if he did have to leave town he could always come back. Have an office in the Bay Road, a name, money, and then he'd come around to Sally Brimmer Mayhew and . . . buy her velvet dresses . . . and stroke her velvet legs . . .

Eight

Sally lay naked on her bed in the Revere Street apartment, all her velvet and chiffon pulled off and scattered carelessly on the floor. There was a glass of Scotch on the bedtable next to her and from time to time she rose on one elbow and sipped from it and then went back to singing this parody of "Love's Old Sweet Song" she'd just dreamed up in a blues time. Her voice rose up, hoarse and mocking, in the empty room:

> *"Just a song at twiiilight*
> *When I'm feeling low*
> *And the flickering people*
> *Shadows that I know . . ."*

No, it won't do my girl, she told herself sternly, pausing in the middle of a note, you'll never make your mark on the world this way. Actually she rather liked the last part in all its awful sentimentality. She sang it straight. Wasn't such a bad song really, even though it didn't fit in this time and place, still it must have had some truth back there in the overstuffed parlors full of cluttered wallpaper and furniture. She had a sneaking fondness for all those old relics like "O Promise Me that someday you and I" and "Pale Hands I Loved Beside the Shalimar" and those two songs from *The Bohemian Girl*, what were they, oh yes, the one about marble halls and "Then You'll Remember Me." And they were great songs to sing, full of lovely swoops and flourishes and simple melodies, a voice could enjoy itself with no matter how spurious and thump-thump the sentiments and the beat. But of course one could only sing them in the shower now. They were too reminiscent of teacosys, gaslight, hand-cranked honking phonographs, John McCormack, Madame Schumann-Heink, a world all bundled up to the eyebrows and in poor taste.

Ah hell, she thought, shaking out her hair and reaching down to grope on the floor for her pack of cigarettes, what a fabulously unconsummated day it's been. And what with no dinner and that waterglass of Scotch, brimful not too long ago and now practically empty, she must be getting drunk singing to herself like a loon, all these maudlin songs. Curious to think that she knew them. All the words and each little uppy-downy note. How had this happened? Ah, of course, she remembered wincing, Maddalena. Her mother, whose style, tastes, and proportions had remained resolutely and embarrassingly Edwardian in the midst of the Jazz Age, playing on the piano and singing "The Last Rose of Summer" in her charmingly accented voice. Oh damn, Sally thought, if I'm going to remember Maddalena now, I might as well be drunk. She drank up the rest of the whisky, punctuating each sip with a line or two of "Then You'll Remember Me" singing it all the way through very seriously, with appropriate pauses and trills:

> "When hooollow hearts
> Shall weeeear aaamask
> Twill break your ooown toosee
> In such a mo-ment Iiiiii buuut ask
> That you'll reeemember meeeee
> That you'll reemem-buh
> You'll reeeemem (way up there) buh meeee."

Kind of a sweet song and, in spite of its antiquated verbiage, quite truly sad. Too bad it had gone out of fashion.

But how was it possible, that with so many good intentions, she'd ended up in this miasmic mire of dreary futility? All occasions had informed against her. First, Mike whom she'd really wanted to see and talk to. And what an utter, disappointing bore to find him bogged down with that extraordinarily tiresome girl. And then, the session. Dear God!

There'd been a mixup in schedules and Kaminsky, Russell, and Freeman who'd been slated to appear and whom she'd wanted very much to hear had been unable to make it. The only other musicians available at such short notice had been hiding their light under bushel baskets for years with, it turned out, very good reason. Mike and Si had then directed some very hard words at the Jazzbo, the impresario of these sessions, for his deliberate negligence and failure to notify those who might've sensibly stayed away had they known of the change. The Jazzbo'd sworn that the whole fraud'd been perpetrated by the Bat Club manager behind his back. That silly, sycophantic Gordon Bruce had backed him up and ill-feeling had filled the air like a murder of crows above a cornfield. Of course, once they were there, no matter how bad the musicians were, it would not have been the thing to walk out on them and so they'd all stayed being polite and doing a lot of drinking.

Afterwards, out on the sidewalk, Si'd summed it all up by saying that good sportsmanship had been unfamiliar to him until today and after this afternoon's dose he would damn well steer clear of it forever.

"But why didn't you sing, Sara?" he'd asked plaintively. "It would damn well have picked things up."

"I'm sorry," Sally'd said. "But I might've made things worse, you know."

"I don't believe that," Si'd protested. "You used to be able to rise above a lot of bad music and wallow in the joy of self-expression. A few years of Californian climate can't've made that much difference."

"Oh let her alone," Mike'd intervened crossly. "If she didn't want to sing, she didn't. I can't blame her. Never saw such a nowhere day."

"Never mind," Sally'd smiled at him as he lighted her cigarette. "Perhaps it will get better. I'm quite free tonight."

"I'm supposed to take Jean to dinner," Mike'd said glumly, "and then, we have tickets to some cruddy comedy."

"I wouldn't feed her." Si had sounded positively vindictive. "I'd drown her. The creative temperament is supposed to be coddled in case you don't know Bo, not exposed to the dagger glances of sour, jealous females. No wonder Sal wouldn't sing. Where is your rayon lady, anyway?"

"Sulking in the ladies' room." Sally had laughed although it was obviously not funny. "We crossed swords in the mirror and then she retired and slammed the john door."

"Well," Si'd said, "I have a reptilian-eyed woman of my own over there, tapping her foot with ill-concealed impatience. Try to make it to Ella's show tomorrow, Sal, and Mike, if you bring that Gorgon sister with you, you'll deserve a good, round drubbing."

"Go to hell," Mike'd said conversationally. "Your cigarette is not making it, Sal. Let me try again." He'd flashed his lighter for her and they'd stood close together for a second while very clearly behind them, Jean Donnelly's voice had risen, nasal and clotted by tears and spiteful anguish:

"Do me a favor Gordie and take that female away for a drink, will you?"

"Take it easy, baby," Gordie'd mumbled. "She'll hear you."

"Oh Christ!" Mike'd pulled Sally away. They'd leaned against the wall on the other side of the club's canopy. "I'm sorry Sal. I wouldn't . . ."

"Your girl's crying," Sally'd interrupted abruptly, bracing herself against the brick wall and gently she moved away from him.

"Dammit, I know it. Well you see how it is. This thing's been planned for a couple of weeks now."

"You always were terribly honorable, Michael. That's one of your charms. Not that I'm not disappointed."

"Then come to lunch at Barings' and to Ella's opening tomorrow, with me. Afterwards we can go out for dinner and have a ball."

"I don't know." Sally'd been deliberately teasing and tentative. "I never know about tomorrows. I'm always more interested in immediate moments. We always run into one another at the wrong times, don't we?"

"One can always make a right time you know," he'd retorted, a trifle irritably.

"I never could, darling. A grave flaw no doubt but there it is. Well, here comes the suave and gallant courtier who, by dint of all his social charms and graces, will divert me from the malicious torment of that appallingly ill-mannered girl."

"Cut it, Sal!" Mike's face had flushed angrily. "It's not like you, this snobbishness."

"You're missing the point," Sally had given the oncoming Gordie a brief, cool nod. "One might be a snob if one simply listened to Bach and not jazz but to dislike both of them and care only for dinner music, and to think the "Ride of the Valkyrie" the ne plus ultra in highbrow music, well, I don't want to belabor the thing but you see how it is. I can't abide ninth-rate people and I am really baffled at your . . ."

"I dig you." Mike had nodded curtly. "They're people too, you know."

"Oh darling!" Sally'd laughed and they'd both ignored Gordie uneasily standing by. "Of course. But you don't need to know them."

"You can't expect," Mike'd said savagely, "to pick up the past exactly where you left it lying in the ashheap, six years ago. And not even a postcard for Christ's sakes. So what the hell did you expect?"

"You're absolutely right," Sally'd drawled. "And now, hadn't you better go? Mr. Bruce is going to buy me a drink and tell me all about journalism, aren't you?" She'd turned and given the nervous Gordie a full, dazzling smile.

"I'm sorry to break in like this," Gordie'd said awkwardly.

"We know," Sally'd said sweetly. "Goodbye, Mike, it's been a delightful afternoon and perhaps I will see you at the show."

He'd turned and gone without another word, striding angrily under the canopy, grabbing Jean Donnelly by the arm and marching her off, up the street.

"Well, let's all have a little drink," Gordie'd said. "Deborah's waiting over there."

Sally'd noticed then that the pretty child with the big, innocent eyes, the one she'd thought, before forgetting about it, would be so awfully appropriate for Dudley's unspeakable purposes, was standing, rather sadly, by the fire hydrant.

"It isn't very nice of you to leave her all alone," she'd said teasingly, "in order to pander to that sniveling female of Mike's. Don't you have to take your girl home?"

"Ah, she lives way out in Winthrop," Gordie'd said dismissingly.

"So you don't take her home?" Quite the little gentleman, she'd thought and made up her mind quickly. This Gordie type didn't count. She would take the little girl home and introduce her to Dudley. Something would then be accomplished at least in this desert of a day.

"Debby's just a kid. She's in one of my classes."

Why, he's making eyes at *me*, Sally'd realized disgustedly. Oh this was too much. She'd grasped him firmly by the arm, leading him in Deborah's direction.

"Your beau informs me that you live in Winthrop and he hates to travel so since I have my car here I'll take you home."

"Hey, wait a minute!" Gordie'd been genuinely astonished. "I thought we were all going to have a drink."

"No thanks," the little girl'd said stiffly. "You two go ahead. I'm expected at home."

"Now don't you start. I couldn't bear to have been the cause of two broken hearts in one day. In any case, I don't want a drink and I'd love to ride out to the beach."

"Well," Deborah'd said uncertainly, "if you're sure it's no trouble."

"None whatsoever. I must make a phone call first and stop up at my apartment to get a coat. I'd forgotten about New England spring evenings. The car's parked right around the corner."

"Well," Gordie'd said, following along, "I guess I could take a ride out to the beach too if you're coming back into town again."

Sally'd paused and looked at him consideringly. "I don't believe I will be," she'd lied coldly. "Do you live on the North Shore too?"

"No. Back Bay."

"Then you're a mere stone's throw away from home. How nice for you."

"Well, wait a minute, Debby, don't you . . ."

"It's very nice of you to offer me this ride," the little girl'd said getting into the car. "I'm awfully late as it is and my father makes a terrible fuss."

Sally'd gone into the drugstore across the street to call Dudley, leaving the obnoxious Gordon to lean on the car door and make his farewells. She'd been able to see them through the window as she dialed the number and wondered what on earth this nothing boy could be saying to make the girl look so uncomfortable. Wants her to go to bed with him no doubt and is having a difficult time of it. Why on earth do these childish mechanical urge-satisfiers always pick out pure snowmaidens to batter themselves against, can't tell which of them I'm sorrier for, in fact, I'm doing both of them a vast favor, not to mention Dudley and myself. Damn, where is Dudley? Perhaps best if he's out, I don't like doing this. Eight rings. Nine. One more. Te . . . Ah well.

"I hope you're up and dressed," she'd said impatiently. "Dudley, what were you doing? I've been ringing for ages. I'll be coming by presently with a girl named Deborah. She seems to fit some of your exorbitant specifications."

"Very drunk and sick," Dudley'd mumbled. "Sorry Sally, no girl."

"Oh you're impossible! Why, if you knew you were going off like that, didn't you call this doctor of yours?"

"Why? 's a psychiatrist not AA. Listen, Sally, little sister . . . you there . . . ?"

"Yes. Must I come home and put an icebag on your head?"

"My own icebag," he'd said with difficult dignity, "but need go . . . you need . . . to go tell Matthew Berman . . . lives near here. He can take the duty for me tonight."

"Why can't you call him?" Sally'd asked, infuriated.

"He'll know the trouble 'f I talk. You come home soon, Sally, tell you his address, what to say."

"Then I'll call him. Nothing wrong with my voice. What's his number?"

"Do's I say, Sally." There'd been a very faint hint of menace under the thick nauseated tones of her brother's voice. "Berman's a good fellow. Can't do this with phone calls from strangers. Ugh!" A strangled noise had followed and a bang as of the phone being dropped on the floor. Sally'd waited for a few minutes and then, in an access of disgust, slammed up the phone and walked, erect and angry, out to the car.

It'd gotten much cooler, an east wind springing up from the harbor, but she'd found an old sweater in the back of the car and they'd driven fast through the Sumner Tunnel. It'd been impossible to talk much there underneath the water, in the pale green gloom, rushing along in roar of tunnelhollow. The little girl called Deborah had sat stiffly upright by the window trying to keep her hands folded by clenching them, Sally'd noticed, wondering why she was so tense.

"I hope," Deborah'd said timidly when they'd wheeled out of the tunnel into the sunny, late afternoon slumminess of East Boston, "driving me home didn't interfere with any of your plans. I mean, I thought you were going to stop at your . . ."

"No," Sally'd interrupted abruptly. She'd tried to calm herself against the interior rage boiling at the thought of Dudley and had begun to question the girl about herself. Looks hideously sensitive, she'd thought, must think I'm cross and silent because I'm sorry I offered to drive her home. Oh, that loathsome Dudley. But she's sweet and seems rather intelligent. I shouldn't do this to her. Perhaps it wouldn't work out anyway. But oh, such a temptation, because all she needed was some money, which he'd give her, he would, he was honorable, if he liked the girl, and then she could get away from him, that horror, little sister indeed, making her a sort of servant for him and a liar too.

The little girl'd been saying rather proudly that she went to Marplot, what on earth was that, oh yes, that weird, little, funny school on the Hill, she was a sophomore, majoring in English. And where had she met this Bruce lout, oh he was a classmate, of course. What a jungle this East Boston was, perfectly hideous, depressing bleakness, little streets and horrid, dirty, little houses.

"You must tell me how to get there," she'd said, "I'm afraid I don't know this area very well."

"Dear me," Deborah had cast worried looks around, "I've never driven over here and I don't . . . oh yes . . . well, I think if you drive up here, this wide street, you'll get to Orient Heights and I know the way from there, that is, if we follow the trolley lines."

"You don't really like this Bruce type, do you?" Sally'd maneuvered expertly around some exasperating truck. "I wouldn't have dragged you off so bodily if . . ."

"Oh no," hastily. "I did have to go home. I like him, of course."

"Mmmmm. He ought to take you home though. Doesn't your father think so?"

"They haven't met." Blushing. "My father is rather, well, old-fashioned. He doesn't think I should go out with boys, well, some boys, I mean, we're . . . well . . ." She'd closed her mouth quickly and looked unhappy.

Secrets, Sally'd thought, how curious with that frank, open, guileless face. Father some sort of old-world tyrant, no doubt would account for it. Still he was right about that Bruce type. She'd changed the subject.

"Pretty skirt you're wearing."

"Oh, do you like it?" Really, a most responsive face, Sally'd thought. The slightest, most conventional praise, lighted her up. Dudley would like that. He was so damn buried himself. "I haven't seen another one like it. So I just couldn't resist it when I saw it in Filene's. In the Basement. There were some books I wanted too but I bought the skirt instead."

About to ask why she couldn't have both, Sally'd suddenly remembered that students often had little money. Still, didn't families usually buy the clothes at least?

"Some of the most fabulous things in that Basement," she'd agreed. "I do love bargains. I got a wild suède jacket there last week. In the Saks sale. It was fur-lined. I really had no use for it but I couldn't bear to let it go. Tremendously cheap."

"Yes," Deborah'd said wistfully. "I saw those jackets."

They'd been getting closer to the water. Sally smelled the salt and the tide ebbing and the seaweed and she'd longed suddenly to be up to her neck in the cold, clear water to wash away the disappointing day. Very rundown neighborhood, boarded-up beach cottages, discouraged-looking bushes, seedy three-story houses, back porches with washing, prevailingly gray.

"If you drop me right here, at this corner," Deborah'd said quickly, "you can get right back on the main road."

"No trouble." But then Sally'd thought, perhaps the old-fashioned father will be waiting and it would get tedious with introductions and being asked in. She'd stopped the car and Deborah had scrambled out.

"Thank you very much. It really was wonderful. The trip is so long, specially on the streetcar."

"Quite all right. I'll call you about swimming. What's your number?"

"That would be very nice," the little girl had said primly. "I work in the library at Marplot. You could just call there and if I'm not there you could, uh, leave a message. Goodbye, thanks again." She'd walked away very fast and as Sally peered out of the window to see if she could safely back up instead of turning around, she'd noted that her former passenger was actually running.

Now why not give her home phone number? Most mysterious. Sally'd looked at her watch. Oh damn. Speeding along toward the tunnel she'd cursed Dudley, Mike, the day, and her ridiculous fate. On her way back to Revere Street she'd toyed for a few moments with the independent notion of telling Dudley to go to hell and tell his own lies. What if she didn't come home? He might have to go on duty with a hangover, that's what, and be urping all over the wards. Or, perish the thought, have to reveal to a colleague that he was stinko. Wouldn't old Grandpa Brimmer writhe and rage to see his favorite heir now? No, Sally'd thought, fuming at the clogged traffic around Faneuil Hall, if I can ever get out of this jam, I'll go back and pull his imbecilic chestnuts out of this fire, but it's the last damn time, you hear Dudley. Of course, she'd thought, if he had a girl, she could do his dirty work, but would this scared little girl with the old-fashioned father who lived in that awful neighborhood and was all tied up in obscure knots at the age of nineteen, be therapeutic for Dudley? There he was on the verge of some madness and only being held together by his own sense of family pride and money and youth. His career wasn't helping by God if he couldn't even meet its obligations properly. Didn't he really need some kind, placid, secure, athletic type girl? Of course he did but he didn't want such a one. But shouldn't one be a little sensible about this? Even though Dudley's deal had not been in the least sensible, did one introduce a brother with as imposing a façade as his, in control of as much money as he was, to a very young nobody girl who lived in a neighborhood like that? Of course that was what Dudley wanted, exactly, a young nobody girl, but she seemed very defenseless, and would it be fair to her? No, Sally'd thought, as, with her car, finally freed from the jam of produce trucks, she got going in the direction of the Hill, I won't mix in this. It's apt to be too utterly messy. If Dudley'd been available in the beginning it might've worked out, but he wasn't and now, on mature consideration, it is seen to be a mistake. At any rate, Sally'd thought, I shall probably not see her again, and perhaps some other type, a bit more possible, will turn up.

But when she'd gotten back to the apartment to find her splendid brother literally reeling around, having just retched all over the bathroom, his face the color of an old, faded tennis shoe, she'd changed her mind, very rapidly. Completely sickened and disgusted, she'd told him sharply that he was a sordid fool and then, sorry for his misery, had persuaded him to take a phenobarb and go to bed. He'd written down Dr. Matthew Berman's address but she couldn't, of course, do anything until that reeking bathroom was scrubbed down. With a strip of gauze tied over her wrinkled nose and a pair of surgical gloves on, she'd cleaned up the mess herself, and then taken a shower. Unsuitable or not, she'd thought, spraying germicide around the bathroom, this girl Deborah is available here and now and she's going to be my passport to freedom from this sort of thing forevermore. At least, she'd thought, flinging the bathroom window wide open, one mystery was solved. Now she knew why her brother didn't live at the hospital, at her aunt's or in a good apartment with a daily maid. It was not mere introversion or New England thrift, but the simple shameful fact that every now and then he either drank himself into sickness and oblivion or had liaisons with women he was ashamed of and he'd as soon no one, not even a servant, should be aware that the dignified Dr. Brimmer was a mess of a man. How lucky I am, Sally'd thought satirically, to be privy to all this secret knowledge and how fortunate Deborah is going to be when I turn all this over to her.

She'd gone to check on Dudley who was breathing heavily, but asleep, his face now a more normal color and reluctantly had been about to put on some slacks and a shirt for her call on the unfortunate Dr. Berman when the phone had rung and produced her Aunt Fan, the unwilling doyenne of a dinner party for a very dull Navy captain cousin of her husband's that evening. One of the guests had been unable to come and could Sally please fill in. It would be a bore, but of course, she'd promised, and, in order to lift her spirits, dressed herself up luxuriously even though her heart wasn't in it and sprayed herself liberally with Diablerie which ordinarily ought to be used in minute quantities, but hell, suppose she turned up at this proper dinner, still reminiscent of her nauseating chores in the bathroom?

It'd been a lovely evening as she'd walked toward Joy Street, with the sun dropping away behind the Common leaving as token only some pink and flame pennons in the rapidly graying sky while the old dark roofs of the Hill stood out solid and solemn and the brick fronts of the houses turned rosy in the pink light, but Sally had been so utterly depressed that no mere sunset could cheer her. She'd thought of all the girls she'd gone to school with and how they must now be getting ready to move to their summer places with their fat healthy blond children who would turn brown and delectable like little cookies in the sun and sand and salt; the sailing races, the lobster, the clambakes, the dances, the cocktail parties, the picnics and the horse shows and what was the matter with her and with Dudley for that matter? Why were they aliens in a world to which they were born and in any other world for that matter, finding no pleasure or attachment anywhere? She had wanted, this afternoon, to be a part of the group at Mike's but Mike himself had rejected her, still nursing old grievances, and, though Si and Tom'd been pleasant, the women had shunned her as though she were deadly nightshade. And she'd been lonely and bored and felt the spring stirring inside her, the wanting of love, the sharp, unchanneled desire to feel a man's hands on her and all the rest of it. But she'd tried not to think about it. It would have driven her wild and there were things she could not do in Boston. She'd felt stifled and angrily rung the bell marked MATTHEW B. BERMAN, M.D.

He'd turned out to be a very handsome young man who'd immediately stared at her the way men did which cheered her although it was a bit boring being so obvious, and they had stood lamely out there in the hall while he'd looked uneasy and she'd wondered, rather annoyed at being put in this anomalous position of messenger, why he didn't ask her in and had finally decided that perhaps he had a wife or a girl inside and anyway, why did she expect courtesy tonight since her whole day had been rife with other people's bad manners and taste, and had been about to turn away feeling bleak at this flat, unprofitable encounter when suddenly she'd been shocked to see the almost perfect image of Benjie standing there behind the doctor, looking her over familiarly in the semi-darkness of the hall-way.

Of course, the way things were that day, the way the fates whirled her around on their stupid merry-go-round, it had to be Saul Berman, the boxer she'd enjoyed watching because he'd been such a big, splendid animal with the most beautiful body she'd ever seen next to Benjie and all tied up in a maudlin way with how he looked like Ben and how she and Ben had gone to see all his fights and how Benjie had teased her for her interest in this pug. You look at a boxer's hands and feet and how he moves, he'd said, not his crotch. Naturally, and by this time, she'd been surprised at nothing, he was the doctor's brother and had lost a leg in the war and he didn't fight any more but still he had that beautiful big body. The whole time in that dark little apartment she'd really noticed no one else and how queer it had been, ghostly almost, to see him sitting there, the way their eyes met, as if they'd known each other before. But it was just because he looked like Ben and all the time she'd kept thinking, would I know Ben now, if he came back and if he'd come back crippled like this Saul Berman had, would he be the same, furious, bitter, and sad? Anyway, after this sort of a visition from the spirit world, it'd been quite impossible to face a dull dinner party. Aunt Fan had nobly understood her sudden headache and now here she was well on her way to duplicating Dudley's afternoon adventures. Oh God, she thought, stroking her bare skin, to have a man like that again. She gulped the last of the Scotch, switched off the bedlamp and lay there, thinking about it.

Dark stillness, suddenly pierced by the telephone, startling and shrill. Sally sat up quickly, her heart beating a little faster. Perhaps it was Mike, she thought, racing barefoot and still naked, down the hall. Might have ditched that cross of a girl and called to say he's sorry. She snatched up the phone. It was a man's voice but not Mike's.

"Sally there?" the voice said roughly, slightly wary.

"This is Sally." Now, who . . . ?

"Waddaya know," the voice said, "first crack outa the box. Listen, you probably won't believe this but this is—uh—Saul Berman. Remember? I met you a coupla hours ago at my brother's place."

"Oh yes." She noted with satisfaction that her voice remained cool. Uncanny though, the way he'd called just when . . . If he asked her to go out, although rather a tough specimen for her, in Boston, still, a man who'd suffered such a dreadful experience in the war, well, one simply couldn't refuse. Actually she'd expected him to call considering his greedy glances but not quite so soon.

"I'm surprised you're home," he was saying. Seemed completely sure of himself. She wondered if she ought to be very cold and indicate that she thought him presumptuous, but no, he would certainly help to relieve the boredom.

"I figured," he said, "the way you were all dressed up you were going some fancy place."

"I changed my mind."

"That's my good luck, I guess. Well say, listen, Sally, I couldn't go into this much in front of my folks but I thought it was damn nice of you to . . . well . . . remember me. You know, cheers a guy up to know that there's a few people around who remember him when he was pretty good. So, anyway, seeing as how you said you liked the fights, well, I got two free tickets to a heavyweight match down at the Garden tonight, men to watch they say. Sports editor gave them to me. I was gonna give 'em to my brother but he says he has to go on duty and anyway I'm kinda sore at him, so, well, to make a long story short, I wondered if maybe you could use them."

"You mean you want me to go with you?" It sounded horribly blunt but she found herself completely mystified and rather annoyed.

"Well now, listen, don't get any wrong ideas. What I meant was I'd drop the tickets at your place and you could, uh, well, I dunno, take somebody, do what you want with them."

"It's a bit late, Mr. Berman, to find anyone at such short notice. Thanks very much for thinking of me. Goodbye." Ridiculous, she thought, as she took the receiver away from her ear, to feel so disappointed.

She'd taken two steps down the hall when the phone rang again and there he was.

"Now wait a minute," he said, "don't be in such a hurry. I suppose I said something wrong. I don't know what though."

"I told you I'm unable to use the tickets. It's very kind of you and all. Is there anything more to say?"

"Yes," he said, "boy, will I feel like a fool but I guess I have to explain otherwise you'll think I'm crazy. I figured that you had a date with my brother tonight. So I was gonna give you the tickets and you could both go, since I'm on the outs with him."

Sally began to laugh.

"What's so funny?" He sounded irritated.

"Men," Sally said, "men are very funny. I have no date with your brother, since I just met him today and don't know him, nor did he ask me. But I think it's very solicitous of you to worry about his entertainment and his social life. I don't know where in the world you got such a weird idea."

"Hell, I don't know either," he said, jovial again. "If you asked Bud, my brother, he'd tell you it's because I'm a no-goodnik. I got a warped mind. In fact, I'm a neurotic misfit. But listen, Sally, if you don't have a date, with Bud or anybody, how about going out with me?"

"I adore boxing," Sally said promptly, smiling, as she thought of the devious ways of men, "I'd love to go."

There was a tiny silence. "Christ," he said, "you really will. You're serious?"

"Cross my heart."

There was another silence, and finally he said, "That bout, the main one, don't go on till ten-thirty or eleven. It's about eight-thirty now. Maybe if I picked you up right away we could make a night of it. You know, drinks, dinner someplace? You like steak? We could go to the Red Lion. Or maybe you've had dinner?"

"No. And I love steak. Give me about fifteen minutes to get dressed. Where are you?"

"Right in the neighborhood," he said, "no flies on me. Say if it's a walkup, you mind if I don't come up? Too many stairs in a round-trip. I'll ring the bell."

Now what did one wear to go out with Saul Berman, ex-boxer, now linotype operator? She stood before the smallish clothes closet. Everything was packed in here like sprats in a can. Really ought to weed it, she thought, things in here I never wear any more. Give them to someone. She wondered, as she made a place in the jammed ranks for the ecru chiffon blouse and its attendant velvet suit whether some of the clothes might not fit this little Deborah. Strange that she'd be wearing her school costume to a session. Didn't undergraduates always get decked out on weekend dates, well, they had at Berkeley. But if pandering sister's plans worked out and she took Dudley's fancy, this plain living style of dressing would have to be changed. He'd be embarrassed all to hell to be seen with a bobby-soxer.

At her aunt's when she'd lived there, years ago, the old maid, Alice, had taken care of her clothes. All of them hanging properly on padded hangers in protective bags scented with lavender sachet. There'd been an absolutely huge closet in her room. Trust Dudley, who seemed to own only one suit, to find an apartment with practically no closet space.

And if they ran into people she knew? She fancied the raised eyebrows. No one cared who you went about with in California but here in Boston if you were Sally Brimmer there were things you did not do. But then, she'd always done them and before hadn't given a damn. Why get guilty now? What if he was sort of a rowdy and had obviously not been in contact with the Ivy League? She hadn't picked him up and her brother did know his. And if he was good enough to lose a leg fighting for his country he was good enough to go out with her. Besides, this was just what she'd been waiting for. Some excitement. It would be fun to go to a fight and Lord, he was good-looking.

She pulled out a sleeveless, tight-fitting, blackvelvet dress and slid into it. Very sexy-looking, she thought, smiling at herself in the full-length mirror and he would probably like it, but for a semblance of

modesty and in case of too much goose-pimpling chill in the drafty
Boston Garden, she slipped on the jacket which matched it. No
jewelry. A black velvet, soft, Cinquecento cap, which she fancied
because it could be worn almost any way, to the back of the head,
pulled down over the forehead or, as tonight, to one side, with her
hair smoothly curling and rippling out from under it. He was not the
sort of man to tell her she looked like a painting, but men usually
liked women's hats to be simple, good-looking or dramatic, but
never, never too conspicuous or silly. They liked the women they
were with to attract admiring attention but no laughter. Women,
Sally thought scornfully, were idiots about hats. Most of them simply
thought of the hat alone, not realizing that a hat should be part of a
costume and a simple but striking frame for the hair and face.

Perfume. She searched around in the jumble of bottles on her
dressing table or bureau. It was hard to tell exactly what this monolithic object was, but it did have drawers and was surmounted by a
mirror. Aunt Fan had suggested that she could have the furniture
from her room in the house in Louisburg Square moved over here
but it didn't really seem worth the trouble since she might not stay
long. Mon Pèche, my sin, yes, that would do very well. As if one
had only one sin. One thousand and one nights of sin would be a
more accurate name. How did they think up these names, anyway?
All sorts of wicked, titillating, sexually stimulating words: TABU,
ECSTASY, WHILE WAITING, BREATHLESS, FORBIDDEN,
SHOCKING, SCANDAL, RUMOR, NIGHT OF LOVE, and all
the nice little girls trying hard to be chaste and catch a good husband
at the same time, spraying themselves with these pseudo-aphrodisiacs,
making ready to go out all over town on a Saturday night. Nice,
sweet little girls whose strength was as the strength of ten because
their hearts were pure and who deep down wanted to be good and
moral but didn't a man always like just a little fillip of naughtiness
even in good girls, and so, on went the perfume and the lowcut
clinging dresses and then they wondered why they had to grapple
to keep their purity and it always ended up that the men were
beasts.

The bell rang and she took a last look at herself in the mirror.
White gloves, small bag, a little high on Scotch, on her way to begin
an unknown evening.

Saul was waiting as she came down the last flight of stairs. She
made a kind of business out of each step, knowing that he was looking her over carefully, smiling as he watched her. Well, why not,
Sally thought, walking slowly toward him, returning his smile, why

pretend, as so many girls did, that this kind of onceover displeased her. Because it indicated a genuine instinctive male admiration and she would have felt herself growing old and ugly if such stares ceased.

"Say," he said agreeably as they shook hands quite formally and he took her arm and led her out to his car, "you are a doll and that's no lie. You really look like a million, Sally, I guess I can call you that, after all your brother knows my brother." He laughed, rather sardonically, at this and held out a pack of cigarettes to her. "How about a drink before we eat?"

"Fine."

He swung the car onto Pinckney Street and they roared away down the Hill to the river.

"These hills are hell to drive on," he said.

It was a safe opening but Sally was not interested in wasting time hiding behind small talk. After the way he'd talked and looked at her this afternoon, she was sure there was more to this man than banal, boys in the bowling alley conversation.

"How about the Lincolnshire?" he asked suddenly. "I feel like some soft carpet slop tonight. Probably your influence. Usually I'm a gin mill boy from way back."

"I'd like that." Obviously, Sally thought, rather amused, they were heading toward the Lincolnshire whether she wanted to or not. Used to ordering women around no doubt. "Although a gin mill would do as well," she added politely.

"Nah. They're for guys drinking alone with blood in their eye. No atmosphere."

"Oh atmosphere," Sally said understandingly, trying not to smile. "Of course." She leaned her head back against the seat and looked at him through her eyelashes. Six foot two or perhaps three, powerful shoulders and neck, massive chest, getting sort of fat around the middle. Black curly hair, lightly streaked with grey, wonderfully imposing head, rather leonine. For someone so large, his movements were quick and impatient. Fascinating profile, nose in high relief, splendidly aquiline but with nicely sculpted nostrils.

He turned his head, looking at her quickly. "Thinking I look like my brother, huh?"

"Why no." Sally eyed him. "Your brother is slighter than you, isn't he? I don't really remember too well." Curiouser and curiouser, she thought. Would he turn out to be slightly cracked, nerves utterly shattered by war and his affliction? Although why this should give him a brother obsession was baffling. She sighed mutedly and added,

"Honestly, I really don't know your brother, Saul. Is there no way I can convince you?"

"Okay, okay, so you don't. Only you'll have to admit it looked kind of funny there this afternoon, you know, coming to see him and all. I figured you had a date with him and then you had it fixed with him to tell us he had to go to work tonight so he could sluff off his family in a polite way. Bud's got good manners. I have to admit that. I suppose it sounds kind of nutty, at least it does now, but that's what I thought."

"You don't have a very high opinion of your brother's honesty." They were sliding up in front of the Lincolnshire and she wondered if the whole evening was going to be as tedious as this inauspicious beginning. Whatever he had against his brother she couldn't care less. Why did all these terribly good-looking and sexy ones turn out to be either boringly simple minded or a bit crazy?

"Let's put it this way. We're brothers like Jacob and Esau."

"And you're poor old cheated Esau, I suppose?" Sally drawled. "How awfully Biblical."

They were sitting in the parked car, making no move to get out and suddenly he turned, brought his face close to hers and caught her hands in a tight grip. "I'm so goddamn Biblical," he said intensely, "that I wouldn't touch you if you were his."

"Or if I didn't want you to."

He laughed unpleasantly. "I may be stupid about some things but I do know when a woman wants you to touch her." He dropped her hand and moved back away from her. "Like, for instance, I could kiss you right now. I know you want it."

"Perfectly true. But that means nothing."

"No, I guess not. Not to your type. Known a lot of guys, haven't you, doll?" His voice was jeering.

Sally sat quietly for a moment. It would be very simple to stop this entire thing right now. The disadvantages were all too plain. But of course she did not want to stop. She wanted him to kiss her. Two such disparate people, she thought, did not come together by sheer chance. Their goals were obviously mutual and of course one could not really tell so soon but she always relied on inexplicable instincts in such cases and right then, all of these hidden, mysterious, sensory presences were doing little snake dances all over her body. Of course if she went on behaving like an icy subdeb in a farce he would assume she was one, and he'd continue to throw up these oafish barriers against his senses and the end for which these twain were met, that beautiful explosive satisfaction, would never be even remotely approached.

"Saul," she said reasonably, "of course I want you to kiss me but it really doesn't have a thing to do with your brother, my past, or anyone's future."

"Ah," he said bending down and putting his arms around her, his voice relieved, "I know it doesn't."

Well, I was right, Sally thought, pleased, as, a few minutes later they were settling themselves in the cocktail lounge. With some men, no matter how much you blunted yourself by drinking, that first exploratory kiss, still remained akin to touching a stone gargoyle or a dead fish with your mouth, and even though, in the interests of experimentation, she might try again, it was never different. But when it was right as that lengthy kiss in the car just now had been, it would stay that way for as long as these things were fated to last. One day, it was not the same any more, not good, and all the rest of it became a weary bore and then you knew it was over and time to go on.

"God," Saul said as he took a big gulp of his first drink, "I needed that." He reached across the little low table and took her hand. "Christ, I'm glad you didn't get sore and ask me to take you home. Just promise me one thing, Sally, just don't listen to me willya? I say crazy things sometimes. I don't know how to act, I guess, any more. To women, that is. And forget what I said about Bud, my brother. He's a good kid. I don't know what comes over me sometimes."

"Of course," Sally said soothingly. "Besides the Old Testament was dreadfully hard on brothers and Philistines."

"Yeah," he said grinning, "that's right. I always had a kind of sorry feeling for poor old Goliath. I mean here he was a good fighter, playing it according to rules and he gets killed by a kid with a slingshot. Damn unfair. Come on, Sally, drink up. I'll order another round."

He drank the way she did, thirstily. She asked him about his job and he told her readily enough but without the slightest enthusiasm and it did sound pretty dull. She watched him as they talked and could see him relaxing perceptibly with each sip of the second drink.

"Let's skip my job," he said suddenly, interrupting himself in the middle of a gripe, "it's just a nothing and we've got more to talk about. That was quite a kiss you gave me."

"You mean you gave me."

"Sure," he said, "we gave each other. Okay. Well anyway, it's a great way to start out an evening. Christ, these drinks taste good. Let's have another one."

"We might never get to the fight if we do."

"The hell with the fight." He signaled the waitress.

"Very well. But we ought to go after this one."

"Don't spoil things, Sally. I'd just as soon stay here and drink all night with you. Waddya say?"

"No," Sally said firmly. "I've spent too many nights like that and tonight I want to go see a fight."

"Look," he said slowly, "I lied to you, because I wanted to take you out so much, I didn't tell you that I don't go to the fights. Haven't been to one in five years. They're poison to me. You can understand that, can't you?" He lowered his head and looked at her. His eyes were brown, smoky, glowing feverishly, set high with an almost Oriental slant above prominent cheekbones. "I figured you for a dame who'd understand. You've been there. Not like most of them."

"Then why did you ask me?" Sally, looking at his blueblack closely shaven cheeks and chin, thought of how the hair would be thick, silky, and black on his chest and belly and . . .

He stabbed an impatient finger at her, "I didn't ask you. I asked you if you wanted to use the tickets, because I thought you were going out with Bud. Remember? Then, when you weren't, I wanted to take you out and someway or other you thought I was going to use the tickets to take you. I let it ride because I couldn't explain over the phone without sounding more of a jerk than I did to begin with, so I thought I'd tell you later. We could do something else," he pleaded, "anything else you want to, Sally."

For a moment Sally wavered. Of course he wouldn't want to go to boxing matches. She could plainly see why. And if they didn't go she knew perfectly well what would happen. They'd sit there, drink more, never go eat and then, quite plastered they'd think of bed. But where? Dudley was home, and what with a sleeping pill and a hangover he might never wake up and hear them come in. But if they had too much to drink they might make an awful lot of noise and later fall asleep and forget the time. She shuddered mentally, thinking of Saul and Dudley meeting each other at the bathroom door in the morning. No, no it'd be too utterly messy. Of course he might have a place of his own . . . No, Sally thought, conjectures and contingencies abruptly crystallizing into opinion and position. If they went to his place, say he had one, it would simply mean that she was a silly schoolgirl who'd been taken in by his ridiculous tricks. Of course he'd asked her to go to a fight, had even mentioned the time the main bout went on. Getting tight and going to her place would be completely ruinous. Normally, she wouldn't give a damn if Dudley did wake up but, right now, considering her knowledge of his sad sex life and the plans she had for fixing him up with Deborah and then escaping, it would be the height of insanity to blatantly parade Saul in under his nose. Besides, as she knew well, a man who'd had too much to drink was apt to perform quite badly.

"But I don't want to do anything else," she said smiling at him sweetly, "I adore fights and I haven't been in ages. And you did ask me to go with you and I did accept. I can understand why you might not want to go, although I think you're being silly, but you shouldn't have led me to think you did. So, if you don't mind, as soon as we finish these drinks, I think I will go home."

"Meaning it's take you to the goddamn fight tonight or nothing."

"Right."

"Listen," he said angrily, "what the hell are you trying to do? Reform me? Maybe you think I'm soft and you're going to try a little therapy on me like my pill-peddling brother and the damn sports editor and a lot of other nosy parkers. Well, forget it, see. I'm on to their little game but I didn't think a broad like you'd fall into that kind of Salvation Army crap."

Poor thing, Sally thought, how awful to have everyone try to rehabilitate him, with no one understanding the irrevocability of his loss. She made her voice very sincere and warm. "I understand, Saul," she said, closing her hand over his and rubbing, delicately, the strong black hairs under her fingers. "Believe me I do." Oh Lord, she thought, sparks again. "And if you really don't want to go, we won't. But I do want to. I've had an awfully dull time lately and tonight for the first time in, oh, months, two of my favorite things are on hand, tall, good-looking men and boxing, so couldn't we try? You know, it might not be as painful as you think. We needn't stay if you find it's too awful. I'll leave as soon as you want to, I promise."

"Boy, you can really pour it on," he said, but he sounded pleased. "What are you doing this for anyway? You don't have to go to all this trouble to get to a ringside. There'd be a thousand guys, falling all over each other, to take you where you want to go any night in the week."

"Perhaps I like you," Sally said reasonably. "And don't want you to fight shadows." It sounded inane and she respected him for his unbelieving snort.

"Chrissakes, you don't even know me. Well, it's all right honey, I know it isn't me you're thinking about, it's one or two other guys. But I appreciate it just the same."

"I wasn't thinking of . . ." Sally began and then stopped.

"Sure you were," he said, "it stands to reason. And I guess it wouldn't kill me to take in a good match, at that. As you say, we could always leave. What the hell, if you can't be in the ring, the next best thing is to have a classy-looking broad next to you in the good seats and you're the classiest-looking one I know. Come on, let's go eat."

At the restaurant, waiting for thick steaks, rare, they drank another Scotch and water.

"You drink a lot for a girl," Saul said after a short silence during which he'd lit two cigarettes, smoked a quarter of each and then mashed them out. "Now don't get me wrong, beautiful"—as Sally raised her eyebrows—"I'm all for it. If we didn't have this damn fight to go to tonight, I'd like to try and drink you under the table. Bet you'd put up a stiff battle, and that's a compliment coming from me." He frowned. "You know something. You're the first woman who didn't look like a pie-faced broad I've seen in years and the first one who drinks right."

"Thank you," Sally said, trying to keep a straight face. "But I'm not really at my best in drinking contests and . . ."

"Think I'm trying to back out, don't you?" he interrupted belligerently. "Well, I'm not, see. A promise is a promise but I never did see a dame so crazy to go to a fight. Well, thank God, here's the steaks. I could eat ten of them."

Being a pie-faced broad might have its advantages Sally thought wryly. Life would be so simple. You simply slapped the face of an escort who talked and behaved like this and walked away from him forever. But probably, if you were such a girl, you never got involved with the Sauls of this world anyway. And yet, what fun they must miss. No, I must have him, she thought, looking at him as he sat across the table chewing vigorously on his steak. He's really too marvelous. But one would have to tame him down a bit. These flashes of hostility were really very unpleasant. She felt his knee pressing against hers under the table. Must be the good one or could you tell? They made them very cleverly these days, she'd read somewhere. But then, perhaps, his real leg had been amputated only below the knee. Never mind the macabre musings, Sally. She concentrated on her steak.

"My God," Saul said, leaning back in his chair, "there isn't a thing in the world like steak." He grinned, seeing her look of surprise at his empty plate. "I eat fast," he explained, "especially when it's steak. I don't know why in hell I don't come here more often except I hate eating alone. You're good company in a steakhouse, you know that, Sally. Most women talk too much. When you eat a good steak you ought to eat it, is the way I feel about it. Want some coffee or another drink?"

Sally ordered coffee but Saul as she'd sort of suspected, had another Scotch.

"Which one were you in love with?" he demanded suddenly after he'd lit a cigarette for her and a cigar for himself.

"Cigars seem to suit you," Sally said pleasantly. "Most men look rather silly with them, like little boys playing politician."

"I asked you a question." He let the ash grow long and trembling until at the very last minute he flicked it into the ashtray. Through the fragrant blue smoke he surveyed her with that lingering look, undressing her through her clothes.

Sally caught her breath and looked down at her coffee. "I don't believe I know what you mean."

"Sure you do," he said roughly. "Was it that cousin of yours you loved or your husband? Or both of them? Maybe neither of them, is my guess."

Sally felt the pressure of his knee, again, hard against hers and abruptly she pulled her leg back against the chair rung. The restaurant suddenly seemed stifling hot and noisy and the lights glared too brightly.

"I don't think I know you well enough to answer that," she said teasingly. "Shall we go now?"

"You're awful damn sophisticated, aren't you?" he said, and again his eyes took her all in. "Why not?" he muttered almost to himself, "why should a good-looker like you waste her time on just one joe."

He was morose and silent during the short drive to the Garden and when they'd parked and gotten out of the car, he said abruptly, "The main bout don't start for a while, there's some other stuff before but I don't want to see it. Let's go to that bar up the street there and have some drinks."

Sally knew perfectly well what would happen. He drank much faster than she did and in twenty minutes had gulped down five

Scotches and was well on his way to being drunk. She looked at her watch. It was a quarter to eleven.

He saw her looking at it and his eyes narrowed. He lowered his head like a bull about to charge. "Lissen, for crisssakes," he said, "I don't wanna go to no damn motherlovin fight see, just wanna stay here and be happy. But you're like all dames. 'Be nice boy,'" he whined, "'be a good boy, do what mama wants, don't drink so much,' ah shit, I heard it all, and I'm up to here with it. Even you, beauty, you're no different, same thing underneath, same tricks, screw you Jack, minute a guy's back's turned. Ain't gonna no fight, see, wanna stay here with me, all right, 'f not go home. What you need's a jerk like my little brother. He'll treat you right. You ain't my meat, baby. Don't waste your time with me. I don't need no Gray Ladies."

"Very well," Sally said. She picked up her jacket which was lying next to her on the padded leather booth seat and held out her hand. "Give me the tickets if you're not going to use them. I'll find someone who'd like to go."

"Too late now," he said cunningly, "you'll never dig up anybody so late."

"Then I'll go myself," Sally said impatiently. "Just give me the tickets please, since you don't want them. They're wasted on you."

"You can't go by yourself," he said in a shocked voice. "There'll be ninety slobs pawing you before you even get sat down."

"That's ridiculous," Sally said crisply. "It's a public event, isn't it?"

He shook his head. "You really gonna go, you must be nuts. What the hell difference does it make to you? You don't even know anything about these boys. You don't know anything about boxing. You just wanna see how far you can push me."

She was putting her jacket on, standing up and looking down at him. "No," she said calmly, "it's true, I don't know anything about boxing, but I like to look at men, the bigger and more naked the better. And tonight I feel like looking at some big, half-naked men and the most uncomplicated way to do it is to see a fight. And the more they hammer each other and batter their brains out the more I'll enjoy it thinking how beautiful and stupid such men are. So give me the tickets."

Saul's jaw dropped open and his face got red and then pale and then he began to laugh and got to his feet. "Oh no you don't," he said, still laughing, "Jesus Christ, you think I'd let a wild babe like you walk into a place like that alone? You'd probably pick up some broken-down fighter at the door who's just hanging around trying to pick up a free ticket and take him in with you and I'd have a hell of a time explaining to the sports editor how a crumbum got into a good seat."

"You mean you've decided to stop this shilly-shallying and are going with me?" Sally demanded coolly.

"You're damn right I am," he said. "She likes to watch big, naked men, does she? Well, baby, I wouldn't miss this spectator sport with you for a million bucks. Let's go."

The seats were very close to the ring. Saul handed Sally into hers and settled down beside her. "The boys are coming up into the ring now," he said. "Thank God we didn't come too early. That schlemiel at the mike likes to introduce old has-beens like me to the crowd. Quite a turnout," he added after a quick, thorough survey of the audience. "I used to draw a big crowd too, if I do say so myself. You know, Sally, there wasn't an extra ounce of fat on me in those days. I really cut quite a figure."

"You cut quite a figure now." She flicked her eyes over him casually and was pleased to see that it embarrassed him.

"Nah," he said, "I'm just an old, fat, crippled hulk now. Wish I'd known you then, might've made a lot of difference . . . But then I wouldn'ta known you anyhow, would I? We didn't run around in the same circles. In fact, we don't even now."

"Then how does it happen we're out together tonight?"

"Because my kid brother got to be a hotshot doctor." He grinned at her. "I must've been blind to think you were his girl. He never had a girl who talked like you. You'd've shocked the pants off him. You know, once, I called a girlfriend of his he brought around, a broad, and you'd've thought the earth fell in, the hell he gave me."

Sally tried not to laugh. Really she felt a little sorry for Matthew Berman. She hadn't found him very interesting in that brief time this afternoon, but the poor thing must have quite a time with this boorish but magnetic brother. And she'd just bet that the girl who'd been called a broad had probably liked Saul a good deal better than the nicer, more well-behaved, more gentlemanly Matthew. Women were weird masochists, herself included of course.

The M.C. was shouting into the mike ". . . And in this corner wearing blue trunks . . ." A lot of men seemed to know Saul and they hailed him with big smiles and slaps on the back.

"You seem to know everyone here." Of course they'd remember him. Not only women. Underneath all the roughness and bitterness there was something awfully likable. Wish I *had* known him before, Sally thought, he must've been charming. Like a big, sweet child.

Saul was silent, watching the fighters, with the tense look back on his face and in his eyes a strange, distant gleam. He didn't seem to hear her banal observation and she didn't speak again. After all this time, she thought, he deserves to be left alone awhile. In a few minutes, the bell rang, the bout began and she was so completely absorbed in it that for a while she forgot about Saul.

It was just as she'd told him. She didn't know anything at all about boxing technicalities. She'd gone to a lot of fights with Ben and then later she remembered going with Mike who kept trying to hate boxing because Hemingway liked it but for some reason couldn't stay away from a good fight. After she'd married Joe Mayhew, she'd been shocked to find that he, unlike other males she'd known, thought all fights were fixed, the whole sport corrupt and he'd be damned before he'd take her to see one. Later, after he'd left, she'd fallen in with a crowd of avid fans at Berkeley. But even after all this time she couldn't tell an uppercut from a jab. It was just watching that excited her, especially the heavyweights. There was something so beautifully savage and powerful about two large, wellbuilt men knocking each other around. Men, the most beautiful animals in the world, the large, brawny ones with broad chests and wide shoulders and heavy muscular hairy thighs particularly, and when she looked at them she got the most tremendous sensual kick.

In the ring, now, was a tall Negro and a husky, hairyblack, piledriver boy and they were beating each other furiously, the crowd yelling, a little interval between bells, then back to hammering and Sally was having a very good time. It was a splendid show.

At the end of the second round, Saul excused himself abruptly and limped up the aisle and Sally amused herself by looking about at the people. There were a lot of men sitting around in groups, mostly chewing on cigars and she collected a goodly set of admiring smiles and a few glances that could pass for leers. She took out a cigarette and a man two seats away leaped clean across and flashed his lighter for her. She was just saying thankyou with her sweetest smile when Saul came back with a thin, balding man whom he introduced as Jimmy Baskerville, the sports editor of the *Beacon-Journal*.

"It's a great fight, so far, Saul," Baskerville was saying, "glad as hell you could make it. And you too, Miss Mayhew. Say, Saul, there's going to be a little party at the Press Club after the bout. I'd like to have you and Miss Mayhew come along as my guests."

"I dunno," Saul grunted sinking down into his seat. "Maybe." He looked sort of pale yellow and his lips were pressed tightly together.

"How about you, Miss Mayhew," Baskerville asked, his hand on her shoulder. "You'd like to come wouldn't you? Good. Try to persuade that old bum Berman." He nodded at them briskly and went off toward his seat.

"I'd like to go," Sally said, "if you would."

"I dunno," Saul repeated. "I don't feel so hot right now. Guess I drank too much."

"Well," Sally said. "We don't have to go."

The bell rang for the third round. Saul took out a handkerchief and mopped at his forehead. It was not warm in the Garden but he was perspiring.

"Listen, Sally, will you excuse me for a while. I gotta go out."

"Do you want me to go with you?" She was slightly alarmed. He really looked hideous, sort of a putty color.

"No. I'll be okay. Back soon." He disappeared up the aisle again and Sally concentrated on the fight. The Negro boxer whose name was Jacob Abbott knocked down the other one, whose name was Mike Marino but he was up again on the count of six, prancing around like a bloodthirsty tiger.

Just before the round ended, Saul was back in his seat.

"Christ," he said and he really sounded disappointed. "I missed the whole damn round. These boys are really good Sally. I don't know if you know or not."

"They seemed so to me," she said, "but I wasn't sure if their technical proficiency matched their aesthetic appeal."

He grinned. He looked much happier now. "Always trust your instinct," he said, "and when it comes to men, I've got a hunch your instinct is terrific."

"You look much better now," Sally said. "What happened?"

"Funny as hell. You know, I was pretty drunk when we came in here and the first round was pure hell for me, the boys up there looked like they were punching in slow motion, everything was in a fog. But that wasn't the worst of it. I hated those bastards up there, God, I could feel the hate right up in my throat. Specially that ginzo, Mike Marino, I know him, see. He was in the Army too, like me, see, but he come out all right, some kind of truckdriver for the Quartermaster Corps, and now he's back in the fight game and doing all right for himself. All I could think of was, it could've been me, could've been me, and now I'm a one-legged nothing. Never wanted to come to things like this for that reason. So, I went out and had a drink at a bar, thinking it'd make me feel better, that's where I ran into Baskerville. Came back here and didn't feel better, so I went out again. And I was just gonna keep on going, right outa here, and leave you all alone. That shows you what a nogood bastard I am. So it's okay, she wanted to come, I kept telling myself, she can take care of herself. But when I was almost to the door, it caught me and I had to make it fast to the can. And I got it all out of my system, damn near puked my guts out, till I was as weak as a kitten and shaking all over. I'm sorry Sally, I'm a crude joe, but that's the way I am."

"That's all right," Sally said encouragingly.

"Then I went out and breathed in some air and stood there thinking and I got sore at myself. You're a damned yellowlivered bastard I said to myself, you're not even a man any more, gonna walk off and leave a girl sitting, she hasn't done anything to you. And it's funny, Sally, I don't even know you, but I thought about how nice you been, going out with me, being a real swell girl, polite, putting up with the cruddy way I act, and I haven't even got the decency to treat you right. So I came back in and I thought, what the hell it's just a fight. I'm not much of a man if I can't watch two guys boxing without getting sick to my stomach. I'll be all right now but I don't think I'll ever get over it hurting. You know what I mean, Sally?"

"Yes. You know we can leave. Right now, if you prefer."

"No," he said, "I'll be okay now. And you know, something else I thought while I was outside. About you. You could resent the guys that're left, but no, you're nice as hell to me, so I'm not gonna be an ape and spoil your time. You had it bad too."

"I'm glad you came back," Sally said and then the fourth round started and by the fifth round Saul was yelling as loudly as all the other men around them even though he didn't get out of his seat to do it.

In the seventh round, Mike Marino hammered Jacob Abbott right into the ropes with tremendous thwacking sounds. Sally winced a little and wanted to cover her ears but the unmerciful beating didn't last long. Jacob Abbott was knocked out and the fight was over and Saul and Sally cheered and whistled for the winner.

Afterwards, they went to the party at the Press Club.

"We'll just have a couple quick ones," Saul said, "and then go.

I don't think I could take it, shaking hands with Marino and him looking sorry for me."

But when they got there Saul was so busy talking to all the men he knew and introducing her and getting them drinks and salami on rye sandwiches with pickles and he seemed to be having such a good time that, apparently, he didn't mind, when the time came, shaking hands with Mike Marino.

The next room was cleared for dancing and when Saul got involved in a discussion with Jimmy Baskerville, Sally wandered in to look over the trio of musicians and immediately was hailed by Bobby Drummond. Bobby was a local white boy, small and undersized, whom she'd known around at the jazz places as a very good drummer. He'd been working with Vance Paley's band the year she'd been singing with them just before running off to get married and although it'd been about five years ago, Bobby looked exactly the same, as if he'd been born wizened.

Now the musicians were resting on the stand between numbers so she went over to talk to Bobby. The piano player was an unknown but Joe Bark the trumpet player had recorded and played behind some of the greatest jazz and blues singers in the country like Billie Holiday and Joe Turner and, after she'd said hello to him, she wondered vaguely what this acknowledged classic was doing here.

"Sally, *baby*," Bobby said, "well, look at you. After all these years and here you turn up with all these squares. What gives?"

She leaned against the piano, drink in hand. "I might ask the same of you." She had a familiar, comfortable feeling talking to Bobby, as if she'd never gone away and lived her strange life. He'd always thought that she was a good, honest blues vocalist and he'd had the dedicated professional jazzman's admiration for her because of it. It made her feel good to remember that.

"Times are hard," Bobby said, "and this Terry Hannigan character on the *Beacon* digs the hot stuff, so he lined me up and I knew that Bark was in town unemployed and Farmer there on the joybox had just come in off a road gig with Bob Crosby and so here we are. I heard you were back, chick, and how you were going to sing at the Bat this afternoon. But I couldn't make it."

"Not even to hear me?" Sally asked teasingly.

"Ah listen," Bobby said, "I'd go miles to hear you but a voice like yours has to be backed up and when I heard the New York cats weren't going to show, well, not for me . . . not those half-hipped cats, oh no. They ought to cut out."

"They were pretty sad," Sally admitted. "Anyway, I didn't sing."

"I didn't think you would," Bobby said grinning wickedly, "you'd need a tin ear to do it. What's with you, chick? Now that you've fallen in on Boston again? Any plans?"

Sally shrugged.

"I heard you once," Joe Bark said suddenly. "Bat Club session during the war. You sang 'Rocks in My Bed.' Knocked me out."

"Oh well," Sally said deprecatingly, "I was only imitating Billie all the time in those days."

He shook his head. "No, you're different from Billie. She has more style but you got something else. Power, misery, I dunno. Blues shouldn't be too stylish, sometimes."

"She does it for kicks," Bobby said. "It's a waste. I used to think even when you were singing that rinkydink stuff with Vance that you could be another Bessie."

"Blues are out of fashion," Sally said. "In fact, singers are. The cognoscenti just like instruments that play notes straight from a refrigerator. Music for robots."

"It's a drag all right," Bobby agreed, "but I don't get salty about it. People still like the happy music. I heard a rumor that you might sing for Vance this summer."

"Well we talked about it," Sally admitted cautiously.

"Listen," Bobby urged, "take him up on it, will you Sal? I'll be there too."

"He didn't seem too certain that he wanted me," Sally said dubiously. "And I don't know myself. It's been so long since I've worked for Vance's kind of band and that sort of audience."

"I've never heard you sing," Farmer, the piano player said suddenly. He was a young, crew-cutted, horn-rimmed glasses type and she'd noticed the cold look he'd given her while she'd been mocking the new music.

"Hey, that's a killer," Bobby said excitedly. "Why don't you give us a tune right here and now. No real blues, these characters are too square here, but something like you used to sing with Vance. 'Stormy Weather,' how's about that, the way I remember it, you almost made it not commercial."

"Here!" Sally said. "Oh no, Bobby, I don't think so. They want to dance. And I'm so out of practice, I couldn't just dash into it."

Saul came up behind her. He looked happy and was carrying a drink for her. "You want to dance, Sally?" he asked. "Mike Marino wants to dance with you, the bum. He asked me if I'd mind. I don't care, you go ahead. I can't dance."

She introduced him to the three musicians.

"We want your chick to sing a song," Bobby said. "Give the squares a few jumps. She's playing coy."

"I didn't know you sang, Sally," Saul said. "No kidding. Christ, go ahead. I'm crazy to hear you."

"There you are," Bobby said. "Make your man happy."

Sally looked at Saul. He'd rather have me sing than dance she thought, even though he says he doesn't care. I can't dance, he said, not I can't dance any more. Anyway, why not sing? It would be all right here. There were at least two good musicians, one of whom she'd worked with before and this crowd here was not likely to be as knowledgeable as the audience at a good session or the kind hellbent on getting their money's worth in conventional entertainment, who would come to hear Vance this summer, and if she made a few mistakes, they'd not notice. Besides if they stayed around here a bit longer and the music began someone would ask her to dance and she'd have to and Saul would be put down.

"All right," she said. "One song. But what?"

"'Stormy,'" Bobby insisted. "Give it that wild, blue treatment."

"She can do better than that," Joe Bark said. "How about one of the real blues?"

"No," Sally said firmly. "It'd be hideous messing up something really good."

"I don't know," Joe Bark said, shaking his head at Bobby. "When you get a good blues singer why waste her on songs anyone can do?"

"A tune's a tune," Bobby said earnestly. "It's what you do with it. And 'Stormy's' not bad. Let's not get so intellectual, man."

"It's only good," Joe Bark said with final authority, "if you can feel it right. It's too easy to fake."

"Who're we playing for anyway?" Bobby wanted to know. "These characters are getting a break hearing her sing even if she gave them 'Mairzy Doats.'"

Terry Hannigan of the *Beacon-Journal* came up just then and held a whispered conference with Bobby. Sally, standing by, only half listening, heard Terry say, "Oh sure, I thought she looked familiar, by all means . . ." She looked at Joe Bark who seemed to have given into Bobby's insistence on the song he thought was too obvious and insincere. And, of course, he was right. On the other hand, feeling as uncertain and rusty as she did, the simulated blueness of the song would serve as a crutch to help her along. She sort of liked "Stormy" anyway and maybe she wouldn't do badly with it, because she was beginning to feel depressed, a depression engendered by the memory of Benjie tied up with that song. He'd always liked it.

That, and "Blues in the Night." They'd been his two favorites and she'd never been able to explain to him why they weren't true jazz blues and how they differed from the honest, lowdown kind. No point thinking about that now and how she'd been imperious and told him his taste was deplorable. Oh the words you'd call back if you could.

"Oh hell," she said aloud and drank her drink down fast because she was seeing shadows again and it was simply the usual quakiness before the first song and whisky scared away goblins. Behind her, Terry was fixing the spotlight so it would shine on her and leave the musicians in semi-darkness and now, she began to feel really excited, hearing soft, warmup chords on the piano and then Bobby whispering to her about where he thought she ought to come in and it was all like old times, good times.

"Better have another drink," Saul said. So it was he who was there looking, in rough outline, so damnably like Benjie. "Here, take mine. I haven't touched it yet."

If Joe Bark would help her, Sally thought absently taking Saul's glass, if he wasn't opposed irrevocably to her as some kind of fake pretty society girl, if he could see that she was honest in her reluctance not to ruin a good blues through ineptness, then he could send her enough to make this a really good job, no matter what the song was or who was listening. Because he was an inspired trumpet player if he cared enough. Even now, listening to an old record he'd done with Billie Holiday was enough to make her hair stand on end, every time his trumpet came on. And she needed something good now. If she didn't sing this well, after avoiding the issue at the session this afternoon because of vile circumstances and perhaps being too scared to, she'd never sing again, not for Vance this summer and not ever again and then what else was there? Why did Joe Bark have to be such a purist anyway?

Bobby came over. "All ready, chick. Make like you ain't had any jelly for ten years. It'll knock 'em out."

Joe Bark laughed behind her and Saul looked suspiciously at Bobby.

"What's he talking about?"

"Just jazz talk." Because he wanted her to sing it hot and low-down. And was it a lie after all? Had there ever been anyone since Ben who could melt away her insides with one look? No but perhaps . . . Saul was taking away her empty glass, and patting her on the shoulder.

Then he got off the stand and Bobby gave out with a few big

rolls and people stopped milling around on the little floor, they were waiting to dance, she supposed and looked up surprised. Other people came drifting in from the bar and Sally stood by the mike wishing she had another drink.

"Ladies and gentlemen," she heard Terry Hannigan saying, ". . . great surprise . . . with us tonight . . . one of Boston's well-known . . . will favor us with a . . ."

She felt herself moving away and out and very cold and high up and Terry was announcing her name and people were clapping and then she heard the piano and a slow trumpet intro from Joe Bark and it was good, he was going to give her a break, just the few notes were great, sending slow shivers of blue sadness down her spine . . .

"Come on, chick," Bobby whispered, "come on like mad."

Then she was alone before the mike, the light on her, just some muted instrumental behind her and she looked down at the faces and wondered how it was that she never found what she was looking for and it came to her and she began to sing . . .

At first it was shaped and formed, the phrases restrained, holding her voice low, pouring in only a little blue, asking a question, husky, mournful but low-keyed, no wild grief, following the melody, keeping with the beat Bobby was giving her, the room hushed and she could hear her own quiet sadnotes dropping everywhere like the rain drops, nodding and rocking with the bewilderment, the question of why it had to be, her mouth only half-open, going lower almost to a whisper, yet feeling it, rich, warm, lingering, holding to the ends of the words, to the edges of sorrow, but slow, slow, plenty of time, he'd been gone long and maybe never come back, a little hoarse on the sky, the protracted, weeping sky, thinned and wavery sky, the Boston, raw, gray way of saying *Stawmy*, harder and ruder here, promise of worse to come, almost humming, drowsy and slow toward the end, all the time . . . the tiiime . . . slowrock, sweet, sad . . . long on the all . . . and letting the time drag out on leaden feet . . . hearing Joe Bark come in with the few theme repetition notes, slow, clear bubbles of sadness . . . spelling out the slow rock dirge of her meaning . . .

Oh he knew, the dark, dour, low, beat, then swinging in louder, an ever-widening circle of blue, a darker, more lowdown blue, a stark cry now to the harpies with the scissors, rounder, richer tones, rocking now, moving her body, harsher, a little improvisation now away from the melody but still within the over-all beat, oh nothing now to cover her, all gone, all naked now to the cold winds, holding onto together because there was nothing left, oh so tired and sad . . . but take a deep breath, go into it now, harsh, strident, loud, defiant, tell them all, tell them what will happen, and Joe Bark there, right there, behind her, approving, assisting, telling her it was great, not loud but behind her all the way, and open up wide because the blues have really walked in this time, the deepest, most passionate, most shoutmaking, griefstricken, bluernblues, hoarse, inarticulate, pleading in her damn rocking chair, no bed, no rocking bed, her voice somber but feeling it come out warm and from way down in her and Bobby softly tapping it out back of her and letting the power come up up and out, not able to hold it back any more. Then pausing holding hard on walk, praying for the sun, because and with almost no pause, only time to hear a few beats from Bobby, and lingering a little on the more, and his whisper, oh baby, baby, and then she hit it, loud, wideopen, with the full force of a real blue wail, because she couldn't go on, it was true, there was nothing, because there was no sun, no Ben, no man, no love, she was more than gone, and they knew it, everyone in the room knew it, she could feel them down there and behind her knowing all her abysmal loneliness and despair, but then the ritual repetition caught her up and held her together a little and she drew it back again toward her, shaking it up a little and embroidering it and trailing off with it in a series of low, blue gutturals so she could step back and let the boys come in now, hearing Joe Bark do wonderful things with it, feeling the crowd sway with the beat, then back again for another chorus, pulling all the stops, as big, powerful and blue as she could, riding with her voice, which seemed adventurously able to penetrate the most magical depths, willing to be pushed into the most elaborate kind of vocal play and never straying off and she was slower now, less with the beat, all to herself, making every word and note count, making that together mean something, shaking it, because that's what together was, not nice, sweet, polite but the end, just all there was that's all and it was raining, but all the time but forever, slower lower deeper sadder, raining like that all the time, with no together, until she deserted words as useless to express it and was just rocking, humming blue notes like a muted brass instrument with only Bobby, the last, the only one there, tapping very very softly the slow lamenting beat and she'd forgotten any audience was there, swaying with her eyes closed and her hands clasped and then her voice faded away into a faint echo and there was no more. Sally opened her eyes into a complete, mesmerized silence and moved back from the mike and the trance was broken.

The light was on her, she heard them clapping and shouting and she made some kind of courtesy bow.

Bobby was patting her arm. "Dreamboat, did you rock me, did you come on. Didn't I tell you?" he said to Joe Bark.

"My apologies," Joe said seriously to Sally. "It was a privilege."

"You were all fabulous," Sally said. "Thanks so much."

"You really sent us," Bobby said. "Joe doesn't blow like that all the time, chick."

"I know," Sally said happily.

"I'd like to play behind you again sometime," Joe Bark said formally.

"Perhaps this summer," Sally said and then realized her mistake.

"Vance uses only ofay musicians," Joe said quietly.

"Maybe he needs a kick in the ass," Bobby said. "Anyway, why wait till this summer? How about now?"

"No," Sally said, "I need a drink now." She suddenly felt very shaky and got off the stand in a hurry. She looked around for Saul and saw him smiling at her, holding up a drink.

"Here's a little reward," he said. "You can really sing, kid. I'm surprised."

"Helen Morgan," Terry Hannigan was saying, "how about favoring us with another number? This time you can sit on the piano. That was really wonderful."

"I'm sorry," Sally said. "I'm a little tired." In a low voice she said to Saul, "Would you mind very much if we left?"

"Sure," he said, "any time you say." He put his arm around her. "What's the matter, doll, don't you like to sing? If I had a voice and a delivery like that, I'd be making a million."

"I like to," Sally said, "but not any more tonight."

On their way out she was cornered by three or four gentlemen of the press and had a hard time getting away. "What's the story Miss Brimmer, babble, babble . . . any contracts for this year, you've been away, where, oh and were you performing out there, any contracts for this year, no, too bad, we really enjoyed it, unexpected pleasure, family objections . . ."

"Make a nice little item," Saul said casually as they got into the car. "You people are always news in this bluenose town."

"I know. Even at parties where they're supposed to relax and not talk shop they're still at it. I hope it misses my uncle's gimlet eyes."

"I'm no philosopher," Saul said, "but after thirty-two years, I come to the conclusion that this damn life is nothing but a bunch of lost opportunities. For one crappy reason or another." He'd lighted a cigar which had immediately gone out and he was now chewing savagely on the end of it, driving slowly down Tremont Street. "What did these legmen mean about family objections? You mean to tell me, when you can sing that great, your family won't let you? A girl like you don't let people tell her what to do, do you?"

"Of course not. Naturally they don't like it, particularly my uncle. But that was simply silly, romantic, reporter nonsense."

"Then you could do it for a living, if you wanted to? But then"— he turned to her frowning—"I was forgetting. You don't need a living, do you? But you like to do it. I could tell, just from listening. So why don't you, even if you don't need the money?"

"It's too difficult to explain," Sally said lazily. "Perhaps when I know you better, I'll tell you." How could one explain such a thing to Saul, who, like many others, simply and directly thought that if you had an ability you just went out and made yourself famous with it. "I'm not that good, anyway," she said, trying to explain almost to herself too. "It's really a terribly competitive business. And I haven't the drive to compete I'm afraid. In Boston, I'm known you see, but nowhere else." She lapsed into silence, thinking about sing-ing, about the fine sense of skill and power she'd had tonight, living with, creating, and controlling her song. It was great to feel that you could do something that well.

"I guess it's not the thing for people like you to do anyway," Saul said suddenly. "You're supposed to get married and have a lot of kids and do charity work and give tea parties and hunt foxes, isn't that it?"

"Something like that," Sally said laughing at his contemptuous tone.

"Damned waste of time and a voice if you ask me," Saul said. "Anyway, I just want you to know I thought you were the best and I'm only sorry you don't do it more so I could hear you again."

"Oh you might. There's a thing in the offing for this summer with Vance Paley."

"You mean traveling around?"

"No. A new club opening around Rockport."

"Now I got a place to spend my vacation," Saul said jokingly.

"It may not work out. Vance was terribly tentative about it, mainly because he isn't sure how much drawing power I'd have now."

"I don't figure that. All anybody's got to do is look and listen."

"Well, you see," Sally explained patiently, "Vance plays mostly for debutante parties and country clubs and the big hotels and when I sang for him before I'd just made my debut."

"Oh, and you mean all your crowd came to hear you because they knew you? Kind of a novelty, huh? Instead of being down there on the floor you were entertaining them. Yeah, but I don't see what's so different now. You're still one of them."

"I'm much older now, for one thing," Sally said thinking how horribly true that was. "And the younger ones don't know me, except as a ghastly sort of legendary, bad example."

"You mean you're some kind of a black sheep?"

"Sort of."

"I bet you are." He turned his head around and looked at her, smiling. "What the hell did you do?"

"It's an awfully long story," Sally drawled, "and not terribly interesting."

"Did you marry one of the wrong people?"

"In a way, yes."

"Okay. I get you. You mind your business, I mind mine. Well, here we are." He turned off the motor. "Home safe and sound. Didya have a good time, Sally, or have I got a lot of nerve asking after the way I acted?"

"I was rather piqued for a while," Sally smiled at him. "But then I thought you came out of it rather well considering how hard I was on you. I had a lovely time, I really did."

"Boy, do I love the way you talk," he said irrelevantly. "I suppose a lot of guys have told you that. I don't mean just your voice but the things you say. You're a damn attractive doll, you know, Sally, but what's even better in my book, you're a real lady and a hundred percent woman. Funny," he laughed self-consciously, "I don't mind telling you now, I wanted to take you out more to steal a march on Bud, my brother, than for myself, but I sure as hell changed my mind. I mean, I had a swell evening, first in years, and though I hated you for a while for pushing me, you were right. I'm glad you did. I just want you to know that."

"Thank you," Sally said. She picked up her bag. "I must go now. I'd ask you in for a drink but my brother hasn't been too well and . . ."

"Oh yah," he said, "I forgot about that. Well, I'll take a raincheck on that drink. How about that? Or was just one night of Saul Berman's lousy disposition plenty for you?" He sounded so boyishly eager in contrast to his earlier lordly assurance that Sally almost laughed aloud.

"Why don't you come and get that drink about seven tomorrow night," she suggested casually, fumbling with the door handle. "Or do you have things to do?"

"I don't have a darned thing to do," he said quickly. "Here, let me get that for you."

He walked to the door with her. "Seven tomorrow night," he said. They were standing close together in the doorway. "I'll be there with bells on. Well, good night Sally, thanks a million."

"Good night," Sally said. But she didn't move, waiting for him to either go away or kiss her. They stared at each other for a long second and then he turned and limped hastily toward his car.

Sally looked after him, biting her lower lip hard and then she ran upstairs and slammed the apartment door behind her, not caring if it woke Dudley, that disgusting obstacle. She undressed quickly, splashed some Scotch into a glass and then drank it down neat and fast.

He's afraid of me, she thought, switching off the bedlamp and pulling the covers up over her. It'd be interesting to know why, after all those licentious, disrobing looks and that kiss in the car outside the Lincolnshire, he'd practically run away from her there downstairs. She yawned and folded her bare arms under her head. He was really a little crazy and sort of wild and would, after awhile, no doubt, turn out to be fairly stupid and impossible, but right now he was just what she needed. She'd had an awfully good evening really. Things she liked to do, sing, meet admiring people, drinking, feeling good about herself, better than in a long time, not that way often any more, but tonight, singing well, and made Saul happy, shouldn't really tamper with someone's interior that way, could've turned out very badly, but her hunch'd been right, that male animal smell emanating strongly from him, a mistake to lose someone of that potential and if she hadn't forced him he'd've retreated into self-pity and that'd've been the end. Love and a song and that old good feeling, smiling to herself in the drowsy dark . . .

Nine

Deborah came out of the subway at Harvard Square and asked one of the crop-headed students passing by her in which direction Lemon Street would be. He told her in a rather lordly mumble and she walked along gazing through the fence at the Yard, beautiful but deserted on this end of semester Sunday and wished she wouldn't be quite so nervous. They seemed like pleasant people and surely Ella Baring wouldn't have asked her for lunch or invited her to the show if . . . If only I wouldn't be so afraid of people, she told herself angrily. It's silly. In spite of Gordie's horridness the day before she longed now for his presence at the Barings'. At least she knew him. And all those people were so, well, clique-y, having all those years of friendship together, so many private jokes and arguments and memories and common frames of reference. Even the most self-assured person might feel alien among them. But wasn't that just an excuse really? They had all been nice and friendly, to her, at any rate, if not to Gordie.

But the way they'd talked about Gordie now though, that hadn't been at all polite. Because after all it could mean that although they liked a person for a while, he or she might just as easily be disliked for no comprehensible reason at all. They could determine that you were square, as Gordie would say, and didn't fit in and could chill you with disapproval as they'd done to Gordie. Maybe I don't want to go at all, Deborah thought uneasily, as she neared the corner of Lemon Street. They were really all older than she was and knew so much more. She might make an awful fool of herself, say or do something wrong, she always seemed to be so unsure of what was acceptable in . . . And then, nobody would tell her what had happened but she'd be left standing in a corner looking at books. One thing about Gordie, he always told her when she did or said something silly, even if he was nasty about it, so she knew enough not to commit the same blunder again. But he wouldn't be there today. He hadn't mentioned Ella's show to her yesterday and he certainly would have, had he been invited. Perhaps, she thought, in an access of charity, he was invited but suspecting that she wasn't, didn't want to hurt her feelings by talking about it. But no, to be quite truthful, that wouldn't be Gordie's way at all. Sometimes, listening to him run on about interesting things he'd done, she'd wondered why, instead of using her as an audience, he didn't ask her to come with him. But of course she couldn't come out and say it. Up until yesterday, she'd had to accept the fact that Gordie led two lives and she'd better accept her place in the lower or square, greasy Marplot one or else. But yesterday's scene, well, my, that had been enlightening. Of course, it didn't mean he actually *lied* about his friends just because this particular group didn't like him. But he had talked an awful lot about how intimate he was with Mike and although Mike was more polite than the others, well, even he had seemed kind of embarrassed by Gordie.

What a muddle people were, Deborah thought, standing uncertainly on the corner. She would never get to understand them or know how to get on with them, not if she lived a million years.

She heard a bell chime the hour somewhere behind her. It was only one o'clock and she was too early. She turned and walked back along the street. I won't go in just yet, she thought, I'll go have a Coke someplace. There was a little drugstore at the next corner. She went in and climbed on a stool, ordering a lemon Coke and lighting a cigarette. How terrible to arrive too early. But then she was always either too late or too early. Someday I'll have a watch, she thought, and then I'll be on time. Sipping on her Coke and smoking, in what Gordie referred to as a very messy way, she pretended to read the book she'd brought with her. It was an old limp-covered, Modern Library edition of Katherine Mansfield's *The Garden Party*, which she'd bought for forty cents at a remainder counter in Gilchrist's bookstore last week and on the subway coming out to Cambridge she'd read the story called "Miss Brill" about the old woman with the miserable little furpiece draped around her withered neck, sitting alone in the park. Then some beautiful gay young lovers had come along and laughed at the mangy fur and, by implication, its owner, and the old woman had gone home and put away her wretched little piece of faded elegance in the box where it was always kept between seasons, not looking at it, not stroking it or being careful with it as she usually was, and as she lowered the lid, thought she heard something crying. It was a terrible story which hit one in the face with its truth about old age, loneliness, pathetic delusions, and spinsterhood. Deborah had been unable to read anything else in the book after that one. That's the way people alone are, she thought now, looking at her Coke. Objects of ridicule from more fortunate, companioned and loved people and always wearing the wrong thing. And age had nothing to do with it either because once you were marked like that, somehow unbeknownst to you in childhood, you'd be the same all your life.

Why did I ever come, she thought. It had been such an effort to get here. First there'd been her mother's disappointment at her not being home for Sunday dinner and the curiosity about where she was going. Well, it was nice that Deborah was going to an art display, her mother's words, but who were these people she was going to visit for lunch, and why didn't she ever meet any of Deborah's friends any more? Then her father had intervened. The daughters of proper people, it seemed, didn't go running off to all sorts of strange places with God knows what unknown wrong kinds. But naturally he'd said with martyred irony, he didn't have a word to say about how his daughter was being brought up because her mother let her do anything and run wild. Because you go to college he'd said, doesn't mean you know everything and mark my words you'll get into trouble someday. So then, of course, her mother had to stick up for her and explain that she was going to look at some paintings with people she knew at school and was going to eat lunch at their house which had only sent him off on a further wild tangent about eating pork and non-kosher food and because the father's word was ignored in the house, her mother would lament bitterly when her daughter ran off with a goy. Nobody could get a word in during this but finally peace had descended when he'd stormed out to take his Sunday walk on the beach.

Then there'd been the inevitable frenzy of indecision about what to wear. If I were really an intelligent girl, Deborah thought now, absently stirring her Coke with the straw, I'd just accept the fact that I only have a few clothes and none of them are really right for anything except school. Then I'd put on what I've got and march around arms akimbo and nose in air not caring what people think. Instead, each time she had to go somewhere outside her usual rut of school and work, she was attacked by absolute misery. If she had one good summer dress it was winter and vice versa. She never had the right shoes to match anything but sweaters and skirts. And there was never enough money for clothes, not even though she was working. This morning, her tiny wardrobe had been piled on the bed while she tried things on, in turn, and discarded them in despair and her mother had counseled and reasoned.

"You could wear your little gray suit, dear. Spring is suit weather."

The little gray suit was about three years old and, having been bought before the New Look, was completely old-fashioned, with padded shoulders, a long jacket and narrow short skirt. Deborah wore it only in winter when she was reasonably certain to be covered up by a coat most of the time. And the price of a new suit, at present, was prohibitive, even in Filene's Basement.

"The lavender cotton dress with the bertha collar that you bought last summer," her mother'd suggested. "With a warm coat."

It was a lovely dress and Deborah had been delighted with it when she'd found it on sale. The color looked fine on her and it was very New Look, with a full skirt and tight bodice but still it was *cotton*. And even though it was May, still it was not warm enough to wear *cotton* and furthermore it was a very pale, summery lavender, just right for hot July garden parties and if she wore it, without the slightest doubt in the world not another soul, either at the Barings' or at the show would be sporting a summer dress.

Then she'd tried on a sleeveless, fancy blacksilk dress with tiered skirt which had been donated to her mother by an aunt but this was completely out of the question.

"It's the kind of dress an old lady would wear."

She had retreated from the insoluble problem for a moment and put on her stockings and shoes. At least she liked her shoes. They were flat, black, suède sandals with a turned-up snub of a toe, pinched in with a little gold bow, rather like Turkish harem slippers.

"You could wear your black corduroy skirt," her mother'd suggested. "That's full enough. And a nice white blouse."

But the only blouse at hand was a short-sleeved one, quite plain with an open collar like a man's shirt and would be all wrong with the shoes. What she ought to have had was a long-sleeved one with plenty of ruffles.

So finally with her back to the wall she'd pulled out an old purple wool dress which although pre-New Look had a full enough skirt to pass. But when she'd tried it on it was too short. Her mother had then pulled the thread out of a short hem and pressed it quickly. It wasn't, even then, really long enough to be fashionable but at least her knees weren't showing. Well, wool dresses were probably just as wrong for a warm May day as a summer one would've been but it was too late to change her mind. And off she'd gone finally, disregarding her mother's warning to wear her warm gabardine coat because it was sure to turn cold before she got home. She'd be warm enough in this awful unsuitable dress. She had pictured herself, red-faced and perspiring, in the middle of a gallery full of cool, beautifully dressed, suave people. But, as a matter of protection, in case her dress turned out to be wrong, or if it really did get cold, she'd taken along her old white, cotton poplin raincoat. Too bad that it was really so shabby because it zipped all the way down the front and made her feel, when she wore it, as no other garment had ever done, completely all right, sporty, dashing, and sophisticated.

That coat had been, since her senior year in high school, armor against all the uncertainties engendered by her inadequate wardrobe, until in fact, the week before when with Gordie, she'd gone to see an old Marlene Dietrich movie in which the most glamorous woman in the world had worn a black, revered, belted trench coat and beret and when the movie'd been over, Deborah, donning and zipping up her by now consistency of a handkerchief raincoat, had recognized its shabbiness and resemblance to a flour sack and felt pretty square.

Well, anyway, there she'd been, all ready to leave, standing on one foot, while her mother hurried around with the iron, making little hurt remarks about how they never seemed to do anything together any more and she knew Deborah had a lot of studying but couldn't they sometime go to a movie together. And on and on about how she liked going to the Museum of Fine Arts herself and hadn't been in a long time and they must do that too. All making Deborah feel quite guilty for rushing off alone like that because she knew her father never went to the movies. Or took her mother anyplace except for walks.

She ought to have friends of her own, Deborah'd thought righteously. If he doesn't like museums, concerts, and movies, she ought to . . . but what was the use? You couldn't live your parents' lives for them and so thinking, she'd managed, at last, to get out of the house before her father returned, thank heaven, and board the streetcar.

Tediously, the trolley'd rocked and plowed through the interminable bleak, shoddy, dullness of an East Boston Sunday where crowds streamed out of churches or sat in the sun on the stoops of their ugly houses, wearing their raw, sherbet-colored spring best, and everywhere like a plague of flies, young, pimply, raucous boys cavorted on sidewalks before dingy candy stores. Now, if only, she'd thought, idly, there were stretches of green, along here, with brightly striped maypoles and flower-bedecked people dancing round them, or just a few beds of pink tulips and yellow daffodils, a person who has to ride this slow, wheezing car wouldn't feel quite so grim. But this eternal depressing vista of shabby ugliness with hardly a tree or blade of grass or flower, just concrete and stores where even the sunlight was tarnished and turned cheap and sleazy, made one want to cover one's eyes. She wondered how it was that when the sea and sky and spring were so beautiful people could be content, living in such barren surroundings. Even the churches which one might expect at least to be attractive were all made of glaring yellow brick, or covered with mudcolored shingles.

She'd continued to feel depressed all the way from Maverick station in the subway to Scollay Square, on the underground bus to Park Street and even just making the subway to Cambridge before the doors closed didn't help. It wasn't just the dreariness of streets and houses, she'd thought, but simply that one knew, looking at the people who lived in such a tasteless way, how really empty and unimaginative their lives must be. It wasn't just lack of money either. You didn't need to have much money to grow flowers or to paint your house an interesting color. Did money help you to tune your radio to the broadcast of a concert so that the air would be filled with lovely sounds and not the loud braying blat of a baseball announcer, the unspeakable noises of hawkers or the yangtangtang of unmelodic harpies? How rich did one have to be to ride a bike into the country or one of the big parks for a picnic instead of hanging around beer joints, pool parlors, greasy spoons, and gangster movies?

Even poor men could be pleasant and courteous to their wives and take them to movies on occasion. And was it sheer poverty that made a man start a disagreeable tirade on his wife's shortcomings and abruptly walk away from her in the street leaving her to go home alone and almost in tears? If it were me, Deborah had thought, I wouldn't walk a step with him. She remembered how when she was small he'd take her to the zoo sometimes and she'd prattle along, asking him questions which he'd answer very impatiently or not at all. Finally, she'd gotten the idea that he'd just as soon she'd shut up, because, in his phrase, he had things on his mind and apparently needed to concentrate on these inner broodings without distraction.

The subway had emerged from its seemingly everlasting gloom, into the sunlight at Charles Street and when they'd run across the bridge over the Charles River, Deborah'd, at last, begun to feel better. Going to spend a good afternoon, looking at pictures. Being with people who were intelligent, imaginative, and interesting. Who know how to spend their Sundays. Not tied down by boring thousands of domestic, drudging details and stupid, empty pastimes and clawing, festering unhappy arguments. The sunlight had sparkled on the river and she could see red-sailed boats skimming. I'm going to have fun, she'd thought vehemently, I'm going to have fun. Then, like a fool, she'd read the story of "Miss Brill."

And now, here she was, sipping at an oversweet Coke, skulking in a drugstore, afraid to go to a house to which she'd been invited, brooding about her clothes and not having a bit of fun. The drugstore wall clock read one-twenty. She took a mirror from her brown leather purse which did not, naturally, match her dress or shoes and looked nervously at her face. Was this new purplypink lipstick she'd bought in the five and ten a little too ridiculous? Several months ago, she'd decided that she ought to try and look a bit more grownup and had bought a pair of small, false gold earrings in the five and ten. They'd hurt her ears but didn't look too bad. Rather arty and gipsy-like, she'd fancied. But when Gordie'd seen them, he'd hooted and said she looked like a peasant and that was the last of the earrings.

She patted down her curls which were unruly as usual, paid for her Coke and took a big gulp of water because her mouth felt dry and persimmon sour. But her throat seemed to have closed up and the water choked her and there she was having an embarrassing coughing fit in this perfectly strange drugstore, with red face and wet eyes and the pharmacist having to come out from behind his mortar and pestle and pound her on the back. Oh, I'm going to have a lovely time she thought grimly as she sidled out of the store after thanking the man who'd helped her and been stared at by several grisly people and bold-eyed children, I'm just going to have a grand day. Absolutely nothing mortifying will be spared me. Her raincoat had suddenly gotten so heavy she could barely carry it and her stomach began a species of queasy antics as she lagged along the street and around the corner to fetch up abruptly before a yellow two-family house. Yes, this was it. Number fifty-four. If I go up the steps, she thought, and into the house I'll probably be sick in the living room. Yes, that was what would happen, beyond a doubt. She sat down on the top step to wait until the inside quaking stopped. The sun blazed in a mid-July fury on the top of her head and she felt the fever heat of her face and body inside the loathsome purple dress. Why did I ever like these shoes, she wondered, looking despondently down at her feet. Not only were they cheap, sleazy, and gaudy but also, they were coy, cute, and . . .

"Hi, Deborah."

She raised her eyes from the miserable, pretentious shoes, as awful in their way as Miss Brill's ratty little furpiece, to see Ella Baring, wearing blue jeans, an outsize gray sweatshirt and torn blue sneakers, coming up the steps toward her carrying a bundle of groceries. Her short, wavy blonde hair was tousled, her round, blue eyes, kind and her wide unlipsticked smile seemed warm and genuine.

"That foul ball of a bell seems to be on the fritz," she said, balancing her brown paper bag on one arm. "I left a note saying to walk right up but you probably didn't see it. What a fine color your dress is."

Deborah's mutinuous stomach subsided immediately, calmed by the friendly, soothing sounds of this clear, r-pronouncing voice. She followed Ella into a hallway occupied by a baby carriage, a stroller, a tricycle, a pair of roller skates, and a gross of several assorted small metal and plastic vehicles.

"Watch the stairs," Ella said. "There's always a lethal little toy tank to trip on."

"I didn't know you had children."

"The neighbors," Ella muttered, "have three. All permissively raised because the parents are both psychologists. The little fiends might be fouled up for life if they're reproved for leaving things on the stairs. Somedays we can't even get out the door."

A door opened at the top of the stairs and Tom Baring ran down lightly and took the bag of groceries from his wife.

"Si and Caro are here," he said. "I had to come down and de-mine the steps before Si'd venture up. Claims he's still crippled from the time he put his foot in the GI helmet and bumped the rest of the way. Hi, Deborah, nice to see you."

He shepherded her up into the apartment and took away her wadded-up coat.

"Why don't you join Si and Caro in the living room," Ella said, "and I'll get you something to drink after I check the spaghetti sauce. Beer or coffee is the only choice, I'm afraid, although we are having some reasonably decent wine with lunch."

"Coffee, please." Beer was Deborah's idea of hemlock. "Can I help you with the lunch or anything?" she asked Ella, afraid to be left unprotected by this guardian angel in the presence of the un-inhibited Si.

"Oh, there's not much to do," Ella said comfortably. "I spent the morning tearing around trying to make this place look habitable so now I'm simply going to relax and try to get into the poised, confident mood of a successful artist."

Deborah tagged after her to the kitchen, a pleasant country-looking place with turkey-red half curtains on the windows and freshly painted walls, two, pale gray and the others stark white.

"What a beautiful kitchen," she said looking around approvingly at the interesting array of copper, wood, and plain white china pots and implements on the table and open wall shelves. The Barings' poverty was obviously of the sell-one-loaf-of-bread-and-buy-a-lily-school so wonderfully different from the kind omnipresent along the trolley car route, or even, she thought sadly, from her own so-called home.

"Isn't this linoleum on the floor the most jarring note?" Ella demanded handing her a steaming brown pottery mug. "The landlord wouldn't let us take it up and sand the floor. Obviously thought we were out of our heads anyway for wanting a gray and white kitchen. Whatsthematter with buff and cream, he kept shouting. Who needs a kitchen with white walls? Believe me, my dear lady, you'll regret it with the grease stains. We did the painting ourselves, of course, although he grudgingly paid for the paint; and were willing to do the same with the floor, but no. If we wanted to sand floors anywhere else in the house, fine—but a kitchen, my dear young people, *must* have a linoleum."

Deborah looked at the despised linoleum. Truthfully she could see it was ugly but up until this very minute she would no more have conceived of removing the linoleum than of taking up the floor. And painting a rented apartment yourself was the strangest thing she'd ever heard of.

"Well," she said, looking around the kitchen. "It must be an awful lot of work, painting it yourself."

"Oh it's fun," Ella said, uncovering a pot on the stove and peering into it. "And it's a necessity in any case if you can't abide other people's dreary tastes."

"Do you come from the Midwest?" Deborah asked thinking of Ella's reaction to the glutty cream color of the kitchen walls at home.

"South Dakota," Ella said, sprinkling what looked like dried green sprigs into the pot. "Tom is from Iowa. Though we met right here in Cambridge when I was in my last year at Wellesley and came to a dance at Harvard with some boring boy from New York who kept saying I was so wholesome. And a friend of his who was also one of those pseudo-sophisticates introduced me to Tom because we were both so wholesome and cornfed and therefore ought to get along well. And we did. Well, that's finished. Let's go sit down."

The living room faced out on a back garden. It was small, flooded by sunlight coming in through uncurtained windows, with its walls painted a pale green and one side of it was dominated by a large marble fireplace. This floor lay beautifully bare, polished and waxed, each board as wide as a plank, with every knot and grain of the wood displayed like a priceless jewel. There was a cot pushed up against one wall and covered by a faded red, cream, and seagreen Indian spread upon which Caroline Lamb was sitting, her shoes on the floor and her legs drawn up, tailor fashion, under her. In a red canvas sling chair by the window sat Si, his arms and legs shooting out in all directions but his head and face completely hidden behind a thick wad of the Sunday *Tatler*. There was one upholstered chair in the room, by the fireplace, and Ella led Deborah there. She herself sat down beside Deborah on what looked like a long, green, garden gate, mounted on dachshund short iron legs.

"You can put your coffee cup down here," she said patting the slats next to her, "it won't fall through."

"Is it a table?" Deborah ventured, puzzled.

"A Daniel, a very Daniel," Si boomed suddenly, casting his paper aside vigorously and grinning at Deborah. "I knew you were a pearl among women the first time I saw you. I've been wondering what the hell that was for years, but never dared ask."

"You know perfectly well what it is, Si," Caroline said, lifting her head from perusal of the clothing ads. "Since I made it but you wouldn't let us use it." She vouchsafed a brief, cool nod in the direction of Deborah who drew back into the sheltering arms of the easy chair while that sensitive barometer, her stomach, curdled. I've done it, she thought, and it didn't take any time at all. Her eyes roamed around the room; at the bubbly green glass bowl of pink tulips in the center of the walnut table across the room, at the straight dining chairs with rush seats, at the marble mantel above the fireplace where a copper pitcher full of yellow iris was flanked on either side by an array of glasses containing peculiar-looking tubers in water which sent out roots and sprouts of green at each end, and finally, at a painting hanging above the fireplace of what seemed to be a very ugly person of indeterminate sex. A man was it, yes, undoubtedly, but what? Of course, she thought triumphantly, it was an Eskimo. But Ella Baring was talking to her and anyway she wouldn't ask another question, not for a while yet, although she was burning with curiosity about the portrait and about the gate and why Caroline had made it and Si hated it and why the Barings had it after all.

"It's a very good piece of furniture really," Ella was saying. "It makes quite a respectable coffee table but actually we use it mostly for a sofa. We have some large, foam rubber cushions we put on it, you see, and push it up against the wall. It usually is where the cot is now, that Caro's sitting on, but we just finished the painting last week and it's all chaotic."

"I think it's a wonderful idea," Deborah said politely and was rewarded by Caroline's mollified smile.

"It's actually an old gate," Caroline said casting a scornful glance at Si who had snorted and turned himself around in the canvas and wrought-iron kangaroo pocket so that his head was hanging down and his feet were draped over the left edge of the chair. "I found it in the street one day and Si and Mike lugged it home for me and I sawed off the rounded end and painted it and put legs on it but we have this old leather couch we bought at the Salvation Army that Si's addicted to. What are you doing, Si? You'll get horribly dizzy in that ridiculous position."

"Madam," Si said with as much dignity as a red-faced man could muster, "I am no more ridiculous than the piece of furniture I'm sitting in. What the hell is one supposed to do in a butterfly net like this?" He sat upright with sudden energy and pointed his finger at Caroline. "You liked that beautiful leather couch, Caro, when we first bought it, fickle female."

"It's too slippery," Caroline said, "although I admit it's wonderful to look at."

"Nonsense," Si said decisively. "It's a good, solid, serious couch, a piece of furniture that takes pride in itself, that knows what it is and what it stands for. Not some kind of a schizoid, multi-purpose object that started out in life as a garden gate and finds itself suddenly catapulted into a living room and told to assume three or four different roles." He whirled and flailed himself around so that his head now rested on one of the chair's lower corners while his knees gripped the center top canvas and his legs and feet hung down limp and straight in back. "Why that poor specimen over there"—he waved a hand vaguely in the air—"is completely confused. When I came in here today it whimpered at me in a little warped, weather-beaten voice. 'Who am I?' it said and 'Why have they taken my lovely, rusty hinges away?' My couch on the other hand has no such problems. 'Lie down, sirrah,' it says to me in a catarrhal but dignified voice, too much snuff I expect, 'lie down, puff on your pipe and brood on your repressed past.' You know, I believe, Ella," he added meditatively, staring up at the ceiling, "that I have finally found the right way to sit in this confounded chair. Here at last I am at peace communing with those rutabagas you have lined up there on the mantelpiece. They're a stolid lot, let me tell you, from this angle. Or are they turnips?"

"Avocados," Ella said and there was a crash as the chair, unable to endure Si's expressive gestures a minute longer, tipped over and spewed him onto the floor.

Tom Baring came in just then carrying an opened can of beer which he handed to the unperturbed Si who picked himself and the chair up from the floor in one movement.

"You ought to send all the furniture in your home to an analyst, Baring," Si remarked thoughtfully after a long swig from the can. He went over to the couch and gingerly lowered himself to sit beside Caroline. "I don't mean to be stuffy but I couldn't spend one peaceful night in a house where the furniture is so insecure. That poor chair there"—he looked at it regretfully—"is so obviously a case of emotional instability, completely unable to withstand the stresses and strains of everyday living, that, out of consideration to your friends you ought not to bring it out among people. I daresay this couch is all right," he said, poking it tentatively, "though it's beginning to show signs of apprehension at having to associate with a gate and a main tops'l."

It was the crash that undid Deborah. She'd wanted to laugh before but when the chair tipped over and Si, poker-faced, continued his whimsy, a wild avalanche of laughter began to pour through her and she pealed like a bell of hilarity and could not contain herself.

When, after much gasping and rocking back and forth, she finally subsided, Si gazed at her with satisfaction.

"Appreciation! Genuine, happy, unsophisticated laughter," he said. "That's what gladdens my heart and I so seldom get it any more. Even my best beloved immediately becomes absorbed in the wedding announcements when I open my mouth."

"I heard you," Caroline said defensively, looking up from the paper, "I was just glancing at the fashion . . ."

"I know your secret vice," he said taking the paper from her and scanning it scornfully. "What amazes me about these nuptial bliss forecasts is the utter, whimpering, toadying craving to tell *all*, absolutely everything about their lives, to the public press. Here's a specimen, for instance, whose name is different and more refined than that of his poor parents domiciled with their electric blue, over-stuffed, mohair living-room set in Allston or Mattapan, and, instead of saying the hell with it and letting the reader figure it out for himself, the announcement must explain that it's okay. The groom is not really a lily-livered hypocrite, ashamed of his ancestral name and its uncouth syllables, he's a good boy, who, *legally*, mind you, went to court and changed it.

"And here's another classic. A girl who spent her junior year in Paris. Now that's like telling the world that she spent her first year in diapers. I mean, my God, how far can you carry this elevation of the mundane? What girl who goes to those Ivy League female institutions doesn't spend her junior year abroad? If she spent her junior year in a whorehouse now, *that* would be something to shout about. *There* would be a special unique distinction that the readers of the newspaper, the friends and relatives of the families would be happy to know about. *That* would be news!"

He turned a page with much noisy rattlings and flourishings and smirked at Caroline who was tapping ashes off her cigarette in a venomous piqued Bette Davis style.

"Hey!" he exclaimed. "How about this, Caro? Here's one you'll love." He began to read in a high, sentimental voice: "Mr. and Mrs. Whitney Fowler Lamb announce the engagement of their daughter Miss Caroline Layton Marchpane Lamb to Mr. Josiah Hunnicutt. Gosh! He only has two names, the poor fellow. Miss Lamb is a graduate of Miss Porter's School in Farmington and of Smith College. She was presented to society at a masked ball and is a member of the Bath, Maine Junior League, the Sisters of the Mayflower Compact, and the DAR. Miss Lamb is descended from seven founding fathers, nine Episcopal bishops, two senators and three governors and had one great-grandfather who was eaten by cannibals while pausing in the South Seas to steal heathen idols for a local museum. Mr. Hunnicutt graduated from the Phillips Brooks grammar school in Boston and is at present attending the Welding and Soldering School in Pittsburgh, Pennsylvania. He is the son of Mr. and Mrs. Lafe Hunnicutt of Harlan County, Kentucky, and is descended from Simon Girty and an unknown bound girl."

"I'm going out to look at the garden," Caroline said abruptly. She got up and left the room, tall and graceful, Deborah noted enviously, in a full-skirted, bright yellow wraparound dress of some cotton knit jersey, encircled at the waist with the same gold chain she'd worn yesterday only today there were several bronze color medallions hanging from it, so that she clanked resplendently as she marched out the door, her red hair wound in a braided bun at the nape.

"What the samhill's the matter with my Boadicea?" Si wondered plaintively.

Tom, who'd been grinning delightedly all during Si's spoof, got up and pulled the table out from the wall, marshaling chairs around it. "Well, dammit, Si, those things *are* ridiculous, but they happen to mean more to her than to us."

"Well, they shouldn't," Si said sulkily. "She's getting so damn supersensitive about this marriage kick that she's totally lost her sense of humor. I suppose a straightforward announcement is okay if every salacious gossip in town has to get vicarious kicks from knowing the name of each virgin about to be deflowered but I refuse to allow my name to appear in a welter of petty frivolous detail. The groom's best man was a pink muff trimmed with his great-grandmother's needlepoint veil type of horse shit. And who cares what my ancestors did? Unless they were robber barons and left me a pack why should I dwell on them? And don't you go and get righteous on me, Baring. I didn't notice that your wedding to the granddaughter of an old sourdough who found gold in the Yukon and robbed the Indians of acres of valuable South Dakota land hit the society pages of the *Times* or the jolly old Boston *Tatler*."

Ella, who was setting the table, smiled seraphically at him. "There *was* an announcement in the local paper," she said. "But since everybody knew us and we had a simple civil ceremony it wasn't necessary to be elaborate."

"You're not with it, Si," Tom said. "Most girls only get their names in the paper when they're born, married and die. So it's important for them. Ella can sign her name to her paintings and have her shows written up. She doesn't need that kind of statistical, ephemeral notoriety."

"If Caro weren't so damn brainwashed by her background and her parent's notion of what the proper young lady does," Si said disgustedly, "she could dispense with all that crap too." He tussled unsuccessfully with the paper again and then flung it aside. "Only one page of book reviews here. In a Sunday paper too. Where's your *Times*, Tom?"

"Mike said he'd stop for it."

"Well where is he? Not only do I have to wait for lunch because of him but I must be deprived of the book review too. He's probably just getting out of bed now. But the question is, with who? Would it be that weepy placebo of a woman he got himself stuck with for the weekend and, if he's not careful, for life, or that lusty, busty, trusty wench that he's got the eternal hots for?"

"It seems strange," Ella said musingly, "that Mike wouldn't have gotten over Sally by now. He's so sound in all other ways I somehow can't see him as one of those sick, Romantic poetry type lovers who puts only one woman on a pedestal forever."

"My dear girl," Si said clasping his hands judiciously over his stomach, "no matter how many times Wainscott puts on his blue serge vest and heads for squaresville, basically he *is* a poet and she is his inspiration, his cruelly changeable tantalizing muse-goddess. She slipped him a few drams of ambrosia when he was young and impressionable and he was hooked for life. Of course, he does try to give her up for Lent every once in a while. You have to give him that."

Deborah, who felt another belly laugh coming on, hastily volunteered to help Ella carry things in from the kitchen, although so fascinated by Si's irrepressibility that she hated to miss a word he might utter.

"I don't know," Ella said, counting stainless steel forks, "how many places to set. Sally didn't say for sure whether she could come or not. Oh, that must be Mike at the door. He'll probably know."

"The book review," Si shouted as Mike, carrying the *Times,* came in followed by Caroline, illustrating Spring in a medieval book of hours, a white and purple iris held out before her. "Where's Sally, Wainscott?"

"I don't know," Mike said indifferently, dumping the *Times* on the couch next to Si and dropping himself into the sling chair. "Was she coming here?" He noticed Deborah who was listening interestedly and smiled, saying Hello, in a warmer voice.

"These mats came out very well, Caro," Ella said. "Have you seen these, Deborah?" She displayed the heavy cotton squares inscribed like quaint, old-fashioned samplers with grotesquely shaped bright blue birds, fat pink roses, and a sprawling motto which said, 'When this you see, remember me.' "Caro made them with silkscreen."

Deborah, who hadn't the vaguest idea what silkscreen was, nevertheless was completely overwhelmed at the thought of anyone making such things by hand and looked at the red-headed girl with a new respect. But wasn't it depressing, she thought, how they were all so talented and clever and she couldn't do anything.

"Caroline met me at the steps and took me for a walk in your eighteenth-century formal garden, Ella," Mike said. "And I saw where the mint, thyme, lemon balm, water cress, and squills were planted. If she'd only had on a damask dress it would've been righteous Amy Lowell."

"I saw a sundial in a junk shop the other day," Caroline said musingly. "D'you think the landlord would mind if you put in a sundial, Ella?"

"Hey," Si protested from behind the book review, "why don't you quit taking over their garden. First you come and plant all these crazy herbs and now you want a sundial. I'll get you a window box if you insist on growing mandrake root. Or at least do something practical with this mad down-East herb-woman obsession of yours. Make love potions, for instance. Something we could charge for."

"Sally called," Tom said, appearing with a basket of Italian bread and the salad bowl. "She can't make lunch but will be at the show. So we can eat now."

"Tchah!" Si said flipping the book review pages rapidly, "I see where another eleven-year-old girl has written a sensationally sexy best-seller."

They gathered around the table and Ella ladled a rich smelling meaty sauce over the plates of spaghetti.

Deborah unfolded her napkin and looked furtively around. All the spaghetti disappearing into mouths was twirled neatly on forks with, apparently, no loose ends. She picked up her fork and, with a wild, clumsy motion, stabbed it into the mass on her plate and lifted it, flourishing her wrist in mid-air. She was rewarded with a catch of three sauce-dripping pieces of pasta, one of which got into her mouth, the second falling onto the napkin in her lap, and the third into a rusty puddle plump in the center of a bluebird on the place mat. How do they do it, she wondered, not daring to look up, because she knew they were all staring at her ineptness. Her mother never served spaghetti at home and though she'd eaten it once or twice in Italian restaurants, it'd only been a small amount, as a side dish with the main course and very easily cut with a knife and fork. She stared in dismay at the lovely place mat now irredeemably stained. Resolutely, she dug her fork back into the spaghetti and tried again. This time, although some of the intractable, squiggly things fell back onto the plate she managed to convey an adequate amount to her mouth but was horrified to see a gaggle of them, still hanging, dripping sauce, inextricably intertwined in the fork. Quickly she put the entire fork into her mouth and tried sucking them off without making any noise. It was impossible. She definitely slurped. In despair, she looked up but no one was paying any attention to her disgusting shambles. They were all talking and eating with gusto and drinking great swigs of wine. Except Mike.

He was sitting directly across the table from her, calmly cutting his spaghetti with a knife and fork. Why hadn't she noticed him before? As she stared at him he looked up and smiled at her. She smiled back gratefully, picked up her knife and hitherto recalcitrant fork and began to, at last, enjoy her lunch. What a marvelous color the wine was. She tasted it. A small sip almost strangled her with surprise at its tartness. They had wine at home of course, on holidays and Friday night suppers but it never tasted like this. She took another sip. Did she like this kind of mouth-puckering wine? Yes, she decided it was very good, making her feel lively and happy. And it went well with the spicy heartiness of the sauce.

"I think the sauce needs more pepper," Ella said. "Would you pass it please, Deborah?"

"Pepper?" Deborah looked and saw a small, pristine, china shaker, directly in front of her plate. She reached for it.

"No, that's the salt," Ella said. "The pepper's in that big wooden mill."

"Oh, sorry," Deborah mumbled passing on the peculiar, tall, wooden object. It had a handle and a large, round head but there didn't seem to be any holes in the top. What on earth did they need so much pepper for? She stared in amazement as Ella turned the handle on the weird thing and pepper came drifting out of the bottom onto her plate. Forgetting to eat, she followed the pepper mill's progress around the table. Imagine going to all that trouble to get pepper when one could simply pour it from the box one bought at the store.

Mike, she was interested to see, simply grimaced at the thing when it came to him and passed it on, unused, to Si.

"Why don't you carry your own pepper with you when you dine out, Wainscott," Si challenged. "In an eighteenth-century snuffbox. What a riot that would cause. Wainscott ostentatiously refuses the pepper mill because it is now the sine qua non among all the upstart nouveau culture vultures and produces from his pocket a small cloisonné box from which he takes a pinch of stale, canned pepper."

"Listen," Mike said, scowling, "there is absolutely no bloody difference between the pepper you get in a box from the store and the stuff you grind out of that stupid Henry Moore Stonehenge. You people are suckers for the snobbish and affected myth that everything handcrafted and European is better than the machine-made and or American stuff."

At this point a spirited argument ensued which Deborah couldn't follow too well but they all seemed to be accusing Mike of being, among other things, an inverted snob, a jingoist who accepted the machine's evils far too uncritically and a selfish verbal intellectual who refused to admit that other people could derive a valuable, creative satisfaction from making things by hand. Mike said that they all ought to come out of the eighteenth century, embrace the machine and all it had done for humanity and stop cultivating European ways and products created by toiling peasants for a few cents a day. Tom said that Mike's kind of thinking had brought about the despoiling and junked-up uglification of the American landscape.

"Ignore him," Si said, "and pass the salad. He's a stubborn hyena who should be left alone in his greasy hot plate lair to scribble poems on paper bags while eating potato chips and corned beef hash out of a can with a spoon filched from the local cafeteria. I think you started this entire jeremiad, Wainscott, in order to avoid the overwhelming question. The poop was that you were to escort the lovely Sara."

"Why don't you change your fortuneteller?" Mike said coolly. "This one's way off."

"Well you do have two to choose from don't you? Where's the other millstone?"

"I'm between two stools," Mike said. "It's not a bad way to be."

Deborah had finished her coffee and was sitting back in her chair, dreamily smoking and trying valiantly not to stare at the painting above the fireplace. But the tiny, cunning, painted, black eyes of the Eskimo seemed to mesmerize her. They were mean, pig-like, little eyes with a rapacious, greedy gleam, dropped like raisins in the upper third of a flat, sallow, pudding of a face. There was a nose, narrow and cruel with fierce, flaring nostrils and a thin, predatory mouth. The head, surmounted by a brush of stiff, black hair, seemed to have no neck and was placed like a small, pointed filbert atop a vast, shapeless garment of a blazing, scarlet color which began at the person's chin and descended to a little below the waist where the picture ended. The massive shoulders and loose, baggy sleeves of this singular cloak were banded in white, the paint laid on there in thick, extruding slabs. The figure's hands, protruding from the huge sleeves, were gnarled, tortured, and grotesque, engaged, as they seemed to be, in a convulsive attempt either to clasp each other or to squeeze the breath out of some throat, mercifully not depicted. The vicious little hammerhead and the relentless elemental mass of the body seemed to be in furious flight from the painting's brilliantly lucid bluegreen background. Deborah sat, unashamedly staring now, a bird focused in a snake's eye. The picture was evil, ugly, and hateful and yet full of a strange, fascinating, brutal power and she could not understand how such a hideous thing could have been painted by a girl who might have modeled for all the small, gold-dusted angels that peek around pink clouds in Christmas cards.

"Oh my," she said involuntarily and then noticed that they were all sitting in silence watching her. She blushed, embarrassed, and turned hastily to Ella. "It's a fascinating painting," she said.

Ella murmured something polite about there being more paintings in the studio if she was interested. There was a scraping of chairs and everybody got up and moved around. Deborah went up to the fireplace for a closer look at the painting and was joined by Mike.

"So you like it?"

"I don't know anything about painting at all. But it seems quite remarkable."

"You looked so puzzled when you were staring at it before. We're all used to it, you know. That's why it's always interesting when new people turn up. You get a fresh light on things heretofore taken for granted."

"You know an awful lot about painting, I suppose," Deborah said humbly, "because of your mother."

He grinned, a trifle cynically. "I always made every effort not to know precisely for that reason. But I suppose there are some things I imbibed unconsciously. Why? What did you want to know?"

"Well," Deborah began hesitantly, "uh . . . well, I wondered how she painted it? No, that isn't right. I mean, did she just make it up or was there a model for it? Because . . ."

"Because if there was," Mike finished readily, "you don't believe it."

"Well, not exactly," Deborah floundered. "I mean, if there was a model, it would have to be a very unusual one, because this person doesn't look well . . . I thought, at first, it was an Eskimo or a Tibetan," she finished desperately, fearful that she'd betrayed herself as a hopeless simpleton to this knowledgeable young man merely because he'd cut his spaghetti with a knife and fork and thus created what was probably only a one-sided bond of confidence.

But he didn't laugh or even look disgusted at her ignorance.

"Every artist, except those way-out abstract characters who claim allegiance to nothing but the paint, has models," he said soberly.

"It's what one does with them that counts. Eskimos don't usually turn up in life classes and Ella doesn't know any personally either."

"Oh," said Deborah rather dashed and changed the subject.

Ella's studio was a large, well-windowed, light room which smelled agreeably of paint and turpentine and was furnished only with an easel, an overstuffed, sagging easy chair, a straight kitchen one and a paint-stained old wooden table. There were canvases stacked in twos and threes against the walls and hanging higher up were more paintings.

"What's this?" Si asked walking over to the easel and peering at the half-finished still life of chartreuse and pink lemons in a basket, stained-glass wine decanter, rosy red intricately angled goblet and small round seagreen and scarlet cheese all set forth on a low, fish-shaped table. "Render unto Braque that which is Braque's. First still life I've ever seen you do, Ella."

"It's good discipline," Ella said. "Besides I haven't seen anyone I wanted to paint lately. Until yesterday, that is," she added in a reflective muted voice.

"Will you walk into my parlor said the spider etcetera," Si said. "She painted my portrait once," he added plaintively to Deborah. "It came on like the real Dorian Gray. Where is it, anyway?"

Ella appeared not to have heard him. She was standing by the windows, her back to the room.

"It's at the show," Tom said quickly. "One of the chosen eight."

"I'd better get dressed," Ella said turning around. "Deborah, you don't need me, do you? Just look at anything you want."

"And I have to put oil in the car," Tom said. "I'll be right back."

Deborah was examining the exciting daubs, splashes, and mixtures of color on what she supposed was the painter's palette which lay on the table by the easel when she heard Mike say in a quiet voice:

"You go too far, man. The joke isn't worth it."

"The hell with it," Si said irritably. "I wasted valuable time, posing for the damned thing with pins and needles in my limbs, didn't I? Haven't I the right to say what I think it looks like?"

"Oh don't be so vain," Caroline said impatiently.

"What do you mean?" Si demanded. "I don't ask that it make me look like Adonis. I just want it to resemble a reasonable facsimile of a human being. What's wrong with that? If it were just her invariable style I wouldn't mind but she's not even consistent, as witness the bewildering variety of approaches to the same model. Now where's the companion piece to that monstrosity in the dining room? I want to show Deborah the other side of the coin."

"I think it's at the gallery," Caroline said. "Please don't talk so loud, Si."

Deborah had looked up when her name was mentioned but they were all grouped together at the other end of the room, looking angry and going on with their argument so she stayed where she was, studying the gratey surface on some of the lemons in the still life, which looked as though sand had been mixed in with the paint. It was strange to hear them quarreling. Their friendship seemed so enviably easy and seasoned and now, here was Si criticizing Ella who was such a kind, sweet girl. One could not take sides on such an issue because of not knowing enough and anyway it would be hard to choose. She liked them all. None of them had made her feel out of it. It was really one of the loveliest days she'd ever spent. A little nerve-wracking, not knowing quite the right things to say and do, but still so exciting.

"I still maintain," Si said belligerently, "that if she hadn't been poisoned with the typical jealousy of new-wedded wives toward their husband's old friends that painting of me would never have turned out like that."

"I think it's a very good portrait of you, actually," Caroline said.

"Oh, you would," Si retorted. "Viper in my bosom."

"It is," Mike affirmed. "Damn good. Not only as a painting but as you."

"My soul looks out of my eyes, eh?" Si sneered. "Well, it happens to be my soul and, as such, I know more about it than any other damn person and I say the hell with it. It isn't me."

Deborah began to move around her corner of the room looking at the paintings on the walls. There was one, of a woman, that she liked very much. The face seemed vaguely familiar. She stood back and looked it over again. Yes, it was Caroline, with her autumn-colored hair hanging down, almost to her waist, wearing a Lincoln-green tunic and holding a large, shaggy-headed, yellow chrysanthe-mum in one long, elegant hand. She'd not recognized it at first not only because of the absence of harlequin glasses but also because, in place of the human Caroline's expression of bland confidence, the painted face had shy, rather timid eyes and a curious, tucked-in, restrained smile.

"I don't know why the hell you have to get all personal and out-raged," Mike was saying. "You're a subject, just as a landscape or a bowl of flowers is. Just a starting point from which the artist takes off. That's all, see. It's the creation that's important, not the subject. So don't sit for any more portraits if you're so stinking sensitive. Just go to Bachrach's and have yourself photographed and then, if you don't like it, you can tear up the proofs."

"Now we have it," Si said sitting down suddenly on the floor. "The artist is sacred, eh, untouchable in his holy grove? He can take his poor, innocent, foolish friends and mock and deride them for all to see; twist their faces into repulsive masks, render their skins as the color of a hippopotamus soaked four days in the greygreen, greasy Limpopo River and no one is supposed to say a mumbling word, least of all the poor slob who merely loaned his body for this auto-da-fé. He ought to stand with a fixed, sickly smile, nod gravely and say, yes, yes, how lucky I am, coming this close, little wormlike me, to the creative process. What the hell do you take me for? A medieval flagellant? Come to think of it, I'd rather do it that way. I'll stand in front of that so-called portrait of me in the gallery this afternoon, strip off my clothes so, and scourge myself with a cat-o'-nine-tails and shout: Despise me good people it's all for *art!*"

"Put your shirt back on, you idiot," Caroline said. "Honestly, Si, you're being absurd. I think the painting Ella did of me is wonderful. There's nothing repulsive about it."

"And if there were," Si said, craning his neck and fixing her with a piercing eye, "how would you know? The job she did on you is a very subtle one. No, the great days of portraiture are over. The old masters, you notice, turned out pretty sensational portraits even though they were hampered by their bourgeois patrons who demanded, at least, a reasonable likeness."

"I've heard you say you don't like non-objective art either," Mike said mildly. "And surely that doesn't hurt anyone's feelings."

"I've no objection to figure painting," Si said jackknifing up from the floor. "Only let them get models they'll never see again. Nowadays, one's ego is held together so precariously by Scotch tape and rubber bands that it just can't stand up to having poison-tipped paintbrushes poked at it."

"Oh, for God's sake!" Mike exclaimed. "You're being deliberately obtuse. Ella didn't just take you whole and put you exactly on her canvas. She also had some personal statement to make."

"Yeah," Si said cynically. "Well, that'll be cold comfort when the reviewer from the *Art Whine* says, Mrs. Baring shows great promise and one of the best paintings is that of a weak-chinned, clothespin-nosed spinster, clad in an incongruous green plaid shirt which is reminiscent of El Greco's St. Jerome Pulling Taffy. And when I'm not around everybody's rolling on the floor in paroxysms of laughter at the thought of old Si who really does look just like a horsefaced old maid, come to think of it, wasn't it uncanny of you to catch it, Ella?"

"Why, Si," Caroline said, truly shocked, "what a horrible way to talk about your friends. You know you don't believe that."

"Ah friendship," Si said gloomily. "When it comes right down to it we're all glad to see our friends discomfited. Makes us feel better because it didn't happen to us."

"When it comes right down to it," Mike said, "you might not be a portrait painter but to be completely honest . . ."

"By all means, be honest," Si interrupted.

"Now don't you two start, please," Caroline said worriedly. She came over to Deborah. "You must be very bored listening to all this."

"Of course not," Si whooped. "She's fascinated. What could be more fun than listening to the sounds of backbite and gossip when you yourself couldn't possibly be involved."

"I've been looking at the pictures," Deborah said politely.

"You didn't finish, Wainscott," Si said.

"Now don't," Caroline pleaded. "Let's not talk about it any more."

"I insist on hearing what this representative of man's ingratitude has to say."

"You've just been accusing Ella of the sort of thing you do so well. Finding weaknesses and foibles in those near and dear and holding them up to ridicule."

"Character analysis!" Si shouted, "elsewhere known as character assassination. Can we never be free of this Freudian devil? Come, Wainscott, you violate the rules of the game."

"Which are?"

"You know damn well what they are. You may disembowel your friends verbally but only when they're not around. And, accept with as much equanimity as you can, the indubitable fact that they do the same to you."

"That's a lovely little slimy rock you live under."

"I am merely more realistic than you are, that's all."

"Ella never slanders you or anyone," Caroline said, "and you know it."

"Oh, I admit that," Si said scornfully, "but she doesn't have to say anything. It all goes into her painting."

"One would think you didn't like her," Mike said smiling ironically at Deborah.

"I abase myself before her. She's a saint. But why did she have to do that to me? It rankles, man, it rankles."

"Furthermore," Mike said, "you've just broken bread with her in her home."

"I'm a boor," Si said remorsefully. "I won't say another word till we get outside." He came to Caroline and kissed her. " 'Nymph in thy orisons be all my sins remembered.'" He turned to Deborah and stared at her solemnly, a hand shading his eyes. "You don't want to get to a nunnery, do you?" he enquired and went right on not waiting for an answer, "I thought not. Well, stop looking so innocent."

"She's just baffled," Mike said. "And who wouldn't be after watching one of your performances."

"It was my Christian duty to warn her," Si said righteously, patting Deborah on the head. "My child, Ella is going to ask you to sit for one of her voodoo images. Be prepared."

"Me?" Deborah said, startled. "Oh, d'you really think so?"

"I'm sorry I took so long," Ella said, coming in hurriedly. "I had to take a few last stitches on this garment I made last night. I can't make any sudden movements though or it might fall apart."

"You look great," Si said obviously trying to make amends. "Just like the girl in green in *Rite of Spring* about to dance herself sacrificially to death."

"Oh come now," Mike said. "Art openings may be depressing but they haven't turned into bloody orgies yet. I think you look like a young willow tree, Ella."

"Thank you, gentlemen," Ella said gravely. "The only trouble is I couldn't find a decent pair of shoes. These towering heels will probably cripple me." She gazed at Deborah's shoes. "I wish I had a pair like those. They're charming and they look awfully comfortable. Did you get them in Boston?"

"In the Buck's on Summer Street," Deborah said, pleased. "I don't like the goldtype bows though, but they don't seem to come off."

"Let me see," Caroline bent down and poked the bows. "They'd look madly exotic if they were plain. Think of them coming from one of those chain stores."

"No," Ella circled around Deborah, studying the shoes. "I think you're wrong, Caro. The bows are an inspired idea. You see, they draw attention to the sickle shape of the toes. I must have some. Would you mind, Deborah? I'll get another color if they have them."

"Thank God, man," Si said to Tom Baring who came in looking

253

hot, harassed and black-handed. "They were talking about little gold bows on their little gold bound feet."

"I'll just wash up and we can go," Tom said. He added worriedly, "I'm afraid there won't be quite enough room for all of us in the car, because Dr. Asch phoned this morning and said there'd be room to show two more paintings which we have to put in the back seat. I think, if either Si or Mike went by subway we could get everyone else in. I thought Sally would be coming with her car . . ."

"Deborah," Mike said unexpectedly, "if you'll keep me company I'll volunteer."

Deborah agreed politely, though she regretted having to leave the safety of a group of people, and especially the loss of Ella Baring's sheltering kindness. Still it was only reasonable that he ask her to go with him because the others were all paired off. Now, if Sally had come he'd've paid no attention to her but then if Sally had come there'd be no problem because she'd have her car. What in the world will I say to him, she wondered, as they all trooped downstairs? Perhaps he'd look at her book and they'd talk about Katherine Mansfield.

She stood on the porch next to Ella Baring who was waiting for Tom.

"If you ever have any time, Deborah," Ella said in a soft, hesitant voice, "could you sit for me? I'd like very much to paint you. In that dress I think. The color's so exciting."

"Well," Deborah began, thinking of Si's warnings, "I'd like to but I . . . don't have too much time now." Would she find something there that I don't know about, she wondered, or something that I do know about but try not to show, like stupidity, fear, unhappiness. And then, just when I'm getting to know her and enjoying them all, most interesting people I've ever met really, and such a pleasant life, so different from mine, would I be as affected by whatever Ella produced as Si seemed to be, so that I couldn't see them again.

"I understand," Ella said pleasantly, but did she detect a note of coolness there? "It wouldn't really take up too much time and you could come over whenever you're free. But if you can't, well . . ."

Don't be such a timid idiot, Deborah told herself. She'd probably never see them again after today. Obviously Gordie wasn't going to be her entree. And why pay attention to Si's mouthings? He apparently liked to exaggerate.

"No, I'd love to really," she said hastily. "I could come some afternoon or evening, depending on my work schedule. I won't know till next week though."

"I just remembered," Ella said disappointedly. "I shouldn't have asked you now anyhow. Because we'll be going away for the summer about the middle of June. Perhaps we can get together in the fall."

Fall, Deborah thought, and the vista of the dull hot summer stretched bleak and interminable like a drought-stricken prairie before her. Hard work. A miserable job. Trying to save her money. How nice it would be to plan blithely to be away all summer. By September she'll have forgotten all about me. When you have a happy, full life there's no time to remember unimportant people.

"You know," Ella said, "I could do some sketches of you before we go and perhaps work from them this summer. And finish it up later on when you have time to sit. Why don't you call me this week and if you can come a few afternoons we can camp out in the garden and you can pose there and we'll have afternoon iced mint tea or something ladylike of that sort."

"I will," Deborah said fervently. Afternoon tea and sketching in a Cambridge garden full of herbs and irises. Her spirits soared.

"Here, I'll carry your rucksack." Mike appeared and took her coat. "We're hiking to Harvard Square, footsoldiers all." He stooped to pick up the book which had fallen from the pocket and glanced at the title. "Aha," he said with a wry smile, "Katherine Mansfield, is it? I haven't read her in years. Are you good at birdwatching? We can do some as we march."

"Goodbye," Ella said, waving.

Even when they were almost to the corner of Lemon Street Deborah could hear Si's loud laughter. She wondered if he was laughing at her.

Ten

The silence between them was as constrained and painful as Deborah had feared. Mike walked lithely beside her, swinging her raincoat easily in one hand and squinting into the sun. The unbearably bright new green of the trees under which they walked hurt her eyes as much as the sun flaming on her head. The purple wool dress was a sweaty prison and she was getting a headache. Why didn't he speak, Deborah wondered resentfully. Had he talked himself dry at the Barings'? She cast around for something, anything to say, to relieve the dull trudging of the walk, the pitiless glare of the sun, the fear of being alone with a strange man and proving herself to be a terrible dud and bore. They passed other young girls, hanging on their young men's arms, out for a Sunday walk, swinging pastel, frothy skirts and wearing little, flowered hats. Girls like that always know what to say, Deborah thought. Bubbling over with bright chatter and laughter that drifted back over their shoulders. It was the laughing that was the worst Deborah thought unhappily, thinking of Miss Brill, in the Mansfield story. It was the symbol of being together, sharing, knowing how to make a walk with a young man a pleasant occasion. Being alone made you so vulnerable to the laughter, because they might be laughing at you, alone, looking funny. Now, she was not alone. She was like all these other girls, out with a man on a Sunday, but feeling just as excluded as if she were by herself. What would happen when they, dumb as stones, glum as winter, in the midst of all the bright Mayday people, reached the subway? Was she expected to assume that he would pay her fare? Stand aside at the turnstile with that protected, treasured, dainty air most girls put on for such occasions? How did one know what to do? Should she suddenly say now in the midst of this dreadful kind of forced march silence, brusquely, that she would pay her own fare. And then, he'd look surprised because he'd never doubted for a minute that she would. But, on the other hand, he'd asked her to come with him, so he should pay, because otherwise she could have ridden in the car with the others. Wistfully, she thought of them now, driving along across the river laughing at some of Si's jokes, with the windows rolled down and green breezes flowing coolly over them.

I ought to ask Mike questions about himself, she thought. That's what girls are supposed to do. They like to talk about themselves, men that is, it said in the books. But questions were personal, rather offensive, when you came right down to it. Too, you might ask the wrong thing. Her headache was getting worse. It would ruin her afternoon if she didn't stop it soon. Only light hammertaps now, but just wait. There was some aspirin in her purse. I'm sorry, she practiced saying in her mind, but I must get a glass of water. I have a headache. They were almost to Harvard Square and surely there must be a drugstore there.

"Do you like going to Law School?" she ventured as they passed by the Yard. Now why had she said that? After all that mind searching to come up with such an inane question.

"What?" Mike stopped walking and looked down at her. "Law School. I thought we were going to talk about Katherine Mansfield."

"I thought so too."

"Yes," he said glumly, "I'm a splendid walking companion, aren't I? I should have let you go in the car. This damn sun is much hotter than I had thought. I'm sorry, Deborah. I meant to be courteous and gallant and burble blithely all the way to Harvard Square and impress the hell out of you. Only when we got to the corner and the sun hit me in the eyes and I realized I didn't bring my sunglasses. . . . Listen, how about a drink? I'm dry and I have a headache and I've got to sit down someplace cool. Perhaps then we can talk about books, facing each other like human beings, and not yoked like oxen in the dust of a tawdry day."

"I'd like to, very much," Deborah said, relieved. "I have a headache too."

"I knew it," he said taking her arm as they crossed the street. "And you have trouble starting conversations too, don't you?"

"Yes," Deborah admitted. "But you don't, do you?"

"Sure, I do," he said leading her into a cool, cocktail lounge sort of place that seemed to be prevailingly chrome and forest green. "Lousy décor," he said, "but handy. I ought to be over it by now. When I was your age, it was worse. I don't know. I got sunk into a morose fog suddenly and felt like an idiot for asking you to come with me. What would you like?" They had wriggled into a green leather banquette and a waitress in dubonnet uniform hovered by the table.

"Whatever you're having."

"That's a nice girl. Well, I'm of two minds. Tom Collins' are green and wet but gin doesn't make me too happy after awhile and who knows what'll be in that arty punch. Whiskey sours, how about that?"

"I've never had any," Deborah confessed.

The waitress looked at her suspiciously, although why, Deborah couldn't imagine. Perhaps she shouldn't've admitted her ignorance. It might have embarrassed Mike. He ordered two whiskey sours and the waitress left a bowl of Spanish peanuts on the table and went away.

"I thought for a second she was going to refuse to serve you," he said, taking a handful of peanuts. "You do look awfully damn young."

"But I'm nineteen," Deborah said indignantly.

"Still a minor," he said smiling. He had wonderful, regular, large white teeth and when he smiled warmly, his rather dour, thin, brown face changed and lightened.

"Oh I forgot about that. I don't usually drink anywhere but at sessions where no one seems to care."

"They don't care around here either," he said. "But Sunday is apt to be a petulant, touchy day. It's been a long time since I've been with a girl under twenty-one."

The waitress brought tall glasses of ice water and the drinks and Deborah passed out aspirin.

"God, what a thirst I had," Mike said after downing his entire glass of water. "Too much wine and argument at lunch."

"This is delicious. Tastes hardly like whisky at all."

"They're lethal," Mike said. "You'll be crocked in an hour."

"Such a lovely froth on top." Deborah regarded her glass fondly. Her headache was in full retreat. She felt wonderful. It was dark, cool and quiet in the cocktail lounge. Venetian blinds were drawn across the wide windows and the voices of the few, scattered customers were muted. "'And all the air a solemn stillness holds,'" she said, and didn't even feel self-conscious.

"Save where the something wheels its droning flight, perhaps," Mike essayed.

Deborah shook her head, "I don't know any more."

"Nor I." He offered her a cigarette and leaned back against the cushioned green leather and stared around. "I always thought this place was appalling but this afternoon it's a miraculous oasis in a sanctimonious, idiotic desert. Shall we have another? I see you're low."

"Oh should we? It's three-thirty and it will take us quite awhile to get there, won't it?"

"Plenty of time," Mike said. He waved to the waitress. "We'll take a cab. This is no day to be dogfacing around on the subway."

Deborah had never heard of such extravagance. A cab from Cambridge to the Back Bay. "Won't that be terribly expensive?"

"I'm determined to throw away my last GI Bill check," Mike said, "and you're not going to stop me. Of course, if we drink any more of these little fruit salads we might not get to the show and I couldn't care less. But you want to go, don't you?"

"Why, yes," Deborah said carefully sipping on her second whisky sour. "I've never been to one before. Besides, doesn't Ella expect us?" Imagine wanting to miss as exciting an event as the first showing of an artist's work to the public.

"Oh, I'll get you there, never fear," he said, suddenly moody. "It'll be awful, you'll see. But since this is your first . . ."

"I thought you liked Mrs. . . . uh . . . I mean . . . Ella's paintings?"

"Oh, I do, I do, but the other cats exhibiting are sure to be abstract types. Still, I guess a person has to rally round. But we don't need to get there on the dot of four. Late entrances are more fashionable, they tell me."

"You know," Deborah said, beginning to feel quite easy-tongued, "I want to see that painting of Si particularly."

"I shouldn't wonder," he said, twisting his lips wryly. "It's a good picture of him, really, whether he likes it or not."

"Was he serious?"

"Sure. I could have kicked him. What a hell of a note. Of course Ella knows how he feels about that picture, has ever since she painted it, but while it drags her, she thinks he's terrific."

"Doesn't he like her? I guess I shouldn't ask though."

"Hell, no, that's all right. I was watching you during that fulmination. You have a very expressive face, by the way, and you looked then, like an Alice who'd strayed into this wonderland where all those crazy creatures were being curiouser and curiouser."

Deborah laughed. "In a way."

"I thought so. Well, sure, he likes her. Except for those damn paintings. Anyone else but Si would have the decency to shut up about it. But he can never let well enough alone. It's the comedian in him, I guess. He's a talker and doesn't dig that some things just can't or shouldn't be talked about. How's your headache?"

"Gone. I feel much better."

"Things are looking up then. You know, while we were walking along there, I'd look at you occasionally, about to open my mouth and croak some dismal message and you looked so depressed and serious, toiling along. And I thought, my God, she looks as though she were being dragged through the streets as a captive in a victory procession or something. Naturally, I thought, she's with the charming, witty Mike Wainscott, why wouldn't she look like that. Then, I decided, I'd better say something, anything at all, or serious lady reformers, in which Cambridge abounds, will begin to think I'm abusing her, or that I purchased her in the Fiji Islands for a few glass beads and she's here under duress and I'll be in jail, next thing you know. But then, I'd look at some of the happy laughing cretins in the passing springtime, courting parade and decided I'd rather have us looking as doleful as we did, than like that. But please, please, accept my apologies."

"Why, you're as funny as Si," Deborah said, after laughing happily for quite awhile.

"Don't let him hear you say that. He guards his status jealously."

"You don't need to apologize," Deborah said, chewing on her orange slice. "I was pretty boring. Don't you like those kind of girls, that kind of toss their heads and say 'Coo,' and are never at a loss for words? I thought all men did."

"Hey, let's have another drink," Mike said. "Well, they don't. But why did you think so?"

"I don't know," Deborah said, suddenly forgetting why. "Well," she rallied. "They looked like girls I went to high school with. They were pretty, peppy, and popular. They were cheerleaders and always went out with football players."

Mike put his head very close to hers. "Deborah, I hate to tell you but you may as well find out now as later. You're not ever going to be the kind of girl football players yearn for. Even on short acquaintance I can testify to that. Closed forever to you are the delights of tossing your ringlets and earrings and laughing in that ear-splitting screech so indicative of the gaiety of youth and the way of a man to a maid. You're great the way you are."

Deborah moved her head a bit so that their faces weren't so close. "I used to care a lot about being like that in high school. I don't so much any more."

"We all must grow up," Mike said, making a long, pompous face, "and stop searching after strange gods. Of course, I never did. I'm still trying to wedge myself into the sheepfold. But I think I'm about to give up, or be given up, to be more accurate."

"I don't know what you're talking about," Deborah said, feeling so completely bemused and en rapport with the world that nothing she said could be wrong.

"Never mind," Mike said. "When I get to know you better, I'll explain it all. How about that?"

"All right." And suddenly, in the midst of her pleasure at his admiration she thought uneasily of the superb Sally Brimmer. And of Gordie. Quickly she said, "Why did Si call that painting in the Barings' dining room a monstrosity?"

"You mean the Eskimo?"

"You're laughing at me," Deborah said reproachfully. "You were, even then."

"No, no, I assure you. Actually, Si and I, though not in Ella's presence, call that painting 'Black Mrs. Behemoth.'"

"Why that just fits it," Deborah said. "How perfect. Did you make it up?"

"No, it's a poem of Edith Sitwell's." He ran his fingers through his hair. "Well, it's a long story and I don't suppose I ought to tell you but I'll rationalize my lack of scruples by saying that that painting is the one flimsy premise upon which Si bases all his cracked theories about Ella's personal attitudes toward people affecting her work. If it were true, it would be a damn good argument for pure abstraction in art, but it isn't true." He waved to the alert waitress.

"It's almost four o'clock," Deborah said. "We'll be awfully late, won't we?"

"Oh, they'll expect that," he said airily, "and it's their own damn fault for letting us slog around on the subway."

He doesn't really want to go see the paintings, Deborah thought, and hazily wondered why. But she settled back against the seat and tried to drink slowly. A person wouldn't be able to look at pictures if this kept up.

"Well, the original model for Mrs. Behemoth was a girl named . . ."

"Girl!" Deborah was horrified. "Oh, you're joking."

"Jane Simms," Mike continued imperturbably, "Ella's roommate at Wellesley for years, old friend, confidante, whathaveyou. I've never met her but Si describes her as a damn attractive female."

"But how could such a distortion . . ."

"It's simple. Ella was engaged to be married to an ex-Navy pilot at that time going to Amherst. Very serious, the whole thing. They were to be married when she graduated. In the interim they saw each other every weekend and what could be more natural than to double date on occasion with her roommate and his buddy. And then, about five or six months before the wedding, he said it wasn't fun any more. Ella was naturally shattered because she cared a lot for this flexible specimen and there didn't seem to be a reason in the world for the breakup.

"Of course, it turned out to be a blessing in disguise, because right after that, she met Tom and as you can see, they're great for each other. That's how Si got to know Jane Simms. And he lost his head about her but kept finding her a mystery. Here was this cheerful, nice-looking, Southern sexpot who didn't seem to have a steady man, who liked bed a hell of a lot and yet sometimes he could make it with her and sometimes he couldn't. The whole thing was explained when the girls graduated and Jane Simms promptly married Ella's ex-fiancée. Can you imagine being hypocritical enough to sit around for all that long a time and listen to one's jilted roommate's confidences, condoling with her and making pseudo-sympathetic murmurs, when all the time you know that you're the reason for her being thrown over? And not saying a goddamn word!"

"I think it would be impossible. Or at least I couldn't do it."

"If you were a greedy, amoral, disloyal character you might do it without turning a hair. And then you'd be Mrs. Behemoth who is not finally the portrait of a person but the artist's conception of evil; a symbolic essence of treachery, cruelty, the seven deadly sins, you know."

"Yes, but if you start out to paint a real person," Deborah said haltingly, thinking of the little bullet head with its rapacious features, "and then turn them into a symbol then isn't Si right? Isn't that kind of a deliberate, vicious caricaturing? A way to get even?"

Mike nodded, his eyes glinting. "The head doctors would call it sublimation," he said mockingly. "But what's wrong with that? Can't a picture be painted with passion whether it be love or hate? Can't one transcend reality and generalize from the particular. That's what makes art, in fact."

"I guess so," Deborah said, feeling that somehow her wits were wandering. "But then why didn't Ella do a portrait of the man who jilted her? I mean it was just as much his doing, wasn't it?"

"Well, for one thing, he didn't pretend to be an old bosom buddy and listen to her sob her secret heart out. And anyway," he added, scratching his head thoughtfully, "she couldn't paint him for practical reasons. He wasn't there to sit for her. But she did have some sketches she'd done of Jane Simms during a ski weekend in New Hampshire with Tom and Si, the deceptively friendly winter before. So when she heard the shocking news after graduation, she just went home and painted from the sketches."

"Then the ski parka is what gives it that Eskimo flavor," Deborah said, forgetting to drink, she was so interested. "I'm glad because I was beginning to think my eyes were crossed."

"It was a takeoff point, yes. You look so worried," he added moving close to her again. "Why? Did Ella ask you to sit for her?" And as she nodded he laughed heartily. "Well, you're a hell of a person to tell that story to. But don't worry, baby. Ella's not going to turn you into a species of primitive Gorgon."

"How do I know?" Deborah said shakily because his carven brown face was so very close. He kissed her. It was a mere brush of a kiss. His lips were very soft. "Oh," she said, "oh!"

"Because you're not," he said touching her face very gently with his fingertips.

"I think we'd better go." Deborah slithered toward the end of the banquette. "It's getting later and later."

"It's very nice here," Mike said contemplatively. "Don't you think so? No maddening crowd yammering about intensities, nasally. Why don't you want to stay, Deborah? I promise not to kiss you again. It seems to have disturbed you."

"I don't know what you mean," Deborah said, patting distractedly at her hair.

"Oh, don't you. You got all flustered when I kissed you. Were you being loyal to Gordie?"

"I don't think he cares enough about me to be jealous."

"I'm glad you have such a clear view of our hero."

"You don't even like him," Deborah said reproachfully. "And he admires you so much."

"Now don't cut me like that," Mike protested. "I like him well enough. But I overheard some of the things he said to you yesterday at my place. Don't let him patronize you, baby. He's a pretty shallow character."

"I know," Deborah said unhappily feeling very treacherous.

"Then what do you hang around with him for? Aren't there any other beaus?"

Deborah shook her head, her lips pressed tight.

"Well then," Mike said reasonably, "why waste this day milling around with a lot of other people in a stuffy gallery. We can sit here and drink the remainder of the afternoon and get to know each other some, and then, when evening quickens in the street as the arbiter once said, go off and be a happy Sunday boy and girl having dinner and holding hands in the movies."

It all sounded very nice, Deborah thought, not minding at all that he was putting his arm around her shoulders, but . . .

"I can't go out tonight," she said stiffly, "and . . ."

"And?"

"You're interested in someone else," she burst out.

"So," he said gravely, "my excellent friends have been talking again?"

"Oh no," Deborah said quickly, "it's just that I think you don't want to go to the gallery because she'll be there."

He waved to the waitress and when she came, asked quietly for the check. There was a silence and Deborah sat with her head drooping.

"I'm sorry," she said as they stood in the street waiting for a cab. "It was terrible of me to say such a personal thing. I think I'm . . . I've had too much to drink, but that's no excuse."

A cab ground to a stop before them and Mike helped her in, gave the driver the address and they were swinging round in a wide arc and away and off with blowaway hurt feelings, sunstruck breezes pouring in the open side windows.

Mike folded his arms and sat back against the seat staring straight ahead.

"I really am very sorry," Deborah repeated, her throat constricted with embarrassment.

Mike turned his head and looked at her. "What for? It was the truth. I don't want to see Sally. But that doesn't mean my invitation to you was a falsehood. Nor my kiss. You shouldn't be such a stiffneck, Deborah. My friendship with Sally is old and in a stinking state of defunctness." He grinned at her rather sourly. "Which explains why I'm such an old rascal as to go around kissing other girls who attract me. That's pretty funny when you think of it. All my friends know I've been chasing Sally for years and getting the shortest damn shrift but it takes a super-innocent like you to come along and get huffy about being kissed because of a supposed other grand passion."

"She's very beautiful," Deborah said. "She drove me home yesterday and was so nice. All the way out to Winthrop, and she didn't even have to go there."

264

"Ah, you've fallen under her spell. My dear little girl, you wouldn't be stealing Sally's man if you went out with me. She's got hundreds, millions, and I'm not one of them."

Deborah said nothing. She was looking out of the window at the shining, bright river and thinking of the kiss. It had been the kiss of a man who hoped to create fire out of the friction of two wet, wooden sticks and had not succeeded. She looked at him out of the corner of her eye. Really it would be nice to go out with him. He was quite handsome, she thought, admiring his pleasant, ascetic, almost monk-like face, the thick black eyebrows bent now in a dark frown over brooding eyes, the straight, narrow-nostriled nose. She liked other things about him; a kind of look of tenderness in the deep brown eyes, a great courtesy, so unlike Gordie who always seemed to be irritated with her and expected her to get herself in and out of conveyances while he stood by as if he wasn't with her. And, as for any of those other manifestations of good manners that to Mike seemed second nature, door openings, chair pullings, listening to what one had to say, politely, why one sometimes wondered what had become of all those special advantages Gordie prated about because he often acted as if he'd been reared in the most indifferent home and was socially shoeless. It would be so enriching going out with someone like Mike. So very sophisticated. She realized suddenly that only yesterday she'd thought Gordie was the epitome of worldly knowledgeability. But next to Mike he was just a little boor.

I should have said yes, she thought, Mike's so nice. She considered all the buts. Wanting to go to the gallery because she'd never been and because Ella Baring expected her. And afterwards, if she didn't go home, there would be some terrible scene. Going out afternoon and evening, no, it was impossible. She quailed inwardly at the thought of her father's wrath. It wasn't worth the trouble just to go out with Mike who kissed her with his mind someplace else. That would be a role for Jean Donnelly, she thought rebelliously, not me. And yet, how did one get to be the kind of girl Sally was, somebody's great love? She wondered if it would ever happen when she got older. Gordie only pursued her because he couldn't bear the idea of there being a girl with the gall to refuse him. And Mike was trying to convince himself that she might be an antidote to Sally, which was ridiculous. But how was it that some girls were completely beloved, treated tenderly, adored, showered with gifts, thought of constantly, all those things, and others, never, others left like Miss Brill, lonely and withered on a park bench with merely an ancient, stringy, furpiece for company. Or, perhaps, worse than Miss Brill, like her mother. At least a furpiece didn't insult you, Deborah reflected, which was probably why so many women never married and had cats.

"How about taking a raincheck on that dinner and movie," Mike said casually. "Later, when Gordie leaves town."

Deborah assented shyly and let him take her hand.

"You know," he went on musingly, "I guess I've forgotten what it's like to be your age. With so many confusing choices and so many hidebound certainties. When you get to be the venerable age of twenty-seven you learn to go along for the ride sometimes. Love isn't really personal or uniquely fashioned to fit just one. It's very adjustable."

"But you don't believe that."

"Sure, I believe it," he said rather irritably. "The trouble is doing something about it. What I mean is, you'll get over Gordie. You already have, only you won't admit it. You'll grieve a while after he leaves and then there'll be someone else. You're still only nineteen and a wonderful world of possibilities is spread before you."

"I don't think it's so wonderful," Deborah said glumly. "Everyone thinks being young is the best time, but I haven't noticed."

"You've been reading too much Katherine Mansfield," he said, picking up her book and flipping through it. "What were you reading?"

"Uh . . . well, the last one was 'Miss Brill.'"

"Now, what was that one . . . oh yes. My God, that's a terrible story."

"I thought it was very good," Deborah said, her voice quavering a little.

"Well, it isn't," he said bluntly. "I hate stuff like that, delicately wrought tearjerkers about loneliness. It's so obvious." He looked out of the window. There was a haze of golden sun on the river. They were on the Boston side now. "Everybody's lonely," he said in a low voice. "Didn't you know that? It's inescapable. Not merely the clichés of solitary birth and death but the interminable stretches of loneliness in between, on park benches like your friend, Miss Brill, or walking solitary in the alleys while the lousy autumn leaves are drifting, like Rilke."

"'Autumn Day,'" Deborah said absently, "'Herbsttag.'"

"So you know that? By heart and in the original language too, no doubt. Come on, say it for me. In English it verges on the sentimental, but it's quite fine in German. An argument against translation, I suppose."

"I'm sure you can say it much better than I can," Deborah demurred. "Since you were raised in Europe."

He laughed shortly. "Baby, if you knew the years of mockery I've endured because people considered I was an affected ass for pronouncing foreign names and words correctly, you'd understand why I've set up a block against any language but English. That doesn't prevent me from liking to hear the poets' original tongue from a voice other than mine."

"Well, I really only know the second part," Deborah said, her eyes averted, her voice a low mumble:

"'*Wer jetzt kein haus hat, baut sich keines mehr*
Wer jetzt allein ist wird es lange bleiben
Will wachen, lesen, lange briefe schreiben
und wird in den Alleen hin und her
unruhig wandern, wenn die Blatter treiben.'"

"Yes," he said glumly, "that's it. But it's just words. You mustn't believe it even though it sounds good." And he put his arm around her and kissed her again. It was a harder kiss this time and, rather timidly, she responded. But she knew that it did not truly bridge the gap for either of them or deny what the poem said.

After awhile he said, "You're quite a girl for a young one, Deborah. I wish I'd met you any other weekend but this one. How did you run across Rilke?"

"In the library. Just browsing."

"You speak German well. Or quote it, anyhow. Did you study it?"

"I don't really know it at all. Just the poems because the Rilke I read had German on one page and the English translation on the other."

"Did that teach you how to pronounce it too?"

"No," Deborah said. She took her hand out of his. In the end, it always had to be said. She didn't know why you had to be defiant about telling people or why you had to tell them. But you did. Somewhere back when she was a child she'd been told something, she couldn't remember what exactly and it had grown to be part of her. Grown in the bone, flowing through her blood, embedded in the viscera and because of it there was always this dilemma when you met a new person. But what was it in her childhood, going to school? Had they said, well, the other children might call you names

267

and don't pay any attention. Was that it? Perhaps. She had a sudden memory of herself, quite small, seven or so, walking the long way to and from school, watching for children who were going to call her names, and for a long time no one had, until one afternoon, she'd heard some of them, across the street, shouting some shocking, abrasive sounds, but she had never really known whether they were yelling at her or someone else. "My father speaks Yiddish sometimes," she said. "It's kind of like German."

"It's a pretty interesting language itself, isn't it? I had a friend in my platoon, Goldberg, who taught me some of the most fantastic words and phrases in Yiddish for which there doesn't seem to be any equivalent in English. Poor damn Goldberg. He was a great guy. Terrifically funny. Although basically one of the saddest people I ever knew."

"Was he killed?"

"Fell down right in front of me. I had to step over him. The only consoling thought I could possibly have at the time was that he was probably glad."

"To die!" Deborah said, shocked.

"Sounds crazy, doesn't it? But his wife'd been killed in an auto accident and he thought he had nothing to live for."

"I guess I can understand that," Deborah said thoughtfully. "Somewhere, in Rilke, I read," she frowned and hesitated, "that to some people life is good and joy runs high or words to that effect and to others it's poison, unbearable, difficult and pointless, finally."

"So you're pro-death wish," Mike said flippantly.

"I'm not," Deborah protested. "I only feel like that occasionally."

"Ah, you're just going through the usual youthful period of Weltschmerz," Mike said. "Sounds patronizing, but it's true. I boggled through it myself. Well, let me tell you, Deborah, I changed my ideas quick enough when I was in combat. When you might die any hour, day, minute, all you want to do is live, any way you can. You know this is a hell of a conversation to be having with a pretty young girl on a bright spring day. We're almost there and I've been talking twenty to the dozen and don't know a damn thing about you. What do you think of doing with your life, Deborah?"

"Me?" said Deborah, taken aback at the direct personal question. "Well, let's see. I'd like to do everything."

"Impossible. Just narrow it down to a couple of specific goals."

"Oh, I'd like to go to Europe, very much. To Paris, I think. And I'd like to get an M.A. and a Ph.D. and teach and do scholarly research, oh, things like that."

"I see," Mike looked at his fingers absently. "So you probably deplored my little outburst about pepper mills and related matters, at lunch?"

"I thought it was quite plain to everyone I'd never seen a pepper mill before," Deborah said blushing. "And that I didn't know how to twirl my spaghetti. It was nice of you not to do it either."

"Don't be so damn thin-skinned," Mike said shortly. "Nobody noticed but me and I did only because I kept looking at you. Why bother, anyway? It's just a fetish."

"The difference is," Deborah said unhappily, "that you know how to."

"Oh well, for Godsakes, if it's that important, we'll go for a spaghetti dinner when we go out and I'll show you how. But I don't approve."

"You know," Deborah said hesitantly, "I knew very little of what you were talking about at lunch so probably I shouldn't say this, but if the way the Barings live is any example of what you don't like, I think you're wrong. Because it makes life so much more interesting. You ought to see the awful way ordinary people live if you think the pepper mill way is so terrible."

Mike laughed immoderately. "The pepper mill way," he said finally. "That's wonderful. Almost Proustian. Now look, Deborah, don't look so offended. I'm not laughing at you. Surely you've read Proust?"

"No," Deborah said despondently. "I know who he is, but that's all."

"Deborah, you're far too serious. I was kidding you. How can you possibly have read everything at nineteen? The reason I laughed is that two of the titles are *Swann's Way* and the *Guermantes Way*, to indicate, after a fashion, the two worlds, of the aristocracy and the rich, fashionable upper middle-class that the narrator, outside them, is possessed to know. Like the *Pepper Mill Way*. What a title. A satire on our times. I might do that next."

"Next?"

"Never mind," Mike said mysteriously. "It was a slip."

"You're writing a book," Deborah said, bouncing up and down excitedly. "I've never known a real writer before. How could you say those things about writers yesterday when you're one yourself," she added looking at him accusingly. "I can't imagine . . . I mean . . . When will it be published? I'd love to read it."

"You do great things for my ego," Mike said looking at her interestedly. "The funniest damn thing about you. Here, I scarcely know you and I'm spouting confidences. Nobody else knows I'm writing a novel, not one of my friends, my parents, anyone. And I don't want anyone to know. So I want you to forget what I said. That's the first thing. Promise."

"I promise," Deborah said subdued. "But why? If it were me, I'd . . ."

"No you wouldn't. You'd do exactly as I'm doing, creeping around, torn by self-doubt. I'm trying not to be a writer, you see, have been for years, and, if this venture ends badly I will have finally exorcised the goddamn devil that impels me to set words down on paper and be done with it, clean and pure and uncreative. Okay, let's talk about Paris. When did you last read Hemingway?"

"Why, last month," Deborah said, surprised. "The short stories. How did you know?"

"I thought it might be *The Sun Also Rises*."

"No, I haven't read that yet. I want to very much. But it's never in the library and . . . uh . . . I haven't been able to buy it yet. This summer when I work, I will."

"That's one book I refuse to offer in loan to you. No, no, I will not contribute to the delinquency of a minor. The funny part of it is, the real sad frustrations of his people never come across as well as the glamor of international high life does. I mean, you know, he keeps going on about how screwed up and lost all these cats are, but to the ordinary joe living a life of quiet desperation, going to a dull job on every sleety morning in the winter, if that's lost, boy, he'd like to be lost like that."

"Well, perhaps so," Deborah said politely. She didn't quite understand his point, except that it seemed far from hers. "But I'm talking about life. Experiencing all those foreign places and people." She shook her head. "I can't explain but I want to go so desperately I can't stand it sometimes when I think I might never."

"I know what you want to do," Mike said, ruffling her hair. "You want to wear a beret and sit at sidewalk cafés and drink Pernod. And go skiing in Switzerland and to bullfights in Spain and have romantic love affairs with painters in little murky ninth-floor Paris rooms on the Left Bank where the bathrooms are on the first floor so that it's easier if you're a woman to keep a chamber pot under the bed. The men do it out of the window, anyway."

"Oh you're teasing," Deborah cried indignantly.

"On my word. That's what Brett in the *Sun* had to do, only the book, naturally, doesn't mention those sordid details."

"Oh stop," Deborah said. "I don't believe a word of it."

"I tell you what I'll do," Mike said. "When and if my book sells, I'll take you to Europe. You'll be all excited with a guidebook in your hand and want to see and do everything. I'll be, like most American men, bored and cynical, because I've seen enough ruins, monuments, and primitive plumbing during the war to last me a lifetime. The churches and cathedrals and museums will either be too dark to see anything or be closed for cleaning and repairs and anyway religious art makes me yawn. We'll know there's an exciting night life going on in every city we visit, but we won't know where it is. So, exhausted and footsore, we'll drop like stones into the movies every night, which turn out to be old American ones of a D variety. Shall I go on? There's lots more I could say."

"I don't believe you'd really be like that," Deborah said reproachfully. "You, of all people, who knows Europe so well. So . . . so . . . joyless."

"I was just joshing," Mike said. "Actually, I think you'd be a fine girl to take to Europe. The thing is, I have a passion to see the United States. In fact, although they think I'm crazy for wanting to go, I've hornswoggled Ella and Tom into inviting me to Iowa and on to South Dakota this summer. Well, here we are, at long last. The gallery of Dr. Asch and don't say I didn't warn you."

Deborah stood on the sidewalk waiting while he paid the driver, nerving herself to ask a question which might brand her as so impossibly ignorant that Mike would never thereafter speak her name without adding a charitable groan. And yet, she must risk it, because he was probably the only man she'd ever met who might understand and answer without wounding laughter.

"I suppose you'll think I'm very naïve," she began as he stood next to her absently straightening his black knit tie, "but I'm afraid I didn't quite understand something you said about . . ."

"I thought I'd straightened you out about everything," he interrupted. He was scowling again, looking over his shoulder toward a red door at the foot of basement steps. Black letters on a white board indicated that beyond the door was the ASCH GALLERY. "Measured out the rest of your life for you in presumptuous coffee spoons, in fact."

"I've enjoyed our talk very much," Deborah said primly. It did sound so stilted, but how else could you say it? "No, it wasn't about me. It was . . . uh . . . well, the way you told the story it sounded as though Jane Simms had sex with Si sometimes, although she was going around with Ella's old . . . er . . . boyfriend. Does that mean that she . . . uh . . ."

"It does," Mike said, twisting his lips wryly. "She went to bed with both of them, though perhaps not on the same weekend. And, it helped in the deception because naturally Ella always knew about her adventures with Si. Don't look so distressed, Deborah."

"Then everybody . . . I mean . . . even Ella . . . uh . . . did . . . does . . ." She floundered hopelessly and gave up, wondering if he could save her from this embarrassing morass.

Mike stared at her and then said gently, "I'm sorry I'm the instrument of your disillusion but very few girls are chaste before marriage now, still less men. I mean, that's the underpinning upon which society rests, baby, the skull beneath the skin, the clinch before the fadeout in the movies. It's the key to all life's bitter mystery and if you don't know that you'll be listening all the days of your life to a foreign language of which you can grasp only a few words. So accept it and don't be shocked because you suddenly have to link up your biology lessons with people you know. And," he added grimly, closing the red door behind them, "if you're tempted to avert your eyes, just remember that the Gordie Bruce way isn't the only one. There are better."

They stood uneasily at the entrance to the gallery looking around the long, basement room, and listening to the loud clamor of many voices. Bursts of color starred the pale yellow walls, there were fluorescent lights in the ceiling and a table at the far end was laden with two enormous cut-glass punch bowls, an outsize tray full of small sandwiches and a pyramid of paper cups. Deborah produced her invitation.

"No one will ask for it," Mike said, his eyes flicking quickly over the knots of people. "Ella's stuff is over there on the far wall, see. God, listen to these clowns, will you?"

To the left of them a tall, gaunt man in a sagging gray suit was exchanging guidebook information with a weedy blond girl whose blacktaffeta skirt hung almost to her ankles. "But I tell you, you make a mistake if you do not go to Innsbruck. Ach Innsbruck! Beautiful Innsbruck." He clasped his hands in the air and wafted his eyes heavenward.

"Come on," Mike muttered through set teeth, throwing Deborah's coat over his shoulder and grabbing her arm. "I see Ella over there by the punch bowl." And he charged across the floor, head down, expertly steering Deborah around a contorted brass object which looked like a century plant. "Looks like a good place to hang coats," he mumbled as they passed it, "but I know it couldn't serve any functional purpose. My God, why didn't Ella warn me."

"But what's the matter?" Deborah asked, alarmed at his outrage.

"Not only do we have the arty phonies," he murmured bitterly in her ear, "but also a generous helping of genuine, honest to God European intellectuals. I should have known, of course."

"Oh, how interesting," Deborah said. There was a group of people between them and Ella and they paused at the edge of it. "You mean that Innsbruck man back there?"

"He's just the beginning," Mike said grimly. "You wait. You'll hear more. They've never been anywhere in the United States but a few big cities, but they'll let you know in no uncertain terms how utterly without grace and charm and beauty anyplace here is, compared to the mangiest village in Europe. We have good schools and colleges here but what is a Ph.D from Harvard compared to one from Wittenberg, Heidelberg etcetera? No dueling scars either, by God."

"Are they all German?" Deborah asked, listening intently to the sounds surging around her.

"A few are Viennese, I daresay."

"But you like German poetry."

"The Nazis themselves burned Heine," Mike said shortly, "which shows where their taste was. Of course, I like German poetry. But latterday Germans give me a pain."

"Oh, the Nazis of course," Deborah said quickly. "But these people aren't."

"No," Mike said. "But they're still Germans, unfrocked though they were by their delightful compatriots. They're here because they have to be but three out of five can't rest till they put down this country in favor of that stinking crematorium they escaped from. Listen to this." He jerked his head in the direction of a tiny white-haired woman with a small, roach-like face who was standing very close to them, settling her lozenge-shaped glasses and fixing a beady-eyed earnest stare on a square-shaped, short-haired woman in heavy, sensible shoes.

"But I insisted, my dear Clara," the little woman was saying. "It was, after all, a catalogue of the utmost importance. The publishers do not send it to me, as they would have in Germany, then how else, I asked of her, am I to know of the important new works in my field and related ones, if the library does not provide me with their copy. But her manner was most insolent. They have no respect for the faculty. It is no wonder that here the scholarship is so slipshod."

273

"She was undoubtedly not one of the trained ones," dear Clara hissed comfortingly.

"They have few trained ones," the woman in the Franz Schubert glasses said contemptuously. "If they did, there would not be always such a difficulty when you ask them to get a book."

"Yes, yes," said dear Clara, nodding vigorously. "I was told I must to use this so confusing catalogue and note down the number of the book and dusty myself climbing in shelves to look for it. But that is for students, I said, not faculty."

"It is probable," gargled the insect-like older woman returning to her earlier grievance, "that my catalogue was thrown away. There is so much waste of paper here. Mountains of it taken out in waste-baskets each day. To think how careful of paper one was in der heimat."

"Come," said Clara, taking the older woman by the arm, "I have not yet told Dr. Asch how nice it is, her gathering, although I do not much care for the bilden."

"Well," Mike said, as the ladies moved away, "and what did you think of them? I've seen the older one before. She lectures at Radcliffe. Dr. Irmgard Leichenschmaus. She's an authority on Goethe."

"I suppose she's a Jew," Deborah said painfully.

"I don't think so," Mike said. "Not all refugees are Jews, you know. Hitler persecuted the intellectuals immediately. Oh my God . . ." He stopped and clutched at his forehead. "I've touched another sore spot, have I? Honestly Deborah, I just think of them as intellectual Germans with all the typical faults of such a group and I wouldn't mind a damn bit of it if it wasn't so critical of and snobbish about America and Americans."

"I'm sure they're not all like that," Deborah said worriedly. "It must be terrible to know that a country you love doesn't want you and would as soon kill you as look at you. I'd probably feel just the way she does if I were as old and had to leave the United States that way."

"You're right, of course," Mike said ruefully. "But anyway, I do stick to my guns on one point. It isn't just Germans or Hitler refugees, it's almost every European who comes to our shores to visit or study, mostly on generous American scholarships too. There's a Dutch colonial joker . . ."

"For Godsakes, there you are at last," Si said thrusting his long face at them over a cluster of shoulders. The rest of him emerged in portions and at last he stood whole before them. "You need to be a

Cheshire cat to make your way around here. Where in God's name did you take this girl, Wainscott? Don't tell me. I know by the wobbly stance and the fixed stare."

"We went to have a drink," Mike said. "It's a hellish hot day outside in case you haven't noticed."

"Noticed!" Si retorted. "Wait till you've been in here awhile with all this press of intellect and people. What d'you think of Ella's colleagues?" He waved his arm at the crowded walls.

"We haven't seen anything yet," Mike said, "except people. How's the punch?"

"It's flying, man," Si said. "Full of mysterious ingredients I have not as yet identified. Kummel, mayhap, and vodka and blackberry brandy among others. And the mysterious doctor keeps trotting out more interesting-shaped bottles covered with cobwebs and pouring them in. Each time a new one appears there are loud huzzas and cries of Prosit. The Museum of Fine Arts was never like this. Have you seen Sally?"

"In passing," Mike said.

"Oh where?" Deborah turned around.

"She's over in that corner, talking to that limp fruit. Sara's very popular with the boys from queer street. I can't imagine why."

"It doesn't surprise me at all," Mike said. "For them, she's the prototype of the highclass whore. They think all women, are either Lesbians, whores, or domineering mothers. You know that."

"You're shocking Deborah," Si said severely.

"I'm not shocked," Deborah said. She'd had a session with her dictionary the night before and now knew what that word meant but the whole idea of it seemed very remote and unlikely and just the sort of thing smutty old Gordie would accuse women of if they scorned his advances.

"I think you've learned enough facts of life for one day," Mike said taking her arm. "Come on, let's have some punch and go look at the pictures."

Ella was deep in conversation with a brisk little woman in a high-necked, blacksilk dress, pearl earrings and a careless pompadour when they, at last, managed to push their way through to the punch bowl.

"Oh," she said breaking off in the middle of a sentence, "excuse me, Dr. Asch, but these are friends of mine. This is Dr. Asch who runs the gallery. My friends, Michael Wainscott and Deborah . . . uh . . . Miller. What happened to you two?"

"So happy to meet you," Dr. Asch said shaking hands with both of them. She had a bone-crushing grip, surprising in so small a woman, Deborah thought. "You are any relation to Araminta Wainscott?"

"My mother," Mike said handing a paper cup of punch to Deborah.

"Sooo." Dr. Asch clasped her hands and beamed at Mike. "I admire her work very much. How are you enjoying the pictures?"

"They haven't had the privilege yet," Si said. "If you'll give Mike some punch, Ella, and a refill for me, we'll get going on the tour."

"Oh I'm sorry," Ella said, ladling the purple-colored liquid into cups. "By the way, Si, Matthew Berman was looking for you. He's over there near my paintings now. Only actually he's looking at Sally."

"I'd better tell her to move away," Si chortled. "She's distracting the viewers. Has Tom gone underground?"

"He's been talking to Dr. Kopfstein," Ella said, "over in that corner by the window. For at least a half hour."

"Oh my God," Si groaned. "Is he still there? Why I was in at the beginning of that brouhaha but I pretended that Caroline was waving at me across the room and silently stole away on little cat feet. Kopfstein was even then laying bare the sexual fetishism of a story in *The New Yorker* last week called 'Johanna and the Biedermeyer Umbrella.' The author didn't know, naturally, those poor bastards are always the last to know what they're writing, but Kopfstein did, that the whole amusing tale stemmed from a repressed interest in the male genitalia on the part of the heroine in childhood which was sublimated by rummaging in her grandma's curio cabinet. I'm not going back, not even to save Tom. By now, Kopfstein is probably analyzing the Gingerbread Boy's Oedipus complex."

"You do not believe in the theories of Dr. Freud, Mr. Hunnicutt?" Dr. Asch interposed looking at him keenly through her shining glasses.

Si quaffed from his paper cup and then said, "I believe only in the True Punch," and laughed loudly. "Anyway, I think people could save themselves a lot of money if, instead of going to analysts, they'd get their portraits painted. Infinitely more revealing and less expensive."

"Come on," Mike said hastily, propelling Si before him against the crowd and looking meaningfully at Deborah. "Let's see some of the paintings."

"You need a keeper, for Godsakes," he said crossly to Si as they picked their way across the gallery. "Where's Caroline? I'm going to tell her to wash your mouth out with soap or else stop you drinking this damn punch. Man, what a mess. It's got anise in it. And potato schnapps."

"The taste *is* pretty nauseating," Si said happily, "but it has quite an effect you must admit. Rather like having a prefrontal lobotomy I should imagine."

"Why don't you stop riding Ella? You're really going to get under her skin one of these days and Tom's too."

"She just thinks I'm joking," Si said carelessly. " 'They could not see the bitter smile behind the painted grin he wore.' " He patted Deborah on the head. "Remember? That was a real acute bit of analysis, sans Freud, happily. And here it is Deborah." He stopped with a flourish before the wall at the far end where Ella's eight portraits were hung. "See for yourself. The quick and the dead."

The portrait of Si was quite unmistakable. Deborah stepped back a few paces and, cocking her head, surveyed it from all angles. Perhaps he didn't like it because of a slight element of distortion in the length of face and nose and a greater prominence of ears, she thought. But it was so obviously him, with its clever, whimsical mouth, spirited eye, uproarious hair and mountain-bred-in-the-bone features that, having looked in his mirror, he could not but honestly have admitted a remarkable resemblance. Then what else could it be, Deborah wondered. The picture's colors were brilliant. There he sat in a straight-backed Boston rocker of a sun-hued yellow against a delicate flamingo pink background, wearing a rough heavy lumberman's shirt of dark green plaid. The long, gnarled fingers, which, Deborah decided, were a kind of trademark of Ella's paintings, lay opened upwards in a lap of what looked to be blue denim jeans and in one hand was a small, round white globe and in the other a tiny pink pig with a curly tail. The iconography of these two items completely baffled Deborah. Could they be toys? Or were they intended as symbols? But of what? She looked up at the face again and this time, the eyes were disturbingly different. This time they looked a little sly and shrewd and although still mirthful, they were laughing at the viewer and not with him. The mouth too, seemed to have changed. It was slightly open in what Deborah had taken to be the beginnings of a smile, but now she saw that the pictured face was about to speak and she knew incontrovertibly that what it said might give joy or pain, but to the speaker, the effect mattered not at all. Yes, she thought, that is the face of one who loves not his fellow men but only their foibles and follies.

"I see you finally got here," Caroline said behind her. She was holding a tray of paper cups. "You must be dreadfully dry. Do have some punch," and she thrust a full paper cup at Deborah and was gone, moving gracefully through the crowd before there was time to refuse and plead the necessity of abstention. Deborah, left with her second cup, perforce took a sip. It certainly was strong and weird tasting.

Mike and Si, she noticed, had been joined by a restless-looking, handsome fellow, with closely cropped, black curly hair who was wearing a rumpled cord jacket. Si and this newcomer were laughing boisterously while Mike stood by rather aloofly, sipping on his punch and staring at Sally who glowed in the corner surrounded by four or five men. Deborah trailed over to him.

"I think there's a rack down there," she said quietly. "I'll take my coat. No need for you to carry it all over."

Mike seemed to come out of a dream. He looked at her blankly. "Oh. Coat. Yes. Well I'll do it. How did you like Ella's stuff?"

"I just looked at the one of Si. What is he holding?"

"I'll whisper in your ear. We don't want a relapse. He's about to speak, you must have noted, and cast pearls before swine which he often assumes he's doing. Ergo, the pig and the pearl. By the way, there's another more reasonable facsimile painting Ella did of her roommate which is here. It's the obverse of 'Black Mrs. Behemoth,' or, 'Jane Simms before the Fall.'"

"Will I recognize it from the other one?"

"I doubt it. 'Between the idea and the reality. . . . falls the shadow' so to speak. My God, why is it that one always ends up quoting Eliot who is always quoting someone else anyhow? It's that last one with a lot of mauve in it. Well, I'll go get rid of your coat."

He moved off and Deborah was suddenly noticed by Si who introduced her to his friend. He was, it turned out, a doctor named Matthew Berman, who flashed brilliant white teeth at her from a full-lipped mouth, muttered something and then continued talking to Si as if she were not there. He would be a doctor, Deborah thought, taking an instant and unreasonable dislike to him. He was so obviously good-looking and as obviously aware of it. He looked just like all the young doctors in the movies. She could just see him posturing around in a white coat. It was the absolutely indifferent, practiced way he'd looked at her during the introduction that irritated her, she supposed, and then after the mechanical, chewed howdedo, the dismissal of her presence altogether, by a slight turn of his shoulder, an utter blankness on his handsome face. She stood by uneasily, half-listening to their conversation and feeling, for the first time that day, the dreaded lack of belonging, where you stay in the presence of people you know, who aren't really conscious that you're there, because you don't know where else to go. Si and the doctor seemed to be discussing someone they'd known at Tufts, some poor straw figure of fun whose very name sent them off into hilarious hoots and she was about to excuse herself and go look at more paintings when Matthew Berman interrupted Si and said:

"Say listen Si why did you shove me in the ribs when what'shisname, Mike, was here when I asked you about that luscious Sally Brimmer babe?"

"She's his eternal itch and he's sensitive about her, that's why. Why? Do you want to meet her?"

"I met her. Yesterday. I was really bowled over by surprise. I thought she'd be like her brother. Look like him. You know."

"Oh sure. You're colleagues, aren't you? How can you stand it?"

"Look, Si," Matthew Berman said in a low, confidential voice. "I've been trying to get near her ever since I got here, but she's got a solid cordon around her, including some fags, which gives me pause."

"You're asking for trouble I suppose you know," Si said grinning. "I can see you do. Okay, come on. We'll do a little scrimmage work."

Sally again, Deborah thought, watching them walk away with not so much as a backward glance. She addles all their wits. She drank some more punch and wondered where Mike was but although she peered and craned and stretched he was nowhere to be seen and in the end she went and looked at all of Ella's eight portraits by herself, hoping he'd turn up before she reached the other Jane Simms. But he didn't and there was no one to talk to about her wrenching discovery of the force of hatred. For this first painting was that of an almost beautiful girl, composed and harmonious against a lovely blue woodviolet background, the exact color of her large luminous eyes. If one had a very tortured imagination, Deborah thought, staring startled at the picture, one might, with great effort, see how this voluptuous-looking girl could be turned through slashing fury into Mrs. Behemoth. Here was a girl, larger than life, bigboned and of Brunnhilde-like proportions, a lovely sculpted face only slightly flawed by a Mussolini-like jaw. Jane Simms, as Ella had painted her in days of friendship sat, wrapped in what appeared to be a thick, textured bathtowel, of a rich, royalpurple, with one wide, creamy shoulder carelessly bared, a vague dreamy smile on her sensual cupid'sbow mouth and her cloud of thick smokyblack hair in tangled disarray. Perhaps Ella didn't just get to hate her all at once, Deborah thought. Perhaps all along she had despised this blatant sensuality.

I hope no one ever hates me, Deborah thought fervently, as she went round the rest of the gallery dutifully looking at the other paintings which seemed immensely unattractive, and that I never hate another person so vehemently. Halfway round, another Hebe with dangling earrings fobbed some more punch into her unwilling hand and since there was nothing else to do she drank it down to the last drop and while standing in a limbo between two obscure canvases of mudyellow and slimegreen Dr. Asch bustled by her with the tray of little sandwiches, and, nodding and smiling, insisted she take one.

Deborah chewed meditatively on what proved to be liverwurst on pumpernickel and listened to the words flying by her. Then someone else came and offered some punch which this time, she bluntly refused. The light seemed to be wavy and shimmering and people began to recede or come forward with odd abruptness. Where was everybody?

There was a break in the crowd before her and she saw Mike standing with Sally. They were deep in conversation, his head bent down close to hers, his hand grasping her round, bare arm. Her golden head was thrown back and her cheek almost touched Mike's near face. So beautiful, Deborah thought, and was glad when the shifting crowd blocked out the sight of them. Of course, he loved her. It was so plain when you saw the way he looked at her. How silly of him to pretend that he was even vaguely interested in kissing a naïve, little girl. If he and Sally were alone then, and not in a mob, he'd have seized her and not just brushed her mouth with his, either. I won't ever have that kind of wild, undying, fierce, protective, burning, marvelous love, Deborah thought, never, and anyway, why should I? I'm not beautiful, nor succulently feminine, nor do I have any of that verve, charm, and personality they talk about or write about in magazines. Maybe she could quote a little poetry but that was all. The sum total. What man wanted a woman who could quote poetry? She couldn't see a soul she knew. But there was Ella still by the punch table. Deborah marched up but by the time she got to the left of Ella, three voluble, enthusiastic ladies had borne in on her from the right. Deborah stood by uncertainly waiting for Ella's chattering admirers to bow themselves off and was handed some more punch by the girl with the earrings. She noticed absently that the punch's color had changed from its former purple to an ink black. Curiosity impelled her to taste whatever new ingredient had done this and she took two sips. Very much like borscht she thought and sipped again and suddenly was miserably reminded of all she'd had to eat and drink in the past few hours. Biting her lip hard, she put down the punch cup and asked the girl with the green face and cable hawsers in her ears, where the ladies' room was.

It was an inconvenient and embarrassing ladies' room, she noticed later, because it was merely a small closet with a john, mirror, and sink, and therefore only one person at a time could enter and lock the door behind. Deborah, flying in through the door had been in no state to think of locking it and when she straightened up, woefully hollow and weak, there, in the half-open doorway, stood the disapproving upright Dr. Irmgard Leichenschmaus. The authority on Goethe looked Deborah over, frowned, wrinkled her small, yellow nose, turned on black, clumpy shoes and went out, slamming the door behind her.

Viciously, Deborah jerked on the cold-water faucet and washed her face. German girls probably didn't get sick in art galleries she reflected bitterly. They had strong stomachs and could make lampshades out of human skin without losing a single meal. She wondered if the good doctor had stood and listened to the gasping noises going on inside. This was the truly ignominious end to a day that had held such promise, Deborah thought, staring blankly at her wet hands. She saw a roll of paper towels above the sink, pulled some off and scrubbed her face and hands angrily with the rough-textured square. To be seen and scorned in such a dreadful state by an eminent lady scholar. How low could one's self-respect get? I must go home, she thought, applying lipstick, before something worse happens. But first it was essential to air herself out. There was a door leading out into a small garden in back of the gallery, with a few chairs where she could sit and let a wind, if any, blow through clothes and hair. To come home reeking of cigarette smoke, vomit, and liquor would cause the sort of scene in which window shades were pulled off their rollers and cast in fury on the floor.

Hurriedly she came out of the bathroom and cast a furtive glance around. No familiar face appeared in the now thinning crowd and she was glad. There was one couple out in the garden and they left as soon as she came out. Thankfully, Deborah sank into a square, wooden, garden seat and lighted a cigarette but the smell gagged her and she crushed it out on a flagstone, carefully picked up the flattened remainder and put it back in her package for later use. I'll wait here, she thought, and then they'll all go away and I can slip out by myself.

Where had it all gone wrong? she wondered dismally. Perhaps

none of it would've happened had she not gone with Mike. If she'd driven over with the others they'd've seen to it that she wasn't neglected. Ella particularly. And of course without Mike there'd never've been all those fatal whisky sours. Oh fool! And on top of that, the swilling of that disgusting punch, simply because of nothing else to do, no one to talk to, because of being an outsider. Which she was. No use pretending because Mike'd flung her a few compliments and kisses. Anyway, I don't really care about him. He did ask me out after all and I refused. He'd probably leave with Sally. But he's nice, he's nice, she thought defensively. She let her thoughts stray, building up pictures of what it would be like to have him as a steady sort of beau. But no, how useless. He could never really care for her.

I don't want to be Miss Brill, she cried in her heart, alone, alone, always. Now Gordie would go away and with him, whether they had sex or not, would go any pretense she'd had, any little flicker of a notion that she might be attractive to men. She'd learned that, right this weekend. Mike had simply deserted her, although it was hard to blame him for that certainly since what woman could compete with Sally. And of course one did not care really about a wolf type like that Dr. Berman still how awful to be ignored by him. How small, unimportant and puny could one get? There was no point in crying about it, Deborah thought, annoyed, screwing up her eyelids tightly. If you were a bookworm prig with no feminine charms, you were, that was all. You would never break hearts or even one heart, except your own, never go to Paris, no one would ever, in your entire life find you interesting and you would live forever with your parents, be browbeaten by your father, always dress like a frump and never get out of the library. It'd been sheer fatuity to think for one moment that you could ever be different.

I'm going home, Deborah thought, patting her eyes with a piece of Kleenex and getting up. I'm going home and endure my father. It's all I deserve. There're always books, after all. They didn't turn on you and behave contrarily. She thought of Mike's story about the man, Goldberg, who'd wanted to die, and wished self-pityingly that she'd been a man and old enough to have died and ended this ludicrous failure, in the war.

In the doorway, she caromed into Tom Baring.

"We've been looking for you," he said. "We thought you'd left with Mike. But he's suddenly turned up wondering where you were. You look damn pale. Did that punch do you in too? I didn't drink much of it fortunately but Si was overcome."

"Don't exaggerate," Si said. He closed in on her from the other side. "I merely felt queasy and lay on the floor for a while under a pile of coats. God, what a rout this has turned into."

"Why, almost everyone's gone," Deborah said. The gallery echoed with their few voices. Uncertain stragglers said goodbye to each other at the door.

"Will someone please tell me what's going on?" Si asked plaintively. "Where's Caro? Did she run off with Kopfstein to have her repressed interest in sexual machinery plumbed?"

"She's upstairs in the kitchen with Ella and Dr. Asch," Tom said. "Washing the punch bowls. And don't jeer at Kopfstein. He's bought one of Ella's painting."

"Which one?" Si asked suspiciously.

"Not the one of you. The portrait of her father. He raved over it. So American, so Grant Wood. Ella didn't relish that part, but his money is good even if his criticism isn't."

"Aha," Si jeered, "so that's why you spent all those hours having your ear pounded."

"I thought he was pretty interesting. He claims, you know, that it isn't the children who're in love with the parents, as in Oedipus and Electra complexes, but just the other way round."

"I don't want to hear about it," Si covered his ears. "Where did Mike go? He really disturbed my slumber, I can tell you."

"He went up to the kitchen too. Thought Deborah might be there. How in God's name could you fall asleep on the floor?"

"You'd think, if the woman was going to serve hemlock, she'd at least provide comfortable couches to lie down and die on. Damned inconsiderate. Anyway, I didn't sleep much, I may tell you. In no time at all, it seemed, came a female straight from a Kafka story, who stepped on my hand with a big, black shoe, which was odd, when I think of it now, a cockroach wearing a shoe, screamed, leaped in the air, shouted Verdammte Amerkanische Naar, pulled a coat from under me, loosed a shower of coathangers and Teutonic abuse on my head, and, in parting, clubbed me with an umbrella. I was about to get up but my head felt so terrible I sank back and outside the window I heard the dulcet voice of my supposedly sensible friend Matthew Berman who'd managed to maneuver Sally out into the garden where he made a big pitch. She told him she was busy, nice as you please, and he made the foolish mistake of pressing her and then she got quite cold in that sweet icecream way that could make your teeth chatter. I got up then and stuck my head out of the window intending to make some cheery remark

283

to lighten the oppressive silence when I saw that Sally was alone, staring glazedly off into space and that a determined Mike was coming through the door. So I pulled back in and knelt to peek."

"My God," Tom said indignantly, "have you no scruples?"

"None," Si said blissfully. "Anyway, he pulled her out of her chair and there was some difficulty because they couldn't stand too well and, in spite of her protests, they had a rubbing match but he was bested. Then he shouted that she was a Christawful bitch and she said he was demented, then he said he was sorry and she said she was too and then they left."

"You're sure you didn't dream it all?" Tom asked skeptically.

"I could have. Pretty pastiche kind of nightmare though."

"Well why ask what's been going on then," Tom said. "You were in the thick of things. Kopfstein would say you were a true voyeur."

"At least I'm well-informed," Si said smugly, "which I can't say the same about him. But where were you all the time?" He turned to Deborah. "You should have kept an eye on our boy lover and not let him get in that disgraceful state. Do you realize, Miss Muffett, that Tom, Ella, and Caro were in lecherous ecstasy when you two didn't appear. You were to be the new twosome of the ages. I, more skeptical and realistic, proved to be right."

Deborah blushed. "We just went to a bar to cool off," she said.

"I'll warrant that wasn't what he had in mind," Si said.

"You're embarrassing the lady," Tom said. "Ah, there's Mike."

"Face like Big Chief Thundercloud," Si murmured. "It was no dream."

Mike came loping down the stairs leading off the gallery and hurried across the room. Deborah looked at the floor.

"I was afraid you'd left," Mike said. "I'll take you home."

"It's too far. I can go myself."

"Where is it?" he insisted.

"Winthrop."

"We can run you home," Tom said. "Si, you and Caro, can get home from here, can't you?"

"I'll go along," Mike said defiantly. "Unless Deborah objects."

"Why should I?"

"More hurt egos per square yard here," Si said cheerfully.

"That lousy punch," Mike said with feeling. "You didn't drink much of it, did you?" he asked Deborah.

"I'm afraid I did," Deborah admitted. She was beginning to feel much better about the whole thing. In fact, rather emboldened and risqué. It was sort of a grownup thing, getting drunk (forget the sick part) at an art gallery on Sunday afternoon, especially when other people seemed to have been behaving tipsily too.

"You're all right now?"

"Fine, thank you."

"Have a heart, baby," he said in her ear. "I told you I didn't want to come. I knew what would happen."

"You're not obligated to me."

"I wanted to be. Oh, I know, if wishes were horses . . . and I'm God's own beggar or was this afternoon. But it's all over, all over. What's that fine, old Victorian phrase? She sent him about his business. You know I'm still a little high. Which is as well because when I sober up, I'll remember with shame what a fool I made of myself."

"Did Sally leave with Matt Berman?" Si enquired with such an air of sham innocence that Deborah was sure Mike would notice.

"She did not," Mike said, oblivious of all Si's sidelong smiles and winks. "I saw her into a cab myself. She's got a new bull, someone she just met."

"It's great being a confidante," Si said ironically. "A close one too, judging by the smear of orange lipstick on your ear. Left one."

"Oh Christ!" Mike took out his handkerchief and rubbed distractedly at the bedaubed ear. "Well, at least I tried."

"There are always fresh fields and pastures new," said Si, folding his arms and staring thoughtfully at Deborah, who felt her cheeks getting red. She was glad to see Ella and Caroline come downstairs bearing the punchbowl.

Mike rolled down the windows in the back seat of the Baring's car the minute they got inside and they both sat quite silent, breathing deeply, while Tom and Ella, in front, discussed the show and what they would do with Kopfstein's money.

"Sally looked so lovely," Ella said musingly after awhile. "All cream and gold and flamingo and peacock shimmer. I so want to paint her, particularly in what she was wearing today. Could you ask her, Mike, if she'll sit for me?"

"Let Tom ask her," Mike said gloomily. "She's a spectre that haunts my dreams no longer."

Deborah's head felt thick and full of cottonwool. She found her eyes closing and was grateful when Mike put his arm around her and pulled her head down on his shoulder. I don't care, she thought welcomingly, I'll be second fiddle. It's not bad. Better than being alone.

After awhile, she was being jogged awake by Mike's gentle hand.

"We're almost there. Let Tom know where you want to go."

She sat up and looked out of the window, smitten afresh by the sight of the dreadfully shoddy neighborhood. "Straight down that next big avenue," she said to Tom. "It's not far from there."

"You remember that Rilke poem about Solitude?" Mike said in a low voice and when she nodded dumbly, he went on, "And the lines in the middle about the people who have found nothing of what they searched for leaving each other sadly. Well, we had a bad start today, and I was a heel and I'm sorry about it. We'll do better next time. Where can I call you?"

"In the library at Marplot," she said and just then saw her father turning the corner of the street a little way ahead of them and her heart began to beat very fast. She smoothed down her hair and rubbed off some of her lipstick with a piece of Kleenex. If he just didn't see her getting out of the car it would be all right.

"Tom," she said in a shaky voice, "could you stop please and let me off here."

"I'll have to swing around," he said mildly. "Is this where you live?"

"No. It's the next street down. But I'd rather get off here."

"I never saw a girl take her lipstick off before," Mike observed.

"My father doesn't like me to use it. Oh yes, here is fine."

Mike got out and opened the car door and handed over her coat and book. He bowed a little ironically and then got back in while Deborah thanked Ella for lunch and promised to call about modeling. She stood and watched the car speed away and wished that she could go with them. With a sigh she turned and began, very slowly, to walk toward home. As she came around the corner, she saw her father who had paused to talk to an old man, a crony from the synagogue. He gave her a cold nod as she went rapidly by and continued his conversation. His voice sounded very jovial but she wasn't deceived. He was always full of smiles and laughter outside the home but the comic mask was doffed the moment he came in the door and so it was this day.

She had locked herself in the bathroom and was washing herself furiously with some strong-smelling soap and scrubbing at the small spots she'd just noticed on her dress when she heard the bang of the front door. It would be her evil luck, she thought, listening to his loud baying, that the moment he'd turned the corner he'd run into this disastrous fool of an old man who'd buttonholed him for a chat. Naturally they'd had to pause right there on the corner for a while and naturally her father had to be facing the opposite side of the road, and so, of course, she'd been seen getting out of the car. And Mike had been seen too.

"Who was he?" she heard him roar to her mother. "He's no good, you can rest assured of that. A decent Jewish boy would come to get her and take her home. She's running around with bums I tell you. That's the way you brought her up. And where does she come to going out with boys altogether? She's a little fool who thinks she knows everything. Lipstick, she had on and smoking cigarettes. I could smell her coming. It's a disgrace to have a daughter like her. I was afraid the old man would see her, my daughter, getting out of a car, all painted and smelling like a whore. He'd ask me, Who's the boy your daughter's going with? What could I say? Some tramp, who knows his name? Just wait. You'll get a reward for bringing up a daughter like this. Some night one of those tramps will throw her out of a car right in front of your house. Here's your daughter, the harlot, all beaten up for you."

Deborah grabbed her toothbrush and brushed her teeth slowly and carefully, keeping the water running so that it might drown out the noise. But it didn't.

"So," she heard him howl in obvious response to some soft remonstrance of her mother's, "Time enough when she's older. I know some fine men with sons. She can meet them and we'll know who she's with and that nobody's fooling around with her. And there'll be some respect for the father, the way it should be. Now I want it stopped. She goes to school and comes home again and if she goes anywhere, it's with you."

Hastily Deborah took off all her clothes and turned the shower on and the noise outside was muted under the gentle, running spray of the water. Presently she heard the door slam. The noise rattled bottles on the glass shelf above the sink. She turned the water off and stepped out of the tub.

She was drying herself when her mother, as expected, came to the door. "Can I come in, Debby?"

"I suppose." Her mother's martyred expression was even worse than her father's tirades sometimes.

"Your father's very upset. Who were you with?"

"If he thinks," Deborah said bitterly, "that he's going to keep me locked up here until he picks out a husband for me, he's crazy. He's not in the old country any more. I suppose he has a dowry for me?"

"He's just worried about you. Were you smoking? That's terrible. It's bad for you and you're too young. I'm the one who gets all the trouble when you go out. Why don't you consider me once in a while?"

"Oh, let me alone," Deborah said bursting out of the bathroom and running into her room. "Let me alone. I'm sick to death of it all. It would serve him right if I did become a prostitute. That's all he ever calls me anyhow."

"Debby!" Her mother's voice was sharp and shocked. "That's a terrible thing to say."

"I don't care," Deborah wailed, her voice breaking. "I hate coming home. I hate it. No matter what I do, he throws a scene. I don't want to live here any more. All I want is to have a little normal fun like any other girl. I'm going to move out or go away. You'll see. Now let me alone." She slammed the door of her room shut and lay sobbing and crying on the bed for a long, shameful time.

Eleven

Precisely at seven o'clock, the bell rang. Sally, all dressed for a quiet, seductive evening at home, in tight black-velvet pants and a clinging, white silk jersey blouse, so artfully constructed that there was more material in the sleeves than the bodice, poured some Scotch into a glass, lit a cigarette and then opened the door. She was leaning casually against the doorjamb, smoking and laughing a little, thinking how trite and badmovie her scene staging was, but then he was a simple sort and the subtle would be lost on him, when Saul appeared finally, puffing up the last flight of steps.

"Well," he said surveying her and grinning, "I guess these damn stairs were worth climbing after all." He handed her a large, spicy-smelling, brown paper bag. "Delicatessen stuff. You know, salami, pastrami, potato salad, the works. I thought maybe we could have some sandwiches to go with our drinks. Okay with you?"

"Of course." She put the bag down on the floor. "It was lovely of you to think of it. I have a drink all ready for you."

"God!" He took the glass from her and collapsed into the ugly green armchair. "I'm no good at this mountain goat stuff on stairs any more. Only do it for you, beautiful." He took two swallows and emptied the glass.

"I'm flattered," Sally said gravely.

"Hey!" He waved his empty glass at her. "Where's yours? Not going to let me get ahead are you? I like company when I drink."

Sally explained that the ice bucket was empty so he followed her into the kitchen and, with one quick, easy movement, pulled out the eternally frozen solid ice tray while she made up sandwiches and dished potato salad onto plates. He'd brought a bewildering variety of spiced meats and a plenitude of pickles and relishes but since both of them seemed to be hungry it all disappeared rapidly.

"How thoughtful of you, Saul. Now we won't have to bother about dinner."

"That's what I figured. This is my favorite kind of meal anyhow. Sandwiches and Scotch." He leaned back in his chair. "I brought another bottle by the way. I put it in the kitchen."

"Well you are a splendid guest, but we don't really need it."

"Yeah, I see now, but how did I know? I figured maybe you people had nothing but sherry around and then I'd have to run down the stairs again."

"Why in the world would you think that?" Sally asked, amused.

"My brother," he said grinning. "He came home one weekend and started telling my uncle he ought to have a bottle of good sherry around for a beforedinner drink. I thought that's what all the best people did."

"I think sherry's a bore," Sally said. "What did your uncle say?"

"He said Bayischern wine was good enough for him."

"Bayer . . . I've never heard of that. What is it?"

"Oh, I forgot you wouldn't know," Saul said, looking a little embarrassed. "It's kosher wine you know, very sweet grape wine. They drink it a lot on holidays, with meals, for prayers. Lousy stuff, it turns my gut."

"Kosher wine," Sally said, puzzled. "Oh you mean Jewish wine. Then you're Jewish?"

"Yeah," Saul said. He looked at her appraisingly. "Didn't you know?"

"How would I?" Sally asked. How mercurial his emotions were she thought. In the space of a minute his expression had changed from cheer to truculence.

"I thought maybe your brother might've said something. But otherwise there's no way for you to tell is there? In Germany they had it all figured out so there wouldn't be any mistakes. All the Jews wore a yellow star. Yellow for coward, I suppose. Sometimes," he said musingly, "I think it was almost worthwhile losing a leg to help beat those bastards. Other times, I don't know if anything's worth it." He leaned over and offered her a cigarette. "Well how do you stand? I mean, maybe you made a mistake asking me here."

Oho, another complex, Sally thought, waiting for him to light the cigarette. Peel one away and there was another, right underneath, just like an onion. She inhaled deeply on her cigarette and blew out smoke.

"I suppose you know you're being very silly," she said. "I couldn't care less about your religion."

"Being a Jew isn't just belonging to a religion," he said broodingly.

290

"If it were just that, I couldn't call myself a Jew since I haven't been near a synagogue in years."

Sally looked at him through the thin veil of cigarette smoke. He sat there, hulkingly attractive, in spite of a rather awful loud checked sports jacket, and eminently desirable. She sighed a little, wondering how the conversation had gotten off into these dull channels, but supposed she must make an effort. "Then what is it?"

"Ah, who knows?" Saul said disgustedly, squashing out his cigarette. "Even the best brains haven't figured it out, so why should I try. It's just something that happens to you by being born one, even if you don't give a damn about it, the way I don't. Well, I didn't mean to get off on that, but I just wanted you to know, since you didn't."

"I still don't see why it should make any difference," Sally said lazily. She wished he'd come and sit by her.

"Because sometimes people say things," he said slowly. "Little things, maybe they don't mean any harm. But I got a lousy temper and I get mad easy."

"But wouldn't you prefer to know how people felt, really?" Sally asked. She sat on the edge of the sofa stacking plates and silver on the tray.

"No," Saul said grimly. "I had enough trouble and enough fights for one life. I don't give a damn what people think about Jews or ex-prizefighters or one-legged cripples or drunks or roughnecks with bad manners or guys whose wives screwed around with other men while they were sweating their guts out in the war or guys who go to whorehouses. Let them think what they like but I don't wanna hear about it." He took the tray from her hands. "Let me have that. I'll put the stuff in the sink and you can mix some more drinks."

"Were all those things you don't want to hear people's opinions about, true of you?" Sally asked him when he came back to the living room. It sounded clumsy and childish, putting a question like that but the part about the wife and whorehouse sounded sort of interesting and might get him closer to the reason she'd asked him over. Boring subjects, such as people's religion, obviously just carried him off into another realm of anger.

"Sure," he said, taking the drink from her. "Didn't you recognize the picture of a first-class bum? The kind you shouldn't have in your house. Well, here's mud in your eye, lovely."

"I didn't know about the wife part," Sally said.

"Yeah," he said, "well, to tell you the truth, Sally, there's damn little you do know about me. Oh don't get the idea I'm still married. That was over a long time ago."

Sally took her drink and curled up in a corner of the sofa and he sat down next to her, for a wonder, his face dark and the bitter lines deep around the mouth.

"You didn't really divorce her because she had an affair while you were away, did you?" she asked lightly. "That sounds terribly old-fashioned somehow."

"Old-fashioned," he said furiously. "I wasn't old-fashioned enough. I shoulda broken her goddamn legs for her before I went away."

"Oh, men are so tiresome and unfair," Sally said, taking a cigarette out of a box on the table beside her and lighting it quickly because he seemed so far off in a mood that she might sit there embarrassingly for minutes before he noticed her again. "You know perfectly well that very few men in wartime are faithful to their wives, but oh, if the wives ever dare to cast a glance . . ."

"A glance!" Saul said loudly. "Well, what the hell, why should I get sore at you. You don't know nothing about it."

"You might tell me," Sally said sweetly, "instead of shouting."

"Listen," he said seriously, "you're a swell girl, Sally. I got a lot of admiration for you. I mean, you're a real lady, you got good manners and you treat people right. It's nice just sitting here with you like this and it was wonderful last night. I don't even know how come a girl like you wants to bother with an old broken-down pug like me. Why, tell me, why?"

"I daresay you know why," Sally drawled. "I thought it was awfully plain yesterday and last night."

"Yeah," he said twisting his mouth a little. "That's old Saul. He's a smart apple all right. He knows everything. Well, let me tell you something, Sally. Yesterday, I was a wise guy. Sure, I looked you over like you was a tart or something. I dunno, maybe I did it to get Bud sore, at first. Maybe to get you sore. That's the way most girls do, you know, they pull the shock act, how dare you sir, I'm an innocent pure girl. Only you didn't. Took me right up on it. Okay, so when I was first with you last night, I figured so she doesn't fool around, she wants it and don't mind if I know it, so okay, where's the harm." He paused and looked at her. "Does this sound pretty lousy? That's the only way I can say things. Straight out. I can't talk around things."

"No," Sally said. "Go on."

"Okay, so you're a beautiful, sexy-looking, high-class doll and it gives me a big kick to think you might go for me. So we go out and

I behave like a bastard and you act like a real lady. So that's it." He snapped his fingers. "I go home and say, Saul, this is no girl for you to fool around with. This is really fire, boy, and you can't afford no more burns." He moved away down the sofa and looked at her morosely, his arms folded. "And believe me, Sally, it wasn't easy coming up here and not touching you. I wasn't even gonna come, you know, but I promised and I wanted to see you again, one more time."

"Oh dear," Sally said. "You're really an awfully complicated person, aren't you?"

"Let's face it, beautiful, I'm doing both of us a favor. I'm a fouled up character and I got one leg. You don't want me. You might think you do, but you don't know what the hell you'd be letting yourself in for. And it works both ways. I don't need any more mess in my life."

"You make me feel sort of like a vampire," Sally said, smiling a little. Really how deadly serious he looked.

He shook his head. "I didn't mean it like that. You're a great girl. It's my fault. I ought to know better by now. Only sometimes I forget and think I'm like I used to be and when I see a girl like you . . . well," he shrugged, "I shouldn't get started on things I can't finish. See what I mean?"

"No," Sally said. She was beginning to feel depressed. It would've been so simple. But perhaps he was right and it was wise not to begin anything. She shut her eyes not wanting to look at him any more. What with the liquor and all she would have to hang on tightly.

"Hey," he said anxiously, "are you all right? Don't you feel well?"

"I'm fine," Sally said. Her voice sounded far away.

"Do you want something, Sally? Another drink or something?"

"I guess," Sally said limply. She wanted to say, rudely, why don't you go away, but was there any point in being nasty? He'd only been honest. Another thought occurred to her, some sort of serious question she wanted to ask him. Now what was it? She opened her eyes and saw him sitting by her, holding out the drink.

"Did I say something I shouldn't? Christ, Sally, I'd cut my tongue out before I . . ."

"What did she do to you?" Sally sat up and took an experimental sip at her drink. It made her feel a little better. "Your wife, I mean. What could a woman do to a man to make him feel so damn dubious? Or is it something you can't bear to talk about?"

"I could talk about it, all right. I could yell about it all night long.

But it wouldn't change nothing. And it'd only bore you stiff. Anyway, what happened between her and me's got nothing to do with it. It's the lousy rotten war, that's all. Tough shit, brother, real sad, but what the hell . . . Whyn't you kick me out of here Sally? You don't want me crying on your shoulder. Such a damn beautiful shoulder, too. You got lovely hair too, you know that?" He moved back to where he'd been sitting, next to her, and touched her hair gently. "Lovely hair," he repeated stroking it down lightly, "real blonde and silky and long. Not dyed. I hate dyed hair on a woman. The damn fool mistakes we make. Because I'd been in the fight game and seen the brassy-haired broads and I thought, that's not for me, what I want's a nice girl, see, a good girl. It was only afterwards I realized that what's on the outside don't mean a damn, underneath, Rose was worse than those dames. And now I know I couldn't have stood her anyway, even if she didn't divorce me."

"Oh," Sally said, shocked. She sat up straight and outraged and forgot about being a little high and frustrated. "She didn't divorce you because you lost your leg did she? You don't mean that, do you, Saul?"

"Another guy, another guy," he said impatiently, "but pretty damn convenient anyway. Oh yeah, maybe it was just a coincidence. That's what they tell me and maybe I woulda believed it before the war when I used to be a big-hearted joe and loved everybody. But when you're in the hospital for a long time and you lost part of your body along with any hopes for hitting the big time in boxing, well, you begin to hate people. It turns out they all got ulterior motives." He pulled his hand away from where it'd been resting on her shoulder and looked at it blankly, then flexed his fingers and tightened it into a fist.

"See this hand, Sally, see how it works, I can use it, I can touch it, I can feel your beautiful hair, I can feed myself with it, I can drive a car. But if I didn't have it, I couldn't do none of those things. I'd lose half the pleasures a man can have. And you take it for granted when you got them. And that's the way it was with my leg. They sent me to war, I'm a patriot, even a little of a hero, but Jesus, I lost my leg, my leg, my God! I woke up one morning in the field hospital and it's gone. Before that, I thought the worst thing that ever happened to me was when my mother died but when I knew my leg was gone, I knew no person dying, no matter how much you loved them, could be as bad as losing part of yourself. And I just lay in that hospital bed and thought about how, without even knowing how to do it even, I got up and took a coupla steps and there it was. Born with it, a year-old kid with two wonderful legs, all those muscles and bones and flesh and the ten toes and the veins, all working together, so I could do ordinary things like walking, running, and jumping and here I was, twenty-eight, and I'd never be able to do any of it any more. Oh yeah, they told me about the great prosthetics they have nowadays and I bet you know all about them and everybody does, but it ain't the same. It's the lousiest facsimile." He choked a little and rubbed his eyes with his fingers.

"Of course it's not the same," Sally said soothingly. "It's a horrid loss. No one can ever make up to you for that, Saul." She took his empty glass and got them both another drink.

"Then there's other things too," he was saying. "Oh, I sure used that old brainpan of mine overtime while I was lying there in that bed, it hurt to do it after years of letting that department strictly alone. I thought about making love to Rose and what woman would want a man with one leg doing it to her, specially since she could remember when he used to be all there. I didn't want a woman to ever see me again, not like that. So I was gonna write and tell her to get a divorce anyway, but the little bitch beat me to the draw. And that's what hurt, because then I knew what a fool I was. Sure, a guy thinks when he's away maybe his wife is shacking but what the hell, he's doing it, and the thing is not to think about it. It's wartime and people are lonesome and I'm not the kind of guy thinks it's all right only for men. But Christ, them others, they were nothing. Ships in the night. And if she had of shacked up like that, I didn't care, long as she never told me and she still loved me. But not her. Not her kind. All they ever think about is things, you know, furniture, a house, clothes, a husband they can brag about to other women. But I didn't know that until I got her letter and all of a sudden, like I was hit by lightning, I knew what she was. And I was only another thing to her. Only no good any more. Broken . . ."

He went on for a long time getting more incoherent and after a while he began to cry, hard, dry, horrible suppressed sounds. It was more than Sally could bear, seeing this big man eaten away with sadness, choking out his rage and misery. She put her arms around him and drew his head down on her breast.

"Don't, Saul, oh don't," she kept murmuring, saying it over and over, senselessly, trying to comfort him, knowing how useless it was, but trying anyway, "oh don't. It's all over, it's all done with." She stroked his curly black hair and after a while he stopped and she could feel him lying there against her, breathing hard, and then she heard him saying in a low, fierce voice, "You don't know, you don't know how it is, how it is with a man to feel like a nothing, like dirt. I was gonna be big, they cheered me, they wrote about me in the papers. People came to see me fight and I can never do it again. I'm nothing but a cripple that nobody wants."

"You're not," Sally said, "you're as fine as you ever were."

"No," he said dully, "I'm a nobody, a gimpy schmuck. Even when I was an officer in the Army, I was something, a good soldier. I wasn't afraid of nobody. I could knock down anybody with one hand behind me, and now, any little punk could push me over like I was a bowling pin and that little whore that was my wife could throw me away . . ."

"Stop it, Saul," Sally said gently.

"Even you," he said, "you don't really wanna go to bed with me. No woman would, only pigs who do it for money."

His body pressed heavily and arousingly upon hers and he was breathing hard, almost panting.

"It's you that don't want me, Saul. You know that I've wanted you since we first saw each other."

"Yeah," he said bitterly. "It's because you feel sorry for me. Because you think maybe it might've been your husband or that cousin of yours you were so crazy for, instead of getting killed they only lost a leg."

"I don't feel sorry for you," Sally said. "Why don't you stop being so damn stubborn? You don't believe in yourself, Saul, and it's silly. And you're afraid of me."

He made an impatient gesture. "Sally, for Christ's sakes, I tell you it's not that. It's well, like I told you, you don't want to get mixed up with me or me with you. It's all wrong. You don't know about me. If you did you wouldn't get near me with a tenfoot pole."

"I'm not precisely a virginal angel myself," Sally said. She leaned her head against his chest and slowly unbuttoned some of the buttons of his shirt.

"Christ!" he said explosively and then he pulled her up to him and kissed her and she felt him holding her, big, strong, impatient, powerful, and in a little while, he got up and went into her room and then he called her to come in. She was in a dream because of the drinking and the long wanting and when she came in the room was dark and she wanted to see him, to look at him and have him look at her but she knew he was ashamed.

"Love me, Sally," he was saying. "Make me feel like something, you feel so beautiful, your skin's so soft and smooth, I want a woman to love me, a real woman . . ."

It was strange being with him, feeling the leg only to below the knee and then nothing, but after a while there in the dark, there was nothing gone or missing. He was over her, heavy, hard, big, the thick black hair on his chest pressing now against her breasts, driving her into an almost unbelievable frenzy because she was so unused to it, for a minute her mind wandered off, never had a man with so much hair before, crazy, wild tickling, exciting as hell. Then the wave of desire mounted and she was almost drowning because he was inside her, big, big, soft, velvety, yet hard, pushing, his tongue stroking hers, they were one, his hands clasping her body tightly to his, pounding, moving fast, and she was on tiptoe, poised, waiting, and then it came in a rush, she wanted it never to stop and yet it must because she couldn't bear it any more, it was so lovely and it was going up, up and she had to cry out and it would end soon, so soon and it was doing, done, did, ended, ended, over and done and at the same instant she felt him going quite wild and then he was finished, lying there, breathing deeply, his head on her breast. Languorously, she stroked his back, her eyes closed and then she heard his voice, a voice of awe and adoration, saying gently,

"Sally, oh honey, I never had a woman like you before, never in my life."

Ridiculous, Sally thought, behind her closed eyelids, a ridiculous, simple thing to say. But, in a way, rather wonderful. And was he ridiculous at all, she wondered, a little ashamed, or could he ever be again, after that. In the dark, his arm went around her shoulders and his hand folded over her breast but they were separate again and he had pulled the sheet up over his waist.

"Would you like a cigarette?" She was impatient to see his body but he would not let her turn on the light.

For a while they smoked silently in the dark, her head against his shoulder.

"You're being silly," Sally said finally. "Why won't you let me see you?"

"Give you a charge would it?"

"I suspect so."

He chuckled. "You're quite a woman, aren't you? You suspect so, huh? You know, Sally, years ago, women like you used to give me a pain. They talked so fancy, I'd avoid them like poison. I'm not boasting but there were a couple of ritzy broads chasing me when

I was in the ring only I used to run the other way when I saw them coming."

"Is that what I am, a ritzy broad?"

"Don't get sore."

"I'm not."

"Oh yes you are. I can tell by the way you pull out your words. Real high-class. Sure you are, you're pretty classy. But no broad."

"Thank you."

"I meant it as a compliment."

"So you don't mind the way I talk?"

"Mind," he echoed fervently. "I love it. It's music to my ears. I was just kind of thinking about how the way people talk don't have a damn thing to do with whether they're real women or not. Or is that too mixed up?"

"No. Quite clear." She was beginning to get drowsy. All that liquor.

"So you liked it, huh?"

"You know I did."

"Sometimes women fake these things."

"You must know some very peculiar women." She yawned and now her eyes were open but it was definitely an effort.

"You tired, Sally? Want me to go?"

"Oh no," Sally said, uncontrollably sleepy now. "Stay till morning."

"What time does your brother get home?"

Sally thought she answered him but couldn't remember. So peaceful and relaxed now. She caught sort of an indistinguishable murmur from him and wanted to make him promise he wouldn't go away, he'd wake her up in a while and then . . .

It was the slamming of the front door that woke her. In a panic she sat up and struggled desperately to shake the deep wool of sleep. Through half-open eyes she could see the cracks of light between the venetian blind slats. She looked at her watch. It was 8:15 and morning and she was all alone. Steps marched along the hall. Dudley, no doubt about that. The awkward, slithery way he had of walking. But how had she slept so long? Surely, she would have heard Saul leave if he'd only gone a short time ago. And wouldn't he have woken her up? A second later her eyes opened a little wider and she saw the note on the table.

"*If you want to call me, the number is . . .*" It was a Cunningham exchange. The writing was almost illegible and she could barely read the number, although the signature, Saul, was bold and plain enough. He must have written it in the dark. How on earth, she wondered, suddenly wide awake, could he have done all those things and she not heard a sound? Oh, my God, she thought remembering, if I were a cat, I'd sit and lick my fur and purr. If only she hadn't fallen asleep like a damn fool. But he should've awakened her. Would've if he'd really wanted to. She looked at the note closely and finally made out the number. Perhaps if she hurried might be time to get him. What did he mean by walking out on her like that and leaving that silly, shamefaced note? She got out of bed and opened the door into the hall before remembering that she was naked. No damn robe anyplace. She pulled the sheet from the bed and wrapped it around her. Dudley was probably in bed by now anyway.

A woman's nasal voice answered the telephone, doubtful and suspicious, and wanting to know who was calling. The funny aunt who'd asked such peculiar questions. Sally tapped the appointment book pencil stub impatiently against the table. She might jump right out of her skin if the woman said another word but her voice was, she thought, unrevealing and cool.

"From the *Beacon*," she explained.

"Well, just a minute, he just went out the back door to the car . . . I'll see if I can get him, is it important hah?"

"We want him to get something on his way in," Sally lied brightly.

"Hold on, hold on." Sally heard a shrill cry. "Solly, it's for you. Telephone. The *Beacon*. He'll be in in a minute, miss." Triumphantly. "I just caught him."

"Thank you so much." Heart was pounding. Was it silly of her to do this? How would he sound? What would he say? She pulled the sheet more closely around her. Her feet were chilly without slippers on the cold linoleum floor. Disgusting mustard-and-brown stripes. Dudley was still in the bathroom. She could hear the shower running. Undoubtedly he would come out while she was talking. Well, let him. She clutched the sheet.

"Yeah, this is Saul. Who's this? Miss McCarty?"

"This is Sally," she said slowly. Her voice seemed to have sunk very low in her throat. "I didn't want to tell your aunt who I was."

There was a brief silence. Finally he said in a guarded voice, "I was just on my way to work. Can I do anything for you?"

The aunt probably standing by listening, hands on her plump hips, ears cocked.

"I want to see you." More than see you, much more. She gripped the pencil tightly, her fingernails digging into the soft wood. Acting like a teenager. Overemotional. But she had to.

"When?"

"Now."

"Listen," he said carefully, "wait a second, will you?" She heard him say then, "Sophy, how about shutting the door? No, it's not important. Yeah, well thanks." Then the unnecessarily loud slam of a door.

"My aunt was listening."

"I gathered."

"This is crazy. You know I have to go to work. I'll be late as it is now."

"Couldn't you take the day off?"

"Well, I dunno," he said doubtfully. "I spose I could call up sick or something. But it's nuts."

"Not at all," Sally said sweetly. "Just some unfinished business to complete."

"Boy," he said. "You don't beat around the bush, do you?"

"You should have awakened me."

"Aaaah, I dunno," he said glumly. "I figured, what's the percentage? You do a crazy thing, once, maybe, okay. But more and it gets to be a habit."

"It's a fine habit."

"Listen Sally. Why don't you sleep on it for a day or two. I mean, I'll be around . . ."

"My, we're so full of prudence and scruples this morning," Sally drawled.

"Oh can that stuff," he said. "I just want to save us both some trouble."

"You're an incredible pessimist," Sally said lightly although she knew that there were tears in her eyes. "Very well, I shan't try to convince you." She heard the water stop running in the bathroom. Dudley would appear in a few minutes and raise his infernal eyebrows at the sheet and the damn tears too, probably.

"What beats me is what a classy dame like you wants me around for?" Saul was saying in a puzzled way.

"I loathe all that false humility," Sally said crisply. "When you find something perfect you don't want to let it slip away. Isn't your aunt listening to you?"

"Probly. Behind the door. I don't care. Listen, do you always get what you want?"

"Usually. My wants are simple."

"Look," he said. "I'll be so goddamn late to work by now, it isn't worth going. So what'll we do if I call in sick? Isn't your brother home?"

"I have the keys to my aunt's cottage in Nahant. If it's warm enough we can go swimming."

"Swimming!" he said incredulously and began to laugh. "Boy," he said after awhile, "you're a real, honest-to-God A number one crazy, you know that? Sure, honey, we'll go swimming. Where do you want me to pick you up?"

The bathroom door was opening. "Here," Sally said hastily. "Downstairs. In an hour."

He was laughing again. "I dunno if I got any swimming trunks. It's kind of early. Sophy's probly got 'em put away in mothballs. Jesus Christ! Swimming! In May, yet!"

"There'll be some there, I expect. Goodbye." She put down the phone. "Hi, Dud." The sheet had slipped down leaving one shoulder bare. She pulled it up quickly and smiled at him as he stood irresolute in the bathroom doorway, staring at her.

Too late, she noticed that one of her thighs was showing and he seemed to be unable to look anywhere else.

"New style in robes?" he enquired.

"Oh, you're too funny," Sally said, sitting there fuming. If she got up the fool thing might fall off completely. Why did he keep standing there?

"I wanted to apologize for the other day," her brother said. "I'm very sorry. About the mess and all." He fumbled in his bathrobe pocket and drew his glasses out. "You really look very charming in that sheet, my dear."

"I couldn't find my robe," Sally said defensively. "No need to apologize, Dud." The last thing she could bear this morning was to have him fumble around, explaining his revolting problems.

"About the girl?" Dudley enquired tentatively, his face a little flushed.

"What girl?"

"The girl you were going to introduce . . . well, that day, when I was . . ."

"Oh . . ." She had completely forgotten about Deborah. "Yes, that girl. You can meet her some other time."

"What is she, that is, what sort . . ."

Sheet or no sheet, Sally thought, bouncing up impatiently, I cannot sit here and listen to him, one moment more. If he could ever come directly to the point, once, instead of circling around like a dog jumping at a shadow.

"She's very pretty," Sally said, moving toward the bathroom, determinedly, holding the sheet up so that she wouldn't trip on it, "very sweet, young, naïve, and bookish. And shy. I'll work something out, Dudley. Very soon. Now, if you don't mind, I must take a shower. Are you finished in here?"

"Yes, certainly," he said standing aside to let her go through the door. "Well, thank you, Sally. It was very kind of you to think of me."

"Uh huh," Sally said ungraciously. She slammed the bathroom door, knowing that his pale, gooseberry eyes were fixed on the bare backs of her thighs, which the sheet couldn't cover and allow her to walk too.

"It's pretty swell, all right," Saul said, as they stood on the porch of the cottage looking out at the bay, glittering and flashing in the early morning sun. The water was as cold-looking and beautiful as emeralds. "But Jesus, you'd have to have some nerve to go into that water."

Sally rummaged through her handbag searching for the key. "I thought you said you didn't swim."

"I used to. But that's one of the little joys I had to give up for my country."

"You could still swim," Sally said severely, turning the key in the lock. "It's silly to give it up if you like it. It's not like other exercise. In fact, you'd probably be more buoyant."

"How about basket weaving? You think I'd be good at that?"

"You know I'm right."

"Sure you're right," he agreed. "But it's too goddamn much of a production, that's all. I'd need crutches to get me down to the water for one thing. And I'd only do it if I were alone. No, I'll just lie around and get pneumonia and a sunburn and watch you, that is, if you're crazy enough to go into that ice."

He waited outside, sitting on the porch steps in the sun, while Sally went in and flung open windows. There was a horrid, musty smell. She changed hastily into her bathing suit, buckled on sandals and draped a toweling robe around her. He was very weird, she thought. When she'd slid into the car, an hour earlier, he'd acted as if he'd totally forgotten the passion of the night before, simply grinning at her and shaking his head. Hadn't even kissed her. What on earth was the matter with him, anyway? Here she was practically flinging herself at his head. Now let's see . . . oh yes. She found her grandmother's sheets, stowed away, lavender-scented, in a teak chest and swiftly made up the old birdseye maple bed in the larger bedroom.

Of course the water would be cold, she thought, picking up her bathing cap, a towel and a blanket, still full of melted glacier, but she must get into it. Somehow, she felt that after five years, her first plunge into the familiar northern waters of her childhood and youth would wash away the sad, dull years and return to her the enchantment of summers she'd spent on this beach with Benjie. Those crazy, wild summers when they'd tried to cool their burning bodies by plunging into the marvelous coldness of the water and come out to lie on the fiery sand, trying not to touch each other, feeling themselves one with the shimmering heat, melting with love, on fire from the sun and how they'd waited for the night when they could lie in the same place, mouths and bodies glued together, hidden in the blue-black, salt-smelling, mysterious darkness. Perhaps it would all come back, she thought, going outside on the porch, and when she came out of the water, she'd feel once again that each day would be wonderful, that marvelous things were to happen. Only, this time, Saul would be there . . .

He was sitting where she'd left him, smoking, his eyes closed against the sun.

"Ready, Saul?"

He didn't open his eyes. "I'm kind of comfortable where I am. Why don't you go ahead and I'll come down in a few minutes."

Awfully damn uncooperative, Sally thought, going down the steps. Acting as if he were the only sensible man in a land of fools. Too bad he wouldn't swim. Probably look lovely in lastex trunks. She'd not seen his naked body completely after all. Modest as a virginal bride. Poor thing, of course, he's afraid, all marred as he is and doesn't trust me. It really was a sensational day, even he couldn't be insensitive to it for long. Suddenly, she felt all excited and happy and went flying down the road to the beach, rapturously sniffing the salt in the air and all the green things growing. Azaleas glowed in gardens full of the blue air that is always purest in little white seaside towns early in the morning. Bees droned in some late-flowering white lilacs and Sally couldn't endure all that smell of lilac around her and none for herself. She broke a sprig from a bush trailing over someone's fence as she passed and tucked it into the belt of her jade-green robe. Heavenly colors of morning. Trailing rainbow showers of spray, she ran in.

At the clean, green, salt heart of the water the coldness was unbelievable, shocking at first, but after the primary gasps and the
feeling that the cold had eaten all her bones away, she began to
stroke strongly and the old wonder started. Her blood pumped pure
and strong through a body shrived, pristine, innocent, and healthy.

After awhile, she rolled over and lay on her back, staring straight
up, floating deliciously on the water, unthinkingly happy in a vast,
blue-green bubble. The water held her safely and strongly and she
felt that it was like being in love again: the tingling excitement of
the water rousing her and then there would be the coming ashore
to lie drowsily in the sun of the languorous aftermath. But no, it
would not be, she thought, shaken out of her inviolable moment,
like that at all any more. Slowly she began to swim toward shore.
Saul would be there with his strange advances, withdrawals and
moods. And love? Well there was no question of that, surely, but
passion was such a simple form of love for both of them right now.
It would solve all sorts of problems with no involvements and after
awhile it would be over. Why couldn't he see that? Surely, after that
shoddy wife of his he'd be leery of love. Obviously, he couldn't
suspect her of romantic sentiments. What then, was it? Wading out
of the water, she determined to tell him plainly that this ridiculous
changeability, this backing and filling, didn't go down with her. No
matter how much she enjoyed having sex with him. She thought,
briefly, of Mike. He was a sweet boy, wonderful really.

Saul was standing by the spread-out blanket holding a leather
flask.

"Here," he said handing it to her, "you'll turn blue in a minute."

She was shivering, because, in spite of all her bravery, the water
had been freezing and the morning air on her wet body was dev-
astatingly cold. She threw the towel around her shoulders and took
a great swig from the flask.

"Marvelous idea," she said. "Should've thought of it myself."

"You can't think of everything," he said grinning. "Here, gimme
the towel. I'll give you a rubdown."

"Are you sure you want to get that close to me?"

"Don't be so fresh," he said rubbing her back vigorously with the
towel. "And take another slug of the brandy. If you lie down I'll
rub your legs for you. Real professional service here. Just like my
trainer used to do for me."

"I'll just put my robe on," Sally said, reaching for it. He pulled the
towel away immediately and she wrapped herself in the green

warmth of the robe and sitting down cross-legged on the blanket began to comb out her wet hair.

With an effort he dropped himself on the blanket beside her and lit two cigarettes. He handed her one.

"You sore at me?"

"A bit."

"More brandy?"

"No thanks."

"I'm sorry about . . . well . . . I get moods sometimes."

"So I see." Sally inhaled deeply on her cigarette and squinted into the sun. He'd taken off his shirt. Out of the corner of her eye she noted it, flung on top of the damp towel next to her. His hand was on her back, slowly caressing it through the toweling robe. She shrugged her shoulders impatiently and the hand went away.

"All right," he said, "okay, I deserve it. No excuse, honey. I'm a little tired is all. When I left you I drove around awhile, had some coffee in an all-night diner. Couldn't fall asleep when I got home. You got me all stirred up and I don't know what the hell to do."

"I'm sorry if I've disturbed your life. We can forget about it."

She stretched out full length on the blanket and closed her eyes against the strengthening sun which stabbed in flashes against her eyelids. Sunglasses somewhere. She groped around in her robe pocket and drew them out.

"Don't put those things on yet, honey," he said softly. "Look at me."

He was lying propped on his elbow, his enormous, naked, hairy chest looming above her, all black and masculine against the white glare of sun on sand.

"You're impossible," she said and shivered again, even though her swimming chill was all gone.

"It's just a climb in the hay to you?"

"What else should it be?"

"What if I fell in love with you and wanted to marry you, what about that?"

"Why would you want to do that?" Sally asked, startled. She noticed that his lips were trembling and he gripped one of her arms so tightly that it hurt. "I should think you've had enough of marriage."

"Sometimes, I think I'd like to have a kid before I die."

"How weird," Sally said. "Still, you do have years. Men can have children till they're a hundred years old."

"I'm lucky if I make forty."

"Why? Are you suffering from some wasting, mysterious disease?"

"Nah," he said broodingly. "Life isn't worth a thing to me nowadays. I don't give a damn about nothing."

"Well, I'm not going to marry you," Sally said impatiently. "I've been married and it was a bore. And I haven't the remotest desire for children."

Suddenly he reached over and pulled her to him.

"Oh, Saul," Sally said, "why must you make things so difficult?"

"I'm in a black hole," he said in a voice of such cold despair that Sally quaked. "Buried in slime and no matter how much I try I can't climb out of it. I figured maybe you'd understand."

"I do. And I could help you."

"Yeah. Only after awhile you'd drop me back in again."

"God! You must hate women."

"Not women. It's just this lousy, rotten life. You know the Bible, Sally?"

"Fairly well. Why? I thought you weren't religious."

"I'm not. But when I was in the hospital, I used to go crazy from thinking about what had happened to me and the only way I could avoid it for a few minutes was to read. And pretty soon I'd read all the stinking Westerns and detective stories and magazines they had around and there wasn't much left but the Bible. The New Testament was too saintly. I liked the Old one better, lotta wars and bloodshed. I used to read Kings. And Prophets. And maybe because I had his name, I liked Saul. He used to have these crazy fits. And I could understand that. 'But the spirit of the Lord departed from Saul and an evil spirit troubled him.' He did something wrong. I forget what. Kept a few sheep or didn't kill someone he should've or some screwy little thing like that. That God of the Jews didn't mince words. Anyway, he was removed from office, like."

"I remember," Sally said. The Sunday school in the church basement. A big pink ribbon in her hair. Shiny black Mary Janes and pink socks. Eight or nine, wasn't she, then? Just come from Europe where she'd occasionally gone to Mass with the maid. Popery, her grandfather'd said, I knew it. They'd seen slides. Samson carrying the gates of Gaza on his shoulders. Bad art. Terrible colors. Brassy greens and bluey yellows.

"I remember," she repeated. "David came and played to him on the harp and he'd feel better."

"How much better can you feel when God has a down on you?"

"If you think that about yourself," Sally said, "you're a little crazy."

306

"More than a little. That's what I keep trying to tell you only you won't believe me."

"Oh, nonsense. You're just wretchedly unhappy and you've a right to be. But you don't need to fight against one of the few pleasant things life offers. Anyway, I don't believe for one minute that you think God is persecuting you."

"Oh, God," he said with a shrug. "I never said it was God, for me, that is. For the other Saul, sure, God did everything in those days. No, with me, it's just being in the way of the wrong luck, that's all. Luck, chance, whatever you want to call it, but I've had it all right. God didn't do it, I didn't do it, there's no one person responsible, but just the same, here I am. In a way, they were better off when they could blame someone unreal like God instead of big systems that make wars where some guys get it and some don't." He laughed, a little short harsh bark. "So when the evil spirit comes on me I just cast my javelins at whos'ever around. So you happened to be around."

"Yes," Sally said. She put on her sunglasses. "But, you know all this moody change of heart and soul searching is awfully tedious. It was so fine last night. So simple. We could have had that for as long as we wanted. But since you don't seem to, I'm sure we can say goodbye nicely after you drop me at my doorstep."

"Okay," he said. He moved away from her. "Guess I'll try to get caught up on my lost shuteye. Since we're here. Good place for a nap as any."

Sally closed her eyes. She smelled the cigarette smoke, heard the soft sound of the waves hitting the shore and knew that all the harsh colors around her were tempered with green, green gold, green green, green blue. She drowsed while the sun flamed pale yellow behind her sunglasses. Her morning idyll and he had spoiled it. She thought of the lavender-scented sheets on the bed. Sentiment and neurotic clods didn't mix well obviously. Silly of her to have thought for a moment that they might. Alone in the afterward. Why couldn't it have been Benjie? A gull screamed overhead. The waves' whisper faded. She fell asleep.

She woke up suddenly feeling his hands on her. He'd opened her robe and pulled the straps of her suit down so that her breasts were completely bared. She stared at him, startled, as he loomed over her and knew after a moment that he had not slept but had finished the brandy in the flask. His face was flushed, his eyes half-closed and the brandy smell was strong around them. She lay there passively for a few seconds while he stroked her nipples and then she reached her arms out to him and his head came down and he was feverishly kissing her breasts with loud, sucking gasps.

"The bed's all made up in the cottage. Let's not be stupid any more, Saul, let's go now."

He sat up and looked at her in a dazed sort of way. "Okay," he said. "You win. I don't care what happens. Because this is glory. I've never seen anything more goddamn beautiful in my whole lousy life, than you, like that. I'd like to pull the whole damn suit off and have you like that, all naked in the sun . . ."

They lay, at last, on the freshly made-up bed in the cottage, and he was kissing her body. "You'll never get rid of me now," he said fiercely. "You woman, you. Oh, my God, what a woman you are."

There was a salt-tinged wind blowing cool from the open windows on their tightly bound together bodies.

"Honey," he murmured, "feel it. It's all for you."

Under her hands were the great, heavy, hairy thighs, the fleshy stomach, the wonderful maleness and everything came alive again. Only more so. More than everything. More soft, but firm, more yielding but hard, white as marble, soft as black fur, full and rich and liquid like white cream and she could feel every inch of her skin as he was feeling it and at the same time she was herself there being taken by him, receiving him, being wide and warm, firm and cushioned, soft and wet for him and knowing that there had never been anything prouder, stronger, wilder, more powerful than he was for her. In an instant's wild fury it was all over and they plummeted down together and lay, lethargically clutching the now not really caring bodies.

That was how the summer began and proceeded. Sally was in such a constant fever of passion that she wanted to do absolutely nothing but see and be with Saul. She couldn't eat. Food choked her. She existed, for at least a month, solely on black coffee, whiskey, gin, and cigarettes. Some nights, when he couldn't come up to stay with her, she would lie awake half the night, biting her pillow and pressing herself against the mattress until it got so unbearable that she'd have to drink herself to sleep with three or four glasses of straight Scotch. One night, in desperation, she'd called him at one in the morning and gotten his aunt out of bed to answer the phone. The aunt had been very rude and not wanted to call Saul and when she finally did Sally could hear her in the background, shrilly castigating women who had no decency and when Saul told Sally he'd come right over and get her the aunt had set up a siren wail. They'd gone to a hotel that night because Dudley was home but Saul's aunt wouldn't talk to him for a week.

"Why don't you move out?" Sally said. "We'll get a place."

"I can't do it, honey. I need someone to take care of me sometimes and I don't want it to be you. Anyway, my aunt wouldn't understand. She's been damn good to me. And I've been kind of bastardly to her."

"Well, darling, I should think if she insists on telling you what to do every second . . ."

"Ah, she just worries I'll get into trouble and not be able to take care of myself. She don't mean any harm. Besides, what's the point of getting a place? You'll be going to Rockport in July."

"Then I'll go stay at the cottage in Nahant," Sally said decisively. "And you come out every night. You'll be a commuter."

"That'd be as bad as living together," he protested. "You'd have to help me out sometimes and . . . see things . . . well, that I don't want you to see."

"Darling, you are an idiot." They were sitting next to each other in a bar booth and she put her hand on his thigh. "You think I care? Don't you know me well enough by now?"

"I guess so. I guess I know you well enough to give you just what you want, don't I? Only how I'm going to explain to Sophy I don't know."

"You could say that you were going off for a vacation, couldn't you?"

"I'm gonna take my vacation in July when you're up in Rockport. Otherwise, I'll only see you on weekends."

"Oh Lord, that's so. I couldn't stand that."

"There'll be plenty of guys up there, keep you busy," he said in the kind of morose voice she hadn't heard for a long time.

"No," Sally said positively. "There'll be no one but you. Don't you know that?"

"How should I know? You're a beautiful doll."

"Well then, I won't go. I'll tell Vance I don't want the job."

"Say," he said alarmed. "Don't be crazy. You know you want that job. It'd be good for you. You got a real voice there, a real talent. And believe me I know how lousy it is if you can't do what you wanna do. I won't let you give up that job just because I'm crazy jealous. Oh no."

"I can't bear being away from you," Sally said leaning her head against his shoulder. He bent down and kissed her till her lips quivered.

"Why did you take your hand away?"

"The guys at the bar are looking," he said in a low voice.

"I don't care."

"Well, I do. I don't want these bums around here to think you're some cheap tart. Let's go. We'll go out to the cottage now, though why you call a fancy place like that a cottage, I'll never figure. I'll move some of my stuff out there tomorrow. Even if Sophy carries on it'll be worth it to stay with you every night."

The month of June was hot. High in the 80s and low in the 90s and for one whole week and a half there was a heat wave when the mercury remained monotonously at 98, 99, and 100.

Every morning after Saul left, Sally would get up naked and put on her bathing suit and at night when he came home she'd be wearing a pair of shorts and a jersey which were her grocery-going clothes. She'd put the shorts on over her naked bottom and drive over to the supermarket in town to buy breakfast and supper stuff, for all the world like any other hasty suburban housewife, at five o'clock, rushing to get dinner on the table before the man came home. She herself ate almost nothing but Saul's appetite was as gargantuan as ever. Some nights in the week they would take a drive along the coast and have dinner in a restaurant. And then perhaps a movie until it became apparent that neither of them had the vaguest idea afterwards of what had gone on in the movies they'd seen and it was too frustrating even in drive-ins to wait so long before getting home to bed.

"The hell with movies and civilization," Saul said. "We can see them anytime when we're alone. Let's just have a bite here and do what we like to do most."

So on week nights they'd simply go to bed after supper, naked between the cool sheets in the hot night with cigarettes and a bottle of whisky and a pitcher of ice water on the table beside them.

"I thought a man was supposed to get sort of tired by the time he was thirty-two," Sally said once when they were lying together talking in the dark.

"For a smart girl you don't seem to have figured much out. We're two of a kind, honey, didn't you know that? I knew about you right away. How come you didn't know about me?"

"I thought perhaps it was because it was the beginning. Things are always more exciting at the start, aren't they?"

"Sure," he said, "but that's not why, with us. Me, I've always been superhot for the skin game. Used to drive my wife nuts. In a way she was glad I went into the Army, though she was jealous, knowing I couldn't do without it."

"Was she . . ." Sally began and then stopped. "I'm sorry. I don't really care."

He laughed. "No, I don't either. But she didn't know anything, see. When I married her she was a virgin and I had to teach her the whole damn business. That's what I wanted so I didn't complain. Except, she never really made it, you know. But some girls don't want to, anyway. Or can't. You know, it's funny but I'm not even sore at her any more. Since I've known you, I feel like I used to. Real great and happy, except when I think it's too good to last. Then it's worse."

"Don't talk about it, Saul. It won't end. Unless you die from lack of sleep. I sleep on the beach in the morning, but you, how do you stand it?"

"Who wants to sleep? That, I can do all summer when you're up in Rockport. Won't be a damn thing else to do. You ought to eat more though," he added seriously. "I'm afraid you'll get sick on me, honey."

"But I just can't eat. Honestly Saul. Sex ruins my appetite. I'll come out of it."

"Been like this before?"

"Sometimes. Not often. Not in years, anyway."

"Not with your husband?"

"Why do you keep asking me that, Saul? I've told you it's not interesting or important."

"Because," he said, "maybe I'm a sucker. I knew I could be if I got the chance. But the only thing I care about now is you. So I want to know all about you. Every lousy little thing. Like what you think about anything. Why you're always brushing your teeth. Why you don't wear a girdle and have your hair curled all the time like other women do. And why you married a guy you didn't love. That's the most important thing."

"What fabulously muscular arms you have," she said, browsing. "And your skin tastes so marvelous. Well, I imagine it's odd, but I don't really feel this consuming interest in *your* past. To me, you came all new and fresh, when I met you. Just created all male and wonderful for me. I don't care about what you did before. All I care about is now." Slowly, she traced the imprint of her eternal desire across the flesh of his groin and then they didn't have to talk any more.

But weekends, when they could be together for two whole days and three whole nights were the very best. On Friday afternoons, Sally would rouse herself from her sun and saltsoaked lethargy, take a scented bath and put on a dress, some gay, bright cotton. Then she would drive around and buy some good wine and flowers and herbs and wonderfully fresh fish or seafood and then come home and make a special festive dinner for him to celebrate the oncoming weekend.

One Friday night Saul'd come home with two tickets for a play at the summer theatre in Beverly.

"They're passing them out down at the paper," he said. "Since you're all dressed up and it's so close, whyn't we go?"

But the play was so pretentious and dull that they'd left after the second act.

"I don't know why we bother," Sally said dreamily as they were driving back to Nahant. "We're so much more interesting than all these dim-witted entertainments."

"You look beautiful in that dress," he said. "I had trouble keeping my hands off you. All the guys were looking at you during intermission. I wanted to wrap you up in a sheet."

"I love weekends," Sally said. "I wish they'd last forever. Do you know, Saul, we've never had sex in a car."

"We're not going to either. I'm too old and broken up for that kid stuff."

"Still," Sally said. "It's fine on the grass too and on the beach on a hot night."

"I remember," Saul said grimly. "How many guys have you had on the beach on hot nights?"

"Oh, darling, now don't. Why should you care? You've probably had thousands of women and I don't ask you, do I?"

"They weren't women. At least for the past four years they weren't."

"Well, good Lord, what were they? Men?"

He laughed hoarsely. "Sure. I'm just the type."

"I'm not the one who introduced the subject," Sally said. "You are." She stopped suddenly. I never wanted to let a woman see me that way, he'd said. And even now he didn't want her to see him. It's just a stub down there, he'd said once, what the hell, are you morbid, you don't wanna see it. They weren't women, he'd said, and then, I couldn't do without it. And long ago, he didn't want to hear the opinions on men who went to whorehouses.

"So you don't think whores are women?"

"No," he said curtly. "They made a business out of what a woman does for love. Let's drop it, huh?"

"I'm fascinated."

"You would be," he said bitterly. "Well it makes me sick to talk about it."

"Ah, now there are things you don't want to discuss. Well I think I have a right to know. You want to worm every tiny bit of my life out of me and you drop all these insinuating hints and then you say you don't want to talk about it."

"All right," he said angrily. "It's my fault. I know it. But it got me sore to think about all the guys who've loved you and you've loved. Like with me. So you're the first real woman I've had since my wife. And so it's deep with me only with you it's just another roll on the beach or wherever. And if you look at it another way it's an insult to you."

"Not at all," Sally said coolly. "I'm terribly flattered. We're quarreling, Saul. Just as we did at the beginning."

"I know," he said, and drove off the road onto a grassy headland overlooking the bay. He stopped the car and there was a small, silver, new moon and they lay back in each other's arms, kissing fiercely. The tide was out and through the car's open window floated the smell of seaweed stranded on the beach and the fertile earth and the sweet, sweet, piercing smell of wild honeysuckle.

"Darling," she said after awhile. "I'm so sorry. It must have been terrible. You're really such a warm, loving person underneath all that façade."

"When I first came home, I hated women and everything so much, I thought I'd never get hot again. Might as well lose that I thought, I lost every goddamn thing else that made it worth while. But after awhile I started getting a hard on every time I looked at a good-looking dame and once, Jesus, I sweat every time I remember this, my car was on the fritz and I had to take a subway which was a bitch with my leg anyhow and it was jammed, so I was pressed up against some real chesty broad and up it came. What a dirty look she gave me and boy I felt like hell. Like one of those lousy perverts you know and I got out at the next stop even though it wasn't mine and took a cab the rest of the way home and when I got there I had to do what I used to do when I was a kid. But that was it. I was no kid. So I hunted up a house, I used to know about when I was fighting though I never went there then. Never needed to. The girls were clean and all. And for awhile I didn't care. You know. I went a lot. Couldn't stand it if I didn't."

"Anyway I kept telling myself what the hell difference did it make? With a whore you pay for them and you're through with them and nobody's pulling the wool over nobody's eyes. And with some of them I didn't even have to pay. For a war hero some of those damn sentimental whores'd do it for nothing. And I never tried to be noble and stop them. But the rest of them made up for it. Some of those money-mad fleabags'd charge a one-legged man more. And I didn't argue with them neither. What the hell it was their job." He stopped and lit two cigarettes and gave her one. "Well, how do you feel about me now?"

Sally kissed him gently on the cheek. "Just wish I'd met you long before. Funny about you, Saul, having these weird guilt feelings. I suppose it's the way you were brought up. I don't think it's so terrible. But you must have loathed it to be so upset about it all. And I don't think you needed to, anyway. I'm sure you could have found a girl to love you."

"I didn't try. I dunno, it's mixed up, but I wanted to make the whole thing cold, a cash transaction. No feelings mixed up in it. Only the trouble was, it got on my nerves after awhile. I'm a soft sap and all the time I wanted somebody to love me. I'd take a few dames out once in a while but I dunno, I was scared to try anything so I'd have a fight with them and that'd be the end of it."

"Yes," Sally said. "I see why I had to pursue you so vigilantly."

"So you see how much you mean to me, Sally. I guess you didn't want to mean that much to anybody, did you?"

"No," Sally said honestly, "I don't really."

"I tried to tell you."

"I know you did."

"Well, it's too late now. I'm crazy in love with you."

"I'm very fond of you," Sally said, crushing out her half-smoked cigarette in the dashboard ashtray, "only . . ."

"Only that's all."

"It's not quite all. You see, I care more for you than I have for any man since Ben. I know there's all this wise talk about how passion vanishes rapidly, but I don't believe it. It can last an awfully long time under the right circumstances. And we're very good together. As you said, we're two of a kind. But I want this just the way it is. I don't want to turn it into something deadly and wrong for us both, like marriage and children."

"You really mean that? About me being the first since your cousin?"

"Yes."

"Okay," he said, "it's a deal. Only don't fall in love with somebody else too fast, will you?"

"I'm too busy now to look at another man." She put her hand on him. "Let's go home. I'm starved."

He pulled up her dress and ran his hand over the insides of her thighs. "We'll go down on the beach now," he said in a strangled voice. "Like you want to."

She drew away from him, straightening her dress. "No," she said firmly. "We'll go home and go to bed. You'll be miserable down on the beach. I don't know what I was thinking of. You'll hate it. And I want you to love everything we do together and not think about other men I've been with. We'll go home and make love and be happy with no stale ghosts around."

Sally lost ten pounds in three weeks. She was brown and dry like a Frost sand dune. Her eyes blazed green and hectic, visionary and wild, like a deluded mystic's. She forgot to wear lipstick most of the time and then one day remembered and suddenly didn't like her usual shade of pinky red and went out and bought a big tube of bright, slashing purple.

"You look like a wino," Saul said, "but even more beautiful than you did before, if that's possible."

It was possible. She knew it. She hadn't been so beautiful and healthy in years. Sometimes, when she lay baking and sundrenched on the beach in the mornings she felt as bare of superfluous fat and trivialities as an old, bleached, white bone in the desert. And she was almost drunk all the time with love and lightheadedness and not eating. All week long her hair would lie long and saltcaked, stiff, bright and brittle, unwashed and sunbleached. She'd keep meaning to wash it but only on blessed Fridays did she manage it. She knew her hair was drying out and the ends would split. She didn't care. That she might get sunstroke and ought to wear a hat in the sun. She didn't care.

During that hot and loving month the beach often became unbearable by one o'clock. There was not even a cool Atlantic east wind to stir the sand in little waves, to lift the strands of her bannered hair. She would have to leave the beach and go home to draw the shades and sit in the cool dimness and drink iced coffee for a long time or gin-and-tonics until she felt sleepy and had a nap on the bed. Often Saul would find her asleep when he came and no dinner ready. She would bob up startled and say she'd fix him something and then find she'd forgotten to go to the store. But he didn't care. He'd have an egg, he'd say, or later they could go to a ham-

315

burger shack. She would open her mouth like a bird and he would put his cool tongue inside. He was milk and honey, frankincense, myrrh, and balm. She loved him, she knew it, she would let herself burn to a tiny, curled crisp on the beach if she couldn't have him come home to her when it was evening and the salt tide drifted out, leaving, as security, a luggage of dead horseshoe crabs, frosted bits of glass and stone and poignant, perfumed, olive-colored seaweed among its lacy weavings on the wet sand. But, with the small remnant of mind left to her she knew that it was essential never to let Saul know how it was with her. He would want to marry her. There was no point in that. Whatever would they do, but hate each other, finally, for being so different.

One weekday, in a deliberate effort to exile herself from lotus land, she rushed around determinedly after Saul had left for work and, all fixed up in a woodviolet cotton dress underpinned by several lacy petticoats, her hair still damp from the shower, drove into Boston.

Dudley happened to be home and awake when she came to the apartment.

"What are you doing out there all alone?" he asked.

"Swimming," Sally said briefly looking over her accumulated mail and the rash of telephone messages most of which seemed to be from Mike Wainscott.

"I told people you'd gone to New York," Dudley said.

"Why do that?"

"Ben Merritt asked me. I was there to dinner the other night. I thought possibly if he knew where you actually were he might pay a visit. I think he has a remonstrance in mind. Rather irritated about this forthcoming job of yours."

"Aunt Fan knows I'm there."

"She obviously didn't tell him."

"Wise Aunt Fan. The old dear. I must call her."

"I don't know," Dudley said, rather wistfully and for a second she was sorry for him. "I think I'd be bored alone out there. But perhaps some of the people we know have come out?"

"No one we know goes there any more," Sally said. "As you very well know. Stop fishing, Dud. I'm not alone as you've undoubtedly guessed."

"I did. You're far too extroverted to have been alone for three weeks. Am I to meet him?"

"Perhaps." She remembered suddenly that Saul had said he didn't want his brother Matthew to know about them. They would have to rechristen him. Saul the Giant Killer, Saul, the Chiefest Among Ten Thousand, anything but Berman for when he met Dudley. If he ever did. The thought of them juxtaposed was ridiculous. She bubbled suddenly with rich, crazy laughter. Poor old Dudley with both legs and feet flat on the ground and nothing else. But Saul, oh Saul and here it was only two o'clock and she had to wait, to endure time till five-thirty when he could leave the paper.

"He must be awfully amusing," Dudley said stiffly, his face hurt. He's always being left out of the joke, Sally thought. She was suddenly imbued with a vast magnanimity. She must share some of this enormous trove of richness with poor, old, starved, sticky Dud.

"I'm sorry," she said. "I just thought of something funny. But I've had a simply marvelous idea. Why don't you put on your best tucker and we'll go over to the library of that school where Deborah works and I'll introduce you. I've been meaning to, you know but I simply haven't been around."

"Well," Dudley said, his face looking suddenly alight like a small boy who's been promised some foolish treat. Then he got gloomy again. "She's probably not there. And what sort of a place is a library to get to—uh—?"

"You ask such pedantic questions," Sally said. "You can take her to lunch, dodo."

"It's too late for lunch," Dudley said dourly. "And how am I going to take a strange girl to lunch? Aren't you coming?"

"I wouldn't be any help at all," Sally said airily, blowing smoke around.

"I hope you're not tied up with any Svengali," Dudley said in such a droll, glum, Yankee way that Sally almost choked on her gin and tonic. "You act very . . . well . . . sort of drugged."

"Oh Dudley, you're such a killjoy. I'm sorry, I can't help it. I'm just happy."

"Spare me the ecstasies," Dudley said frowning. "I wouldn't know."

"Perhaps you will," Sally said cheerfully. "What does your analyst say?"

"Nothing. I'm stalemated. Blocked."

"Poor darling. Well, perhaps Deborah is just the thing to freshen you up. And, if you must, I'll go have lunch with you. But I warn you I shall not chatter. You'll have to overawe her all by your wee self."

So they had another gin and tonic to help Dudley's courage and he put on his properly wilted seersucker coat and they strolled over to that funny Marplot place.

"She's eaten lunch probably," Dudley said in a depressed way that Sally found irresistibly funny.

"I daresay she could eat again. She doesn't look very well fed to me."

By the time they'd walked up to the third gloomy floor, however, Sally'd begun to wonder why she'd been asinine enough not to telephone. All this lightheaded bravado. Dudley might be disappointed. Perhaps the girl had quit working or achieved another beau. But no, there she was, and obviously flabbergasted at seeing Sally again.

They ended up having lunch at Locke-Ober's because Deborah had certainly not eaten, working, as she explained, from 10:30 to 2:30, there'd been time only for breakfast, but insisting that they shouldn't take her to lunch and there was a very nice drugstore nearby where they could have hamburgers. Dudley was magnificent. Sally was overwhelmed at the sight of him, being courtly and firm and overruling Deborah and saying he needed a good lunch and they must go to Locke-Ober's and bowing and ducking and being charming and masterful and oh so man of the world. Deborah, very sweet, shy and embarrassed, was patently impressed. She looked quite lovely in a simple sort of Grecian-cut brown cotton with sandals. Dress must be quite old, Sally thought, but Dudley didn't notice that grayness around the armpits. He was giddy with delight to be seen with two such lovelies and he whispered to Sally that Deborah was one of the prettiest, most natural-looking girls he'd ever seen. You always did have excellent taste, Sally, he beamed, she's just the sort of girl I like, unspoiled and charming.

Ha, ha, brother, Sally thought rudely, we know how you like them. Innocent and scared all to hell of being deflowered. But, in a way, she herself was fairly cute bringing these two lacking types together and they did seem to be getting on well. She smiled benevolently at them and went to call Saul.

"I'm pining away for you in Locke-Ober's dining room."

"You sound drunk," he said. "Are you?"

"Perhaps I am," she said, realizing suddenly that technically she ought to be drunk having had nothing to eat all day except a piece of toast and a smidgin of bratwurst. But many gin and tonics.

"I'd be the same," she said, "if I hadn't had a drop to drink."

"I wish I had you here."

"In two and a half hours or three," she chanted deliriously, "I'll fall upon you and drain the blood out of you."

"What are you wearing?" he asked seriously.

"Lots of petticoats and a violet dress. Why?"

"Good. I'll lift each one up separately."

"The whole composing room must be listening to you, you lecherous man."

"Too noisy," he shouted. "If I stood up on a machine and yelled that they were all motherlovers they wouldn't know it. Hang up beautiful or I'll float away like a balloon. The whole evening edition is already full of errors due only to me."

She hung up and as an afterthought called Mike Wainscott. He had boat races in mind, it turned out.

"It's tomorrow," he said. "Where have you been? Been calling you all week. Have dinner afterwards. There's a new band in at the Bobo. We'll have a ball."

"I can't have dinner," Sally said. "But perhaps I could make the races. Can I call you in the morning?"

"Sure. I'm not booked up."

"Had a fight with that lovely girl?"

"She's just a dear, dull days that are no more girl," he said. "You saw to that."

"Whatever do you mean? I made no move to break up that starcrossed love."

"No," he said, "you didn't do a bloody thing. It was me. What I mean was, I saw you. Anyway, I couldn't care less. And I'm drunk I want you to know, Sara, la belle dame sans merci has thee in thrall. I'm sitting here writing great undying prose and drinking up my father's gin."

"It seems to be a plague all over the city," Sally said happily.

"I knew *you* were," Mike said. "I could tell by that crazy, wonderful husky laugh, like the gurgle of Cointreau over emeralds."

"But I'm with my brother," Sally rebuked him. "I'm respectable. I'm not getting drunk with a lot of bad metaphors. I'm glad you're writing though. You sound lots better."

"I feel way up there. So I don't even care to know why you can't have dinner with me, or don't think I can't guess."

"You needn't guess."

"Publishing it in Gath, eh?"

"Oh everyone's so drunken and Biblical these days," Sally said. "It's the heatwave don't you think?"

"Yes," Mike said, "it frizzles the brains and only the poor overworked genitals are left to carry the entire load. Hey, that's a good line. I must get it down. Call me tomorrow, huh? My heart at thy sweet voice."

Perhaps I will go with him, Sally thought, steering her way back to the table. She had a dress and hat scarcely worn which would be eminently suitable for a boat race. Would Saul mind, she wondered. Yes, undoubtedly. Well, he'd get over it. There was no reason for him to be jealous of Mike Wainscott for heaven's sakes. Oh how marvelous life was. It was like a thousand childhood Christmas mornings, it was like reciprocated love at first sight every day with the most wonderful man in the world, like New Year's Eve and the end of the war. Everybody, all over the city, was probably sitting in air-cooled restaurants and bars, getting drunk and holidayish because of the heat and all the offices closed early. Locke-Ober's was oddly crowded for the middle of the afternoon.

She smiled brilliantly at Deborah and Dudley. "Darlings," she cried, "isn't it a magnificent day?"

"It's a vile day," Dudley said. "It was ninety-eight this morning at ten o'clock."

"You haven't eaten your lunch," Deborah said looking gravely at Sally's untouched plate.

"You eat it," Sally said. "I'm not hungry. I'll have another drink though."

"Seems to me you might be having too many," Dudley said, officiously brotherly suddenly.

"Ha, ha," chortled Sally, "listen at who's calling the kettle black." But they were not with it. Deborah's expression was blank and Dudley's eye cold with reprimand. Poor dear, she thought, trying to make a good impression with drunken, rowdy sister balling it all up.

"You seem very happy," Deborah said and then was obviously afraid she'd been too personal.

"She's in love," Dudley intoned, as if she'd gotten leprosy. "Which accounts for her euphoric description of the worst day of the summer as magnificent."

Then they, sobersided as hell, ignored her unseemly frivolity and returned to what they probably thought was an animated discussion of music. Sally, sitting there on a pink-aquamarine and ginsoaked cloud, heard stray phrases: "Oh yes, I heard him conduct that but I couldn't see too well . . . I was in the rush seats and it was behind a post." And Dudley going on draggingly about oratorios and fugues and counterpoint, making Bach sound like some species of melancholy ague. Oh bore, Sally thought, wishing she were with that gay, jolly crowd of summerstock actors in the corner, but at least he had gotten around to asking her to attend a concert with him.

"I don't really care for Pops," he was saying, "the music is far too anemic. However if you've never been you'll find it an interesting experience, once at least. Rather festive. Of course, I prefer chamber music, but in summer . . ."

And he droningly expounded on the virtues of Beethoven's string quartets. Ah, lucky Deborah, thought Sally. Next fall when Symphony season began again she would not have to sit in the Friday afternoon rush seats any more. No, all uplifted and improved and dressed up in black velvet and pearls like a fine lady, she would accompany the noble scion of an ancient name on Saturday evenings in the orchestra, in the family pew, no that couldn't be right, that pew, seat was better. And she was quite sweet too, poor child, what did I do to her, what did I wish on her? Anyway, Sally thought, she's getting a meal out of it, or a meal and a half, because old Dudley who would rather eat a breadcrust himself than throw it out to the birds, had neatly divvied up her untouched lunch between himself and Deborah who protested that she couldn't eat another mouthful but managed to put it away nevertheless.

Outside in the street, there was suddenly a social problem because Sally was deserting them. There was a good deal of uncertain dancing around on the corner of Winter and Summer by Dudley, in an agony of indecision, with Deborah trying to look unconcerned and fixing her gaze steadily on a store window. Sally, behind her sunglasses, watched her brother derisively, wondering how he was going to get out of his bag.

"Goodbye, Deborah," she said airily, "you must come out to Nahant and swim sometime . . ." (Sometime when I'm not in bed) ". . . before I go to Rockport. I'll call you about it."

"Why that would be very nice," said she, in a voice that betokened she knew perfectly well Sally didn't mean a word of it, that nobody ever did, that they were both just dying to get away from her.

Imbecile Dudley, Sally thought impatiently, I give him a perfect opening and he stands there, rubbing his nose ruminatively.

"How about a weekday," she said to Deborah. "I'm usually quite free during the day. I could drive over to your house and pick you up."

"I mostly work every day," Deborah said, plainly confused by all this insistence.

"Why I'll take you out there any day we're both free," Dudley said finally coming through, Hallelujah, but sending Sally a stern steely glance to remind her that there should be no monkeyshines when he triumphantly led this innocent child out to that Sodom by the sea she was operating.

"Great," Sally said with such false, social cheer that she was almost ashamed of herself. "Then I shall leave it to you, Dudley. Only do give me a call beforehand. I might be engaged in good works."

"Oh we shall give you fair warning, shan't we, Deborah?" said he, suddenly hearty and full of masculine confidence now that he'd finally spoken. In a second, Sally thought, he'll chuck her under the chin and I shall be sick.

"I think," Deborah said contemplatively, addressing a mannequin in the store window and earning Sally's vast admiration because instead of answering Dudley's inane Victorian-uncle blat, she simply gave him a small, shy, one-sided smile and went on to higher things, "that one feels hotter after airconditioning than before."

"Well goodbye you two. I must go," Sally said, turning hastily away.

But only Deborah said goodbye because Dudley was too busy saying gallantly, "Well, there's a good cure for that. More airconditioning. There's a very good French film at the Exeter. Do you like foreign films?"

And to her muted reply of "Yes I do, very much," she was borne away in triumph up Winter Street, like a tiny Sabine woman who wasn't quite aware of how the hell it had all happened, or, worst of all, the awful fate in store for her. Ah Sally, she thought, picking her way through the wilted evening crowd hurrying for the subways, you're a doll no doubt about it, as sweet and noble as a female cobra, no that cobra wasn't really true. I'm a nice girl, she thought righteously and anyway, perhaps she'll think he's fine. They had both looked happy enough in their square way going off up the street arm in arm, Deborah appearing slightly perplexed, as if men hadn't taken her arm often enough. Why the poor, funny little kid, Sally thought, in a burst of warm, patronizing enlightenment, she doesn't know anything about men. I bet that Gordie type never took her arm. Why she undoubtedly thinks Dudley is a glass of fashion and a mold of form. And perhaps for her, he would be. He might stop that loathsome, sloppy, secret lushing and, happy day, desist from leering at sister's legs and other appurtenances. What was that kick, anyway? Was he so sexstarved? Only his analyst could figure it out, God knows, she wouldn't even dare.

Someday soon, Sally reflected, stopping to stare in Filene's Little

Shoe Shop window at a pair of pink and purple sandals that she simply must have, I must tackle Dud about that allowance increase, now that I've done what I promised. Hastily, she checked to see how much money there was in her purse, dashed into the store, tried on the sandals and bought them. They looked wonderful, classically strapped but at the same time, irresponsibly carnival-like. Must get some more mauve, pink, lavender, purple, rosy summer clothes to go with them, she thought, and told the clerk she'd wear them right this moment.

And went out, skimming all amethystine through the crowd of sweaty, weary, shirt-sleeved people, and by some miracle not even having one of her bare toes trod upon. And there was Saul, looking eagerly along the river of people flowing down the narrow street. He saw her and smiled and waved. His teeth were very white and he was chewing on a cigar and he needed a haircut and he was wearing a wrinkled and depressed short-sleeved sports shirt but oh, wasn't he lovely, Sally thought, all her senses soaring like a flight of singing birds, wasn't he altogether the most lovely, exciting sight in the world?

Part Two

One

Mike

Blithe June morning with the windows open to the one spindly backyard tree. Sam, peevish over bran muffins and marmalade.

"What were you typing all night, steady as a bloody woodpecker? Copying out all of Mr. Justice Holmes?"

Mumble, cagy, mumble through helpful mouthful of toast.

"Speak up, boy," boomed the phony old autocrat, bending a keen eye out from under theatrical, uncombed mane of grey hair.

Pompous jokester never spoke like a human being if he could help it. Always a minor Dickens character.

"I said, Aged Parent, that I was writing a self-help book. Pick up a bit of extra cash you know. It's called *How to Be a Feeder at the Public Trough in Nine Easy Lessons.*"

The folded-up Boston *Herald* landed fat and flat on the floor.

"I can do without the sophomoric Si Hunnicutt variety of waggishness this morning, thank you, Michael. Where's the coffee? Minta!"

Minta, high priestess of the café au lait ritual appearing, eyes heavy-lidded, skin sallow, all neck and collar bones showing in a longskirted, tightly braced orange cotton housecoat affair.

"Araminta, do you know I don't remember seeing my son at breakfast for almost twenty-five years, back in the days when I fed it to him myself from a blue china bowl ornamented with hyperthyroid ducks."

"School's out, Sam, and I'm at liberty or at large, whichever suits you." The coffee being very good, another cup was in order. A little toast, another strip of bacon, more butter to melt on his third bran muffin. When, after all, would he eat again?

"Indeed. Where is the toothpick you usually flourish when you revert to the taciturn Yankee I hurried across an ocean to prevent you from being. I know school is out. Why should that keep you fastened to the dining table of a pair of French cuisine fanciers."

"Well, coq au vin's better than nothing."

"Translated from the Ungracious that means you have no money?"

"You might put it like that."

"Sam!" Minta, truly scandalized, large dark eyes wide awake and flashing now, "Mike is on vacation. What is so unusual about his eating here when he has no classes to go to?"

"And no cigarettes either?" Pleasantly fiendish smile recognizing the gesture toward Minta's pack lying just out of reach.

"Take them darling, do. I demand to know what this heavy, paternal hand is all about? What deep, subtle significance do you read into the fact that he has no cigarettes this morning. Is he a boarder here or our son?"

"I am simply trying to ascertain a few facts if you will allow me, Minta. He eats here constantly now, with a sour expression, and we know he doesn't like the food. He has no cigarettes, not only this morning but consistently. He doesn't go out much. That female does not call him on the phone any more, fortunately. From all this, I deduce, that my only son, a poor thing, an arms akimbo idiot, but mine, is on his uppers but isn't planning to mention it to me . . . I must say I thought you had better sense Mike. You know, I'm sure, that if you need money until summer school starts and you get your next check or your pension money comes in, Minta, and I would advance it to you."

"I'm not going to summer school, Sam. So there won't be any check." Flicking a crumb of tobacco off his lower left canine and inhaling deeply on the cigarette. You never appreciated them properly until they got scarce.

"You're not? Perhaps I'm mistaken then. I thought you said you'd take advantage of the speededup program and thus have income during the summer too. You'd be ready to begin your career much sooner, too, a particular concern of you veterans who've lost time in the war."

Well, here it came. The horse laugh. The smug I told you so. Hold your nose now, take a deep breath, keep your temper tightly wrapped around you, as it's ho for a plunge in the bitter, briny bath of paternal ridicule. "I did say that, Sam, but that was before I flunked out of Law School. The notification came last week right after I'd spent up all my last check. Anyway, I thought I'd have enough money to tide me over till I decided what to do next but . . . uh . . . all my bonus money seems to've vanished and, since

I never had any luck at poker games in the Army, here I am, the well-adjusted prodigal son, living temporarily on your bounty."

The most talkative parents in the world but not a word between them. Silent as eleven o'clock on Armistice Day. It was his star turn obviously so he ground out a little more dialogue.

"The truth of it is that I thought, up till a few days ago, that I could loaf this summer and eke out on my disability compensation. But at the physical the other day the doctors decided my hand was in superb shape, which cut my compensation down considerable. I thought they'd just declare me ineligible but it seems they're afraid to. Too many aroused indignant veterans complaining to their congressmen. Of course I was damn glad to hear the good news about the hand."

"Yes, it is wonderful." Minta, mechanical, coffeecup hiding face.

"You flunked out of Law School!" Sam, finally coming to the forefront of the battle. Now why the rising, incredulous note? Hadn't he foretold doom all year?

"Now, Sam, please." Warning glances raining across the table. The pestilence that flieth at noonday. And the male parent going through an obvious mighty struggle for control. Of course, the lousy ego again. His son, HIS SON, no less, flunking out of anywhere.

"Well!" Cup clashing against saucer, much brushing of muffin crumbs and leaning, classically well-fed and making like FDR, fitting a cigarette into a holder. "And what, if it is not too much to ask you to dwell for a moment on your future, do you plan to do now? And don't bestow on me that twisted, feckless grin. You are no longer a boy, Michael. In three and a half years you'll be thirty and wondering just where you made the wrong turn, with a whole lifetime of the consequences of the wrong choice looming irrevocably, before you."

"Oh Sam, really." Minta kneading her forehead with long ivory, yellow-stained fingers. "Isn't it too early to discuss eternal verities? Particularly when you should have been in your office fifteen minutes ago."

"All the signs and portents indicate a man-to-man talk, Minta. Sam probably wants you to retire gracefully to your sitting room and paint flowers on sugar bowls."

"Oh God! Aren't you ever going to grow up, Mike? Minta and I have no money to leave you. You've got to earn your living. Now, all I ask is that you be serious a moment and tell me what your plans are. Are you going to marry a rich girl? Is that the reason for this aplomb?"

"Who's being funny now? Look, Sam, I'm old enough to take care of myself. You're not going to leave a penniless orphan to the mercy of the world."

"Indeed. Of course. Forgive me. You're extremely mature and responsible. If your mother didn't send your laundry out, I doubt if you'd have a clean shirt. What would you do if we weren't here? Where would you live? And now that you've lost your GI Bill through this flunking out what would you live on?"

"I'm going to get a job."

"Doing what? In the present day and age your B.A. will get you a nice clerk's job. You seem to have rejected writing, which is, God knows, an impossible way to earn money but at least, if you were trying that, I'd do my best to help you. But you don't want that. Whatever it is, you do want you must begin now, to get training and experience. Would you like to try publishing?"

"No thanks, Sam. Nice of you to think of it. Like I told you"— a pause, allowing Sam to wince at the use of *like* in place of *as*— "I'm going to get some sort of half-ass job for the summer. Then, in the fall, I'll try to reinstate myself with the VA, and enroll in Graduate English. For an M.A. and teaching."

"I thought you were planning to visit the Barings in Iowa and South Dakota this summer?" Minta rushing in to give Sam time to digest this new idea and frame a strongly colored picture of Mike as a teacher. The famous eyebrows were furling and unfurling.

"Well, I'll have to pass it up, I guess."

"Teaching, eh? The genteel refuge. You need a Ph.D. now, I gather to get a job. The field's overcrowded. It's more in your line I suppose. Have you enough GI Bill to get through a doctorate?"

"Probably not. I'd have to start on a fellowship and get experience while I was working on it."

"You'll enjoy writing academic criticism, I daresay. They call it New but it smells of scholasticism to me." A silence. Then Sam's nostrils dilated, because the uncanny old buzzard had started smelling printer's ink last night in his sleep through the typing. "What the hell were you doing on that typewriter all year? It wasn't Law School stuff or you wouldn't have flunked."

"Hand exercises, that's all. Quick, brown fox, you know. It paid off, see, because now, I'm technically not disabled."

"Why don't you show it to me, Mike?"

"Nothing to show, Sam, honest Injun."

"All right, Mike. Have it your way." Scraping his chair back, eyes shadowed with rueful memories of how he fed this serpentine-toothed, thankless child, the most elegant, savoir-faire cereal out of a blue bowl. "But if you insist on going to that flat, hot state this summer I see no reason why you shouldn't. Do you, Minta?" The two of them exchanging odd smiles. Childish secrets at their age too.

"No, of course not. I just sold some paintings and we're rather rolling."

"I don't want any money."

"I'll write you a check and leave it on the hall table. You can pay it back whenever you're ready. Where in God's name is my briefcase, Minta?" Stomping out and pausing in the doorway to survey his son with the same odd smile. "Put it in the bank, will you? Your Grandfather Wainscott used to hide money around the house and you're a hell of a lot like him. Ornery."

"More coffee, Mike?" Minta returning to the table.

"Sure. What were you and Sam smiling about?"

"No particular reason. Have another muffin and butter. You really look awfully thin. I hope you haven't been depriving yourself because of your stupid, stubborn pride."

"Clucking over me like a real mother, Minta."

Her turn to look pained now. "You're really dreadfully unkind sometimes, Mike. Aren't you ever going to stop thinking we were terrible to you?"

"Oh forget it, Minta. I was just kidding."

"No, you weren't. I don't think you'll see things in a less distorted perspective until you marry and have children of your own. Then perhaps you'll discover we're not quite so hideous, and perhaps even wish that your child be a bit like you, because by then you might like yourself more than you do now."

"Hey, Minta, for Pete's sake. Freud's passé at breakfast now. Didn't you know?"

"Nevertheless. You think you'd prefer to have had parents who were stuffed shirts and dullards but you don't know how deadly it can be. Well, have a good day, darling, and try not to kill all the joy you see. And, by the way, Sam and I are going out to a new shore place for lobster dinner tonight. Please join us if you like."

Now what could you do but say sure, swell, and kiss her, so she went up to her studio, flushed and smiling. If he'd only been an adult all his life she would have been a great mother. When, elaborately unconcerned, he came to the hall table, there was the check. For seven hundred and fifty dollars. Why that damn Sam! How could he ever pay that back? With this, he needn't work all summer.

Just write. No, he ought to give it back. It was too much. Cagy Sam. All suspicious, quivering editorial antennae, that parent. Keep it, boy. It means a whole summer for the book. My blood for the book. My pride. My love, my sex drive, my bones, my flesh, my bowels, my all. My sweat and tears, my prayers, my fasting, and all for what? A heap of rubbish. A weed. But just to do it. One vast spasm of creative agony. No good. Then, all done, no more, never again.

Suddenly Sally on the phone. Would he die if he didn't go watch Harvard and Yale regatta-ing. Because there was an absolutely marvelous thing she'd been invited to this afternoon, by an old friend of her aunt's, which he would enjoy and which was, he gathered, about to vanish into the archives of the past, like horsecars, equine turds in the street, and all the wonderful things you used to be able to get for a nickel. It was a sort of a garden party, she slurred, but much more attractive, more of a fête, really. Whatever you say, baby. It was no day to quibble and after all the madness of the brain about her, who cared where they went even though it was masochistic of him to want to see her again after that furious whirl and disappointment in the gallery.

Feeling good in spite of half the night writing and the oncoming hot day and going to meet Sally on the corner of Louisburg and Pinckney. A sheer miracle the way his fingers flew on that keyboard, could scarcely go fast enough to keep up with that other wonder inside himself whose brain was teeming with crystal insights and shapely words. Whoever he was, this secret superior person, he certainly was not old, shambling, half-baked Mike who had heretofore failed dismally at love and at writing and what, after all, else was there?

Yes, today he believed in himself and that his work was superb. But what about the other sable days such as last week when the other self, let us call him Malte Laurids Brigge after Deborah's old friend Rilke, deserted him and went spaziehren off to some walled German garden and a countess no doubt and he was left on his lousy, left-handed own. Oh he sat there and pecked slowly, thinking rationally but it all turned out dry rot. Then his gut would get all in an uproar thinking of the pressure of time and all the days running away from him. And about the mess of Jean and the sneaking, cowardly way he'd behaved to Deborah, a sweet, bright chick who needed more time for sympathetic cultivation than he could give. And the big thing. How he would live, make money. But the check from Sam, goddam his eyes, what a father, what a man, how

332

I love and hate him alternately, had fixed that little ulcer. At least for the summer.

Show it to Sam. He's helping you, damn it, he's giving you money, no strings. Nobody did it for him. His eyes asked you. No, NO, NO. Interference, next thing you know. Perhaps you could cut it down here. Build it up there. This doesn't quite say what you want, does it? He couldn't help it, he was an egotistical father and an editor. A fatal combination. Because it would kill it. The whole fragile trembling feeling about the life and continuance of his characters would shrivel. But a promise. Give it to Sam, first thing, if it ever got finished and no more to say about Them, his people, his place, the little world at war that he was making, then give it to Sam and whatever he thought about it, it wouldn't matter any more.

Sally was late. Standing on the corner, waiting, hands in pockets. Old iron streetlamps. Red brick, nice, pink red brick. Little iron-paled park of the square. How he loved Beacon Hill. Where else was there to live? At least time hadn't succumbed to omnipresent vulgarity here. Now, if he'd ever been weak enough to be ensnared by Jean into marriage he'd be living in a little ranch house, everything new, tacky, and full of picture windows and phony knotted pine. These old houses are so hard to keep clean, was one of her little sayings when she came to see him. Well, poor girl, she'd never have to climb the Hill for him again. But why, why, in the name of common sense couldn't she've accepted the end of the season gracefully? But over at last. No nooky, boy, Si's comment when he'd heard. Better no nooky than having it with Jean.

A horn honking. There she was, Sara, the heart's desire, wearing a flame-colored, thin, floaty dress and a white straw bonnet tied under her chin with a yellow ribbon, waving, of all damn things, a ruffled flame-colored parasol or sunshade or all like that. Oh, she was beautiful. She knocked him out. Off they went down the Hill in a triumphant sweep.

"And whose little painting are you?" Staring rudely down the front of the lownecked dress.

"You know perfectly well."

"Isn't it time you stopped being a Renoir? Just because my mother typed you at the age of eight. And your skin's the wrong color. A Gauguin red sarong is what you want, not that oddball parasol."

"Don't be such a stickler, Michael." Laughing up at him so that he couldn't help it but had to lean down and kiss her warm round honeycolored cheek while they were idling at a light. "We're going to visit a Henry James lady and my costume is quite appropriate."

A friendly, brotherly kiss. She had another guy. When didn't she? Passing lawns like deep green velvet beds. Be nice to lay her down on one of them and bury his face in her Impressionist dress and adjacent bosom. Crème fraiche. But a want he couldn't have. Somebody else doing it tonight. Doing well by her obviously, whoever he was. There is a garden in her face and her body is a thousand and one fecund summers.

The day and Sally were one, both in the full bloom of summer, together perfect and rare. My love is a fat, pink peony, bursting shower petals, a scarlet rose, and so is the day, happy, healthy, a sunburned outdoors, a renaissance of a day, a girl and he was mad, poetical, strawhatted, and full of honeydew and paradise milk, which was green and pink. Correction. Not my love. His.

"Am I gonna meet this guy?"

"What is this violently slangy kick we're on, Michael? You were, in my admittedly faulty memory, a well-spoken young man."

"I was a jerk. A pedantic, dumb, young jerk."

"I deny that absolutely. I could never have made love to such a creature."

"Let's skip that huh, Sally? I learned the right way to talk in the Army. The hoi-polloi veneer it's called, only after awhile it's essential protective covering. A poor thing but all you've got to prevent being murdered for a lousy, knowitall, rich, Harvard-talking swell. Anyway, what's he like? Pretty phallic I'd say from the looks of you."

"La!" Her face blooming at him from under the whimsical bonnet. "Does it really show?"

"Well never mind. Keep your skeleton in the stable. Minta ought to see you. She'd blow a gasket and reach for her paint tubes. Where are we going, anyway?"

"To Arabella Random's."

"Why Christ, Sally, she must be a hundred and two. I've never seen her of course but I've read enough about her in memoirs and newspapers and Sam went to interview her once for the *Pilgrim* but that was just before the war. Wasn't she a friend of Mrs. Jack's?"

"Michael, you're witless about time. She was one of Mrs. Jack's much younger, sort of polite rivals. She thinks Mrs. Jack's taste was very messy and rails about how badly the Museum is arranged."

"You're sure you're not taking me to a funeral?"

"Don't be so suspicious, darling. Arabella's place is one of the last of the really fabulous ones hereabouts, and you ought to see it before she dies and the builders rush in with the ghastly little gimcracky bungalows and neon shopping centers. Every year within hu-

334

man memory she's given a big June fête cum musicale. Chamber music out of doors, no less. Aunt Fan always goes and this morning when I came in from Nahant to dress for the boat races, she called me, and insisted I must come and take you. Arabella apparently was very ill the last two years and there were no fêtes, but this year, she reared up and charged about on the lawn making ready. She's eighty-five and frail but no doctor on earth could dissuade her. Rather admirable, don't you think?"

"Great. That's the way to die. Doing what you want. What good is a meeching little life if you can't live it? Like Bunny Berigan. Remember?"

"Yes. That was wonderful, wasn't it? So right."

"I don't know though. When you're young you can talk blithely about dying splendidly because it's far away, but I wonder how we'll feel when the old icy shadow is breathing daily down our backs?"

"Did you feel that way during the war?"

"No, weirdly enough, because it was absolutely essential for over-active imaginations like mine, to never consider the possibility of death. I mean of course it crossed my mind but I kicked it right out. Otherwise I'd've gone into paralysis even when I wasn't near a gun. And a guy has to maintain some respect for himself in a situation as basic as that. I'd rather have been shot to hell than've become a poor, slobbering thing, devoid of reason."

"Oh dear. Well, I don't want to think about it at all. It's grue-some being as old as we are now. Of course, Michael, I must say that six years haven't made much difference in your case. You're exactly as I remembered. Brown and spare and kind of limber with that wonderful, enlightening, sudden smile. And the dark, with-drawing frowns and moods too. A few sunsquint wrinkles around the eyes is all I can see."

"I wish you'd changed. That you'd turned into a skinny hag with long walrus teeth, grey hair, and a seamy skin. But I'm afraid not. You're still a tree of ripe peaches and I won't complete the image."

"I have though." Seriously. "Perhaps not to look at. But you'll see. As you get to know me better."

"The only answer to that is a hollow laugh. I've known you, as the man said, in another country."

"We might try being friends, which we've never done. Perhaps we'd be better at that than the other."

"Tell me about what's likely to happen at the Random acres so I don't blunder around making wisecracks."

"You'll see." Mysterious, secret, sidelong glance and a wise

335

smile and she began to sing something about if you don't want to be my friend don't shake my tree, so naturally he had to laugh and then they sang a chorus of Berigan being an international success but never being able to get started with his truelove only it got too pointed for Mike so he stopped and just listened because her voice was as great as ever.

When she'd finished. "Very obliged to you for taking me to see history before it melts."

"I think it will be sort of interesting. And we don't need to stay if it isn't. It's rather sad, don't you think, that people like Arabella are dying off and there'll be no replacements. Like the buffalo. They'll be read about in the books and perhaps there'll be a mannequin in the Smithsonian made up to look like her."

"Oh now listen, Sal, don't tell me you've succumbed to the popular nostalgia for the graces of the Edwardian era. Her descendants'll be like her although maybe they won't dress the same way."

"They never had any children. People like that don't. Either they don't marry or they don't breed. They're too busy collecting art or travelling or doing good works or being public servants."

"Cheer up, Sal, there're some good people coming up from the ranks. I never knew you had all this pride of family."

"My family!" Scornfully. "Don't be silly, darling. I don't identify myself with the Arabellas of this world. My family were businessmen, congenitally opposed to art. You know there *are* some people who have no taste for good living, who actually are sickened by richness, not just money but beauty and fullness and vitality. They prefer la vie empty and skim milk. It isn't even part of that talked-about Puritan heritage either. Just a basic personality thing. Narrow, small, frightened minds who use all sorts of excuses, economic or snobbish, to disguise their fear of the chaos that might ensue if they accepted all the enormous confusing possibilities of a life fully lived. Of course, if the Brimmers had been rich for a very long time it might've been different. But my great-grandfather and my grandfather were too busy owning property and far too unsure of themselves to spend ostentatiously. And as for collecting art and patronizing musicians, heaven forbid!"

"But your uncle's on the board of the Symphony."

"Doesn't mean he either likes music or understands it. It's just the proper thing to do."

"I should think after a few generations of piled up income the money would have to be spent somehow, perhaps even on ostentation."

A burst of ribald laughter. "Oh, I'm perfectly willing to be horribly nouveau riche. But I'm not given much of an opportunity. Well you're right of course and in other families if they don't cotton to art they go in for horses and boats and dogs. But Brimmers had really only one passion and that was business, money-making, financial power. I discount my father, whose passion seemed to be for self-destruction. As for me, I just want to live and have all the kicks I can and Dudley, well, shall I just not spoil the day by talking about him. Did you know that the Brimmers were comparatively poor until the city began to expand with immigration because they owned a lot of, until then, undesirable land and falling down buildings."

"What about that fine old public-spirited family the Dudleys?"

"It's always been my idea considering the remoteness of the connection that my great-grandfather must have been an arrant social-climber when he bestowed that name on my grandfather. Conjures up an illustrious founding father past which I doubt if we're really entitled to. The Pyms, my grandmother's family, were more respectable. Clipper ships. Of course, there are some who say the slave trade and opium contributed to their fortune."

"Who says?"

"My late husband for one. He was terribly up on the debunking history of the Commonwealth."

"You must have had a very instructive married life." Why was her tone so acid? Shouldn't her eyes have filled with tears or something? The great love of her life, died in the war and all. Best not foul up this so far rare day though by pursuing this mystery. Still it was an odd one. Couldn't she've been happy with him for Godsakes? How could anyone not make Sally happy if she loved you enough to run off and marry you?

"You don't look much like a skinflint Brimmer to me."

"Wasn't caught early enough. But Dudley was. He couldn't spend a lot of money for personal pleasure if he wanted to. They call it admirable Yankee thrift but it's merely the classic miser habit."

The economic foundations of Boston society the last thing he'd expected her to talk about. Yes, changed, as she said. Getting smarter. Before she'd been, truly, kind of a spoiled, oversexed, frivolous, deb type who thought everything she did was so damn dashing. Breaking men's hearts and hanging around pretending to be decadent. Now she seemed to have a more definite style, three quarters femme fatale still, but not hiding her native intelligence. Husband must've had something to do with that. Thinking back to the one time meeting

Sally with Joe Mayhew at the session. Very tall, lean. Hard to remember because the Navy officer's uniform, when they were all still civilians, obscured a lot. Kind of a general feeling exuded that they were not only slackers but kids frittering away time in unimportant pursuits, whereas this Mayhew cat was a grown man who'd already been torpedoed and lived to take Sally to bed. Had forgotten about that part, hating him anyway because of Sally. Remembered a hawk-like face and nose. Cold golden eyes. Rufous face. A blond Indian. A twist to his smile. Pretty laconic. Patronizing way he'd said he didn't know much about jazz, implying it wasn't worth knowing about and impatient, brusque way he'd dragged Sally off when she seemed to be having a good time. Pure prejudice probably. Dead now, though. De mortuis.

"You must have had a great time in California to have stayed so long."

"After awhile it got to be sort of fun. The first year was vile."

Now how was he supposed to take that one? The first year. She was married only one year for crissakes. Leading up to something. Looking sideways at her face. The soft, round chin set determinedly. For a moment, a craggy granite look, fleetingly like Dudley.

"Oh." Politely. "What happened?" He wanted to hear her say it. With his vengeful little mind. Tell him of her comeuppance. And kind of sore too that anyone should've treated her badly. Gallant to the end.

"Marriage happened, that's all. But I hate confidences. Particularly to old lovers. Even if you're not a dance on the grave type. It's all over and done with. In another state."

"And besides the man is dead."

"You catch all sorts of nuances, darling, yes. I don't know. Suddenly, since I've been back I keep having this dreadful maudlin desire to tell someone about it. But I don't want to really. And I don't know what good it does to think about it. Nothing to be done. You look so sort of shocked, Michael, though why I can't imagine."

"I dunno. Thought it was a grande passion, I guess."

"Well, it wasn't." Flatly. "But that was all right. It was fun and he was impressive and, I thought, confident and worldly."

"Everyone else being a sophomoric Harvard kid."

"Yes. And I was fairly giddy and careless, and oh well what's the difference, if there's no Benjie, it might as well be him. And thought it was rather dazzling to elope when he got his orders. And we seemed to enjoy the same things and liked going to bed. So it all seemed fine until after we got out there."

338

"And got to know each other?" Probing, prodding.

"Oh it's a fairly typical, sordid tale, I suppose. It must happen in most marriages I daresay, particularly hasty wartime ones. At first, it was just sort of minor things. He'd make fun of me. Of the things I liked and thought or didn't know about. It wasn't nice fun either. Then I became a stupid little nympho rich bitch. And the things I liked were foolish little frivolous pursuits and he'd only indulged in all the dancing and jazz joints and sport things because he was making himself agreeable to me. Now he didn't want to be agreeable any more. It bored him. And the nympho bitch part was my fault because in a moment of foolish confidence I'd told him about a few others. He didn't care but it was simply part of his arsenal of weapons. Then it appeared that he didn't really approve of me at all but that he'd decided to mold me. Which didn't go down with me at all. I thought I was fairly splendid just the way I was. Then my allowance used to come every month you know and that was always good for a fierce dispute. Because I had too much money, he said. Incredible, you know, because he knew I would have some then and much more later. But later didn't matter because by then I would've been molded."

They were turning into a long driveway which rose steeply up a high, grassy hill. Elaborate iron gates stood wide open, a small untenanted cottage to one side, half hidden in high overgrown privet hedges which bordered the driveway on either side. Bowling swiftly up, up the hill. What was there to say? Only her side of the story anyway.

"Sorry I talked so much, Michael. Very boring for you."

"Not at all."

"And what have you been doing while I was having cliché marriage troubles? Did you really ditch that acidulous girl?"

"She had marriage on the mind. My thoughts lay elsewhere."

"Poor thing." Looking at him consideringly. "You look half-starved. It must've been like dieting on curds and whey with that girl."

Showed what a bad way he was in that he had to laugh at that. But principles demanded more. "She wasn't a bad girl, Sal. Don't be so bitchy."

"Of course. I'm sorry. I'm glad you didn't marry her though. No one should be married. It's just the most neurotic estate. Now don't smile in that bland, sourgrapes way. It's quite true. I have all sorts of theories worked out about it."

"You must tell me sometime."

They had reached the top of the hill and she slid the car deftly in amongst a pride of variegated vehicles. Small foreign cars, sleek expensive long ones. Ancient, high, carefully polished ones. They sat for a moment, looking at each other. Her green eyes mocking him, she laughed, bubbling spilled over laughter.

"Wouldn't you just love me to? It might get awfully personal. Because I've often thought and wondered, while I was out in California, about what might've happened if I'd married *you*."

"So you remember me? Or is it just something outrageous to say in the ever useful past conditional."

"You've become dreadfully cynical with the years, Michael. I suppose it's part of that camouflage you spoke of. Of course I remember you. Very well. Why?"

"Oh, I thought I was just one of those 'others' you told your husband about. Which gave him such a misleading impression of you."

"You needn't be mean, darling. Now that I've placed my moist, hot little heart confidingly in your hands. No, I never told him about you. You were different. Come, let's go meet Arabella."

There was a formal boxhedged garden with neat, flagstone paths, centered by a sundial and laid out in elaborate patterns of blue, yellow, and pink flowers, varieties unknown to a non-horticultural nature, and full of people more flowering and infinitely more pretentious than the flowers.

"No spats on those pearlgray gentlemen? 'Christ what are patterns for?' "

"Oh, you are nice, Michael. And you know everything, don't you? Even the right time to wear a yellow linen waistcoat with pearl buttons."

Arm linked in his and soft roundness pressing against his arm.

"I didn't know it. I'm a social imbecile. Minta brought the damn thing from New York and I've never worn it. In fact, I'm ashamed of it."

"Is that why you have your jacket all buttoned up? Don't be silly, it's lovely. Ah, there's Arabella by the sundial. We'll pay our respects and then wander around. I don't see Aunt Fan anywhere. She was driving out with one of her little group of serious thinkers."

"Everyone suddenly burst out singing," was the way of it. Because she'd said "You were different." Nice little thought to hug to one's cold groin on depressed nights.

Mrs. Smithcraft Random was receiving graciously before her thirteenth-century French sundial when they elbowed their way up through devoted, caroling admirers. She was small, birdlike, and frail in a lavender silk dress and her high clear voice in two tones pierced commandingly through at least two sycophants when her sharp, blue eyes caught sight of Sally.

"My dear Sara!" A regal wave of hand and a way to the throne was opened for them. "Child! Do come here and let me look at you. Lovely as ever. Turn your head and take that charming bonnet off. Ah yes. Still Titian. Your aunt said you were coming and I wondered if I should recognize you after so many years. But I thought you would fulfill your earlier promise. The oldgold Renaissance coloring. None of that dour, bleak Brimmerness. Very much like your mother."

"I didn't know you knew her, Mrs. Random." Sally's cheeks pink with an unexpected blush.

A small, wry smile and under the frizzy, grey bangs Arabella Random's eyes were frosty blue, very impertinent and lively for such an old woman.

"I didn't *know* her my dear although I met her several times in Europe. Knowing her would not have been as productive, I fear, as looking at her was. Those who painted her never did justice to her, I always thought."

Sally smiled politely but her puzzlement was obvious. "I'm sorry. I'm afraid I've never seen any portraits of her. I remember that my father wanted her once to sit for a portrait but she said they never looked as real as a photograph and it would make her too restless."

"That's quite understandable, I'm sure," Arabella Random said and her smile was now frankly sardonic. "You must forgive an old woman for a bit of possibly addled reminiscence." She turned her promontory of a nose toward Mike. "And who is this young man?"

"My friend, Michael Wainscott."

She extended a friendly hand but those marrow-probing blue eyes raked him over and categorized him within a second's blink.

"How do you do. I'm happy that you could come. Someone of that name wrote a piece about me once for *Pilgrim's Monthly*."

"My father."

"Indeed. I rather liked the article although there were overtones of journalese which surprised me in the *Pilgrim*. But, like all periodicals, it has changed. Come, I must speak to the musicians. We're about to begin." She linked arms with them and, rather embarrassed and glancing furtively at each other across her cavernous lavender front, they trailed slowly out of the garden across a vast sweep of green lawn toward two enormous copper beech trees where the musicians were assembling.

A small, bald, sallow man rushed up to them. "Oh, dear Mrs.

Random," he enthused, his large, dark eyes soulful, "how kind of you to ask us. My wife and I are enchanted. It is such a charming idea. So gala. It is a pity that your pictures cannot be on view also. We too are collectors but in a very modest way."

"Too kind of you Mr. Stefanotis." Arabella's voice, vague and mannered. But she smiled quite pleasantly and took the man's proffered hand. "Of course you must come and see the pictures. I am very quiet now but if you wish to call and notify me as to when you can come, I'm sure it will be possible."

"Kind of an odd guest for our grande dame, isn't he?" They stood a pace behind watching the conclusion of the boongranting.

"He's probably the Greek consul or something. She spent a lot of . . ."

"No he's not." Succinctly interrupting. "He owns hell's own amount of movie theatres here in town and a peck of other related enterprises like amusement parks, bowling alleys, honky-tonk dance palaces."

"Well, how peculiar." Sally's eyebrows went up. "Do you think she's giving in to vulgarity and selling him some land for a drive-in?" A girlish giggle which was interrupted by the firm voice of Arabella Random who had sent Mr. Stefanotis off in a burst of beams and thankyous and had obviously caught the last words.

"I am surprised, my dear girl, to hear you indulge in such callow snobbery. I am not in the least interested in the native origin of people or in the manner they earn their money as long as it is honest. But I am devoted to people who are eager to use their money intelligently in the service and love of the arts."

"Sorry," Sally murmured. "Very thoughtless of me."

A gracious nod. "I'm sure you are, my dear." She turned and raked Mike again. "I just remembered. Your great-grandfather was a Senator from this state, was he not? Yes, of course, I met him once, years ago in Washington when I was a very young woman. He was a rigid Republican. Well, I trust you will enjoy the music and you must come and see me later." She marched away, erect and stanch and it was surprising to note how small her feet were and how frivolous and modern her elegant gray low-heeled shoes.

Gay little red-and-white striped canvas camp chairs were drawn in circular rows around the beech trees.

"Shall we find seats, Sal?" He'd never seen her looking quite so discomfited. She was biting her lip.

"Am I really that awful, Mike?"

"Of course not. It's just that she's overpowering. Good thing the grande dame *is* going out. What d'you suppose she meant about the old Senator being a rigid Republican? Isn't she?"

"No. They were ardent Democrats. Odd, isn't it? Her husband, Smithcraft Random was ambassador to some Near or Middle Eastern country, I forget which, during Wilson's administrations and later they were out of season politically until Roosevelt came in. I think he died right at the beginning of the war." The faint sound of violins scraping into tune drifted over to them. She shook her head impatiently. "It'll be a bit before they start. Shall we walk around? I want you to see the house from the outside. It's quite weird. We can hear the music while we tour anyway."

They wandered slowly through what seemed like a small pine grove. Pungence and green quiet. Silent, arm in arm. The little crooked path they followed led them gently farther up the hill. Sally absently trailed her sunshade through the pine needles.

"I haven't seen her since I was about seventeen. What a baffling female. What on earth could she have meant about paintings of my mother? There were some elaborately posed photographs but no paintings. I'm sure. And did you see that horrid, malevolent grin when she said it?"

"People that age get things mixed up." Giving her hand a comforting squeeze.

"You're right, I daresay. Now this is it. Isn't it wild?"

The path came out of the firs and they with it onto a wide, blue-flagged terrace in full sunlight. Beyond it, on the very crest of the hill, bolstered by a brilliant, terraced rock garden, loomed the house.

"My God! What's a mosque like that doing here, in New England, of all places?"

It was a definitely Near Eastern house. Long and low and stretching wide over the brim of the hill, its white stone dazzled the eyes in the sun. There were many narrow, arched windows and a lapis-lazuli dome. To the left, the house was curved in the arm of what seemed like acres of rosypink and purple blue hydrangea bushes.

"This is only the back. Let's go round. I was told that they were both so wild about Turkey or Lebanon or wherever it was and so unhappy at leaving it that they bought this place and tore down the Victorian Gothic monstrosity on it and had this one built. I wish you could see the inside. It's even more fantastic. There's an inner courtyard with a small pool and a fountain and olive and lemon trees in pots and carp swimming around in the pool. There are acres of glowing old Persian rugs. And elaborately scrolled columns and and arches and whatnot. And all these absolutely uncharacteristic

343

modern and Renaissance and impressionist paintings everywhere. Much more mad than the Gardner Museum. That little window on the side there's genuine medieval stained glass. Then there's a dark little room full of nothing but Persian tapestries and miniatures and copper things. And a Byzantine room and mosaics. She has one whole series of small rooms full of Indian, Tibetan, and Chinese items. The only thing she lacks is a collection of armor. I'm sure there's much more but it's mercifully suppressed in my memory."

"What are all those trees there with those hairnets on them?"

"Mulberry trees. And that's mosquito netting to keep the birds away."

"Does she weave silk too?"

"I shouldn't be surprised."

They came around to the front of the house. Here there was a larger terrace paved in striped black and white marble, and set at intervals along its periphery were large purple or oldrose jars each of which held odd, stiff little trees or shrubs with thick, oily leaves. All over the terrace in neat little groups were painted, curly-backed, white iron chairs and small, round, marbletopped tables.

"Ye Gods! Is this a bistro? Sally, I'm damn glad I can't see the inside. The exterior alone causes me to wonder if I'm sunstricken."

On a distant, vagrant breeze there floated to them the wispy, shredded sounds of cerebral Beethoven.

"They've begun, Michael. But I don't care. I'm suddenly very hungry. Let's go around the corner here. I think that's where the cloth is being laid. We might be able to wangle something although the real spread won't come till after the music."

They followed the Florentine marble trail. On this side the terrace was bordered by a row of umbrella-shaped, feathery trees and in the pleasant frondfingered shade of these, several long tables were being set up. Lurking while Sally intercepted a lace-capped maid and came away triumphant bearing two heaped up plates.

"I'm ravenous really. If you'll get those two glasses of iced mint tea there's sort of a summerhouse on the other side of the hill that's a relic of the Victorian period."

The area sloping down behind the house was as overgrown as the other side was carefully tended. They found the summerhouse, a small, shabby green latticework structure overgrown with wild honeysuckle sitting forlornly in a small clearing under the dense shade of tall old trees. Beside it was a mosscovered stone bench supported by crumbling stone lions and before it was a small, slimecovered pool dotted with lily pads. They sat down on thick grass starred with daisies, beside the pool.

"There used to be all sorts of sculpture all over the grounds." She was wolfing in a variety of small, crustless sandwiches. "She must have removed some. I remember giving my shins a nasty bark on a lecherous little Cupid when I was here last. You're not eating, Michael. The cucumber ones are very good."

"Cucumber! I thought they were served only in Wilde plays." Lying on his back crushing daisies or was it pushing, no that was death when you did that, tall grass tickling his ears, what was greener than green elm leaves against a china blue summer sky? "What else did you manage to scavenge?"

"Oh, deviled eggs and petit fours and some smoked oysters. There'll be more grand stuff later. But I got these few loose things. They were making up a huge punch too. I saw them throwing in strawberries."

"The word punch has been cast out of my vocabulary. Iced mint tea will do well enough." Rising on one elbow to sip at his finely beaded cold glass.

"That conglomeration at Asch's was hideous, wasn't it? I'm surprised there weren't more people urping all over the pictures."

"I'm sorry I made such an ass of myself that day."

"I might've taken you up on it really so there's no need to prostrate yourself. Except I had this date and I was all hot about it."

"And you're in the full flood tide now?"

"Oh well. If you really want to know it's quite tremendous. But by the same token it won't last. One would turn into an ash. Very exciting now though. He's a little bit mad actually. Very intense. I like that now but it would be very wearing as a steady thing."

"And you're never going to get married again?"

"No. I told you. I have all these theories. I probably read them somewhere. They couldn't be original. But I believe I was married for use as a sort of personal target. And I think that's what marriage is. Everyone having their own little crazinesses. They get involved with people whose particular madness works in with theirs. In every marriage one of them is armed and the other is the target. Some people like being victims. I didn't."

"Your disillusionment must have been very swift and shattering. You used to pretty much glow when you looked at him. I, of course, thought it was to puke."

"You needn't remind me. I remember all those sweet and squiggly moments very well. When I think of them now it's as if they happened to another person. One hates to remember being a fool."

Munching a cucumber sandwich. "You couldn't have been that much of a fool. There had to've been something."

"May I have one of your sandwiches? I am so hungry."

"Of course. What sort of a target were you?"

"I don't know why you want to be betediumed by all this. Shouldn't we go listen to music now that we've eaten?"

"I'd rather listen to you. I hate to do this but it's so damn apt and I'll probably never have another chance again so I'll change Shakespeare around a little and say that I'd rather feed on cates and talk to you in any summerhouse in Christendom than live on cheese and garlic in a windmill far."

"You do know the loveliest literature. That's one of the things I remember so clearly about you. All the poetry you used to quote to me. I even went out and read up on some of the things later and learned some of them. Or when I'd run across one in some class I'd think, oh yes, that's one Mike quoted to me. But I don't know the cheese and garlic one at all."

" 'I brush a tear away from my eye you touch me so deeply.' It's *Henry IV*, Part 1. Hotspur, who has had his ear bent for nine hours by a windy Welshman finally cries out: 'Oh, he's as tedious as a tired horse, a railing wife; Worse than a smoky house. I had rather live with cheese and garlic in a windmill far than feed on cates and have him talk to me in any summer house in Christendom.' "

"Oh that's mahvlous. I must remember that. And, someday, when I'm very peeved with Dudley, I'll use it on him. I'm a very unkind sister aren't I but I do think it's dreadfully applicable to him don't you?"

Malicious mirth shaking both their sides. Then gravely, "You're not a nice girl, Sara. But then, your brother has always been beyond me."

"Beyond everyone, darling. May I lie beside you? The grass looks so cool."

"Your dress will get all green but if you don't mind." Her head on his shoulder. Together chewing companionably on blades of grass. "Now come on, tell me. What put you down so out there?"

"I can't fathom why you're so interested."

"Might want to put you in a book someday."

"You're seriously writing books, Michael? You said you were the other day when I called but you were drunk and I wasn't sure. But it is true? I'm so pleased."

"Never mind about that."

"Oh well if it's for art, I'd be more than glad. Only I won't if you don't stop tickling me under the chin with that green blade."

"You don't understand. It's a highly symbolic gesture."

"If you're going to be that kind of writer I won't read you even if I am in the book."

It wasn't that. Who would put her in a book? Lay his soul bare. When it was too real and raw. Years later when it was truly distant and she could become someone else, a created character. No, it was wanting to grasp the filaments of her life in the lost six years.

"You can't be in this one, baby. For men only. A war book." Must be getting more sure of himself. Being able to talk about it. First to Deborah and now Sally.

"Masculine chauvinism," she said which made him laugh because it was obviously a phrase borrowed but not incorporated by her. And began to talk.

Listening he was more aware of the sound of her voice than the words. Should be enshrined for her voice alone. Even if crow ugly, if didactic, if stupid. Which she wasn't. The voice was a lovely lagniappe.

How it was when the war was on, she was saying, Orpheus at Eurydice's grave, with the gloom and the cypresses and the rich, subtly shaded voice mourning lost love, dead illusions, and youth never no more. You remember, everything exciting and a little sad and all the boys going away.

"I remember." Darkly. One of the crowd around the grave.

"I wanted to get involved in the war some way. Not patriotically. But for excitement. Spoiling for a whirlwind, a real storm, something to blow me out of the doldrums."

"You had a glamorous sorrow. Couldn't you have capitalized on that and stalked around in a black veil like an F. Marion Crawford character?"

"It was too real to be glamorous. And then—oh—there were so many parties and *Gone with the Wind* farewells and tiresomeness."

Joe Mayhew, then, the wind that filled out her sails and sent her scudding gloriously, hair flying like a Maenad into the eye of the storm she'd wanted. And damnnear wrecked her. Lived like a clamdigger half his life, her uncle Ben Merritt, narrow prig, had said, and that tells on a man, but she was all admiration. Because he was not only truly learned, but tough, wild and self-sufficient and unlike any other man in the world, even Benjie, which she did not say but it was there between the lines, who, for all his hulk was fundamentally soft. Almost the first date, Mayhew had treated her defiantly to his Horatio Alger history, and she, a Desdemona, had considered him clever and objective when he said he was from a family of old stock gone to seed, and very old stock too, much more antique than Sally's. Wheelwrights and shipwrights and yeomen and coopers and cabinet makers and bakers and psalmsingers and sailors and whalers and not one of them ever went into business and sat behind their desks in the countinghouses. No, the Mayhews were out there climbing the masts and harpooning the whales and making the wages and the boats and the oil and the barrels and hardtack and the money so that Sally's johnnycomelately, shrewd ancestors could shore it all up in trust funds for expensive coming-out parties, the best finishing schools and colleges, economic and social security for ever and ever.

And so, down into the present they'd come, marching militant, nasal, trueblue Yankees, every Mayhew, to Joe's father, stiff, touchy, unreliable, and alcoholic who worked at odd jobs and handymanning when he felt like it and when disinclined they lived even more meagerly than usual on the salary his mother made teaching the elementary grades in the smalltown school. The hands Joe Mayhew had held and touched Sally with were large, heavy-knuckled, hard, the hands of a boy who'd spent many youthful summers under broiling sun, picking berries for hire and the big white scar across the left palm was where the knife had slipped when he was ten and had started an earnest, annual summer's labor which was later to become afterschool labor too, gutting clams for ten cents an hour. He'd had no free time, no dances, proms, parties, or innocent flirtations around sodafountains with girls. Every moment was full of working and studying for a scholarship to Harvard. His dream and his mother's. Because his family must be redeemed. Then there was the scholarship but he had to live and buy books and eat too. His father had died by then which made one less person to drain his mother's salary and she could help him a little. But he scrimped and scrounged and worked after classes or between them. Summers, he went out with the fishing fleets from New Bedford and later to Europe and South America on big ships as a deckhand, making big money and saving and squeezing each penny.

At Harvard he lived as lonely as Thoreau at Walden until somehow it came to his attention that the DAR gave a small, personal fund scholarship for which he could qualify and did. One of the august, worthy ladies of that institution who lived in the best,

348

archaic Brahmin tradition, took a personal interest in him and he was invited for dinners, lunches, and teas. He suspected that, to her, he was simply a monument which must be preserved, but she was kind and he went often to her house because he was hungry, not only for good food and glimpses of a cushioned life but for people. There, he met others of her persuasion, their sons, their daughters, their husbands and brothers and from there he was whirled into coming-out parties, dinner dances and tennis matches. He had to borrow money to buy decent clothes, he slept little in order to keep studying, working and still go to where all these young and happy people sported, splashing their ancestors' money around.

But it was too late for him. The people were kind but he was tired and arrogant. He said nasty, curt things and thought dancing, tennis, and riding were child's play and said so. Besides he wanted a Rhodes and had to work hard for it. There were some lovely girls. They looked at him rather nervously but fascinated. But he preferred to be simple and matter of fact and go to bed and not fool with romance which he couldn't afford. There were girls who worked in five and tens and lunchrooms who would go have a few beers with him and had a room someplace. Sex meant a few words in the dark, the pleasant briefness and goodbye and when he'd accomplished his aims he'd get a wife.

But after awhile he wasn't invited to the parties any more because who knew what harm it might do to introduce him to sheltered daughters when he was so patently a poor, stiffnecked boy, with only a Colonial name to line his pockets and no manners. He might become president but until then he was not eligible. But he was cold and hard and matter of fact and it didn't show if he was hurt, only somewhere those Boston girls at the parties and playing tennis at Longwood must have become an ambivalent symbol.

He could not marry them. But he could marry Sally, when he came back years later in his Navy uniform with carefree money and an extremely promising academic career waiting, to be resumed when the fool war was over. He could marry Sally because she was flawed; only a halfbreed Bostonian, by her grandfather's will cut down to mere ribbons of a fortune, almost alone in the world, belonging nowhere, and wild.

He probably did not know why he wanted to marry her. She was beautiful, yes, but as she found out later, he cared little for mere beauty. He preferred women who were ugly, bucktoothed or fat, incapable of protesting his indifferent attitudes because they were lucky to get anyone. Well, then, why? It was love, he would say wryly, a scrofulous disease which renders one helpless. And what had changed him from a sympathetic, exciting lover in Boston to an indifferent, ridiculing, punitive husband in California? He didn't change, she said, her head nestling in the crook of Mike's arm, it was me. I was a newborn and one day I opened my eyes and there he was, with a whole lifetime of deprivation to pour on my head like boiling oil.

You know nothing, you Boston society girls. Not educated. Fashionable girls' schools and coming out and getting married and that's it. You don't even go to college. You don't have to. That's for the grubby, ambitious poor, the children of immigrants. Why, you people with your society that's based on money alone, made by merchants, before a certain date, and marrying each other to keep the money from going out to untouchables, you've inherited a pattern of living, safe, shrewd, thrifty, and God, so provincial. She'd been humble because that was one of the first diatribes. It was true about college but all those other things, she wasn't like that. She would have been, he'd said triumphantly, his American eagle eyes glowing, obsessed, but he had saved her, only now he didn't know if it was worth it. The pain of living with and educating a frivolous, oversexed child, who'd always done exactly as she pleased and had maids pick up after her. He might be able to forgive her for throwing her clothes all over the apartment and burning the coffee if she had read anything, but she was stupid too.

She learned to cook to please him and liked it, but it was hard to get anyone to come and clean in wartime California and she tried, she tried to be neat, to dust and sweep and wash dishes. But it got boring and after awhile she went and took a job singing in a nightclub and they had a large argument about it and he moved to the BOQ on the base and the apartment just gathered dust. They made up two weeks later and found a cleaning woman and she stopped her job and took some literature courses at Berkeley.

You'll never be a Margaret Fuller, he said. Boston doesn't produce them any more. Everyone's dead there, intellectually and politically, and the city, the beautiful city stagnated, tied in knots of reaction, strangling in dirt and corruption, debased, empty, narrow. Books are banned and plays are censored. Why, you people with all your generations of advantages haven't given the nation a President since John Quincy Adams. All dead and walking around smiling at themselves because salespersons scrape when they hear their names.

New England is dead and rotting away and everybody talks about its great past. It's just a place for tourists to come to now and admire its monuments. If you're poor in New England you'll have to go to some other state to go to school or else break your balls to work your way through. The culture and thought is mummified. No more Concord.

Nights were better but then the corrosion crept in there too. At night he said he was too tired to have sex all night long and too old to have a constant hot. I'm not going to wear myself out and be exhausted all the next day on duty because you're a greedy little animal. And he'd turned over and gone to sleep and left her lying there. She'd thought it would be nice to put a pillow over his head and hold it there till he smothered. She had considered crying. Instead, she'd gotten up and gone out to a bar and picked up a Marine and let herself be good and pawed and then taken a taxi home, sans Marine, and gone to sleep, drunk and obscurely revenged, on the sofa.

She had not gotten up to make his breakfast that morning but lay on the sofa pretending to be asleep. If he said he was sorry. He didn't. He acted as though it were the most normal morning in the world, whistling cheerfully while he shaved. So she'd told him about the Marine. He'd been very calm. He'd expected it. He'd been thinking seriously for a long time about their marriage. She was not the wife for him. An English instructor's wife could not be a jazzy tramp with a boudoir lampshade mind, no matter how illustrious her ancestry or how covered with doubloons she was. He had not worked all these years to be dragged down, pitied, or mocked at or even, very probably, cuckolded.

Nothing happened with the Marine she said and you shouldn't say crazy things like that about going to bed, and it won't happen again. Don't bargain with me, Sally, nothing happened this time but it will, because I see the way you look at men. And bed is just a natural function and you have it and it makes you feel better and it's over and it shouldn't become either an idol or a disease. I don't want to hang around dissecting it or ornamenting it with rococo.

Three days later he was unexpectedly ordered to sea duty and then he went off before they'd had a chance to sew up the wound decently. For months and months she tortured herself to find the answers, to know whose fault it was. She remembered the good moments, the good love, the sweet words, the friends, the talk, the music, the picnics and swimming and sailing, the lying in bed together talking over parties and movies and love. Remembered the pleasure at the sight of him waiting to meet her in Boston, the passion of his kisses, the mutual delight in waking up and finding each other.

But the night she heard he had died, she was alone, lying in bed, drinking and went down again for the last time, the long, long flight of tormented, riddle-strewn steps. She would find him and ask him what pride had prevented her asking: What is it? Why did you turn the face of coldness and hatred to me? When did you stop being my friend? Was it me? I tried to please you but I couldn't change my being for you.

And he'd risen before her, his face burning, glowing like a coal, surrounded by other Furies in torment, writhing and screaming in the fires of the damned but their faces were all the faces of young men whose lives have been thrown away before they've lived. She thought to see Benjie and she'd looked for him but there were too many of them. But why, she pleaded, her lyre voice all grief and love, why, tell me? Even now, you see, he said, even now seeing me, the way I died with lumps of charred flesh falling around me, you are still looking for someone else. You know why, because you had everything and I had nothing and yet you could not give me love. But he hadn't wanted love from her. He'd only wanted her to give him the youth he'd never had and when he got her, he saw what a silly dream it was and only hated her more. Then they'd all banded against her and driven her back up the steps crying NO, NO, NOooo! NOoooo, it's too late for all of us, we have no answers here, we can only burn forever with the memories of our mistakes and the regrets for all the things we'll never have. And if you are guilty and sorry and tormented eternally with questions so much the better. Although you live, you will live remembering us. She had stumbled back up the interminable, enigmatic stairs with their mocking jeers at her back and turned once, one last time, flinging out her arms, calling, asking her question, pleading with them to understand, telling them that she would remember them always, crying hot tears at the sight of their yearning, stretched-out hands. But a sheet of flame rolled, cut them off and they were gone.

"I'll never know now," she said to Mike in the green coolness by Arabella Random's slimy pool. "They wouldn't let me pass and the flame was molten lava and it hardened and became enormous rock and I woke up and I never even tried to move the stone till today."

"I'm sorry I asked you to talk about it. I didn't know it was that bad."

"If he hadn't died it'd've been just another foolish marriage between two people who were wildly incompatible. But death does odd things when there was hatred in life. It leaves a mystery and a complete feeling of helplessness. You can't talk or apologize or make amends. Anyway, it doesn't matter. I'm glad I talked to you about it. You're the only one I could see telling it to, somehow."

"Thank you."

They began to walk back to where the music was, silently.

Finally, "All marriages don't turn out like that, Sal."

"Yes, I'm sure they do. Sooner or later, the walls go up and you can't remember where it all began or what caused it but you know you're living in a thick fog of beastliness. It's rather like a poem you read to me once. Back there in San Francisco, it came to mind and I tore through a few books looking for it. It was by Wallace Stevens. It was in the spring and we'd gone on a picnic and sat under an apple tree."

"'Peter Quince at the Clavier,' yes, I remember." He hadn't been able to read that poem for a long time without an agony because after that she'd gone away and it was all over.

"The part that begins, 'Beauty is momentary in the mind,/The fitful tracing of a portal,' which is really the way love is and it never lasts and it's hopeless to pretend it ever will and I shall never be blind enough to think it might again."

"It isn't . . . uh . . . it doesn't quite mean that, Sal."

"Oh you needn't go explicating it to me. I expect it means whatever people who read it and like it, feel it means. Tell me the rest of it."

They walked through the pine woods swinging clasped hands.

> "*Beauty is momentary in the mind—*
> *The fitful tracing of a portal;*
> *But in the flesh it is immortal.*
> *The body dies; the body's beauty lives.*
> *So evenings die, in their green going,*
> *A wave, interminably flowing.*
> *So gardens die, their meek breath scenting*
> *The cowl of winter, done repenting.*
> *So maidens die, to the auroral*

Celebration of a maiden's choral.
Susanna's music touched the bawdy strings
Of those white elders; but, escaping,
Left only Death's ironic scraping.
Now, in its immortality, it plays
On the clear viol of her memory,
and makes a constant sacrament of praise.'"

"That's it," she said, "death's ironic scraping."

She took what she wanted of anything and tailored it for her needs. For an instant, he understood a little how aggravating a careless kind of mind like hers might have been to Joe Mayhew. And if her story were true, or even just remotely distorted by hatred, by disillusion, how damnable, how sad, to hear what his rival had really been like. All that brilliance, driving ambition, hard, fanatical perfection, all that herculean labor to attain goals that lesser, softer people had thrust upon them had left him without human emotion, choked by hellfire and damnation and perhaps death had come to him early and mercifully before the mind he'd valued above love, had cracked in half. And of course he'd have to marry Sally. Someone like that would always search for impossibles.

They drifted up behind the circle of canvas chairs just in time to hear the closing notes of a Haydn trio. The musicians put away their instruments and Sally saw her aunt waving at them.

"Aunt Fan is coming out of a rapture. Please don't tell her we didn't stay for the music. She takes these things very seriously."

With Frances Merritt they followed the crowd back to the terrace where the white-linened tables were now spread lavishly with huge platters of food. They sat at one of the small, marble-topped tables consuming quantities of cold, sliced turkey and ham and coffee ice with whipped cream and some ethereal wine punch with sliced strawberries bobbing in it. They were almost finished when Arabella Random bore down on them and they both sat quietly and listened to a monologue delivered in a rapid, breathy chant on four or five unrelated subjects, the thread holding them together, obviously only Mrs. Random herself.

"Have you been to Alaska, Mr. Wainscott?"

"No. I always . . ."

"Fascinatin' place, Alaska. We went up on the boat, my husband and I. He had to go on some government business and I always remember some horrid man who chased us around all over the boat as he wanted Mr. Random to intercede . . . well . . . it was something totally out of the question, at any rate. Were you in the service, Mr. Wainscott?"

"Yes. In the Army."

"Ah, well of course I've always preferred the Navy. What commission did you hold?"

"I was enlisted. A tech sergeant."

A silence, a blessed one. He wondered how she'd get out of that. Sally's lips were quivering but she continued to spoon up whipped cream. Frances Merritt looked distressedly at him and then gave attention to an obscure forkful of salmon in aspic.

"How curious. A sergeant. Then you are not a university man."

"Harvard."

"A matter of choice then, I see. Of course, there were some excellent young men among our private soldiers, particularly during the First War. I was one of the first Gray Ladies in Washington in 1917. At the hospitals, you know. There was one young Irishman, I remember him particularly, the son of a saloonkeeper, I believe. He'd lost part of his arm at Château-Thierry and had to undergo several more operations. He begged me to stay with him in the operating room during one of them and I thought that he'd undergone so much pain, had given up so much that if he wanted me to do this small thing, I would. I had no son to send myself. Our family has a long tradition of service to the nation but we are the end of it and if the sons of immigrants can lay down their lives and limbs for our country, I, I told myself, can control a mere distaste for blood. So I was with him. Unfortunately, I was overcome and had to leave the operating room once. He was under anesthetic and didn't know. But I remember standing out there in the hall trying to control myself and chiding myself for my lack of fortitude and in the end I went back and was there when he woke up. When I saw his face, I was glad that I had."

They all murmured the expected things and shortly thereafter she left them to enthrall another table.

When they came to say goodbye to her she smiled at Mike and said archly, "Now you must take good care of our Sara. True beauty should always be cherished, you know."

"Now, what inspired all that?" They were driving back to Boston together. "My God, she's fantastic. But why pick on me?"

"Oh darling, it's most odd but I think she thought you were my beau."

"Well even if I were does it signify that I care how good she is about distributing tracts and baskets to the needy poor."

"Mike, for a writer, you're really dreadfully obtuse. Don't you see? You went to Harvard and yet you were an enlisted man during the war. For Arabella that means that you're just overflowing with noblesse oblige and liberal notions. Of course, you are, I know. So, therefore, she must needs tell you that she too sympathizes and understands and had her moments. Just a social convention darling."

"So if I do happen to marry you, she won't hold it against me that I was just a poor, bloody sergeant? The whole thing sounded awful damn patronizing to me."

"Oh, you're such a churl. Don't you know that true beauty should be cherished. And here you are such an indifferent guy."

"Well, that's the way it is with Harvard men, so the song says. But they love their Vincent baby till the day they die."

"I'm no longer a member of the Vincent Club. That's a wonderful song isn't it? Wish I could sing it but it's a man's song. You know, seriously, it gave me rather a turn to hear Arabella talking about watching an operation on a man's arm. I think it was wildly gutty of her to do it. I'm not sure I could. The man I'm with now lost a leg, and, well, not to go into gory details, to watch it come off must've been incredibly sickmaking."

He couldn't help whistling. "Does that make you more noble than Arabella? Or could it have something to do with that dream of hero Furies in hell?"

She only smiled and told him to stop behaving like a parlor analyst and let him off right at his door, zooming on up the Hill before he thought to ask her when they could have another friendly little talk. He got himself cleaned up and had a drink with Sam and Minta and then they all took off for the lobster dinner which he was afraid what with the select kickshaws he'd consumed at Arabella's fête he'd be unable to do justice to but by the time they got a table and had a few more drinks his appetite had returned.

The place was in Marblehead, quiet, many-windowed and they sat at a table with candles flaring against the oncoming dark, looking out over the water. The lobster shells mounted in pink piles, the drawn butter sauce lay in fat streaks on the plates and over coffee he told them about his afternoon.

"You're really mixing with plantation folks boy," Sam said, making a face.

"I guess you didn't like Dame Arabella."

"Personally, no. When I interviewed her, I felt that she was patronizing me as a ghoulish representative of the yellow press. However, viewed objectively, as a sort of period piece, a portion of social history, I found her quite wonderful."

"She made Sally feel that the guillotine was waiting because she let off some careless wisecrack about that Greek theatre owner who was there, Stefanotis."

Sam snorted. "Yes, I'd noticed that she's a fine example of the think-with-the-liberals, eat-with-the-Tories school. I don't know if she's aware of it though. She comes from a different age when it was considered all right to be philanthropic to the great unwashed as long as they didn't expect to be entertained in your home. It wasn't going to deprive you of anything and, in fact, it did wonders for your ego to have all that gratitude and beaming faces and touching of forelocks when you came around. It's the only thing the American rich could have, in a so-called democratic society, in place of the European titles, great feudal estates and curtsying peasants. That's one reason I've always preferred Europe. Much less pretense."

"And this much touted devotion of hers to the arts is another hypocrisy," Minta said acidly. "She doesn't really know a damn thing about art. Absolutely the worst type of rich, shrewd collector, the kind who thinks of art as an investment and loves bargains, which is why she buys pictures and objets d'art instead of stocks and land, having enough of those already, I daresay. I absolutely loathed having to sell any of my work to that smug beldame who actually couldn't understand how a woman of my background could become a painter."

"I didn't know she owned anything of yours, Minta."

"Well, she doesn't any more fortunately. It was the one of you actually, as the little fat baby in the tin bathtub. She gave it to the Chicago Art Institute several years ago for a whopping fat tax deduction, no doubt."

"Oh yes." He'd seen photographs of that painting and it could have been any other baby. Still, it unnerved him a little to think of a picture of himself sitting around on The Random's Turkish Delight walls for years, all unbeknownst to him. "Seeing as how this was a picture of the apple of your eye, Minta," he couldn't resist saying, "how could you stand giving it into her care?"

"It was sheer necessity, if we wanted to eat," Sam said, hunting lobster meat with fingers, forks, and care. "Some of those years at Meudon when you were a baby were damn lean, you know."

"Her horrid money paid for your gruel for months," Minta agreed happily slopping butter on her baked potato. "I suppose it was for-

tunate really that she was such a pennypincher. You know, she didn't
go through dealers as most collectors do, at least not at that time.
She knew that there were hordes of probably very good artists starving all over Paris whose work might be worth something eventually,
people who didn't show or have dealers, which I didn't at the time
either. All she had to do was plod through miles of garrets and
studios and pick up the paintings for a song. And darling Jack
Brimmer whose father was a friend of hers told her about me and
she came out to Meudon . . . Sort of grimly ironical for Jack when
you consider that because Arabella saw all those lush nudes of
Maddalena, his wife, on practically every wall and floor in fifty
studios . . ."

"Sally's mother was a Montparnasse model?" His voice cracking
like an adolescent who's had his first brush with pornography. "A
sort of a Kiki?"

"She was much better-looking than Kiki," Sam said smugly. "Almost the perfect prototype of one of those Titian Venuses. More
buxom if possible."

"I didn't think well brought up pre-World War I young ladies of
the Italian nobility went in for that sort of thing."

Sam made a derisive noise. "Paris, after the war, was crawling with
penniless, decayed and declassed nobility who, in order to live, did
anything. I gather that Maddalena's mother had been brought up
with some pretensions and a lady's education but her father was
some sort of minor civil servant who died early and then there was
a stepfather who owned a small restaurant. What could a beautiful
and untrained girl do in those days but . . ." He stopped abruptly,
looking harassed. "Minta, for Godsakes, why'd you let me run on
like that? The whole thing about Maddalena was supposed to be a
secret. So the kids could hold their heads up in stuffy Boston. God,
it was so long ago, I forgot all about it."

They clammed up while the lobster debris was being carted away
and parfaits, coffee and B&B ordered and he waited edgily, thinking about Arabella Random's crack that afternoon. All the paintings
of your mother, my dear. And Sal, obviously not a party to the
secret, very put down, having, for the first time in her life, been
shown the tradesmen's entrance only not knowing why. Well, dammit, he would con this arcane tale out of Sam and Minta and someday he would tell Sally, so she could be forewarned and not fall
innocently into traps set for her by shrikes who knew her mother
when. Someday when he knew her better. The real Sally he was be-

ginning to see, after today, was a hell of a lot more interesting than the old one, up to and including her mother.

Yes, someday when she had gotten tired of this new passion, he might undertake a voyage out to the spice Indies. A newfound girl. "How blest am I in this discovering thee."

Minta, warmed by B&B and indignant anyway about the dunder-headed rich's haughty and snobbish attitude toward artists and their models, needed very little encouragement. Every now and then her petitpoint style unraveled into a few silky green streaks of jealousy because Sam, apparently, had not been immune to Maddalena Brimmer and then they'd have little acid exchanges as to the accuracy of each other's memory, while he tried not to laugh.

It was a depressing story though, involving a girl brought up to believe that her heritage entitled her to better things than cooking and waiting tables in her stepfather's greasy spoon in Firenze and a soulful-eyed Czech Jewish painter who wandered in to eat one day and found her blazing there like a forgotten masterpiece. Painting her in all her gold and cream and velvet flesh was not enough. He had to love her too and take her away with him to Paris. She was a good mistress and model and to make extra money because he was poor she modeled for other painters and for student's life classes. But inevitably, women whose beauty is their only fortune, have to think about dreary facts like old age and no more beauty and after awhile there was Jack Brimmer.

"Have you ever noticed," Minta said, "how these cold, repressed, shy people are magnetized by warm, emotionally free and easy types. Well, that's the way he was about Maddalena. An icicle until she smiled at him like the Mediterranean sun and he melted away to nothing. Before he met her the only way he could loosen up was to drink too much and after he married her he had so many troubles with his father and money that he drank even more. Still, I've never seen a man so in love. For awhile there in the beginning, it almost seemed as if there was some hope for him."

"Your harpy hostess at the fête champêtre this afternoon managed to foul that up," Sam said. "Of course, old Brimmer wasn't too pleased that his only son had married a foreigner but he was told that she was the granddaughter of a Venetian Count and, after all, there was a grandson, Dudley being born about seven months after the wedding. Old Brimmer being one of those dynasty-mad business-men was all prepared to forgive his son for not coming home after the war, restore and increase his allowance, get the whole inherit-ance business sewed up legally and properly. In fact, Jack, Maddalena, and the baby were due to go over and be welcomed and Jack would probably have settled down and led a staid business life. Maddalena was even willing to remove the old man's one objection to her and become Protestant."

Enter Arabella, returning homeward, the memory of all those lovingly rendered nudes engraved on her virtuous mind, and after all it was only her duty to tell a respectable father-in-law what his son had married, wasn't it? And back there in Boston everyone knew how morally loose artists were. Rapprochement after that was, of course, impossible. The redoubtable grandfather ordered a divorce and said that born Brimmers could come home but not That Woman.

"Jack wasn't his usual wishy-washy self then," Minta said, "and he refused to give up his wife. It was very brave of him, poor darling, because he was deathly afraid of his father and one of those unfortunates who didn't know how to do anything to earn his own living. Finally the old man realized he couldn't let his only Brimmer grandson starve to death in Paris so he made a deal with them. They could have all the money they wanted, they could stay in Europe all their lives but they must send Dudley back to Boston alone when he was housebroken. His very words. The old ogre."

"I think," Sam said gloomily, "they thought it would just be for a short time. But then, Jack's drinking got worse and she was neglected more than a frankly sensuous woman ought to be and their marriage became a mess and then they were dead."

"I always thought," Minta said, stubbing out her cigarette while Sam tried to decipher the check, "that Jack really became an alcoholic after Dudley left. Maddalena was a little sterner about it. She had some crazy European theories about not wanting to jeopardize her son's great inheritance before he could choose for himself. Consistent enough, I daresay, considering that she married for money. Still, children can survive the most ghastly treatment. Sally seems to have come out all right and I hear that Dudley is a doctor, so he couldn't have been too damaged."

In the car on the way home unanswered questions hovered. Had Sam slept with Sally's succulent mother? Or did he merely lust? And so what if she was a nude model and artist's mistress and waited on tables? Why all the secrecy? Because it meant little now but in the twenties it must've really panicked that bluenose grandfather. Kind of explained a little about Sally too. Everyone was so enlightened nowadays they didn't believe in inheritance or blood or family but he'd just bet that a little of that lusty earthiness had leaked through from mother to daughter, tempered by Brimmer intelligence and the rich girl environment and the Boston bringing up. And from where pray tell had come the emotional romanticism that'd displayed itself in those curious flashes, this afternoon, in the dream about the dead soldiers in hell? Not from the old, cold, hardheaded Brimmers that was for sure."

"I think we better swing off on to the other road now," Sam said suddenly. "We're approaching Revere Beach and we'll be running over America enjoying itself."

Sitting up with sudden excitement and peering through the car window, Mike could see, glimmering tipsily spangled in the salt-scented night, the lights of a Ferris wheel and hear the roar of a roller coaster whooshing down dizzy heights. The thin sounds of screams and shrill laughter hung in the air.

"Hey," he said and in his voice was an eager note, regrettably, but he couldn't suppress it. "Let's go up there and go on the roller coaster and one of those things where the little cars hit each other and eat some fried clams and popcorn. How about that?" He knew it was a stupid suggestion when he made it. But suddenly the lights and sounds and the buttered smells wafted to him, made Revere Beach boulevard infinitely glamorous. The kind of expectant excitement he used to have about carnivals and amusement parks and circuses when he was a kid.

"Roller coasters make me deathly ill," Minta said.

"Damn fool idea of amusement," Sam said. "No thanks, Mike. I hate all amusement parks, midways, carnivals etc., on principle. You go. We'll wait for you."

"Never mind." Slumping back. He remembered now. They'd never taken him. A couple of times to circuses where, in spite of all the splendid acrobats and bears riding bicycles their boredom and discontent was apparent. "It was just an idea."

"If you want to go on the roller coaster, Mike, I'll go with you," Minta said. "And wait below. Then we might ride the carousel. I've always thought they were rather charming. There was one in the Luxembourg Gardens that you used to love when you were small. All the animals had lovely names even if they were shabby."

"No, I don't want to. Forget it." He should've shut up. It'd been good before that. As if they all liked each other and had a family feeling. And he'd wanted to continue it. To go back. Should have known you couldn't. Couldn't be a kid again, only this time going off on an outing with them, not being sent off with somebody else, a special thing they were doing for him, even if they didn't like it.

Clambering into roller coaster cars and shooting up and down canyons of air, staring into the little machines where you saw old Mack Sennett comedies when you turned the crank or got a fortune card from the wax grandmother, or went round and round fearfully, high up in the air in the Ferris wheel, with all the people far below, faces tilted upward, white blurs, and the lights going and the world spread out before you, perilously hovering over nothing, but safe, safe, because they were with you. And the European amusement parks didn't have all that crazy stuff to eat, all the buttered popcorn and frozen custard and hot dogs and clams and by the time he got back he was too old and it didn't mean the same. It wouldn't now either but for a passing instant he had wanted to try.

"I never liked Fun Houses either," Minta said. "Your skirts blow up around your neck and you feel like a fool. And those mirrors are really depressing."

"The whole business," Sam pontificated, "is predicated on the eternal gullibility of people. All that tinsel enchantment and simple-minded laughter and screeching makes people think that there must be happiness and pleasure with that much brightness and noise. Only when they get there in the midst of it all they find that it's not at all like that. People are screaming in fear, afraid of falling and smashing like china out of those precarious junk machines. And the laughter is only because when they look fat and ugly in a mirror it's better to laugh at themselves than have other people do it. Scott put it very well in one of his stories, I think. I've forgotten the name but it's the one about the priest. He equated it to the realities of life which the priest could not share and was afraid of and yet drawn to and it's very exact, I think."

"Yeah, I know the one." Weary now and back to this morning when his father seemed no more than a southern senatorial fake. "'But don't get up close because if you do you'll only feel the heat and the sweat and the life'" Lousy name-dropper! Scott indeed! A wonder he could associate with ordinary people, like his son, having known so many exalted personalities.

"I know what I would like," Minta said positively, "I'd like one of those ice cream cones of exotic flavor."

She didn't care what it was as long as it was sufficiently weird, she said, so he got out of the car, abruptly and walked a way down the boulevard to the Howard Johnson stand. He got himself a pistachio cone and one for her called chocolate banana which ought to knock her out. Sam, remaining in death's head at the feast character, had refused. The ice cream stand was right by the merry-go-round and while he waited his turn, he looked and saw the gilded horses whirling by and the red and gold and blue and the children laughing. They were playing some canned music, "Roll Out the Barrel," it sounded like. Mobs were streaming up and down the sidewalks which were covered with papers and scum of food and spilled bags of popcorn. Sailors and soldiers with young, overpainted chicks, hair dyed and cheap, gaudy clothes, lots of wild-looking adolescents, boys with overly long hair and shiny jackets, girls wearing tight, obscene-looking pants, weary-looking parents, badly dressed, trailing a lot of tired, whiny kids, holding the refuse souvenir stuff you get when you throw three balls and hit a straw man. There was a kind of a glare over it all from the unshaded bulbs in the myriad stands and the crude colored lights on the façades of the amusements. Across the narrow boulevard there were benches with necking couples and farther down it was black dark and you could hear the vague whisper of water slopping on the beach and you knew the sand was gray and wet, sprinkled with the leavings of the day's beach outings and that boys and girls were lying down there feeling each other up, and farther out the bay was utterly indifferent and across the water there were some dim lights in Nahant and Sally was over there lying in a bed with some other man. A vacant, mocking, eternal noise irritated his ears and when the sweating, pimply kid in the ice cream stand handed him his cones, he walked back a way to see where the noise came from and there was a big, pâpier-maché, fierce face stretched wide across the front of a shanty bedlam called Bluebeard's Palace and out of the big, red horror mouth, came this crazy, shrill, unending HO, HO, HO. He went back to the car where his damn, always right parents were, glad to escape from the tawdry jangle. The time of wonder had long gone but if he ever had a child, even though he couldn't stand it, he'd take him, either here, or someplace like it, as soon as ever he wanted to go.

Minta and Sam had evidently been talking about him because when he clambered into the back seat there was a silence and then a flurry of meaningless chatter.

"You never liked trains," Sam said suddenly turning around and looking at him, sitting there licking on his fast melting pistachio ice cream. They were inching along in a slow line just outside the Sumner Tunnel.

"What do you mean I didn't like trains?"

"Toy electric trains. I bought a whole set for you in Germany, with everything, tracks, the whole kit and caboodle complete. You never gave a damn for them. And lead soldiers. I had a whole army of different kinds when I was a child. I sent all the way back to Massachusetts and had your grandmother wrap them, each one carefully and ship them all the way to Paris. They were all mine when I was a boy and I bought some other ones in Paris for you. I remember there was a whole regiment of Hessian mercenaries. Soldiers in 1812 uniforms. Some French ones in armor. Miniature cannons, muskets, perfect replicas. You'd pick them up and look at them and that was it."

"I vaguely remember that. Well, what happened to them then? Where are they now?"

"I sent everything back to Stockbridge. Your Cousin Ned played with them. He apparently appreciated them. If there's anything left of them, they're probably in your aunt's house. I don't know. I put them out of my mind."

"Ned got my trains and soldiers? That hyena!" It seemed shocking now that someone as impossible as his cousin had ever played with and owned his toys.

"That's why we never saved any of your things," Minta said. "It's too heartrending to have wonderful memories of things you loved as a child, which gave you so much pleasure and you think of your children loving them as much as you did and they don't. I didn't want you to undergo the same disappointment when you trotted them out for your children and they turned their noses up."

"I had some books I remember, that were yours, Sam. *Treasure Island* and all like that."

"Yes," Sam said grudgingly, as they sped along through the tunnel. "I decided that you weren't completely hopeless when you pounced on it and even liked the illustrations."

"I don't remember the trains at all and damn little about the soldiers."

"Sure you don't," Sam said. "You have a very convenient memory. You can remember that we never took you to carnivals but nothing about our positive aspects."

"All children are different," Minta said. "Perhaps Mike might have a son who'd like lead soldiers and trains. You really ought to see your cousin Ned and ask him if they still exist."

"No," he said grudgingly, "they're his now. He can give them to his oafish kids if he has any."

"There's no point talking to him about children," Sam said. "He's going to live with us until we die and then he'll frequent hall bedrooms."

"Hear, hear!"

"Don't be so snide," Minta said. "You don't want him to marry just anyone, do you?"

In the back, he yawned and stretched out on the seat and tried to picture all the little, lead soldiers in the different uniforms that he hadn't wanted. And a sudden awful image of Sam, kneeling on the floor, eagerly lining up regiments of them in battle position, explaining about the various insignia on the soldiers' uniforms and the parts of the cannons, trying to entice a show of interest from a recalcitrant, sullen, little boy who only wanted to run between his parents, holding hands, up and down the gaudy, tawdry streets of a raucous, amusement park.

Two

Sally

In Nahant on Sunday mornings most of the people from the big old deep-porched, diamondpaned windowed summer houses along the shore went to church. Many of the same people didn't come there any more but still the bells tolled their invitations and on clear days you could hear the light sounds of upright singing.

The bell's owlish warnings came muffled in mist, this particular Sunday, their last together in Nahant. They were going to get her settled in Rockport that afternoon.

"I'm going swimming, Saul. There'll be no one down on the beach today. Want to try?"

"It's a hell of a day honey. There's a fog coming in. Whyn't we just stay warm in bed awhile? I hate this goddamn dampness. My leg aches."

"If I were a native I'd tell you that likely the fog'll burn off after awhile. But I'm going anyway."

"I know better than to argue with a wild one like you once you get your mind made up." He took fishing gear along and while she was in the water stood up above on the rocks with a few other diehards, putting out lines for flounder they didn't want.

Swimming was all right even though the water was gray and rheumy but getting out into the cool, dispiriting dampness, the clamminess of her wet suit, the thin, sad, struggling sun, all made her sorry she'd decide to give her votive offering body to the usually inspiring sea. The mist was thicker now, rolling in over the water, creeping right up the beach, webbing her sandy, wet feet. Pulling her jersey on over the goosepimpled bareness of her arms and shoulders, she ran briskly up and down the deserted sand to dry her suit, pulled on a pair of blue jeans shorts and, buckling her sandals, raced down to the end of the beach, scrambling up the face of the rocks where Saul stood among the company of shrouded, ghostly monomaniacs. He waved at her, but he too was intent, mesmerized in the nether world of fishermen, straining all senses toward that challenging pull on the line.

Sitting with her back against a rock, smoking quietly and waiting, looking out to the disappointing, queasy gray swell of sea. Silly of her to have gone swimming on a day like this, with packing and getting ready to go and why? To propitiate Neptune for what he had given her, that wonderful month with Saul the Triton and his wreathed horn and because it was the last day and who knew what falling apart thing would happen now?

The poor, feeble sun finally giving up the ghost, the mist thickening into an unmistakable fog and the fishermen reeling in their lines preparing to go. Only Saul remained, apparently undaunted, his shirt open to the increasingly chilly dampness, his eyes fixed on the water. How deep brown he was, how imposing, all his bones and muscles and flesh so marvelously made for her pleasure and she knew every hair on his chest and arms, and God would she always want him in the same incensed way, every gesture arousing her, the way he was holding his fishing line now, was sexual to her informed eye. Jaundiced eye really, remembering how she used to have notions that jazz saxophonists and bass men were making love to their instruments when they played. Reeling in his line now and waving his hand disgustedly at the fog. Good, they would have time to go back to bed for a while and if she hadn't been so stubborn that's where they'd've stayed the whole morning.

"Did you catch anything, darling?"

"Nah. Not a nibble. Just as well. What would we do with it? Anyway, I wasn't concentrating too much to begin with. Watching you down there on the beach. Can't keep my eyes off you, honey. And the other guys up here couldn't neither. Nobody said anything though. I guess they knew you were mine. Wish I could've said you were my wife. You know something, I keep wishing that, everywhere we are, that I could tell every sonovabitch we see. This is my wife, mine."

"Saul, don't. You promised."

"Okay, I promised. But I can't help what I feel can I? Want some beer, Sally? I got a coupla cans in the car. I'm kind of dry."

"I thought we'd go back to bed for a while."

"Changed your mind, did you? Well, so did I." He stomped off to get the beer. Piqued, obviously, but he knew he shouldn't talk about marriage. It spoiled everything.

They drank from the cans. "Why don't you want to go back to bed?"

He made a face. "It'll depress me, that's all. I wanted to stay there this morning because I never wanted to get up and leave the way we two have been together all this month. And with you up there singing, things'll change. There'll be other people hanging around. And if we go back to the happiest bed I've ever been on, for a quickie, for five minutes and then go, it'll just remind me of . . . well, the hell with it. Let's stay here a few minutes. Kind of nice, alone, the two of us with the fog creeping in."

"But you'll be with me, Saul. All next month. You'll be on vacation." Inwardly sighing. Was he going to be jealous now, up there? How difficult and provoking just when she was worrying as to whether she could sing at all any more. She might prove a dreadful flop.

"Listen, honey, you know it's true. Won't be the same. Here, we didn't talk to nobody, nobody saw us or knew us. There, you'll be in the middle of a crowd. I just hate to share you, that's all. Okay, so it's a kid feeling. If you were my wife, I wouldn't care, other guys looking at you, laughing with you, talking to you. Who can blame a guy for getting into an uproar about you. Not me. But you don't belong to me, so I got no rights. Makes me nervous, that's all." Slanting dark eyes regarding her watchfully, hopefully from the heavy, sensuous face. Must take a firm hand with him. He got the jimjams so easily.

"Other people, my singing, won't change a thing. You're still all I care about. It will be better than here, you'll see. We'll be together even more, a whole month, not just nights and weekends. Just a few hours of rehearsals and you can come to the club when I sing and we'll loll on the beach."

He drained off the last of his beer and threw the can over the edge of the rocks into the foggy face of the sea. A long way off they heard it splash. "Okay. So you're not the marrying kind. You just want to play around. And you can afford to, I grant you that. But what happens after July? I can only come up on weekends and Christ, Sally, I know you. You want something, you take it."

"Darling, please give me some credit for discrimination, can't you? I don't want everyone. And I can last till the weekends, if that's what's worrying you."

He lay his head down in her lap and she stroked his brooding face.

"You'll want to get married sometime again, won't you, honey? I can wait. Years, if I have to, if I know I'll get you in the end."

"It would be silly for you to do that, Saul." Lightly.

"Is it me? Or just marriage in general? We have it so good together."

"Marriage is a terrible drag, darling. I can't fathom why you aren't completely off it."

"I'd love to know what that husband of yours did to you. Was he some kind of a pervert?"

"That's not very respectful, is it? It was nothing really. Just all wrong for each other. And we'd be too."

"I don't see that. We get along fine."

"Sex isn't marriage, darling. They're two utterly different things."

He wouldn't understand of course. It was like their trip to New York, last week. He'd wanted to go see the champion heavyweight fight between Louis and Walcott and he'd been able to get tickets and a few days off and reluctantly she'd allowed herself to be persuaded. They'd flown down and he'd reserved a double room and bath in a hotel near Macy's. She'd have preferred the Plaza but to him the Hotel Penn-Hudson was the acme of luxury and indeed it was very new and gleaming. There'd been a huge vase of gladioli ordered by him beforehand on a table when they got up to the room and she'd had to say, how lovely, when gladioli were her idea of funeral flowers which simply accentuated the depressed mood induced by having to pretend that she was his wife when they'd registered. Should never have done it, either, that's what gave him all these possessive my wife ideas. But he'd been so happy how could she disillusion him. Pranced around the room, which was big and full of glaring, vacant, modern furniture and ugly swollen lamps. Talked his head off as they'd had drinks in the hotel bar.

"Beautiful," he'd said exultingly, "I'm gonna give you the best weekend you've had in years. Nothing to spend my money on for a long time. Just mention anything you want, we'll do it. Dinner in the best places. God, I got an itch to see this town with you. I used to come here a lot years ago and loved it. Then, acourse, after the war I didn't give a damn about going anyplace. But with you, God, I bet you're the most beautiful-looking dame in this entire town of dolled-up, painted-up women."

He'd had a good time anyway. They'd gone to any number of well-known tourist traps, to jazz joints on 52nd Street, to a musical which was appallingly dull and pretentious with not one decent song to its name, but since Saul'd paid such a huge price for the tickets and seemed to revel in the tedious gaudiness, she'd kept silence.

There'd been some pleasant moments riding up Fifth Avenue in a bus and shopping in some of the wonderful stores near the Plaza but Saul had spoiled that too. He'd wanted to buy her expensive negligees, an insanely florid black lace nightgown and improbable pieces of jewelry he'd seen in windows. And when she'd told him that she couldn't accept such things and that she didn't like black lace nightgowns and that if he wanted to buy her a gift it should be something very simple and impersonal he'd said that it was all a lot of phony hypocrisy and if she could sleep with him he could buy her underwear and jewelry and this was so uncomfortably true that they'd had a near quarrel under General Sherman's horse and he'd gone off sulkily to drink in the men's bar at the Plaza while she finished shopping. Dudley'd given her a whopping fat check several days before, the newly raised allowance, and she'd spent very lavishly in Bonwit's, Bergdorf's, Hattie Carnegie's and a sinfully expensive boutique fantasque and almost forgot he was waiting for her, she became so engrossed. When she'd finally met him, he'd handed her, without a word, an enormous bottle of Chanel Number Five, which of course she never in this world used, but obviously had to enthuse over.

She'd wanted to go to the Modern Museum since they were so close and although he didn't like museums or modern art he agreed to come along and see *The Blue Angel* which was showing there that day. The film had moved her almost to tears of horror and depressed her inordinately. She'd wanted to talk about it, when they came out; the plump, frizzy-haired German fraülein with the shrill voice who was the early Dietrich, singing those marvelous songs, the whole decadent atmosphere, the sickness of Jannings' obsession, but Saul wanted to forget the whole thing.

"Goddamn crock of crap," he'd said brusquely. "Well, there's no fool like an old fool, I guess. Why the hell did you want to take me to that, Sally? To show me what saps men can be? Don't you think I know it?"

Trying vainly to explain to him that having never seen it before she couldn't possibly have known what it was like but it'd been obvious that he was unable to view it objectively as a piece of cinema art; that the songs, the macabre realism of sets and atmosphere, the masterly dissection of an outwardly rigid, arrogant society full of pus and rot inside, meant nothing to him and could not compensate for the story. He saw her as another cruel, uncaring siren, à la Dietrich, even though she'd just rejected his efforts to throw money away on her.

And, had she not, in truth, been a hypocrite? Actually, wasn't he treating her exactly as she deserved to be treated? Was she much different from those other brassy haired broads as he called them? He had meant no harm. Only trying to show his fondness for her and that was the way people like him did it. All those people they'd seen at the fight and in the Latin Quarter and those places with their women, all decked out in costly summer fur stoles and jewelry that the men had given them and not a wedding ring in sight. And Lindy's and the wild, spicy, many-layered sandwiches and the fantasia of strawberry cheesecake and the flamboyant, generous, flashy, loud vulgarity that fight and entertainment people went in for because it was full of vitality, why, she liked all that. It drew her.

But the naïveté of those people, their lack of breeding, the innocent, loud boasting, showiness, lack of manners. And yet who had been more overbearing and rude, acting as if politeness cost money, than her Grandfather Brimmer? She didn't want that either, that inbred cold narrowness. But she'd not been able to help wincing at the high, shrill, uneducated voices of those beautifully dressed, perfectly made-up women who'd been with the fight and show people even though they'd had hearts of gold. And the men, the beautiful bodies themselves alone were fine but they had a taste for the most flashy clothes and cars while their promoters, managers and trainers were the same and not beautiful at all.

She'd brooded sitting with Saul in these places and knew that was one reason why she'd never tried very hard to become a professional jazz or pop singer. The whole entertainment world was like that and she could not ever be completely part of it. The only people who seemed right in that sphere were the Negroes, with their dark skins beautiful in bright colors, their laughter rich and warm and natural, not shrill, nervous, a means of being noticed having a good time like the others, and the gusty, lusty way they told jokes. With them it was real, and only when they adopted the white man's so-called restraint did they become not quite so impressive. The staid, conservative blacks and grays of ofay clothes drained all the vitality from their lovely color. Sometimes it crept into the music too and the more dignified and intellectual the composer or musician got, the colder the music became.

All the way home in the plane sitting next to Saul who slept, she'd thought and wondered. What do you want, Sally? Where is it you belong? Not really the stuff that brassy haired broads are made of nor yet a staid Boston wife and mother, a doer-of-good-works type. Not an intellectual, not a career woman, not even a consistent, decent singer. A nothing. A nowhere chick who'd better straighten out and fly right.

It'd been a painful few days all around and certainly not calculated to put her into a radiant tremulous bride mood. It'd been a bad mistake to go, but she couldn't tell him and now, she could say only,

"Let's go, shall we? I'm growing mold sitting here in this dampness."

The fog had thickened by afternoon and they drove along up the coast cosily enclosed in the weird, gray light, suspended in a timeless, private world. The foghorns burred and the mist dripped down from the trees along the road and in Salem the statues of the witch and Nathaniel Hawthorne were wet and shiny with moisture.

"When I was in California, I missed this North Shore coast more than anything else." Looking affectionately out the window at the witch. "Perhaps because my family have lived along here for hundreds of years and even though I wasn't born here I've spent so much of my life around it and it's a thing you can't forget."

"Is that right?" Ominously. "And because your people were witchburners you think you own the place?"

"I didn't say that." If she was going to have to walk on eggs talking to him now that they'd left the bower of bliss where he'd had her all to himself how silly, stupid and quarrelsome it would become all over again.

"That's what you meant though. Well, I want to tell you that my grandfather didn't get to Boston from the steerage till the nineties sometime, but I think it's a great piece of coastline too. We didn't have no summer home either. Bud and me and my uncle used to come here when we were kids and go swimming and take out a boat and go fishing. Boy, we really looked forward to the summer for things like that. And we thought all the towns here and the water and the sand and the fish and rocks and gulls belonged to us too. And whaddya know. All the time they didn't. All the time it was the sole, exclusive property of people who got here first and grabbed it all and we were just nasty little trespassers."

"Saul, on occasion, you sound so much like my late husband that it's uncanny."

"Yeah, well if you said stupid things to him, like you just said to me, no wonder he got sore. Now look, honey, I'm sorry. Don't look that way. I didn't mean to shoot my mouth off. Now I reason this way. Remember when we went up to Gloucester to see the fleet blessed that day?"

"Yes. It was lovely, wasn't it? But didn't you think it was strange to see something so old world in the streets of an American town?" The procession of fishermen marching from the church to the waterfront, carrying on their shoulders the carved image of the Virgin and the crowd along the docks, while the Archbishop gave his blessing, the fishing boat whistles shrilling and reverberating and the little, white-frocked girls dropping their pink and white flowers into the water and the flowers flowing out to sea with the outgoing tide. "I mean, it was like those church processions in the streets in Europe, the Catholic countries, Italy and so on. But it looked, well, awfully anachronistic in a basically New England, founded by Puritans, image-haters town. I'm not opposed to it, it just doesn't seem aesthetically in keeping."

"Well, Jesus," he said helplessly, "I, honest to God, don't know what you're talking about when you dig out those five-dollar words. What my point is, is that those Portygees who knock themselves out taking out those fishing boats in all kinds of lousy weather, and it ain't the safest job in the world either, so that Massachusetts has a fishing industry, my Christ, they're just as much part of this place even though they didn't stake their claim till later, as you people. And about whether it looks good for Catholics to be carrying the Virgin Mary around the streets of a town founded by people who hated Catholics, if I get you right, well that's just a lot of bull. They operate the boats, they're the ones who're worried about dying out there on the water, they got a right to use whatever religious business they want to help them out."

"Well, naturally they have. How can you distort things so? You make me sound arrantly prejudiced which, as you perfectly well know, I'm not."

"No prejudices you know of, that is."

"I will not continue this pointless discussion any longer. No matter what I say, you'll turn it inside out. You're a horrible romantic, Saul, saying that people operate fishing boats just so the Commonwealth can have a fishing industry. That's sheer nonsense and you know it. They do it, because that's how they earn their living."

"Sure, I know that. And did you ever stop to think that all this ancestor worship about the pioneers who built up our country is the same thing. You think they figured they were making the U.S. into a great power or were they maybe just figuring out how to get enough food into their families' bellies."

"Very probably, the latter." Yawning. "Darling, do stop or write a letter to the DAR, why don't you? I'm not one of your ancestor worshipers."

"No, I know you're not. Come on over here. What are you sitting so far away for? You're a great girl and I feel lousy because . . . well, you know why."

"This road is far too slippery for . . . Saul, don't. You'll wreck the car."

"I guess you don't remember," he said reproachfully, "but a couple of weeks ago in bed in Nahant I was told by a young lady who ought to know that a real gentleman does what he wants when he wants to. He makes his own rules, you said. Acourse, if you're worried about accidents we can stop."

They were parked on a deserted, dirt, side road with the dank, woolly fog all around them.

"Let's see your lovely chest. There are some buttons missing here."

"Makes it easier, doesn't it? Ah honey, honey."

She slid her fingers down the black line of hair on his chest. "Your belt is too tight, you wicked, tempting man and you have no underwear on. I can tell."

Very clearly the foghorn's boom came through the grey ooze outside the car windows and then new noises, the sounds of hysterical sirens.

"Some fool's capsized out there. That's the Coast Guard. Honey, it won't be too good this way. You want to wait till we get there?"

"I can't now." She couldn't stop it and she couldn't stop it and now it was too late to try. They never learned, did they, not to start things? Clumsy, but it would be all right soon, it always was. All lost and gone inside, dissolving, melting away, it was everything, no, perhaps nothing, then really everything, the only real thing and she couldn't stop it and dreamily hearing the first swish of rain on the roof of the car above her head.

"Oh Christ, rain!" A big sheet of it dashed itself against the windshield. "Well, let's go, baby. And now we've done it in a car. Damn it, what a lousy mudhole. Okay, here's the highway. Just like you wanted, in a car. Sooner or later I'll do everything you want. Even maybe like art. Even do it on a beach at night. Just give me time. I'll do everything you want, Sally, I love you so much."

"Yes, I know, darling, and you're very sweet but do pay attention to the road. I wouldn't want us to die while we're still so good together."

Vance's band wore unbecoming maroon jackets, white trousers with a braided stripe down the side and black bow ties as their summer uniform.

"Don't these bring you way down?" Bobby Drummond said. "And how about these rinkydink arrangements? Still, it's a swinging band even if Vance is nowhere."

Even Vance turned out rather well. From the beginning, the club had been a success, crowded every night with young collegiate dancers who spent money freely, so both Vance and the owner were pleased. The first night singing, the very first number, she'd been shaky. But the band was behind her all the way, they liked the way she sang and the audience really listened to her and clapped loudly and enthusiastically. So after that it all went beautifully even if she didn't much care for the cheap, June, moon songs sung in that dull, standardized way, still some of the songs were tailor made for manipulation by her kind of voice and she squeezed as much style out of them as possible. Things were going so well indeed that Vance began to have visions inside his glossy, patent leather head of himself as the Benny Goodman of the North Shore and decided to have a trio with vocalist, on occasional nights. He said they could figure out what they wanted to do themselves, stipulating only that whatever they performed shouldn't be so jazzed up, whether hot or cool, that the customers wouldn't know what it was. The first night the trio was on view they did "Old Black Magic" because, as Bobby said, although it was a gummy tune it was just right for Sally to turn inside out. Saul was sitting drinking at a table beside the stand as he did every night and she sang it to him, to make him happy because he hadn't been really, except in bed, since they got there.

Singing it slow, deep, accenting, sliding, styling, stressing, keeping her voice in, pouncing on every word, caressing it, loving it, her shoulders and hips moving with them and it was all there, the whole feeling, when they looked at each other and when it was the same old tingle that she felt inside, the word was made to not only shiver but shake and when it was down and down I go, oh but she did, lowdown blues, with her mouth hardly open. Then, pausing and waiting so they could do an imaginative fill in and then Bobby's encouraging signal, and then going into it, knowing she should stay away but what can I do, opening up with the volume, then snaking down again almost to a whisper, because now a flame, burning and wanting and not having, then picking it up, beating it out, fast and accented and now the whole body moving with the rhythm and they were all behind her, not loud but right with her, and opening up again loud and every time, oh every time your lips meet mine, then slowing down again, dropping down, melting away, drawling it out, dragging it, heavy, wanting, pounding it out, in a spin, hitting it hard, but the power restrained, loving the spin I'm in, black magic called love, leaving it hanging there, stepping back and letting them have a ball with it and Bobby being frantic, and really coming on, and then back again for another chorus, knowing now she had it, could do anything with it, almost feel the crowd moving with it, making love to it, it was love, we were with it and it wasn't just a song any more, it was herself making love to Saul with her voice, not just a cheap tune, it was the two of them together and they were beautiful and they made it and they had it and it would never go away and she looked at him when it was done and hoped he knew.

The break came up then and she stepped down from the stand with Bobby and they went over to where Saul was.

"I tell you," Bobby said, "you really came on. I don't know how you do that strictly for crooners tune and make me feel that real jelly roll but you do."

Saul kissed her lightly as they sat down. "Here's a drink for you, honey. That was very good." Soberly. He got up. "Excuse me, willya, honey?"

"Better put your coat on," Bobby said smirking. "You really got sent, didn't you? Not that I blame you."

"Never mind, darling," she said quickly. Saul's face was red with embarrassment and anger. "You look splendid. In full battle position. Bobby's all teaed up and lacking inhibitions."

"I knew it would be like this," he said furiously, pulling on his jacket. "Everything in a goldfish bowl. You tell that jerk to shut his mouth or I'll fix him so's he can't play the drums any more." And marched off to the men's room.

"Hey, what's he so salty about?" Bobby said innocently. "What'd I say? What the hell? Did he want to march across the dance floor with his love coming down? Just tried to do him a favor is all. How'd a sharp chick like you get tied up with such a big, salty, square mick?"

"He's not Irish, Bobby, and you might stop teasing him. He doesn't understand half of what you say."

"Well, I don't care what he is if he wouldn't pull such a long face all the time when any other cat gets near you. What's he want to do? Put you in his pocket?"

The Jazzbo and a new foamrubber wife who was wearing an unbelievable array of costume jewelry with her simple summer cotton, came over to enthuse and Bobby slipped off somewhere so that when Saul returned, things were reasonably pleasant, although he was obviously suspicious of the Jazzbo's thick, secondhand Harvard mannerisms but at least he managed a semblance of good fellowship and bought drinks all round.

Two days later Bobby came to morning rehearsal with a copy of the Boston paper folded back to the entertainment section and Jazzbo's story.

"Now is the summer or more accurately the era of our discontent. For we, the true aficionados of that happy, creative musical expression known as jazz, have had to sit huddled with our old records underground in little rooms, while above us, is that barren, sterile, wasteland inhabited by the faux-monnayeurs of American music.

"All this is by way of suggesting that if you are tired of listening to old records and want to hear a good, jazz singer and some excellent, instrumental work, you take a run up to the Sandbox outside Rockport where Vance Paley's dance band disports itself. If you can close your ears to the tired old thumpthump dance music and be patient you will be rewarded by the trio and the sensitively authentic and sorrowfully blue voice of the stunning Sally Brimmer who has been too long gone from these parts and whose singing, even of pop tunes, shines out from the rest of it all, like a good deed in a very naughty world."

Her uncle rose like a hungry fish to this laudatory publicity and sent one of his tediously predictable notes from Bar Harbor wanting to know why she persisted in trading in on her family name when making a public show of herself. What was the old rockbound Mayhew good for?

Jazzbo's piece also increased the attendance enough for an extra performance on Sunday afternoons which caused Saul to sulk about lost time but made one feel quite wonderfully successful. Vance offered her a job singing in the fall at his usual stands but after some thought she turned it down. It wouldn't be any fun singing in Boston hotels now that she was a superannuated postdeb gone wrong, and would cause no end of family dither. If the band were going on tour, it might be different. Still, it made one feel good and rather worthy.

Jazzbo's eclectic style evoked some caustic comment from Dudley who called and said he would make it his business to come and see her being a good deed and that he'd bring Deborah who was, in his own weird, whimsy words, a charming elfchild, quite a breath of fresh air etcetera, etcetera, and he was eternally grateful, yammer, stammer and drag.

Feeling very setup that halcyon peach of a July then, what with grateful brothers, impressed audiences, publicity in Boston papers and her own trio of dedicated musicians. The only shadow being the daytime moroseness of Saul who couldn't seem to get with it.

Summer then, the unleashed, softly padding king of beasts, the madness in the zodiac, the fire, temper, and fury of perpetually aroused lust, the cracks of thunder, crazy, quicksilver flashes of heat lightning, the lowering deepgreen gloom pressing in the windows just before, the white sand and marsh grass swept by winds, the gay umbrellas, striped beach towels, pails and shovels all gathered in clumsy heaps and the figures running for shelter and then the sluices open, the wet, wet sheets of downpouring rain, so soon over, so quickly done, the freshened sun smiling now and a little bounty of rainbow drops of water carelessly scattered everywhere.

And the hot sun on the warm sand, in the peaceful days, half asleep, sun, gold moidores on closed eyelids, hearing small cries of children playing at the edge of the water, gulls greedy shrieks, knowing that the eyes would open on sand, rocks, little white houses, candystripes of umbrellas, naked brown sturdy tops of children with red and blue bottoms and sneakers to match, the sweet blue of the sky, coarse feverish green saltgrass, motif no. 1, fishing nets, rocks of breakwater, how picturesque in the distance the wharves and fishing boats and if there was a surf, the purest white, crashing on the shore from out the greenblue sea.

Improbable summer when more people go crazy and fall in love and the salt life fluid, the source and the beginnings surrounds and permeates, breathing the whiff of salt, nostalgic and unbelievably perfumed, better than anything in bottles, more stirring to the senses, the taste of dried salt on the sweetfleshed brown skin and the heat and the clothes just dropped anywhere and the loveliness, and, in the middle of the night, the east wind coming to stir the lovers in their sleep, bringing them close again, under the suddenly pulled up sheet.

And what are the fixed round of stars in their courses and what the scientific inquiries of generations and all the dry statistical tables unctuously incised on sheets of tin pomposity by sociologists and all their sawdust ilk. All poohbah and nonsense and pay no mind to the fable of grasshopper and ant and oil and water can too mix because this is summer and in that time one knows that the truths of signs and portents, miracles, gipsy palm readers, horoscopes, transmigration of souls, nay, even witchcraft, certainly white magic, are infinite. The lovers at night have not only known each other all their lives, but in many other lives, back to the beginning of time, cave days or whatever, the beautiful, lost, paradise garden perhaps.

Yes, so what did it matter if he was silly about wanting to stow her away in his heart in the daytime and let no one else see her, because the nights more than made up for it and they were not long enough and the memory of them filled her days with a prodigality of zest and euphoria. When he left in August it was singing the emptybed blues and taking pills to sleep and the first weekend he was due to come up, he arrived early and found her taking a late afternoon swim. Wading ashore and suddenly seeing him there standing on the beach and an unexpected, a ridiculous fit of trembles in her wet bathing suit at the sight of him.

"Honey, Sally, I've missed you so."

"Oh so have I. So have I."

"Don't ever leave me baby. Just a week away from you, almost drove me nuts."

No, no, never, what did words mean when all the colors of the day were melting and running like bad dye, everything dim and faded only he standing out clear and strong and vivid.

"Marry me, Sally, say you will, now, now, so we'll always be together."

Say anything, what difference did talk make, yes, perhaps, we'll see, later, later, darling, only hurry, hurry, let's go, let's not waste any more time, magnificent, lustful, standup, all ready, all ready for me.

Three

Deborah

Because she didn't know anything. Well, there were men who loved men, and women each other, and there was the right way, men and women, so that there'd be babies because the same sex couldn't and it sounded pretty creepy anyway.

So then there'd been Biology and she'd sat next to Gordie and they'd learned all about how the egg is fertilized by the sperm and how the embryo grows and goes through all these stages like salamander and pig and frog types. It was very interesting. She was glad to know about it but afterwards when they were sitting around in the Rec Hall, it was puzzling. Gordie wanted to know what she was frowning about.

"Well,"—it sounded funny but she hated gaps in her knowledge—"I know what happens after the sperm gets inside the woman but what I don't know is how it gets there. He didn't tell us that."

Gordie went off into what sounded like an asthmatic fit but finally pulled himself together.

"You really don't know?"

She really didn't so he asked her if she knew what a naked man looked like.

But she didn't, thinking as hard as she could, no. He was scratching his head and half-laughing and half mock groans. Then, finally,

"You've seen naked baby boys, at least?"

"No. Oh wait, yes," she said, happy to have remembered. "But it was only a picture. A photograph of a painting by one of those German expressionists. Of a fat, little, naked boy." Remembering the convoluted folds of the little, twisted squirl between the baby's legs.

"Oh God," Gordie said seriously, "you really knock me out sometimes, Deborah, you know that. I mean, all this German expressionist jive and not even knowing what you're looking at."

"I only asked. You don't have to be so superior."

"Well anyway, it's a small penis and only a photograph at that, of a painting, ye gods, how secondhand can you get—"

Penis. Well there was nothing new about that. The chart in the biology text. All drawn and labeled.

"I know about that," she said loftily. "Of course. That's what men use to . . ."

"It's used for both," Gordie said calmly.

"But that's impossible. How could it?"

"Waddya mean it's impossible. If you aren't a killer of a chick. It's not only possible, it is."

"But it's just a little limp . . . I mean . . . how could it . . ."

He began to laugh again bending over his folded arms and almost choking with his shoulders shaking and she was very offended and almost got up and walked away but he pulled her back in her chair.

"It doesn't stay limp, baby, see, it gets all stiffened up by passion."

"Oh, I see. Sort of a bridge. But it's so small, I don't understand . . ."

"Stop thinking about that baby in the picture," he shouted and she was very embarrassed because some of the other students, upperclassmen too, had stopped playing Ping-pong and turned around to look. "When a boy grows up it grows too. And it's expandable. It's a wonderful invention. Stop staring at me like that. Oh my God, classroom instruction is lost on you. What you need are some field trips."

So then he'd gone on and told her more, very carefully explaining, and it sounded awful and just terribly personal and for several days after that she kept trying not to think that that's what her parents must have done and it seemed highly unlikely and not their style at all. But after about a week she decided that it probably was true and the only thing was not to think about your parents in relation to this.

After awhile, when she'd gone around a lot with Gordie she began to understand more fully how it could come about but not actually in detail and Gordie could not seem to understand ever, why, although she liked to kiss him and have him touch her and why, although she sometimes got a strange, weak feeling when he did those things, she never wanted any more to happen. He'd shake his head and say, "You're just not human baby." But that was in the beginning when he thought she'd get human in time.

But now it was summer and waking up at five-thirty the menacing Poe-like whine of a mosquito magnified to a siren sound of horror there in the early quiet half-dark and Gordie had gone away and before he'd left she'd allowed herself to become humanized, just once, and now she knew. She lay, unable to fall back to sleep, remembering her stupid promise, her curiosity, listening to the screech of a gull who'd strayed inland in his predawn hunger, the sleepy, cross squabbling of a family of bluejays in the tree of the next door yard, her father's choking snores floating spasmodically through the closed door. Yes, she could tell them all, now, in her knowledge, that her parents did not merely lie in the big, double bed next to each other, as a brother and sister, as relatives, as she'd thought when she was younger, not knowing that strangers married each other, always thinking there had to be some closer bond, you couldn't simply creep into bed with a stranger, they didn't just lie in bed and talk to each other or quarrel or read newspapers or, as her father did, snore or be sick in the bed, with a handkerchief around his head, or smoke cigars when he was feeling better. And the bed wasn't just for sleeping.

It had happened two days before Gordie went to Maine. He'd taken her to his house because his mother and sister were away and there in his mother's bed in the hot afternoon, with the yellow downdrawn blinds only increasing the thick, sun-baked heat, on top of the white chenille bedspread it had happened, her curiosity thus forever appeased.

Had it happened because she'd promised, because she was sorry he was going away, or because, in truth, she'd been so rootstricken by what Mike Wainscott had told her; that this sex between male and female was the fundamental axis upon which humanity revolved? And to be ignorant, shut out, unable to understand the secret language every other grownup spoke would have been unthinkable.

Gordie was very careful and told her she shouldn't worry. First it was brown and then it was white and she didn't understand that and closed her eyes and that's to prevent us making little babies, with a laugh. But it hurt and hurt and wasn't even pleasant and no matter what he said she was still afraid of getting pregnant. And there wasn't a thing good about it. It was just savage and animal-like and Gordie looked different and sounded strange. He perspired and his eyes didn't even seem to see her and he was red-faced and his hair was all damp with sweat and plastered to his head. He didn't even look handsome any more and before, no matter how mean he was, he always had. And afterwards he just fell asleep without saying a word. He'd even bitten her tongue which hurt too.

She lay beside him while he slept, smoking a cigarette and not looking at him and wondering if perhaps his mother might come back unexpectedly and ought she to get up and dress. And feeling just like somebody's dirty underwear that had been thrown in a corner. Glad he was going away and hoped she'd never see him again. And the silly little hope that maybe if you did it, this thing he talked about incessantly and obsessively desired, he'd care deeply about you and be thoughtful and generous and kind and pleasant, was just as she'd suspected all along, a mistake. So even in the midst of her regret she was triumphant that she'd never done it before. She wasn't quite a fool after all. Because a girl might as well be a chamberpot for all he and his kind cared. So it was hatefully true, all the little banal Victorian mottos your mother mouthed about a girl being a lily and how there was only one thing a man wanted of a girl.

Now she knew and would never go to bed with anyone again unless she was married or definitely going to be married. If he, whoever he would be, thought enough of her to marry her, only then would she think enough of him to go through that again. And, she put out her cigarette and got up to dress and wake up Gordie and tell him coldly that she was leaving. He grumbled but moved by some obscure notions of gentlemanliness left over from his St. Paul's days he threw some clothes on and took her to the subway. And said goodbye. And that, she told herself on the way home, is what everyone talks about and makes fools of themselves for and gets into all sorts of trouble and misery for. What a fraud! And Mike Wainscott with his big, literary talk about the deep running tide of its elemental importance was another one and she was glad when he didn't call her. Then she'd waited anxiously to see if perhaps she'd get pregnant but four days later she was all right and could finish with the whole disgusting memory. Only now it was true, she was initiated, and when she read passages in books that had heretofore been slightly obscure, she could understand what they meant, and now she puzzled as to why they went on about this empty hollow nothing, pouring all sorts of fine words over it to disguise its essential nonsense until she noticed that the books were all written by men. Of course! Because it was obviously a man's sport, pleasure and game.

And they could have it too, she thought, this summer dawn, seeing under the green window blind's edge, streaks of pink tinging the gray sky and, cornering the mosquito on the wall above her head where it was whirring away, about to take off on a dive and draw blood from her face, she thwacked it murderously with a rolled-up

New Yorker and watched, satisfied as it fell dead to the floor. Probably a male mosquito and went to sleep.

Waking up again, this time to sunlight and noises of her father and mother in the kitchen and looking around her room. There was linoleum on the floor which Ella Baring would think horrible but otherwise it was a pretty good room, in the summer, anyway. There were the few books she owned in the bookcase she'd made herself from two orange crates nailed together and painted red, rough and splintery but it was good enough, and, on the pale gray walls, her pictures, ripped, with many qualms from the book she'd bought on sale for thirty-nine cents, Significant Moderns. Significant enough, in respect to her sex education as well as art appreciation, since it was in this book that she'd seen the picture of the baby boy. Hateful to rip pictures from a book but how else would she have them? Color reproduction from the cover of the lovely, round, Renoir bathing girl. Nice Picasso family, father in his clown's suit, child on his shoulders, quite naked mother, sweet, classic face, piling her hair up on her head. Matisse head, gaunt, haggard-faced woman, burnt-eyed, frazzly Marie Laurencin girl, Utrillo, "Cafe Lapin-Agile," what made French buildings so much more beautiful than American ones, too bad they were only black and white. Funny scribbled Klee, "Little Fool in a Trance," which she loved and could not explain why except that it made her happy although not much to it as her mother said. An eternal conflict with her mother about the Renoir and Picasso nude ladies. To her, free untrammeled soul that she was, they were Art but to her mother they were indecent. Every now and then for the sake of peace she'd take them down and put up something else, Art but not nude and time would pass and she'd sneak them back up again. It was her room after all.

Above the bookcase, appropriately, the writers' gallery. Pencil sketch of Ernest Hemingway, magazine cover, newspaper photograph of Thomas Wolfe tall and huge, standing by one of his favorite trains, another one of Jack London, hair windswept and blowing in his eyes, she didn't like his books but such an exciting life and so terribly handsome, picture of Robert Graves from some book review magazine, rugged honest sculptured face, mane of shaggy hair, looked as if he paid no mind to it, contrast to Hemingway who looked slick and sleek. Graves lived in a village in Majorca. Someday she would go there and perhaps meet him. How do you do, I've admired your work for years. What nonsensical gaucherie. What did you say in such a situation? You didn't. Busy writers had no time to be bothered by callow, worshipful, tonguetied schoolgirls.

Well, I liked the autobiography and Claudius of course and Belisarius, especially, and the "Antigua Stamp" which was very hard to get in the library and all the poetry. "The Climate of Thought" is one of my favorite poems. I know it by heart. Well, well, fancy that, and who are you? Still, he sounded like the sort of person one might meet quite casually in the village street or in a local café, wearing a beret, rope-soled sandals and carrying a market basket on his arm and have almost any kind of interesting friendly conversation. That part in his autobiography where they were living in the cottage at Oxford and he was trying to write and take care of children at the same time, with baby diapers all over the place. Great contrast to Hemingway whom one could never conceive of meeting anyplace except in the most exalted expensive circles or in some unlikely spot chasing lions or bulls, pastimes both unsuitable and uninteresting in her view.

Across the room, above an old chest of drawers, the advertisement of a map company, featuring a particolored map of one of the Midwestern states with a train streaking across it and Benét's poem, "I Have Fallen in Love with American Names" and next to it, a Van Gogh reproduction, mounted on cardboard, "Stem of an Almond Tree Flowery," which she'd bought in a dingy West End store in some rare moment of extravagance and enthusiasm about Van Gogh after she'd read Lust for Life. Nothing else in the room but the folding cot she slept on and a small brown painted table with claw feet on which she did her homework.

Sitting up in bed and pulling the window shade halfway up so the sun shone full on her face, she peered around the white net curtain, a concession to her mother's constricted notions that windows should be as covered up as the human body. The sun dazzled away on the gnarled old peach tree beside the house, planted by her grandfather many years ago (he simply threw a peach pit did he, well anyway, however it'd begun nothing much had been done to it in the intervening years and the peaches were small, wormy and unfit to eat) on the neat, green awnings of the white house across the street, on the pink and white striped petunias and heavenly blue morning glories nodding in a small morning breeze in its accompanying neat garden and in the spaces between the houses, she saw stretches of the field where the boys played baseball and then there was a little creek and you crossed it on a wooden plank and went over the old narrow gauge railway tracks, over which no train had run in years, and up a little rise to where the bay would be waiting, dusky blue water, flashing back the sun.

It was nice waking up in this sunny room on summer mornings but it never made up for the winter when, because it was a beach cottage and had no cellar or heat, you woke up all bundled up in blankets but still freezing uncomfortable cold, all curled up and stiff in the cold sheets, with your nose like a wedge of ice and had to gather all your will to hurl yourself into the kitchen to stand by the oilstove and dress. There was one tap in the kitchen sink which ran only cold water and every scrap of water for washing had to be heated on the oilstove. Sometimes in the winter the pipes would freeze and then there would be no water to wash with but snow gathered in a pail by her furious father and melted down on the stove. There was a little toilet off the kitchen which was so icy cold to sit on in the winter mornings that it was almost worth while waiting till you got someplace else, if you could, but no bathtub and for two years she'd had to take baths, standing before the stove with a pan of water and washing herself piece by piece. It was the shame of her life and she never felt really clean.

Her parents minded it all very much but to them it was not really very unusual. Her mother remembered living in a big house as a girl when there was no heat except that of the big woodstove in the kitchen and how all the children rolled out of icy beds way up on the third floor on winter mornings and tore all the way down to the kitchen to dress. And in the cold northern Baltic country where her father had spent his childhood everyone seemed to spend the entire winter on top of one of those tile stoves drinking hot glasses of tea to warm their hands.

Yes, but to live this way now was an unthinkable indignity and yet they did and had done so for two years since her father had suffered his first heart attack and they'd not been able to keep up the mortgage payments on a house they owned and so had come here just to spend the summer, they'd said then, till they got straightened out. It was a family cottage, owned by her grandfather, the land bought many years ago and the little cottage built so that his wife and children could leave the hot city, the West End, where the drunks rolled out of the saloon across the street and spend healthy summers swimming and fishing. Even later when they were older and had moved to big houses farther out in suburbs where there were yards and trees, they still came every summer, and to hear her mother talk it must've been one jolly party all summer long. And then they grew up and married and they and their children took turns using the cottage until they made more money and took to going other places because the beach wasn't as good as other beaches and the place was changing for the worse, and all their children's friends were going here and there.

But she and her father and mother always came. It was rent free for two weeks or a month and she had lovely memories of coming here as a child. Eating a Hershey bar with almonds which seemed to last forever and melt messily all over her small hand, standing with her mother on the ferry that ran from that enchanted name Rowe's Wharf across to East Boston, peering through the railing at the water swirling white against greenslimed pilings as the ferry edged into the dock. The little, never-failingly exciting, hints of summer to come Narrow gauge railway with the straw seats and a little whistle that went toot toot at each magic station and which they never could ride all the way to her sorrow. In the summer sun, with the blue saltflash of water waiting at journey's end, white fine sand and the green marsh grass, with the gulls calling and rocks. The field they walked across to get to the beach, crushing little hardheaded yellow weeds under foot which gave out a spicy noplaceelsebutthere smell. The pungent smell of privet hedge outside the cottage in the rain. Playing pirate on rainy days with her cousins in the beaverboard partitioned attic which smelled of years of damp sandy sneakers and bathing suits and sun baked into the roof. Her grandfather going swimming even on the coldest grayest days, bobbing solemnly up and down in his striped, old-fashioned bathing suit, his bald head wet. One of her younger uncles cutting up for a family photograph on the beach with a pail on his head. Her grandfather telling her how it used to be really country when they first came out there and no other beach cottages around and then people started to build year round houses next to them because it was such a choice spot and he'd had a chance to sell his land many times but he hadn't because never again would he be able to buy a vacation for himself and his children and grandchildren at that price and that was why theirs was the only beach cottage on a street full of houses and it was important to keep it looking good even though it was just a cottage because although the neighborhood around it had run down, that part of the street was still as good as it had ever been and he remembered how beautiful it'd looked years ago when he was young and he hoped it would always stay that way and the cottage stay in the family.

And she had thought how it must have been then, helping herself reconstruct from pictures in her mother's photograph album, when it had been pristine with patches of woods and farms with cows and all the ladies and gentlemen coming out from Boston on their highwheeled cycles, the men in straw boaters and the ladies with huge plumed hats and shirtwaists and long skirts and her grandfather with a huge walrus moustache and his hair parted in the middle and her uncles in sailor suits and the little ones in long white dresses and her mother and aunt with big ribbon bows in their hair and dresses with sailor collars and copper-toed high boots with tassels. And how covered up they were in their bathing suits with the long stockings.

But when they'd lost their boring yellow brick house in the monotonous suburb and summer lengthened into cold, sparkling October days and dismal November ones and they couldn't go swimming any more and the water of the bay was steely and sullen, it was hard to remember all the beautiful summers stretching back not only to her childhood but to her mother's and the gaslight youth of her grandparents. Nevertheless they lived on through two winters in that cottage which was permeated with the smell of bygone summers exuded through the furniture which had been there with the bureau drawers sticking since her mother was a young girl.

There was a great deal of carrying on by her father as to how they'd gotten into this shabby pickle and it all had to do originally with the simultaneous impact of the depression and the hard heart and ignorant head of her grandfather but Deborah, by this time, had ceased trying to sort out the reasons for the steady progression of disasters which had befallen her father. She just did not want to hear about any of it, nor did she want to hear about other people's daughters who worked in offices and contributed to the family income. Her father's daughter, instead, had to put on the airs of a college girl which not only demanded whatever wages she could make but also caused her to deliberately flout her religion by going to school on Friday nights and working on Saturdays.

"There are plenty of real brains who go to Harvard," he would shout at her, "and yet they keep their religion."

The real brains, she would think, smarting with anger, had fathers who paid their tuition and could afford to get an education and observe the Sabbath too. Her mother who, right now, was the only breadwinner, had perforce to work a half day on Saturday although she noticed that her father had very rarely done so even when they were in the severest pinch. Religion, she'd concluded, was for the rich.

She ought to have a job and help out and yet, what in the world could she do? In high school, her mother, forewarned of imminent economic and physical collapse had made her switch from the college preparatory course involving useless Latin and algebra to a business course replete with shorthand, typing, and bookkeeping. Deborah had immediately flunked all three hateful subjects the first semester and changed right back again, even though she knew it was futile because in Massachusetts, home of the endowed Ivy League colleges, the poor native student like the proverbial shoemakers' children, went barefoot. In the Greater Boston area to which Deborah was limited by having to live at home the accredited schools were either too expensive or too crowded with returning veterans. Scholarships were impossible unless you were a foreigner or an A average student from kindergarten on. If you had to work fulltime days and go to school at night which was Deborah's only hope you had three choices; one cost too much, one was oriented mainly toward engineering and one was this eccentric place on the Hill that no one ever seemed to take seriously.

Pure chance had brought her to Marplot the day before they gave their yearly scholarship exam and she'd never been sure whether the full year's tuition she'd been awarded came as a result of how well she'd performed in the exam or simply by default. Other people who'd taken the exam, undoubtedly much cleverer and more proficient in math and science than she was, had perhaps not wanted to go to an unaccredited college. Nevertheless, the summer day she'd been notified of her scholarship was still ensconced in her memory as one of the happiest, most triumphant days of her life. And Gordie's sneers, the implausibility of the school, the penury at home, her father's rages, the real struggle to keep working constantly in order to make living expenses and after the first year, tuition, the fact that she knew guiltily that whatever small sum her mother squeezed out to help her was dearly needed elsewhere, none of these things mattered, because Marplot which had continued to be good to her by giving her a job in the library, had started her on the road. She was never going to look back. She would go on and get that unaccredited B.A. and then an M.A. from a better school. She would be useless working in an office job or anywhere else. She must have a degree; others might not mind being workers of the world, sloppy waitresses, frustrated bookkeepers, marginal factory workers all their lives. Not me, she prayed, not me.

So now, on this summer morning when the sun told her it would be a beautiful day on the beach, she got out of bed because there was no time to waste. The job in Marplot's library was over for the year. She must go to the U. S. Employment and offer her wretched lack of skill, to get some sort of job, any kind at all. Preferably a permanent one, with evening hours so that she could take morning classes in September, but failing that, anything. It was essential to save money for next year's tuition and she simply had to have at least her own living expenses. In the past year her father had been feeling better and had begun to make occasional forays out to the mills and into the lofts and factories of Boston's garment district in search of the odd lots of textile remnants, which no one seemed to want except him. He always schemed up a useful purpose for this stuff and then induced some manufacturer to take a chance on both the material and the idea. This was his business, a sporadic one, which had provided him with a good income one month and nothing the next, but at least it was his own and someday he might make the big strike, and then one day he'd gotten sick and there he'd been with nothing. A hat with no office in it, a business which depended solely on his energy and resource. And now, he was trying to pick up the threads again. The doctor had told him it would be all right if he went about it very slowly but had cautioned him against living through another winter in an unheated flimsy summer cottage. Therefore, they had recently arranged with a local grocer, two streets away, to rent the two-room furnished apartment above his store from October to May, at a low rent. From June to September, when the summer people came and paid double rent they would return to the cottage. This dual-purpose cubbyhole had steam heat, hot water, and a bathtub, but all her mother's wages and whatever her father could scrape together, after paying off drugstore and doctor bills, must go for rent.

Deborah hated looking for jobs. It wasn't so bad at the employment office. The interviewers were kind and pleasant. But the employers were gruff and suspicious and she knew they thought she was unworthy and she was. Feeling small and insignificant, she would slink in, knowing she needed the work desperately and yet would probably do it badly, feeling too good for its dullness, stupidity, petty, grubby detail and overbearing supervisors who were far more stupid than she. Yes, and generally employers disliked college students. What was the point of wasting time and money training them when they'd never stay, and didn't pay attention to the work.

Ah, how complicated life was when you were poor, young, ambitious, frightened and a girl to boot, she thought hastily dressing and gulping down some breakfast, ignoring her father's complaints as he lay in bed reading a newspaper and telling her mother what a bad night he'd had and how he was sure he was going off any minute the way his heart fluttered. She rode into Boston with her mother and they parted at the Atlantic Avenue stop, her mother hurrying, very fresh and trim to her job. Wondering idly how her mother always managed to look so neat and pretty in spite of her hellish life.

The employment office sent her down to the Blood's Creamery Lunch on Summer Street for a job as a bus girl. The hours were terrible, 7 to 3:45, but it seemed to pay a little better than the few other choices she was limited to. It would do for the summer and in the fall, well, something better might come along. She was hired, shown a uniform and locker and told to report at seven the next morning.

"Bussing is the poorest paid job here," the woman who seemed sort of intelligent said cheerfully, "but nobody stays at it long. There's always openings at the counter or at the salad and sandwich table. You look like a smart girl and you'll probably get promoted soon."

The steppingstones to higher things at Blood's interested Deborah not at all but she smiled agreeably and wandered out along Summer Street to Filene's, happy because the day was hers. She prowled around in the Basement, having no money to spend, but there was always a chance that some of the merchandise she had eyes for would not be sold and thus, in Filene's wondrous plan, would be marked down lower and lower, until by the time her first wages at Blood's were paid, she would be able to buy at least a blouse or cotton skirt or a pair of originally ten dollar sandals.

It was noon in the cool, shadowed, twisted streets of Boston, where the sun had not quite found its afternoon way. She sauntered up Winter Street and loitered along Tremont amid the bustling lunch crowds, the noise of bells and whistles and the whir of pigeons' wings. She was to meet Dudley for lunch and although they were going to a Swedish place on Carver Street to eat, he'd asked her to wait for him in the Parker House lobby. She was early and went to the ladies' room to comb her hair and look over her best mauve cotton dress to see if it were still fresh and unwrinkled. Then she went out and sat in the lobby, counterfeiting poise by smoking a crumpled cigarette and placing her fresh white unworn cotton gloves carefully atop a little straw basket purse on the leather couch next to her.

The bus girl job'd probably be dreadful but it couldn't be as awful as some she'd had. Last fall, when she'd first met Gordie in one of her night classes before they'd both been fortunate enough to switch to day school, she'd had a job working for a dental laboratory. She did a little dusting around the office but her major function was to deliver neat little packages of dentures to dentists' offices all over the city. There was a great deal of trolley and subway riding and she usually maneuvered her trips so that she could have lunch with Gordie. Sitting on the grassy Common, they'd eaten sandwiches brought from home, and Gordie'd found her job irresistibly funny.

"Put that package behind you, will you, baby," he'd say, because usually someone's future chewing apparatus would be in her possession, waiting to be delivered after lunch. "It ruins my appetite to have those teeth grinning at me while I eat."

"Why, you can't even see them," she'd protested.

"My imagination's very strong though. You shouldn't take such menial jobs, baby. A girl of your intelligence ought to be able to do better than be an errand girl for a bunch of false teeth."

She'd been hurt but had tried not to show it and laughed with him. Somehow it seemed to be a reflection on her that her jobs were so ridiculous to him. Still, after all, he himself was only a copy boy and she'd not been able to resist saying stoutly:

"Gertrude Stein said once that no task was too menial for her, or something like that and if she could feel that way why should you or I be any different."

"Bully for Gertrude Stein," he'd said ironically. "She only had a private income of a damn sight more money than you or I will ever see, so it's easy enough for her to say, or was. Anyway I think she's a lousy writer."

The dentalplate job had lasted only a month which was too bad, in a way, because the work was easy and she studied a lot on the subways. But one day there was a Jewish holiday which she'd forgotten all about and her father had refused to let her go to work, and when she called up to explain, the boss'd been very annoyed, saying that she ought to have notified them beforehand. The next day, back at work, everyone was very sour toward her and her father said they were anti-Semites and she ought to quit which was all very well for him to say, but then came the wonderful opportunity of the job afternoons in the school library which paid less but allowed her to go to morning classes so she'd left the laboratory anyway.

It was twelve-twenty. Dudley was always punctual. Deborah looked anxiously toward the revolving door and smoothed down her skirt, wriggling a little in a nervousness she hated to acknowledge. She took the mirror from her small purse and examined this painful face of hers whose very bones reflected all her feelings and, knowing that she must look extraordinarily silly, nevertheless, was driven to attempt several facial arrangements which might pass for bland sophistication, custom, ease, and gracious delight. The kind of face she wanted was unattainable because it would reflect what was completely untrue; that she was the kind of person that rich, intellectual, older doctors always clamored to be seen with. She put the mirror away, twisted her ankles together and opened the book she'd carried from home. It was U.S.A. and she'd just started it this summer and found it terribly exciting and interesting but today the words made no sense at all. Still, it had stageprop value, at least, so she kept it open in her lap, feeling its trilogic heaviness, her eyes glued on the words of one of the earlier camera eyes, so that when Dudley came through the revolving door he would see her reading calmly, Bluestocking in the Parker House Lobby, or somesuch and she would not have to see him enter and perhaps catch the dread expression that one of these days would cross his face at the sight of her.

But, of course, it would never be like that. If it ever occurred to him, to the enigma that was Dr. John Dudley Brimmer, that he was unsuitably spending a good deal of time with an odd little nobody, he would certainly never show it. No, one day, very soon, undoubtedly, his grave, polite, and miraculous attentions would cease and she would never see him again, nor would she be surprised. That was the way of the world. The surprise, a never ending one, to her, was in the now.

She'd seen him once a week for a little over a month now, since the wholly amazing afternoon when his sister had brought him to the library. After Sally had left them that day and he'd taken her to the movie at the Exeter, she'd thought that her tongue would tie up in knots being left along with someone so really awfully dignified and equipped with such a beautifully superior sort of speech but somehow her delight at the wonderful lunch and the good movie had overflowed and she'd found herself enthusing over coffee. Too late, she'd realized in the midst of fumbling to say what she really thought of the film that she was using high school slang at great length to mouth almost exactly what he, in a few choice, Latinic words, had declared when they were coming out of the theatre. So she'd stopped, just like that, and they'd sat there in, to her, an uncomfortable silence, and she'd fastened her eyes on her coffee cup.

"Your impressions of the film are very interesting," he'd said finally. "Do go on."

Raising her eyes, hoping he wouldn't be looking at her, she'd been startled at the glance he bent on her. It'd lasted a mere second, but she'd almost felt that her misery was answered by his, that he was sure, but it was ridiculous, that she found *his* presence a dead weight, which must've been some trick of mind's projection and so unnerved her that she went off into a totally unnecessary incoherent tangent about her favorite movie, *Henry V*, and how she'd seen it four times.

Yes, he'd liked it too and then he'd talked a bit more about various other movies *he'd* seen, in a detached sort of way, as if he wasn't convinced of the importance of a word he was saying, and all the while he'd looked at her, studied her really with his cool, eyeglass-masked eyes, his face expressionless.

"You're a beautiful child," he'd said suddenly interrupting himself in mid-sentence. "Or do you mind my saying that? I feel quite venerable when I look at you."

Deborah hadn't known where to look, her confusion was so immense. He'd given no overt sign that he'd noticed her blush but she knew he had and that he'd ordered more coffee at that precise moment to give her time to recover. Because it wasn't what he'd said. It was simply that suddenly as he'd looked at her with his strange eyes, she'd felt exactly as if she were a little tiny child, and if, at that precise moment, he'd taken her hand and said Deborah I'm taking you with me only you musn't ask where, she would have gone with him willingly, unquestioningly, and in the same spirit, she'd have done almost anything he asked. Her heart had begun to beat very fast, and somewhere, way back, there stirred a little tiny flicker of fear. Then, the whole senseless nonsense had gone out of her head when she'd noticed the time and realized that her mother would wonder about her lateness.

She'd sipped slowly on the fresh cup of coffee and while he'd talked about music, she'd looked at him, a little bit, through her eyelashes. He was really dreadfully distinguished-looking, his hair cropped very close for the summer, his casually rumpled cord suit, the confident way he smoked a cigarette in a holder which Gordie would have deemed a silly affectation and on Gordie it would've looked silly. The funny thing was that his face, which she'd never seen before this afternoon, looked almost familiar, with its commanding nose, square jutting jaw and thin determined lips, rather like a personage in a history book, brought up to date with horn-rimmed spectacles. Oliver Cromwell? No, not Cromwell, his nose was pictured as bulbous and Dudley's was more like the Biblical, thy nose is a tower of Lebanon looking toward Damascus. But someone of that period, yes, he would've looked suitable in a round steel helmet at Marston Moor or under a high steeple crowned hat and large, stiff white collar, walking sedately to the church of a snowy Sunday morning, carrying his flintlock or pinning some hapless miscreant in the stocks on the Common, what an awful image . . . Why he's a Roundhead, she'd thought, almost breathlessly, of course, a descendant of Roundheads. Sitting across the table from American history. A small moment of defiance thinking that he too was sitting across the table from not only religious history but world history but that rebellion hadn't lasted long. She was an American, a member of a minority group, absorbed into the melting pot, born and brought up in a city where reminders of who'd founded the country were everywhere in sight, where April 19 was Patriot's Day, a holiday to sound again the alarm and celebrate the bravery of those who came to fight at the rude bridge of Concord. It was also the city which remembered as no other city could that the 17th of June was the day of a battle at Breed's Hill and on that day, in these times, the streets resounded again to the marching of soldiers, schoolboy soldiers from the various Boston high schools. And, to make it finally known whose city this really was, March 17 might simply be St. Patrick's Day in other places and perhaps too in the hearts of most latterday Bostonians, but for those who came first and for those who cared not a fig for Irish saints, March 17 was the day the British left Boston forever.

So then, Dudley had driven her home in a funny old tan business coupe and, without question, let her off at the corner, a block from her house. Consummate tact not to ask why she preferred it to being driven to the door. Only in the very last moment he'd leaned toward her and gently run his hand across her hair and again, that queer feeling, impossible to understand, because really he wasn't terribly attractive to her, not nearly as much as Gordie or even Mike, but if he'd wanted to kiss her, she'd have let him easily, and glad he hadn't attempted anything of the sort because what in the world would he have thought of her. He was not a boy but a man and a very important one at that and she'd wanted his good opinion and respect, for some obscure reason, more than anything. Then, he'd gotten out of the car, said goodnight, opened the door for her, they must do it again. But of course she'd never hear from him again because hadn't Mike said the same.

Four days later, he had called her at the library and taken her to dinner at the Union Oyster House, to an Esplanade concert and then there'd been the summer theatre evening at Marblehead and some more movies and one Sunday afternoon at the Gardner Museum and a Saturday afternoon sailing on the Charles. That afternoon she'd gone to his apartment for the first time. Although the day'd begun summery and fine an east wind had sprung up, the river'd grown choppy and gray and she, sitting up in the bow of the boat, had suddenly been soaked in a rush of water.

Dudley'd been all solicitude and although she'd protested, he'd insisted on going ashore at once and taking her up the Hill to his place to get dried off and warmed. Not the right thing, of course, going to his apartment, but beginning to shiver by then and the fool sun disappearing completely and the day in one of those sudden Boston whims growing quite chilly and, after all, it wasn't very sophisticated to be fearful of going home with a man, and ridiculous to suspect that after all these times together when he'd done nothing more than hold her hand well. . . .

He'd given her a pair of shorts and a jersey of Sally's to wear while her own clothes were drying and insisted she drink some Scotch and ginger ale and played some records, a rather nice bouncy Haydn symphony was all she remembered and every now and then he'd look her over and say things like how happy he was that the day had become so foul because she brightened up his living room amazingly. Funny about Dudley. He'd almost never asked her personal questions, just about her classes at school and what she was reading and her opinions of it. And they talked about music. He knew so much and explained things as the music went on, that day, in his raindarkened living room, with one lamp on. And she'd listened and desultorily read the backs of the albums. When they were together they never talked about themselves so she really knew very little about him, either. She'd liked it just that way. They were just Deborah and Dudley who were friends and had similar tastes and enjoyed each other's company. She could just forget about her father and no money and poor clothes. She was Deborah, that he seemed to like and took out to wonderful places that she could never have gone to ordinarily and he was never really dressed up himself.

But that afternoon, in his apartment, was different. Dudley drank more for one thing. He'd offered her a second Scotch, but she'd refused and after asking her if she minded, he'd gone on to another and then another and perhaps another, she'd lost track. Not that it mattered. Sophisticated people could drink and not get silly but one Scotch had put her in a dreamy, lassitudinous state. Anyway, suddenly he'd asked her if she had a boyfriend, though not in quite that crude a fashion. In fact, it'd taken her a little time to figure out what, exactly, he was asking her. Finally, stammering and blushing, she'd explained there'd been someone but he'd left town.

Wondering why he'd asked. Undoubtedly had other girls, more his own sort. Since she only saw him once a week it was very likely. And completely taken aback to find that incredibly he was kneeling beside her, had seized her hand and kissed it. She hadn't even yet gotten over the shock of that. So unlike him, so undignified. She hadn't known what to do. And he'd been talking, his head against her knees, murmuring.

"Dearest Deborah, please don't mind my asking you. You're so young and pretty and I was sure you had many beaus. It's none of my affair, I know, but I somehow hated to share you."

So embarrassing and unbelievably she'd been almost sickened but unable to move just letting her hand lie limp in his. Then, in a rush of words, seizing anything to say, knowing her hectic utterance to be of classic irrelevancy,

"I like your apartment, Dudley."

There'd been a moment's silence, outrageous in its implications and he'd sat still as a tombstone, his face hidden, then she'd heard sort of choking noise and he'd tilted his head back and he was laughing, shakily. He'd gotten up and pulling her to her feet, holding her at arm's length, the laughter gone, his face grave—"My sweet Deborah, I'm afraid I frightened you. Can you forgive me?"

"It was nothing Dudley, please, I . . ."

"Of course. You were startled. It's quite understandable." And, very gently, he'd stroked her cheeks, her chin, her throat. "So soft," he'd murmured, "so young and vulnerable. You must promise you'll come and see me often. And now, would you like to hear the Goldberg Variations? It's quite superb. Another drink?"

"No. I really must go."

"Nonsense. It's very wet out. I should feel quite guilty if you caught cold." He'd swept her firmly back into her chair, tucking a cushion in behind her back and lifting her feet gently onto a hassock.

"But I must go home, Dudley. My parents are expecting me."

"I'm sure they'd not like you to be running about in the rain." Glancing at his watch. "I hadn't realized the time. I've asked one of my colleagues here for a drink."

"Well, of course, then, I'll go."

"But I asked him here especially to meet you. You'll like him. He's a very good doctor and a good fellow all round. Interested in music too."

So she'd stayed and thought how kind and good Dudley was and cursed herself for being such an idiot. Just because a person was a doctor and very serious most of the time didn't mean he couldn't be human on occasion. Still, she'd been glad that someone else was coming. The dignified Dudley was preferable to the person out of an old-fashioned French novel. That Dudley had made her very uneasy. Perhaps because she was only used to brash boys like Gordie and couldn't understand the way mature people got romantic.

Dudley's colleague had turned out to be, of all people, the young Dr. Kildare she'd met at the gallery that afternoon, Matthew something, the one she'd disliked immediately because he'd ignored her. But up at Dudley's what a change in his manners.

"Why hello," he said when Dudley introduced them. And his eyes had taken her all in appraisingly, just as before in the gallery, only now, because she was Dudley's girl, there was none of that indifferent dismissal. Wouldn't you know a fresh wolf-type like that would say hello instead of howdeyou do.

"How do you do," she'd said primly, firm in righteousness, "I've met you before. But you don't remember."

He'd been looking around the living room rather uneasily as if in search of some unknown quantity which apparently, he'd found unsatisfactorily missing and Dudley on the far side of the room, mixing drinks, his back turned. Matthew Mumble's eyes had taken on a rather guilty look.

"I don't know how I could've been so forgetful," he'd said with that fake gallantry that she abhorred. "But I plead guilty. Where was it? At the Mardi Gras? Monte Carlo?"

It'd been baffling to contemplate how Dudley could possibly be friendly with a person who had such pretensions to inept wit and was so generally all around shifty and fake.

"At Dr. Asch's art gallery. But you were rather busy that afternoon." With a deliberate cutting edge to her voice, showing him that she knew he was a lecher and even implying, which was not nice, but he really wasn't nice himself, that she knew all about his disgraceful chase after Dud's sister. Which was probably why, when she came to think about it, he was a friend of Dud's at all. Dudley being so courteous and innocent would never know it.

Well, that'd put him in his place right then and there. He hadn't made any more indulgent masculine jokes for her benefit after that. Muttered something about how art galleries gave him the willies and Jenni made the darndest punch didn't she and after that Dudley'd come over with the drinks and the conversation'd gotten on to music and a bit of gossip about the hospital and some talk of medical State Boards. Every now and then she'd noticed him rather covertly studying her with a kind of surprised look on his face and, sort of sitting on the edge of his chair, casting glances at his watch and then down the dark hall, as if he had another date or something, but when Dud'd asked if he had plans for later, he said No. Which'd left one wondering about his carefully shined shoes, the knife-like creases in his trousers, the too-perfect knot in a vile, thick, green satin tie. He and Dud'd arranged to go somewhere for dinner after they'd driven her home. To all his other faults Deborah'd added the fact that he didn't know any better than to dress up like a department store dummy for a simple drink.

After that, unfortunately, she'd seen him several times and although it was a silly sort of triumph, how righteously satisfying to note the marked difference in attitude displayed by such a pretentious, conceited fellow as soon as he'd seen that Dudley liked her. Idiots like that Matthew, his last name was Berman, were only impressed by beautiful, well-dressed, socially secure women, but no one could fail to be impressed by Dudley and therefore his choice in women would have to be good.

The clock over the door of the Parker House lobby said quarter to one. Deborah sat up quickly and *U.S.A.* thudded to the floor. He'd never been late before. She stared hard at the door but no sign of him. If a man stood up a girl, well, what could that mean but the irrevocable way of telling her that he didn't want to see her again. Best way to do it really. You didn't have to face her and tell her but if you didn't appear, she'd know all right. It wasn't a nice thing to do, making a person wait and wait and then know slowly and sinkingly that the person awaited wasn't ever coming any more but at least you didn't have to see her doing it. But gentlemen never pulled cheap craven little tricks like that. No, Dudley'd write her a note or just not call any more but he'd never leave her waiting. Should she call or would that seem too anxious?

But there he was, pushing the revolving door before him and looking around for her. She waved and he came, walking fast, looking unusually pale.

"I was afraid you might've gone. I overslept you see. Woke up earlier, feeling hellish and then burrowed back you know."

"Oh, I'm sorry. I wish I'd known. We could have called off the lunch if I'd known you were sick." He certainly looked odd. He was sitting exhaustedly on the seat next to her and his hands shook as he tried to light a cigarette.

Finally, he inhaled deeply several times, squinting as if the smoke hurt his eyes. "Just one of those damnable sinus headaches. Nothing for you to concern yourself about. I'll be all right shortly. But I do need a drink unless you're too hungry."

He took her arm and piloted her up the steps to the Lounge Bar. "A drink!"

"People do drink before lunch," he assured her smiling rather grimly. "You look very lovely in that color. Very Persian, rather like a lilac, or the original lilac I presume since the American ones are quite prim."

She watched him sipping on a pale martini and said after awhile, "I thought I was fairly prim."

"My dear Deborah, what odd ideas you do have about yourself. Would you call a rosebud prim? Scarcely. And that's what you are. Warm and glowing but still untouched and v . . . But here I am and I haven't yet given you your present. It was your birthday last week, wasn't it? Well, Happy Birthday, lovely child." He kissed her cheek gently and handed her a beribboned, gift-wrapped package and a crimson rosebud on a long, green stem, nestling inside a fold of grassgreen oiled paper.

"But how did you know it was?" She gazed delightedly at the rose and the gift. "It's a lovely rose, a beautiful color." She lifted the half-open bud to her nose, sniffing rapturously. "Roses are marvelous, aren't they? Nothing in the world smells quite like them. I wonder why people prefer awful scents like gardenias."

"Because they're fools," he said. "I knew you were the sort of girl who liked roses better. The ass in the florist's shop tried to persuade me to buy an orchid. One seemingly is not allowed to purchase a single flower any more in these vulgar times. He wanted me to buy a whole bunch and when I grew impatient he began to push the value of a single orchid. You don't like them, do you?"

"Why I've never seen a real one," Deborah said, still gazing dreamily at her rose. She wasn't going to tell Dudley but no one had ever given her flowers before. She beamed at dearest, most thoughtful Dudley who'd suddenly conferred upon her the most delicate accolade and made her one with all the cherished women in the world whose men in gestures of extravagant luxury brought them flowers. "Do they smell as nice as roses?"

"They have no scent," he said gravely.

"Well why does anyone want them then?"

"Because they're expensive and showy and proclaim the giver's bad taste and large bankroll. Aren't you going to open your package?"

"Oh, I completely forgot about it. You shouldn't have, Dudley. The rose is so lovely it's quite enough." But she tore open the wrappings eagerly and took out a book. The Modern Library copy of *The Sun Also Rises*. The shiny jacket was bright yellow and blood red. A new book. She held it, smelling its ink.

"I knew you hadn't read it," he said forestalling her question, "because I asked you in the bookstore that day. That's when I bought it, hoping you wouldn't see me. Open it. There's something written in it."

"For Deborah," she read. Small neat handwriting. " '*On the first birthday. From Dudley.*' First? I don't understand. It's my twentieth."

"But the first with me. And I hope there will be many more."

"They're lovely gifts, Dudley. Thank you so much. How is your headache now?"

"Much better, thank you. For which I must thank not only pills or the drink but the sight of your happy face at these small gifts. You never have any difficulty expressing your feelings, do you?"

"Difficulty?" Deborah asked dubiously wondering if he was teasing her. "My trouble is concealing them. I've always wished I were more reserved and dignified. Like you."

"Like me?" he queried sharply.

"Why yes. Is that too personal a thing to say?"

"Personal . . . uh . . . oh no, of course not. I was hoping that with you, or to you, I didn't seem quite so . . . well . . . it's unimportant. Shall we go to lunch?"

He was silent as he steered her through the lobby and driving down to the restaurant. She must have hurt his feelings saying that about his dignity. But how else could he be? People wouldn't feel much confidence in a doctor who wasn't. She mentioned this to him as he was parking the car by the restaurant and suddenly he took her in his arms and gave her a hard rather brutal kiss on the mouth.

"Is that undignified enough?" he said rather angrily when he'd released her. "Why are you looking at me with those saucer eyes? Isn't that what other men do who aren't so damnably dignified?"

"I don't know," Deborah said shakily. "I haven't been kissed by that many men."

"Of course you haven't. I'm sorry. I'm afraid I'm rather a bad companion today. I shouldn't have come out but I did want to give you your present."

After that he sat through almost the entire lunch sunk in a gloomy silence, punctuated by a few deep sighs, and when she ventured to make some species of polite conversation, he seemed to come back from far away.

"Have you read the book, Dudley?"

"Uh, which book? I'm sorry, I'm afraid I was thinking of something else and didn't quite . . ."

"The one you gave me. *The Sun Also Rises*."

"Oh yes." With a twist of his lips, his eyes basilisklike behind the glasses. "Yes, yes, quite intensively. Rather my Bible at one point."

"I read somewhere that a whole generation of people were influenced by this book. They all cultivated despair and went to Paris and acted lost."

"Indeed. Well the more fools they. It's really a very trumped up tale but one should, I daresay, read it in one's youth in order to acquaint one with certain inescapable facts of life, fictionalized though they are."

"I'm looking forward to it," Deborah said carefully, wondering what could be wrong with him. He really looked quite bad. If he weren't Dudley he'd look almost seedy. He took off his glasses then and rubbed his eyes which she saw were bloodshot.

He looked at his watch and then waved for the check. "I'm sorry, Deborah, but I'm afraid I won't be able to spend the afternoon with you. If I take you to the subway will you be able to get home all right?"

At the subway entrance he said an abrupt goodbye and plunged into the crowd. For some reason, she paused before going down and saw him disappear into what surely was a garish hole-in-the-corner bar. Probably to make a telephone call, she thought. Surely Dudley would never drink in a place like that. But didn't illness make a man behave weirdly though. And that kiss. She wondered if he'd been feverish he'd been so wild about it. But how sweet of him to remember her birthday. She carried the rose carefully through the subway crowd all the way home and spent most of the ride wondering whether to start on the Hemingway or continue with *U.S.A.*, a dilemma which resulted, of course, in reading neither.

After her first day as bus girl at Blood's Creamery Lunch, Deborah, coming home exhausted and convinced that the sour smell of the cheesecloth rag she carried constantly from 7 A.M. to 3:45 P.M.

clung insidiously to her street clothes and had caused people in the subway to turn away from her, saw Dudley's rose in a glass jar on her bookcase. At least, there would be Dudley, or at most. Even seeing him only once a week would make the boring galley slave job bearable. The first week dragged its hours slowly, each day clanking its chains. It was only toward the end of the week when she hadn't heard from him, that realization flashed sharp and cold. There was no way he could call her. Her job at the library was over and there was no phone at home and they'd parted so abruptly last time that she'd forgotten to make some alternate arrangement. The library at Marplot was closed until the first of September while the librarian took her vacation.

So she called him, feeling embarrassed because girls shouldn't call men, it made them appear far too eager, but it was only logical after all since he didn't even know her home address. The first time she tried was a Sunday afternoon and the phone rang and rang countless times unanswered. She went through it again in the evening. No one there. Of course, he'd be at the hospital. On her lunch hour, the next day, in a great rush because she was allowed only forty-five minutes to eat and relax before the miserable grind began again, she renewed her attack on his telephone. This time, there was a continuous busy signal, but at least he was there. She tried again after work, every ten minutes for two hours, and was rewarded by the same busy signal. How could he talk so long?

And then abruptly she remembered their last meeting and his peculiar behavior. That was it, of course! He'd given her a gift as a farewell which also explained the kiss and the distant style over lunch. And then, to make it tactfully final, had simply taken the phone off the hook and left it that way. Very well, she thought proudly, the implications were understood. She'd expected it and here it was. But why, why? What had she done or said to cause him to drop her at just this time? He didn't want to see her any more, that was all. Anyway, what difference did it make? She didn't really love him. Just being a coldblooded little opportunist who simply wanted him around because he was a man who took her out and who would've made life at Blood's a little less hard to take. She thought wistfully of how he'd mentioned going up to Rockport one Sunday to see Sally. She'd been terribly excited the day Jazzbo's piece about Sally came out. In fact, she'd shown it to Dudley herself. He read only *The Christian Science Monitor* and the Sunday New York *Times*. Knowing someone who performed publicly and was written up in the papers made her feel almost on the threshold of glamour and fame. Well, glamour and fame be damned. They were not for her, only Blood's tables to be cleared and mopped, that was her portion. The month of August coiled in glaring, heat-stricken sweat around her and she came to work every day at seven or thereabouts o'clock in the morning, carrying *U.S.A.* with her for surcease on the long trip back and forth on trolley and subway and during her miserable lunch hour. She tried, one afternoon, in an access of despair, when leaving work, to call Dudley at the hospital and was told disapprovingly that Dr. Brimmer was away on vacation and they could not say for how long.

Only one thing now to look forward to, she thought, one morning coming hastily out of the subway at 7:15. The opening of school late in September. A whole month away.

The air was still damp this early in the morning and the sun not yet too hot. Boys in long white aprons were washing out doorways and swabbing down sidewalks. Dirty water flowed by her feet, muddying the cracks, rolling into the gutters. Blood's opened officially at seven to cater to the early-morning breakfast rush although its wheels were set in motion at 5 A.M. when Grischa, the caretaker, dishwasher, and man of all work came, turned keys, mopped floors, set up chairs, and chased stray rats. At 5:30, the cook, Hertha, came creaking and complaining every step of her descent to the kitchen. At six o'clock one of the counterboys appeared to make coffee and set up the counter, accompanied by his crony, the cook's helper. At seven, when the doors were opened for all who were hungry to come and batten on Blood's mouthwatering (so the posters pasted on the windows said) breakfasts, four counter girls, pert and whiteuniformed were behind the counter ready to sing out orders in bored voices to the two steam table girls.

"Wun dubble scrammeled! Sinngle bra-an! Coffee to go-OO!"

Deborah was the one bus girl on duty at seven but for the past two weeks she'd never gotten herself on the floor until twenty minutes past and this morning she'd be even later. In anticipation of the soulsearing day ahead of her she had clung to her peaceful bed a little too long. Maybe they'll fire me, she thought hopefully slipping in through Blood's back door. If fired, she could collect unemployment while hunting for another job. Even Blood's was preferable to job hunting and if she just quit with no unemployment compensation, in desperation she might end up taking something worse.

The hostess, Miss Masters, was fortunately sitting with her back to the door, writing out the day's menu. Spared for a few more minutes, Deborah hurried down the dark stairs to the locker room, pulling off her dress and sliding into the coffeestained uniform, white yesterday, fitted a net over her hair, pulled off street shoes and, unable to stand the sight of herself in the full-length mirror, hastily donned ripped stockings and dirty rundown saddle shoes. Now where was this vile rag, the badge of her profession, this thing, this rank cheesecloth? And why, why was she such a fool, since the job provided free lunches and breakfasts if you came early enough, not to get there by ten to seven and at least have coffee and Danish? Today, as usual, she'd go weak and hungry until the midmorning lull when one could snatch a minute and a donut behind the counter.

There was a knock on the door and a startled mouse ran across a pipe overhead and disappeared into a hole above the lockers.

Grischa was outside attired in long apron and equipped with mop, his small, putty-colored monkey face creased in a simple smile.

"How are you this morning, hah?" He didn't wait for her answer but began to gather lipsticksmeared Kleenex, old newspapers, and scraps of hairwads from the floor, muttering, "Yah, yah, the girls throw papers. Old Grischa's back they don't think of. Dirty girls. Pfoo!"

"Why don't you give us a clean roller towel?" Deborah said, incensed, since although the other girls were sloppy she never was. "That one's all filthy. And there's no toilet paper." It made her feel a little better to tell him off since he was practically the only one in the place lower in the social scale than the seven o'clock bus girl.

He mumbled something in Polish which was undoubtedly a curse and she slammed the door and pounded hastily upstairs. There were only four sleepy-eyed people sitting disconsolately scattered at the small wall tables spooning cereal into their foolish mouths, as she took a sticky plate and coffee cup from one of the tables in the back and walked down to the front dishstation. Three men were standing at the counter exchanging jovial imbecilities with the three girls getting their breakfasts. I bet they love their jobs, Deborah thought, eying her fellow workers with hostility. I bet they think it's swell working in a place where they can bandy smart chitchat with all these paunchy fools in leather goods.

The fourth counter girl was busy putting donuts, fruit muffins, bran muffins, date and nut bars and Danish pastry on plates, ready to slide them into the glass pastry cases along the counter. Blood's had its own bakery downstairs adjoining the kitchen where all the delectable brownies, brambles, hermits, fudgecakes, angelfood, and sundry other delights were made. Deborah looked hungrily at the array of morning muffins. It was very quiet and she might be able to . . . A hand fell on her shoulder. Miss Masters.

Deborah smiled falsely. "Good morning."

"Deborah!" A great business of ominous watch glancing and comparing notes with largefaced clock over the door. "Do you realize it is now seven-thirty and you've only been on the floor five minutes. If it happens again I'll have to let you go. I'm surprised at you, Deborah. You're a bright girl and you could do so much better here, if you'd only try."

"Well, I've been helping the cook," Deborah said defensively, feeling it essential to say at least one word or two to show that she didn't totally lack ambition.

Miss Masters smiled patronizingly, dismissing this feeble pretense with a wave of her long, well-manicured fingers.

"You know that's only because our second cook has been out sick. That's not getting you a raise in pay. Mr. Deacon spoke to me about trying you on the counter only the other day. I didn't tell him about your habitual lateness but I had to say I didn't think you were ready. Now you'd better get busy and put out the salt and pepper shakers." She nodded and marched away on her white nurse's shoes to the back of the store.

Two by two, every day, Deborah put out the salt and pepper shakers, two by two, walking in her meniality up and down, her mind elsewhere, every day, two by two. Today, for once, her mind stayed with Blood's Creamery Lunch. Perhaps Miss Masters didn't tell Mr. Deacon, the manager, about the girls who were late but he didn't tell *her* everything either. Because Deborah had been aware for a week now of Mr. Deacon's plans for her advancement. One day, when she was working down in the kitchen, he had come up behind her and said, as she was making meat patties:

"You'll have a lot of experience making mud pies after this now, won't you?"

The thing to do was laugh at this because both Hertha the cook and Chuck Lonigan her helper had thought it very witty. Deborah never had sense enough to laugh at the boss's jokes until it was too late but in this case Mr. Deacon hadn't seemed to mind but had engaged her in lowvoiced conversation about how he'd heard she was going to college in the fall and was she going at night or in the daytime?

"Well, I don't know," Deborah had said helplessly thinking about the new apartment her parents were getting and how she hadn't really any money to pay tuition. "I might have to take night classes the first semester anyhow."

"And work during the day?" Mr. Deacon had pressed eagerly, his fat, round, unctuous face beaming.

"I guess."

"Well now, let's make it just between us two but what I'm getting at, is, well, it isn't easy to get good hostesses and dietitians and so a college girl like you could work your way up here if you had more experience in all phases of the work and in no time at all you could probably qualify as a hostess here or in one of our other stores. Blood's is expanding all the time. You'd make good money too, after awhile, and you could go on with your schooling at night. That's what Miss Masters has been doing. Studying dietetics at BU at night. Bet you didn't know that, did you?"

Deborah had shaken her head numbly as he'd paused and smiled, delighted that he'd edified her.

"That's what education does for you. Gets you ahead and out of the dirty jobs. I've always wished I had one myself and I certainly give a lot of credit to people who're trying for one. So what do you say?"

"Well, I don't know . . ." The thought of spending years of her life in Blood's, no matter in what capacity was so appalling she couldn't face it, but of course it wouldn't do to say so to Mr. Deacon who thought of it as his lifework. Nor could she point out to this round, smiling man who apparently assumed he was offering her a choice plum that there was a vast difference between studying dietetics and becoming a literary scholar. A dietitian, she'd thought with suppressed scorn, he really thinks a dietitian is learned, poor man. "I don't understand what you want me to do," she'd said finally.

"Just think about it and when you get a few minutes try memorizing the prices for some of our items. You'd have to have more experience on counter for one thing and there, you have to know the prices just like that." He'd snapped his fingers. "That's the first step. After that, we'll talk some more about it. Okay?" And without waiting to hear her answer he'd taken off which was none too soon as Hertha had been casting baleful glances and muttering. Even the manager couldn't cross Hertha. A restaurant with a disturbed cook might as well close its doors.

Since that day whenever he caught sight of her he'd pad up behind her on his rubber-soled shoes and purr softly, "How much is a brownie?" or "What's the price of bacon, eggs, and toast?" or "How much would two date and nut bars, an apricot square, a bramble, and four containers of coffee to go be?" Of course she never knew the answers and at first, thinking he was joking, because surely no one could be expected to keep all that stuff in their head, she'd smile and say, "I'm afraid I don't know, Mr. Deacon."

After a few times he'd look very disappointed and question her about whether she'd been doing as he'd asked, so she'd tried to memorize some of the prices of the baked goods, particularly, since that's what he seemed hepped on, but the amount of a brownie or a bramble simply would not stick in her mind. So then she'd guess and he'd say "Wrong," rather sadly, tell her the correct price and shake his head as he went away. If only Miss Masters had told him she was an unreliable, unpunctual employee this badgering would cease, but no, they had to go play cat and mouse with each other.

Eight o'clock now and more people thronging up to the counter for their breakfasts. The eight o'clock bus girl now on the floor, pretty, redheaded girl with enviable starry blue eyes. They rushed around like vultures in their dirty Blood's uniforms clearing off the dishes and wiping the tables so that more hungry factory owners, bookkeepers, saleswomen, stenographers, typists, accountants, bank tellers, and lonely men in shirt sleeves could sit down, gulp their coffee and run out to begin the day.

By nine o'clock coffee was out at Blood's English houseparty breakfast, there were some vacant tables and Deborah breathed again. She paused by the front window which looked out on the street and, making an elaborate business of flicking crumbs off a table, stared outside. In ten minutes she would have to go cut pies and cakes, put them on plates and distribute them to the glass display cases. She longed instead to throw down her dirty rag and rush out into the street, to tear off her hairnet and let the wind blow her hair around, to feel the sun warming her arms, to wear new, clean clothes, to be free to come and go as she pleased. Now, some of the newspaper people were coming in and a few portly men who looked prosperous enough to be owners of wholesale and retail clothing and shoe businesses, smoking cigars and talking of unions and deals. She turned from the window as Miss Masters swooped down then on her.

"Deborah, you'll have to go downstairs to the kitchen and help Hertha, right away."

"Can't you send someone else, Miss Masters? When I get through I feel as if I've been in the oven all day myself."

Miss Masters laughed, because bully for her, she appreciated wit.

"I'm afraid not. Hertha wants you. My little one with the nose in the book, she calls you."

Deborah did not laugh and went on downstairs deciding bitterly that her uniform was so dirty now, it would be senseless to get an apron. She paused on the march to Golgotha and went into the ladies' room to wash her face and hands and take a few puffs on a cigarette. If I ever get out of here, she thought, throwing her half-smoked cigarette into the john, I never want to see another dish or coffee cup again, unless it's in a good restaurant where I'm being waited on. For I have known them all already, known them all, have known the evenings, mornings, afternoons, measured out my life with dirty coffee spoons. It didn't even help to be literary about it, because it only brought to mind how quiet, clean, and peaceful it must be to sit and write poetry about life instead of really sweating in the midst of the stinking grease.

Hertha, fatly monumental in a white uniform, wore gold-rimmed glasses and a white winding sheet on her head and moved ponderously through the hellfired heat of the kitchen like an Easter Island statue set into petulant motion.

Deborah took a deep breath of whatever air there was and said with pseudo-cheerfulness, "Good morning Hertha."

Hertha peered at her blindly through her steamed over glasses. "Goot morning, my darling." She mopped at sweat running down her face with a dishtowel. "Run to the bakeshop pet and get the brush to grease the pans and get two more pans. Here iss the scoop for the meat patties. Do them just like I showed you. No sloppiness. I hate sloppiness. Now moof as fastest as you can, pet. We got lots work to do. Chucky! Come here to taste my tomato sauce."

Chuck Lonigan, whom Deborah secretly thought was pretty good-looking, with a kind of Greek statue profile and short brown ringleted hair, was stripped to the waist, slicing meat on a machine. "Sure, Hertha, sure." He stopped the machine and, winking at Deborah, went over to taste the sauce. "Perfect, Hertha, the best."

The bakeshop was reasonably cool and Deborah ate a hermit and talked about the weather with the sirup boy before going back to the kitchen where now the electric fan had unreasonably stopped working and Hertha was in a fury. "Iss not bad enough," she raged, "that all night long I wass up with mine foot. Iss sore as hell and all night long I soak in water and salt. Unt now, busy day, four people's work to do, shoemakers I got for helpers, now iss kitchen smelting pot."

"Now, now, Hertha," Mr. Deacon said pussyfooting in, smiling cherubically, "I'll have it fixed right away." He beamed at Deborah and hissed sottovoce, "How much is fudge cake and ice cream now?"

Deborah knew that one because it was her favorite dessert.

"No, no," he said ruefully, "we raised the price three days ago. You've got to keep on your toes."

"Mr. Deacon," Hertha, majestic, with hands on her hips, "iss meat patties to be underdone for lunch?"

He snuck away and Deborah dragged out the jar of grease from under the work table, greased four pans, scooped hash out of the bowl, making interminable rows, flattened them with her hands, and slid the pans one after another into the oven. Sweat rolled down her face, made her eyes sting and trickled down her neck. Her uniform clung like another wet filthy skin to her body. She got out the carrots and potatoes, preparing to dice them when Hertha ordered her to the icebox for butter. Deborah looked around for Chuck who was nowhere in sight.

"Why don't you ask Chuck to get it? He's in there now."

"Ha ha, my little one. Chances I give you to go hold feet with Chucky and you don't want."

"Feet! Why would anyone hold feet?"

"Dice well the vegetables pet, like I show you. In Lithuania, holding feet iss love." And when Chuck, shivering and shirtless came out of the refrigerator carrying a bologna and a chicken, she shouted across to him, "I tell my little one to go get butter the more to hold feet with you and she says no."

"She don't know what she's missing, ha, Hertha?"

Kitchen romance, Deborah thought ironically, peeling potatoes and hoping Hertha, full of her obscure Lithuanian jokes wouldn't notice how thick the peels were, and in the kitchen, the proper place for love would naturally be the icebox, the only private cool retreat from the inferno. But, trying to join in, she said, "It's too cold in there for anything to happen, Hertha."

"Love make you warm," Hertha said and suddenly noticed the potato peelings on the work board. "Mind on love all the time," she shouted in one of her lightning mood changes, "nowadays all girls think of. I show you make potato peels nice, thin, now look. Waste, sloppiness. Go, get butter, go!"

Deborah stayed in the icebox room a few goose-pimpling seconds longer than actually necessary in order to cool off. She had just picked up the butter when the door slammed and there was Chuck Lonigan, smirking at her, his curly hair twisted by sweat, like a fiend's horns above his forehead.

410

"Hey!" He detained her swift rush past him with a hand on her arm. "Howsa about telling Hertha I let you hold my foot."

"Don't be silly."

"Come on," he said rubbing her arm. "You're a girl, aren't you? Whyn't you act like one?"

"I'm sure you have no trouble finding girls." She pulled her arm away angrily. "I'm freezing and I've got to get out of here."

"I bet you spend every night home reading books, kid, don't you? You know, you're not too bad. A guy wouldn't mind giving you a feel."

"He might not," Deborah said, shivering but trying to speak in tones of crushing dignity to conceal her revolting blush. Blushing in an icebox of all things! "But I would."

Outside in the heat of the kitchen Hertha stormed like a lion who hadn't been fed. "Shysters, politicians, shoemakers! Hot day, everybody ask for cantaloupe and not enough cantaloupe do they buy. Go for Mr. Deacon, Chucky. More cantaloupes!"

The scullions in the kitchen who started their day at dawn ate lunch earlier than the upstairs help but Deborah with her foot in both camps never knew whether she was going to have to stay in the kitchen during lunch or go back upstairs to bus dishes. As a result her lunch hours had become erratic and today at 11:30 here came Miss Masters scattering sunshine.

"You'll have to eat later today, Deborah. I hired a new girl yesterday and she can take your place upstairs. Hertha needs you here."

Suddenly Deborah realized that, in spite of the hermit, she was furiously hungry but it was too late to complain. Miss Masters had gone off and Hertha was shouting at her not to forget the meat patties in the oven.

The noise from the dishroom and slide increased. Hertha exhorted and issued contradictory orders in a steady stream. Chuck whistled and Hertha told him to shut up. She was building up to her usual lunch-hour explosion, raving as she stood, melting and monolithic, over the stove, stirring in huge pots, using her favorite epithets about everyone, the managers of Blood's, the owners, the people who didn't buy enough food, or too much, the customers who were all uniformly unworthy of her cooking and most of all her helpers who were so useless that all they could do well was get in her way.

Deborah, having burned her tongue tasting one of Hertha's culinary marvels, armed herself with potholders and pulled open the oven door to remove the meat patties. Three came out easily but while extracting the fourth she stumbled on the slippery brick floor and inadvertently pressed the almost molten side of the pan against her arm and, with a scream, dropped the pan on the floor. The meat patties fell and scattered on the wet, dirty floor, Hertha stepped on one and, as Deborah, in roaring pain, was picking them up, a barrage of Lithuanian and English billingsgate ricocheted about her ears.

A long ugly red burn covered a good half of the underside of Deborah's arm. "I burned my arm, dammit, Hertha," she said loudly interrupting the storm of abuse.

"You think I have not burned myself many times crybaby? Put on butter and go quickly to make up another pan of the meat patties or we run short."

"You're in luck, kid," Chuck Lonigan murmured in her ear. "I just finished making up another batch of hash. If there wasn't any more, boy, would you get it."

There was a lot Deborah could have said in self-defense such as that she was weak and hungry and it was long past her lunch hour and that the floor was slippery. But she said nothing. No one cared whether she'd burned her arm or not. Her head was spinning and she felt faint. Numbly she put the new pan of meat patties into Hertha's care and announced that she was going to lunch. Just to get out of there and do die somewhere.

"Ho, no," Hertha said menacingly. "Grischa has brought the cantaloupes. You will cut. Otherwise, I tell Mr. Deacon and you will go. You lose your job, you hear. Make trouble for Hertha, she makes for you but good."

Well, why not? Just turn around and walk out and then be fired. Mr. Deacon would have to do it. The cook must be pacified at all costs. Then she'd get unemployment. Why put through another afternoon here? Could sleep late tomorrow. And having worked it all out neatly, Deborah took a cantaloupe and poised the sharp knife over its approximate center. Because it was cowardly to run away from a job just because it was hard.

The cantaloupe was cut and for a wonder both sides came out exactly even. The buzzer rang and Chuck went to the slide.

"Hey, Hertha! They're screaming for cantaloupes."

"Tell fools to keep shirts on," Hertha yelled. "We haf soon. So hurry, pet. Cut quickly." She had recovered from her temper as Deborah had known she would but it was small comfort when you were the target of the insults, to know that Hertha got over her fits quickly.

"So what keeps you? Only two cantaloupes cut in all this time." Hastily, Deborah attacked another cantaloupe and this time, in her rush, she judged wrong. One side was small and puny, the other enormous.

"My Gott!" Hertha, screaming like an ambulance siren. She snatched the knife from Deborah and waved it around in the air. Deborah backed away from that slashing knife which was about two inches away from her head and Hertha gave her a giantess' shove. "Go from my sight, go! Never do I want you here again. One whole cantaloupe, murdered, useless. You are stupid fool, never let Hertha to lay eyes on you again."

Deborah fled from the kitchen, washed her face quickly in the ladies' room and, taking *U.S.A.* from her locker, pounded upstairs. She got some lunch and sat down at the help's table, in the back. It was the height of the rush hour and everyone else on the staff was working. She chewed on a tomato and lettuce sandwich steadily although it tasted like sawdust and kept staring at the print on the pages. All around her roared the clamor of the animals' feeding time at the zoo. Her ears remained deaf to it, she could not really taste, hear, or see. The pain in her burned arm was worse and she felt only a vast throb. The red streak was beginning to blister. She drank a chocolate milk shake. Its cold sweetness helped a little.

Quit now. Go on, stop being a worm and a slavey. No, I can't, said the other part of her, the person she despised, who always cautioned, don't listen to insults, don't give in to your pride, swallow your self-respect, because you need unemployment compensation, because you need whatever it is, you have to put up with it, your dignity trampled on by boors and swine because of your craven need.

People passed by her with laden trays, looking for a place to sit down in the crowded cafeteria, stared at her filthy uniform and edged away.

Chuck Lonigan came and sat down opposite her with a Coke. Deborah was aware of his presence but kept her eyes on the book.

"That Hertha's a riot when she gets mad. And, boy, the scared way *you* looked when she waved that knife at you, I almost split a gut trying not to laugh or she'd've gotten after *me*."

"You have a remarkable sense of humor." Deborah closed her book and stared at him bitterly. The pain in her burned arm was now so terrible she knew herself to be on the verge of tears.

"Don't take it so hard," he consoled. "She'll forget all about it by tomorrow. You know how she is."

"Well, I won't. No crazy old woman can threaten me with a knife."

He shrugged. "What're you gonna do about it? Cooks are worth plenty these days. And put the lousy book down. Say, kid, don't you know you make a fool of yourself and everybody laughs at you, sitting around on your lunch hour, reading a goddamn book, big as the Bible for crissakes. You know, nobody even knows your name here, except the boss. They just call you the girl who reads the big book. I mean we know you're a college kid and all that but if you take a job in a place like this, you don't have to go around acting like you think you're better than other people. See? And I'm only tellin'ya for your own good and because I think you're kinda cute from watchin'ya down in the kitchen."

Deborah was aghast. To think that all these types talked and laughed about her. Just because she read a book in her free time. She had read *U.S.A.* on the beach, on the trolley and subway, at home, whenever there was a free minute. Couldn't stop reading it. So tremendously exciting, all those technical innovations, new to her, which at first she hadn't understood and then after a while, rereading, finally grasping Dos Passos' intentions. The only pleasure, after all, she'd had since the Dudley fiasco.

"I don't think I'm better than anyone else," she protested, feeling betrayed and miserable because, all along, she'd thought she fitted in pretty well. Even managing to make small talk with the other girls when they were all washing up after lunch, even laughing at Hertha's jokes.

"Well, you sure act like it," he said, shrugging again. "Anyway, howsabout going out with me? Maybe tonight. I can borrow my brother's car. Go down Revere Beach, get some clams. You know, live it up. I'll show you a few things ain't in books." He winked at her.

Just this morning, Deborah mused, she'd thought this oafish chimpanzee was rather nice-looking.

"No, I'm afraid I can't."

He stiffened. "Yeah? Don't tell me you got a boyfriend?"

Deborah felt much better and began to eat her fudgecake and ice cream with relish. "That's exactly what I mean."

"Yeah," he repeated suspiciously, "one of those college jokers with glasses and big snow jobs. Hell, kid, they don't know nothin'. What you need to wake you up is a real man."

Deborah shook her head.

"Well, okay," he said. "Only I don't ask twice." He got up and swaggered away, waving carelessly at Miss Masters who was heading purposefully in the direction of Deborah's table.

"I've just been talking to Hertha, Deborah."

The fudgecake was impossibly sweet. Deborah pushed the plate away.

"Hertha's very upset," Miss Masters was saying, her eyes fastened on the wall above Deborah's head where a livid yellow poster advertised Blood's superscrumptious meat patties and tomato sauce. "She's threatening to quit if she doesn't get more capable assistance. And of course we can't lose her."

"I wasn't hired as a cook's helper," Deborah said.

"No, that's true, but to be frank with you, Deborah, you haven't worked out well at all here. Even the pastry you cut comes out awful. Uneven and ragged. And now, you've driven Hertha crazy, and slowed up lunch and—well—I'm afraid I have to let you go. I talked to Mr. Deacon and he was very disappointed because he'd hoped that a girl of your intelligence could really get on in the Blood system."

I'll bet he was, Deborah thought, I'll bet he was furious when it turned out that I didn't even care enough about his precious store and the tremendous opportunity for advancement in it, to come to work on time.

"So tomorrow," Miss Masters went on, "will be your last day. I'm sorry, Deborah, but it's for the best. I'm sure you'll be happier elsewhere."

All the fires lit for heretics and martyrs were licking with greedy savagery at Deborah's arm and her eyes burned and stung from the smoke and the flame. Her unemployment compensation turned to ashes.

"I'm not going to work till tomorrow," she said in a small voice. "In fact I'm not working any more today."

"Now Deborah," Miss Masters said severely, "we're not going to take that attitude, are we? You'll have to work out the week, otherwise I'll consider that you've quit and you won't be able to claim compensation. Besides you'll have to get your pay."

"You can send me my pay."

"Very well," Miss Masters said. "If you want to be a bad sport about it. Leave your locker key on my desk." She walked away.

It was two o'clock in the afternoon and Deborah walked free up Summer Street, her hair blown by a gentle warm wind, her hands and face clean, the sun hot on her shoulders. She crossed at Washington and strolled up Winter, looking in the shop windows. And, passing by Locke-Ober's, she suddenly thought of Dudley. Well, she'd humbled herself quite a bit for a month and a half and after today's terrors with Hertha, nothing seemed very important. If he was cool, or didn't answer, what did it matter? But if he was there and by some remote chance wanted to see her, she'd be glad. Just to talk to someone like him, after all those slobs, would be an exquisite relief.

He answered on the first ring, almost as if he'd been sitting by the phone waiting.

"This is Deborah," she said. From the Russian novel, the Insulted and the Injured.

There was a silence. "I hope you enjoyed your vacation," she went on politely.

"Deborah!" he said and it was balm, manna, sandalwood, and wine merely to hear his voice, the voice of educated intelligence, properly enunciated consonants and vowels, so modulated, so full of breeding and gentility and, let's face it, money. "I . . . don't know what to say except to apologize. I'm very glad . . . you called . . . I'd like to see you. But if you're angry I'll understand."

Deborah giggled. Angry! He'd obviously never seen anger in the raw, nor Hertha, ready to slice one's head off, à la cantaloupe, or he wouldn't prate of anger.

"You find my circumlocutions amusing, no doubt. Understandable, of course. I had hoped . . ." He trailed off into a deep sigh which unfortunately reminded her of the Mock Turtle, and sent her off into another outburst.

I must be getting hysterical, Deborah thought repressing herself sternly, delayed shock or something. "I'm not laughing at you, Dudley. I have a bad burn on my arm and . . ." How could one explain Blood's, to someone like Dudley. One might as well describe life on another planet. "I've had a bad day and I'm lightheaded I guess. Except I'm not angry with you at all."

"Burn?" he asked sharply. "Have you had a doctor look at it?"

"No, of course not. I only got it about two hours ago. It's nothing really."

"Stay where you are," he said shortly. "I'll come and get you. And where are you? . . . Liggett's drugstore on Tremont. Very well, I'll be there in a few minutes."

Back in his apartment, in the closed, hot, indoor afternoon with the sun slanting vengefully bright through dusty Venetian blinds onto the faded rug, he dressed the burn on her arm with a soothing, yellow ointment and after he'd bandaged it, sat her down in a chair

416

before an electric fan and gave her a cold drink, gin and tonic with a frosty lime slice floating in it. Then he knelt before her, took her shoes off and slid the hassock under her legs.

"My feet aren't very clean," she said leaning back. Now that the nagging pain in her arm had abated she felt limp and almost ready to cry from the sheer bliss of feeling better and having someone care about her.

"Your feet are beautiful," he said and he sat on the floor and massaged them gently.

"Oh, Dudley," she said and burst into tears at the gentle touch of his healing hands upon her. "Thank you. You've made me feel so much better. I'm sorry," she sniffled. "How silly of me. I'll be all right in a minute."

He gave her his handkerchief which smelled nicely of something minty and stared at her soberly while she dried her eyes and dabbed at her nose.

"Why didn't you get that burn looked at before?" he demanded. "The blisters had opened. You might have gotten a serious infection. Where did you get it?"

She told him about everything. It poured out in a rush. Before she could stop and realize how dreadful it would sound to him. Last month he'd simply considered her a college student. But a bus girl! It was like a bad movie. The Doctor and the Bus Girl. He probably saw patients like her in the outpatient clinic all the time.

Finally, when she'd finished, he said, "I don't want you to take a job like that again, Deborah, do you hear. That's no place for you."

"I have to earn money for school, Dudley. You wouldn't understand. Lots of people who have to work their way through school do restaurant jobs."

"Not that sort of job," he said wryly, twisting his mouth a little. "And don't patronize me, Deborah. Of course I understand that many college students work their way through school. At all the resorts up and down this coast there are whole crowds of college students working in restaurants, hotels, and inns every summer. But at least they're with people of their own sort. Don't you see, Deborah, how important your difference from the others in that place was? You probably didn't do the work well because of your nature, thank God, and your intelligence, but even if you did, you'd be watched more closely because you were different. Why do you want to humble yourself so?"

"I don't," she said, mustering a little more spirit than she was really capable of. "I just need money. I'm sorry I talked about it. Tell me what you did on your vacation."

He looked at her amazed as if he were seeing her for the first time. "My vacation. Yes. I think you'd better lie down. I'm going to give you something to calm you down."

She shook her head. "I'm all right, really."

"You're not. You're almost green under your tan. Now don't argue." He picked her up and she protested feebly, but oh, it did feel good because he truly cared about her. Someone did.

"You're so light," he said, "so little to have so many terrible things happen." He laid her down gently on his bed in the back room where she'd never been and brought her a glass of water and a green capsule to swallow. Then he sat beside the bed in a wicker armchair and held her hand. "This will put you to sleep for a few hours, which is what you need."

"I must go home," she protested. "I can't sleep."

"I'll see you get home in plenty of time." He lit two cigarettes and handed her one. Presently he said, "I ran away from you. Did you know that?"

"But why?" she asked feeling rather unreal. Nothing he said could really surprise her. "I wasn't chasing you."

He smiled rather grimly and rubbed the palm of his hand across hers. "Of course you weren't. I was afraid of the feeling I was beginning to have for you. So, I simply withdrew. It's an old pattern of mine. Began to drink too much, took the phone off the hook, spoke only to people I had to. At the hospital. My analyst. You didn't know that I'm undergoing analysis, did you?"

"No," Deborah said. It didn't seem to matter. She felt quite fuzzy now and all the things he was saying were interesting but not important. He would take care of her. That was important. She could trust him.

"You see," he was saying, "I need you very much, Deborah, and I didn't want you to be burdened with my need. But now I see that you need me almost as much. At any rate, last month, my analyst went on vacation so I fled even farther away from the temptation of seeing you to Bar Harbor to visit my uncle and aunt. That was no help at all. I kept seeing your face when I gave you the rose and the book. So when I came back I tried to call you. But you weren't there any more . . . I obtained your address and was planning to write you a note but I couldn't decide . . ."

He seemed to go on talking but after awhile Deborah couldn't make sense of what he was saying and presently she felt the soft pressure of a mouth on hers and the room got darker and there was no one in the darkness but herself, all wrapped up and lapped in warmth and cherishing.

Later, when she woke up, it was dark and Dudley came and brought her some scrambled eggs and toast on a tray and said did she think perhaps she could go up to Rockport with him on Sunday to hear Sally sing. They could drive up in the morning, go swimming and have dinner and did she like to dance?

"I don't dance very well. And besides I'm afraid I don't own anything sort of proper for dancing in a place like that."

He insisted then that she try on some of Sally's clothes but she demurred. He became very imperious and said, very well, if she was going to worry about whether Sally wanted her to take the clothes, he'd call her.

He almost barked into the telephone at Sally, way up there in Rockport, which apparently didn't bother her, because Deborah heard her laughter rippling huskily and then Dudley handed her the receiver.

"Of course, darling, you must take some clothes," Sally drawled, sounding lovely, careless, and amused. "Shoes too, anything you like. I've been planning to give you some things anyway. So, if you don't take them I shall simply throw them away."

Deborah muttered, feeling horribly humiliated really by the whole thing. If she hadn't been so dopey from that dumb pill she never would have allowed Dudley to be so presumptuous.

"Now look, darling," Sally said finally, stemming the stammering tide of apologies. "Everyone knows that students are ill equipped for any expense but foolscap and a goose quill pen. And you can't go about with my august medical brother in sabots and an inkstained smock. Why don't you look at it from Dudley's point of view? He's much older than you are, and do you want to simply emphasize his grey hair and wrinkled visage by your attire?"

"Why, he's not that old," Deborah protested. "But I never thought of it that way."

"Of course you didn't," Sally said smoothly. "And I'm so delighted that you and Dudley are getting on so well. Surely a few clothes that I can't use shouldn't stand in the way of you both having a fine day, now should it? Good. Farewell, then, see you on Sunday."

Deborah hung up the phone, wondering how it was possible that a girl like Sally who looked as though she oughtn't to have a brain in her head could be so, well, smart. Foolscap and a goose quill pen, well, well, how very interesting.

"Your sister is very clever," she said to Dudley. "She just sort of knows exactly the right way to put things."

Dudley looked at her gloomily. "Yes, she is very articulate," he said, "and she has an awfully good mind too, appearances to the contrary. It's a pity she doesn't utilize it more."

Which was an odd sort of statement since why in the world should a girl with so many physical and economic attributes need to use her mind at all, Deborah thought, as she tried on several dresses before the full-length mirror in Sally's room. Only the Deborahs of this world with nothing but minds and not grand ones at that had to use them. Now, this white cotton lace dress with the crimson silk sash and the full rustling petticoat to go with it, would be the very thing to wear. It was very loose in the bodice but she could fix that. Sally must wear a 38 bra she thought, why you could put another Deborah down the front of this dress and there'd still be room to spare. But the skirt was fine and she could take the waist in with the sash. She came out and showed herself to Dudley.

He stared at her. "You look lovely in it," he said softly. "It becomes you more than it did Sally. That white shows up your dark skin marvelously, and the sash is exactly the color of a rose. Yes, you must have some roses too."

"I think it's a little long," Deborah said anxiously. "But I don't want to make a hem because that would ruin the dress for Sally."

"You must keep it," he said. "It's just right for you."

She went back into Sally's room and found a delightful little pair of shoes on the floor of the closet, flat, black kid ballet slippers, with long laces which tied round and round the ankles. They were about a half-size larger than her own so she was regretfully about to put them back when her eye caught a brilliant, yellow cotton dress of some stiff, crinkly fabric, full skirted and very plain. It was a wonderful color, like a flood of spring sunshine. Just try it on, she thought, and posed in front of the mirror, on one leg, her arm upflung, like a Spanish dancer. The dress had a lowcut rounded neckline and with very little to fill it up it gawped wide open and drooped almost uncovering whatever there was of her bosom. I'm so skinny, she thought regretfully, staring down inside the dress at her body.

The door opened and she jerked her head up quickly and saw Dudley looking at her. He didn't seem embarrassed at having come in without knocking.

"You look like a lovely little gipsy in that," he said. He came over and held out his hand. "I have some earrings here that you might be able to wear. They were my mother's."

The earrings were tiny gold circlets, a little bit smaller than the fake five-and-ten ones which Gordie had twitted her about. Apparently Dudley didn't care if she looked like a peasant. How nice he was. His mother's earrings. She looked at them closely, bending down a little. "Oh, Dudley," she said disappointed, "they're for pierced ears. I can't wear them."

"Oh, stupid of me, of course. Well, perhaps some other time, if you'd like, I could pierce them for you." He dropped the earrings into his pocket and looked at her. He was biting his lip.

"My mother was very beautiful," Dudley said abruptly. "She wasn't a Boston woman who would have looked ridiculous in those earrings. She was Italian and they were quite natural to her. Sally looks a good bit like her."

Deborah said something polite and waited for him to go out so that she could change her clothes but he didn't move.

"I must change," she said uneasily.

"Yes," he said and he walked over to her slowly. "Let me help you."

"No." She whirled away from his touch which was no longer gentle.

"Yes," he said softly, insistently. "Yes, let me. I want to see you, Deborah. To look at your little breasts, like plums."

"No, please." But it didn't do any good. He was strong and firm and good and he would take care of her. She leaned against him helplessly and he sat down on the bed holding her on his lap. She hid her face in his shoulder and felt him pull the dress down to her waist and unfasten her brassiere.

"Don't be afraid of me, Deborah." He fumbled awkwardly at her breasts. Then he pulled off the yellow dress. All the while she could not look at him, her head burrowing against his chest.

"What a young body you have, like a little girl in white cotton pants. Will you kiss me, my little girl?"

"Yes, Dudley," she murmured obediently and she clasped her arms around his neck and kissed him swiftly and chastely on the cheek.

"Sweet," he whispered and he parted her legs and began to stroke her there, still holding her on his lap, clasping her firmly against his chest.

Deborah began to tremble at the touch of his fingers against her pants but she could not open her mouth to utter a word or lift her hand to push him away. She lay curled in his lap, completely enervated, and yet feeling a peculiar topsy-turvy sensation way down there where his hand was and then the light went off and she ought to object but it was too much trouble.

"We won't do anything, Deborah," he mumbled in the dark in her ear and he stretched her out on the bed and she heard noises of belt buckles being opened and zippers pulled. "Just lie quietly close together, like brother and sister, all pure and clean."

She lay against him, feeling his bare chest, but he still had his shorts on, she knew that, and he kept pressing against her and calling her his baby sister girl but she felt remote from it all, only warm and safe, and even the silly things he said were all right because he was taking care of her, he wasn't doing awful things to her the way Gordie had. And then he stopped saying things and he didn't press against her any more and there was silence and she felt water on her face, because he was perspiring there in the darkness and then he groaned and after awhile he turned on the light and sat her on his lap again and dressed her and kept kissing and hugging her and saying never to go away from him because she was his little rosebud, his pretty doll and took her by the hand and led her downstairs and lifted her up and deposited her gently in the car and she slept all the way home on his shoulder, even though he was driving, but he didn't seem to mind.

When they went up to Rockport on Sunday it was a beautiful day. They went swimming and spent two hours on the beach with Sally and some man she had who was a big, dour-looking, silent brute named Saul to whom Dudley was coldly courteous. Deborah took one dip in the water but it was too cold. She came out shivering and fell asleep on the beach because she seemed to be so tired these days and Saul Something who'd been drinking stoically from a leather-covered flask and not bothering to talk to anybody had gone to sleep while she was in the water. Dudley and Sally talked desultorily and later Deborah woke up halfway to hear Sally say,

"I hope you haven't been hypnotizing her, Dud. She looks sort of heavylidded and wan."

Dudley muttered something which she couldn't catch and Sally laughed and said, "Well. Father image, right? You must love that. Terribly convenient too. And admitting it bravely. Wonderful! No repressions at all are there?"

"It wouldn't hurt you to have a few," he retorted angrily. "And I don't like it but at least I'm trying to change. Frequently it's a strain, saying things I feel, which sound inane coming out. But I'm happy, very happy now, can't you see that? I won't tell you about it if you're going to jeer."

"Oh, you have to tell me," Sally said mockingly. "Aside from the good doctor, I'm the only one who knows. Of course I can see you're happy. You look like a vampire who's recently had a good, nourishing bowl of blood."

What an awful thing to say to a brother, Deborah thought, they really were the most curious family. She closed her eyes hastily, as Dudley turned his head in her direction, even though she was lying a little way away from them and wearing sunglasses. What on earth could they be talking about? All she could gather was that Dudley was happy which might or might not have something to do with her, although that seemed unlikely, anyway, it was so comfortable and pleasant and warm in the sun and she was just, oh so sleepy . . .

"I didn't think you'd still be hanging about with that type," Dudley said in a low-pitched, determinedly pleasant voice. "It's rather a long siege of bad judgment, isn't it?"

"Ah, but it's my own judgment, which makes all the difference. I didn't need to go crawling into some Viennese confessional box to ask if it was all right please."

"You know nothing whatever about the subject," Dudley said coldly. "Had I known you were going to be so hostile I'd never have . . ."

"Oh, yes you would," Sally interrupted rudely. "All neophytes undergoing analysis are the same. It's no fun going if other people don't know it. How else would they become aware that the secret smile crossing your lips when they talk or act indicates a million hidden meanings that they, poor fools, little suspect, whereas you, who have been anointed, are infinitely more aware of the slime pockets in their subconscious than they are."

"Well, it's true," Dudley said stoutly. "If you, for example, were only aware of how clearly your behavior indicates. . . ."

"Oh pooh!" Sally said blithely. "You'll get over it, Dudley, and begin to take your new religion cum grano salis in time, I trust. The beginning is really the most tiresome period, all full of crusading zeal. Very fretting being around such people. You don't dare say or do anything natural for fear they'll pounce on it with a triumphant AHA!, and pull up out of the murk, a wriggling halfaborted case of penis envy or some such claptrap. In pink bootees for girls. For men they have it in blue under a different brand name, castration complex, I believe."

Dudley snorted, in a sort of half-protesting laugh and Deborah smiled up at the sky. Sally was quite remarkable, she thought. The kind of girl you were sure you'd hate and envy when you first met her, because of her looks, but how kind and warmhearted she really was and what a refreshingly scathing tongue in her head.

"You're very clever, I'll admit," Dudley said grudgingly, "but it's much easier to tear down something of which you have no knowledge than it is to discuss its beneficial aspects seriously. I daresay you have some splendidly frivolous and orgiastic solution of your own?"

"I simply think people ought to live as much as they can. A Jamesian character's notion, I believe."

"Henry James himself might well have profited from an analysis," Dudley said musingly.

"But perhaps he might never have written some of those lovely novels if he had."

"He might have written better ones."

"We'll never know now, will we?" Sally said teasingly. "So many great men and women in the past, so many enduring masterpieces that could have been even more superb if their creators had only submitted to Freudian brainwashing."

"They might've been happier and better human beings," Dudley said. "Don't you understand that? It isn't essential to have a wretched personal life in order to be a world shaker."

"Yes, but everyone's idea of happiness is different," Sally said. "And here's mine waking up right now. Hello, darling, did you have a good snooze?"

Deborah sat up too, all eager to listen to the good talk and perhaps get in a quote she'd read recently, that to the Romantics of the nineteenth century the goal of life was not happiness but activity, but the conversation seemed to have died with Saul's reappearance and Dudley asked her if she'd like to see the town before the afternoon performance. So of course she had to say yes and that was the end of that except just before they were leaving the beach, Sally said to Dudley,

"It might comfort you to know darling that I feel psychoanalysis is a great deal like other imports of its type. It loses something in the translation." Upon which she laughed immoderately and Saul looked bewildered and even Dudley smiled.

"And where did you read that?" he demanded.

"I don't know. Could I have made it up?"

"Dubious," Dudley grumbled and led Deborah away in what seemed an awful hurry.

Later, at the Sandbox, they danced three or four fairly sedate dances together. Dudley danced very well, Deborah thought, leading her correctly around the floor, but she felt strained and tense in his arms and was sure she was about to trample on his feet or miss a step or stumble. That none of these things happened was due solely, she was sure, to his excellence as a partner. Then too, she was convinced that she looked ridiculous in Sally's dress, that it hung on her and the hasty hem she'd basted in, would come dangling down and cause her to be a public object of ridicule. She much preferred sitting at their table sipping on a Tom Collins and talking to Dudley who kept assuring her that she looked wonderful and no, the dress was not too loose at all, skintight things made a woman look cheap. This, with a distasteful glance at his sister who was walking toward them on her way up to the stand to sing.

"Sally looks beautiful," Deborah said, staring.

"There's no need to emphasize the obvious," Dudley said crossly.

Men were very prudish where their female relatives were concerned, Deborah thought, admiring Sally's sleeveless milkwhite sheath dress, which accentuated the gold color of her tan and the bright shine of her hair. It was tight of course but entertainers had to dress that way and those terrific green satin shoes with the very high heels and the wide flashing bracelet on her brown arm, real emeralds or costume jewelry, Deborah wondered, no matter, how could Dudley think she looked cheap? He probably didn't know. Men were sometimes very dumb about what constituted good taste in women's clothes.

"You look charming in that dress," Sally said to Deborah, pausing at their table. "I never liked it on me. Too littlegirly, but it's quite accurate for you. And an American Beauty rose to match the sash, too. My, how well you're doing, Dudley. And do give me a cigarette and a sip of that Scotch will you darling? I always get jumpy before the first song."

She bent over to get a light from Dudley and Deborah noticed Saul, was his name Milman, at a table close to the stand, staring rather angrily over at them. So she missed whatever byplay there was between brother and sister which caused Dudley to say impatiently, "Here, light it yourself," and push the lighter rudely into Sally's hand.

"Steady on, surgeon," Sally said, flicking the lighter and smiling coolly down at him.

"Do you have to flaunt yourself like this?" Dudley said, not even troubling to disguise his irritation.

"I'm paid to look like this. They expect it." Sally didn't look amused any more. Her nostrils were dilated and her eyes cold. She doesn't even wear any make-up, Deborah noticed. How scrubbed and shining her tanned face was. Looked so clean compared to most girls.

"You ought to watch yourself, Duddy. Sometimes that poker mask slips and I'm not receptive to what I see beneath."

"I can't make much sense of what you're saying," Dudley said contemptuously. "Hadn't you ought to go see your boy over there? He's looking murderous."

"Because of your brotherly expression, no doubt." She smiled at Deborah and said cheerfully, "Don't mind us darling, we go on this way all the time. It's an inbred family trait," and sauntered away.

After that, Dudley went off into one of his morose clouds, staring at his drink, not even looking up when Sally came onto the stand in a spotlighted hush, leaning against the piano. In fact, he acted exactly as though he was sitting at a bar all alone and Deborah, quick to take a hint, turned her back on him and concentrated on the music.

She had heard so much about Sally as a good blues singer that it was disappointing to find that the first number was to be "September Song," of all things. Not real blues, she thought scornfully, not real jazz, just sentimental musical comedy stuff. But by the time Sally, in a voice as golden and honest as Sidney Bechet's saxophone, had turned the autumn leaves to flame, Deborah knew that she was in the presence, not only of a great voice but also of the artful mastery of a medium.

For this was a voice that was not ashamed of itself. It had riches and passion, and with each phrase, each line, another facet of opulent treasure disclosed itself. And she gave it all to her audience with effortless ease, with smiling grace and they sat, entranced, mute, receptive and all in love with her, as if she were a sun who lighted them up for a little while. Not even an ice cube tinkled in a glass, not a chair scraped . . . "These gold-den days, I'd spend . . . with . . . you." Then, the sun went away, the spell was broken and it was winter. It took the audience a few seconds to face the end of the season and break out into a roar of applause.

"God!" said a crewcutted, horn-rimmed glasses youth at the next table, taking out his handkerchief and wiping his brow, "I come up every Sunday to hear her ever since I read the Jazzbo's thing and each time, I think, it won't work today, she can't do like this each time, make a creative thing out of one of those tinpan songs. But she does. It's fantastic!"

"It's more on the order of a wet dream," said his companion who was robust and redheaded.

426

"Why don't you go to a burlesque show?" his friend said unsympathetically. "My God, don't you understand, she has an amazing true jazz voice. And all you think about is . . ."

"I suppose you didn't notice the way her breasts shimmy?" the redhead said tauntingly.

"Sssh, they're starting up again."

It was announced that the next number would be "I Got It Bad and That Ain't Good." Miss Sally Mayhew and Vance Paley's trio.

She sang it first in a kind of harsh, semi-talking growl like a muted trombone, with many suggestive breaks which roused some of the more hip members of the audience to happy laughter and encouraging murmurs. But, on the second chorus, her voice got softer and more reminiscently caressing and she was smiling down at the table where Saul sat:

> "But when the fish are jumpin'
> And Friday rolls around
> Mah mann and meee weee gennn some
> And 'brace some . . .
> And send some . . ."

Then her voice rose again from its depths for the last chorus, "He don't love me lahk I love him, nobuddyy could," and then finished with ornate little thematic embroideries on the lost, weeping willow, her voice moving easily up and down.

"Now how about that?" demanded the redhead at the next table when the song was over. "She almost as good as told you that if she didn't get it every night she'd die."

"Oh don't be a square," said his friend, polishing eyeglasses vigorously. "Do you think lyrics are of any importance? Technically, she's even more flexible than I'd thought. Did you hear all that last part? Very cool, man, very cerebral."

"Yes, but listen. She sang the words wrong in that middle part. It should be something about the weekend being over and Monday rolling around. Her version was Greek to me."

"You've only heard the censored version. It's the only way they can play it over the radio to be respectable. It's simple enough. Just means, generate, embrace and send, meaning sex that's all."

"Rubbish!" Dudley said loudly ignoring the offended and pained glances from the two boys. The performers were now taking a break and Sally had gone to sit with Saul and a Tom Collins.

427

"They are sort of silly, aren't they?" Deborah said in a low voice to Dudley. "But Sally is so impressive, really remarkable."

"I think she sounded like a cat on a back fence," Dudley said. "But then, I find this sort of music appalling. It affects me exactly as if it were fingernails scraping on a blackboard. And I don't enjoy hearing my sister being bandied about in the mouths of any imbecile with the price of admission."

"You mean you don't like her singing?" Deborah asked astounded.

"Precisely. I don't like her voice and I don't care for her getting up before a mob of louts and displaying herself halfnaked. When you consider that she doesn't need to do it, it's a clear case of exhibitionism and, as such, quite disturbing to me."

"Then why did you want to come?"

"Because I never have heard her sing and I thought I ought to. But it's exactly as I feared. I'm sorry, Deborah, I'm perhaps a killjoy, but I can't bear to watch her further. So, if you don't mind, I'll go out to the bar and you can stay till she's finished. Then, we really should leave so that I can get you home early enough."

"We can leave now if you want to," Deborah said, trying not to sound disappointed.

"No, no, I insist. You stay."

Sally sang two more numbers, "Am I Blue" and "Rocks in My Bed" while Deborah sat enraptured, forgetting to finish her drink. When they were saying goodbye, she tried to tell Sally how much she'd enjoyed it but found herself rather intimidated with Dudley by her side.

Driving home, Dudley said to her, "My sister is very dazzling to you, I'm sure and I can see why you'd admire her. But she's rather reckless and self-destructive and overdoes things at times. I hope she won't regret it some day."

He said no more about Sally, and Deborah, after thinking that it was kind of too bad the way they didn't seem to like one another remembered that tomorrow was Monday and she was out of a job again and thanks to her own badly-timed recklessness must perforce, once more, begin the weary old pilgrimage of humiliation in search of bread and knowledge.

Part Three

One

Sally was dreaming that she had murdered the old man in the derby hat who sold lavender on Park Street. He had a little tray of sachets hung round his neck and was there in mostly all weathers and wore a high, old-fashioned collar and her bureau drawers were stuffed with sachets because she couldn't resist buying them when she went past him. It seemed such a dreadful way to make a living when one was so old and frail. Just why she'd murdered him was very vague. One blow with a big wooden club and he'd fallen down dead. No one knew it yet but it was only a matter of time. She saw herself walking along Tremont Street and everyone passing stared, their whispers were louder, that girl's a murderer . . . was that a policeman shining his light in her eyes?

A logical dream for one who'd fallen asleep reading a mystery story, she thought, logily opening her eyes, seeing the bed light on and herself fully dressed, the Dorothy Sayers lying face down on the floor. She shook her head, conscious of a heaviness behind her temples and a slightly peculiar sensation somewhere. Always so healthy and never got headaches or fell into little catnaps. Damn weird. Or was it? This moony seasick nonsense which, if she'd been drinking a lot, could've been fobbed off as hangover, but what could be more decorous than the day just gone by.

Saul had taken her driving out into the country to look at the glory of the turning leaves and afterwards to a movie. Then they'd had an early dinner and he'd gone home to sleep because now he was on the midnight shift. They'd each had only one drink, hers an innocuous whiskey sour. Sour. Complaining to Saul that it was the sourest whiskey sour she'd ever had and he saying that maybe it was her. And they'd gone on. So odd really. Not any real quarrels between them since those first few disjointed days back last May. And what had they quarreled about anyway? He'd been sort of moody all day but of course that might be the result of those new, gruesome working hours. Probably the excess of his complaints on that subject had irritated her. And since she felt sort of moldy anyway it was very tiresome listening to him and his self-centered conversation.

"You haven't mentioned the worst drawback," she'd said, "that your hours are far too similar to Dudley's."

"Sure, so we're frustrated. But I've been that way since we got back after Labor Day."

"Then you ought to get an apartment," she'd said dismissingly, taking lipstick and mirror out of her bag and doing a little public paintwork. This was a deliberate vulgarity which ordinarily was unthinkable at a restaurant table but suddenly she was so bored with the conversation, with him, with his childish egocentricity, with her dinner which she'd scarcely touched, with her whiskey sour which must've been actually poisoned, so overwhelmed with lassitude that all she wanted to do was get outside and breathe in the cool autumn night.

"Let's not go over that again," he said, biting hard on the end of a cigar. "I'd be some laughingstock if I moved out on Sophy and Moe and you threw me over."

"You'd still have the apartment," Sally'd said, knowing she was being impossible and not caring.

"Ha, ha," he'd said grimly, picking up the check and glancing at it, "it might mean nothing to you honey, since you're a daughter of the lousy rich, but I contribute something to the upkeep of my aunt and uncle while I live there and it helps out, believe me. Not that they'd starve if I didn't but it gives them a little extra and I owe them something. And while we're on the subject of money, next time you don't feel like eating, don't order a four-dollar meal and leave it lie there. Or have you forgotten that I'm a working stiff and not a guy who just clips coupons?"

"No," Sally'd said coldly. "I have not forgotten because you're constantly throwing it in my face in the most boorish and vulgar manner possible. And as for that sad tale of the poverty of your aunt and uncle I shall not get out my handkerchief and wipe away a tear. I know the amount of money you give them because you've told me and I also know the way you eat and I'd be perfectly willing to swear on a stack of Bibles that your food bill alone comes to three times that much. They'd undoubtedly be at no loss if you moved out. It's simple selfishness, not altruism, that motivates you."

"Well, you wouldn't take care of me," he'd said defensively. "Because you couldn't live with me, could you?"

"Of course not. That would be much too obvious. But I'd be there a lot. I could cook suppers for you and things, although you'd have to send your shirts to the laundry."

"And have a cleaning woman come in, I suppose."

"Of course."

He'd laughed at that and they'd gone to the cashier's desk, where she'd waited, pulling on her gloves while he paid the bill.

"I'm sorry about the untouched four-dollar dinner, Saul," she'd said contritely when they were in the car. "I just feel hideous suddenly."

To her surprise, he'd switched on the light in the car and examined her face keenly. "You look all right to me. What's the matter with you?"

"I don't know. My head aches. It's nothing though. A minor germ or suchlike."

"Or an itch."

"Yes, that must be it."

"There's lot of that going around," he'd said. "I've got a bad case of that myself. Any other symptoms?" he'd asked his voice suddenly so jovial that she was taken aback.

"You're so damn mercurial. Oh, a few, but I always feel if you don't dwell on ailments, they'll go away. Unscientific no doubt but . . ."

"You're crazy," he'd interrupted, smiling at her in an odd, triumphant way. "Sometimes you have to get worse to get better."

"Oh Saul. I'm just too muzzy to follow you tonight."

"I could fix you up fine if I didn't have to go to work."

"I know." Wearily. "But you do. So take me home, please."

He'd turned the light off and in the dark, grabbed her, putting one hand up inside her skirt, squeezing her breasts with the other, kissing her so hard that her mouth felt raw, and biting her neck. "I want to love you all to hell all my life," he said in a muffled voice. "I can't stand this kid stuff any more. Say you'll marry me, Sally. You will anyway, one of these days."

Angrily, she'd pushed him away. For the first time in her life she'd felt no answering response when a man she liked touched her like that. Instead she'd had the fantastic and overwhelming desire to be sick. Her head spinning and hands, unusually clumsy, she'd straightened her skirt. Must be really ill she thought and touched her forehead to see if there might be a fever flush.

"You have an awfully short memory, Saul."

"I know." He'd started the car. "Don't worry, I didn't forget about it. Just thought you mighta changed your mind, that's all."

"Well, I haven't."

"Okay, okay. Forget about it. I won't say another word. But we'll just have to work something out. I'm trying to get off this goddamn shift, but this other guy's sick, see, and everybody's supposed to take a turn on it, you know. Naturally, nobody likes it."

"Naturally," she'd murmured, closing her heavy eyelids and leaning back against the car seat, wondering why suddenly for no apparent reason his bad mood had vanished. He sounded marvelously cheerful considering her nastiness in pushing him away and all. And then when they came to her door, he was all tender solicitude, kissing her gently, hoping she'd feel better and going away smiling.

It was that smile that lingered with her now when she sat up in bed after her dream, feeling not much better, after an hour's nap. Why? Why had he smiled? Why had he grown so suddenly pleasant and gentle and happy? And proposing to her again for the fourth time and then acting as though she'd given him a birthday present instead of a fourth emphatic refusal? Why, dammit, why?

She went to the mirror and stuck out her tongue at the girl there. Being nasty to Saul who loved her, you're really a great chick and so blah too. But it was true. She was suddenly very bored with him. Nothing now seemed to have the shining rightness of their summer. Oncoming winter, perhaps, she felt dim when the sun went away. Winter! Why it was only the end of October and she hadn't . . . oh my God, she thought, in swift, startled panic, I must have. It was so long since she'd bothered to keep track, never any reason to worry, always been careful. No, no, silly to consider it.

I've just forgotten, she told herself, looking around her disordered room with distaste, really must speak to that sloppy cleaning woman. That's it, bad memory. Take a shower and clear all these old wives' fidgets out of my head. Not a thing the matter with me. She opened the door of her room and noted with dismay that Dudley must have guests. There were sounds of murmured voices and a record clicking onto the turntable and ice trembling in glasses. Hell, she thought, hastily shutting the door, and went to hunt for her robe, found for a wonder hanging over the back of a chair by the desk under a heap of discarded underwear. And while standing there looking at it full in the face, wouldn't hurt to glance at the desk calender, just to make sure. Frowning, she sat down on the bed, holding a fountain pen and swiftly, turned the calendar leaves. What was that they were playing out there, sounded familiar, chorus "Come away fellow sailors, come away . . ." Dido and Aeneas. Deborah. Undoubtedly. Dudley, teaching Deborah all about Purcell. Must go out after the shower and say hello. Deborah proving damn good for Dudley. He showed some signs of thaw.

Now let's see, when was the last time she could remember. It was awfully hard. She leaned against the wall, sitting on her feet, chewing on the end of the pen. Concentrate, idiot, this might, just might be important. Ah! The second last weekend in August. She remembered distinctly now what an annoying, frustrating weekend it'd been and Dudley had come with Deborah and behaved loathsomely, but Saul'd said never mind, they'd make up for it over Labor Day weekend and he'd taken the Friday off too so they'd had four days together. Next time, therefore must have been second last week in September. She counted off twenty-eight days from the first date in August, added a few days give or take. She tried to think back a month ago. She jogged, she cudgeled, she performed every cliché known to bring one's brains to heel, but there was only a blank. Well then, she thought brightly, it was so important that it happened and I just can't remember it, after all, it's happened every month for twelve years, by this time, I can't possibly remember each and every time. I don't remember every meal I've had now, do I? The thing to do was skip along and count off to October. She counted very slowly, one day after another, twenty-eight, well twenty-nine, oh, it could be thirty. But no matter how she stretched it and went over it and counted again, the sober dates admitted of no release. It should have happened last week. That was it, plain and clear. No way out of it. You couldn't juggle those days around and get the answer you wanted. And I might not remember last month, she thought honestly, but there was no forgetting last week. Not last week, nor, if the truth fits wear it, last month either. And what does that mean, dear girl? Ho, ho, she thought, and flung both pen and calendar across the room. It means you're feeling miserable old girl, means you're coming down with the grippe.

She knew, all at once, with great certainty, that it was true. In vain, she told herself, sitting in a sort of evil trance on the bed, lighting one cigarette after another, that one couldn't actually be sure until a doctor said so or one of those frogs or rabbits popped out with a yes. That it could be all in the mind. She failed to convince herself and even knew now how it'd happened. And spelled it out carefully and painfully for her own edification. Not that first night, that Friday when he'd come and after two weeks they'd been ravenous for each other. No, the third night, Sunday, because there'd

435

been a sort of wild, drunken party given by some young bloods of the summer season around there and she'd gone with Saul and the whole band had been there. And she'd gotten very high although Saul had remained carefully and, she'd thought, rather squarely sober and when joshed about it, he'd admitted it and said he had to take care of her, and he kept wanting her to go home but for the first time since knowing him she'd been in a real party mood and wanted to stay, dance barefoot, drink and have a time. So, of course, by the time they finally got home, she'd been pretty much out but he'd wanted it and she remembered now being sort of collapsed on the bed and murmuring drowsily that she felt too dead to do much about it but he'd said it would be all right because he'd use . . . I should have known, I should have known, she thought now, drearily. If I hadn't been drunk I'd've realized that on the beach that very afternoon, he'd asked me if I'd ever change my mind about marrying him. No, she'd said, then, no, never. Treacherous bastard, I trusted him, I trusted him, like a fool. Reading up on the fertility cycle all summer, no doubt. No, he was a good gambler, always said so, very lucky at cards. Ah, that smile, she thought, that happy, inexplicable perking up when I suddenly, for the first time, showed signs of illness. And so now, he was sitting back waiting for her to confide her shy secret and they would live happily ever after. And he'd continue to wait, she thought, girding on her robe and plunging out into the hall, because . . . She almost careened into Dudley coming along with the ice bucket.

"Deborah here?" she asked, putting on a casual face.

"No. She's working tonight. It's Matthew Berman. You've met him, haven't you? Well then, come in and say hello. I have some new records."

"Perhaps." She looked at her brother speculatively. He'd be terribly happy to hear her news, now, wouldn't he? One might think that with a doctor brother one would be all fixed up. For a fraction of a second she thought of telling him and then dismissed the idea.

"I'll fix you a drink," Dudley was saying. "Matthew'd like to see you again. He's always asking about you."

He ought to, Sally thought, I need a keeper. "Very well," she said. "I'll come in after my shower. I could do with a drink."

A glance in the full-length mirror when she'd finished dressing convinced her that tonight was one of her Lauren Bacall nights and that Matthew Berman was probably crazy about Lauren Bacall. A bubble of absurd and shaky laughter rose up irresistibly inside as she strode rangily, conscious of her sullen, purple-lipsticked mouth, long hair falling perilously close to one eye, and new close-fitting purple knit dress, into the living room. It won't fit me soon, she thought, smiling closemouthed and secretive at Matthew Berman, who sat looking a bit uncomfortable on the sofa. No, I don't care if he is Saul's brother, doesn't know about us and he's the only other doctor I know.

"Don't let me interrupt this serious panel discussion on Purcell," she said sprawling unladylike and stretching out her fine, nyloned legs for Matthew Berman's reluctantly admiring inspection. He's still annoyed because I refused to go out with him, she guessed, interpreting his stiff smile and bare nod of greeting. Dudley gave her a drink and old, keen-eyed Saul's brother took in thoroughly the way she guzzled half of it in one swallow. By now, he must know we're a family of old stock gone to seed and alcohol. She put her half-finished drink down on the table. Too much whisky too quickly with no dinner and feeling vile might send her reeling back to bed before she even made up her mind about talking to Matthew Berman. Then how about the rumors one heard that drinking a bottle of some strengthening spirit at one sitting might bring a girl, as the distasteful phrase had it, around? Sounded too easy, at any rate for her. Dynamite, she thought cynically, alone, would do it. Just let one not want a baby and only stern measures could get rid of it, whereas, of course, a happily married woman, invariably had trouble holding on to them.

She toyed with a heavy piece of spurious gold and amethysts at her wrist and listened with one ear to a mild argument between Dudley and Matthew who didn't it appeared, really relish Purcell.

"Oh rubbish!" she interrupted, "put on the Hafner symphony or something, Duddy. Matthew's been hungrily eying all the Mozart."

Matthew gave her a grateful but embarrassed smile.

"Sabotaged by Philistines within the home," she said, winking at him over her raised glass behind Dudley's resentful back. Wish I *had* gone out with him, she thought, instead of picking the other brother, bet he's much too cagy to knock a girl up. When you knew they were brothers he really looked quite a bit like Saul, although smaller, neater, more fine-boned, but with the same crisp, curly black hair. Eyes set the same way but Matthew's were larger and a rather wonderful amber color. The eyes were obviously a bit shocked at her rowdy wink. She drained her drink quickly and held her glass up to Dudley. Beginnings of wooziness. Who cares, she thought, what else is there but to get drunk and try to forget this disgusting pickle. But in the next second, the fear clutched at her again and her heart

437

pounded alarmingly. Two months, that's what it meant. By four months it was too late, she knew that, there'd been the girl, that blonde waitress in the club in California where she'd been singing, who'd let it go too long and had to end up having the baby. She'd been living with some Air Force captain who'd promised to marry her and then taken off and when he did it was too late.

"That's an overwhelming bracelet you have there," Dudley said. He was always quick to point out what he referred to as her West Coast vulgarities. He was still victim of the simple Boston idea that the only jewelry one wore was a single strand of great-aunt Hezekiah's pearls. "A little baroque though. One of the Mayhew heirlooms?"

"A Filene's Basement heirloom, darling. Just like that lovely shirt I bought you from the hoity-toity New York men's shop sale which you spat upon." She'd bought one for Saul too and he'd been very pleased although she'd seen that he thought rounded button down collars shamefully effete.

"Pink," Dudley said. "I will not wear a pink shirt."

"Dudley buys all his socks at the Army surplus store," Sally explained to Matthew, straight-faced, "and his shirts and ties at Sears Roebuck. Sometimes, when he's in the mood for something terribly fancy and extravagant like a suit or sweater he wanders into that old Yankee cracker barrel emporium down there on Washington Street. You know, Unkle Obadiah's."

Dudley frowned at her. "They have good, serviceable clothes at Obadiah Lindsey and Company," he said defensively. "They don't go in for this current plot to make men dress like pimps and gipsies and their prices are reasonable. I've been going there since I was a boy. Grandfather bought most of *his* clothes there. He had them for years."

"Of course," Sally said glimmering at him, "and because he always used to take a sandwich and some leftover wilted salad along with him as a lunch every time he went on a longish car trip so he wouldn't have to spend money in highway hash houses, you, naturally, must do the same. But we're boring Dr. Berman. He thinks it's all a quaint old family joke. But, alas, no. Or haven't you taken him to your favorite eating place yet, Dudley?"

"Locke-Ober's?" Matthew asked nervously.

"Ha," Sally said. "Tell him where you took Deborah to lunch yesterday, darling."

"Grant's cafeteria," Dudley said. "What's wrong with that? She wanted to eat quickly and I must say you can get a good inexpensive meal there and none of this nonsense of waiting for seats." He looked irritatedly at both of them who were smiling broadly. "Well, she liked it very much, anyway."

"He eats there every time he's downtown," Sally said to Matthew.

"If you ate there on occasion," Dudley retorted, "you wouldn't always be running out of your allowance."

"Dear, dear, we're back to that, are we? Why don't you play some Bach, Dud? It will make you feel better."

"I'm about to. You people can sit here and play Mozart as long as you want but I'm on call tonight and have to sleep in hospital. And," he announced pettishly, "I shall have my breakfast in the hospital cafeteria where the food is much worse than Grant's."

"And a diet of hospital food would do wonders for my fatted soul, I know," Sally said. "I'm sorry, Dud, I didn't mean to tease. But you are such an awful old Yankee, you know. Lucky for Deborah that she's studying American Literature and understands the Yankee psyche."

He gave her a steely glance and put on a Brandenburg Concerto. Matthew, obviously unnerved by all this ohsopolite family bickering, jumped up and offered her a cigarette. She knew she was behaving badly and that Matthew probably thought she was a bitch, but really, she felt so impossible. The burny sensation noted earlier while drinking the whiskey sour had returned twofold with this second glass of Scotch and it was hellish. I hate it, I hate it, she thought, smiling her thanks at Matthew after he'd lighted her cigarette, I won't have it, I won't feel rotten like this, I must talk to him, the sooner the better.

She sat listening to the music, trying to frame in her mind how she'd explain her problem to Saul's unknowing brother. He'd probably be shocked, a man who could sit and drink with Dudley and not know he was pretty much of a drunk and look at the way he dressed and not know he was a miser. And what if he says, well, why didn't you ask your brother. No, even he couldn't avoid noticing that Dudley was not, but not, the sort of brother one leaned on in such a crisis.

"You don't need to leave simply because poor old Dud has to go drudge away tonight," she said to Matthew pleasantly when Dudley was getting their coats. "Or do you have something to do?"

"No, it's one of my nights off," he said. "If I'd stayed on with the Med residency I wouldn't have the duty so often but, now I'm right back where I started from, every other night."

"Oh," she asked lazily, not really caring, "you and Dudley both changed then. Are you in surgery too?"

"No. I'm in obstetrics now."

"A baby doctor," Sally said and smiled at him brilliantly. "How absolutely fascinating. Now you really must stay and tell me all about it. Are you hungry? Because I am and I'm going to fix us some scrambled eggs."

"Matthew's going to stay," she informed Dudley when he reappeared. "He's going to tell me how babies are born."

"Indeed," Dudley said, staring. "It should be an exciting conversation. I regret that I must miss it. Well, goodbye you two, there's a plenitude of Mozart and Scotch and I hope, Sara, you won't get carried away by the lecture on obstetrics."

"Now what did he mean by that?" Matthew asked when the door had shut. His face was a little red. "I guess I shouldn't've stayed."

"He wasn't accusing you of planning to trifle with me," Sally said laughing. "It was just a little underhanded thrust at me. Come along into the kitchen and we'll have our eggs."

"You must've been pretty busy this summer," he said when they were sitting cozily at the kitchen table forking up eggs and crunching on toast. "I thought of calling you a few times but Dud said you were away. I didn't know you were singing till I ran into Si and he told me."

"Yes, Dudley wouldn't tell anyone that his sister was in show biz. Tantamount to walking the streets." Sally buttered a piece of toast. "You should have come up to hear me sing though. I was quite good, people told me."

"As a matter of fact," he said, "I was kind of sore for a while. About you refusing me a date, I mean. Not that I expected you to give me a tumble but you were a little, well, abrupt."

"I was?" Sally said innocently. Cast your bread on the waters, darling, she thought, and then contritely, "Well I didn't mean to be. I was having my problems that day and you were just the last straw. But I'm sorry if I was rude."

"It's okay. Anyway, maybe I imagined it. Well, you know, I did think about going up to hear you sing. I read a thing on you in the paper . . . What's the matter, Sally? You look a little strange."

"It's nothing." It will go away, she thought. She held herself together tightly and tried to keep her eyes from blurring. Bloody eggs. Blasted Scotch. "Excuse me," she said, quickly getting out of her chair, and ran wretchedly to the bathroom.

What, after all, could be funnier, she thought when it was over, leaning weak and red-eyed against the basin, looking at her pale face in the mirror, what could be more ironic and ludicrous and double-crossticky than to get morning sickness at night in the presence of Saul's brother who was learning to be an obstetrician. So this was what happened, she thought, washing her face and combing her hair, this was woman's joy and lot in life. To be sick, to not enjoy a mouthful of food or drink without regretting it, to have a good body that was admired and to have it grow obese, distorted, and ugly, and eventually after a few babies, to lose its lovely, clean lines forever. And I would, she thought, surveying herself in the mirror. I'm not exactly a sylph now and my mother ran to Rubens proportions. But it was mad to let her mind run on this way. She was not going to be trapped. She turned the bathroom light off decisively and went into the living room where Matthew was starting up the phonograph and said there was something rather important she had to ask him. And asked him, in a great big rush before he managed to say one word.

He was embarrassed. He shifted his feet around and looked all over the room, anywhere, but in her direction. Poor thing, Sally thought charitably, after she'd finished and leaned back in her chair, he'd gone for a walk on Beacon Hill looking at the lavender bow windows and wasn't it all too quaint and suddenly an uncouth bear had grinned at him through one of the storied old panes. She smiled, a little grimly, at this ridiculous conceit and watched him struggle to get his bearings, having recovered much of her aplomb now that she felt better.

He was frowning and looking quite serious now and, no longer uneasy, had taken a pipe and oilskin pouch from his pocket and begun to stuff the bowl intently. Rather nice with a pipe, not fake tweedy as so many did.

"I'm sorry to be so slow on the uptake," he said finally. "I admit that it's not what I was expecting. Did you tell me this, by the way, because you found out I was doing my residency in OB?"

"No. I would have told you anyway. You're the only other doctor I know. I couldn't tell Dudley."

"Well, in the first place, I don't think you should get all worked up about it." He struck a kitchen match inelegantly on the sole of his shoe and grinned at her boyishly. He's on home ground now, Sally thought interestedly, and isn't worried about how he ought to act. Probably an awfully good doctor or will be someday. Quite sure of himself, confident and skillful. It was a quality she admired.

Something Dudley would undoubtedly never have. Or she either, not really knowing how to do anything important.

"You've no idea how often this happens," he was going on. "I mean women getting nervous about delayed menstruation and the very worry about it delays it more."

"I've never missed two months before," Sally said calm and positive now very much as if she were talking to a sympathetic and polite doctor in his office, and not someone she was so entanglingly involved with, although he wasn't aware, fortunately, of all the nasty nuances.

He was puffing steadily at the pipe and finally the tobacco in the bowl glowed red. He took it out of his mouth and looked at it thoughtfully. It was one of those cheap drugstore briars and Sally wondered how he would look with a good English one. I must get him one, she thought, because even if he can't do a blessed thing for me he's terribly sweet to sit here and listen and make me feel that it's all quite normal.

"Well, if you're sure of that," he said, "then the first thing to do before you get more worried is to go to an obstetrician, have an examination and take a test."

"Wouldn't the examination be enough?"

"Two months," he pursed his lips. "Oh, usually they can tell by that time, but if you want to have pretty certain corroboration, the tests are pretty much ninety-nine per cent infallible. If you don't know any good OB's I can arrange for you to go see a friend of mine. Jenni Asch."

"The German lady with the art gallery?"

"Oh sure. I forgot. Well, then, you know her, so you can just call up and get an appointment."

"I don't really know her," Sally said twining an end of blonde hair around her finger. "I saw her at the opening that day but I wasn't introduced. My aunt knows her. They're messing around with Planned Parenthood. But I scarcely want to introduce my aunt's name into this, since it wasn't really planned." She smiled at him and he began to look uncomfortable again.

"No, I can see that," he said hurriedly. He rubbed his forehead a bit, opened his mouth and closed it. Finally he took the plunge. "Look . . . er . . . Sally . . . D'you just want to . . . uh . . . discuss . . . the medical aspects with me, because that's all I have to say about it. You go see Jenni and get the straight dope."

"What other aspects are there?" Sally said teasingly.

"Because, frankly, I don't know why you're telling *me* about it.

I mean, all you said was that you thought you were pregnant and you don't seem too worried about it so, for all I know, maybe you're well, married, or are planning to get married, so naturally you'd like to know for sure as soon as possible. I mean that happens all the time . . ." His voice trailed off and hung questioningly in the air.

"Does it? I'm happy to hear how reassuringly normal I am." Sally took a cigarette, lighted it, inhaled a few puffs and felt sick again. She squashed it out quickly, breathing deeply and noticing as she did so that her bra seemed too tight. It's begun so soon, she thought, and in no time at all, I'll be getting thick in the middle, my breasts will be as enormous as an unmilked cow's udders and everyone will know. "I'm not married," she said, "and I'm not planning to be. And I talked to you because if I find out that I am pregnant and I have no doubt about it, because, to be perfectly honest, I know how it happened, then I shall be wanting an abortion."

He turned his head and looked at her directly. "All right," he said pleasantly, "I thought something like that might be the case. You want me to be honest with you?" He didn't wait for her nod. "Okay then. I won't do it for you. I don't know if that's what you had in mind, but if you did, it's out. I don't know enough and even if I was already a licensed OB, I wouldn't do it. And very few reputable doctors, particularly in this town, will."

"But it's not impossible?"

He chewed on his thumbnail and looked at her speculatively. "In Boston it is, just about, as far as I know."

"Then I could go somewhere else."

"That's not the point," he said, getting heated. "Abortion is a lousy business for everybody concerned. Have you had one before?"

"No, dear heart," Sally said shortly. "I've always dealt with honest men before."

"What exactly do you mean by that?"

"Precisely what I said," Sally flashed.

"You mean, it's the—uh—the fellow did it on purpose? Does he want to marry you?" He looked baffled as if he'd never heard of such a thing before.

"Yes, unbelievable as it might seem to a man," Sally said coolly, "it's all quite true. And I don't like being tricked."

"Well, whoever he is, I can see his point."

"What about my point?"

"Look, Sally, I don't know the ins and outs of the thing and it's none of my business. But I will tell you what I do know something about and that's abortions. On the whole they're dangerous because the majority of them are illegal and because of that, most of them have to be performed without anesthetic which is goddamn painful and without much aseptic care. A doctor can go to jail if he's caught, so very few of them dare do it, which leaves the work to the foulups and they can, by not using proper precautions, kill a girl. And they have. So, if you want to take my advice, if you like the guy at all, and you must've, marry him."

"That's quite out of the question, I'm afraid."

"He's married, you mean?"

Sally gazed at him severely. "I didn't know they considered experience in marriage counseling a requirement for an obstetrician."

He flushed, quite noticeably. "Well, you wanted my advice and that's it." He stood up and put his now cold pipe back in his pocket. "I'll be getting along now. If you'd like me to call Jenni for you, tomorrow, I will. Let me know. Although you could probably do it yourself."

"No need to get your back up," Sally drawled. But there was a shakiness in her voice that she knew he noted. "So you won't help me?"

He came over to her and stood looking at her concernedly. "I'm trying to only you don't want to listen. Look, I don't know you at all, Sally. But I'd say the same to any girl who was in your fix. It's not worth taking a chance on if there's any other way out. I mean, look"—he swallowed and raked fingers through his hair, as if, by all these intense gestures he could make her understand what his words obviously couldn't—"I'm a friend of your brother but even if I weren't, even if I were a complete stranger, I couldn't take a chance on sending you to some quack, provided I knew of one, who's on the shady side of the law, who'd maybe only do it halfway, or leave you in a mess of infection. It's like asking me to send you out to get murdered. And I won't do it."

Sally examined her fingernails. "You're painting this ineffably sordid picture simply to frighten me. I'm perfectly sure that there are many women in this country who have abortions performed by reputable doctors who do it properly, though I daresay the price comes high. Now all I ask you to do is to tell me if you know of any. Is that too much to ask? You said something before that interested me about most of them being illegal. Meaning that some are legal. Now why couldn't I get one of those?"

"A legal abortion," he said pedantically, "is usually performed for any number of good reasons on women who shouldn't have children, because the birth of such a child would either be dangerous for the mother or the child. For instance, if the patient has a seriously damaged heart, or vomits so much she can't take in any food at all and no other treatment helps, or possibly, if the mother is a really serious psychotic. In which case, not only does a medical doctor have to advise and sign for it but also a psychiatrist or two."

"I'm sure," Sally said with studied carelessness, "that it would be horribly dangerous for me to have this baby. I might get to be awfully psychotic. Could I see a psychiatrist and convince him of that, do you think?"

Matthew Berman smiled at her grimly. "If you'd ever seen a psychotic you wouldn't ask a damnfool question like that."

"You're awfully stuffy, do you know that?" Sally said coldly.

"And you're awfully ignorant."

"You've got a lovely temper, Dr. Berman."

"I'm sorry," he said, a little shamefacedly, "but you're so damn sure of yourself."

"I'm not," Sally said seriously. He wanted her to tell him she was afraid. So she would. It was quite true. If abasement was the price she had to pay for his help then she would grovel. Why he wanted her to do this she couldn't imagine. Was it that a fallen woman must act like one and not give herself airs and graces? "I'm really quite upset."

"It doesn't show."

"You really think people should show their emotions."

"Sure," Matthew Berman said. "I don't mean they should tear their hair, but there ought to be some way to be honest about how you feel without getting embarrassing. I don't go for this stiff upper lip, oversophisticated junk."

"Perhaps you're right," she said thoughtfully. Why, she thought, looking at him carefully, seeing for the first time that familiar once-over, only respectfully, of course, why the poor lamb is smitten. He wants to put all this on a personal basis, he wants us to have a common ground. I'm to like him for himself, not merely consider him a doctor to whom I turn for medical help of a sort. Sitting here like Queen Victoria conversing with the gardener isn't going to open up the floodgates of his warm, giving spirit. "You do know of someone," she guessed.

He compressed his lips and shifted his eyes away from her. "I'd have to ask around," he said guardedly.

Sally smiled at him warmly. "You're very nice. Why did you have to be so poisonous about it before?"

"Now listen," he said hastily, "don't get your hopes up. It might come to nothing. And this whole discussion could be completely academic anyway. Maybe you're not pregnant. So there's no point in even thinking about it until you go see Jenni. I think the fastest way is for me to call her and try to get her to fit you in tomorrow."

They stood at the door rather awkwardly. "You're terribly sweet to do all this for me," Sally said. In a way, she meant it, and wondered whether to give him a gentle, sisterly kiss on the cheek as an incentive. Fill him full of extra zeal. But no, he was awfully serious. Might take it amiss and abandon her to her fate worse than death.

"I haven't done anything yet. And there's one thing I want to tell you Sally, right now. If I can't turn up someone who operates with every precaution, every safeguard taken against infection, then you might as well count me out." He looked suddenly very angry. "Then I suppose you'll start making the rounds of all those dirty little offices, full of the fat, old drunks that somebody thinks might do it for you because they're so obviously down on their luck. Oh, they'll tell you they have to examine you first to make sure, with their crummy, dirty fingers, because they like having a chance to feel up a beautiful young girl, but after that they'll say no, Christ it's a sin and what dyou take me for kiddo and it's against the law and go get married. They're the ones I'd like to lock up because compared to them an abortionist with a wealthy practice that does it all very carefully and aseptically, is a saint."

"And what if some of them say they will?" Sally inquired. Her stomach was beginning to turn over and she wanted to shriek at him to stop but she had to keep standing there all poised and interested, because she wasn't going to be frightened. She was not.

"If you're very lucky," he said, "some guy will either do it for you some night in his office with a minimum, an absolute minimum, of precautions and no anesthesia, so, well there's no point in kidding you, you'll suffer a hell of a lot of pain, and maybe you'll be all right, maybe. Or he could do it another way, inserting a, well, there's no point in going into it medically, but you're supposed to go home and expel the foetus yourself, and hope to hell there's no hemorrhage. Sometimes it works. Sometimes it doesn't. You get a little pain, a little bleeding, a few cramps, and then, everything stops. You think, oh that's all there is to it, I'm okay now and you wait a month for your regular menstrual period to start. It doesn't. You go back to this doctor you paid a damn good sum of money to and he says he's sorry it didn't work, that's the chance you take, if you'd only come back sooner he could have done it over but it's too late now because you're about four months and he wouldn't chance it,

446

that late. So there you are, defrauded out of your money and still pregnant and not a damn thing to be done about it, because you've been operating outside the law."

Sally drew a deep breath. "Are you a deliberate sadist, Dr. Berman, or do you simply want to subvert the confidence of laymen in the medical profession?"

"I'm in the medical profession," Matthew said, "and lice like that shouldn't be. That's all I'm trying to say. And, if I'm frightening you, it's only because I want you to see reason."

"You honestly think," Sally demanded indignantly, "that an impossible marriage or an illegitimate child is better than an abortion?"

"Better than some kinds," he said firmly. "Anyway, even if you don't want the child, there are plenty of people who would. So think it over, Sally. Birth, the life of a child, a human being, is a serious business, not just a shopworn story."

"And where would an obstetrician be without it?"

"He wouldn't be. There wouldn't be any obstetricians. There wouldn't be any people."

"You think I'm a horror, don't you?" Sally felt herself almost near to tears. He was so damnably clear-eyed. But he wasn't having a baby. So why should she care what he thought. Just nerves, she thought, just foolish, female, pregnancy nerves.

"You know better," he said and there was that look in his eyes again. "Well I'll call you tomorrow and we'll go see Jenni. Maybe everything will be okay."

"I hope so."

So now your nasty secret is out, dearie, Sally told herself as, cynical and sickened she went back to her room, undressed and crawled into bed, after taking one of Dudley's large collection of sleeping pills. And whose bosom should this knowledge be nestling in but the uncle of this tiny foetus in her womb. She flung herself on her side angrily. No sense thinking about Saul now. She wasn't going to tell him at all, ever. Would this strong-minded brother of his think it funny to go telling all about Dudley's indiscreet sister to his medical colleagues? No, he seemed somehow, terribly trustworthy. She thought of the way he'd looked at her with long-black-lashed, gold eyes. And how all the warnings and lectures had been delivered, the first ones with great conviction and then, after she'd caught his furtive desirous glance and sent it back with the slightest hint of invitation, he'd broken down and said he'd try, albeit with many hedgings and contingencies. Because he had his own little ideas about her and probably had entertained them since the day at the

447

gallery when he'd asked her for a date and there, providentially, she was, right in his hand, like ripe fig, oh so at his mercy. Or rather, they were at each other's, in a convoluted web, the inner meshings of which would appall him if he knew. Well, let him, she thought, it was his brother who had done this to her, even if he didn't know it, let him hope and try, I don't care, if he only helps me get rid of this illness in the safest possible way. Oh madness, Sally thought disgustedly and pulled the yellow silk comforter over her head.

He called her early the next afternoon. "If you go down right away Jenni can see you. She's finished all her office appointments and is waiting around for word from the hospital about a delivery so she might have a lot of time and she might have a little. She wants to talk to me anyway, so I said I'd bring you down and introduce you, because she's giving you an appointment outside office hours as a kind of favor to me."

"How darling of her," Sally said, flip again, with the sunny new day.

She picked him up on the corner of Joy and Myrtle. It was a brisk, nippy gold-and-blue fall day and he was standing with his hands in the pockets of a gray tweed burberry, his dark hair all ruffled by wind and the tips of his ears red, quite handsome and smiling as he climbed into the car.

"You're looking much better," he said, settling back. "This car really suits you."

"Mmm," Sally said trying to decide whether it would be best to take the car up Joy and down along Beacon or more easily down into Cambridge. "It is rather nice, isn't it?" Easier to go down hill. It was a silly argument she and Saul always had, this which way to go one. Saul. He'd called her earlier and there'd been a stupid row because she'd had to cancel their date and he'd banged down the phone. "It's one of those old houses on Commonwealth out by the Bay Road, isn't it? Well, we'll circle around on Charles then. What on earth did you tell Dr. Asch?"

"I just said you were a friend named Mrs. Mayhew and you were new in town, not knowing any obstetricians and you thought you might be pregnant. And she was so busy shouting Ach and Good and telling me why she wanted to see me that I doubt if she even heard half of what I said."

"And how do I explain the missing Mr. Mayhew?"

Matthew shrugged. "I'll leave that up to you. I don't see, frankly, why the subject should ever come up. All she's going to do is examine you. She probly won't bring up the male in the case unless you do."

"Tell me," Sally said, "what do you really think the chances are that you'll know of a doctor who'll perform an illegal abortion with all the preventive measures you mentioned last night? Doesn't anesthesia and so on, increase the risk of being found out because of having to have more people in on it?"

"That's right," he said laconically. He took out a pack of cigarettes and lit two, giving her one. "So the chances are damn small."

"Otherwise I'll have to go to one of those horrid people you mentioned."

"Yep. Only not through me."

"Then," Sally said decisively, "I shall have to try to get it legally."

"Huh! She won't do it for you if that's what you're thinking."

"One can only try," Sally said. She stopped abruptly at a red light at Commonwealth and Newbury and they both jerked forward a little.

"Take it easy," Matthew said. And then. "I wouldn't even ask her if I were you."

"You're not me. That's the thing. No man would understand."

"Uh huh. What about the guy? What does he think about this?"

"I haven't told him and don't plan to."

"Listen," he said and his voice was really shocked, "you can't do a thing like that. He had a right to know. It's partly his too."

"The decision is mine," Sally said coldly. "Because I'm the one it's happening to. And if he'd played fair this wouldn't have happened. He didn't and so he must take the consequences, minor ones in his case, major ones in mine. Haven't you seen enough women in labor to know that I'm right."

He sighed. "I suppose. Only I feel kind of sorry for the guy without even knowing him. He must've wanted you a hell of a lot. I can understand that although it is kind of a crazy thing for a man to do."

"Would you go to extremes like that if a girl you liked wouldn't marry you?"

"Of course not," he said in amazement. "Only someone a little sick would do a thing like that. Is he?"

"I didn't think about it before, but I suppose he is."

"Well, you're not an everyday kind of woman," Matthew Berman said, "so maybe he just went temporarily off the beam about you."

Sally drew the car up before the white door which bore a discreet, little brass plate JENNI K. ASCH M.D.

"That's a courtly speech," she said smiling at him, "and you didn't even ask me how I got mixed up with someone who's a little, as you put it, sick."

"I could guess, but I won't."

"You mean you don't know me well enough."

"Well, there's nothing like a little medical conference to change strangers into intimates."

"What does the K stand for?" Sally whispered as they pushed the door open to the tune of the buzzer.

"Oh some funny name like Kunigunde."

Jenni herself, bustling in a white starched coat, threw open the inner office door to them. "Ach, Matthew," she cried in her shrill, cheerful voice, "so good to see you."

"This is Mrs. Mayhew, Dr. Asch. Here, I'll take your coat, Sally." He hung both coats up on the rack. "You've still got your rubber gloves on, Jenni."

"Yes, yes. I have been making a small hemoglobin test."

"She doesn't have a laboratory," Matthew explained grinning to Sally, "sends all the big work to a technician near here, but she's got one of those girl doctor sets, a couple of little test tubes and slides so she can putter around in her spare time."

"Ha. Funny joke," Jenni said indignantly. "Would it not be silly to send someone to the technician for a simple hemoglobin test which here I can do easily and accurately and not have the poor patient charged extra. So, Matthew, now we be serious, I have not much time perhaps. Mrs. Mayhew and I will go into the examining room and you will either sit here and read or go back into the house. The door is open and today we have received a package of new records from England. The Glyndebourne Festival which we attended last summer. Wonderful. So you may listen, as you please."

"Is that the 'Orpheus'" Matthew asked interestedly, "with the contralto who gave you ecstasies?"

"Yes, yes, Ferrier. A marvel. The voice of a true angel."

"I'll go listen then. Though I don't know how I'm going to get caught up with all my reading. I do some of my best reading here," he added to Sally.

Sally sat down on a low, modern easy chair upholstered in a frieze-like pumpkin-colored material and looked around; at the couch covered with black corduroy, the pale brown and turquoise pillows and some pieces of old copper in the few bare spaces between books, at the low teakwood coffeetable before the couch piled high with the only concession to a conventional doctor's office, *Lifes* and *New Yorkers*, at the delicate, abstract landscape watercolors framed on the walls above the bookcases. But most of all, she looked at the books. The waiting room glowed, quietly burnished like an old, beautiful, autumn colored, Persian rug because of all the books. Except for an area grudgingly allowed the couch, each wall was lined three quarters of the way up with books; contemporary books still in their bright jackets alternated with heavy, serious brown-and-gold leather volumes and side by side they jogged for position, spilled over, were crowded out of oldfashioned glassfronted cases into low, more modern shelves. They were piled up in precarious double rows on top of the bookcases and they threatened the lives of the copper trays and pitchers, the ceramic ashtrays, and some small wooden figure sculptures.

"Amazing," Sally said.

"You'll never see another doctor's waiting room like it." Matthew said grinning. "Jenni figures to throw the patients off this way. They think they're in some potentate's library where drinks or coffee'll be served any minute so they don't get nervous waiting."

"You like it, hah, Mrs. Mayhew?" Jenni Asch said, smiling at Sally.

"It's quite wonderful."

"It is different, is it not? But I like it better myself than the kind of the dark leather chairs, so uncomfortable, with the dim lights and the heavy greens everywhere and the torn magazines about how the ladies saved their marriages. Ugh!" she shuddered, "dreadful. So goodbye Matthew, I see you later."

"Do you read all these books, Dr. Asch?" Sally followed her into the examining room and, in its clean, white, medical glitter, she began to be afraid again.

"As to that," Jenni Asch threw up her hands resignedly, "that is another question. No, I do not get the time for the reading that I would like to. And sometimes, I may confess to you, the sight of all the books makes me very angry. They sit there and I want so much to read them, but I am so gottamn busy all the time. No, it is Gregor, my husband, who does much of the reading and the buying of them also. Where he finds the time I do not know." She began to strip off her rubber gloves and then went to the sink to wash her hands. "But even if he does not read them, he buys, always he buys." She scrubbed at her hands busily, as if they were recalcitrant vegetables, with a rough brush and a great deal of lather from a plastic squeeze bottle.

"So, Mrs. Mayhew, you will please to take off your panties and girdle and blouse and loosen your brassiere and get up on the table." And still talking rapidly, she dried her hands on a sterile towel and pulled on a fresh pair of gloves. "If I knew I were not to be called to the hospital at any moment you would first go to the bathroom to deliver for me a urine specimen and then I would take in writing for my record a history. But I would like to do the examination first and the other things may be done at another time. However, of necessity, I must ask you *some* questions now. When was it your last menstrual period?" She switched on a glaring lamp and moved it close up to the table where Sally sat uneasily blinking in the light. "You please to move yourself forward on the table, so, lie down, and put your legs in the stirrups here. And relax. Do not so tense up the arms. It was the end of August you say, so you have missed two periods, hein? Good, then one should be able to tell. We will also of course have you take a test at the laboratory. It will cost perhaps ten dollars. You do not mind?"

"No," Sally said in such a low voice that she could hardly hear herself. "I'd like to be sure."

"Just so."

She squeezed some colorless jelly from a tube onto her rubbered finger. "Now make yourself loose. This will not hurt."

"I know." But in spite of herself she could not control an involuntary shudder at the brisk, probing exploration of those hidden, secret parts of herself that she would never see.

"So. It is finished. You may sit up now." She moved quickly, taking off her gloves and hanging a stethescope around her neck.

"Am I . . . ? Sally didn't really know how to ask.

"Yes, I would say. Two months pregnant. Now I will listen to your heart and take your blood pressure."

"You're sure?" Sally murmured, feeling sick again, after the cold touch of the stethescope on her naked breast had made her wince.

"As sure as one can be at this stage," Jenni Asch said briskly, palpating Sally's half-covered breasts. "Yes, the breasts seem enlarged, the nipples darker than normal. Do you not feel a tingling there sometimes and the brassiere is perhaps tight?"

"Yes," Sally said unwillingly. "But I've had those sensations before menstruation very often."

"Just so. It is not a conclusive symptom. Nor, this early, is the uterus. I would say that you are pregnant, yes, and in another half month I could tell completely but since you wish to be absolutely sure you must go take this test. You may get dressed now, Mrs.

Mayhew, and then if you will please sit in that chair by the desk we shall put something in the record."

"Some of those old tooled leather volumes, your books, I mean," Sally said, desperately searching for something, anything to say to avoid the horrid, black gulf yawning in her mind, "they look quite heirloomy. You know, nineteenth-century bindings and goldleaf topped pages." This small, pale, thin woman with the mass of light brown hair pinned carelessly on top of her head, who was so competent and brisk and cheerful, acting as if it were an everyday occurrence, which it was for her, of course, this annunciation. How could she possibly ask her about such a thing as a legal abortion? And yet she must . . .

"Brought them from Germany," Jenni Asch was saying. "Of course we had much more, but many were sold. There was so little room for them and they brought a good price which was necessary when we were first here, beginning. You must look at the art books. The reproductions they make now are wonderful. Gregor is completely insane for art books. You are interested in art, Mrs. Mayhew?"

"A bit," Sally said vaguely. "I know very little really." She'd finished dressing and sat down in a swivel chair by the desk, nervously fumbling in her bag for a cigarette. She doesn't remember me from the gallery opening, she thought, just as well.

"So, now," Jenni Asch said briskly, sitting down at her desk and uncapping a fountain pen, "a few particulars please."

"Of course," Sally said, shaking out her hair, straightening her skirt and looking around for an ashtray which Dr. Asch, after scrabbling around the desk under some papers, finally found and handed her saying pleasantly, "Well, from now on, perhaps less smoking."

She began to write busily in the large black ledger before her, occasionally throwing out questions about childhood illnesses and age and were there any operations or long term ailments. Sally answered mechanically, waiting for the big question, the husband kick. What shall I say, she wondered, perhaps I could lie, I could say that my husband goes to school or some such thing and he doesn't make enough money to support a child and couldn't I please, Dr. Asch, have you certify that I need a legal abortion and perhaps if you'll be so kind and non-law abiding, perhaps *you* could give me such surcease from pain. She couldn't really make much money. Her office for all its entrance's intellectual charm was part of her home and didn't look wildly well equipped. But then paying a fat fee for an abortion wasn't consistent with the poverty-stricken husband theme.

Still abortions couldn't cost more than having a child. But Dr. Asch peering questioningly over the light horn-rimmed glasses perched crookedly just below the bridge of her sharp, bird-like nose was asking something.

"I'm sorry," Sally said, "I'm afraid I . . . didn't . . . I wasn't . . ."

"I ask," Jenni repeated, her voice cracking a little with loudness, "if you are happy to be having this child because it is your first."

Sally took a deep breath. It was time now. There would be no more polite fictions between the happy, roseate mother and the obstetrician who was to help her along to the great and ennobling moment of lying-in and childbirth. It was practically implicit in Jenni Asch's manner that that was how she considered matters and Sally hated to disillusion her . . . "No," she said, "I'm not."

There was a sudden silence and Jenni Asch's pen stopped scratching illegibly on the clean, blue-lined pages of her ledger.

"And your husband," she asked quietly, "how does he feel?"

Oh, she's keen, Sally thought, feeling all hard and cold and rejecting, she's sharp, she smelled corruption and lack of proper credentials on me from the beginning.

"My husband was killed in the war," Sally said dispassionately looking at the glowing end of her cigarette. "Early in the summer of 1945, to be precise."

"So," said Jenni Asch and she screwed the cap back on her fountain pen, very slowly and carefully and leaned forward and looked at Sally, her small, clever blue eyes behind the glasses, unmistakably serious. "I may tell you now that if you want to get rid of it you have come to the wrong place."

They looked at each other steadily. "I want to try to get an abortion legally," Sally said.

"It is impossible," Jenni Asch said quietly. She shook her head, "I am sorry. I can do nothing for you. Matthew should have told you. I am surprised at him." She picked up the telephone. "I call the laboratory now and arrange for your test." She dialed, her small, peaked face grave and unsmiling now and spoke rapidly into the receiver in German. "He will see you in an hour, Mrs. Mayhew. It is quite near here. I write the address and he will send me the results by day after tomorrow. If you call here, I will tell you. He will expect to be paid after the test and my bills are sent monthly."

"Thank you," Sally said, taking the slip of paper from her. She stood up. "Will you tell Matthew goodbye for me. I'm sorry if I disturbed you and it isn't Matthew's fault because he did tell me."

"No, no," Jenni Asch said abstractedly leaning back in her chair.

"It is I who have given you offense. I am sorry. But you have no idea how many, many times I am asked this. In your case, I confess I was very surprised. Will you sit down please, Mrs. Mayhew. I would like so much to help you but I do not think you realize the difficulty of your situation."

Sally sighed impatiently. "Dr. Asch, you mean well I'm sure, but there's really not much point in discussing all this. I cannot have this child."

"Listen to me," Jenni Asch said rapping authoritatively on the desk. "If you would want a doctor to certify that you need a legal abortion you cannot be so closemouthed. There would have to be some better reason than your health which is excellent. How did this happen to you? It is not a prurient curiosity that makes me ask this. I haf better things to do with my time. You were not raped?"

"No," Sally said. It was so absurd that in spite of her gloom, she laughed. "By no means."

"No," said Jenni Asch, glancing at her shrewdly, "I did not think so. But it is wise to canvass all possibilities. Then it is because of this foolishness of the laws against birth control in this state that encouraged your carelessness?"

Sally stood up again, picking up her bag. "I have all sorts of jolly equipment, Dr. Asch," she said flippantly, "which I got in California when I was first married and which is in excellent shape, just checked over and replaced last year and which I'm ordinarily quite faithful about using. And I sympathize with you about Planned Parenthood but none of this applies to me. I regret having wasted your time."

"You are very honest. I admire that. You were careless and do not deny it. So many of the girls who come to me pretend that they are fools to whom men can do anything. In most cases it is as much their responsibility as the man's. But they will not confess to it."

Sally smiled, feeling rather friendly toward this odd type of a woman. I'll make one more try, she thought. "Dr. Asch," she said, "is there any way I could get a legal abortion if I tell you what truly happened? That I was tricked into this pregnancy by a man who wants very much to marry me and simplemindedly conceived this the way to do it, by lying to me, the one time I did not use the contraceptive and telling me that he would. And because I was sort of drunk, I didn't notice."

"Sooo." She looked Sally over from head to foot, very quickly, then pursed her lips and nodded. "Yes, I could believe that. And you do not want to marry him because he is not . . . hochgeboren

. . . I do not know quite how to translate that, but, in sum it means he is not of the same class as you."

"I'm afraid I don't quite know what you mean."

"You are very polite. Yes, in America I realize such unsuitability is not discussed. They pretend that it does not exist. Nevertheless, it is true, no?"

"We are very different," Sally said carefully, "and a marriage between us, particularly with a child, wouldn't be at all right. I don't think it has much to with the other thing you were talking about though."

"You are thinking that it is impolite of me to venture such a guess about this man, no?" Jenni Asch insisted. "But I am correct, am I not?"

Matthew didn't tell me she was a witch, too, Sally thought, hochgeboren indeed.

"It is curious," Dr. Asch was saying almost to herself, "the similarities that exist between groups no matter in what country, even in a democracy. The highest and the lowest have much in common. The middle-classes are left to their own dull moralities." She shook herself slightly and bounded out of her chair. "But these vague theories do not give you the answer you wanted hein? Still, the answer is not of any use to you either."

"You won't then?"

"I cannot. These are not sufficient grounds and no doctor would consider them. It is not even possible for me to send you to a psychiatrist, although you may go yourself if you wish and simulate a strong crise de nerfs but you would have to be a very good actress, very, very good, and even so I doubt whether you could convince any trained person that you were mentally unstable. Come"—she slammed shut her black book—"you go to the bathroom and leave for me a urine specimen and then you will come back to the apartment with me and we will, with Matthew, have coffee and listen to some music and we will talk. There are perhaps other ways to solve your problem."

"I can't imagine what else there is to say, Dr. Asch. If you can't help me then I shall simply try elsewhere." Sally closed her lips tightly to check the disappointed words which would surely come tumbling out.

"Aha!" Jenni said with magnificent scorn. "You are, my dear Mrs. Mayhew, very young, very beautiful, and very arrogant, I am sorry to say and perhaps I am rude to say it, but nevertheless . . . A child, a life, is not so easily dismissed. What does the father think of this? Or does he not know? I thought not," as Sally nodded her head. "You must have really great contempt for him."

"Dr. Asch," Sally said coldly walking toward the open door of the bathroom, "you are really quite unpardonable."

"I am aware of that," she said cheerfully. "But sometimes it is vital to shock rudely in order to help. The jar for the specimen is on the floor. We see you in the apartment. You must hear the Gluck. It is marvelous. It will make you feel better, particularly since you are a singer yourself, hearing such a voice as Ferrier's will inspire you."

"How did you . . ." Sally began but Dr. Asch had turned out the office light and shut the door.

She's uncanny, Sally thought, alone in the bathroom, looking grimly at the glass jar and thinking how messy all medical procedures were. How did one do it without getting it all over one's hands or anyplace but in the jar. She's horrible, I loathe her, I shall not go and have coffee with her. How did she know I sing, I didn't tell her. Perhaps Matthew did, but then why should he? The only answer must be that she really knows who I am. That must be it, all those sly hints about different classes, she knows all about me, that I'm Aunt Fan's niece and all, why she's a horrible little pry, a supernatural witch and so smug too. How dare she lecture me like that when I'm utterly strange to her? Such presumption. No, she may keep her coffee and her music and overbearing sermons. Hell, Sally thought, having a terrible time with the jar, oh hell, I mustn't cry, I really must not.

Matthew was standing in the outer hallway smoking. "I thought maybe you wouldn't know which door to go into."

"I don't want any coffee," Sally said shaking off his detaining hand. "Please thank Dr. Asch for me. I have this test to take, you know."

"You've got almost an hour." He looked at her closely. "She gave you a rough time, didn't she? Damn her. I was afraid of that. You shouldn't have asked her. Y'see Sally"—he lowered his voice—"it's like a red flag to a bull asking her a question like that. She's crazy about children and couldn't have any."

"And all the girls who come and ask her about abortions are responsible for that?" Sally asked angrily.

"Of course not. And that's only part of it anyway. When somebody comes around and says they're determined to kill themselves one way or another, any doctor worth his salt tries to prevent it. Jenni's just more honest than most. She always says what she thinks. Sometimes it gets me sore too, but she's usually right you know.

457

She's got a kind of extra-sensory perception about some things. Come on, Sally, come on in and have some coffee for Godsakes, she wants you to. She feels very distressed about you."

"Indeed. That was not apparent in her office. Anyway, she doesn't even know me."

"Listen," Matthew said earnestly, "take my word for it. I know her better than you do. You came to her for help. Anybody who does that immediately gets some part of Jenni's heart, corny as it may sound. That's the way she is. She gets very involved and interested in her patients and worried about them even. Look, I mean I know that she's offended you and it's hard for a girl like you to understand her but she's a sterling character, she really is. She does more real good in this city than twenty-five doctors put together. Her fees are very low and although she could charge some of her richer patients more, she doesn't, and the poor ones, half the time, don't pay her anything at all."

"I'm sure she's very noble," Sally said, "and for those who enjoy having a doctor play God to them it must be grand. But I can do without all that personal touch. My problems remain as messy as ever and all the coffeehouse discussions of life's philosophy aren't going to straighten them out."

"You come on back and have a cup of coffee," Matthew said, taking her arm with assurance. "She puts whipped cream in it. It'll make you feel very Continental." And as Sally hung back, he added quietly, "Look, we knew she wasn't going to help you. But I'm still the guy you asked first and I said I would. And I prescribe coffee. If you don't come in, she'll feel quite rightly of course that she's been too sharp-tongued and then she'll get guilty and brood and be hell to have around the hospital. And since I'm directly in line of fire it's only enlightened self-interest."

"Oh very well"—Sally gave in and followed him across the pseudo-marbled floor of the hallway—"if it's essential to preserve your professional peace. Did she tell you her horrid suspicions about my state?"

"Yup. She also asked me if, by chance, I was responsible. I said no, but . . ."

"And then she sniffed, I suppose?"

"She said I should stop looking so wistful."

Sally laughed. "Still, how can you put up with her? Don't you mind?"

"Oh sure. She tries to crawl inside your guts sometimes. But she's such a warm, generous woman I ignore the rest of it. And the big thing is, I'm learning a hell of a lot from her. She's one of the most competent, careful OB's in the city. Here we are . . ."

Jenni was sitting on a tweedy low sofa when they came in, her ear to the phone. She waved at them to sit down.

"Yah, yah," she said impatiently, "yes, well you may tell her for me that if she thinks these far apart pains hurt now and she must have the drug for them, she will be sorry later when they are worse and unrelenting and too much of the drug early will make no effect when she needs it. So, of course, I shall be notified immediately if anything occurs within the next hour or so, but this is very unlikely. In any case, since she is nervous I come to see her soon and talk to her. So goodbye, I see you." She slammed down the phone and said, "Zum Teufel," loudly, whether because of the conversation or a hairpin that had just slithered down her neck bringing with it a clump of hair, Sally didn't know.

"The primiparae." She stabbed the hair back in place, indignantly. "Such a lengthy procedure, such boredom and fears while they wait. I always like to keep them at home as long as possible but this one, the membranes ruptured at six o'clock in the morning so she has been there since seven and nothing has happened. A few faint contractions which go away and return sporadically. I have been to see her at nine and now I shall go back again but I fear it will not happen until the middle of the night."

"What are you giving her?" Matthew asked interestedly.

"Some sedatives now to calm her and let her rest for the hard time ahead. Later, when the real pains begin she will have Demerol and for the birth, gas. She is a young, healthy girl and I do not believe in too much of drugs or anesthetic. Unless some complications ensue but I do not foresee them. I hope however the birth occurs before the other patient of mine who is due tomorrow, I believe, goes into labor, because she is a primipara of thirty-seven and to make things more difficult it will as of now, be a breech. So, although I shall try with her a short test labor, I am afraid I must do a section."

"You think that'll happen while I'm on call? I'd like to watch but if I'm on call I won't be able to."

"Such boyish enthusiasm," Jenni clicked her tongue. "It does you credit, no doubt, but if you miss this one, there will be, believe me, many opportunities to both observe and participate in the future."

"Anyway," Matthew said, "I don't understand why you bother to give an elderly breech primipara a test labor. Why not schedule her for a section before she even goes into labor?"

"That is a matter of opinion. I myself prefer to give a test in most cases because I think it is always better to have a normal birth if possible. Although I am not happy to have her suffer pain for naught."

"I still think it just causes everyone more trouble," Matthew argued. "And then you run the risk of uterine infection."

Jenni shrugged. "My dear boy it is so easy to theorize. Each case is different. But we bore Mrs. Mayhew so now we stop this shop, do they call it, talk, and you will go to the kitchen for the coffee. The woman has set all the things on the tray. If you will simply pour the coffee from the percolator to the white pot and bring it, we will be ready."

"Sure," Matthew said, getting up and casting an uneasy glance at Sally as if he just remembered she was there. "But you generally give Scopolamine for such a labor, don't you?"

Jenni pursed her lips and nodded her head ever so slightly in Sally's direction. "Yah, yah," she said hastily, "sometimes. Go for the coffee and do not make my guest nervous."

"Oh I think it's all very fascinating," Sally said drily.

"I am afraid the conversation has upset you," Jenni said soberly when Matthew had finally left the room. "That one is so eager to learn he forgets his manners."

"No," Sally said. "I found it very useful actually, to make me more resolute."

"Either way it is not easy. But with birth you have a child which is a wonderful thing."

"Not for me." She remembered, looking at the doctor whose energy seemed to have waned suddenly and left her limp, crumpled and small against a corner of the sofa, what Matthew had said about her wanting children and felt again a warmth and sympathy toward her. I'm sure she's really good, Sally thought. "You don't know me at all," she said, "though you've made some awfully good guesses about me. I know it sounds cruel and silly. It's no good trying to explain. There are certain limits beyond which I can't go, just as you can't."

"You could not perhaps consider marrying him for a short time until the child is born?"

"That would be a hellish thing to do to anyone. What you don't seem to understand, Dr. Asch, is that I don't want this child born at all. It would be the result of a mistake and wouldn't belong anywhere."

"How do you know?" Jenni Asch demanded sitting up and staring at her fiercely. "How can you know such a thing in advance?"

It seemed suddenly very important to Sally to try and convince this woman that she was not a complete bitch and perhaps, in the process, drive away the lingering tiny doubt somewhere in the shadows of her own mind. "Because," she said, "I know this might sound completely crackpot to you but that's how I was brought up. Not really fitting in anywhere. My brother and I were both the result of a mistake my father made, it's not important what or how, and neither of us are terribly happy because of it."

"And your mother, she did not make the mistake?"

"No," Sally said, wondering why in the world she was being so damn confiding to this disapproving strange sandpapery woman. "I don't think she ever conceived of life in terms of mistakes or choices. She simply lived the best and easiest way."

"As a vegetable you would say."

"Perhaps." More like an animal but let us not be disrespectful to the dead, Sally thought, remembering the few times she'd been allowed around, when her father was supposedly sick, either lying in a darkened bedroom or off in some sanatorium and her mother was always going somewhere with one man or another or being all perfumed and lush and cushioned, having parties with very few women and the inevitable eternal admiring men. "I'm afraid," she said trying to sound light about it, "that my mother didn't have much maternal instinct. She had children and felt it was all right to send them off for strangers to take care of."

"Ah," said Jenni, "that is what the rich do. But all the same it does not sound like an American mother. So many I have met here are wonderful, conscientious, interested . . . But I digress. You are afraid of behaving like your mother?"

Sally laughed. "I am very much like her, which is all right when I'm by myself but it wouldn't be if I were married and had children. But that's not important. What I am concerned about is having a child grow up, confused, with feet in two different worlds."

"So," Jenni said, "you have your own little private psychology all worked out. And yet, it has happened to many children and they have survived and done well."

"But you don't know. You simply say those things. I do know. Not only because I lived through it and have not, as you so optimistically put it, done well, but because it happened in an even worse form to someone I loved very much and it ruined his life and perhaps, even contributed to his death." She paused, rather embarrassed. "You have a bad influence on me, Dr. Asch. I don't usually go on so personally."

"It is good sometimes to break down the reserves. That is why the psychiatrists and priests do such a plump business." She sighed and thwacked her hand tensely against a pillow. "Ach! They used to say, the religious ones, that the sins of the fathers were visited on the children and we pooh-poohed such ancient, unscientific moralities and yet, sometimes I feel that perhaps they knew more of the truths than we with all our equipment, clarity and reason." She stood up, "Very well then. You do what you think best. I disapprove. As a doctor I am committed to life. But perhaps for you it is necessary. I don't know. Sometimes there is no right answer no matter how much we think we know. Only you must be very careful. I will not tell you of the pitfalls because I have been grim long enough. So now we listen to music." She went over to the phonograph and clicked the switch. "This is the 'Dance of the Blessed Spirits.'" She put a record on. "You know the story? Orfeo searches for his dead wife and must go through Hades to Elysium . . ."

"Yes," Sally said in a low voice, "I know it very well." She felt chilled and haunted. How the hell had she gotten into this witch's gingerbread house? Compose yourself, she thought. Nothing uncanny or weird about it. Normal. She likes music. So do you. That you should like the same music, know the same stories, even have the same bad dreams is not at all unlikely.

"Sorry I took so long," Matthew said, holding the door open with his foot. "What's the matter with that maid of yours, Jenni? She unplugged the percolator before the coffee perked, so I had to wait. Said she was sure it was getting overheated or at least that's what I thought she said . . ."

"She is very nervous, poor thing," Jenni said. "She has not been here long and understands not much English. She was Gregor's mother's, how do you call it, lady's maid, and when all her family died in the war, we sponsor her to come here."

"That's a switch," Matthew said setting the tray full of eggshell white china down on the coffeetable. "You believe in turning the other cheek, huh, Jenni?"

"The family was kind and helped us in many ways when we were in trouble," Jenni said softly. "Not all the Germans went crazy. Do you use cream and sugar, Mrs. Mayhew?"

"I drink it black, usually, but I think I'll try some of that whipped cream, please. What a beautiful pot."

"I am not an artist," Jenni Asch said handing one of the bluish-white cups and a saucer to Sally, "but my aesthetic sense is often pleased by such simple things as deep brown, strong coffee being poured out of a plain white china pot. It is very old china, it was in my family for many years, over one hundred fifty, I think. But this means nothing, this worship of things, several pieces have been broken when we brought it here, after being cherished so long. My family," she added, sipping at her coffee, "and Gregor's too, have been in Germany for no one knows how many hundreds or thousands of years longer than the china and then—poof!"—she snapped her fingers—"we are one day dirt and vermin and must flee to avoid digging our own graves. So the things do not matter, it is the living genes, the pieces of oneself one passes on to one's children. The Limoges, even so, will be here many years after Gregor and I die and we have no one to leave it to so it will be sold at auction, so I do not care if it is all broken while I live. I use it always."

"You could leave it to me," Matthew said, spooning some more whipped cream into his coffee. "Maybe some nice girl will marry me if I come equipped with Limoges china as a dowry."

"He is a fool, is he not?" Jenni said looking impishly at him, "but I take you on your word, Matthew, this way. You marry a nice girl, and I give you the Limoges as a wedding gift. So, now, I take better care of it, now I know it is to be passed on to your children. I will have one of my rare cigarettes, Matthew, to seal the bargain."

"You can have a cigarette," Matthew said, lighting it for her, "but there's no bargain. I was just joking."

"I was not. Ssh! She is about to sing the 'Che Faro.'"

Music was a sentimental trap, Sally thought, mesmerized against her will by the soulsearing voice. It left you wallowing in a wash of pent-up emotions, with easy tears in your eyes and gulled you into accepting all kinds of ridiculous melodramatic situations and people. Crude, irrational. The Perils of Pauline with that old silent film piano accompaniment was at least unpretentious. But aloud, when the aria was over, to please her hostess, she was all praise.

"I knew you would like it," Jenni said eagerly. "A contralto always appreciates another one, more than the sopranos. Their ears are tuned to the lower notes from their own voices. What do you sing? Opera, lieder?"

Matthew laughed. "You're an unreconcilable German, Jenni," he said.

"Actually," Sally said, "I'm a kind of blues singer. I don't work at it much. I've always wanted to sing the other sort of thing but I never studied."

"Why not?" Jenni demanded. "If you have the voice and the desire it is a crime not to train it."

"Oh, it was a vague notion and I don't believe I ever spoke of it to anyone. I don't think I would've been encouraged in any case."

Jenni gave her a compassionate look. "Yes, I understand. It is unfortunate that to take up a serious study for a career and pursue it is not considered necessary and proper for a girl like you. It is a great waste."

"I daresay I wouldn't have been any good," Sally said, "so perhaps it's as well. I've been wondering, Dr. Asch, how did you know I had these slight pretentions toward singing? Did Matthew tell you?"

"Not I," he grinned at Jenni. "It's the old seeress herself who figured it out. I told you, she's just alive with ESP."

"There is nothing supernatural about it," Jenni said. "What nonsense. I use my eyes and ears, that is all. You have the voice of singer, the chest of a singer. It is very simple."

"Why don't you give up medicine, Jenni," Matthew suggested, "and offer your services to Scotland Yard or the FBI. There are plenty of OB's around but human bloodhounds are scarce."

"You are a grinning imbecile," Jenni said pleasantly. "Patients will flock to you and you will become very rich just because you are so witty."

She saw Sally to the door. "So goodbye, my dear. I am sorry we have so many harsh words. I hope all goes well with you. And, remember, I shall be very happy to deliver your baby, should you change your mind. Perhaps, anyway, I am wrong and the test will say so . . . We will know in two days. So call me and come sometime as a friend to listen to music."

Sally drove furiously downtown after parceling out another urine specimen to the laboratory and wandered aimlessly through three department stores and one shop, looking for the proper pipe to give Matthew. She found nothing that suited her capricious taste. Why buy him anything, she thought, it'll just be a bribe and he'll know it. He was her only frail hope and what if he couldn't do anything? What will I do, where will I go? The music from the *Orfeo* aria haunted her but it's very beauty only made her feel more miserable, more out of touch with the pleasant normal world where people listened to music and drank coffee and were not in any danger of having to traffick outside the law, or suffer pain or bleed to death. Oh yes, she thought, leaving the store and wondering what to do next, they've frightened you, any moment now, you'll tuck your tail between your legs and marry Saul. If she went home Saul would call her and want to know what was the matter. He'd want to see her and suddenly the thought of his touch was unbearable. She crossed the street and went into Loew's Orpheum.

In the darkness of the movie the people on the screen flickered by her. What they were doing from one reel to the next, or who they were or what artificiality they were contriving themselves into she didn't know. Couldn't stop thinking about herself. It was as if she were all alone on an island.

I used to think my life so dull, boring and empty, she thought ruefully, and now, this very minute, if I could only have back one of the most ordinary days of my life, I'd sell my soul, granted I have one. Just to sit in a movie, lighthearted and careless, nothing to think of but what's happening to these insubstantial people, to have no shadow of an unknown, horrendous terror, a ponderously moving inevitability, hovering over her. Matthew, he must help, he must. She began to feel sick again and at the same time, quite hungry. This vile body of hers with the blight inside it. She left the movie quickly and drove home. The sick feeling had disappeared by the time the car was parked and now, she was intent solely on food.

She met Dudley on the second landing, wearing his best or only mildly shabby tweeds.

"Your inamorato is here," he said. "Been here for an hour waiting for you. I told him I rahlly didn't know where you were or when you were to return and he pawed the ground and snorted."

"I don't wonder," Sally said, "if you talked to him in that rahlly tone."

"I am going to the theater with Deborah, and won't be home till after midnight so you two peevish people will have only yourselves to vent your spleen on. Seriously, Sara, I know it's none of my affair, but hasn't he begun to pall on you yet?"

"Oh!" Sally said furiously and rushed past him up the stairs.

"Baby," Saul said when she whirled in the door, "baby, where've you been?" He got up from the sofa and limped quickly toward her holding his arms out. "What's the matter? I've been going crazy. I couldn't sleep. Are you sore at me?" He pulled her close against him and kissed her face and neck as if his life depended on it.

"Don't!" She pulled away.

"Waddya mean, don't? What's with this don't now and last night and this lousiness over the telephone all of a sudden. I've been going nuts all afternoon since I talked to you. I've been running around trying to get hold of an apartment. I can't stand this any more. And I came to tell you about it. I'm moving in tomorrow. And now you're giving me the cold shoulder. What is it?"

465

"Nothing," She flung her coat on the chair. "You look dreadful." His eyes were red-rimmed and there were smudgy dark shadows under them. His face, looking at her, seemed crumpled in agonized despair. She noticed for the first time that there was a wide streak of really grey hair by his right temple. All this intense emotion, she thought distastefully, really impossible, how did I ever get involved in it. "Come into the kitchen and tell me about the apartment. I must eat. I'm starving."

"Eat," Saul muttered following her. "I could eat you. I want you so damn much and here you are talking about food."

He sat silently in a cream and red kitchen chair and watched her as she made a cheese sandwich and bolted it down along with a tall glass of milk. "I guess you're not in love with me any more huh?" he said twisting his mouth into one of those miserable smiles that Sally despised, the asking for sympathy, oh don't bother about me smile. "You got your appetite back."

"Oh, don't be an ass. I haven't eaten all day, that's all."

"Yeah. What've you been doing?" His voice was casual but she noticed that he was having trouble getting his lighter to work. He sat there, absurdly pathetic for such a large man, with a bravado cigar gripped between his teeth, looking downward and pressing desperately on the lighter with a shaky hand. "Been with some other fellow and too busy to eat?"

"Here let me do that." Sally put down her milk and went over to him, taking the lighter from his powerless hand. The flame spurted up blue.

"Are you giving me the brush, honey?"

"Don't be absurd."

"I've been feeling that cold wind for a couple of days now. Today, on the phone, I felt it right here." He slapped his stomach. "Maybe I'm crazy, I dunno, maybe because I been expecting it to happen ever since I met you." He held her hand tightly. "I thought I could stand it but all afternoon when I thought, maybe now, maybe this is it, I knew I couldn't. Is it true, Sally, have you got somebody else?"

"No. Saul, must you be so melodramatic. I saw you yesterday and because I had things to do this afternoon you go off madly and imagine all sorts of wild nonsense."

"I'm sorry, honey, honest I am." He pulled her down in his lap. "But you just seemed so kind of distant the past coupla days and you didn't seem to want me to touch you." He put his arm around her. "Honey, I know you get sore at me when I talk like this but you're my food and drink, my life, you're everything to me. If you left me, I don't know what I'd do. There'd be nothing left to live for."

"Tell me about the apartment," Sally commanded, "and no more silliness please." Again, with the pleasure-arousing hands on her, the wonderful exciting body against hers, she was beginning to feel passionate and happy, not sick, not grey and dreary. That wonderful, alive sharpness. Perhaps Dr. Asch was wrong, she thought, almost gaily, perhaps the test will prove I'm not pregnant at all. To feel good again, to enjoy going to bed with this marvelous bull of a Saul, to love eating and smoking and buying new clothes. What joy. Oh, let it be true, so I won't need to hurt Saul, who makes me feel so good in bed, and myself, especially, the horror of pain and bleeding to death.

"This racketeer I know," Saul was saying, "he's been married and divorced twice, you know, and he's going to Florida for the winter and I can have the apartment for as long as I want. It's behind the Statler. So you can come and be with me all day and in the evening. Willya, honey, will you?"

"Of course. A real racketeer?"

"As real as they can get."

"I didn't know you knew people in the underworld." She rubbed his mouth with her fingers and he kissed them.

"Sure," he said. "They ain't the kind of associations I'm proud of, although I've never done anything wrong. But I had plenty of chances to. It's a sucker's game. Oh, I don't see these guys much, once in a while, in a poker game. When I was fighting is when I ran into this guy. He was always around making fixes or trying to. Never fixed any of my fights though. He likes me although he tells me I'm a stupid, honest sonovabitch that'll never get anywhere."

"How marvelous of you to resist temptation so manfully," Sally said.

He put his hands on her breasts. "God, they feel so big and full. Maybe because I'm not used to them any more. It's like a thousand years since last time. Let's go to bed." He began to unbutton her blouse.

"It was only last week. Do they seem that much larger?" They're not, she thought, afraid again. Why did he have to say that?

"Like the biggest melons, the sweetest, the juiciest in the world. God, I'm crazy about you, Sally. It's worse than it ever was. Hurry up baby, get ready . . ."

There was no need to bother, Sally thought, stricken with the absolutely sure knowledge, the happiness had been temporary, she really knew, had known all along, the test would be positive, but let us have this one perfect time now, she'd not think about it, now, when really wanting in the old way, before the evil days came. She went to the bathroom and brushed her teeth slowly and carefully and when she came to him, lying naked on the bed, half his body covered with the sheet, she sat down on the edge of the bed and deliberately pulled off her shoes and lay, fully clothed beside him.

"Sally," he said feverishly, "what are you doing?"

"I want you to undress me. You never have."

"I can't wait."

"Yes, you can."

"All right. Anything you want."

She lay passively, feeling more and more aroused as his impatient, wild hands tugged at her clothes. There were ripping sounds and she shuddered, fiercely excited, as he seized her and now she became completely uncontrolled and tasted blood from his mouth and knew vaguely that she'd bitten his lip but that he didn't know it and for one clear instant before merging unidentifiably with him, she thought, this is the best I shall ever have, in my whole entire one life and I am going to kill it, along with part of myself and perhaps all of him who gives me this wonderful gift, generously and humbly, I am going to do it, to be cursed and doubledamned, through the sin of pride. Saul, o my love, my darling, I am so sorry.

But he didn't hear her and what good would it have done anyway?

Two

Matthew was beginning to feel a little clotted with whipped cream and the heavily unusual silence of Jenni's living room after Sally's departure. He'd drunk up all the coffee and they'd played through the whole final act of *Orfeo* and still Jenni hadn't uttered more than four words. Talked herself out, giving Sally hell, he thought wrathfully.

"It is nice," Jenni said finally rousing herself ten minutes after the last note had died away, "that Eurydice is brought back to life, but always, though I am glad for the happy ending, I know, regrettably that it is unreal, too simple. Please to turn off the phonograph, Matthew. I had planned to go over with you certain aspects of some of the patients I expect to be in hospital tonight, as assistance for you when you are there. But now I think it is more important to speak of more personal matters."

"What could be more important than my career?" Matthew demanded.

She peered at him cynically and pushed her glasses back up to the bridge of her nose. Clear autumn light glittered ice-like through the tall windows facing them, catching on the glasses and hiding her eyes, making her seem for an instant both blind and sinister. "That is precisely what I consider to talk to you of."

"All right Dr. Caligari," Matthew said resignedly, "go ahead."

"You are disrespectful. It is for your own good, I speak." She pointed a bony finger at him. "You are going to do a very foolish thing and try to get that girl an abortion because you have forgotten that you are a doctor and are suddenly only an oversexed male. Please"—she held up her hand in a theatrical request for silence as he opened his mouth—"do not think I blame you. Men are very simple in structure and a girl who looks like this one—"

Matthew lit a cigarette irritatedly. "Jenni, if you're going to rake me over I've got a few things to say to you first. I brought Sally down here to have an examination, to be treated with courtesy as befits a patient who pays you a fee, not to have the Articles of War read to her. You're so wrought up with this Planned Parenthood and agitating for birth control laws you forget it's patients you're talking to and not politicians and churchmen."

"Ach!" Jenni said disgustedly. "They are so selfish, so pigheaded. If they have seen so many sad, poor women in my office and in the clinics, and so many poor, deprived children as I see, not a minute would they hesitate."

"You overestimate them," Matthew said acidly. "Also the power of religion."

"No, no," Jenni said, shaking her head. "We will do it yet. I do not give up hope. But your friend, Mrs. Mayhew, it is girls like her that make me most angry. She is intelligent, no fool, she is educated, for her to be careless is worse than the ones who do not know."

"I gather it was the man's fault," Matthew said almost apologetically. He leaned back in his chair sighing a little and looked hopelessly at his cigarette.

"Oh yes," Jenni said loudly, "she told me this with great hauteur. That he would dare, this peasant, to deceive her into marriage."

"How the hell do you know he's a peasant?" Matthew asked with great interest. "Honest to God, you just meet the girl and most of the time all you see of her is her female organs and already you know her whole story. She didn't tell me anything about him."

"And you would like very much to know, eh?" Jenni said shrewdly. "It is pure envy."

"Sure it is," Matthew admitted, "I asked her to go out with me once and she refused."

"So by getting her what she wants now you think you may succeed this time."

"Well, if you're so well-informed, tell me this, Jenni, mein schatz, why won't she marry the guy? Because he's a peasant? And she told you that?"

Jenni made an impatient noise. "Stupid boy! It is just such innocence on your part that gives me to worry about you. Of course she did not tell me. I simply look at her, at her clothes, at her manner, I listen to her speech. I hear one word and I know much about her and the man. She is from a very good, wealthy family, yes? What they call here a Yankee?"

"Sure," Matthew said grudgingly. "That's not hard to figure."

"Very well," Jenni said triumphantly, "if then such a girl would say to you that the man 'simplemindedly' thought of this trick of making her with child in order to marry her, you would not know that she looks down on him, that he is not of her group?"

"Oh, hell," Matthew grumbled, "all this European class structure stuff."

"You may sneer," Jenni said complacently, "but it exists here, as you will find if you get your way with that girl."

"The hell it does," Matthew said heatedly. "That's why Americans can't understand Europeans. People do move up and down here, you know. Horatio Alger still exists and so do silverspoon radicals."

"Yah, yah," Jenni said nodding emphatically, "there I agree with you. Nevertheless the fences are in place unless you are rich and public. But to return to your friend, for such a girl it is quite correct to go to bed with the chauffeur, but it is not done to marry him."

"Ah," Matthew said feebly, "she's not like that. I mean, she's not a snob."

"You hope not," Jenni said crisply.

"Anyway, I don't see her taking up with a lout. From what she told me he sounded a little bit crazy."

"You do not like to think that your precious Mrs. Mayhew is more inclined to use her glands than her head, do you? No, you do not, you are turning red."

"Listen," Matthew said, annoyed at her impossible perception. "Doctors aren't supposed to make value judgments, remember that sometime, will you?"

"I do not make moral pronouncements," she said emphatically. "Never!"

"Only every two minutes."

"My dear boy," Jenni said scornfully. "You are blind to all else but the magnificent body and the sweet, blooming face. Have you told her how she can ruin all that loveliness, deeply told her? Or failing that, even the possibility that she may after, never be able to have a child when she wants one."

"I threw a bad enough scare into her as it was without adding that. In fact, I overdid it a little."

"Then why are you planning to help her?"

"Who said I was?" Matthew asked warily "Jenni, listen. I'm not going to do anything to get myself into trouble if that's what you mean."

"Well, I should hope that you would not be that crazy," Jenni cried. "I admit that it entered my head but I knew you would not be so foolish. No, there is more to it. I beg of you, Matthew, leave this thing alone. There is something, I sense, of, no, I shall not say the word I wanted, let us use instead, destructive, yes, yes, she can destroy that girl. She will bring you only to grief, someway, I do not know how."

"Hey, Jenni," Matthew said gently, "take it easy will you?" He leaned forward, offering his cigarette pack. "Step inside ladies and gentlemen, see Madam Doctor, the famous clairvoyant. Leads two lives. On the one hand, an apostle of science and reason, with the other dabbles in the occult. A tea leaf reading with every spontaneous birth and a horoscope after every section."

"Hah!" Jenni said, puffing inexpertly at her cigarette, "you think I am a little crazy, no Matthew? But it is . . . ah the phone."

At last, Matthew thought gloomily, why didn't the darn thing ring ten minutes ago and save me from her gipsy keenings. As if he wasn't in enough of a pickle, having committed himself for some crazy reason to help Sally without the least idea how to do it, he had to listen to Jenni, the self-appointed voice of his conscience, crying woe and doom. Here he'd been going along, minding his own business, happy enough, in a half-ass sort of way and suddenly he was in the midst of a lunatic comic strip like that one in the Sunday *Tatler* with the two disapproving professors, one bearing a book called WHAT TO DO and the other one holding a companion volume entitled DON'T DO IT. He read it every Sunday and had since he was a kid, had never seen it anywhere else but in Boston and it was never funny and neither was his predicament.

"Ten minutes apart," Jenni was shouting, "and they are hard you say?" Yes, you must go immediately and I shall be there very soon. So, you must be very calm. All will be well."

"Now that," she said as she hung up, "was my thirty-seven-year-old primipara. I must go at once."

"I'll get your bag," Matthew said with relief.

"I have not done with you yet," Jenni said struggling into her coat. "Why do you not drive to the hospital with me? If you want to hank around there, I will let you know if I decide to do the section."

"And I suppose you want me to drive so that you'll be more free to burn my ears?"

"Since you must be back in the neighborhood anyway," Jenni said practically as they got into her unpretentious Chevvy, "you might as well come with me. The subway will not be as entertaining. Yes, you laugh. I know I could as well be talking against the wind as advising you. You will do as you wish, I know, but at least I have tried."

"So if I go to the dogs it's on my own head, huh?"

"It is very amusing, hah?" Jenni shouted above the roar of a truck starting up next to them at the light. "Well, we cannot tell the young. They must suffer the pain as if it were handmade with each generation. But I want to tell you, Matthew, you have a something that is rare. This is what impresses Gregor and I about you from our first meeting. You wish to help. No matter what you would have done, anything you have specialized in, you would do with heart. And with women too, you will be very good, you will answer questions patiently, give them time, advice sometimes, let them talk as I do, not rush them out with the big bill in hand. This, before Freud, many doctors knew was necessary, not only to treat them organically."

"You embarrass me, Jenni, honest to God, you do. I think you project a lot of virtues on me that you want me to have. It's all part of your talent for seeing things that aren't there."

"Your humility is charming," Jenni said drily, "but it also can be dangerous. You wish to make yourself out as a nothing and there are many people in this world who will be eager to accept you in your own estimation and make even less of you, in order to aggrandize their own worthlessness. They are not happy unless they make of all they come in contact with as miserable a dry stick of a wretch as they are. Because if it were not for goodness and strength and vitality and, you laugh, love, the wicked, the haters, the malcontents, the corrupters, the weaklings would not be so obvious. Do you know that the devil is not just a funny, ancient story?"

"You're way over my head, Jenni. Such things to me are crazy."

"Huh," she said angrily, "again you mock, you pooh-pooh, you pretend ignorance. The devil is a word, a symbol used to signify the bad impulses within us that cause us to lose our capacity for the good work we may do. And there are many in this time, in this world, who have no capacity for good, nor indeed for anything. They are the empty, those who make small, who jeer, who do not want to see enthusiasm, love of life in people around them. Who do not understand goodness, joy. To them, it is all a pose, a fake and they try to kill it if they find it. They have no ideals, no love. They fasten onto those strong ones who have all this and suck from them. They are the users and destroyers of people. And the terrible thing is, they know not what they do. They laugh if you try to tell them. They call you phony, a bleeding heart, a do-gooder, a poor fool. Oh yes, I have heard all those words and you can prove nothing to such people. They are deaf to all but what they want. They take and take and give nothing."

"If you're trying to tell me Sally is . . ."

"I tell you nothing about her," Jenni said shortly picking up her bag as they rolled into the driveway of the hospital. "I say merely that this that you have within you should not be destroyed. It is important for your work, your future, your usefulness to others that you do not get involved personally with such a girl."

"You're raving mad," Matthew said slamming the car door and following her up the walk to the pillared entrance. "You act as if Sally were some sort of vampire. If I do a favor for her, that's all it is. I'm not compromising my career. And if I happen to like her a lot, it doesn't mean I'm going down the road to drink, drugs, and suicide. Half the time you act as oldfashioned as my grandmother who shaved her head and wore a wig."

"I will put it to you simply," Jenni said turning her w's into v's as she always did when excited. "It is not that I think that she is wicked in the way we think of it. It is that she does not care. She has a strange emptiness within her, that one." They stood by the elevator. "Do you not think it odd," Jenni demanded, "that she will not tell the father of her child that she has it? Is that not a natural feminine reaction to seek the protection of the male?"

"She explained all that."

"However she explained it, it sums up only that she despises him. I, myself, would think twice before tendering my love to a girl who feels thus about a man she's slept with."

"I tell you what, mein herz," Matthew declared frowning at her, "you think I'm too soft for her, only you don't want to say so, that she'd get rid of me too after I'd been her errand boy. And I think that's a damn unflattering thing to think about a guy you pretend to have such a high regard for."

"Oh that would happen. I have no doubt of that. But not because you are soft. For more social reasons. And from that you would get hurt. It is nothing unusual and you would recover. Although if you had sense and not a pain in the groin, you would not need to even be scarred in such a fashion. No, it is another sort of tangle which you as a doctor should not have to shoulder the burden of, because you need all your head and mental clarity for your work."

"Okay, Jenni, okay. I read you. Now let's drop it, huh? I'll go have coffee and call you on Maternity in about an hour to see how things are."

"Well, you will see," Jenni said, glancing exasperatedly at the elevator man who stood by the open door of his cage. "Perhaps she is not disturbed enough to warrant a legal abortion for mental health but there is something there you should not fool with. And, finally, as a doctor you are forsworn to life. You should not, therefore, try to get her an abortion. Let her get what she wants from laymen."

"There are two sides to that story."

She threw up her hands helplessly. "Ach! Well, I have done my best. You may call me later but I do not know if I want you in my OR today. I am so bothered by your stubborn stupidity."

Matthew bent over and clicked his heels, picking up her gloved hand and kissing it. "Auf Wiedersehn, Frau General Doktor. We will meet in some better, kinder world."

She pulled her hand away quickly. "Goodbye, clown. Someday you joke on the other side of your face." She marched into the elevator, her slight body bent a little to one side by the weight of her heavy medical bag and disappeared behind the swiftly clanging doors.

It never paid, Matthew reflected, as he stood in line by the coffee urn of the cafeteria, to have too much respect for anyone's judgment. Take Jenni now. As an obstetrician and gynecologist she was sure and skillful and knew what she was doing but the minute she strayed out of her own territory, it was pathetic. She became naïve and simple, reverting to all sorts of feminine silliness, crazy mysticism, traditional morality, falling back on simplicist labels. He hated to admit it, but she was just as woolly-witted as his aunt who talked about sticking with your own kind. And Jenni, in a way, was worse because she was crawling with notions derived from living in a European world of rigidly marked class boundaries. He ordered a piece of ratty looking prune Danish to go with his coffee and sat down at a coffee-stained table near him, to avoid being knocked down by a hurrying nurse. From Army mess hall to Army mess hall in three years, he reflected, the story of his generation . . .

Now, he thought, taking his pipe out, I am here, a man with a mission. Ask around, he'd said, who . . . where . . . why had he made a crazy promise like that? Meant asking almost every guy he knew in hospital and perhaps some of the nurses, and of course, no matter what he said, everyone questioned would immediately assume that he was the moron who'd put it in the oven, so either he'd be a cad, or, since doctors were a cynical group, by and large, a careless boob, a glomp, a schlemiel in a classically funny situation. On second thought better not ask any nurses, not even Peggy, who, of all people'd be likely to know, because nurses gossiped like hell and he didn't need any such reputation following him around all his life. In fact it'd be infinitely better if he didn't have to ask anyone in Bay Colony. Some members of his class were doing residencies in other hospitals. He'd tap them too but still . . .

How about some non-medical people? Let's see, there was Si, he might, just might, but what an unmerciful ribbing he'd have to take from that joker. Who else? Saul . . . Saul knew a lot of very shady specimens who'd be sure to have an acquaintance with all the sleaziest outside the law doings in the city. Well, it'd only be if worse came to worse that he'd ask Saul for anything and for something like this, God . . . he could imagine his brother's laughter and jeers. Come to think of it he hadn't seen Saul much for a couple of months, maybe longer. Sophy said she thought maybe he had a girlfriend because his temper had certainly improved and he was never home. Impossible to contemplate the kind of girlfriend Saul might have, in front of Sophy anyhow. It might mean Saul'd be a better person to approach now. But only if it was the last avenue and it might well be.

Jesus Christ, he thought in a kind of unbelievable, unlikely nervousness, this is serious! I'm it. If I don't find that girl somebody decent to go to, she'll offer herself to a butcher and it'll be my fault. Oh don't be a goon. Since when are you so damn important? She's got money and contacts in places you never even get near. People like that always land on their feet and saps like you always waste a lot of sympathy and time worrying about them. Jenni's right. Why be a fool and burn your hands taking somebody else's chestnuts out of the fire? Why didn't she tell the man responsible? Let him get her the abortion. Why throw her burdens on Matthew Berman M.D. an unknown, non-suitable escort? But it was a useless kind of mental ranting. He knew he was going to try his damnedest for her, even though he didn't approve, and what's more, he knew why. Damn that Jenni, she knew too.

Thinking of Jenni again, he noted that it was past the hour of waiting so he left the cafeteria and paged her on the phone in Maternity.

"You need not remain around here, Matthew," she yelled happily into the phone, "it will take a while but the birth will be spontaneous. I am so pleased."

He felt depressed and aimless as he left the hospital and walked slowly up Cambridge Street. Ordinarily, he walked around on Charles and up Pinckney or Mount Vernon because it was a better walk and he liked to look at the old houses and the view of the river from the Hill and think how good it was to be living here and how swell it was not having to take dull subways out to Mattapan but today, he didn't care. It was almost six o'clock and a damp, strangling dusk coming on and he knew he ought to go eat somewhere and go to the hospital library and study or home to do the same and sleep but the lousy Danish had ruined whatever appetite he had which wasn't much.

Here he'd spent the whole damn summer in a sweat about Sally, crazy to see her again, until finally he'd given up hope and then yesterday, for Godsakes, after all this time going up there, casually expecting to see only Deborah and Dudley and all of a sudden there Sally was, looking more terrific than he'd even remembered and they'd seemed to be getting along so swimmingly and he'd been imbecilically encouraged because she'd asked him to stay after Dud left until he found out why. For a few minutes there, after she'd told him, he'd hated himself and as for her, boy did she make him sick. But that hadn't lasted very long. All she had to do was look at him. She was just oozing with sex, every glance, every movement of hers was freighted with a thousand messages to that old, primitive, hairy-chested id. But it was a special kind of sex, he couldn't define it, but he knew he'd never had quite the same speculations and fantasies about any other girl. She looked like she could make a man jump through hoops and think he was in heaven doing it . . . Jenni's right, he thought, irritated with himself, I'm using my genitals for brains.

He was almost to the corner of Hancock and Derne when he remembered that Si Hunnicutt lived in the house just opposite him. Now that was an idea. He'd drop in on Si and maybe see what he knew. And even if he didn't, there'd be some cheering up which right now was badly needed.

"Ah, what timing," Si said, after going through a pantomime of intense joy on the landing as Matthew came up the stairs. "You have just missed our workhouse supper of ancient stew embellished with abominable canned soup. You may, however, partake of the dessert, mocha fudge ice cream, if you promise to help me with the damnable dishes. Caroline"—he jerked his head at the closed bedroom door—"is getting ready to go to a grisly female rite known as a baby shower and thus has no time to attend properly to the duties of her hearth and home."

"Are you having a fight or something?" Matthew sat down and lit a cigarette while Si dished out the ice cream. "Want me to leave?"

"For Godsakes, no. There's nothing two quarrelsome people like more than having an uninvolved third party around to provide a disinterested arbiter for grievances. And if you leave I'll have to think about or work on my thesis since Caro won't be here to distract me and I couldn't stand that."

Matthew reflected as he savored two helpings of the ice cream that the supper Si was still grumbling about had probably been a hell of a lot better than anything he'd get in the hospital cafeteria or any local greasy spoon because Caroline was a terrific cook so, in one way, it was too bad he hadn't dropped in a little sooner. On the other hand he'd been through this wrangle about weekday meals with them before and tonight he was too jumpy to enjoy it. Caroline claimed, with justice, he thought, that she was too tired when she came home from work at night to cook elaborate meals and that Si, whose classes were usually over by four in the afternoon ought to make the suppers once in a while as Tom Baring frequently did if Ella was involved in painting. Si said that Baring was a subversive who was bringing about the downfall of the ordered universe, that cooking was a woman's game and that Caroline was a deceitful jade who had inveigled him into love by inviting him to little dinners of beef Stroganoff and home-baked lemon meringue pies before they actually began to live together. After that, they usually had a fight about Caroline's cat, a supercilious Siamese who, Si said, was fed lobster and paté, while he starved to death and the mice overran the apartment. The cat was nowhere in evidence tonight. Caroline had loaned her to the Barings, Si explained, rapturously licking his spoon, because he had threatened to throw her out of the window.

"Say, Matt. Guess who I ran into the other day? Joe Bernstein as ever was. Remember him?"

"Very well." Matthew lit a cigarette and accepted the cup of coffee, Si sloppily poured for him, from a large Italian pottery pot.

"From the grimace of distaste I gather it is a memory you do not dwell on."

"Oh, he's not a bad guy. It's just that I spent so many years bigbrothering him through Med School that he got to be a big bore with the perpetual crisis and lovepangs over girls. Still, that was a long time ago and maybe he's grown up and stopped being such a general allround foulup."

"The tale of woe about a girl in New York that he unfolded to me, telling his beads all the while, would not indicate that he has changed a whit," Si said, helping himself to more ice cream. "He was doing a residency in pathology there, you know, and although he says he didn't dig that specialty, it was plain to me that his heart was too broken to concentrate on mere medicine. He was probably eased out."

"But it's amazing how he never learns. I mentioned that you had an apartment around here and his eyes got wistful and he said he'd have to look you up, followed by, to the uninitiated ear, a seeming irrelevancy about lack of privacy in hospital resident quarters and his family in Mattapan. No place to take girls. Obviously having started in again with fresh zeal since he got back here. So expect to hear from him. He's got a residency now in opthamology at Beth Israel. Bubbled happily about strabismus until even my well-focused eyes crossed."

"That won't last," Matthew said cynically. "He approaches medicine the same way he does girls. A wild crackbrained enthusiasm followed by disillusion and grief. Thanks for the warning, Si, I'll try to avoid him."

Si poured out more coffee for them and gazed at him grinning. "You mean you're not going to loan the poor mewing tomcat your apartment for his amorous sport? Sometimes, I wonder about you, Matt, whether you've ever felt the hot liquorous blood rise to your head? You're always so damn cosy. Ever lost your head over a girl?"

"Have you?" Matthew countered.

"I'm not the type," Si said seriously. "Unbalanced love makes people look ridiculous. Of course I'm in love with Caro but I'm just not sentimental and although she'd like me to I'm not going to tear my passion to public tatters."

"Well, I've never found a girl to unbalance me either," Matthew said. Liar, he told himself, you've found one all right, but better not acknowledge it, specially not to yourself.

"That's the way to be," Si said nodding. "Marry a girl with dough and no temperament. Medicine is a taxing enough profession without having wife problems."

"You'll regret all those ashes you're dropping into the plates, Si," Caroline said, appearing all dressed up, "when you finally get to do the dishes. Matthew, it's lovely to see you but how provoking of you to come when I have to go out. How do I look?" She whirled around in front of them.

"Swell!" Matthew said. She did too, he thought. Her red hair was rolled up in a fashionable bun, topped by a flat black hat and she wore a demure gray suit, a few pearls showing at the neck, handsome high-heeled green shoes and, a final note of elegance, a little fur piece, coiled over her shoulders. "Stylish as hell," he added admiringly.

"Oh, my ears and whiskers," Si said disgustedly, "you call this style? Caroline, tell me you're not going out masquerading like that. Why I won't be able to hold my head up in front of the man in the coke and wood logs store if he sees you. Where'd you get that outfit anyway? You must've been hiding that fur piece on me. You know damn well I'd've given it to the Salvation Army if I'd seen it."

"I might've known you wouldn't approve," Caroline said severely, drawing on white gloves. "I suppose you'd think it fine if I wore my burlap skirt and a babushka around my head?"

"Sure, why not?"

"Because," Caroline said coldly, "everyone at the shower would think I was out of my head. Furthermore, if you want to know, I'm very tired of burlap, corduroy, denim, and black turtleneck jerseys. And thick leather belts. And these clothes are rotting in the closet and I have no place to wear them, not even to work because they'd get too messed up there. And I certainly can't when I'm with you. This will be my last chance before they go completely out of style and are motheaten."

"My own dear girl," Si said, "I'll make a bargain with you. If you'll take off the hat and that piece of dried codfish you've got around your neck and the earrings that match your mother's real pearls, I'll promise, cross my heart, to cook one meal a week."

"No."

"Caroline," Si said, quite seriously for him, Matthew thought, wondering what he was getting so wrought up about, "I mean it. My God, isn't it bad enough that for some obscure reason you have to go to a fatheaded, dull piece of conventionality with a gaggle of clacking geese you haven't seen since you developed some intelligence but do you have to dress like those idiots too?"

"My reasons are not obscure although you pretend to think they are, Si. If I don't go Liz's mother will write her sister that I didn't come, and Mrs. Blackwell will tell my mother."

"Fine! When the barrage of indignant and curious letters hit us we'll throw them out unread. If you want to be scrupulous, you can write and say that you don't go to baby showers any more. They're passé. Demodé. Not chic. Even the truth. That all that sentimental, middle-class, henparty suburban tosh is from endsville. Aren't you listening to me? What are you scrabbling in my desk for?"

"I'm looking for my present. Ah, here it is." She drew out a silver tissue-wrapped package tied with elaborate curlicues of pink and blue ribbon.

"We live in a land of lies," Si said to Matthew, pointing at the present. "If any of those bitches were honest they'd tie their offerings in bleeding umbilical cords. You're really going, Caroline," he added sardonically, "dressed up like a square suburban matron carrying that monstrous commercial-looking package so that your mother way up there in Bath, Maine, won't worry about you? In spite of all I've tried to teach you you're going to revert to type. Pah! I thought better of you."

"I'm sorry you had to bring this up before Matthew," Caroline said, picking up her purse and adjusting her fur piece, "but since you did, I want to tell you something and I hope Matthew will forgive me."

Matthew muttered something but Caroline rushed on in a fine sweep.

"First of all, Liz was my roommate at college and we were very close. I've been invited over there hundreds of times and hardly ever gone because you said they bored you. And if I did go, I'd have to ask them over here. You know I can't do that. She'd never understand in all the world. Maybe that's square of her, I don't know. Sometimes it's not so bad being square, I'm beginning to find out. Naturally, the information would eventually filter back to my mother. And I'm not going to hurt her. Now this baby shower has come up and it's a perfect excuse to see her, there'll only be women there and I won't have to worry about problems raised by you, either your non-appearance or your constant appearance and the usual questions as to when we're going to be married. And, best of all, it doesn't require a return invitation. And the final thing is, that if I didn't go, not only would my mother hear of it and write, but she'd get really upset and come down to visit."

"That's another thing," Si said, turning to Matthew unperturbed. "One of the things that haunts my days is the dread that someday Caro's mother will come to visit, in which case I have to move out and go live with my friends. Expect me, any day, Berman, to take up the rickety couch in your front room." He turned back to Caroline who was now at the door. "Very well, my dear, if you yearn for a world full of fur pieces, baby showers, engagement parties, and frosted cakes from caterers which turn out to be little coy party sandwiches all along and shoddy weddings in a hired hall with orchids for all the lady guests and corsages with tinsel ribbons and at the cake-cutting ceremonies everybody sings 'The Cheese Cuts the Cake' to the tune of 'The Farmer in the Dell,' get ye gone. I'll have none of it."

"Oh, you're loathsome," Caroline said, opening the door.

"All the same," Si said admiringly, "no matter what kind of lousy garden club clothes you put on to destroy your beauty, you're still a lovely wench." He ran to the door and blew a kiss out into the hallway. "You're sure you don't want to take Matthew along to deliver a lecture on the fundamental facts of birth. He'd be a bigger attraction than all the pink and blue bootees. Dope straight from the disgorging point. What every baby shower needs."

Matthew heard Caroline laugh irrepressibly and then Si disappeared from view for a moment and sounds indicated a kiss and make up conference.

Si returned whistling cheerfully. "Caroline said to tell you that if you came over more often you'd have a better chance of catching us on a good day. Well, comrade, shall we hit those dishes?"

"For a while there I really thought you two were having an argument," Matthew said as he stood armed with a gingham dishtowel waiting for Si to stop slamming the crockery around and put something in the drainer.

"Never underestimate the powers of your unblemished instinct, old man," Si advised, frowning at a plate. "Now how did that crack get there? Caro will hate me. It's her own fault though, for using this flimsy, foreign pottery. I advocated the purchase of a few of those divided tin trays we used to have in the Army, but no . . . You know this lousy thing is still greasy."

"You might try using some hot water and soap."

"Ah, the aseptic medical mind." Si turned off the cold water tap and rinsed dishes under the hot. "You're right. Much better. I'll have to remember that little trick."

"You're a nut," Matthew said laughing. He polished the plates vigorously hoping that the lingering grease might come off on the towel. "You mean you were serious about the way she was dressed."

"As serious as she was, which was plenty, believe me. You might as well make up your mind to it, Berman, life with a woman is not easy. Thank God, that's done." He threw a handful of silverware into the drainer and turned off the water.

"You forgot the pot."

"Mother's little helper," Si said with a dark glance. "I'm going to ignore the pot. A little myopia is a convenient thing, you uninitiate you. When charged with not completing a distasteful task properly, you plead ignorance, blindness, helplessness. The female then is convinced of your complete idiocy and uselessness and does all the drudgery herself, while you have time for more agreeable matters. Come on, let's leave this greasy scullery and sit down with beers like gentlemen. How would a cigar suit you?"

They lolled and chewed and puffed smoke from their cigars and Si speculated as to what it was about cigars that turned boys into men by the mere act of putting one into their mouths. "Pipes don't do it," he said, turning the cigar around in his fingers and staring at it happily, "cigarettes don't do it, but the trusty old cigar makes of a male a he-man and, in many instances, he assumes almost a city hall aura too."

Matthew only half-listened. He yawned and wondered about going home to sleep. It was unnerving spending a day with so many dogmatic people. Jenni and Sally, and then Si, picking on a girl as fine and handsome as Caroline for some imbecilic reason. What the hell was the matter with Si, anyway? Didn't he know he was being impossible?

"No, I'm serious, Si, this was really it. This was *the* girl," Si launched into such an accurate imitation of Bernstein's nasal protestations that Matthew woke up enough to laugh.

"It's been years since I heard that song but I'd know it anywhere. And he always said the same thing. Every time. Every girl. It was monotonous."

"In a way, he's a kind of classic," Si said, "because he believes himself. He always means it. Anyway, this girl he knew, in New York, was not only a beautiful pneumatic piece to hear him tell it, but her father, was just a couple of nickels short of being a millionaire. He owned a department store or something . . ."

"It's even the same girl," Matthew exclaimed. "They're always rich and zaftig. What an obsessive! And how did he get the brush this time? Used the old man's car and expense account too often, I bet."

"The trouble is, I don't really know," Si admitted ruefully. "My uncontrollable funnybone got the best of me just before the denouement of his lovesong. I mean, like you, I was overcome with dèja vue and was remembering the time he had to mark off all those girls' fertility cycles on a Boy Scout calendar because he was so superlatively careless. Anyway, my uncontrollable guffaws offended him mightily and he clammed up. I was too thick-skinned and hard hearted to understand about *love*, it seemed. Now there's a cat who should've been an obstetrician. It would come in damn handy sometimes, I vum."

Bernstein, Matthew thought, squashing out his cigar and getting up to look for his jacket, his veins suddenly infused with instant energy, *Bernstein*, of course. The sacred, magic name of power. Whether he had gotten careless again and knocked up a girl in New York or not, didn't matter. That schlemiel would inevitably know all about abortionists.

"You're not going, are you?" Si demanded. "It's still early. Don't leave me here alone with my cruel mistress, the thesis."

"Well, at least open the window for Christ's sakes, Si. I'm about to fall asleep with all these cigar fumes." Would Bernstein be at home now? It'd probably be better if Sally had it done in some other city anyhow. Less risk of anyone in her family finding out.

Si flung up the window with a crash and sniffed. "Real post-nasal drip weather," he said. "Weird, but even in the city in the fall, you always smell the smoke of leaves burning in a thousand suburban gardens." He stood looking out and yawned. "A heavy-headed Poe-like night. Can't you just see the stalactites and stalagmites quivering phosphorescently in the greasy air? Although," he added reflectively, "since this is New England, I suppose it's more like an Eliot night than a Poe night. All that yellow fog rubbing its back on . . ."

"That was London fog," Matthew objected.

"Hey," Si said, "you hypodermic pushers aren't supposed to know anything about literature. You're a narrow specialist, remember?"

"I used to like Eliot a lot when I was in pre-med," Matthew reminisced. "Funny, I haven't read a line of his in years but I still remember all of that Prufrock one."

"Ah, you were led astray by that 'patient etherized upon a table' image," Si said. "Just think if I'd stopped there I'd be a doctor now, God save all the people alive now because I didn't. How about another beer? Kill another half-hour with me. That thesis is lying there on the desk looking at me with reproach. You know, I don't think I'd want to live any place else but Boston or Cambridge. Though if I ever do get a teaching job, the chances are skinny that I'll get one here, so I'll have to go someplace else, but will I be in exile, man, dreaming of my Dublin. You figure on staying here?"

"I don't know," Matthew sat down again, feeling the cold beer trickling, pleasantly gassy, down his throat, "I like it here, but sometimes I think it's a little narrow, kind of small."

"You're really free, man," Si gazed at him and shook his head. "No woman and her dreams of home, family and mortgages tying you down. I don't dig it though, Matt. I'd've thought a guy like you would be snatched up long ago. I remember when we were freshmen at Tufts. I used to have to talk my head off to get a girl to go out with me, but with you, one look and the girls swooned."

"The hell with that," Matthew said. "I wasn't that successful. Anyway," he shrugged, "I never really ran into anybody special."

"That's what happens to you Adonises," Si said. "Your heads get turned by success and you end up all blasé and jaded."

"Let's can all this crap about me and go back to your thesis and *your* girl."

"At last!" Si said, "Didn't you know I was longing to pour out my unwashed soul to you, Berman, and you've been avoiding the issue. I could see the sympathy and pity you were wallowing in for poor old abused Caro. Well, for the record I want to tell you she likes living in sin."

"Then you're lucky because *I* never knew a girl, who, basically, truthfully did."

"I'm serious," Si insisted. "All that stuff about her clothes. Well, that's all part of it. When I first met her, the poor putupon girl dressed like that all the time."

"And I don't understand what's wrong with it?"

"Because she didn't like it is one of the things wrong with it. She didn't like anything about her life. When I first met her she was working in one of the offices at Harvard and taking a few ladylike Fine Arts classes at Radcliffe. Oh, she was dicty, man, with her little well-cut suits and real pearls and her Smith accent and her family up there in Bath, Maine, rolling in solidly invested dough from lumber and shipbuilding, all of them wondering why Caroline, two years out of one of the best women's colleges in the country, hadn't made a good marriage but had to knock around in Boston being a badly paid career girl."

"Say, you don't have to tell me about this," Matthew interrupted uneasily. "After all, it's none of my business."

"You walked in on it, buddy boy, like the poor Wedding Guest, so now you're mesmerized by my glittering eye and you have to listen."

Christ, Matthew thought, ironically, leaning back and crossing his legs, if I'd only had the time and the money to become an analyst, I'd've made a good fat sum in the past two days, just listening to all the dark secrets on this Hill, which now are coming to me gratis, dammit.

"Anyway," Si was going on, "after a few dates, Caroline showed me some sketches of clothes she designed, kind of sketched while watching slides in Renaissance Art courses. Beautiful arty things. The

485

poor girl had a terrific commercial art talent, all sorts of ability that there'd been no opportunity to use, ideas for textile designs and wallpaper and interior decoration. Honest to God, Matt, I talked her deaf, dumb, and blind for weeks before I finally convinced her to leave off fooling with this Fine Arts stuff and her little correct job and go to a commercial art school. What a revelation! She started to make her own clothes, arty as hell, looked wonderful in them, stopped going to beauty parlors and having her hair crimped and burned in the latest style so she looked like five thousand other girls, let it grow and from a correct, schoolgirl nonentity she became a beautiful original woman. And you wondered why I got sore to-night. It was an act of rebellion, that's what it was, because she doesn't really like all that claptrap she used to be part of."

"You mean she wants to get married?" Matthew asked.

"She thinks she does," Si said gloomily, "but only, mind you, because she recently received a letter from her mother enclosing a mental stiletto about her age and how everybody to home is married. By God, Matt, do you know that men haven't the vaguest idea of the inherent medievalism, the blasted, bloody ignorance of the way so many girls are raised."

"Maybe you didn't," Matthew said, amused at Si's vehemence, "but I've been miserably aware of it ever since I started going out with girls." He pitched his voice into a falsetto, "'All you ever think about is *that*.'"

"Exactly, exactly," Si shouted. "When I ran into Caroline at twenty-three, she was completely unawakened. She was figuratively wearing a widow's veil, because some 'boy' she'd known for years, somebody she didn't even love, mind you, had had his last date with her before he went off to war, and begged her to give up her virginity for him and she'd steadfastly refused. So, the poor cat got killed, and when I met her, she'd almost talked herself into believing that he was the great love of her life and since he hadn't gotten it, nobody else was going to. It took an enormous amount of effort on my part to dislodge such craziness but I did it, I did it. She flowered, she bloomed, what was marriage but a conventional pattern, she'd learned at last of love and desire. And she knows we'll be married eventually, so why the hell she's getting into such a sweat now, beats me. But she is and we've been wrangling for days. Which is where you came in."

"Well, why not get married then?" Matthew asked. "If you're going to anyway, sometime, why not do it now and save yourself all these battles."

"It's not quite that simple, I'm afraid," Si pulled at his long nose and looked irritably around the room. "Living with Caro and her family not knowing, is one thing. Marriage is a connubial couch of a different color, because I can't support her on the GI Bill. Caro's old man gives her a nice allowance, you know, and she works, so we don't do badly, but if we got married, the pressure on her to stop supporting this carpet-slippered loafer would be terrific and maybe she couldn't take it. She's pretty fond of her parents. Also I dunno if I could stand all that being looked over and found wanting."

"What's the matter with you?" Matthew asked, puzzled. "You a leper or something? You go to Harvard, don't you? What more could her old man want in a son-in-law?"

"Not only are her family rich and conventional," Si said musingly, "but they're also provincial. It's an unbeatable combination. I mean, they patronize the arts but basically they distrust artists and intellectuals and people who make jokes. So, I wanted to put off this Rubicon crossing until I got my M.A. and maybe snared a teaching fellowship. Caro was agreed. I was supposed to receive the damn thing in August. I took all my exams and passed. Everything Captain Hunky and Lieutenant Dory. Only thing left to do was write my thesis. And I haven't done it. So no degree. No wedding. Now, don't, don't for Hippocrates' sake, ask me why I haven't written it."

"I guess you've got a block," Matthew said equably. "Is it on Eliot?"

"It's been on four different guys and three wild ideas, so far," Si said bitterly. "Each time I get what I think is a real angle and throw myself into it with frantic enthusiasm, the same thing happens. I plow through a million books, take cornucopias of notes and then sit down to write and suddenly I find my splendid idea has either been dealt with far better by pro's, or there wasn't much there to begin with. Last spring, I wrote one whole chapter on Joyce's influence on the contemporary American novel. There it stands." He waved at a spring binder on his desk. "In addition my dead husk collection contains half a chapter on Fitzgerald and eight pages on Nathanael West. My adviser keeps telling me impatiently to do a bibliography or a concordance but I can't stand the thought of the tedious research and every morning I wake up, thinking, *today will be the day*, the day I have the brilliant insight, which will become *the thesis*, and will practically write itself. Caro says it's all sinister and Freudian and that I didn't write the thesis because I don't want to marry her. In the meantime, I avoid all issues by continuing to go to classes in preparation for doctoral credit and every time I should sit down and wrestle with this black devil of a thesis I play poker or drink or have a fight with Caro or go to the movies. I should've been a doctor after all, I'm beginning to think."

"Well, I don't think so," Matthew said, having recovered from a mighty yawn. "You'd go through the same hell not only every time you took an exam or State Boards but also when you had to figure out what to do with a patient. You'd be hopping from one foot to another, saying, what marvelous decayed Poe-like insides that fella has, it'd be a shame to fix them up."

"You're probably right," Si said, walking to the door with him. He began to laugh. "I'll have to tell Caro that even if it is at my expense. She thinks you're terrific. If we ever broke up and you were free, well . . ."

"Stop being a jackass," Matthew said, "and marry her."

"I will one of these days," Si said airily.

"You're a changeable bastard. Two minutes ago I'd've sworn you were ready to crawl to the nearest analytical couch."

"I always feel better after I blow off steam," Si said cheerfully. "Thanks for lending your ears. I'll be hosting the usual Friday night game. Can you come?"

"Depends on the birth rate."

"Listen, speaking of Poe-like decayed insides, do you ever see that ghost of Halloween past, J. D. Brimmer, now you've changed residencies?"

"Hey, what did he ever do to you?" Matthew protested.

"I know, I know," Si said, "I was impressed with him too when I first met him." He patted Matthew patronizingly on the shoulder. "The trouble with you, you sunny, clear-eyed youth you, is that you never saw enough horror movies. Well, how is he?"

"Fine," Matthew said. He added reluctantly, "I was at his place last night, as a matter of fact. But I don't see him much any more. He's got a girl."

"Oh, I know about that revolting mésalliance," Si said darkly, folding his arms and lolling against the door jamb. "Isn't that from messville?"

"Deborah? She seems like a nice kid."

"Damn nice," Si affirmed. "A little beauty and smart, too. But her knowledge of men is obviously nowhere. The first time I met her she was in the company of a cheeky snot that Mike Wainscott couldn't shake off and then he disappeared to poison the air in some other city and, lo, the poor child falls into the clutches of our badly repressed gentleman friend. I'd give a handsome bon mot to know how that happened."

"Well, she's not the easiest girl in the world to talk to," Matthew said, "so she and Dud have that in common. I had a hell of a time trying to start a conversation with her at first till I figured out that you could talk about books, music, medicine, art, but never anything personal. Nothing in the least off color either."

"Hmmm. That's not the way I remember Dud. He always had a disgustingly furtive interest in pornography."

"Well, she hasn't. One night we were talking psychology and I made the mistake of quoting one of Freud's case histories. She lowered her eyelashes, and he got the signal and that conversation was whipped around to something else in two seconds. Of course they're damn nice eyelashes, so I don't blame him if he wants to keep them from distress. I've sat and looked at them quite a few times and those tremendous eyes of hers and one time I made the asinine mistake of interrupting a discourse of hers by telling her she looked very pretty when she got intense and, wow, what a look of pure hatred I got."

"Why don't you make a few overtures," Si suggested. "Give Dud a run for it. She's no girl for him although I don't know who, living, would be."

"I think she's great for him," Matthew said firmly. "She's really livened him up. He's even given a few parties for the hospital crowd. I don't go around stealing other men's women, granted I could, but even if she wasn't Dud's girl I wouldn't get near her. She doesn't appeal to me. Too priggish and childish."

"Oh well, if your heart isn't touched by beauty in the toils of the beast I can't convince you. I'm just trying to fix you up to be as blissful as I am. And since you seem to be a familiar of that weird household, what's the splendid Sara doing lately?"

"I've only met her a couple of times and very briefly at that," Matthew said truthfully, backing out into the concealing darkness of the hallway, "so I couldn't say."

"Now there's a woman," Si said enthusiastically. "Even my dried-up devoted-to-Caro heart beats faster when I see her. Isn't she fantastic?"

"She's certainly very beautiful," Matthew agreed, "and—er—very unusual."

"Hmmm," Si said, peering at him sharply. "Do I detect a quaver of irresolution in that usually matter-of-fact plainspoken voice of yours? Disabuse yourself, my boy. In her presence a man of sense wears dark glasses or keeps his eyes closed. Blindness is the punishment for those who dare to look with the naked eye on such radiance. What are you grinning like a Cheshire idiot for? Do you see me laughing? I'm in grave earnest. She keeps a factory running twenty-four hours a day where men are turned first into lumbering Frankenstein monsters, then gibbering idiots, and finally stone."

"Give up on the thesis," Matthew advised as he started off down the stairs "and start a psychological Lonely hearts column instead. Dear Miss Dix, I cannot write my thesis because I'm too interested in other people's sex lives."

"Touché! touché!" Si shouted. "And believe me I know when I've drawn blood, too. Take care! Big Brother will be watching you."

Matthew dragged himself home yawning so hard the tears stood in his eyes and his head pressed heavily on his neck and he felt rotten. He lay on the couch and looked at the ceiling and thought about his summer which hadn't been bad except that he hadn't really enjoyed it. Not really surprising that Sally'd turned him down and what the hell, good old Peggy had been free and he'd slept with her off and on for most of the summer. Easy, casual, fun, no problems, just the sort of thing he used to like a lot. The intensity of her ardor at first had surprised him and maybe even worried him, but one night, in a loose moment of warm bed confidence, she'd explained it. The worm in the apple.

A whole month, she'd said, and nothing happened. After awhile, she'd thought maybe there was something the matter with her. I'm not his type, she'd said honestly, I was surprised when he took me out the first time. You shouldn't talk about it, uneasy Dr. Berman had answered, it's not the sort of thing you spread around especially not about a guy like Dud Brimmer. It might not mean a thing, Matthew thought lying there, maybe a free and easy type like Peggy made him feel insecure. I never ran across anybody like that, she'd said, truly bewildered, what causes a thing like that, I was going crazy for a while there, I was so glad when you called me up. I don't know, said the answer man, just don't talk about it, it's a lousy thing for a man. Probably just temporary. I only told you, Peggy said, in a hurt voice, because I wanted you to know that you made me feel so much better.

Then, at the end of the summer, she'd gone off to Salisbury Beach for a two-week vacation and come back all reformed, chastened and demure and engaged, for Godsakes, to some simple, worshiping, Southern petty officer stationed at the Fargo Building. Well, it'd been nice while it lasted, and he wished her well, she was a good kid, though it'd left him with a lot of unchanneled lusts and a disturbing bit of information. He wished Peggy'd never told him about Dud Brimmer, now very happy with a childish little girl who was afraid to hear the word sex mentioned. What were they planning to do with each other anyway, have a chaste marriage? Very unlikely, she wasn't his kind, to use Sophy's orthodox vernacular, what was Deborah's last name anyway, Miller, yes, he wondered if she were Jewish, might well be, looking like that with a Biblical name, though the name didn't mean much because now, there was the other side of the coin, Profane Love herself, Sara Brimmer Mayhew.

He sat up instantly, and pulled the telephone over to him, sleep forgotten. He was in luck. Joe was home and happy as a pig in mud to hear from old Matthew, a lucky stiff of a bocher with an apartment. Before he got around to making the pitch about using the apartment as a small-time cathouse, Matthew cut in and asked him pointblank what he knew about New York abortionists, adding quickly that it was for a friend.

"That's what they all say," Joe Bernstein snickered. "Well, Matt since you're an old friend, I guess I can help you out. It's an address worth a fortune, boy. The guy charges plenty but he does it with antibiotics, anesthesia, the works. It's practically foolproof."

Matthew took out his fountain pen. "I'm waiting for the name and address, Joe."

"I'm telling you, this is worth money, Matt. When a guy gets into a jam like this he can really be desperate."

"Are you planning to become wealthy by capitalizing on human misery, Bernstein?" I wish he were here, Matthew thought, I'd like to punch him in the head.

"Well, after all, Matt, I had a lousy time," Bernstein said in a voice full of self-pity. "This address cost me a girl I loved."

"Okay," Matthew said curtly, "you can use the apartment once in a while, only not too often and I have to be notified in advance."

After a little more hypocritical palaver he gave out with the address and name of the doctor and Matthew wrote it down, adding to it the name of Bernstein's former girl for purposes of reference.

"Price?" he inquired briskly.

"Well, I guess it varies. I know he charges nurses around two hundred fifty. Maybe college girls, too. Everyone else pays three hundred or maybe more if they look plush. I'd say three hundred. You're sure it's not your girl?"

"Hell no! Sorry I can't keep you company in your misery."

"Well, I didn't really think so," Joe said despondently. "You always were a cagy wiseguy."

"Thanks a lot, Joe," Matthew said. "See you around." I hope to hell he keeps his mouth shut, he thought, lying down again and closing his eyes, I hope he doesn't come bounding up to me at Si's poker game and start shouting around. Beautiful Sally, because of you, I am now committed to having Bernstein in my hair, running in and out of my apartment. He groaned and wondered whether to call her now. No, test results won't be in till day after tomorrow. Might be negative and it'd all be a waste of time and there he'd be, stuck with Bernstein. But if the test was positive, wouldn't she consider him her knight in shining armor though. How it would be going to bed with her . . . a damnfool, adolescent, dangerous fantasy and after a few, dry-mouthed minutes, he made himself stop by sternly and arbitrarily fixing his mind on the kind of questions that might be on the State Boards next year which proved so mentally exhausting that he was driven, in self-defense, to sleep.

Three

"Why, you wonderful man," Sally said, turning her seagreen eyes on Matthew. "I simply can't believe it. I can't really believe that you've done this fabulous thing for me. And so quickly. You cannot imagine what a hideously crushing time I've had. I was sure that you'd try but equally sure you wouldn't succeed or that it would take forever and be too late."

"It was just luck," Matthew said lamely. They were sitting in the living room of Dudley's apartment having a martini. Matthew didn't like martinis much but he sipped at his bravely, stealing sidelong glances at her. It was seven o'clock and she was all dressed up to go out to a dinner dance. He thought enviously of all the men who'd be privileged to see her and talk to her and sit next to her and dance with her during the evening, whose eyes could linger on those naked, milkwhite shoulders and arms, who could hold her close on the dance floor and look down the front of her strapless, crimson velvet dress. Oh God, he thought, keeping his gaze fixed on the olive at the bottom of his cold, rotten-tasting drink, if I don't go to bed with that girl just once, only once in my life, I'll never be really happy again.

"I wish I didn't have this boring thing to go to tonight," Sally was saying, pouring herself another martini from the frosted pitcher, "because we really ought to celebrate my redemption. But then you probably are taken up anyway, aren't you?"

Matthew wished she wouldn't cross her legs like that. Her dress was short, full, flared, and underpinned by what appeared to be layer on layer of crisp, rustling petticoats in a rainbow array of reds, roses, and pinks. Si would like the way she dresses, he thought, irrelevantly, especially those pointed, towerheeled, red satin shoes, although if you asked him, frankly, he thought they looked a little whorish.

"I'm going to eat a hamburger and go to a poker game," he

493

said, rousing himself from the contemplation of her beautiful, sinuous legs and the unseen, desired core they were joined to underneath all those petticoats. "At Si's."

"Darling, mad old Si. I haven't seen him in ever so long. Haven't felt like seeing anyone or doing anything. But now, Lord, I feel as if I were recovering from some terribly debilitating illness." She stretched luxuriously, flinging back the long skeins of burnt gold hair and kicked out her redsatined feet. Her arms were stretched high in the air and her full, white breasts rose and overflowed from the red velvet calyx. Damn exhibitionist tease, Matthew thought, and drank his drink off fast, making a sour face.

"I couldn't ditch this party though," she drawled on, "but we must do some merry-making when I get back. Something splendid and lavish. My treat. Although I really can't imagine anything superlative enough to match what you've done. When I called you this afternoon burdened with the inevitably positive news from Dr. Asch, I felt so down, so low you know, I thought, silly to call him, he couldn't find anyone this soon. And I thought, well I'll go to this dinner and dance awhile and get horribly drunk and disgrace myself before all those people because I'm in hell and they're not and wouldn't know hell if it opened before them and they'll say, well, what can you expect of Sally, she was always wild." She laughed gleefully. "And, instead, here you come to me, bearing such glad, golden tidings. I'd like to kiss you Matthew. May I?"

"No," he said scared to death that if she approached to give him the sisterly little peck of gratitude he'd lose his head and grab her.

"That's awfully churlish of you," she pouted but her eyes glinted and he knew she was quite aware of his discomfiture.

"Let's be sensible," he began pontifically.

"I hate being sensible when I've been saved from a dreadful fate."

"All I meant was that you don't have to kiss me for what just fell in my lap. Anyway it isn't over yet. You've still got a lot to go through before you can start shouting. Now . . . I've told you about what price he'll probably expect so you can take well, enough money in cash, with you and then . . ."

"Of course I know I don't have to kiss you," she interrupted, "but what if I wanted to? Or isn't that enough?"

"No," he said startled into honesty by her direct approach.

A slow smile curved her mouth. "Ah," she said comfortably, "I thought that's the way it was."

"You brought it up, not me." She's the craziest girl I ever met, he thought, they aren't wrong, all those people who think she's wild.

"I always pay my debts, you know," she said, looking him over appraisingly, "although in this case the creditor will have to be patient."

Matthew couldn't believe his ears. "I don't know what you're talking about, but it sounds damn rude to me."

"Why is it rude to be honest? I owe you a debt of gratitude. I'm willing to pay it in the way you want it paid. Isn't that fair? And don't protest please that you had no such idea in mind."

"You don't owe me anything," Matthew said coldly. She could really make you feel lousy, he thought, just plain lousy, what the hell do I want to get mixed up with her for, just a bitch, Jenni's right. "Not a damn thing. Got that? Things like that aren't matters of gratitude. So now let's get back to business because I have to go and I wouldn't want to keep you."

She wriggled out of her chair and in a flash and rustle of red was sitting on his lap, kissing him gently on the cheek. "Don't get so salty," she said softly. "I feel so elated and I simply wanted to tell you that I'd rather enjoy having you collect the debt. But of course, it's up to you." And she was up and back in her own chair before he'd even had time to touch her.

"You're the damnedest girl," he said, knowing he sounded as foolish as he probably looked.

"I know," she said, picking up the martini pitcher lazily and tilting the last of its contents into her glass. "But I'm really just light-headed and delirious with joy. I shall not offer you another drink because you made such dreadful grimaces over that one. It's very canny of you, Doctor, not to like to drink, rather refreshing actually, but I do think you'd know more of the pitfalls of this wicked world if you'd participate in some of them, don't you?"

I'm crazy, he thought, his head spinning from the martini that he'd hated, and the pressure of her naked flesh close to him for just that second, I'm a meshuggineh to even get near this girl. In a way, he hated her for knowing his unworthy, lustful mind so completely but at the same time he was grateful for her unpretentious forthrightness. So what if it was flinging a dog a bone? What more did a dog want? Why fool around with sentiment? She obviously didn't. Should a fortunately chosen dog complain? Anyway, it might never happen, maybe she was just saying it. Apparently she did or said anything that came into her head.

"You were about to tell me something vital, Dr. Berman, but you seem to've gone off into a trance."

She was laughing at him. He bet she just loved stirring up trouble and shocking people. He tried to pull his dignity together and explained about bedrest and having somebody around to take care of her for two or three days. "D'you know someone there you could stay with?"

"Not really. Relations are obviously out. It won't be difficult however. I know of a little sort of apartment hotel, quiet, in Greenwich Village, where I've stayed before. I think it will do very well. I loathe large hotels where the chambermaids are always running in. And I shall take Deborah with me. She's never been to New York and I think she'll enjoy it. She can see that I get my meals and keep a weather eye out for me and then sightsee the rest of the time."

"Deborah! Are you nuts, Sally? That kid?" He closed his eyes for a moment, exasperated. "Maybe I'm wrong," he added, "but I have the distinct impression that Deborah hasn't the vaguest idea about how she got into this world, so how are you going to explain to her what kind of a little sightseeing trip you're planning for her?"

"I don't think you're being terribly flattering toward my brother, Doctor," Sally said, lowering her eyelashes demurely.

"Stop twisting things around," he said crossly. "Your brother hasn't got a thing to do with this. That kid will be shocked and worse, useless. Don't you know anyone else you can ask, someone older and more responsible? What if something goes wrong? What good'll she be to you? Anyway, I don't think she'll go if you tell her the whole story."

"I don't anticipate anything going wrong," Sally said, lighting a long white cigarette. "If the man charges that much money and uses all those vaunted precautions I fail to see why there'd be any slips. And if some mishap does occur I shall go to another doctor. They can't refuse to treat you after an abortion, can they? Please don't be so grisly. And as for Deborah, naturally she'll be shocked. But she'll go."

"You're sure of that?"

"Certainly. It's quite simple. I'll tell her tomorrow and we'll go Monday. There's very little time to lose."

"I don't know." Matthew shook his head. "I don't like the idea of you going off for a thing like that with just a kid like Deborah. Don't you have any other women friends?"

"No, I do not have women friends," Sally said impatiently. "I've never had any need of them and women don't usually like me very much." She smiled at him teasingly and moved her body around in what he thought was a needlessly provocative manner. "I'm sure

496

I don't know why. Deborah's one of the few girls I've met that I can bear or who, apparently, can put up with me."

No competition, Matthew thought, sure. "How about the . . . er . . . the father? Maybe he could go with you. You know, in a way, this whole thing's on my head. I mean you're going off to a strange city and I'll be the only one who knows where you are and what you're doing there. And if something happened to you . . . well . . ."

"Yes, I see. It's very good of you to worry. But I assure you all my sins shall be on my own head. And, as for the man"—and for a second he thought she looked a little rueful, but it was probably just his imagination—"I have not told him and I shall not."

"You still seeing him?"

"Is there anything else you want to tell me?" she asked blandly.

"Okay. I still think it's a lousy thing to do to a man who cares about you."

"It probably is," she said courteously.

"Are you ever going to tell him?"

"Whatever for?"

"I don't know. I think maybe if I were him I'd like to know."

"No, you wouldn't," she said staring intently at her cigarette. "Would you please not, not, ask me any more questions about it, Dr. Berman. I'm not quite a fiend, you know. I do have some scruples."

"Dr. Berman," he repeated. "You just kissed me a few minutes ago and now suddenly I'm the old family physician again. If it hurts you so much to think of doing this to him maybe you'd better not go. You might even hurt yourself more by doing this than you think. Forgive me for being nosy, Sally, but I just don't think it's right."

"You want to know too much," she said in a low voice. "Although I suppose you're entitled to, having done so much for me."

"I repeat, there are no strings attached for Godsakes, Sally. I just said that because you seem to be a little confused."

"No," she said hurriedly, the words seemingly forced out of her, "I think, perhaps, because, except for Deborah that you will be the only one who knows what I'm doing and, although I refuse to consider it, there is always the remote possibility of some mishap, that I ought to tell you. For future reference if it might help. I do love the man. If I told him about this and what I'm to do, he'd be so tremendously upset that . . ." she trailed off. "I don't want to be melodramatic."

"I don't understand," Matthew said. "If he did it on purpose, won't he suspect?"

"I'm sure he did," Sally said drily. "He kept asking me leading questions and was obviously sort of waiting. But time passed and since I didn't go running to him, screaming hysterically, I believe he's decided that he picked, a, shall we say, unfruitful time."

"If you're planning to continue this relationship," Matthew said, trying to sound disinterested, "you'll have to be damn careful because if he's that determined and emotional about you, he'll get you sometime or other again."

"I must look disgustingly fertile. No, you're quite right although for someone like me, it's quite a difficult thing to give up. I daresay it'll peter out though, shortly. You needn't worry Doctor."

"I'm not involved in this," he said angrily. "I have no claim on you."

She sighed. "Oh Lord, I wish the whole thing were over and I were back here now. Adjusting claims." She smiled mockingly, more at herself, he thought, than at him and got up. "I really must go. Can I drop you somewhere, Doctor?"

"No, thanks, I'll walk." He picked up his coat. "I want the address you'll be staying at. And I want you to call me after you see the . . . doctor and after it's over. Okay? It would relieve my mind."

"It's terribly sweet of you to . . . worry so . . . about me. I'm sure I don't deserve it." In the lamplight, he saw that she was blinking and realized that her eyes were wet.

"Hey," he said, "what's this?"

"Isn't it ridiculous? I'm so damply emotional these days." She brushed at her eyes quickly. "I'll write the name of the hotel for you. Does pregnancy always make a weeping willow of a woman?"

"There's a chemical and hormonal change that often can affect the emotions."

"I shall be awfully happy to get my own emotions back, then. I don't like this new sniveling me."

"An unwanted pregnancy of course can add to the emotional conflict. But psychologists have theories that abortions affect the psyche too, a sense of guilt, other things. So don't expect to get off scot free."

"That's absurd," she scoffed. "But then I think that all this Freudian nonsense is fairly stupid anyway."

"Mmm," he said carefully. "Well, be that as it may, another thing I want you to do, is give Deborah my name and phone number so that if by remote chance you can't call me she can. And here"—he pulled a little black notebook from his pocket and tore out a leaf—"I had it written down and I almost forgot it, is the name and address of a doctor in New York. He's a friend of mine, was in the Army with me, good guy. I want you to call him if you need treatment. And mention my name. He'll help you."

"How nice of you." She took the proffered paper. "How terribly nice. You've thought of everything, haven't you? In a way, I wish you weren't being so kind. It makes me feel simply snakelike."

"Now you're just giving way to typical morbid pregnancy fancies, all that ordinary stuff you despise." He grinned at her.

"No," she shook her head and folded her arms on her breast. "I'm shivering you know. Isn't that silly? It's not cold is it? No it's not a morbid fancy. I wish it were. But this is quite, quite real. I wish I could explain, but I can't. Perhaps someday when I'm eighty years old and we can sit around in our wheelchairs and swap memories, when no one can be hurt any more by telling truths."

"Buck up," he said gently. "You're just a little nervous that's all. It'll be okay, I'm sure. This guy sounds very careful. By the way," he added hoping that a changed subject would lighten her depression, "does Deborah know the man?"

She smiled thinly. "She's met him. He got dreadfully jocular with her and told her she was cute and after that she looked at him as if he were a strange beast in a zoo."

"So you think she'll approve of your action?"

"I can't say, but she's very loyal. At any rate, you have all sorts of incorrect ideas about Deborah. She's not a prude. In fact, she's sort of a romantic and I think sometimes she sees me as a character in a book, one who has *lived*. And it's all right if people in books or those real ones who resemble fictional characters have affairs and abortions. It's only when old raw life gets too close to *her* that she runs the other way."

"You're probly right," Matthew said. "Kind of too bad, isn't it?"

"De gustibus," Sally said casually. "You'll hear from me then. Goodbye," she said as they stood at the door, "and thanks. Kiss me once for luck, will you, Matthew?" Her voice was husky.

The passion in him rose strong but was mixed with a sad amalgam of fear and foreboding. He grabbed her by her beautiful naked shoulders, kissed her closed mouth hard and ran like an arrant coward down the stairs. All the way down, he kept saying under his breath, some nonsensical repetitive chant, and it was not till he was out in the street that he realized it'd been a prayer: Don't let anything happen to her, let her be all safe and well again for me.

* * * *

The little suite at the Mimosa Hotel near Washington Square Park had peach-colored walls and chintz in overwhelming profusion. There was a bedroom with a three-quarter bed of veneer maple, a tiny sitting room with a studio couch, a pink tiled bathroom and, behind the screen in the sitting room, the elements of a kitchenette.

"This must cost quite a lot of money," Deborah said, inspecting everything eagerly. "I've never seen a refrigerator built under a gas range before."

"At least there's a good view of the park," Sally said, standing by the window. "I'd go mad if I had to stay here for four days inundated by this color scheme."

"I suppose it's a nice enough park for New York," Deborah said scornfully. "Although I'm glad you decided to stay in Greenwich Village instead of near the station. The houses and things down here seem much more like Boston."

Sally was thinking about Saul. Yesterday, she'd come to his apartment, bearing the Sunday paper and woken him up. They'd had a late breakfast and made love and read the paper. She'd been lacklustre about the lovemaking not only because it was hard to summon up passion when you felt seasick but also because of what she was about to do. But he had not noticed any of this. He was full of plans about how now that winter was coming on maybe he'd quit his job. He had enough pension to live on and money and bonds saved, he could manage quite well. They could take trips. Would she like to go back to California? How about Las Vegas? His eyes had pleaded with her to tell him that she'd love to go, driving across country, doing glamorous things and she had said only something curt about how it would be impossible. Then he had made everything worse by becoming humble and tender. I'll do anything you want. Only let me love you. Don't let me lose you. Naturally, at that point her gorge had risen but she'd kept tight hold of herself. And, cravenly, the speech she'd planned, about visiting in New York, had been left for the telephone that morning at the station. Getting to him just as he was going to bed after a night's work and being gay, full of mad impulse and tired of tedious old Boston. Friends pressing me, you know, darling, send you a postcard, see you on Friday. And tata and bless you, beautiful, lost, impossible, hopeless, damnfool, allwrong love, sleep sweetly and hung up blithely protesting undying devotion, cutting short his baffled, sleepy exclamations.

"We'd better go," she said now to Deborah, "and get the embarrassment over with."

Dr. Lucas Phillips' office turned out to be in a large, ordinary-looking office building in what seemed to Sally, who knew little about New York, to be the heart of the city.

"Funny," Deborah said, in a low voice, as they stood waiting for the elevator. "I thought it would be way out on a lonely country road."

"So did I. But this is much more convenient."

Although empty of patients, the waiting room of the office looked completely usual. There was a desk with a thin, poker-faced, shrewd nurse in the orthodox white uniform, a bench, a chair and a table with magazines. Deborah sat down on the bench and picked up one of the magazines while Sally gave her name and the hotel's address to the nurse and glibly rattled off, as referral, the unknown female's name which Matthew had written for her. Then the nurse disappeared behind one of the two tightly closed doors beyond her desk.

"Why did she want to know who I was?" Deborah whispered. It seemed quite meet to whisper even though no one was listening.

"They need to be careful and suspicious, I suppose," Sally whispered back.

She still felt nervous. The nurse had seemed so calm and matter-of-fact that she wondered if, perhaps, the whole thing wasn't an awful blunder. Perhaps it wasn't the right man or the right address. There might be any number of Dr. Lucas Phillipses in New York. She took out a cigarette and lit it. At least her hand was steady, which showed that she wasn't really about to go to pieces. Still, here she was, sitting next to an unwontedly quiet Deborah and she felt an enormous gulf stretching between them, for all that their skirts touched on the bench. I'm here, she thought and this is going to happen to me, not to Deborah. I might as well be encased in a block of ice at this moment for all that she can reach me or I her. It was undoubtedly the right Dr. Phillips she decided but that didn't mean he would automatically hand out an abortion. Perhaps he only did it for special people. And for others, why he could be simply as bland as his nurse who behaved as if she were any other doctor's nurse, and say, yes, yes, you think you're pregnant, well, we'll examine you, you are, how splendid, go home and drink a lot of milk and your baby will be due on such and such a day. That will be ten dollars please, my nurse will see you out. What will I say then, she wondered, feeling the sickness of panic again. Will I argue with him, plead, say no, no, you don't understand, I was told that you could give me an abortion. And he could laugh, get angry, outraged, righteous, indignant, why who ever told you that, I wish I could help you but, my advice is, better have the baby. Marry. Why the hell didn't the nurse come back? Ah there she was, the door was opening. And with her came a rather overmade-up girl, wearing a dull hat, who walked quickly to the outer door, swinging her skirts and looking straight ahead of her.

"All right, Miss Mayhew," the nurse said routinely. "Dr. Phillips will see you now."

"I'll wait for you here," Deborah muttered pulling the magazine up around her face.

Dr. Phillips stood, tall, ponderous, and imposing behind a large walnut desk in a booklined office full of clear daylight. There was a Persian carpet on the floor.

"How do you do, Miss Mayhew. Sit down please." He waved at a brown leather chair beside the desk and waited courteously while she obeyed and then sat down himself. His hair was completely white, his face pink and healthy and his eyes, under shaggy white brows were pale blue and eagle-like. "It is Miss Mayhew, isn't it?" He toyed with a fountain pen and looked her over in a friendly, casual way.

Sally returned the look with composure and explained that her husband had been killed in the war. She was no longer nervous. At first sight of this man in his conservative, dark blue business suit, complete with vest and Phi Beta Kappa key, draped from a gold watch chain, at his initial words, delivered in a rumbling, pleasant, and familiarly correct voice, she had felt immediately herself again. He looked and spoke so much like members of her family that it didn't occur to her then, explaining about Joe, that perhaps it was not the proper sort of thing to mention to a man to whom she'd come for an abortion. On the wall behind him she noticed the framed Harvard diploma.

"And what did you want to see me about?"

"I'm pregnant," Sally said, wondering why the word itself was so embarrassing. "About two and a half months."

"Mmm. How do you know?"

"I was examined by a doctor and took one of those frog tests."

"I see," he said noncommittally. "I'll examine you later myself.

You're not a New Yorker, I think, Mrs. Mayhew." His eyes fixed on her interestedly, taking in, she knew, every detail of her dress, gestures, and manner. "Boston, if I'm not mistaken. I thought so," he went on in answer to her nod. "I have a good ear for accents and particularly that one, since I spent so many pleasant years in your city. Many years ago of course. Do you smoke?" He extended an open silver cigarette box and lighted the cigarette for her.

Sally waited while he went through the routine of cutting the end of a cigar and inserting it into a small, amber holder. She found herself trying not to smile, thinking about her picture of a furtive, shifty-eyed abortionist, mumbling nervously in a sloppy New York accent, his little hole-in-the-wall, out-of-the-way office, poorly equipped and dusty and his degree from a third-rate medical school accounting for his choice of this illegal activity. And here, instead, was this prosperous, solid-looking office, this urbane and assured gentleman, who could have been a senator or a judge or some such symbol of vested and enlightened authority. Matthew would never believe it, she thought delightedly. I can hardly wait to tell him.

"Now the man who is responsible for the pregnancy," Dr. Phillips said. "What about him? I'd like to know why you've come here."

"Is it essential?"

He smiled at her benevolently. "Yes, I consider that it is. I believe that I might guess why but for various reasons which perhaps you can understand I think you'd better tell me about it briefly."

Yes, Sally thought, he is attempting to make sure that I'm not a spy from some agency determined to smell out corruption and the best method is to get a candidate's story. He's dreadfully shrewd, she thought, in spite of his easy, pleasant manner. He'd undoubtedly be able to discern a trumped-up tale from a true one. So, carefully and in a clear, unhurried voice she told him about Saul, about his blind determination to marry her and finished off with details of Matthew's research on her behalf. Afterwards, as she sat silent, waiting for him to speak, she wondered if it'd been foolish to mention marriage. Mightn't it have sounded better, made her appear more desperately in need of his services if she'd implied that she was that cliché object of pity and ridicule, the girl who has fallen prey to an unscrupulous male, one who has robbed her of honor and left her to face alone, the castigation of society. Feeling so completely at ease with this doctor, as if she'd met him at her aunt's dinner table, might have led to cutting her own throat.

He was staring meditatively at the smoke from his cigar, turned round in his swivel chair, legs crossed. "So you'll be getting no financial aid from this fellow?"

"No."

"What do you do?" he asked abruptly. "Do you go to school? Have a job? In the past, I'd've said from the look and sound of you, that you didn't do much of anything but grace the social scene but in this fluid day and age it is no longer safe to hazard such a guess."

"I do some sort of blues singing in nightclubs occasionally," Sally admitted. "But you're perfectly right. Mostly I do very little of the workaday and I've been to school."

"Smith? Bryn Mawr?"

This conversation is getting more weirdly evasive than I ever believed possible, Sally thought. "I'm sorry," she said, "you've missed, this time. California. Berkeley."

He gazed at her regretfully and shook his white-maned head. "You shouldn't step out of context that way," he said. "It upsets my assurance. However, I daresay, that if you'd gone to the school you should have, you wouldn't be here, brightening my office."

"In difficulties, you mean," Sally said, determined to bring the conversation back to the point. "And my place of education has little to do with it."

"But your departure from the norm does, doesn't it?" he asked softly, smiling at her. And, before she had a chance to mull over this unexpected bit of analysis he was going on. "Did you do any reading in the Victorians?"

"A survey course," Sally said vaguely. "I'm afraid I always preferred the Romantics."

"Their poetry was perhaps not as good," this astounding man said, gesturing professorially with his cigar, "but the prose, my dear girl, is superb. I advise you to do some reading in it. Carlyle, Macaulay, Mill, Arnold, Darwin, Huxley. Oh magnificent! The great Victorians were so full of belief in the perfectability of man, in progress, in reform, in education, so sure that mankind could not fail to rise from the chains of ignorance, through reason, technology, and science. And now we see," he sighed, "that they were naïve. Mankind has become, if anything, worse. It would have been better to have lived in an age which still had cause to hope, to cherish their illusions. I'll examine you now," he finished abruptly, "and desist from riding my hobby horse."

While the nurse was being called from the outer office, Sally, still baffled and unsure of the outcome of this amazing interview, went into the next room, got partially undressed and clambered up on the examining table. While the dryfaced nurse stood alongside, Dr. Phillips perfunctorily examined her under a concealing sheet.

"Yes," he said. "Two and a half months. Come back to the office when you finish dressing."

He was sitting at his desk when she returned, and smiled at her. "We'll perform the operation tomorrow afternoon," he said. "My nurse will notify you of the time and there are a few minor tests to be done before you leave today. The price will be three hundred dollars. You will have an anesthetic, of course, and we'll give you some antibiotics to ward off infection. The money must be in cash, which I trust will be convenient for you."

"Quite," Sally said, feeling an immense, soaring sense of relief. "Thank you, Dr. Phillips."

"You're quite welcome," he said blandly. "It has been very enjoyable talking to you, Mrs. Mayhew. I shall see you tomorrow." He rose and bowed slightly while pressing a buzzer on his desk. The door opened and the watchful face of the nurse appeared.

Silently, she ushered Sally into a larger room and handed her a labeled glass jar which Sally recognized and opened another door of this apparently endless warren into a little bathroom. Sally emerged, after leaving the jar on a tray, and was shown by the still silent nurse over to a small table in the large room, where a middle-aged man in a white coat, listened to her heart, took her blood pressure and pricked her finger with a needle, drawing the blood off into a small tube. This entire operation was conducted in complete dumb show. The silence in the large, bleak room was overwhelming. It's like a weird, mechanical ballet without music, Sally thought, unwontedly chilled and depressed. And for some reason the smell and sight of blood seemed to permeate the room and her pores, although the only blood she could see was her own, a tiny red drop staining the piece of gauze clapped on her finger. The nurse beckoned her again, like that fearful phantom ghost of Christmas Future, raising her bony hand and Sally obediently went and stood on a scale, noticing, out of the corner of her eye that there was now another girl in the room, entering the bathroom with her glass jar. An assembly line, she thought grimly and looked inquiringly at the nurse who was writing on a small card.

"That's all for today," she said, her face as expressionless as ever. "Be here tomorrow afternoon at two o'clock. You'd better come alone or have your friend meet you nearby, not in the building though. The best arrangement would be to get a cab downstairs when it's over. You'll be able to. Don't worry."

The next minute Sally found herself out the door and back into the waiting room where Deborah was sitting, wriggling on her bench, the magazine fallen neglected in her lap.

"I feel rather reprieved," Sally said when they were out in the street, "and we ought to do something together because after this I'll be Mimosa Hotel ridden. I'd feel rotten if you didn't see some of New York when you're skipping school and quitting your job for me."

"I wanted to quit anyway," Deborah said happily, "and this was the best way to do it because when I told them I had to take three days off from their precious sodafountain they just fired me so I'll get some unemployment for a while. And it doesn't matter if I cut a few classes. I've never done it before and it'll be easy enough to get the lecture notes from someone. You know, it's good that I'm living at the Franklin Square House now because if I were still at home there'd've been immense amounts of arguments and explanations before I could go off with you."

Sally had a moment of silent mirth trying to imagine Deborah explaining the purpose of her visit to New York to her parents. Really, she was a very oddball child. It turned out that she knew all about abortions. In *U.S.A.* one of the female characters had had several. Very poised and knowledgeable, she'd said, of course she would go and take care of Sally. She'd not been shocked at all. Perhaps, Sally thought, in her naïve lexicon those were the expected wages of sin but in any case Deborah had agreed that it was clearly out of the question for Sally to marry as unworthy a man as Saul. Particularly since he'd planned it in such a low, mean, underhanded, conniving sort of way.

They went and strolled on upper Fifth Avenue. At the Plaza, Deborah wouldn't go in to have tea as Sally suggested they do because, as she said mournfully, she just wasn't dressed right for that romantic literary experience. When pressed for an explanation of what her costume ought to be she said only something silk or cloth of gold with beautiful, pale, sheer, blue, gold or peach stockings and satin shoes and a mink coat would do, because that was her impression of how Scott Fitzgerald heroines dressed when they went to have tea at the Plaza and nothing less would do for her. Sally forbore to mention that they were around twenty-five years too late to approximate such an experience so they ended up going to look at dresses in Saks Fifth Avenue and Bergdorf's but Sally couldn't concentrate on shopping and Deborah refused to let Sally buy her anything and they left the stores and went into the violet autumn dusk when the soft lights were coming on all over the Avenue and looked into glittering windows and then had dinner in a French restaurant. Here Deborah gave in to the power of Sally's affluence and allowed herself to consume an enormous meal of onion soup, snails, poulet au vin blanc, and three pastries.

"Oh I've eaten so much," she gasped delightedly when they were having coffee, "but it was all so good. But you didn't eat anything. You didn't even finish that wonderful onion soup."

"After tomorrow," Sally said, trying not to look at the tray of pastries beside them, "I shall eat every hour to make up for this sick starvation I've suffered from for aeons. You've no idea how awful it is to lose your appetite and always be afraid you're going to be publicly sick."

"It must be terrible," Deborah said sympathetically. "I don't know why women want to have children anyway, ever. It seems to me they never enjoy anything while they're pregnant or afterwards. I don't believe I shall ever have any children."

"If you marry Dudley you will," Sally said cynically. "He'll have to have an heir or two, head up a dynasty."

Deborah blushed and said hastily, "I don't like the idea of you going to the doctor all by yourself, tomorrow. Couldn't I go and wait for you around there? There's a coffee shop place, two doors away, I noticed."

"I haven't the remotest notion of allowing you to sit and drown in coffee," Sally said firmly, "because it might take hours. That stick of a nurse assured me I'd be capable of ambulation and I'll simply get a cab."

"Once you're out of there," Deborah said, "I bet they don't care what happens to you. I still think I'd better come."

"We'll see," Sally said, signaling the waiter for their check. She handed Deborah twenty dollars. "Will you pay the bill please. I must either get some fresh air or careen to the ladies room."

Once outside, she felt better and they decided to try for tickets to the theatre. They ended up seeing an evanescent musical comedy and while all the lovely flowercolored costumes kicked and bounced all over the stage and the handsome hero sang melting and inane songs, Sally thought about going under anesthetic and how you lose control over yourself and your life. No danger, painless, but all the same she was, yes, ashamed to admit it, squeezing the knowledge down into her queasy stomach which could ill afford to hold it, yes, she was indeed, afraid.

* * * *

The phone woke Matthew at six o'clock in his darkened, lumpy wallpaper, bedroom, with the cracked, green, downdrawn blinds. He dashed dopily in its direction, stumbling over shoes and furniture, picked it up and gargled hoarsely into it. It took him a few seconds to realize that the worried, apologetic voice at the other end was his Uncle Moe but the gist of the conversation was beyond him.

"Moe, look," he interrupted, "I just woke up. Could you take it a little slower?"

"I figured," Moe said sadly, "I might wake you up and believe me I'm sorry I had to. I would never do it but after all he is your brother."

Matthew listened with growing consternation as Moe explained that Sophy had called him an hour ago, hysterical.

"At the shop, you know, I was just finishing up. Go get your shikker nephew, she tells me crying, but don't bring him here. I don't want to see his face again. He was always a bum. Me, what do I know about taking care of drunks, even him. But I went down to the bar anyway. It's in the South End. He came in there, the bartender told me, already drunk and he starts an argument with one of the customers, but the bartender, who's a friend of Saul's breaks it up and tries to get him to go. But he keeps sitting there, drinking and yelling insults at everybody. That's when the bartender called Sophy. Then Saul gets up to go, only he falls down. So they try to help him get up you know, the bartender and a couple of the customers only he won't let them near him with punching and cursing. So they were just picking up the phone to call the police when I come. And then, a glass of beer in my face he throws when I tell him to come home . . ." Moe stopped and there was the sound of a long, shuddering sigh.

"Jesus Christ!" Matthew said, in a fury. "The sonovabitch! Where is he now? Where are you calling from?"

"From the bar, where else? He got himself up, God knows how, and he's sitting back in a booth with his head down on the table. The bartender, a fine man, says maybe he's passed out now but if he starts any more trouble he'll *have* to call the police. I don't know what to do with him. I know it's not right to be ashamed of my own nephew and he's a war hero with one leg, but that's the truth. One of the customers, a big man, a longshoreman, he wanted to hit him when he threw the beer at me. An old man like that, he kept saying, his own uncle. I had to push him away, to explain he was crippled . . ."

"I'll come right away," Matthew said. "Give me the name and address of the place. If he is out cold it's all to the good. I'll bring something to quiet him if he isn't, and tell the bartender not to do anything drastic even if he does start in again because I'll be responsible for him."

"You're a good boy," Moe said. "I wish I didn't have to bother you with this." He hung up and Matthew dressed hastily, completely unaware of what he was doing and had gotten out the door before he remembered that both his doctor's bag and overcoat were still in the living room.

He told the taxi to wait a few minutes when they drove up in front of the bar and went inside feeling insulted and furious. There were only a few customers and Moe, with his topcoat still on, his felt hat shoved to the back of his head, was sitting at the bar, drinking a glass of brandy, smoking a cigar and talking in a low voice to the bartender.

"Thank God," he said when he saw Matthew and got down from the stool. "I been afraid he'd wake up any minute."

"I've got the cab outside," Matthew said. "We'll have to take him to my place since Sophy's so worked up. Anyway, it's closer."

"His car's outside," the bartender intervened. "I was looking outa the window when he got here and I saw him park it across the street. The keys fell outa his pocket when he was swinging. I didn't wanna take 'em but somebody mighta stolen them." He handed them to Matthew.

"Thanks. I'm sorry about all the trouble he caused. Any damages?"

"Ah, he broke a coupla glasses," the bartender said easily. "But it's okay, forget it. I mean, I was in the war myself and it's just luck I got all my arms and legs. I never seen Saul this stiff for a long time. Something real bad must be eating him."

"How will we get him out of here?" Moe asked, looking in dismay at the behemoth bulk snoring in the booth.

"That's some dead weight," one of the customers, a redfaced fat man in a worn mackinaw, who was chewing gum in between swallows of beer, offered jovially. "You ain't got a block and tackle in that bag widya, Doc, haveya?" He laughed uproariously, and alone, at his joke.

"Doc," the bartender said, "if you bring his car over in front we can drag him, like we used to do wounded men in the Army. You figure it'll hurt his leg?"

"I don't think so." Matthew went out to pay and dismiss the cab driver and get Saul's car. It took four, large, strong men, with many muttered curses and much heavy breathing, to propel and heave his brother out of the bar and fling him like a ton of old, soiled potatoes into the back of the car. Matthew looked in silent contempt at the huge, inert mass stretched out pale and snoring. Moe had arranged him tenderly so that his bad leg rested on the seat.

"I think I better sit here in back with him," Moe said. "Otherwise, he'll roll off."

"I wouldn't mind if he fell on his goddamn head," Matthew said bitterly, starting up the car. "There's no room for you to sit there anyway."

"I'll just sit right on the end here," Moe said gently. "It's all right, I'm comfortable enough."

"You're too damn good to the bastard. Look at him! He looks like he's been on Skid Row for years. How the hell did Sophy ever let him go out looking like that?" He stopped for a light and cast a disgusted glance over his shoulder at Saul's unshaven face and old rag and bone man clothes.

"Sophy didn't see him, that's why," Moe said simply. "He took an apartment of his own. I don't mind telling you, in a way, it was a relief. But I guess it wasn't such a good idea because look what he does. That bartender was right, though, he must be in some trouble. He hasn't been like this since right after he came from the Army."

"Well, he's going to be in more trouble if he pulls a thing like this again," Matthew said angrily. "The next time the cops can have him. He'll end up in some psycho ward and maybe then I can manage to get him to a psychiatrist or hauled into one of the VA hospitals for some mental rehabilitation."

"Listen, Matthew," Moe said, "don't be so hotheaded. You don't want to put your brother into any mental hospital. He'll be all right. I was thinking of him when he was a boy," he added in a faraway voice, "a handsome little boy. In knickers, with his stockings always wrinkled and falling down. And you. When you both came to live with us, so sad and missing your mother. Such wonderful little boys. And how glad we were, Sophy and I, we could have you, with none of our own."

"I don't want to hear about it," Matthew said rudely. "Other guys have straightened up, war or no war. Why can't he?"

"Maybe it ain't so easy for him. Some people are more nervous, excitable, you know more about this than I do, than other people. He was not a calm person even as a boy, Saul."

Matthew remembered, all too well, how Sophy and Moe had kissed them and looked at them, he and Saul, with wondering, unsure eyes, when they'd come there to live and how they knew, young as they were, the way children know, that Sophy and Moe wanted to love them, and how satisfying it'd been for those poor orphans (how he hated that shabby, poorhouse word) to be cruel to Sophy, to turn away from her kisses, her love, her warmth, because she was not their mother, because nobody ever would be again. How they'd plotted and schemed for a long time to disobey her, to speak ostentatiously of how their mother did this and that and never did such-and-such and the quick, fiendish joy at seeing the disappointment in Sophy's face. After awhile, he had begun to forget and to think maybe Sophy was all right, but Saul had never really forgotten and kept egging him on. Then later, it'd all dissolved and Sophy and Moe were their family. To him, but not really ever to Saul probably, although he'd stopped talking about it. And, after all the lousiness they'd perpetrated as kids because they had been hurt, his rotten, stinking brother had thrown a glass of beer in Moe's kind face. Maybe insanity does run in families, emotional instability if not downright insanity, that was what Moe had meant in his tactful way by saying that some people were more excitable than others, wasn't it? Well, I'm going to lay down the law to that roughneck, Matthew thought, if and when he wakes up. He felt afresh, the rage that'd possessed him when he'd come into the bar and seen his brother passed out in that stinking dump and later at the wisecrack of the old scum who'd joked about his doctor's bag.

"He's awake," Moe said softly.

Saul's eyes were open. He was staring at the roof of the car, mumbling to himself.

"How the hell did I get here?" He sat up clumsily and painfully.

"A fairy godmother brought you," Matthew said, "in a pumpkin. Moe, I'll drive up in front of my place and you two get out. Probly no place to park there."

"What're you doing driving my car?" Saul demanded belligerently. "And be careful with it. Do you have to bang around so much? My head, Christ!"

"You shut up," Matthew said wrathfully. "Just keep your goddamn trap shut, that's all. You'd be in jail now, which is where you belong, you lousy ingrate, if it hadn't been for Moe. Can you walk?"

"Sure, I can walk. Who the hell says I can't walk?"

"You couldn't before. Or don't you remember?"

"I don't remember nothing," Saul said sullenly.

Matthew snorted and left Moe to take Saul up to his apartment while he drove around and finally found a parking space halfway down Temple Street outside the Episcopal convent. When he came upstairs, Moe was on the phone to Sophy and Saul was washing up in the bathroom. Matthew started some coffee and waited, skulking in the kitchen till it was done, hearing Moe and Saul out in the living room, talking in low voices, Moe's soothing and Saul's blurred, still thick, and interspersed with groans.

"Here, drink this." He thrust a large mug of hot, black coffee at his brother who was slumped moodily in the armchair.

"Thanks," Saul mumbled. "Thanks for everything, Bud. Moe's been telling me."

"It's Moe you should thank, not me. And apologize to."

Saul was chewing on his lower lip, looking embarrassed. "You think I would've done a thing like that, Christ, if I crawled on my knees, I couldn't show how bad I feel about it. I didn't know it was him, everybody all of a sudden seemed like enemies."

"It's all right," Moe cut in. "I don't hold it against you Solly. Only you shouldn't drink so much, you know you got to be careful." He was putting on his coat as he spoke. "I'm going home. Sophy's all upset. Solly, why don't you stay here tonight? If it's all right by Matthew."

"Sure," Matthew said indifferently.

Saul shook his head. "I got to go to work pretty soon. I'll be okay. I'll go to my place and take a shower."

Moe muttered dubiously about how maybe Saul should call in sick and how he shouldn't stay alone and if it weren't for Sophy's nerves he'd insist Saul come home with him and finally was persuaded that Matthew would watch over Saul with brotherly tenderness and medical solicitude and took himself off.

"Now that he's gone," Matthew said coldly, "we don't have to be polite any more. You can stay here tonight if you want. I'm going on duty. I don't care. If you want my advice you won't go to work the way you are now. Sleep it off. But you don't want my advice, do you? So just go to hell your own way, with my blessings, because as of right now I've forgotten who you are. In fact it hadn't been for Moe I'd've let the cops have you, and I wouldn't be in any rush to spring you out of the tank, believe me." He waited resignedly for the indignant bellow, the string of curses, after which he would try once more for the positively last damn time to get his brother to Gregor's office. But Saul just kept sitting there hunched in his chair, silent, rubbing his eyes in a dazed way, the spiteful sneer gone from his face which was now as unprotected and anguished as, in Matthew's memory, it had been only once before on a shocking day, twenty years ago.

"I've got to talk to you, Bud," he said finally in a low voice. "Can the doctor crap, will you? I don't care what you do with me. I just gambled everything I had on my last card and I think I lost so I don't give a damn."

"You should have gone on the stage," Matthew said. "Everything's always a big, dramatic crisis. Okay, go ahead. Talk, if it'll help you any."

"I don't want any of your creepy sympathy. But I got to talk to somebody, somebody like you, because you understand people like her and I don't."

"I knew it was a girl," Matthew said disgustedly. "You're such a screwy extremist. For years you hate women, treat them like dirt and all of a sudden you go off the deep end over some whore. You're unbalanced."

Saul laughed grimly. "A whore, huh? If I wasn't feeling so lousy I ought to belt you but I won't because what a shock you got coming. In fact, it's funny."

"All right," Matthew said flippantly, "I could use a laugh. Let me in on it."

"Well, hold on to your pants wiseguy. It's Sally Brimmer, the sister of that high and mighty doctor chum of yours. We were away all summer together. In Nahant and Rockport. She went for me in a real big way and I . . ." He choked and his face which had been a triumphant mirror of reflection for Matthew's obvious shock, suddenly changed, twisted and he put both his hands over his eyes as if at a sudden stab of pain. "We had a beautiful relationship," he went on finally, his voice hushed and holy. "I'm crazy in love with her like I've never been with anyone in my life. And I know she loved me for a long time. What're you looking at me like that for? You don't think a girl like that would go for me, do you?"

"Sure, Saul," Matthew said soothingly. It must be a joke, he thought, things like this couldn't happen to anyone. He's really nuts. I haven't seen him to talk to since last May when she came here for the first time and he's crazy enough to hold on to the same riling jokes.

"Don't give me that baby in wet pants routine," Saul said. "You don't believe me, do you?"

"No," he sighed. "Saul, look, I know you're in some sort of mess.

But try not to get carried away will you? If you'd been going out with Sally don't you think I'd've heard about it from Dud."

"You're always so goddamn reasonable, aren't you," Saul said contemptuously. "Well, I got my pride too, you know. I didn't want you poking your nose in my business and apologizing for me because you think I'm not good enough for your friends, so my name is Saul Milman to Dud Brimmer."

"This whole story is fantastic," Matthew said angrily.

"I wish it were but it ain't, boy." He'd gotten up from his chair and was moving about uneasily, prowling around the room, standing by the dusty window, pulling a shade up and down. "Bud, look, for a minute, forget you don't like me. Forget I disgraced you. I wouldn't talk to you, I wouldn't bother you, only I need to. I'm sunk, I tell you, if she leaves me, I'm washed up. Look," he pleaded to Matthew's stony face, "just let me talk, let me finish. Sure, I knew I wasn't her kind, I didn't want to get started with her. But she wanted to, and who could resist her anyway, you've seen her, you know. So, at first, well, it was just the best damn kind of sex a man could want, I, believe me, Bud, I'd sooner cut my tongue out than talk like this, but I got to be honest. I'd never had anything like that before, so . . . so . . . perfect. And before I knew what was happening, I was falling for her, the real thing. I began to think, it was so right, it couldn't be just an ordinary shack job. Nothing like that could happen more than twice in a lifetime. With most people it don't happen at all. I mean, she loved me, I knew she did. She took care of me." He paused trying to control the tremor in his voice and Matthew listened, cold and stricken as a man who has just looked into the eyes of the Medusa. "She saw me, just as I was, with my damn stub and she loved me as much as a whole man. I can't never tell you how it was being with her, how wonderful and loving and kind and beautiful. So I thought she had to love me the way I loved her because nobody could be the way she was with me and not love them. So I asked her to marry me. And she wouldn't."

"And then you finally got it into your cockeyed fathead that she didn't love you?"

"No sir." Saul shook his head with bullish determination. "I knew she did. I'd stake my life on that. And then, I figured, well she's just a kid, she don't know her own mind, or what's good for her. So I pulled a pretty lousy trick on her. If it worked she'd have to marry me. I . . ."

"Never mind," Matthew said, "pass over the details please. I have a good imagination. Although in my wildest mental gymnastics, I could never make up a simpleton like you. You goddamn golem!"

"Well," Saul was saying obliviously, "I guess it didn't work anyway. But when she got back from Rockport she started acting funny, different. And today, this morning, she called me up, just when I got home from work, I ain't had any sleep all day, that's one reason I got so loaded, and she was going to New York. So right away, I knew, that was it, the end, she was going off with some other man, she'd never just have gone off that way, without telling me beforehand, if it wasn't something like that."

"So you reacted in characteristic fashion by getting soused in every dump in town?"

"Yeah, I guess so," Saul said vacantly. "What the hell else is there to do? When you get the ax, you get it, that's all. I can smell a bad ending from way off."

"Saul, you're a grown man. You're thirty-two years old. A girl gave you the heave-ho and you react like an adolescent. What do you expect me to do about it? Why tell me? I can't mend broken hearts."

"Thanks," Saul said bitterly, "thanks a lot. I might've known what I'd get from you. You don't remember when you were a kid and you didn't want to let me out of your sight and I used to take you with me everywhere, even when my gang used to complain they didn't like babies tagging along, I used to say that I was all the family you had left and you went where I went. And you forget about all the fights I fought for you and when I was working after school how I'd give you some dough so's you could buy candy and go to the movies and buy a baseball mitt. And when you was in high school and college how I used to help you so you'd have enough to take girls out once in a while and buy smokes and books. I never begrudged you anything I could give you."

"Saul, stop it, for Godsakes. I remember and I've always been grateful. You know it. But what can I do for you now? Anyway, you're always building a mountain out of nothing. So she went to New York? What's so terrible about that?"

"I don't know," Saul said. "Maybe nothing. But you go see her brother all the time. Maybe you've seen another guy up there, with her, some slick Arrow collar guy. And I want you to tell me."

"I haven't gone there much. But when I have there's been no other man there."

"So you're admitting it now," Saul said cunningly.

"Admitting what, for Godsakes?"

"That it is Sally. Before you thought I was crazy. Making up a dream."

"Oh, I believe you," Matthew said tiredly. "Even you couldn't imagine anything that screwed up. You'd have to live it. What I don't understand you damn ignoramus, is why you wanted to get her pregnant? Don't you realize the . . . the . . ." He gave up the search for a word to express the enormity of his brother's idiocy.

"I don't see what's so wrong about it? It happens to a lot of people. That's how most kids are born. I love the girl, I wanted to marry her. I wanted to have a kid, a family, and for her to be the mother of them. She'd make a wonderful mother."

"We must be talking about two different women. I've never noticed anything maternal about Miss Brimmer."

"You don't know her," Saul said stubbornly.

"I guess not. You know, Saul, if you want to have a family there are plenty of women who'd be better choices."

"She's the only one I want."

"And what if she has thrown you over? What're you going to do about it?"

Saul turned and faced him, his hands in the pockets of his filthy pants. Matthew realized with a sudden shock that he was the living picture of a desperate man, with his red-rimmed eyes, unshaven face and seedy clothes. He never had so much grey in his hair before, he thought, and then, he needs a haircut. The disreputable coat sweater was buttoned tight across his thickening stomach and, in addition to the barroom smells of stale beer and cigarette smoke, there arose from this huge, towering body, the impalpable odor of strength decaying, of the mind's deterioration. He's my brother, Matthew thought, and he's rotting and he had all the lousy breaks in the world and then there she was, a beautiful mirage, a tantalizing rainbow in the dust and he has to believe she's real. Sara, steadfast at the well of the green oasis.

"If I've lost her," Saul said grimly, "there's a couple of pretty good ways out of this shit of a life. You could help me there, huh? Pills, maybe."

"Now take it easy," Matthew said perfunctorily. "How about another cup of coffee?"

"Why not? It all tastes like hell anyway."

In the kitchen, Matthew stood holding the match to the gas burner but forgetting to turn it on until the flame burned his fingers. If I were him, I'd like to know, he'd said to Sally and she'd laughed and said, no you wouldn't. The memory of how he was lulled, caressed, duped by her laugh, her presence, her voice, made his stomach squirm. What a jolly horse's ass he'd turned out to be. And yet, wasn't she right, now that he knew it was Saul, wasn't she? But my brother, poor, lousy, rotten, hardluck Saul. And he didn't want much, did he? All the simp wanted was a girl who'd give her body to be burned by every passing flame of passion but her hand in marriage, please, he wanted that too, the mother of his children yet.

He came out carrying the coffee. It was very quiet. Saul was sitting by the lamp, reading, of all macabre touches, the Bible.

"I didn't know you'd taken to the Good Book. Since when?"

His brother barely glanced at him. "I started in the hospital. Any objections?"

"No, no," Matthew said hastily. "It just seems unusual, that's all."

"At the time," Saul said musingly, "the idea of an eye for an eye appealed to me. I used to think how I'd like to go and cut off some German's leg, personally. I'd think it all out, every detail. Then I formed a kind of a habit. I carry this around with me, it's small, one I got in the Army, and I turn to any page, to see what it's got to say. And I was just going through now and I came to Proverbs. Listen, do you want to hear this?"

"Sure," Matthew said bewildered. "Sure, Saul. Only drink your coffee huh?"

" '*In the twilight, in the evening in the black and dark night*
And behold there met him a woman with the attire of a harlot and
  subtil of heart . . .'

"I'm skipping some of it, see.

" '*So she caught him and kissed him and with an impudent face said*
  unto him
I have peace offerings with me . . .
Therefore, came I forth to meet thee, diligently to seek thy face
  and I have found thee
I have decked my bed with coverings of tapestry with carved works
  with fine linen of Egypt
I have perfumed my bed with myrrh aloes and cinnamon
Come let us take our fill of love until the morning;
Let us solace ourselves with loves . . .

He goeth after her straight way as an ox goeth to the slaughter or as
  a fool to the correction of the stocks
Till a dark strike through his liver as a bird hasteth to the snare and
  knoweth not that it is for his life . . .

Let not thine heart decline to her ways go not astray in her paths.
For she has cast down many wounded: yea, many strong men have
been slain by her
Her house is the way to hell going down to the chambers of
death . . .'"

"Very nice writing," Matthew said exasperatedly, "but how does it tally with the mother of your children image?"

"I don't know," Saul said despairingly. "She's like both see. But I know that with me she's the best woman can be. I wanted a son," he added feverishly, "to watch grow up, give him a happy life. I thought I could give her one and she'd give him to me. And I'd love her and work till I dropped for her and for him. There's nothing else I wanted but I couldn't even do that. Any damn little jerk in town could put one in the oven but I couldn't even do that."

"Why the hell can't you be reasonable? Forget about her and find another woman who *wants* to have a son for you."

"*She's* my woman. But you wouldn't know about that. You've never been there, Buddy. Even if she went off with another guy for a while, I don't care, see. Just so she comes back to me. I got no pride any more. Maybe you can talk to her, Bud. Would you do that for me? You can talk her language. When she comes back. Kind of smooth things out. So she'll know I'm not sore. I'd be afraid to see her first, in case there was somebody else. I couldn't take it cold like that."

Matthew walked around tensely, his hands shoved, fisted, into his pockets wanting to shout, shut up, to that exhausted, pleading voice, which had lost all its brave pretense of bellicosity. Stand up and be the man you once were, Saul.

It's nuts to tell him, he thought, it's too late anyway, she's right, it might send him over the really deep end, but she won't leave him, no, she likes his bed all right and he's got to know what she is, because she can't get away with it, he *is* my brother and she insulted both of us, not only as brothers but as men, laughing up her sleeve, rotten, spoiled bitch . . .

"I have something to tell you," he said. "Put down your Bible. This is a true-to-life story." And if, he thought, in cynical wretchedness, the fierce, moral old Jehovah with His simple, breach for breach justice that Saul believes in, exists and can look into my heart and tell me why I'm doing this, He's the only one who can.

Four

The sky was a whitegray over Washington Square Park where brightly jacketed students scudded across the paths, clutching their books, backs to the cold wind, under the naked trees.

"Where do you suppose they're all going?" Deborah was standing at the window holding her coffee cup. "It's ten o'clock. Too late for public school classes."

"New York University is somewhere hereabouts," Sally said. She yawned and pulled her scarlet wool robe tightly around her. "Why in the world did we ever get up so early? I feel absolutely dreary. What a vile morning."

"It's going to snow," Deborah said dreamily. "When I went out to get the groceries, I could tell right away, the way the wind was, uncompromising, and the way the air smelled."

"You're just an old Yankee weather prophet," Sally said, pouring herself some more coffee. "It's very pleasant though, having breakfast here. And awfully sweet of you to've gone and gotten all this, Deb."

"We have this kitchenette," Deborah said practically, "and we ought to use it. Anyway, I wanted to go out and look around a little. It's really quite nice here, like the Hill, only not so steep. Or handsome and historical," she added loyally. "It's more commercial too, you know, lots of shops, funny ones. They sell leather work, sandals and weird-looking copper and silver jewelry."

"Why, this is Bohemia," Sally said gravely. "In Boston, Bohemia is frowned on, which is sort of too bad. Although, here, it's degenerated into a rather regrettable artsy-craftiness."

"There were quite a few bookshops too," Deborah said. "But they weren't open. You know, if there's a college over there they probably have a library. I might be able to do some reading while I'm here."

"You really miss being in class, don't you?" Sally said wonderingly. "You've been looking at those students out there with a positively green face."

"A little," Deborah said. "I mean, I hate to cut any of my Seventeenth-Century Lit classes because they're so interesting. We're just starting on Milton this week, but I brought a paperback edition of Milton with me. So that doesn't matter. But you see, Sally, I'll just never catch up. Not with classes, but with all the books I want to read, even if I live to be ninety-five and my eyes hold out; so I have to spend every spare minute doing as much of it as I can."

"Nevertheless," Sally said firmly, "I don't think you ought to read while you're here. Loaf and invite your soul as the man said. Sightsee. Museums if you must. We'll reverse roles. You can be the social flibbertigibbet and I shall curl up in bed with the books. Perhaps we can go out presently and tour the bookstores and I'll indulge my frivolous tastes."

"I'll get lost if I go sightseeing alone," Deborah said. "I know I will. This city scares me it's so enormous. I won't mind going around here by myself. It seems sort of casual and friendly and people dress in an interesting way and not in that frightening elegance we saw on Fifth Avenue. And I really do have to read some in *Paradise Lost*, because that's what he'll be talking about in class when I get back."

"At Berkeley," Sally said, "I was awfully surprised when I found I liked that epic. I had a dreadful prejudice against old John, dating from my years at Miss Folsom's. All those stuffy sonnets about his late lamented saint and Hence loathed fun and games. Then, of course, Joe was a Milton scholar which made the man even more abhorrent to me."

"He was?" Deborah asked eagerly, her face lighting up. "Your husband? I didn't know that. But then why . . . I mean . . ."

"Oh yes. He wrote his doctoral dissertation on *Paradise Lost*. Frightfully brilliant, I've heard tell. I didn't understand a word of it when I read it. I still have a copy around somewhere in a trunk."

"Oh, I'd love to read it," Deborah said excitedly. "He must've been terribly, terribly smart to get his doctorate so young."

"A fearful brain," Sally said flippantly. "Overpowering in fact. You'd've been quite struck with him, Deborah, and he might have admired you more than he did most women. He hated stupid women. Like me. Once called me a mindless succubus. I've never forgotten it. Don't look so incredulous, darling. Rotten marriages happen all the time. Now, since I'm responsible for you missing your classes why don't you get old Milton and read some of your stint out loud to me while I finish up the coffee. Then we'll dress and go bookhunting."

"Well, if you're sure you want to. I don't read very well." She came back carrying her book and plumped into a chair, slipping on her glasses. The frames were black and oddly shaped. She looked at Sally like a solemn young panda and said earnestly, "Just the same, I don't see how anyone could despise your mind. Because you're awfully smart, I think, but not one-sided, as so many intelligent people are."

"You know," Sally said, sipping on the coffee, "in one sense I suppose that Joe was good for me. He did touch my pride and I decided that my brain was every bit as good as his if I wanted to apply it, so I did. Only then, of course it was too late to challenge him. Now I know that even if he had come back, my new learning wouldn't have impressed him at all. He had an overweening sense of superiority. A god complex. One of those Baal-type gods that needed human sacrifices to keep them going. Innocent maidens principally. Like you or me, as I was. Let it be a lesson to you."

"Of course I don't plan to get married or fall in love," Deborah said, opening her book, "but if I did, I don't know if I'd recognize a . . . a . . . sense of superiority in somebody."

"No," Sally said, "that's the hell of it. You probably wouldn't. Or else, as I was, you'd be in such a hurry to rebel you wouldn't care." She closed her eyes. "Go ahead and read, Deb, so I can stop being presumptuous."

"This is the beginning," Deborah said and began to read in a soft uncertain voice which became more strong and sure as she went along, taking each one of the heavy, ornate, golden, baroque words and setting them correctly into their foreordained niche of that huge structure of the Puritan vision of God and man:

> "*'Him the Almighty Power*
> *Hurld headlong flaming from the Ethereal Skie*
> *With hideous ruine and combustion down*
> *To bottomless perdition, there to dwell*
> *In Adamantine Chains and penal Fire,*
> *Who durst defy the Omnipotent to Arms.*
> *Nine times the Space that measures Day and Night*
> *To mortal men, he with his horrid crew*
> *Lay vanquisht, rowling in the fiery Gulfe*
> *Confounded though immortal.'*

"Isn't it interesting, Sally, how spelling changes. They spelled rolling with a w then. But probably the pronunciation was different too." She went back to her reading becoming more and more absorbed and Sally half-listened, only a few phrases catching her ear. What if she started bleeding and couldn't stop? Blood, what color was it? Not bright red, but almost a wine color, thick, pouring out of her and no way to stop it . . .

"Go on," she said sharply, suddenly aware of the silence in the room.

"I didn't think you were listening."

"Of course. I love all the evil angels although my favorite is Belial."

"Who's he?"

"Look ahead. I believe there are descriptions of most of them." Deborah flipped pages. "Oh yes. You mean this?

> "*In Courts and Palaces he also Reigns*
> *And in luxurious Cities where the noyse*
> *Of riot ascends above their loftiest Towrs,*
> *And Injury and outrage: And when Night*
> *Darkens the Streets, then wander forth the Sons*
> *Of Belial, flown with insolence and wine.'*

What a marvelous line, 'flown with insolence and wine.' "

"I knew you'd like it," Sally said, adding diffidently, "I read in Joe's dissertation that it was well-known that this picture of the sons of Belial was Milton's Puritanical description of the Restoration. Well-known that is, to scholars. I hadn't the faintest inkling." She laughed. "Deborah, really, your eyes are like saucers. What's so astounding about it?"

"But it's fascinating. I just thought of it as an awfully long poem about religion. I didn't dream it could have . . . a contemporary application, for Milton's time, that is. D'you suppose Lucifer was based on a real person?"

> "*If thou beest he: But O how fall'n! how changed*
> *From him who in the happy Realms of Light*
> *Cloth'd with transcendent brightness didst out-shine*
> *Myriads though bright:*"

The small gold watch at Sally's wrist imperiously pushed aside the minutes. Quarter of eleven. Soon time. "So from hour to hour we ripe and ripe and then from hour to hour we rot and rot and thereby hangs a tale." Dramatic Society's play, junior year, when she was, ridiculously, Rosalind, with the least boyish figure in school. Why be frightened? Dr. Phillips, very capable, did this sort of thing, twelve times every day. Gray-faced, dying, the sheets soaked and red.

> "Farewell, happy Fields
> Where Joy for ever dwells: Hail horrours, hail
> Infernal world, and thou profoundest Hell
> Receive thy new Possessor: One who brings
> A mind not to be changed by Place or Time.
> The mind is its own place, and in itself
> Can make a Heav'n of Hell, a Hell of Heavn.
> What matter where, if I be still the same,
> And what I . . ."

The phone rang. "Now who could that be?" Deborah lifted her eyes from the book, frowning slightly. "No one knows we're here, do they?"

"Matthew. Oh! I promised to call him last night and completely forgot. Perhaps he got anxious." Sally hurried into the bedroom and picked up the receiver.

"Honey," Saul said, "Y'all right? I'm right near here. Gotta see you."

Sally looked blankly at the phone in her hand. I don't believe it, I just don't believe it. Yes, but there he was, his voice crackling off in the distance. "How did you get here, Saul? How did you . . ."

"Now what do you think? My brother turned out to be a good kid after all. At least he let me in on your little plan which is more than you had the decency to do."

Sally sat quietly, struggling with the rage that boiled up inside her. "I don't know what your purpose was in coming here, Saul. But it won't do any good."

"Ah have a heart, for Godsakes, Sally. I was the guy you loved last summer, remember? Now, all of a sudden, you're gonna get rid of my baby and I'm not even supposed to talk about it with you. What the hell kind of a fair shake is that?"

"My memory is excellent, thank you," Sally said coldly, "And I also remember that you weren't very fair to me."

"We don't have to argue about it over the phone, do we? I wanna see you. I'm in a ginmill round the cawner from your hotel."

"I don't want to see *you*. Particularly not in a bar when you're drunk at eleven o'clock in the morning. I'll see you when I get back to Boston."

"Lissen at who's talking about drunks," he scoffed. "Now you come on over here, Sally, if you don't want trouble."

"You needn't bluster," Sally said, thinking quickly. "Why don't you go back to your hotel and sleep off your little drunk and I'll see you tonight."

He laughed nastily. "That's a good one. In the first place, baby doll, it won't work. Because I have no dough. No hotel room. I'm broke, stony, and I owe the bartender money for at least four drinks. In the second place don't think I don't know why you wanna postpone our little meeting. Oh no you don't! Either you come over here and talk to me, or I'll get the hell out of this bar somehow and come over there and bang on your door till you let me in. And it won't look good for you, baby, because believe me, right now, I don't look like no surprise package." There was the sound of a coin dropping and the operator's conventional interruption. "I gotta hang up," Saul said desperately, "I ain't got another cent. Honey, help me out, will you? You owe me at least the right to talk it over with you. It's a bar called La Verne's. Right around the cawner."

"Don't you want me to go with you?" Deborah asked nervously as they stood by the elevator waiting. "You might need help."

"Darling, no one would allow you into the sort of bar Saul is obviously in. No, you go book browsing. I'll be quite all right. This is my own little dram of hemlock and only I can drink it."

I have only two hours to get rid of him, she thought, diving into the cold wind outside the hotel door and letting it toss her around the corner and down the street. The bar was a small, narrow, dark place and, as might be expected at that hour of the morning, Saul was the only customer. She saw him through the window. He was leaning gloomily over a beer glass. I don't have to go in, she thought, pausing in the act of pressing the door handle. His back was to her and he couldn't see her there. I could just turn around and go away. Leave a message at the hotel for Deborah to meet me. She could get us packed while I'm at the doctor's and we'd get another place. He'd keep calling and after awhile he'd get tired and go home. Yes, that would be perfectly lovely, thought Sally, standing irresolutely by the door, he doesn't even have enough money to pay his way out of a bar, how could he possibly get home? Yes, it would be grand and easy to desert a man who was half-drunk and in a dreadful emotional state, and leave him to limp along the streets with nowhere to go, dragging his aluminum badge of courage. The police would probably pick him up, that unpaid bartender would see to that. The fact that he deserved it for behaving like a fool and tearing down to New York, half-cocked and so stirred up by liquor and rage that he didn't have sense enough to bring money along, didn't alter or solve the problem.

Saul turned his head toward the open door and gazed at her blankly for a moment as she came toward him, her heels clacking loudly in the silence of the bar. Then he smiled and make a move to kiss her as she came next to him but at the incredible sight of him, she drew back. Could this disgusting loathsome-looking derelict be Saul? And, as she continued to stare, unable to take her eyes away, she realized that it not only was Saul, but also that it was truly Saul. The real thing. All the time underneath. The hairy ape had rent his garments and come into the open.

"Honey," he said thickly, his bloodshot eyes, peering at her uncertainly, "am I glad to see you. I knew you'd come. I knew it. Come on, give us a little kiss, huh? I come miles for you to give me a little lovin' kiss and you're looking at me all stiff. Cold as a witch's tit. What you need's a drink. Hey, bartender!"

Sally shook her head at the bartender who appeared suddenly and responded with an almost imperceptible nod, looking at Saul with a professionally inured poker face. "Nothing for me, thank you," Sally said. "What do you owe here?"

"A buck, two bucks, what's the difference. Come on, baby, why you being so standoffish?" Saul put his hand on her shoulder. "This here's my girl," he said loudly to the bartender. "Isn't she lovely? But I come all the way to New York to see her and she won't have a drink with me," he added in an injured tone. "Whatdya think a that?"

"Two dollars," the bartender said to Sally, barely moving his lips.

Sally shook off Saul's heavy grimy hand with its black, filthy nails and handed the money to the bartender.

"Another beer here," Saul mumbled.

"No more," Sally said firmly. "Finish what you have there and we'll have some breakfast."

The bartender disappeared as silently as he'd come, back into the tunnel-like gloom at the rear of the bar.

"Who the hell wants breakfast?" Saul demanded. "I'm not hungry. What's the idea, Sally? I wanna talk to you. Why can't we talk here, have a drink?"

"I'll be outside. Come out when you're done." She clamped a hand over her mouth and plunged out the door, leaning against the window of a dress shop, breathing deeply of the precious air, and in a few seconds began to feel more normal. The smell that all cheap bars have, she thought, of uncleaned johns and spilled beer, but that alone wouldn't have done it, because standing next to Saul she'd caught also, the stale, sickening odor of someone who'd not washed or put on clean clothes for several days, who'd been drinking and smoking and sweating in those same clothes in those same cheap bars for endless hours. Kiss him, Sally thought shuddering, at the thought of putting her mouth anywhere near that rank, fetid breath, that scraggly, dark mass of bristles on the unshaven face, my God, I'd rather be buried alive. She felt some cold drops on her face and looked upward to see that the snow, predicted by Deborah, had come, and even as she watched, the white swirls got wilder. It was not to be a tentative snow. Silently Saul came behind her and took her hand.

"You left your coat in the bar," Sally said, noticing suddenly that he was wearing only a faded green coat sweater, stained all down the front, the elbows of which were non-existent, except for ragged fringes of wool. "You'd better go back and get it."

"No coat there," he said indifferently. "Who needs one? I'm not cold. I got you to keep me warm, don't I, honey?"

"Saul. It's snowing. Now where did you leave your coat?"

"Waddya talking about?" He looked at her in surprise. "I'm telling you. No coat. Mighta had one yesterday, but that was Boston. This is New York, see. No coat."

"Where's your car?" Sally asked practically. "Perhaps it's in there?"

"Yeah, maybe. But that's in Boston too."

"You came on the train looking like that?" Sally could not keep the disgust out of her voice.

"Well I didn't walk. Don't walk too well these days. Sure, on the train. I was in a hurry. With a lot on my mind. No time for coats and luggage and toothbrushes and all that crap for jerks. What're you getting so worked up about whether I got a coat or not for? You think I came here to talk about my clothes?" He pulled at her arm. "Quit stalling, Sally. You can't do this to me. It's my kid and I want it. You're not getting rid of any kid of mine. Over my dead body."

The icy snowladen wind knifed in quick, menacing little thrusts around them as they stood in the doorway. Sally shivered in her warm coat. What will I do with him, she wondered, looking prayerfully at the falling snow, what will I ever do? Just walking through the streets with him was unthinkable.

He held her arm tightly and glared down at her. "All right, I'm waiting to hear what you got to say. That's why I traveled all night on the stinking train, going nuts all the way. Now just tell me how you think you can do this to me?"

Looking at his awful face, down at his dreadful clothes, hearing his cracked, desperate voice and the tears rising unbidden to her eyes. A wave of pity and tenderness washed over her, melting the hard glitter of anger and aversion. I must love him, Sally thought, because, in spite of what he looks like now, and what he is, I still want him, want to take him in my arms and comfort him. He was like a big tree, half cut down, swaying crazily in the wind, soon to crash down and lie utterly still, all the power and grandeur quite gone. Eleven-thirty. Take a cab to the doctor's at one-thirty. Two hours.

"Saul," she said softly, "if you want to talk we will. But first you must come to the hotel with me and take a bath and get some sleep."

"I feel swell now," he said sourly. "And I'm not going anywhere with you or do anything unless you promise to come home with me, now, and marry me and have my kid like an honest woman."

"How utterly mad you are standing there, coatless, risking pneumonia in the snow and talking like a fool. I'll promise nothing of the sort and you know it. But I will get you a razor and toothbrush and then you come back to the hotel with me and we'll talk about it quietly. I shall not argue and shout in doorways in the cold. If you don't come with me I shall walk away and leave you here and you'll be picked up as a vagrant. Do as you choose, I don't care."

He laughed wildly, thrusting his hands deep into the sagging pockets of his dirty, baggy pants. "You think you'll get across the lobby of that hotel with me, sister? You don't know hotels too well, do you?"

"You're a guest of mine. They wouldn't dare do anything."

"They'd throw both of us out," he said. "No, that won't work, baby. Anyway, what the hell do you care how I look? What am I, a suit of clothes to you? I can remember a time when all you wanted was no clothes on me or you."

Sally saw a small bow-windowed chemist-type shop down at the corner, presiding quaintly at the junction of three winding, tiny alleys. "Come along, darling. I want to get something."

But he walked so slowly, steering a zigzag course, head down into the wind, that she hurried ahead of him and was in and out of the store with her purchases in time to deflect his oblivious, bear-like stumble toward the curb.

"Can you go back to that bar and use the men's room to clean up in? I've bought you a razor, soap and . . ."

"You think of everything, don't you?" he sneered. "Except what I want to know."

"Will you do as I say? Because until you get to look a little less like a wild animal I will not be seen with you or talk to you. Is that clear?"

"You always have to be the boss, don't you? And since when is it ladylike to stamp your foot in the street like that? Okay, okay, if it makes so damn much difference to you, I'll go shave. Only you better give me some dough. I'll have to tip the lousy bartender."

She gave him all the loose change in her purse and told him she'd be waiting in the cafeteria around the next corner. The nurse had told her not to eat any food for several hours before the operation, sometimes complicated the anesthesia apparently, so Sally lighted a cigarette and sipped a cup of bad coffee, watching for Saul. If we must talk, she thought, this is as good a place as any. It was moderately full and noisy enough to drown out any shouting Saul might feel called on to indulge in. But the best thing about it, surprisingly enough, although why should she be surprised when cafeteria-going was not her habit, was that Saul would not stand out in seediness. Costumes here ran to disreputable-looking sweaters and coats, and beards were as common to the many young, blue-jeaned men as to the old red-nosed ones.

When Saul finally came through the revolving door she saw at once that it had been a mistake to give him money and leeway in a bar. Although shaved, he had also obviously tucked away a few more drinks and not beer this time. He sat across the table and looked at her sullenly. His curly thick hair was blown about by the wind and wet from the snow. She drew a comb from her purse and handed it to him. He looked at the comb belligerently but took it and combed his hair down.

"I'll get you some coffee," she said.

"Don't want coffee." He thrust the comb at her. "Say listen, Sally, what is this? When did you get into the Salvation Army? Now I did what you wanted. I got shaved and washed. And I cut myself too, dammit." He fingered a bloody smear on his right cheek. "N'I brushed my teeth too. Even washed behind my ears. I musta looked like a real ass to that bartender. Had to ask him for a towel. But I'm not taking any more of this, see! You're going to tell me what the hell you're up to and do what I say for a change instead of running me around by the nose. Where you going? I said I didn't want any coffee."

Petulantly he pushed away the steaming cup she'd brought.

"You'd better drink it," Sally said evenly. "And when you've finished that, we're going to buy you a coat and hat and some underwear and perhaps a shirt. Then we'll go to the hotel and you'll sleep. You look exhausted."

"Sure I am," he shouted. "Haven't been in bed since, oh Christ, I forget. The lousy train bounced the hell out of my bones. I caught a coupla winks for an hour on a bench in Penn Station and then some cop came along and told me either to sit up or get moving. I been drinking since yesterday morning and I forgot about eating. But I don't care, see. I don't need any sleep or food when you're planning to rob me of my whole life. So we don't go nowhere, we sit right here, till you promise me not to do this goddamn thing. It's murder that's all it is and you know it."

Sally folded her hands carefully and stared at the bare, whitefaced clock on the opposite wall. Twelve o'clock. "Very well," she said patiently. "Drink your coffee and tell me how you and Matthew worked out this jigsaw puzzle."

"What's it to you? You don't seem to think I have any rights. Why the hell didn't you tell me you were pregnant? Why did I have to find out from my brother?"

"You know why," Sally said coolly. "Because you'd have behaved exactly as you're doing now. Quite out of your mind. Or as you did when you gave me no choice and got me pregnant without my consent."

"I love you," he said and he put his head down on his folded arms and stared intensely across the table at her. "Don't that mean anything to you, Sally? Sure, I'm out of my mind. About you. I can't think straight any more."

He went on in a halting, digressive, thick flow of language to tell her the story of his maudlin odyssey through Boston, including the painful insult to the kindly little uncle which somehow was the worst part. Sally listened, saying nothing, smoking, and staring out of the window at the snow. Talking seemed to calm him, and although the time was dribbling away, she would not stop him. Every now and then, he'd remember his grievance and burst out in anger against her.

"Why'd you pick my brother to help you? All the doctors in the world and you tell him. I thought you loved me, Sally. How could you love a guy and pull such a stinking trick on him?"

"Oh you're so righteous," Sally said, finally angered and tired of recriminations. "You and your brother." She stabbed out her cigarette. "I wish I'd never seen either of you, particularly you."

He drew back as if she'd slapped him. "You really mean that, Sally?" His eyes fixed determinedly on her face, searching, she supposed, for a sign that she'd simply spoken in a moment of temper. She gave no such sign.

"Certainly I mean it." She chose her words carefully, shading them with overtones of freezing malice. "You knew I wouldn't marry you. I told you that when we began. Then you do this unforgivable thing to me and come here raving, drunk, looking like a Bowery habitué and penniless, swaggering, and claiming your rights. Well, you have no rights, none at all, over me and anything I choose to do. And, as for your brother, he helped me and I'm grateful to him. He was the only one I could turn to. I wasn't planning to embarrass either of you, and all of this trouble and dramatic anguish wouldn't have occurred if you both hadn't become so suddenly damnably brotherly. But in any case he might've seen to it that if you must come here to plead your case you were at least in decent condition and had some expenses with you. Now, in addition to having to pay for this abortion, which is your responsibility and which you should pay for, I am saddled with the care and feeding of an irresponsible fool. I suppose you know, or you ought to, if you had any objectivity, and weren't wallowing in self-pity, that if I'd had any objections to you as father and husband before, your appearance on the scene here has completely confirmed them."

He rubbed his hand across his eyes and his massive chest heaved up and down in short quick gasps. Was he going to blubber? she wondered disgustedly. But that indefinable element, manhood, finally came to his rescue and after a minute he said soberly, "Okay. I got the message. I'm twelve kinds of a fool. Only don't blame Bud. He didn't know I was coming. I made out real quiet with him after he told me. He gave me the hotel's name and address because he thought I was gonna go home and call you up to find out how you were. I mean, he'd've broken his pecker in half trying to stop me if he knew I was coming down here this way. He'd be mortified. Not that he isn't already, by me, all the time."

"You seem to have a talent for it," Sally agreed.

"And he had to tell me, you see," Saul plowed on. "Once he knew it was me, he had to. He wouldn't be much of a brother and a man if he didn't. A man should know these things. He should be consulted when . . ." His voice broke and quickly he took out a gray handkerchief and blew his nose. "It's mine too," he said defiantly, "and you can't get rid of it unless I say so. You don't have to rub any more in, Miss Brimmer. I'll pay you back for everything when I get home. And I'd pay for this lousy thing too, if I thought it was right, but I don't. So don't give me that stuff about how rich and great you are. I got the whole picture. You don't love me, you never did, I was just a good lay and you can't live without that. I was a moron to think it could be any more. Okay, so now we know where we stand. But the thing's done. It's in there and I want my kid. If you don't want to marry me, you don't have to. But I want you to have it and give it to me. I'll pay for everything. I'll take care of you till it's born. I'll take you away somewhere so nobody'll know. I got enough money. Now, there's just a few things I want to know"—flourishing a crumpled cigarette which he'd been unable to light properly—"like, have you seen this guy, this abortionist, and made an appointment? Because you better cancel it. The sooner we get back to Boston and make arrangements to leave town the better. We won't live together or anything like that, so you don't have to worry. Or maybe it'd be better to take a house, people get suspicious if a woman's alone when she's in the family way, and each have a floor to ourselves. I won't bother you, I swear, just so I can keep an eye out for you. I was thinking of out West some place, maybe Vegas or Reno, I could probably get a job in one of those gambling joints. I'm about fed up with Boston anyhow."

"My, we're so dreadfully businesslike in our ragged sweater," Sally said mockingly. "Have you quite finished working out your mad fantasy? Then I may tell you that your proposition is quite absurd. Particularly since you don't even know whether the operation's been performed or not. I might be quite sans baby. Or didn't that occur to you?"

"Can the classy dame stuff, will you, Sally," he said quietly. "This is me, remember, the boy who's been right down there with you in bed, and learned things from you that not only no classy dame should know but that even me, who hasn't been cherry since he was fourteen, didn't know. I'm no prude, believe me, but you shocked me more than once, only I never let on, because I was crazy in love with you. I'da walked through hell's fire for you and down deep I thought, well she's just a kid, she's been hanging around with niggers and perverts and she thinks stuff like that is something new.

She'll straighten out. But I see how wrong I was. You look clean and lovely but you're lousy and rotten. So don't try to laugh me off. I know you didn't have that damn murdering thing done yet, because you'd be lying in bed in that room, if you did, not running around in the snow."

"That beastly word 'nigger' ill becomes *you*," Sally said, standing up. "There's a men's shop across the square where we can get you a coat. Then I'll give you some money and you can take the train home. After that, I don't expect to see or hear from you again."

He followed her to the cashier's desk. "Yeah, well I hope you're keeping an account. I admit I was a damn fool to come here without a coat, but at the time, I was in love, clothes didn't matter. Only I don't go back to Boston without you, just so you know that."

They went out into the street and were whipped along to the corner to wait for the light. Saul, in spite of himself, cringed against the cold, whirling snow and for a moment as the wind hit him, he staggered and she had to hold his arm as they crossed the street slowly.

"So I'm a cripple," he said bitterly, shaking her hand off as they reached the curb, "do you have to remind me of that too?"

"The street's slippery."

"What the hell do you care? You wouldn't be bothered by me any more. Some car would've run over me and taken care of the whole problem."

The snow now formed a thin sleety layer over the streets, trodden and mushy in places but still a formidable obstacle for a man navigating in his condition, drunk, tired, heartsick, angry, crippled. And it was cold and getting worse.

Sally drew him along toward the men's shop where they paused and looked in at the suits, caps, tweed coats, ties and elegantly cuff-linked shirts of the window display.

"Leave me alone," he said furiously. "What the hell do you care about dirt like me?"

"I'm afraid you'll fall," Sally said, her voice catching absurdly in her throat.

He put his arms around her and in spite of herself she was glad. The big body pressed against her was shivering.

"Oh you damn fool," she cried. "You're freezing."

"So you do care? Honey, you do care, don't you? Why are you so proud?" His voice rose exultantly and he held her gently, close, sheltering her with his back to the windy street.

"I'll always want you, Saul. Why couldn't you have left it that way?"

"It's not enough, not for me, not now. When you've got something inside you that's mine, you think I can just settle for a lousy roll in the hay whenever you can make some time for me? I never could give you anything, Sally. But now, you got part of me in you and it's growing all the time. It'll be a good kid, half of you, too, somebody, a person, who'll be both of us as well as himself, for as long as he lives, and when he dies, his kids and their kids will still have some of us. And you want to kill that. Don't do it, Sally, please, I'm begging you, the only way I know how, don't do it."

Sally backed away from him. "I don't think you need to come into the store. The largest size ought to fit you, wouldn't you say? Where will you wait for me? Some warm place, I'd suggest."

His still outstretched arms fell slowly to his sides. "Is that all you got to say?"

"I don't want to talk about it any more, Saul."

He nodded curtly. "Yeah, you got your mind too full of drygoods. I'll wait for you in that bar down there."

Sally watched him limp perilously, still unable to keep a straight course, buffeted by the wind, down the street and did not go into the store until she saw him turn into the bar.

"He's a lucky person, whoever he is," the store clerk, who was dreadfully pansy, chirped gushily to Sally, after she had, in rapid succession, chosen a gray cashmere crew neck sweater, a T-shirt and shorts, a pair of leather, fur-lined gloves, black wool slacks, a canvas rain hat and the coat, a dark green of the color worn by Army officers, trench affair with a zip-in alpaca lining. "Getting a complete outfit like this and selected so quickly, too. Women usually take ages to buy things for men. He must be enormous"—the clerk rolled his eyes and smirked at the delicious thought—"we seldom have many calls for these very large sizes." He emphasized the last three words deliberately, looking roguishly at Sally, pencil poised. "Now, where shall I have them sent?"

"I shall take them with me." Sally gave him her best Boston codface. Terrible little vulgarian. Need they be this way, she wondered, while the clerk busily added up the sales slip, occasionally glancing at her in ill-concealed astonishment. It was this type who tarred them all, by dragging lewd, sexual allusions into every ordinary little everyday action. "Put the coat, gloves and hat into a separate parcel please," she added as he began to bustle busily and hippily toward the wrapping desk.

She paid for the clothes in traveler's checks, cashing an immense amount of them, in order to have cash ready for the sub rosa Dr. Phillips, and sank down into a chair. Twelve-thirty and it was to be hoped that Saul had shot his last bolt of poignant argument. All this emotion and wandering about displaced, in this Eliza-crossing-the-ice weather. And yet, to love someone, like Saul, in this degradingly passionate, this is my cross to be borne, way. But to know very clearly that it was over. She'd never forget him though, that was certain. Worthless as he was for her and contrary to all reason, the memory of him would occur to her in all climes and seasons. Years later, she would wake up in the middle of the night, lying in bed next to some other man, a husband perhaps, and she would think of him and want him all over again, freshly, strongly, with the same sharp fury of desire. And in the shop, waiting for her parcels and change, full of clairvoyance, and nostalgic rue, it was equally plain that right now all she wanted of him was to go away and let her keep her excising rendezvous in peace.

Perhaps it was not only Dudley who needed to probe into the Brimmer psyche. Perhaps she too needed to see an analyst and have him exorcise forever this devil of easy attraction to huge, handsome, muscular, stupid toughs, the sort of thing that had been getting her into various complicated broils, since Ben, who might've bridged the gap between passion and reason, had died. The nightclub owner in Frisco who verged perilously close to being Mr. Little in the underworld; the smokey-eyed, inarticulate gambler who went to sea as a waiter only because of the big gambling games on ships and who, when ashore, drove her absolutely wild, as she lay in bed waiting for him, by calling up every half hour to say he'd be around a little later, he just had to play one more hand because his luck was turning good for a change. And the football players at Berkeley and the musicians and the Air Corps pilots and all the beautiful big men just back from overseas who'd wandered into the clubs and heard her sing, or the bars, where just by chance their eyes met and, then it had been either good or bad but always temporary and nobody cared. Then why should it be different with Saul? She'd forgotten all the others, except as a rather amazing memory. Why should she love him and care if he was cold, sick, or sad. In the beginning she'd expected it to follow her pattern, but with him all the gaiety had gone awry. Because he had a depth of feeling the others did not, was it, and because he truly loved. Oh, I'm the idol of his day, Sally thought, rising to accept the two heavy packages the clerk handed her, but I didn't even ask for the honor and what a wretched, boring burden it is too.

Slowly she went up the street toward Saul who waited for her, a man denuded of all civilized, masculine appurtenances, a bit more presentable than before but still employing none of the suitings, the busy self-importance of the masculine workaday world, the men who were now calling for checks in lunchtime restaurants, flourishing their expensive, good leather wallets thick with money, family pictures and cards of identity, membership and authorization to help prove that they were men among their peers.

In their pockets were silver cigarette cases on which they affectedly tamped king-size cigarettes, monogrammed lighters, keys on chains. Their shirts were white, starched at the collars, fresh from the laundry, their faces, clean-shaven pink, their hair neatly trimmed, their heads underneath full of shoptalk, business deals, ambition, and competition: In three years I went from 8000 to 20,000 and if I swing this deal it'll mean capital gains, tax deductible, shares of stock, real estate's where the money is, the car went crazy on the way to the station this morning, garageman says it'll cost a fortune to fix it up, cheaper to get a new one, so we had to sink a well, had to get a gardener for this new place but it's worth it, expense accounts . . . Glad I wore my rubbers this morning. Lousy wet snow, the stock market . . . Rubbers, Sally thought suddenly, I didn't get any, his feet are probably soaking, one rubber or two, nonsense, wore two shoes didn't he, too late to go back now. And why should she have been so shocked at first seeing Saul this morning? True, he'd usually appeared before with a suit and a wallet and money and a lighter, and shaven and washed, but he'd never made any of the gestures, indulged in none of the conventions of the man's world. Her boy, a fool for love, a casualty of war's impersonal rage, sat slumped over a beer in a half-empty bar, unaware that all around him in the city, the country and the world, other members of his sex were rushing, shouting and pushing for power, money, and food, to keep them going in the business of getting ahead in life.

Saul was standing, illumined in the shifty bubbling colors of the jukebox, feeding nickels into it, a glass of whisky in his hand. "They got a record of 'Stormy Weather' here," he said when she came up to him. "Lena Horne. Wish it was you singing. Remember you sang that the first night we went out. Here." He took the packages and steered her to a booth in the back. "Whatd'you want to drink? Nothing? Boy, you're getting so damn respectable, I hardly know you. Now what's all this stuff here?"

Sally opened the one package containing the outdoor clothes.

"Say, that's a swell coat," he said, hardly looking at it. "You're a good kid, Sally."

What a juvenile he is, Sally thought, he's forgotten seemingly, all about his tragic problems and thinking only of playing reminiscent tunes on jukeboxes like an adolescent let out of school.

She took a ten-dollar bill from her wallet and handed it to him.

"Is this the kissoff?" he asked contemptuously throwing it back at her across the table. "I don't want your money."

"If you're going to keep on drinking," Sally said, sliding the bill to the center of the table, "and you obviously are, you might as well have the funds to pay for it. I daresay you owe money for what you're drinking now." She felt his hand on her knee, under the table and pulled her feet back quickly. "The other package has trousers and a shirt and things," she said keeping her voice impersonal, "you could change your clothes in the men's room here if you want."

"Never mind about that stuff." He held her hand, deliberately caressing the palm. "Honey, honey, you know I was here, waiting for you and standing looking out at the snow and remembering some of those days last summer, when it was so hot and we were frying on the beach there, and honey, remember that foggy day we took the ride along the coast and we made love in the car and it was so damp but with you how hot I was, oh my God, I looked out at the snow," he groaned and pressed her hand in a bone-crushing grip, "and my God, I couldn't stand to be reminded of all those beautiful days, it was like cutting my heart out. And now it's cold outside and snowing and I'm like that inside. Honest to God, I could die, and you don't even care, you don't even care enough to listen to me." He got up quickly, seizing the bill from the table and went to the bar, returning with two tumblers of whisky. "Here, drink this," he said, plunking one down before her.

Sally shook her head at the glass.

"Whyn't you look at me," he demanded, sitting down heavily beside her. "Why you keep looking at your watch all the time?"

"I have to leave soon," Sally said quietly. "I'm to meet someone uptown. If I were you I'd stop drinking now and go to the station and buy a ticket to go home. If you don't want to do that, I'll be back at the hotel around six and you can come up."

He clutched at her, one hand going up inside her skirt, stroking her inner thigh, the other enfolding her breasts tightly. "No, not later, now."

"I have to go now," Sally repeated wearily. She pushed his hands away. "Saul, really I do."

He looked at her suspiciously. "Where you going? To that doctor, after all I said?"

"No," Sally lied, reaching for her purse and gloves. "I'm having lunch with an old friend."

"Well, if you're not going there now, when are you going?" His eyes peered like a cunning animal's into hers. "Tell me, tell me." In his urgency he shook her slightly. "I'll see that murdering doctor in hell first before he kills my kid. I'll see that the cops get him, if it's the last thing I do."

"Don't be absurd, Saul. Now, will you let me go?"

"Sally honey, look at me." He took her face between his hands and kissed her mouth gently. "You love me, you know you do. For the love of me, if there's even a little bit, don't, don't do it, it'll finish me and you'll regret it as long as you live."

"Must I climb over this table to get out of here, Saul? Or shall I shout for help?"

Sullenly, he got to his feet and Sally swept past him quickly. I won't run, she thought, or give way to panic. One-thirty. Get a cab. Deborah, poor Deborah, must get a message to her, wandering around alone in the city, hope she went back to the hotel.

She dashed out into the street, her hand held high, waving at cabs which, as evil luck would have it, roared past her, all seemingly full of passengers who, on fair days would be walking or riding subways or buses, now seeking refuge from the snow. This is truly hell, she thought, gazing despairingly after four cabs tearing along toward the next light, a special hell invented for me, pursued by an avenging fury, plagued by a thousand tiny fiendish torments. She felt his hand on her arm and overcome by a feeling of hopelessness, of a dread conspiracy, she allowed him to draw her back up the curb.

"You wanna get killed," he said. "Standing right there in front of all those cars. Come on in here, out of the snow."

They were out of the mainstream of people on the avenue, now, on a side street, huddled in the doorway of a picture frame shop which was closed. Sally stared at the Renoir and Picasso reproductions, feeling an unwilling pleasure at the solidity and strength of his arms around her.

"What do you want of me, Saul? Let me alone, please. I have somewhere to go and I shall be late."

"I know where you're going," he said, "and I won't let you. Come on, honey, let's go back to the hotel so I can hold you and love you, that's all I want to do. Then we'll both take the train and go home." He held her tightly, his hands feverishly unbuttoning her coat.

"Let me go," she said struggling to free herself, "you crazy idiot, let me go."

A man and a girl, wearing trench coats and rubber boots passed by laughing under a purple umbrella. Shuffling past through the slushy ice, they turned curious eyes on Sally and Saul and then quickly looked away.

"People are staring, Saul. Let me go."

"Who cares about them." He swung her around to face him so that her body was crowded against his and her back to the street. "This is me, remember," he said bullishly, "and I say you're not going to do this to me, not after all we've had together. Maybe you forgot but I'll make you remember."

He began to kiss her mouth with a kind of ravening intensity, so that her compressed lips yielded and she opened her mouth and when his hot, moist, curled tongue joined hers, even in the damnable doorway, almost in the street, the feeling began. It was all there, the mounting excitement, the fast breath, the melting lurching dropping away. In a minute, as his skilled hands moved over her as, with his legs set wide apart, he pressed and rubbed against her, she'd not be able to stop it. He knows that I'm going to do it this afternoon, she thought, and this is his way of stopping me. Weakly she leaned against him. It was too late now, all she wanted to do was get to the hotel with him as fast as possible. Their bodies seemed welded together.

"Feel it," he muttered frenziedly, looking wildly into her eyes, "I've got to have you. You know we have to."

It was his voice that probably did it, Sally thought afterwards, although then, she had no time to analyze what caused her, in the midst of her uncontrollable passion, to think suddenly that while being an animal in the privacy of one's own bed, might be a delight, cohabiting with animals in broad daylight in strange doorways was certainly the way of a tramp and though she might very well be one, surely there were more subtle means.

He thought he had her now, his guard was down and he was lost in his own sensations. She broke free of him and ran down the street to the corner as though her life depended on it, and didn't it, didn't it, and there, like an angel and minister of grace, was an empty yellow cab, stopped for the light. She yanked the door open and leaped in before the driver was aware that he had a passenger.

The bald man behind the wheel turned around to gaze at her in astonishment. "Boy, I never saw anyone get in a cab that quick."

"I have to be uptown in fifteen minutes," Sally said, trying to catch her breath. "Let's go."

As the cab jerked forward she saw Saul, gesturing crazily at the corner. It would be part of his melodrama to hail another cab and follow her. Like a detective story. "There might be another cab following us," she said. "Would you know if it were?"

The driver grinned. "Who? That guy who was on the corner waving at you? Hell, lady, he won't follow you. He looked like he'd been hit with a wet fish and got sobered up after a four-day hangover."

It was exactly two o'clock when Sally clambered out of the cab before Dr. Phillips' office building. No time to call Deborah and would Saul bother her at the hotel, now? The hazards of friendship. Coping with drunken obsessed lovers. She overtipped the driver hideously.

"Hey!" he said beaming.

"You've been reassuring," Sally said. "I'll be needing a cab again in about an hour. Is there a cab stand around here?"

"I can be back in an hour," he said.

"It might be longer."

"So I'll wait," he shrugged. "Here's the cab number. I'll go have coffee. I can park across the street."

Dr. Phillips' nurse did not seem perturbed at her lateness and presently she was on the operating table, trussed up, with a white sheet over her, the nurse at one end, efficiently shaving her and behind her someone she couldn't see, putting something over her face.

Lying on the table, the mask came to her nose, breathe they said, breathe deeply now, she didn't want to, it was an unbearable sensation of not breathing for a minute, then she didn't resist and suddenly she was swinging somewhere in outer space, it was black, no, it had colors, there were many-ringed moons and suns. Fancy, these were the planets and she was looping light and bodiless through them. She was flying, freely, eaglelike, familiar of the sun, friend to the moon, and as they swung and circled, she performed marvelous trapeze-like swoops, diving down to catch on to one ring of Saturn, holding on effortlessly, dangling, then with an easy gliding rush, springing up to catch an opalescent circlet and float on it as a child she'd floated in the sea on an inner tube. The colors shifted to red, to orange, to unearthly burning yellows and disappeared into an all-embracing deep midnight black but then there were fires and stars, and she, godlike, whirled above and about them. Ah, what a sight, what a grand and splendid spectacle and suddenly she knew that she alone possessed the whole secret of life and death. She knew, positive and secure in her knowledge, what happened after death, and what the soul was, the answer to the riddle of the universe, the enigma of God's existence, and how everything had begun and who'd started it. Yes, yes, she knew it all. Only give me time, she thought, as she rushed on through the void, her hair flying in a roaring but exhilarating wind, in a little second, I will be able to enunciate it. Yes, it was coming nearer now, not far, on the tip of her tongue, it was the most wonderful thing that had ever happened to her. She wanted, in the pride of her fabulous knowledge, to cry out, and say that she knew more than all other beings. Who is like God? It was marvelous, yes, that was the word, it was a marvel, that she should be, marvelous, wonderful, surpassing all understanding, marvelous, marvelous, she said and she heard a voice replying, quiet, quiet now, you're just coming out of the anesthesia, Oh, but it was, it was, she cried, and the voice came nearer, saying, quiet now, it's all over, you're all right and she was back down in the here and now again, lying on the operating table, over her and shining down into her eyes was the bright, hot, white light, steadying itself back into its place and she was all gone and empty inside and she had lost all that she knew up there, she would never know what she'd been within a hairsbreadth of knowing, the tantalizing secret that had revealed a bit of itself and now, was gone forever, leaving her with no pain, feeling nothing, only a vast sadness. Something wonderful which had been almost within reach, was gone from her and she would never have it again. And after awhile she remembered what she was really there for, that, in her fall through space, like Lucifer, she'd forgotten and now she lay like that bright, beautiful but too proud angel, enchained in the burning lake of hell, and dully, she remembered.

"Is it all over," she asked. "Really?"

"All finished," said Dr. Phillips, suddenly looming up before her in a white gown. "You don't have it any more."

He disappeared and the nurse came bearing a hypodermic to give Sally a penicillin shot and then ushered her into another room, handing her a gauze pad and two pins and advising her to lie down on the leather couch for a few minutes. Sally lay with her eyes closed, not thinking at all, and presently Dr. Phillips reappeared, in his blue suit, the Phi Beta Kappa key hanging honorably from the heavy chain across his dignified vest. He pressed her stomach routinely.

"You'll be bleeding for a few days," he said. "Not much. Think of it as a menstrual period. My nurse will give you some sulfa pills to take back with you with instructions on their use. She'll keep in touch with you for about three days to see how you're progressing. You shouldn't have any trouble. No intercourse for at least four weeks and take showers in place of baths. How do you feel?"

Sally sat up, clutching the sheet around her naked body. "Really fine. A bit dizzy." Her purse was lying on the table beside her. "That's right, isn't it?" she said, handing him six fifty-dollar bills.

He looked at them casually and tucked them into his vest pocket. "I'm sorry we can't give you a receipt," he said gravely, "but I'm sure you understand."

"Of course," Sally said. Impulsively, she added, "Thank you very much, Dr. Phillips."

He smiled a little grimly but his pale eyes under their beetling white brows surveyed her appreciatively. "You seemed to enjoy the operation," he said. "I seldom get such compliments from patients coming out of ether."

Sally flushed a little, remembering her simple-minded words at return to consciousness. "I had a strange dream."

He looked at her thoughtfully. "I trust it will not be a haunting one. No, I don't think so, you're too intelligent for that. Well"— he extended his hand—"goodbye and good luck. You can get dressed now and then I'd lie down again till the dizziness passes. It won't be long. My nurse will see you out."

With two bottles of pills in her purse and the nurse's instructions about staying in bed more or less for three days, still echoing in her head, Sally boarded the elevator ten minutes later, feeling a little dazed. It'd all gone so fast that she couldn't quite believe everything was over and could not, as the elevator lurched down to the street floor, resist pressing her coat against her stomach, a foolish gesture because it proved nothing, but still, was it possible that, a scant hour ago, she'd ridden up in this same elevator bearing a foetus in her womb and now this irrevocable growth had been stopped and she was alone? It was strange. But undoubtedly true because he was not the sort of doctor to lie and take money under false pretenses. It will take awhile to get used to, she assured herself, it all went in such a hurry, and I probably still feel odd from the ether. She hurried across the lobby and almost caromed into Deborah who leaped at her from a phone booth where she'd been sitting.

"Oh, I'm so glad to see you, Sally. I've been worried sick."

She had, it appeared, gone back to the hotel about one, preparing to meet Sally and go uptown with her, growing more and more nervous as time went on and then at ten minutes of two, Saul had called.

"He was wild," Deborah explained excitedly. "Said he was going to break your neck. So I just told him you weren't there and hung up. And he called back, right back. Well, in a way, I was glad he'd called because at least I knew you weren't with him. I was afraid he'd . . ."

"My Lord," Sally interrupted, "I've a cab waiting. Come on. You can tell me the rest going downtown."

The cab driver was just coming out of the next-door coffee shop. "Perfect timing," he said grinning, as they settled themselves in the back. "That guy ever catch up with you, lady?"

"Not yet." Sally lit a cigarette and leaned limply against the seat.

Deborah looked worriedly at Sally's nervous fluttering hands. "How do you feel?" she asked in a low voice.

"Fine." Sally nodded slightly at the back of the driver's head. "Tell you all about it later."

"I wouldn't go back to the hotel yet," Deborah continued in the same near whisper. "He might be there. After he called the fourth time and I said you still weren't there and I didn't know where you were, he laughed in a bloodcurdling way and said to tell it to the Marines and that he was coming over to get you. So I came up here only I stopped and left my key at the desk. And I told them we were both going to be out so that if anyone came they wouldn't send them up, would they? D'you think we should move to another hotel?"

"No," Sally said tiredly, "I don't care any more and I daresay I ought to see him and tell him. But right now, I'm very hungry."

"Gee," Deborah said, looking at her concernedly, after the driver had dropped them off in front of a pleasant, small, tea-shoppe place a block down from the hotel, "you look awfully pale, Sally. Don't you think you better go to bed and I'll bring you some food?"

"He might be there," Sally said, "and I couldn't face him right now until I have some food and perhaps a nap if he will spare me the time. I suddenly feel completely unvital."

She ordered scrambled eggs, toast and coffee for both of them and described her morning with Saul.

"Honestly," Deborah said. "Isn't he just too creepy for words? I suppose it's terrific to think of a man being so in love with you that he'd go out of his mind like that but weren't you afraid?"

"Of Saul? Darling, he's a miserably unhappy type but not dangerous. Really he wouldn't hurt a fly. It's me that's hurt him and I was sorry to do it but there was no other way."

"What I don't understand," Deborah said, attacking some gooey fudge cake and ice cream predatorily, "is how he found out where you were. How could he have known?"

"He's Matthew's brother," Sally said succinctly and smiled rather sourly at Deborah's expression of stark disbelief.

"Oh Sally, you're kidding. He couldn't be."

"I daresay it puzzles Matthew too. But nevertheless, pet, it is so."

"Then Matthew shouldn't have given you away," Deborah cried indignantly. "How awfully sneaky of him. I don't think I'll ever speak to him again."

"You're so wholehearted," Sally said. "For a time this morning, I too, was more than annoyed with Matthew, but it doesn't matter any more, does it? I'm safe and if it hadn't been for Matthew I wouldn't be. And I can quite understand why Matthew told him, not only because of the old saw about blood being thicker and so on, but because Saul can be incredibly overpowering. There was a tiny moment during our snowy chase this morning when he almost convinced me."

"Well, I'm glad you had sense enough to ignore him," Deborah said emphatically.

"Darling, for a young, innocent girl you have some awfully unorthodox ideas. Even Matthew didn't think I ought to have an abortion."

"It's men, you'll notice," Deborah said darkly. "Or women like Dr. Asch you told me about, that can't have children. I think a woman ought to have the right to choose her own destiny and not be forced into a life they don't want just because they're . . . well . . . biologically impressionable. What are you smiling for? Have I said something funny?

"Anyway," she went on, "when I look at the women in my neighborhood, I think, why, they're not even people, they're like cows. Their whole lives are physical. Sex, childbirth, drudgery. And it seems to me that it's no wonder men didn't think women were people for so long and didn't want to give them equal rights or the vote because how can you have any respect for people who allow you to enslave them so easily. All a man had to do in the past," Deborah said bitterly, "and they're still doing it really, is get a woman pregnant and he's got a slave and a mindless drudge for life. No wonder men looked at women and laughed when the intelligent ones demanded suffrage. Because compared to the few women who stood up and demanded to be considered as human beings, there were the vast mass of those who might as well have been living in the barnyard, oh, brought there by men of course, and told to lay their eggs properly, but not minding it, not noticing that they were different from all the other animals, dropping their calves, suckling their young, eating the leftovers from the man's table after they'd served him, like the pigs do and even pigs don't have to wait table for a man."

"Why, you're a rampant feminist," Sally said, smiling broadly now. "I didn't realize. But I got confused there, somewhere. Is it the men who are the villains here or the unthinking vessels, the women, who are at fault?"

"Oh, it's better now," Deborah conceded. "Sometimes, I feel I really ought to get down on my knees and thank whatever gods there be that I live nowadays instead of in the past. How sick-making to have been a woman even fifty years ago. Still, although we're better off than we were, we've a long way to go. Men are still really in control. There ought to be a woman President. In fact," she said seriously, "it is my considered opinion, and I know you'll laugh, but I don't care, that the world would be much better off if women were in charge of governments. I bet if they were there'd be no wars and no atom bombs to radiate us to bits any time some man got aggressive. I think men are just as primitive as they were in the cave days when they had to go out and kill their food. They like war, they like blood and thunder and empty bombast and threats and stirring up trouble and inventing crazier and bloodier weapons. They call it drive, ambition and progress but I think maybe it's just frustration because they can't go out and fight saber-toothed tigers any more. So, that's why I approve of what you did."

It was snowing very heavily now. Snow was piled thick underfoot quite covering the earlier slush. When they got to the hotel Deborah went in first to look around the lobby and see if Saul was there.

"I don't see him," she reported to Sally who was standing outside suddenly ennervated. "I hope he's not upstairs."

"I couldn't care less," Sally said as they went up to the desk to get their key. "I simply must lie down and if he's there, well, you can entertain him or is he in the category of saber-toothed tiger to you?"

"There was a party here looking for you," the desk clerk said. "Couple of times. About an hour ago was the last time. He didn't want to leave a message. Quite some weather we're having, eh ladies? The radio says it'll be a blizzard by tonight."

Happily there was no sign of Saul in the corridor of their floor. Sally took one of the prescribed sulfa pills and a phenobarbital, undressed and crawled into bed.

"I can't believe you're really all right," Deborah said anxiously. "Aren't you supposed to have some aftereffects?"

"Remarkable, isn't it?" Sally yawned and closed her eyes. "I'm really very well, just tired. How would you classify Dr. Phillips, Debby? Do you think he believes in the enslavement of women?"

"I wish I'd met him," Deborah said mournfully. "He sounds like a fascinating man, the way he likes Victorian literature and all. I don't know what to think about him. I suppose he makes an awful lot of money this way, with less work and worry than ordinary obstetricians."

"Oh come," Sally said drowsily, "just because he's a man you refuse to give him any credit. With your ideas you ought to consider that he's a benefactor of womankind. I do. And I don't know if it wouldn't be easier for him to practice legitimate obstetrics. He runs a dreadful risk, you know, and he must have to pay somebody for cover up and protection occasionally. Not to mention how nerve-wracking it must be to know you're on the wrong side of the law. No, having talked to him and seen him and knowing he must come from a good family, I prefer to believe that he deliberately, with intelligent, enlightened cynicism, chose this line of endeavor in order to rid the world of a lot of people who shouldn't be born anyway."

"How do you know he came from a good family and all that?" Deborah asked curiously.

"Oh, you just know," Sally murmured. There was a click as Deborah turned off the light, and then no more sounds.

Once, she was half-roused by the noise of windowpanes rattling and saw a beam of light from the next room. There was a lull between gusts of wind outside and she heard what sounded like pages being rustled far away. She lay there quietly thinking in a disconnected vague way about Dr. Phillips. A murderer, Saul had called him, and the law, religion, and the whole man's world of conventional unfeeling lip-service blatherskites despised him, hunted him and yet, quietly and competently he went on saving foolish, young, loving girls and boys, and the consequent sad little children from the everlasting misery of a life committed to paying for one stupid mistake.

Unbidden, the face of a little faun child she'd seen on the train, yesterday, a boy who ought to have worn a flower hat and a *Mid-summer Night's* name like Mustard-Seed, swam into Sally's half-asleep memory; he'd been in the ladies' room with his mother who was fruitlessly trying to wash chocolate from his face while he wriggled and announced to the world that the train was so noisy it made his penis wiggle. Usually she never noticed children so it was odd that she would remember this one, after such a brief glimpse. His hair had been curly, his ears pointed, his smile elfin and sweet. Why, he looks like a little Saul, she thought now. Why didn't I realize that yesterday? Never mind, little tremor of regret she told the child's face, it's only because I'm free and well out of it now that I can permit such fancies but I will have a child like you some day, only it'll be a legitimate one with a proper father. And with this sentimental resolution she receded again into sleep.

The wind woke her again several hours later. Its demoniacal howling penetrated deep into her dreams and she sat up in bed startled, calling for Deborah who came in quickly turning on the table lamp by the bed.

"What is all that racket outside?" Sally looked at her watch. Only nine o'clock.

"It's a tremendous blizzard," Deborah said, pulling up the Venetian blind. "See."

Sally drew on her scarlet robe and went slowly to the window. The face of the night outside was blinded by whirling gusts of snow. A bleak white blur in the distance marked by a buffeted tree striving to hold itself together was the park. The only thing that seemed alive in the wilderness was a street light on the corner by the hotel, a baleful eye only partially veiled by snow. Was Saul out in this?

"The heat's on," Deborah said, touching the radiator by the window, "but the wind's coming in this direction. That's why the windows are rattling so and it's cold in here. You better get back in bed, Sally. I got some beef bouillon cubes and things this morning, if you want to eat."

"Saul's been calling," she added a few minutes later, appearing like a genie with a bowl of steaming soup and bread and butter. "He kept calling and calling and I kept telling him you were asleep. He was just so drunk. I don't think he understood me. I was afraid he'd wake you up so I told them we were taking naps and didn't want to be disturbed. I didn't know what to do. I've been sitting here, trying to read Milton and afraid every minute he'd come here. I can't think why he hasn't."

Sally spooned up her soup slowly. So groggy and feeble. Difficult to think. "Call down and tell them to put calls through now, Deb."

Deborah looked at her mutinously. "What do you care about him?" she said.

"Do you know," Sally said conversationally, "that in weather like this he can't walk well, particularly when he's drunk. He could fall down in the snow and freeze unless someone found him. That's why he hasn't come here. Now, call them, Deborah."

"Very well. But he's a grown man. He can take care of himself. And you're sick. I don't understand you, Sally."

Sally lay back against the pillows. "It was his child too, Deb. He didn't have very much and I took what little he had away." Where was he? In some snowdrift, passed out in a bar, or had he finally seen reason and taken the train home? And if he had, she wouldn't know. Why am I so weak, she wondered, the bleeding was very minor.

"You're getting sentimental," Deborah said. "I didn't expect it of you."

"Nerves," Sally said lightly and then the phone rang.

"Saul? Good. This is Sally."

"Oh honey, honey. Where've you been? That damn kid wouldn't tell me nothing. You went and did it, didn't you?"

"Yes. Where are you?"

"Some bar. I've been in different bars all day, since you ran away. Around here."

"Listen," Sally said fiercely, "you come up here right away, do you understand?"

"Nah," he said despondently. "I'll just go up to Penn Station and sleep in the waiting room. I'm so tired out from calling you and not knowing what happened and now I know. So that's the end of that. How do you feel?"

"Never mind that. I won't have you sleeping in the station. Don't you have enough money to get a room?"

"It's all gone. Everything's gone."

"Come here right away then. I'll expect you within half an hour. You can pay for a cab, can't you?"

"I guess," he said indifferently and hung up.

Sally looked at Deborah's stony face. "He won't be any trouble. He's simply worn out and cold and probably hasn't eaten all day. I don't want him wandering around out there any more. I've done enough to him as it is."

"He's drunk and dangerous," Deborah said. "Haven't you the slightest sense of self-protection?"

"He's no more drunk than you are," Sally retorted. "Now don't argue, Deb, I can't bear it."

"I'll let him in," Deborah said coldly, "and if he gives the slightest trouble, I'll call the manager, I don't care what you say."

"You're so militantly righteous, Deborah."

"Dudley would never forgive me if anything happened to you." Deborah's voice quavered a little. "He thinks a great deal of you."

"I hadn't noticed."

"Oh, he does," Deborah said with intense conviction. "He talks about you all the time to me, with admiration. But I don't think he likes to reveal his true feelings about people to their faces."

Just as well, Sally thought, his true feelings might turn out to be ghastly, but she said nothing.

"If Saul seems peaceful," Deborah went on, "do you think it'd be all right if I went to the movies for a while? There's a theatre about a block away that's showing a French movie I've been wanting to see. *Volpone.*"

"Fine. You go right ahead."

"I hate to leave you alone with him," Deborah said dubiously, "but I shouldn't hang around either when you're together."

She busied herself washing the dishes and Sally lay with her eyes closed and waited and after awhile there was a knock on the door and presently, Saul came slowly into the bedroom.

"You really did it?" he asked, standing by the bed, looking down at her face intently.

Sally couldn't look at him. "Yes."

"It's no more, my kid? What we made together out of love."

"Yes, darling." The bitter sting of ridiculous tears at her eyelids. "I'm sorry but it wouldn't have worked any other way."

He looked around the room in a vague confused way, holding the rain hat in one hand and the wrinkled, wet paper package of clothes in the other.

"Put everything down on the chair, darling," Sally said, "and take your coat off. Sit down, Saul, please, you look so tired."

"You see, I still got everything you gave me, Sally. I left them in a bar once but I remembered and went back. Even the razor and tooth-brush, in my coat pocket right here. I didn't lose a thing."

"That's good," Sally smiled at him and patted the bed beside her.

He sat gingerly on the edge and took her hand. "Are you all right, honey? Do you feel bad? You should have let me go with you."

"It didn't hurt," Sally said. "And it wouldn't have done any good for you to come."

"Yeah," he said slowly, "I was pretty stiff, I guess. I don't remember too well. Was I pretty lousy?"

"It doesn't matter," Sally said. He sat on the bed, swaying a little, his eyes half-closed. "Why don't you take a bath?" she said. "And put on the clean underwear and then you can sleep here with me."

"Don't want to bother you any more." Holding her hand tightly, his eyes anxious. "Honey, you all right? You don't look so good. Don't lie to me please, Sally. I couldn't stand it if anything happened to you."

"I'm fine," Sally said, with more assurance than she actually felt. "And if you get cleaned up and sleep some I'll feel even better."

"Okay. Whatever you say, if you're sure I won't bother you, staying here."

"Oh Saul, of course not. Would I have asked you here if I didn't want you?"

"I'm going now," Deborah said, coming in with her coat on. "Will you be all right?" She looked suspiciously at Saul fumbling at the wet knotted string on the clothes package.

"I'll take care of her, kid," he said. "Don't worry."

Deborah looked resolutely away from Saul's unbelievable sweater and happily forbore to voice her obvious disbelief that this wreck could look after anyone. "I'll see you later then, Sally."

Sally took another sulfa pill and listened to the water running in the bathtub. All the fight was gone out of him, she thought, and that was worse, far worse, than his earlier belligerence. Now, he was like a child whose spirit'd been irredeemably crushed and she had done it, a kind of crime performed through necessity but for which there was no redress.

After awhile he came to lie beside her, his hair still damp, and without a word she took the towel from his limp hand and, pressing his head against her breasts, she rubbed the crisp, curly hair dry.

"You know," he said almost inaudibly, "when you ran away from me into that taxi it was like somebody threw cold water all over me. I was cold sober in a minute and went and puked my guts out in the lousy gutter. And no matter how much I drank after that, it couldn't kill the feeling. It ain't easy to see, all of a sudden, what a bum you are."

"Don't talk, darling. Go to sleep."

"I wish you hadn't of done it," he said faintly. "It makes me feel lousy, like I was nothing."

"Don't please, Saul, don't talk about it."

"I'll take care of you," he whispered. "I'll take you home. Wish I had my car."

"I can't leave for three days. You'd better go back yourself, Saul. Don't you have to go to work?"

"I'll go home and get my car and drive you back."

"It's not necessary, darling. I'll be perfectly fine. We'll fly home. It will only take an hour."

"You won't even let me do anything for you."

"You can hold me," Sally said, feeling more savagely lonely and empty than she ever had in her entire life.

Wordlessly and sadly they lay in each other's arms. She heard him breathe deeply and saw his eyes close and she reached over and turned off the light. In the dark she lay, hearing the snow and wind hissing and bubbling outside like a witch's caldron. At least, she thought, he's here, warm and safe, with me. I've done that for him. . . .

When she opened her eyes again the sun had replaced the street-light's artificial streamers on the opposite wall. Beside her, the bed was empty and she heard Deborah moving around in the next room, clinking dishes. The phone rang and she picked it up. Dr. Phillips' nurse scrupulously inquired about various aftereffects, changed instructions about the sulfa pills, told her to stay in bed and would call tomorrow. Deborah came in bearing breakfast on a tray. Sally picked up the folded paper next to the coffee cup. Her name was scrawled on it.

"Saul left you a note."

"A note? Where did he go?" Around her the room sprang to life in the brilliant sun pouring through the window now that Deborah had raised the Venetian blind. The coat was gone and the package of clothes.

"I guess he went home," Deborah said indifferently. "He woke me up by his stumbling around out there about seven o'clock. He was looking for paper and a pencil and he was all dressed. He said to throw out all his old clothes."

"How could he go anywhere?" Sally demanded. "He didn't have any money, the fool. I should have given him some last night but I fell asleep and forgot. Oh why didn't he wake me, dammit?"

"I asked him about that, assuming he'd be broke," Deborah said airily, "and although I didn't want to take money from your purse while you were asleep, I thought in this case you wouldn't have minded. But he said he didn't want any money and was going to hitch. I made him some breakfast though. It's horribly cold out and I didn't think he ought to go without eating."

"That was good of you," Sally said shortly. "You know perfectly well you ought to have awakened me. Because he's a fool is no reason for you to be. How in the world could a man in his shape hitch rides?"

"He seemed to know all about it," Deborah said, biting her lip and lowering her eyes.

"I'm sorry," Sally said. "But really it's so provoking. Now, of course, I shall be brooding until I get back to Boston for fear something hideous happened to him."

"It's none of my business, of course," Deborah said in injured tones, "but I do think you're carrying all these guilt feelings to an extreme. He's a man after all, not a baby, even if he is crippled, and, honestly, Sally, they do know how to shift for themselves, no matter how much they pretend not to. And what you don't seem to understand," she added, her voice becoming more kindly, "is that he didn't want any more money from you. No matter what you think, I'd have woken you, but he insisted that I shouldn't and then I offered to get money from your wallet, because I knew you'd take on about him going out penniless, but he absolutely refused. Said he'd taken enough from you and while he might've fallen pretty low he was no gigolo. I knew you'd be furious, so I ran after him to the elevator, and gave him five dollars of mine. The elevator door was opening so he had to take it or look like an idiot struggling with a girl over a five-dollar bill. Why don't you read the note and stop fretting. He'll be quite all right, you'll see."

"Feminism hasn't quite destroyed your human kindness, I see," Sally said. "Thank you, Deb. Five dollars ought to be enough for a bus ticket." She unfolded the note and read slowly. Saul was left-handed and his handwriting suffered from the attendant peculiarities of writing more or less upside down, which, added to the general illegibility of an impatient person who found verbal expression difficult, made reading a letter from him, a slow, exasperating procedure.

"Honey," she read, "this is to say goodbye. And thanks. I'm cold sober now and feel like hell about everything. Guess I didn't know what I was doing. I shouldn't have come down here looking like that but all I could think of was getting here to try and stop you. I didn't want to wake you up and bother you any more and please don't worry about me, I'll be okay. I'll put a check for you in the *mail when I get back for all the money you spent on me. Please call me up when you get back and let me know how you are because sometimes these things cause trouble. I want to see you again, I'll always want to see you but I don't know if we should. Because when you did that to me, after you knew how much it meant, something went out of me and the way I feel about you. You know what I mean, maybe you feel the same way. I'm thinking of leaving Boston soon and going somewhere else. I couldn't live there any more without you and knowing you were in the same city. I don't know what the hell to think or do. I'm all mixed up. But no matter what happens I'll always love you, nothing can change that. Saul."*

Sally threw the note on the floor and went to the window. A snow plow had been through, clearing the street, traffic was normal and the snow, melting slowly on the streets was now just a coffee-stained reminiscence of a bad night. But in the park across the street, it lingered on the earth, in patches, still a clear blue-white, sparkling in the sun like clean sheets laid out to dry on the grass and plastered in wet clumps on the branches of trees, dribbling diamond drops on the walks below. The park was inhabited this morning, mostly by children in gay, primary colored snowsuits; fat, little, padded figures who tumbled and bowled through the remaining snow and shouted and scraped up small, soggy snowballs with their wet mittens and howled, gleefully vindictive, as the snowballs smacked their watchful mothers or unwary passersby.

Five

Crazy Saul was sitting on the steps of the Joy Street place one lousy night when Matthew came shambling home for a change to have a few hours off. Just sitting there quietly in the wintry dusk like the Rodin statue and if it hadn't been for the warning orange light of his cigar, Matthew might have stumbled over him, being too tired to notice anything except maybe if it was hung on the end of his nose.

"What the hell? Oh . . . Saul!"

"Where've you been shacking, Bud? Been calling you for two days now."

"At the hospital. Where else?" A new third year med student was on OB with him now and every ten minutes women were having babies so it was either duty or call. "When I do get to sleep," he added severely, "it's by myself. In that hard bed they provided for me down there."

"How about asking me up? I've been freezing my ass off down here. Everybody making babies, huh?"

"Uh," was the only answer to that one, thrown over the shoulder as they went up the stairs. Nowadays the word baby had to be avoided with Saul, just like boxing used to be, even if he brought it up, you had to quick talk about something else because he just wanted an audience for his grievance. "Want a drink?" he added, more cordially when they got inside, both of them umkaffing catarrhally because of all the dust. "I've got to get a woman in here to clean up this place."

"I can't figure why you want to throw your money away paying for this dump. If you had a girl it'd be different."

"Don't be so damn patronizing. I've got the dough for it. And I want it. My business."

"Sure," said Saul pouring himself a shot. "But get a girl, why don't you? They work wonders. Sweep the floor, let you lay them, put poison in the food. Rub shit in your face. I tell you there's nothing like it."

Matthew sighed. He kept telling himself to try to be patient with Saul. Poor bastard'd had a lousy time. "What's up?" he asked trying to keep a friendly tone going. "I'm about dead. Had a bad afternoon." So tired in fact that he'd quit the hospital wearing the clinical jacket under his coat and it should've gone in the laundry. "Delivered a thirteen-year-old girl." The baby had only weighed two pounds and had died a few minutes later. The mother wasn't in very damn good shape either but there was a pretty fair chance she'd recover.

"You're kidding," Saul said. "Who'd do a thing like that to a kid?"

"Her brother." Even now, thinking about the pisspot parents made him sore, and the whole lousy scene when the poor, scared kid had been brought in just starting labor and her father, who had standards, had kept yelling at her, to tell who the father was, because if she didn't the doctor wouldn't help her have her baby, that she'd suffer terrible pain and the poor kid kept crying and he'd ordered both parents out of there, telling the little girl that he most certainly would help her and he didn't care who the father was and trying to undo the mess, being very reassuring, but it was too late by then, she'd had visions of hellfire closing in on her, so she said, *Bill!* The magic name which caused the fatuglified mother to faint and really got rid of them. So who was Bill to cause such consternation, Matthew'd wondered, but didn't care, only it was a long hard labor and he'd spent a lot of time with her, coming in and talking to her and holding her hand, and telling her not to worry, sure it hurt but it would be over soon, and she'd be glad later when she had a fine baby which was a stinking lie but what else could he say? She'd told him off right then and there with his shoddy medical shibboleths. No, she wouldn't, she'd never be glad again, only it wasn't her fault, doctor, it wasn't, because Bill was her brother and he'd started in on her when she was little and didn't know what it meant, it was play, only don't tell mama, don't ever tell her.

"Lousy pervert," Saul said, taking the whole story personally. "What are they gonna do with him? I'd shoot him if he was mine."

"How do I know?" Matthew said indifferently. "I'm not a psychiatrist. Just an obstetrician, or trying to be." He went to start the water running in the bathtub and came back to find Saul pouring himself another drink.

"When are you taking off for Las Vegas? Let me know and I'll try to come to the airport and see you off."

"Oh, a week, maybe two, I dunno. I'm not planning to come back to this goddamn town for a long time so I got plenty of odds and ends to tie up and I gotta see about shipping the car. That's what I came here for. I'm sorting my stuff and packing and I left a couple of things here. A coat and my Bible."

"Oh yes." Left over on that fateful night which they didn't talk about. "Well, hell, Saul, I could have brought that over to Sophy's when I come for your farewell dinner. You didn't have to sit down there in the cold. You didn't even know if I'd turn up."

"Sure I did. What do you take me for, some kind of dope? When I couldn't get you here I called the hospital and that sourvoiced dame there said you were going off duty in ten minutes and you'd told her you were going home. And I was in the neighborhood anyway."

"Yes? Doing what?" He knew already, why did he even ask?

"There was a light in her window," his brother said. "So, she's home. Not running around. Suppose she's sick?"

"Listen, if she needed help she'd've called me or Jenni Asch. What kind of a schlimazl are you, anyway? She'll always land on her feet. Worry about yourself for Godsakes."

"I still think you ought to call her and find out how she is," Saul said stubbornly.

"You mean you want me to?"

"Who me? Nah! I just think it's, uh . . ." searching around for a non-giveaway word as if his face didn't expose him completely, "uh, the kind of thing a good doctor would do."

Matthew let this snipe at his professional standing slide. It must be hell to feel that way about someone. He hoped the disease would never strike him. "Okay," he said, "I'll call her tomorrow." In a few impersonal words he'd remind her that she ought to see Jenni for a check-up. Hello, howareyou, goodbye. Didn't mean a thing but if Saul wanted another crumb to add to his pathetic hoard he'd get it.

"You know something," his brother said broodingly, "this whole world is full of degenerates. Like that brother who knocked up his own kid sister. So if Sally's home that's not so good either. Living there with her brother like that. You know he's got a case on her? I bet you didn't know that. She don't know it either. Maybe he don't even know it. But I could tell. When you love somebody the way I love her with every goddamn part of you, you, I dunno, feel things stronger, other people's feelings too. And sometimes, the way that cold fish looks at her, boy, it's no way for a decent brother to look at his sister."

Matthew scratched his head and watched his brother down a third straight shot of rye. "Take it easy on that stuff, will you? You'll be seeing pink snakes pretty soon." Incestuous fantasies on that encrusted brain of his now, too. God, if he'd only get out of town. Damn that girl. Saul thought everyone wanted her because he did, up to and including poor, innocent Dudley.

"Say, Saul, I don't mean to rush you but I'm bushed. If you want to stay here okay, but you'll have to excuse me." He went to turn the water off in the bathtub.

His brother was limping around restlessly looking like a decadent Roman emperor. Since quitting his job and hanging around, drinking too much, he'd taken on a kind of bloated, unhealthy appearance. His belly protruded under the starched white shirt and the pants of the good Harris tweed suit were damn tight. His strong, arched nose flared out from between the now deep-etched lines running from nostril to mouth and smudged circles under his eyes looked almost like bruises in the ivory pale face. No time for barbershops either, evidently. That shaggy mane of half-grey black curls made it all worse.

"I'm going, I'm going," Saul said absently. "Where's my stuff?"

"I left it right on the couch there." Matthew noticed, at first casually, a familiar-looking piece of material, white silk, bluestriped, befringed, protruding from his brother's pocket. He looked at it again, more intently.

"Did you ever lay a girl every hour all night long? And every one perfect?"

"Okay, so you're a giant and I'm a pygmy. What's it prove?" "It don't prove anything. I just miss it that's all. I'll never get over missing it. But at the same time I hate her. Pretty funny, huh?"

"No. It's a common reaction. What are you carrying your tallith around for?"

Saul plunged a hand into his pocket and brought out the prayer shawl and a black skullcap. "I've been in shul, that's why. I'm not ashamed of it. A guy's a Jew, he's a Jew and if he wants to pray he does it the way he knows. What's there to remark about?"

Matthew shrugged. "Nothing. It just seems funny that's all. I bet you haven't been in a synagogue since you were thirteen. But, okay, granted you think differently now, what are you doing in a synagogue in the middle of the week? It isn't even a holiday, is it?"

556

"I been going twice a day now," Saul said, with dignity. "Early in the morning and at sundown. That's when they say Kaddish."

"Kaddish! For Godsakes! Who died? You suddenly decided to go say Kaddish for Pa? He's only been dead for a year and a half now and you wouldn't even go to the funeral Sophy said."

"That sonovabitch! No. For my son." Saul fingered the lapel of his jacket and Matthew saw in utter disbelief that the material had been slit. There was no doubt about it. His loony brother was in mourning.

"Saul," he said quietly, reasonably, "you're not serious are you? I mean, Jesus Christ, I don't know much about this sort of thing but I'd swear that if you told a rabbi that you were saying Kaddish and cutting your clothes for an embryo which undoubtedly had no sex characteristics why he'd tell you that you were not only wrong but probably committing some sort of insane sacrilege. Don't you understand? When there is movement, quickening, at about four months, it's then that we consider the embryo is actually animate. You can't mourn something that wasn't alive in the first place. I doubt even if you can do it for stillborns."

Saul shook his head. "Who cares what you hairsplitting rabbis and doctors would say? I know more about this than you do. It was my kid."

Matthew rubbed his eyes which were burning from lack of sleep. "Okay, Saul, have it your way. But listen, could you do me a favor and before you go have a checkup, you know, a complete physical. After all, you're going pretty far away, be on your own and all."

"There's nothing wrong with me," Saul said, looking at him suspiciously. "Who do you think you're fooling? Doctors! You want to ship me off to a headshrinker, that's what it is. Don't try to railroad me to cover yourself. None of it would've happened if it hadn't been for you. But I got a right to do and think what I want and you keep your hands off me, see!"

He gathered up his stuff and went out, slamming the door. There wasn't any point in thinking about it. Matthew sat in the tub till the water got cold and he almost fell asleep, thinking in circles all the same.

* * * *

There was nothing to get up for in the mornings but at night, trying to sleep was fearful. If you cut the mooring ropes the boat that was you would swing silently out on the tide and it would drift, now swift, now turned round and round, to perhaps fetch up on a nightmare shore, but no, you could not bear to try, because underneath you knew there was no way to get back, and you couldn't cut the ropes. You would fight the sleep that had to be induced with such effort by too many of the little pills Dudley had gotten for you or too much Scotch and mystery stories and your heart would be jockeyed swiftly, swooping up and down and come to rocketing stops like a badly run elevator. When this happened, you had to move, fling your arms out, roll over, sit up, turn on the light, because if you didn't stop that flight, didn't resist that pull, your heart would fly out of you, there'd be nothing in the morning, but a cold body in a disordered bed.

You don't want to die, Sally, but yet, when the day comes, what is there to say or do?

You come back to Boston and the days are cold and gray and the sun's praise is damnably faint, the wind comes from the gray water maliciously bringing tears to your eyes. When you get out no furs can warm you, lights hurt your eyes and you have to sit down all the time because you are dizzy. So it is better to stay indoors and there it is ugly and there's never enough warmth and you stay in bed for three whole days and Dudley is suddenly a gentle, understanding person, who asks you no questions and buys mystery stories for you and makes eggs and toast and tea if he is around. Deborah comes and says maybe you're having a reaction and ought to go see Dr. Asch. So you do, one day, and she is much kinder than you had expected and says you are anemic and gives you some foul-tasting iron pills and you have to eat liver which is awful and there is a good deal of so, you have done it, I am sorry but perhaps it is better if you wished it, and on no account, sex, for five more weeks, as if you were some sort of sex maniac, but you have not enough energy to be annoyed. She tells you to come back at the end of five weeks to be examined and asks, her eyes shrewd, if you have seen Matthew.

No, Sally has not seen Matthew, dear Dr. Asch, so fearful of your protégé, nor yet the other Berman brother. The Berman brothers are picketing Sally who is unfair to organized masculinity. One Berman brother has sent you a check for two hundred dollars in the mail which is absurd and you send it back with a brief note saying that you most certainly did not spend that much on him. The check returns to you, this time accompanied by a highly neurotic letter, in which words are left out and there are blots:

"*Well maybe I am no good,*" it starts without any preamble, "*but neither are you. No good woman would've done what you did. Maybe if you did marry me and we had that baby I wouldn't be no bum because I'd a had something to live and work for. And you robbed me of that chance to even try it. Treated me like dirt. You sure showed me what you thought of me and any kid I made in you. Something to get out of you fast as possible and throw in the garbage can. Well, I don't forgive you for that Sally. So take the damn money. Buy yourself black nightgown with it to lift up for some other sap or a dress to knock out someone else's . . . Burn this goddamn letter will you. I would've called you but I couldn't stand to hear your voice. I don't even want to see you again and I'm going away in a few week to Vegas, I think. I bet you're laughing right now reading this. Well I don't care if you are, I'm as good as you are any day. Ah, hell this isn't what I wanted to say. My brother says that instead of being sore at you for the lousy you pulled on me I should be sore at myself for doing it to you in the first place. Maybe I ought to be, but I'm not, because what I did was right, real, the way men and women ought to. I wish I were religious and could forgive you but it's too late to start now. Christ, what's the use of going on. Excuse blotting, scratching out. My hand is shaking like leaf. I love you. Saul.*"

You tore up this incredible missive obviously and sat in front of the telephone for half an hour shivering and crying and wanting to call him. You didn't nor did you acknowledge his note finally after trying several times and throwing each attempt away but you cashed the check several days later, knowing it was essential that you at least do that.

The sleeplessness started then. The first few days it had been difficult not to sleep but after that letter you began to want again. Nothing sentimental about it, just pure, unashamed animal want and not anyone, a particular want. Saul. Completely ridiculous. Unable to now anyway. Leave him alone. But still there and you lay in bed at night and thought of him lying in his. So then Dudley got you some pills.

You couldn't understand any of it. Why did it suddenly seem as though this life you had yearned for, to splash in and enjoy without encumbrances and illness, was a dreadful desert, where the heat parched by day, and your body was scraped eternally by blown sand, and where you froze in a tiny, pitiful tent at night. Where there was no book that could hold your attention for long, no newspaper that bore anything but the most evil tidings. The larger world was as empty and chaotic as you were and each page bore tales of the victims or perpetrators of tyranny, evil, misfortune, and death and you didn't want to hear about it. There were no people you wanted to see, there would be no comfort in them, conversation was a dead end, there was nothing to say after all.

You keep sort of expecting Matthew Berman to call and inquire as to your health but he doesn't which is fairly irritating because after all dammit you're not in too splendid shape and considering his previous unctuous solicitude, it meant that he was cutting you and how dared he when so good at pouring oil on troubled fires.

One evening when you had managed to spend most of the day catnapping and thus felt a bit better than usual, Mike Wainscott called after a silence of months and wondered if you felt like going with him, Si and Caroline to dig some bebop in a new place up by Kenmore Square. Well, it was something to do, so you went but the music made your nerves do a shimmy and you got a headache but kept right on drinking hoping to summon up some love of your fellow men, but none came. Mike was glum. You asked him politely what he was up to and he reluctantly proffered the information that he was taking a few courses in English at the Harvard Grad School and writing on his novel but it was going sour on him and life was shit and he drank as much as you did. Neither of you got even slightly high, which was, as he remarked, symbolic of how unpleasant everything was. It didn't help at all to know there was someone else in exactly as bad a way as you were. Two nihilists with a single thought sitting at a table together could refine themselves out of existence with a mere whisper, he said, when you told him. But he was tasteful enough not to ask why, which you could not have answered anyway. All Sally is divided into three parts only the rest was lost because there was no trot.

And Si, who could generally have been counted on to provide some sort of mental pickup, was also in a state, generated, you gathered, by a family fight occurring just before he and Caroline had left the house concerning the cat which had clawed Si's best sweater and he'd issued an ultimatum that the cat must go. Caroline had then said that the cat would stay and he could go and take his morbid thesis with him. Because the thesis was obviously behind it all, Si having been told sternly by his adviser that since he couldn't seem to find a topic to write on, one would have to be given him. And he'd buckled down but with ill grace to writing and researching but about what, you never knew. He said merely that it was a pure wasteland of a subject enlivened only by clumps of poisonous toadstools. Caroline was cold and fishy-eyed, addressing most of her conversation to Mike and nursing one bottle of beer the entire evening as if it were a grievance.

You came out of the ladies' room at one point and ran into Tommy Rogers who was at the bar with a few other musicians and he asked you to have a drink with him which you did. He played alto sax in the Baron's band and you'd known him quite a while and gone to bed with him once in San Francisco two years ago. He was extraordinarily handsome, very tall, with that beautiful coffee cream skin, a straight narrow nose and a very impressive body. He told you that he'd just left the Baron's band and was looking for some smaller group. He wasn't making any overtures but he had no girl with him and you knew if you wanted to . . . But you didn't and couldn't and anyway this was Boston and too close to home to go to bed with Negroes so you said good night and he said he'd be around awhile and shortly, any more bop was unbearable and you all left.

So home early, feeling more deadly if possible, meeting Dudley on his way out who told you Matthew Berman had called and you called back and he was curt.

"Are you feeling all right, Sally? Any repercussions?"

"Must you have only a medical reason for calling Dr. Berman?"

He almost snarled. "What other reason would there be? Because you're a friend of my brother's?"

"You really oughtn't to play God, you know, Matthew. It can be dangerous."

A silence. Then with difficulty. "Do you think I wanted that to happen? I'm sorry about it but what more can I say? I'm sick of apologizing for him and anyway, if you want the truth, I don't think he was so wrong. Naturally, I never figured he'd be fool enough to go raging down there like that. And . . . uh . . . I want to thank you for taking care of him." In a tone which indicated a complete lack of gratitude.

"Look, Sally, I didn't call to talk about this. It's senseless. But just let me ask you something. Have you ever in your whole life given a damn about anybody? So now, tell me, how are you feeling?"

"It's rather late to ask, isn't it?"

He sighed. "Then you *are* all right. Good. You should go see Dr. Asch in about three weeks."

"I know. She told me."

"Then you have been there?" He sounded as if she'd trekked over to the Bay Road simply to plague him. "What was it? An infection?"

"No, no. Merely mild anemia and advanced boredom. But all is peachy now and your belated solicitude ill becomes you."

"Listen," he said now thoroughly irritated. "I can do without all the shivs, thank you. If you must know I wouldn't have called at all but my dumb brother is brooding about your health."

"Oh. That's kind of him. And you will tell him I'm splendid won't you?"

"Naturally."

"He's going out West soon, isn't he?"

"Yup!" a bad, bored imitation of Gary Cooper.

"And how is he now?"

"He'll get along, I guess."

"Oh Matthew, do try to be human please. Will you tell him for me that I hope he has . . . oh . . . fun."

"Fun," he said. "And you want me to be human. Okay, I'll try to remember those brave words. So take care of yourself, Sally," and there was the terminating click.

The next day your aunt calls you to ask if you want to go to Friday afternoon Symphony which seems to be where you came in but you go and in the course of the afternoon Aunt Fan, apparently stimulated by Dudley's vague remarks on the subject of how you're in a funk, inquires as to whether she can give you a luncheon, inviting old school friends, etcetera. It's a tepid idea but then perhaps it's time to grow up and stop helling around with Negroes, Jews, and bohemians and go back where at least half of you belongs.

But the luncheon proves that if there is a warm welcome waiting for you somewhere it is not there. Of all the females there, your dearest friends at Miss Folsom's only two, in addition to you, are unmarried. One is a rather sweet but dull sort whose bombardier husband was killed. She fills up time doing lots of volunteer hospital work and is especially enthusiastic about some new work she's taken on recently with retarded children. You are supposed to feel selfish and rush to emulate her, but you make it plain that losing a husband in the war does not automatically cause you to shed a basically frivolous personality. Aunt Fan is disappointed because she'd obviously counted on this fellow war widow to convert you to good works. The other unmarried female is the ghastly Betsy Howle, big and muscular, with her plain, pudding face. Contrary to the complacent assumptions of the beauty industry and the dicta promulgated by fashion, you reflect, as you listen to her girlguide conversation, nature cannot be improved upon in the case of Betsy. Both of these unattached females are, of course, full of questions about Dudley.

The other chicks at the luncheon are either married, with children, who, of course they cannot resist talking about or with child, or just married and furnishing their homes. When it becomes startlingly and impolitely clear that any conversational gambits concerning silver, period furniture, girlish reminiscences and social and sporting do's, are bound to glaze your eyes and naturally, a discussion of childbirth and formulas must be severely restrained, you wonder when they'll get to it and finally:

"We heard you were singing at a place near Rockport this summer, Sally. That must have been sort of fun."

"It was." You are perfectly sure that the one who asked about it, had she been spending the summer in Siam, would have managed to rush to Rockport and hear you, to provide her with a whole summer's supply of conversational bitchery on the beach and at the club.

In desperation, you fix your eyes on the centerpiece of purple grapes and yellow chrysanthemums and conjure up a ribald image of Saul as a lean, well-built, hairy, naked Bacchus. You can't decide whether he'd be more effective as a centerpiece sitting down astride a barrel or standing up in full battle array, holding the grapes aloft.

You finally pull yourself out of this madness to find that lunch is over and there is much drawing on of gloves and little tentative invitations are tendered. You must come to tea or cocktails and you watch them combing their memories for unattached males so that they can invite you to dinner. Too risky to invite a single, unaccompanied widow when there are hardwon husbands around.

One rather interesting thing came of it though, because the terble Betsy Howle had actually pressed you to come to her mother's for tea the next day and you, knowing that it was a sadly naïve bait dangled for the wily Dudley were about to mutter of a pressing previous engagement when she let drop that her brother Peter had just taken a leave from his job at an advertising agency in New York because of an imminent divorce and was therefore, lo, at loose ends on River Street.

So, of course you went to tea at Howles and Pete, intrinsically no more exciting than years ago when you knew him vaguely through Dudley said cheerfully, wasn't Boston terrible with everyone married, but knew all sorts of dreadful raffish and café society people in

New York and was full of flip chatter and gossip. So there was much fast riding around in his Jaguar and dancing and drinking every night which was sort of fun if essentially empty but then who cared and what else was there to do? Pete was the sort of drinker who felt he must counterbalance it by keeping fit so there were foolhardy sorties out in bitter frosty mornings with hangovers to go riding, always ending up with more drinking at the club bar. Actually all of this dashing about made you feel a little bit more healthy and less of a zombie and you were too tired not to sleep.

Why Pete's wife, who was the heiress of a suppository fortune, was divorcing him you never quite ascertained and he certainly didn't seem riled over it, being a lukewarm soul whose only passion appeared to be sitting in "21" or the Stork or Sardi's drinking martinis with famous names. Pete kept telling you that you were not the sort of girl for Boston. It was the one sensible thing he did say. It's well enough to live here if you're a nobody, he said, and then you can do what you like. But if you're not, it's dead. Why are you here now, Sal, he wanted to know, you keep doing all the wrong things such as marrying that bloody solemn brain he said with that highpitched laugh of his which I always thought was a mistake when I heard of it, a girl like you marrying a brain. If it'd been a musician, now, that might have been fun. So he seemed to know everyone in New York who was of any importance at all and he was going back soon and advertising was the heart of the American world, he wouldn't give up his career in the agency for anything and he advised you to come to New York, get an apartment, and if you found things boring and lonely at first, why he could get you a job at his agency.

"I knew you'd end up in that cockeyed world," Dudley said when you mentioned it to him. "Of all the pretentious emptiness, spending one's life persuading fools to part with their money for things they don't need. And as for Howle, I didn't mind him when he was simply a solid bore but now that he's a young advertising executive, he's covered up the hollow with clown's patter. He turns my stomach."

All this said bitingly because, unfortunately, the price of Pete's company one evening had to be the arrangement of a foursome including sister Betsy and brother Dudley.

"I can't get out of it," you said. "Pete asked me. I've told them you work constantly down at that slavedriving hospital till I'm purple. Now it's embarrassing. You must come."

"I've spent years fleeing that girl and her obtuse mother," Dudley fulminated, "and now, with little enough time to spare from my work as it is, to see Deborah whom I really care for, you must inflict this on me. Why don't you go back to your phallic symbol? He was a sullen lout but at least he did not have dreadful sisters."

But he went and was as ungracious and noncontributing as he could be and reminded you very unfavorably of Grandfather Brimmer, all of which you pointed out the next afternoon as you strode back to Revere Street with him, walking fast from Louisburg Square in the cold, sooty dusk.

"Never again, never," Dudley fumed. "I've never had a more depressing evening. I don't drink enough now to desensitize myself to such crashing dullards. Then, to add the icing on this soggy cake, *you* persisted in getting drunk, knowing full well that Betsy will gossip about it."

"Reformed rakes are always so righteous, dear brother. Pete got drunk too, may I remind you."

"He's a fool. You're not."

"I'm not? How odd, Dudley, I've distinctly felt many times that you thought I was."

"No," seriously. "You're too intelligent to throw your life away."

"Indeed. You weren't doing too well with yours awhile back."

"I had enough sense to enter analysis and was lucky to find Deborah. She doesn't know about drunks, you know. I met her once last summer and she was completely unaware that I was thoroughly stoned. She'd have been most shocked. Which is one of the reasons I've stopped. And I'm very happy. What would you say if I told you I was thinking of marrying her?"

"I'd say, to use some of your more moldy words, that you were indulging in fantasy and to be more concrete that you were sixty different kinds of ass."

"Not now, naturally, but later when I'm through with analysis." Obliviously.

"Scoff, scoff."

"I am prepared for your eternal derision."

"I'm not derisive but it isn't nice to hurt people who have no defenses."

"You, of course, have always abided by this golden rule."

"I'm not nice at all. But you know that, don't you?"

"I know nothing of the sort. What I do know is that you made me very tired prancing around at Aunt Fan's this afternoon looking horsy," Dudley said crossly. "Do you think it was mature to turn up there in your riding clothes?"

"Of course it wasn't. I don't want to be mature. Maturity is simply a new gobbldeygook name for resignation. I had no time to change when we came back from riding, is all. At any rate, today was Aunt Fan's day for cultured oddballs and I'm sure I looked much more like their idea of a travesty of a Boston girl all breeched and booted than if I'd been dressed. And it was sort of fun watching their eyes light up. So typical they thought."

The temperature was dropping rapidly now. It was below freezing and the stars were coming out over Boston. The wind blew papers and grit along the streets and although the short corduroy coat you wore over your riding clothes was furlined you were shivering and it was good to get indoors where there was heat and Deborah baking potatoes in the oven. You broiled some steak and Dudley made whiskey sours but only drank one and Deborah drank just one so you did for all the rest and after dinner crawled into bed with Scotch on the rocks and an Agatha Christie which it turned out you'd read before. Dudley left soon after because he was on call at the hospital that night and was now so eager that he liked to be there early. Deborah said she had to go to the library before it closed and she left too and the house was very quiet, with all the clocks ticking on like mad, merciless time bombs and your head began to ache.

Pete wanted to go skiing in New Hampshire this weekend and he'd asked you to come, which meant that he would try fumblingly to take you to bed and how could you explain your inability without sounding like a simpering virgin. You could say you didn't want to, which would be perfectly true, but if you went to New York you'd need someone until you met other men, so there'd be no point in cutting him off right now.

Then, all the other superfluous thoughts were blown away like crumpled November leaves. The wind of passion rose up in you, roaring through the gray, ennui emptiness of the past weeks. There, beyond it all, still standing, was the naked essential skeletonic tree, which was Saul. You'd given him up for all this nonsense, this boredom, this nothing. Had hurt his pride, his honor and disdained the only gift he could give you. He would not burrow at your breasts again nor do any of the things that made you so perfect last summer. Yes, he will, you think in fury, swinging out of bed and running to the phone. He'll make you marry him. No, he won't. Now he knows what it's like losing you he'll do what you want. You'll live together, go to Las Vegas. You need only be scrupulously careful. But never, never lose him till you really want to. Not ready to give him up yet. Can't. Grimy, gray, cellar kitchen full of rats and lit only by an unshaded 25-watt bulb. It was like that now. You hadn't known before what it could be but you did now. Make it up to him, all the awful things you did. Hold him, love him, be with him, let him be proud when people think you're his wife. You dial the phone and it rings and rings in emptiness. Of course. Moved back to his aunt's. But the uncle who answers says he isn't home, and no, he couldn't tell you when he'll be back and who is this, warily. A friend and thank you goodbye. Matthew would know. Will he tell you? Yes, eventually, but no one answers there either. These cursed people who were never home. In another hour try again. Back to bed.

"Baby it's Christmas time and I wanna see Santa Claus . . ." All that holly and the ivy and ah the boar's head and the tinsel and the shopping and the canned carols pealing through the streets and stores. "Santa Claus, Santa Claus, listen to my plea, don't send me nuthin' for Christmas but my baby back to me."

* * * *

In the hospital medical library where it was very quiet Matthew looked up for an abstracted moment to rest his eyes from the new issue of *Surgery, Gyn and OB* and saw Dudley Brimmer down at the end of the room, studying a tome on the lung. On an impulse he put the journal back on the rack and gumshoed over. Hadn't seen Dud in a long time due to this Sally-Saul whirligig. At the risk of disturbing him, at least, he ought to say hello.

"What's up?" he asked, indicating Brimmer's reading matter, after greetings.

"Melnikoff's doing a resection tomorrow morning and I'm going to scrub in and watch even though I'm off duty," Dud said, taking off his glasses and rubbing his eyes. "From the biopsy it seems to be a benign tumor and not carcinomatous. I was just reviewing the area. Are you on call too?"

"No. I was at my aunt's for supper and got away early so I thought I'd drop by here. There were some lab reports I wanted to look at. One of Dr. Asch's patients who's had her third spontaneous abortion. It's an interesting problem but nothing enlightening's turned up so far. You just have to keep trying everything."

One of the reasons he'd taken off from Sophy and Moe's so early was the lachrymose nature of the dinner due to the nonappearance of the guest of honor. He knew, the bastard, that Sophy was going to all this trouble to make a special meal with all the things he liked, in honor of his Western journey. Sophy's brother and his wife had been invited, the whole thing'd been postponed twice because of

Matthew being unavoidably busy at the hospital, and on this night of nights, with all the elements working well, Saul doesn't show up. So they wait dinner for him and it gets later and not a word, not a phone call. Sophy is getting more and more nervous and irritable and running to the kitchen poking in the pots full of overcooked food. They even got presents for him, a new wallet, a pair of leather gloves with fur linings, a British wool scarf. Sophy's brother pompously suggests there must be some place to call and see if he's there . . . Well, sure there are, only nobody tells him it's a whole long list of unknown gin mills, whorehouses, pool parlors, gyms, bookie joints, and wherever bigtime crap or poker games might be going on. Sophy keeps saying, pretty runny-eyed, by then, that he went in town right after breakfast to get himself some few clothes, telling her he'd be home in the middle of the afternoon. Moe finally goes and calls the joint in the South End where Saul passed out that evening, quietly so that Sophy's stuffed shirt brother shouldn't hear about it, and the bartender there says, yeah, Saul was in during the afternoon but he didn't stay long and he wasn't stiff. So they finally eat. Moe wonders to Matthew sub rosa if maybe he's in trouble and they should call the police. Troubled in mind all right, but aloud, don't worry, Moe, he'll get home, he always does.

"Got a rotten headache," Dudley was saying now. "How about a cup of coffee?"

In the cafeteria he talked a blue streak about a gallbladder operation he'd performed under Melnikoff's supervision and how he could kick himself for the time he'd wasted as a student and intern in surgery, when he could have gotten so much more out of it that would've been immensely helpful now that surgery was meat and drink, etc. Matthew listened perfunctorily, nodding in agreement, because it'd been the same for him with obstetrics and they agreed that there ought to be some way for a student and intern to know beforehand what specialties would later become absorbing but there wasn't.

"Some men know," Dudley said. "Many fellows in my class knew they wanted to be surgeons or psychiatrists or internists, certainly by their fourth year."

"The Army dulls you," Matthew said, "at least it did me. By the time I got through puttering around there I didn't know what the hell I wanted."

There was a squawk from the callbox. "Dr. Brimmer! Dr. Dudley Brimmer! In Emergency please!"

Hastily swallowing the last of his coffee, Dudley stood up. "This is only the second call from Emergency tonight. The intern on duty there is very capable. Dick Schaeffer. I went to school with his brother who was killed in Kwajalein."

Not wanting to go home because probably Moe would call to ask if he'd heard from Saul, or Saul would call or be there, maudlin drunk, having been hanging around under Sally's window, Matthew wandered over to the Residents' quarters planning to take a nap in his so-called room. A poker game was in progress two doors down so he paused there, hung around to kibbitz and finally sat in on the game. He'd just won a quarter and was beginning to enjoy himself when his name was called on the PA.

"Hey, that's you," said the guy who was dealing.

"I'm not on call," Matthew said, turning to the other OB resident. "But you are." He'd really gotten a good hand for a change. He went back to looking at his two kings. "Are they fouling up again down there?"

"It's not maternity," the other OB said, frowning and listening intently. "They want you in Emergency."

"Trying to fluff off a taxi delivery on me," Matthew jeered.

"Well," the other resident said resignedly, throwing down his cards, "I suppose that's it. Why the hell doesn't that switchboard get the duty straight?" He went off and one of the bystanders took his place and the game went on.

Matthew was dealing when the PA began to blat his name again. This time the chant went on for a while, very particularly, "Dr. Berman! Dr. Matthew Berman. Emergency Ward, please."

"You're a marked man," the guy next to him said. "Here, I'll take the deck. This'll teach you to stay out of the hospital on your nights off."

He'd just turned the corner into the corridor leading to Emergency when he ran into the other OB resident, a jolly plump bastard ordinarily, but now with the cherubic moonface creased into serious lines.

"It's you they want, Matt. Brimmer had you called."

So right then he knew. Somehow he was not surprised. Maybe'd even been expecting it for a long time.

As he paced quickly down the ward, Dudley intercepted him, catching at his arm. "I was afraid you'd left the hospital, Matthew. Your brother has been rather seriously hurt. Bad auto smash." Frowning and grimacing. "I didn't know he . . . well . . . He's over there."

On a bed in the corner, the duty nurse wrapping a blood-pressure cuff around one of his arms and pumping it up. They had started the IV infusion going through a vein in the other arm and medicated a big deep gash by his temple but it remained to be seen what they could do for the blue lips, the moist, sweaty forehead and that paper white face on which every bristle of hair stood out. Saul's eyes were closed. Even at the foot of the bed you could smell the whisky. An orderly had just wheeled up an oxygen tank and Dudley got busy connecting up a nose tube, inserting it and taping it down with adhesive on the upper lip.

"Seems to have received it all in the abdomen," he said conversationally. "Presumably hit the steering wheel. Any luck?" he asked the nurse who'd finished pumping and was writing her findings down on Saul's chart.

She shook her head. "And pulse rate's still the same, too, Doctor. Very weak and thready."

She bustled off down the aisle between the beds and Matthew took Saul's limp, icy hand in his, placing the tips of his fingers on the broad wrist. There wasn't even a faint flutter at first and then, after a second, he picked it up, racing crazily, then away, nothing and then back. Rapid. Thin. Irregular. Classic.

"Hemorrhaging internally," he heard himself reciting to Dudley in a kind of textbook singsong. "Shock. What else?"

"That's about it," Dudley said lightly. "Possibly a broken rib or two. We'll take an X-ray later. Blood's been typed and cross-matched and we're waiting for it now. After we pour some of that into him he'll be in better shape for surgery and we can do an exploratory laparotomy." He pulled his glasses off, looked at them with annoyance and polished the lenses vigorously with a piece of treated paper. "We had rather a bad time at first getting the infusion started. The vein was very flabby. That was when the intern had me called. He was sweating it out and thought perhaps he'd have to do a cut."

"Very interesting," Matthew said mechanically. He couldn't get over Saul looking like one of Madame Tussaud's star attractions. But the transfusion would help. Sure it would.

"I'm sorry," Dudley said quickly. "How stupid of me. Now, we're going to begin the transfusion here and then send him up to Surgical. But I wondered where you wanted him. In a ward? Or a room? And what kind? I've just checked and they have one bed free in the ward, two private rooms and one semi-private."

"Better get him a room," Matthew said. "Then I can stay with him. How much blood d'you think it will take?"

"No idea. All that alcohol isn't going to help matters, you know.

Of course he's a fairly powerful fellow." Dudley stared at Saul abstractedly. "Considering the nature of the accident, I think he's doing rather well. When I examined him he was conscious enough to recognize me and respond. A less vital man would, I believe, have been more profoundly . . ."

Down the end of the ward came the orderly wheeling a cart.

"Here we are," Dudley said briskly interrupting himself. "After we get him upstairs I'm going to have the Resident look at him. And if there's anyone else you want?" He paused delicately.

"Who do you suggest?"

"We'll see how he reacts to transfusion, warmth and so on. Then, if you like, I could call Melnikoff. He's undoubtedly the best in the city."

The cart trundled to a stop by the bed and Dudley went over to shut off the IV solution in order to begin the transfusion.

Dudley said he responded, Matthew thought, but where? Those delicate fingers probing, and palpating, had examined Saul and couldn't they guess pretty well? He unhooked Saul's chart from where it hung on the end of the bed and squinted at the tiny script. Dudley's handwriting was worse than his own.

"*Patient brought into Emergency Room at 11:50 p.m.*" he deciphered, "*in severe shock—semi-conscious—BP 60/40, weak, irregular pulse, clammy, cold sweat. Responds by grunting, indicating tenderness to pressure over right upper quadrant. Presumptive diagnosis: Ruptured liver.*"

"You might bear in mind," Dudley said suddenly appearing behind him, "that I am a very junior Assistant Resident and that my diagnosis is merely my own rather inexperienced idea."

The heavily blanketed mound on the bed stirred slightly.

"Two lungs," Matthew said musingly, "two kidneys, two legs, but only one liver."

"Perfectly true," Dudley said coolly, "but if not too severely damaged, there's quite a good chance of patching it up. Rather a long job of surgery of course."

"Sure you're not trying to shoot any placebos into me?"

The eyes of the death mask facsimile on the bed opened halfway, heavy-lidded pits of darkness, lustreless. The lids blinked slowly.

"I'm being completely honest," Dudley said rather touchily.

"Funny, you know, all the times I've gotten p.o.'d about frantic relatives daring to question my judgment and now I'm acting just like one of them."

"Of course you are," Dudley said patting him awkwardly on the shoulder. "And so would I be. One's professional knowledge is no protection against this sort of emotional shock."

"Saul," Matthew said, leaning over his brother. "It's me, Matthew."

The hazydark eyes met his and the bloodless lips moved.

"We're going to get you fixed up, Saul. You'll feel a lot better soon."

There was some sort of noise vaguely resembling a human voice from down in Saul's throat. Matthew bent lower but couldn't make anything recognizable out of it.

"He wants to see my sister," Dudley murmured in a careful, noncommittal voice. He was on the other side of the bed checking the tape which held the needle fast in the vein. "I think we'd better strap the arm down. He might get restless." He waved at the nurse officiating at a dressing cart several beds down.

"Your sister?" Matthew couldn't keep the surprise out of his voice.

"Yes. He asked for her before when I was examining him. I knew him, obviously, but when the nurse and intern went through his wallet and found an ID card listing you as next of kin I admit I was puzzled. I had thought his name was . . . uh . . . well, I can't remember, but certainly not Berman. Perhaps you had best call Sally. She'd want to know in any case."

"Are you sure?"

Dudley peered at him, eyes narrowed but face bland. "Quite."

Matthew clasped his brother's hand. So nerveless and inanimate. More like a glove than any human's hand had a right to be. Wanted to see Sally, did he? The whole kit and caboodle of them together, he wanted, all the families, all the embarrassment. Poor, poor guy. Well, Matthew thought, Dudley doesn't know the half of it, but let's all be gentlemen together, shall we? "Sally'll be here soon," he said, bending down again, his lips close to Saul's ear. The eyes had closed again but the mouth worked.

If I can find her, he thought. Always the big If. If they pulled Saul out of shock. If he survived the operation. If the liver wasn't too shot to begin with. But hadn't he ever learned, in medicine, not to look too far ahead? Wasn't it always touch and go, maybe yes, maybe no, peculiar, unaccounted for reversals and upswings depending often on factors beyond their control, constitutional, psychological, otherwise. And looking upon the face of death as a doctor, impersonally, he had recognized all these factors, but as a brother, Christ! Why were women allowed to cry easily, turning tears on constantly, and children, but a man, hell, he might as well put a dress on and parade through the streets. He came abreast of the phone booths in the lobby and dived into one just in time to prevent himself from being unmanned in public. Get hold of yourself, ass, he thought, dialing his uncle's number with a shaky hand, there's always a chance, you never know.

It didn't take more than five words to make the business plain to Moe who had anyway been sitting by the phone waiting for some alarm. He didn't envy Moe's job of telling Sophy. She shouldn't come of course but wild bulls couldn't keep her away. Sackcloth and ashes and shrieking and have to turn her out in no time. Embarrassing. Maybe give her a sedative.

He'd be very damn surprised if the whore turned out to be home. Dancing her red-slippered feet off was his guess. Pressing her half-covered breast against some black dinner coat, driving some other tool into the delicious ecstasy before the fall. He was about to hang up after five rings but then he'd promised Saul. She answered on the eighth, acting very dazed and said she'd just been sleeping and would he please say it all again and who was he anyway? So he went through it again, slowly, each word heavy as lead.

She was so quiet.

"Are you there, Sally? I'm in a hurry."

"Is he seriously hurt, Matthew? Tell me. Please."

"No. He's just there for the good food. Of course he's hurt. Why? Is he someone you know?"

"Oh God!" she cried. "You bastard!" and banged down the phone. She'd probably sniffle a little and then take four hours making her face up to where it was suitable for a middle of the night visit to a sick friend. He went into the Blood Donor's room and had himself leeched, changed into his whites over in the Residents' quarters where the jokers were still rolling along with their constantly interrupted poker game, got his equipment together, stuffing the stethoscope into his pocket, called Dudley down in Emergency, who said they were ready to take the patient up to his room, and finally stopped for a hasty, tongue-scalding cup of coffee.

Somebody was playing Brahms, a record, softly, behind one of the closed doors. Matthew paused by the closed door and listened. Passionate sounds, the clangor of chords, the First Piano concerto. Why was he skulking here like a dilettante, delaying, when every minute was so important? But there was nothing he could do, it was all being done, and if it didn't help, because medicine was now the biggest, the only miracle there was, then what did a few minutes matter?

But often music had been able to tell him anything he wanted to know, if he only understood its particular language. Sometimes he did. But not tonight. Tonight he was tone deaf and he went away from the music which seemed to be spinning out long dreams about the majesty of man, his beauty, goodness, his love for all things living, his kinship with the angels. It was all a lie. Man and his life were lousy and there was no love. The petaled piano notes might make some order for themselves and the few happy listeners but beyond that, it was all chaos, black death, foolish mistakes, blind luck, hangdog contingencies. False pride. Irrevocabilities. I had to tell him, Matthew thought, getting into the elevator and he supposed that Saul had to and Sally had to and one thing led to another, just as Brahms had to write music like that to pluck at your guts as if you were just a fiddle and the banshee who'd been running the night elevator in Surgical for some thirty sour years had to chitter like a gibbon about the poor bleeding drunk who'd just come up in the car, him smelling like a distillery and it'd be the priest they'd be calling for that one soon enough.

They'd put Saul's bed on the shock blocks, and a probie in charge of keeping the water bottles hot and the blankets piled up and tucked in tightly. The first pint was almost empty but so far the reaction wasn't too favorable and then the Senior Resident came to examine him, agreeing with Dudley's diagnosis about the liver. Anyway, too early to tell, so continue treatment, give him a hypo of adrenalin to help boost the pressure, get him out of that shock first and the blood trickling down the tube into the vein, the faint, dim whisper of life. His lips anyway were getting a little less blue and his speech was more understandable when he whispered, hello bud, howmIdoin? So the answer was a hearty, swell Saul, have you up in no time. Sally, he kept mumbling, Sally, and when he didn't see her his eyes would go vacant again.

They were pretty rushed up there what with the omnipresent shortage of nurses so he arranged with Dudley to take the BP, PR, and Resp. every fifteen minutes. The latest reading showed a slight improvement in the vital signs but nothing you could really celebrate. Sophy and Moe came, Moe talking to Saul tenderly, softly, as if he were a baby but Sophy couldn't get near the bed without a fresh outburst, so finally he had to pack them off with a phenobarb for Sophy's nerves. Moe went to donate blood because the inevitability of a second transfusion was coming up and it looked like they'd need a third too. He'd come back, Moe said, after he took Sophy home to bed, but Matthew dissuaded him. No sense hanging around till something really happened.

They had just connected up the second blood bottle when she came in, in her damn fur coat which she dropped on a chair near the door, standing uncertainly there waiting for Dudley to give her the nod. She was all straight and shining and lovely, her hair wind-tossed, her cheeks pink from the cold, no hat and hardly any lipstick, her mouth pale pink and demure due to the solemn nature of the situation and wearing a tweed skirt and a soft, clinging lavender cashmere sweater which with her build could be almost enough to make the near dead sit up. And why not? The hell with all this uptodate sanitary antiseptic procedure, let her crawl in with him. If that didn't warm him and quicken the sluggish blood, nothing would. Dudley whispered to him that he'd come back and look in every now and then but he was pretty busy and so was the intern and would it be all right for Sally to stay. She was a stalwart sort who didn't go to pieces easily and, pause, she was very fond of Saul.

"Yeah. I heard about it. Sure she can stay. She might make better medicine than we can."

"Very likely," Dudley said in that clipped, dry way of his that left a person wondering how much he knew, and went on to discuss a new theory; that shock let loose bacterial riot in the system and if so antibiotics were maybe helpful. Anyway, it couldn't hurt so he shot some penicillin into Saul whose eyes were open again, looking around. It wasn't hard to tell who he was looking for so when they'd finished with the hypo, Matthew beckoned to her.

She came hesitantly into the circle of light by the bed and Saul saw her and the next minute she was kneeling by him and kissing those colorless lips. It was hell to watch. The semi-inert mass moved a little, his eyes fixed on hers like a kid who'd lost his mother and finally found her again. She had his hand in hers and was holding it tightly. Dudley avoided the whole overripe nature of the scene by writing busily on the chart and drawing Matthew aside for an old physician's consultative huddle, recapping what everybody already knew.

Later, when he'd gone away and the probie had clumped in and fixed up the nest of bottles and blankets and Matthew had taken the readings and wasn't jumping for joy over them and checked to see that the arm hooked up to the transfusion apparatus was tied down good and tight, he asked the Madonna of the Bedside if she wanted some coffee. She shook her head no, and asked if she could talk to her all of a sudden beloved who'd been making some motions with his mouth, pursing of lips and kind of creaky noises back in his throat.

"Sure," said the attending physician, "talk is cheap."

She slid right over that. As far as she was concerned deferring to the doctor was a gracious whim on her part. And, as for Saul, when he did have his eyes open the fact that he had a brother around meant zero because all he looked for was this shining example of bitchery.

"I wondered," she was saying, "if it would be too great a strain for him. There's so much I . . ."

"I wouldn't expect an intellectual discourse from him if that's what you mean. But he's conscious enough to listen, understand, and maybe answer a question. No serious topics. Just idle sweet chatter. You're pretty good at that. I'm going to get some coffee. Back in a few minutes."

She came to the door with him. "Will you tell me please, truly? What sort of condition is he in? Dudley was terribly noncommittal when I asked him."

"There's every chance of improvement with time," smooth Dr. Berman began as he'd done countless times in his professional capacity to countless people. "That's the theory anyway." He looked at her, suddenly resenting her unruffled health and beauty. "Would you like to hear what I think?"

She nodded dutifully.

"Well, to be brutally frank, he's not responding to transfusions and adrenalin as well as he ought to and he's a mess inside. And the more time he takes pulling out of this the less chance there is of doing anything surgically. See! But what do you care? You didn't want him, anyway."

She drew her breath in sharply as though he'd just stabbed her and let him go without another word.

When he came back ten minutes later Saul was shifting restlessly about on the bed and had pulled his hospital gown partway off and she had her head down on his bare shoulder, rubbing her lips against the flesh. He was muttering some barely audible words about a star and a son and a promise and she was crying, the tears falling down her face and wetting the rough cloth and all the time she couldn't keep her hands off him, stroking his chest under the gown.

So the doctor on the case told her brusquely to pull herself together and she faded off into the background while he went through his little charade with the readings. No change. Holding his own an optimist might say but who was an optimist? He turned around to tell her she could come back and play handsies again when he noted out of the corner of his attuned eye that Saul's free arm was underneath the blankets, poking around down there. Hell, Matthew thought, nothing like the wrath of a nurse who has to remake a wet bed. He pulled up the blankets a little to take a quick look and there sure enough was a lot of it coming out in a strong, steady stream. He turned to get the urinal out of the cabinet which wasn't there of course but on the other side of the bed, where she'd suddenly materialized, looking alarmed.

"Anything wrong?"

"Get the urinal. Right beside you. In the cabinet. Just pull the door out." He flung the blankets back partway while she fumbled at the drawer. Soaked sheets all right. Oh well. Urine stayed warm for a while and Saul wouldn't notice a little more dampness.

Miss Bunberry was behaving very efficiently, sliding the urinal between the patient's legs and with tender, loving care and a lot of unnecessary fondling, maneuvering the fountainhead into place. She seemed quite unconcerned, as if it were the most natural thing in the world to do but it made Matthew feel like a voyeur. She stood there, very alert by the bed, just like a little soldier ready to go over the top, her eyes fixed steadily on the unromantic neck of the urinal. Matthew pulled the blankets back over it all, hearing the sounds of piss hitting the metal sides and went to stand by the window.

It was so agonizingly quiet in the room that you could hear every tiny sound even when the poor sonovabitch dribbled off finally. Matthew made a great show of looking at his watch, shooting out his hand and holding it up. In five more minutes, be time to check again.

"I think he's finished," she said in a small, shaky voice. "Shall I empty it?"

"That's the nurse's job," he said nastily without turning around. What was this damned humility suddenly? "I'll ring for her. Just remove it and set it somewhere out of the way."

He waited, leaning his arms on the window sill, peering through the open slats of the Venetian blind at the lights in the opposite wing, the women's Surgical Ward. He heard the sound of metal hitting metal as the urinal was placed probably on the table top and of liquid slopping over a little and then nothing, until there was that noise, a little noise, a familiar melange of deep breath, whimper and . . . That sound unfroze him, recalled him, and he whipped around almost snapping his jaw out of place.

She hadn't covered him. The fact that he was supposed to be kept warm meant nothing to her. The reaction had set in. If, before, she'd been merely intent on the sight and sound of his stallion brother pissing, she was now in a little world all her own, mesmerized, seeing nothing but the naked lower half of the body on the bed, her lips parted and her breast heaving. With one swift, almost lunge, Matthew came to her, grabbed her back and yanked the blankets up covering what Sally wanted more than anyone's good opinion.

So Lady Macbeth was stopped dead, drew back her hand, stared around wildly, the crazy sleepwalker, at the now inaccessible cloaked treasure on the bed and finally at him who could do nothing but stand and look at her wordlessly because although he'd heard about this kind of thing it was very queer to actually see a woman, her breath coming fast, in the throes of passion standing on her feet, almost falling to pieces in her need for a guy she'd made crap out of and who was very possibly dying. For a second, she met his glance, but her eyes were tranced, and then she turned and ran out of the room.

Matthew rang for the probie to come and take the urinal away. She was an awkward, bulky girl with some remnants of acne on her face but it did him good to see a female right then who wasn't straight out of a surreal fantasy. He didn't even mind the blood in her eye when he told her about the wet bed nor the little reminder that it was the orderly's job to empty urinals. She took it away anyhow without much loss of caste as far as he could see and he made the readings. The BP had begun to drop again, almost imperceptibly, but still lower than before. Saul mumbled every now and then, Christ, cold or dark or Sally. When the probie came back followed by the orderly bearing dry sheets and they began deftly to remake the bed, he told the nurse to stay there till he came back and went out to call Dudley and get more blood.

He hoped Sally had left town but that wasn't likely and he didn't want to leave her alone in the room with Saul. God knows what she might do. Of course it was his fault but honestly he could plead ignorance. Who knew she was that crazy? He hadn't meant for her to put the urinal in place to begin with, only to hand it to him but when she'd done it, he figured, well let her minister to him, maybe she wants to do any little thing she can. Instead she needed ministering herself. In a public place from a dying man. He'd seen some peculiar things in his time but there wasn't much to beat that. And maybe he did feel righteous and shocked because it was his brother being used but so what? There was nothing sacred to that bitch, nothing at all.

Dudley was just leaving the OR and called back saying he'd bring

Melnikoff. Matthew stopped on his way back to Saul's room to take a leak. Standing in the can, he stared at himself. Well, some were made better than others for certain purposes and there was no denying that his brother was one of them. But what good did it do him? He'd just been paid the highest compliment a man could receive from a woman, or so most men would think, and it was highly likely that he didn't even know it. Nice to think so for his sake but pretty dubious. The circulation would be pretty poor except in the most vital areas.

Sally was back, sitting by the bed, when he returned, avoiding his eye, with her lipstick freshened, whispering to her darling but whether he heard her or not was a good question. The BP had dropped a fraction again and Dudley came with Melnikoff who recommended another adrenalin infusion and the use of a new drug they were experimenting with. Matthew said sure, why not to the new drug and Dudley suggested an oxygen tent but Melnikoff thought the nose tube was enough. And they hooked up a third bottle of blood while Matthew went to call Moe.

They had to wait awhile to see what the reaction would be and now there was a lot more bustle and a bigger cast of medical characters and Moe came and in the diet kitchen where she'd been persuaded to come and have coffee, Sally cried and cried. And Matthew held her in his arms and wiped her face with his handkerchief because, what the hell, just because she was a crazy nympho who was in love with a guy's genitals but thought she was too good for him personally didn't mean it wasn't real to her. But he was feeling lousier and lousier and he couldn't talk to her or Moe.

Because it was a lost cause, no matter what they tried. His brother had suddenly become a statistic, one of that small percentage of cases that defied analysis. After awhile it got worse. Once Saul opened the eyes that'd been closed for the last hour and Matthew, standing there, pumping up the blood-pressure apparatus knew that the eyes saw nothing. It was a sightless frantic stare like that of a blind man. The world, for his brother, had narrowed down progressively from Sally and Matthew's faces, to a cold blur fringed with dim spinning lights and then to black alone. Somewhere dimly the mind, the warranty seal of man, was perhaps aware enough to know that he existed. Saul's mouth opened emitting a kind of very low gasping gargle in an impossible attempt to leap the ever-widening distance, to communicate. I'm still here. Where are you? And a few minutes later, he was unconscious. Dudley told Sally she ought to go home and Matthew went and puked in the can.

When he recovered he went back and Dudley reported that the blood pressure was unobtainable although the heart was still beating and Moe was off in a corner saying the Shema over and over again in a whisper since that was the only prayer he knew. Sally was still there, sitting with dazed eyes, holding the hand that would never pleasure her again and he told Dudley he couldn't take it any more and went down to his room in the Residents' quarters where his roommate woke up and handed him a bottle of brandy without saying anything.

And the only thing he could think at all over and over, was that he couldn't break down the whole damn night and say, Saul, I'm sorry about everything, I didn't mean to hurt you, I've always thought the world of you, no matter how I acted, discount all I ever said, will you? But he hadn't, he couldn't, and now he never would.

* * * *

Dudley and Matthew speaking in sort of chloroformed voices and terribly impressive in their little white starched outfits with the stethoscopes and the grave intent looks and all their absolutely impenetrable language, being so efficient rigging up all that apparatus and knowing exactly what to do, when, as they moved about so surely and quickly, apparently full of skillful assurance, their hands strong and capable, generating in toto, a feeling of such complete confidence that you rode along with it, thinking for quite a gullible while that it was merely a question of waiting till things improved. Soon, he would be better, you told yourself, the dreadful face as white as the pillow he was lying on would begin to draw some sustenance from that hanging bottle of wine-red blood which flashed and glowed in the dimmed light like a great dark ruby but was infinitely more expensive and vital than a mere jewel. It had been shocking at first, to see him lying there in that unnatural position with his head lower than his feet, all trussed and bundled up and attached to rubber tubes and what with the marble face and colorless lips and the uncombed black and gray curls he almost looked like a stone effigy on a tomb but he could speak even if his voice was almost inaudible unless you got very close. And he could see you and clutch your hand and except that he seemed to be running almost entirely in slow motion, he really looked in quite good shape. You had sort of expected him to be completely swathed in bloody bandages, with perhaps only an eye showing and his leg, the other and only leg and an arm perhaps hung up in pulleys. So it was fine and he was all there almost intact and you would have him again, soon, soon, and you would never let him go.

Dudley said he'd been drunk and speeding down Cambridge Street from Scollay Square when he hit this other car and you wondered whether he'd planned to come and see you which might account for the close proximity of the accident to the foot of the Hill and you thought of how futilely coincidental things were in that case, because there you'd been lying all alone up there wanting him and if only he'd gotten there instead of into this silly mess, why there you'd both be, having a fine time in bed. It was quite unseemly to feel so excited this particular night, all that chaste abstinence beginning to tell probably, but there it was, all quite wasted with nothing of Saul to be seen but his head and a hand. Still, you could kiss him even though his lips were so cold but they were firm and sweet as always and you could stroke his forehead and whisper in his ear that you would go away with him, that you loved him, that he was your dearest darling and they would never be apart again, that all the badness was over and it would be good again. He understood, you knew, and looked at you with his heart in his eyes and you longed to fling away all the blankets and the tubes and glass and things that separated you and take him in your arms, holding and loving him till he got warm again. But all you had was this damn cold hand and that only intermittently and Matthew circling around looking disapproving and Dudley every now and then casting a fishy glance of embarrassment in your direction. You pressed the hand against the softness of your sweater, not caring what Dudley or Matthew thought. But of course, aside from them there was that silly striped rustling curious nurse who came in and out with rubber bottles and you knew such lack of restraint would do you no good at all.

So you just held the hand, trying to be content with that and the look of trust in Saul's eyes and wondered what Matthew and Dudley were talking about over there by the door. You felt as if you'd never really known them until tonight, that you had treated them as ordinary men, when in reality, they were not. Instead they seemed with their skill and knowledge and their jugglings with immortality to have transcended humanity and become instead a pair of minor Saviors. You loved them both dearly because tonight they were not just the men you'd known in coats and ties, eating, drinking, and talking in colored, patterned rooms, men whom you'd thought rather ridiculous, one because he was your pompous stick of a brother who couldn't utilize his maleness and the other because he was a rather brash vulgarian and a hypocritical lecher to boot. No, tonight, instead, they were magicians who would save this lovely flesh and blood body on the bed for you and your further delectation and delight. And, you thought, smiling at Dudley who'd given you a sympathetic pat on the shoulder and was leaving the room, never again would you feel contempt or perhaps a soupçon of pity for your brother who could recreate and sustain whereas you could only muddle.

With Dudley's going, Matthew became strangely fidgety. He moved his stethoscope around on Saul's chest, listening intently, frowned, bit his lips, drew back some of the blankets and poked at Saul's stomach, waved her away from the bed, pumped hard at the green rubber ball of the blood pressure tube until the gray cloth cuff was tightly wound around Saul's powerful forearm, held Saul's wrist and stared it nearly out of countenance, his ears sort of cocked for apparent noises, probed around the great column of Saul's neck in which you could see the veins standing out large and blue, felt under the blankets to see if the hot water bottles stacked around the body were warm, looked at his watch, put it to his ear and then wound it. And with a kind of fond, boyish gesture he mussed up his brother's hair which made you suddenly aware that they were actually members of the same family who'd grown up together in the same house, had probably tussled and fought as boys, rolled on the ground, pummeled and bickered, played baseball, drunk milk and stolen cookies, had eaten at the same table and slept in the same room for years, sharing possessions and secrets, clothes and parents and thus, how extraordinarily new in time you were to both of them.

You couldn't help noticing though, how nicely Matthew's white clothes set him off. With his straight short classical nose and the nicely shaped head of graven curls he suddenly seemed as inspiring as Michelangelo's David, and you looked and admired, perhaps because you were receptive to all maleness tonight, even marking the contrast of black, wiry hairs on the backs of his clean, scrubbed white fingers. He stood for a moment looking down at his brother with a kind of tender melancholy on his face which was strange to see and made him look so vulnerable suddenly that you turned your head away. But when he spoke, asking if you wanted some coffee, his voice was perfunctory and utterly without emotion.

You flew back to the bed when you saw Saul moving his lips and heard, when you bent over, the faint, labored voice:

"Stay . . . honey." The large hand searching for yours.

"Yes," with an answering pressure, "always darling."

"Coming for you. But I hit."

"I wanted you too, Saul. I was trying to call you. But it's all right now. I'll never go away from you again."

You could almost trace the movements of his every breath.

"Promise."

"Yes, dearest, yes. Forever."

"Marry me?" Squeezing her hand tightly, his eyes intent on her face. "Promise."

"Yes, Saul, I promise." What madness this was. He'd probably remember and hold her to it. Still, if that was the only way to have him, you would. You'd given your word. And marriage, after all, was not irrevocable. Lord knows one could not go on suffering this tormenting desire and having to poultice oneself with facsimiles. He was trying to speak again. You leaned very close and finally heard it.

"All alone. Nothing left."

"*I'm* here, Saul and I'm with you."

"Baby!" The word came out clearly in a kind of anguished hiss.

He'd never called you baby before, Mike, jazz musicians, almost any other man and then, with a sickening, hateful throb, you understood.

"We can have another baby, darling. As soon as you're better."

He closed his eyes again, breathing deeply, and you wondered, ashamed of the facile way you could say what he wanted to hear, if he believed you. You were not so sure now that Matthew had been unnecessarily gloomy. It was sickening to see the struggle this strong man was putting up to speak a few halting words.

"Too much trouble," he mumbled. "Everything. Always could before. My star. Sally. My . . . star. You have it."

What wild gibberish was he talking now? You wondered whether he was going out of his head and should you get Matthew. But he'd pulled his hand away from yours and was clutching at his neck. Then it became clear.

It was a tiny little gold star, six pointed, two wee triangles, superimposed with weird little symbols on it and you'd first noticed it this summer when you'd given him a key to the cottage because he had it on his key ring. You'd wanted to know what that darling little thing was and he'd been surprised at your interest but explained that it was a Jewish religious object like a cross was to Christians and it was called the Star of David. The letters on it were Hebrew although he couldn't tell you what they meant. Used to know, he'd said, but forgot. You'd thought it was rather funny that someone as completely irreligious as he was should be carrying around such a thing but he'd said diffidently that it'd been his mother's and she'd worn it on a chain around her neck. Rather sweet of him to have such sentiment you'd thought and several days later passing by Shreve's you'd gone into the jewelry store and bought a fine gold chain and that night you asked Saul if you could borrow his star for a moment and then strung it on the chain and as he'd been kissing you had bound it around his neck. And he'd been very peculiar, saying men never wore jewelry, did she think he was a pansy or something. But you'd insisted because it really looked lovely, sort of barbaric and splendid hanging down on his broad naked chest, against the thick black hair. So he'd finally given in saying you were the craziest girl in the world but if that's what you wanted, only the points of the star might hurt you. But you said nonsense and afterwards you'd made love together and the star on its chain had swung back and forth. Now he wanted to give it to you. He was turning his head, fumbling with limp fingers at the back of his neck.

"Darling, no. You keep it. We'll be together again soon."

"No. Wear it. For me. There. Warm."

So you unfastened the chain from about his neck carefully and while he watched intently you hung it around yours and dropped the star inside your sweater. It hung cold and damp between your breasts.

"Instead of me," he said and closed his eyes again and now you were really afraid. But the star had a life of its own because the moment you had hung it there, where he had once lain saying it was glory you could not equate the memory of him as he had been then with what was there now on the bed and you closed your eyes feeling again the old languorous warmth, moving a bit in the chair but your thighs clenched tightly together. If Matthew would only stay out awhile longer, if you could just kiss a small part of his body, perhaps . . .

It was frightening that the skin was so cold when you kissed his shoulder repeatedly and licked your tongue along it but still the old memories would not go away nor the sensations they aroused. You scarcely saw or heard Matthew when he came except that he had something to do and wanted you to go away.

You'd always been excited at the sight of men doing that perfectly normal thing. The big ones particularly. Ben and you in the bathroom. He always wanted to watch you too. Saul thought it was funny and used to laugh. But don't put it away yet darling. Honey, it's all for you any time. And now, there'd be no other time. Not again, not ever. You knew this all at once, incontrovertibly and you could not wait now that you'd heard the slashing sound of the harpy's scissors, so clearly, so close. They would be there soon and you must hurry. Greedy Death, give me a last chance. Just once more, darling, let us have our lovely little death together before you go away alone . . .

Then suddenly what you'd been watching was not here. Shattered like a torn film, the image erased, the screen you'd been almost part of quivering into darkness and with a sick shiver, still wild with longing, you awoke as if from a dream where it had almost happened and you were all ready and couldn't stand it a moment longer only you moved, ending the lovely frenzy and saw real-life Matthew staring at you. So you ran away, away from his accusing, disgusted eyes, his face which told you that you were some sort of incredible necrophiliac, an insane, diseased female. But it wasn't that way, you told yourself, sick and guilty in the bathroom and you'd never done this before in your whole life, it was horrible and loathsome but you had to do it, and it was joyless and all over in a few seconds and the only thing that saved you from absolutely despising yourself was the thought that Saul would have understood.

Back into the room again there was nothing to do but let him know you were there and loved him. And after awhile he knew less and less, he could only murmur fuzzily of chill and then darkness and then, where was she, he couldn't see her and after that he didn't know she was there at all. There were a great many people coming and going in the room and around his bed but no matter what they said or did, he just flickered out, all that huge strength and vitality, like a spent, cardboard match.

Sitting there, wrapped in your incredulous pall, all you could think of was the dream you'd had under anesthesia on Dr. Phillips' table. The marvel you'd been seeking in the stars and fires of infinity had finally made itself known to you as well as the reason you'd not found it then. Because it was life, the creation and the sustenance and the joy and you knew it now, when you saw this common, ordinary, completely priceless gift taken away from Saul. Saul, who'd known in the simplest, most unquestioning kind of way what the cherishing of life meant, was losing his while you, who'd gone along blindly and stupidly for twenty-four years, unaware of the exact, precise nature of this until now, were still there, full of knowledge, now that it was too late, on this dreadful night. A member of the myriad moles and pack rats who were foolishly deluded into thinking that money and power, jewels and pride were all more precious than one human life. And if you told them they would only laugh as you had laughed and pushed Saul away in the snow with his pitiful ludicrous plea.

You must have nodded, exhausted in the chair for a while because suddenly the lights in the room had been turned off, the shades at the window raised, and you could see the washed out winter dawn creeping like an old, cold palsied man shakily up the sky. And there was Matthew, terrible and dark, his eyes heavy-lidded, shadowed, with a smell of liquor on him and the uncle's sad, gnome-like face, his eyes unashamedly red-rimmed. He's dead they were saying and you must go. Dudley was there too, ready to take you home and he held your hand as you stood and looked and bent down and kissed the snowwhite forehead and the lips, all cold. You had kissed ice and your heart froze. You pulled the sheet up over his face and then they made you leave. It did not seem right but that's what you had to do.

Saul's uncle in his quiet, humble voice said something to you out in the hall and then repeated it. The funeral would be this afternoon and would you come. This was unbelievable. Bury him. They were going to bury him.

"We don't embalm," he explained apparently understanding your look of consternation. "We bury our dead before sundown. It seems too quick to you maybe but believe me it is best."

"Maybe she doesn't want to come, Moe," Matthew said. "Don't bother her."

"It is a good deed to go to a man's funeral," the uncle insisted. "And why shouldn't she come? Saul loved her."

Matthew muttered inaudibly and then said rather gruffly that she was welcome to come if she wanted and hurried away down the hall with Dudley to sign some papers.

So you said of course you'd come, thinking, how unbearable but aware that you must and what else, in any case, was there to do? It was not until you left the hospital that you remembered the little gold star and wondered if perhaps you should've given it to the uncle. It might be the sort of thing they buried with the body. But no. He had given it to you to keep. And so you would. Even now, you could feel, around your neck, the burden of its simple power.

* * * *

The funeral was not, it so happened, until the next day, at eleven
o'clock in the morning and even so it was a terrible hustle getting
things done. Moe and Sophy were kind of sore at Matthew because
of the delay. They thought it should've been that same afternoon,
but he'd given his permission to have Pathology do an autopsy and
that slowed things up to begin with. Sophy, in fact, was furious
when she found out. The idea of them cutting Solly up like that.
It was disrespect to the dead and orthodox Jews didn't have it done.
As if she was orthodox. He explained to her as much as he could
because his tongue was thick with brandy and his head fuzzy from
no sleep and the bloody hell of it all, and words didn't come easy,
that Saul never came out of shock, and maybe, just maybe, doing
an autopsy on him might help some other guy later. This only infuriated her still more because according to her, if doctors hadn't
been able to save him with all the things they knew already, as far
as she was concerned, they could keep their knives and hands off
him, now that they had let him die. Well, in spite of her tongue it
had to be his way because he was next of kin.

And then a further snag developed when it came out from Moe
that Saul had told him he wanted to be buried in a Veterans cemetery. Sophy then started riding away on that one. Of course Saul
should be buried in the family plot alongside his mother, grandfather, and grandmother and where she and Moe would finally be
laid to rest. She was about to spring to the telephone and get hold
of the cemetery to make arrangements but Moe, pretty gentle and
quiet but firm, said that Saul'd been positive about it. He even
quoted him, to the effect that he lost his leg for his country and
therefore his country could damn well pay for his grave and its upkeep and furthermore he wanted to be buried like a military hero
since what other glory did he have left. So it was Matthew's decision
and of course he made it the way Saul wanted. And the nearest
Veterans cemetery couldn't accommodate them till the following
morning. Well, at least it gave Sophy a chance to put a notice in
the evening papers.

Funny thing about people like her. She couldn't be allowed in a
sickroom because of her hysterics and had spent the whole night
lying prostrate, awake and moaning despite the sedative, not even
knowing what was going on, for Godsakes, but the minute she
heard of the actual death, or passing away which she thought was

the refined way to refer to the end of a life, why she was on her feet, rising to the occasion so to speak, running to the undertakers and all, while all he and Moe could do was just sit around and drink schnapps and try vainly to sleep.

A beautiful sheaf of bronze and gold chrysanthemums had come from Sally and Dudley. Sophy eyed it suspiciously as he unwrapped the oiled green paper and wanted to know what he was going to do with them and didn't his fine friends know that Jews didn't have flowers at their funerals. That girl, she kept saying, as she looked at the simple white, black-bordered card accompanying the flowers, that girl was what caused him all that trouble. He was a good driver, Solly, it never would've happened if she hadn't made his life miserable. Moe chimed in to say that the girl seemed to be nice and Saul was a heavy drinker already before he knew her. It was a technical argument which Matthew was in no shape to involve himself in so he carried the flowers and one of Sophy's ugly old vases into Saul's room and put them up on top of the chest of drawers where his brother had kept shirts and stuff. They sat there, bright and crisp, smelling of damp earth and autumn mornings. From the best florist's shop in the city too. Nothing but the best for her, he thought, and he'd bet she picked them out. Yes, that was her handwriting on the card. The names and another word. *Immortelles.* Now what did that mean? Immortal, wasn't it? But the "s" meant plural. More than one immortal? Maybe it was the name in French of the flowers. Damned if he knew. Have to ask her sometime. Yeah, and when would that be? In some other life maybe. He'd live to a ripe old age with his curiosity about other names for chrysanthemums unsatisfied. Or did she think Saul was immortal? Oh sure, that was it. She was going to live devoted to his memory for the rest of her life. He wondered how long it would take her to get a new shack job. Wasn't going to be easy finding someone so completely suitable in a hurry. Still, you didn't have to worry about her. She'd make it.

He remembered, with a kind of nervous shiver up his backbone, what she'd said that morning when they'd woken her up and told her Saul was dead.

"Thou canst not think," she'd murmured to Dudley, "how ill all is here about my heart."

She'd said it in a kind of ordinary way, her voice husky and full of sadness but not self-consciously, not the way most people would who were quoting Shakespeare, but as if she were saying the kind of things other people would say, like, It's so terrible I can't realize it, which was Sophy's line. He'd almost jumped when he heard her saying that, his heart had rung like a bell, because it expressed exactly how he felt. If you didn't know her and you just heard or saw her that minute when she spoke, you'd think she was the most sensitive, warmhearted, wonderful girl in the world, full of poetry and love. Only on further acquaintance all it meant was that she should've gone on the stage.

There were a lot of people at the funeral even though it was a weekday morning. The entire crew who worked with Saul at the *Beacon* turned out; the paper's sports editor, a whole crowd he didn't specially recognize but who were obviously fight characters, Saul's old trainer, manager, etcetera, a batch of shifty-eyed types in sharp suits who sat in back together and looked very out of place and couldn't be anybody but his drinking and gambling friends. The Disabled Vets sent a delegation although Saul had stopped going to meetings years ago. Saul's former in-laws were there too as well as every relative available including a lot of old second cousins, female, who probably made a career of attending funerals. It was a pretty motley crew in general that filled up almost all the seats in the funeral chapel but the strangest sight in the midst of that collection was Sally, wearing a brown fur hat, Russian style, to match her coat. Moe'd met her at the door and wanted to escort her down to the second row behind the immediate family but she'd apparently preferred to sit somewhere in the middle among the undifferentiated fringe friends of the deceased. Which was as well, Matthew figured, as Sophy beside him, might have been damn rude.

The young rabbi of the synagogue Sophy and Moe sometimes went to was to deliver the eulogy and he didn't know Saul at all naturally so Moe and Matthew had to prep him a little which seemed a pretty phony thing but what were you going to do? Matthew was surprised at the sight of the rabbi when he met him to talk to in a little room off the chapel. He was as big and tall as Saul in his prime and looked more Irish than Jewish, with blue eyes behind his horn-rimmed glasses, a pug nose, freckles and none of the unctuous orotund tones or beard, gravity and air of solemn scholarship that Matthew was accustomed to equate with rabbis. But what the hell kind of speech could he deliver about the departed's good qualities or about the nature of his life, which was what was expected at these affairs, when he didn't know Saul, had never seen him or spoken to him? The man he had to pronounce the good word over had obviously never been a member of his congregation, not even on holidays. And as for the cause of death you couldn't make too many silk purses out of that. Still less did you want to bring up the departed's sunrise and sunset appearances with the mourners in the last three weeks. But it wouldn't hurt, thought Matthew, as he was sketching a brief biography of his brother for the rabbi's enlightenment, to include mention that although Saul was not a synagogue-goer he'd been an ardent Bible reader. And for the rest it was the rabbi's worry and he probably had whole books of speeches to be tailored for any occasion.

All the same, Matthew thought, as he made his way back to the front row, it was kind of a lousy thing having to go through all this cut and dried ceremony. Making up a speech out of thin air about an unknown man. Who would ever know Saul's true nature? Even he, now a putrefying corpse in a coffin, hadn't known it. Little bits and pieces, that's all anyone living would now remember. He was big and handsome and highly sexed. He was awarded a Silver Star with a couple of clusters for bravery in combat. He gambled and swore and drank and crashed around over the top of the earth like a lot of other guys and lived for the physical until one day his body failed him and he didn't have much else. He loved not wisely but too well. He'd been shortchanged by life and was a little crazy as a result. He was good to his brother and helped him out with an education. He was a patriot and a hero, and never a coward or a bully.

He was my brother, Matthew thought, coming down the aisle past all the people sitting vacantly in their seats waiting for the business to begin and listening with half an ear to the tallith draped old man who was sitting up by the coffin reciting prayers in half-drowned Hebrew as he'd been doing all night, he was all I had for years when I was little and alone and afraid. He used to wake up at night when I cried because I wanted my mother and sit on the bed and talk to me and tell me he missed her too but it was all right because they were together and Saul would always take care of him. He was my brother and he never said a bad word to me when we were younger, never played any rotten tricks, acted as if I were in his way, shared all his things with me, never selfish, never teased me, picked on me, beat me up or pushed me around. He was my brother and later on when he came back from the war and things were bad for him, I talked down to him and was embarrassed by him because he was such a roughneck. Because it didn't look good for a superior, educated doctor to have such a brother. How could he ever aspire to the tone of a Dudley Brimmer with a specimen like that around to remind the world of where he sprang from? Nobody could ever say that Dr. Matthew Berman wasn't good to his brother. Only jealous, that's all. Because Sally had climbed into bed with Saul not Matthew who was so damn superior and respectable. Was it family solidarity or male pride that'd impelled him to tell Saul where Sally was that night? Or was it just that he wanted Saul to know how little Sally'd really cared for him?

He saw Sally just then, sitting a little way in from the aisle, right next to, of all people, the bartender of that gin mill in the South End. She was staring straight ahead, looking, under the fur hat, suitably tragic and like, maybe Garbo in an old costume movie. She was pale and her hands were folded primly in her lap. Now where did all these other people come from, anyway? Did they all spend their time reading obituaries?

He slid into his seat just as the rabbi came out and clambered up on the little dais. What was Sally making out of this kind of funeral with no flowers or organ music, and only the plain wooden pine box up there in the front, covered simply with a blue cloth marked by a large gold embroidered star.

And, for a man who'd just grabbed up a few facts ten minutes ago, the rabbi didn't do badly, mainly emphasizing the heroism in wartime of the dead and how beloved he'd been in life among many sorts of people, something he could figure for himself by noting the size and curious mixture of the crowd in attendance. It was over in a short time, after the rabbi had concluded with a short prayer in Hebrew of which Matthew caught only Saul's full Hebrew name coupled with that of their father and then outside there were limousines waiting for the long drive to the cemetery.

Sally came up to him as he was handing Sophy into the car behind the hearse. She had her convertible it appeared, and wondered if she could come to, as the undertakers would say, the interment. He said sure, if she had time to kill, and just follow the crowd and she nodded curtly and walked away.

"She's coming to the cemetery?" Sophy said shrilly when they were all three seated. "Well, of all the nerve! Cossack!"

Matthew noticed, when they were stopped for a light and he looked out of the window, that there were quite a few cars lined up behind. He could see Sally's yellow flash about three down behind the red sports car belonging to Saul's former manager. Sophy, in the limousine by the other window, was crying noisily and mopping her eyes. She controlled herself finally and began to remark on the turnout of people.

"Who would've ever thought Solly had so many friends? But half of them I never even knew. Some of them were so nice. You can't imagine the fine things they said to me about Saul. All the people at the newspaper. And there was one man, I've never seen anybody look more like a racketeer, but he came up and shook my hand and introduced himself and said how sorry he was, that it was a terrible loss and if there was ever anything we needed or wanted I should call him. He gave me his card. Such a fine-spoken man, so it just shows you should never judge by appearances."

She showed them the card which bore the name of one who was notorious as having his finger in every shady pie in the city. Matthew didn't bother to disillusion his aunt and again they rode along in silence and he thought how strange it was that Saul'd had that knack of attracting everyone. He had never done anything dishonest or hurt anyone nor would he even though he consorted with all sorts of crooks and they remained his friends in spite of divergent views on ethics. A sudden image of his brother as he'd looked years ago, before the war, rose before him; one summer day at the training camp where he'd been working out. Standing in full sunlight, near the ring, having just pulled a gray sweatshirt off and dropped it on the grass, the sweat running down his naked chest, his stance confident, tall, smiling, tanned, in full health and manhood, his vitality, strength and happiness apparent in every wide, sweeping, expansive gesture of hands and the flash of white teeth in the brown face and then throwing his head back and giving vent to a big, roaring laugh because of a joke Moe had just told him.

"What's the matter, Matt?" Moe asked softly. "You don't feel well? Why are you all bent over like that?"

"Nothing," and he straightened up. "Just a cramp. I'll be all right."

So it was all over, wasn't it? The hope that perhaps things might go well for him someday had gone off with him. He had left nothing and died nothing and that was the end of it. Who would remember him after all except his brother who would die, too? Matthew could see why people wanted to believe in immortality, in Heaven, in a wise Providence. It would help but the hell of it was, he couldn't. How cosy, if maybe he could think, as probably Sophy and Moe could, of the comforting picture of Saul and their mother meeting in heaven, talking, smiling, embracing, looking down on all that drear procession of black hearse and cars winding out to a lonesome cemetery. Nice but untrue. If that were so where did someone like their father fit in? If he was there had their mother forgiven him? Would Saul like him better? Maybe he wasn't there. And yet, had he actually been so wicked? Then who was to say what was actual evil? If fornication outside marriage was the test for his father, Saul himself would be only a shade less black. No, no, it wouldn't work. He was dead and soon they'd put him in earth and the ground would grow cold and hard through the long winter.

It was a damn cold day out there in the wide unprotected spaces of the cemetery where the wind bowled along above the crosses and stars and down the paths. The sun was dim and the sky full of massed gray clouds moving in on it. There'd been a light snowfall two days ago which hadn't even been noticed in the city but out here, tiny shreds of it clung to the grass between the graves.

There were two soldiers in uniform standing by the coffin, which was now draped with a flag. The rabbi stepped up and said a few more prayers and then Matthew, his uncle, and Sophy's brother came forward with their skullcaps on and read the prayer about God having mercy. Matthew'd been practicing it under the supervision of Sophy's brother the night before but even so he faltered along feeling ashamed of himself for his ineptitude. Then they stepped back and the soldiers came forward, removing the flag from the coffin, folding it reverently and handing it to Matthew. It was now his to keep. The coffin was lowered slowly into the open grave, and Sophy began to cry again and call Saul's name. The soldiers fired their guns into the air. Echoing volleys rolled back from the silence and Matthew, looking up, saw Sally standing on the other side of the grave from him, staring down into the open hole. There was the sound of a bugle. It was taps, long drawn out, agonizingly slow, melancholy brass notes, repeated twice. Funny, Matthew thought, staring at Sally, how he used to hear this bugle call every night at eleven in various Army camps and never realized how it could harrow up one's soul and make the stomach churn. He saw that Sally's fur shoulders were shaking. She looked up and saw him and took a handkerchief out of her pocket and poked at her eyes with it, and mercifully then, the mournful, muted bugle ceased and the gravediggers came with shovels to fill in the new-dug hole.

There was a movement of people turning toward the gates where the cars were. He saw Sally up ahead walking swiftly along, hands in her pockets. He wanted to talk to her and see her with red eyes, her composure cracked, so he caught up with her at the gate just as she was getting into her car.

"Thanks for the flowers," he said. "They were very nice."

Her eyes *were* red too and so was the end of her nose, in fact she looked lousy, which pleased him in some obscure way.

"Glad you liked them. Why in the world was he buried with all those military trappings? Of all people."

"He wanted it."

She was silent. Then, "Yes, I see that he might. Perhaps he did die years ago, really. You know, *'Dulce et decorum est pro patria mori'* and all that."

They stared at each other for a moment and then she started up the car and roared off.

So they went away and left him all alone with nothing in the dark.